THE ADVENTURES OF
SHERLOCK HOLMES

THE ADVENTURES OF SHERLOCK HOLMES

Sir Arthur Conan Doyle

WORDSWORTH CLASSICS

NOTE TO READER

This volume constitutes part of a trilogy of Sherlock Holmes adventures. Each of the three volumes, *The Adventures of Sherlock Holmes*, *The Return of Sherlock Holmes* and *The Case-Book of Sherlock Holmes* can be read independently, but the books have been paginated consecutively from volume one through to the close of volume three to create a complete chronological record of the great detective's exploits as originally published in *The Strand Magazine*.

This edition published 1995 by
Wordsworth Editions Limited
Cumberland House, Crib Street, Ware,
Hertfordshire SG12 9ET

ISBN 1 85326 852 6

Printed and bound by Mackays of Chatham

INTRODUCTION

SHERLOCK HOLMES is perhaps the best-known of all fictional characters. From the first appearance of the short stories in the *Strand Magazine* chronicling his extraordinary deductive powers, Holmes became a larger-than-life figure whose devotees were stricken when it seemed that the great detective had perished at the Reichenbach Falls in *The Adventure of the Final Problem*. Young men put mourning crepe in their hats, and the author was forced by public demand to resurrect his hero. From that day, a literary cult was born and continues unabated to this day. Perhaps it is best exemplified by The Baker Street Irregulars, who exist to perpetuate the memory, methods and iconography of the great detective. Its members comprise diplomats, judges, academics as well as great numbers of ordinary readers who enjoy the romance and atmosphere of Conan Doyle's creation.

Sherlock Holmes's methods may be traced back to one of Doyle's teachers at the Edinburgh Infirmary. Joseph Bell used to enliven his lectures by encouraging his students to recognise a patient as a left-handed cobbler or as a retired sergeant of a Highland regiment who had served in Barbados, by the simple processes of accurate observation and rational deduction. This inclined Doyle to attribute these qualities to a detective, and to cast that detective as a hero, which was unusual, if not unique, in English stories of the time. The first appearance of Sherlock Holmes was in 1887, in *A Study in Scarlet*, which was presented as 'a reprint from the reminiscences of John H. Watson, late of the Army Medical Department', and so the happy pairing of the deductive Holmes, with the down-to-earth Dr Watson as foil, was established. *The Sign of Four* followed in 1890, but Holmes did not really catch the public imagination until the first of the short stories, *A Scandal in Bohemia*, was published in the July issue of *The Strand Magazine* in 1891. These stories were illustrated by the remarkable Sidney Paget, who used his brother Walter as model for 'the tall, spare figure of Holmes', standing before the Baker Street fireplace, looking down on Watson in his 'singular, introspective fashion'. It was Paget who equipped Holmes with his famous deerstalker hat, though he never gave him the meerschaum pipe which became an icon following a stage production of one of the stories in the 1920's.

As well as being fast-paced detective stories, the Sherlock Holmes adventures provide a fascinating glimpse into 1890's London. The domestic arrangements at 221B Baker Street are the focal point of the metropolitan civilization that encompasses November fog and hansom cabs, frock coats, silk hats and hurried railway journeys on trains that run on time, scandal in high places and murder in low ones.

From textual evidence, Sir Sidney Roberts concluded that Sherlock Holmes was born in 1854 of an English father and a mother descended from a line of French painters. He seems to have been someting of an aesthete at university, probably Oxford, but certainly not Cambridge. On coming down from university he took rooms near the British Museum to study those sciences relevant to his subsequent career. In 1881, in a laboratory at St Bartholomew's Hospital, he met Dr Watson, and they decided to share the rooms in Baker Street. We know that Holmes refused a knighthood, but he did accept the *Legion d'Honneur*. He retired to Sussex, kept bees, but of his life after 1914, there exists no record.

Arthur Conan Doyle was born in Edinburgh in 1859. He was educated at Stonyhurst and Edinburgh University where he qualified as a doctor. He practised at Southsea from 1882-1890, but from that date he devoted himself entirely to writing. Without doubt, the Sherlock Holmes stories are his finest work, but Doyle himself always preferred his other writing, especially the historical romances such as Micah Clarke, Sir Nigel *and* The White Company. *He had considerable success with these, as he did with* The Exploits of Brigadier Gerard *which recount the preposterous adventures of a vainglorious officer of Napoleon's cavalry, and the Professor Challenger stories, the first of which was* The Lost World *(1912). In later years, Doyle's increasing obsession with spiritualism clouded his judgement. He was knighted in 1902 and died in 1930.*

Further reading:
J D Carr: *The Life of Conan Doyle*
R Pearsall: *Conan Doyle: A Biographical Solution*
S C Roberts: *Holmes and Watson*

CONTENTS

Introducing Sherlock Holmes
(1887, 1890)

The Adventures of Sherlock Holmes
(1891-1893)

INTRODUCING
SHERLOCK HOLMES

*The first two Sherlock Holmes stories, first published
in 1887 and 1890*

A Study in Scarlet

CHAPTER 1

MR. SHERLOCK HOLMES

In the year 1878 I took my degree of Doctor of Medicine of the University of London, and proceeded to Netley to go through the course prescribed for surgeons in the army. Having completed my studies there, I was duly attached to the Fifth Northumberland Fusiliers as Assistant Surgeon. The regiment was stationed in India at the time, and before I could join it, the second Afghan war had broken out. On landing at Bombay, I learned that my corps had advanced through the passes, and was already deep in the enemy's country. I followed, however, with many other officers who were in the same situation as myself, and succeeded in reaching Candahar in safety, where I found my regiment, and at once entered upon my new duties.

The campaign brought honours and promotion to many, but for me it had nothing but misfortune and disaster. I was removed from my brigade and attached to the Berkshires, with whom I served at the fatal battle of Maiwand. There I was struck on the shoulder by a Jezail bullet, which shattered the bone and grazed the subclavian artery. I should have fallen into the hands of the murderous Ghazis had it not been for the devotion and courage shown by Murray, my orderly, who threw me across a packhorse, and succeeded in bringing me safely to the British lines.

Worn with pain, and weak from the prolonged hardships which I had undergone, I was removed, with a great train of wounded sufferers, to the base hospital at Peshawar. Here I rallied, and had already improved so far as to be able to walk about the wards, and even to bask a little upon the verandah, when I was struck down by enteric fever, that curse of our Indian possessions. For months my life was despaired of, and when as last I came to myself and became convalescent, I was so weak and emaciated that a medical board determined that not a day should be lost in sending me back to England. I was despatched accordingly in the troopship Orontes, and landed a month later on Portsmouth Jetty, with my health irretrievably ruined, but with permission from a paternal government to spend the next nine months in attempting to improve it.

I had neither kith nor kin in England, and was therefore as free as air—or as free as an income of eleven shillings and sixpence a day will permit a man to be. Under such circumstances I naturally gravitated to London, that great cesspool into which all the loungers and idlers of the Empire are irresistibly drained. There I stayed for some time at a private hotel in the Strand, leading a comfortless, meaningless existence, and spending such money as I had, considerably more freely than I ought. So alarming did the state of my finances become that I soon realized that I must either leave the metropolis and rusticate somewhere in the country, or that I must make a complete alteration in my style of living. Choosing the latter alternative, I began by making up my mind to leave the hotel, and to take up my quarters in some less pretentious and less expensive domicile.

On the very day that I had come to this conclusion, I was standing at the Criterion Bar, when someone tapped me on the shoulder, and turning round I recognized young Stamford, who had been a dresser under me at Barts. The sight of a friendly face in the great wilderness of London is a pleasant thing indeed to a lonely man. In old days Stamford had never been a particular crony of mine, but now I hailed him with enthusiasm, and he, in his turn, appeared to be delighted to see me. In the exuberance of my joy, I asked him to lunch with me at the Holborn, and we started off together in a hansom.

"Whatever have you been doing with yourself, Watson?" he asked in undisguised wonder, as we rattled through the crowded London streets. "You are as thin as a lath and as brown as a nut."

I gave him a short sketch of my adventures, and had hardly concluded it by the time that we reached our destination.

" Poor devil ! " he said, commiseratingly, after he had listened to my misfortunes. " What are you up to now ? "

" Looking for lodgings," I answered. " Trying to solve the problem as to whether it is possible to get comfortable rooms at a reasonable price."

" That's a strange thing," remarked my companion " you are the second man today that has used that expression to me."

" And who was the first ? " I asked.

" A fellow who is working at the chemical laboratory up at the hospital. He was bemoaning himself this morning because he could not get someone to go halves with him in some nice rooms which he had found, and which were too much for his purse,"

" By Jove ! " I cried; " if he really wants someone to share the rooms and the expense, I am the very man for him. I should prefer having a partner to being alone."

Young Stamford looked rather strangely at me over his wine-glass. " You don't know Sherlock Holmes yet," he said; " perhaps you would not care for him as a constant companion."

" Why, what is there against him ? "

" Oh, I didn't say there was anything against him. He is a little queer in his ideas—an enthusiast in some branches of science. As far as I know he is a decent fellow enough."

" A medical student, I suppose ? " said I.

" No—I have no idea what he intends to go in for. I believe he is well up in anatomy, and he is a first-class chemist; but, as far as I know, he has never taken out any systematic medical classes. His studies are very desultory and eccentric, but he has amassed a lot of out-of-the-way knowledge which would astonish his professors."

" Did you never ask him what he was going in for ? " I asked.

" No; he is not a man that is easy to draw out, though he can be communicative enough when the fancy seizes him."

" I should like to meet him," I said. " If I am to lodge with anyone, I should prefer a man of studious and quiet habits. I am not strong enough yet to stand much noise or excitement. I had enough of both in Afghanistan to last me for the remainder of my natural existence. How could I meet this friend of yours ? "

" He is sure to be at the laboratory," returned my companion. " He either avoids the place for weeks, or else he works there from morning till night. If you like, we will drive round together after luncheon."

" Certainly," I answered, and the conversation drifted away into other channels.

As we made our way to the hospital after leaving the Holborn, Stamford gave me a few more particulars about the gentleman whom I proposed to take as a fellow-lodger.

" You mustn't blame me if you don't get on with him," he said; " I know nothing more of him than I have learned from meeting him occasionally in the laboratory. You proposed this arrangement, so you must not hold me responsible."

" If we don't get on it will be easy to part company," I answered. " It seems to me, Stamford," I added, looking hard at my companion, " that you have some reason for washing you hands of this matter. Is this fellow's temper so formidable, or what is it ? Don't be mealy-mouthed about it."

" It is not easy to express the inexpressible," he answered with a laugh. Holmes is a little too scientific for my tastes—it approaches to cold-bloodedness. I could imagine his giving a friend a little pinch of the latest vegetable alkaloid, not out of malevolence, you understand, but simply out of a spirit of inquiry in order to have an accurate idea of the effects. To do him justice, I think that he would take it himself with the same readiness. He appears to have a passion for definite and exact knowledge."

" Very right too."

" Yes, but it may be pushed to excess. When it comes to beating the subjects in the dissecting-rooms with a stick, it is certainly taking rather a bizarre shape."

" Beating the subjects ! "

" Yes, to verify how far bruises may be produced after death. I saw him at it with my own eyes."

" And yet you say he is not a medical student ? "

"No. Heaven knows what the objects of his studies are. But here we are, and you must form your own impressions about him." As he spoke, we turned down a narrow lane and passed through a small side-door which opened into a wing of the great hospital. It was familiar ground to me, and I needed no guiding as we ascended the bleak stone staircase and made our way down the long corridor with its vista of whitewashed wall and dun-coloured doors. Near the farther end a low arched passage branched away from it and led to the chemical laboratory.

This was a lofty chamber, lined and littered with countless bottles. Broad, low tables were scattered about, which bristled with retorts, test-tubes, and little Bunsen lamps with their blue flickering flames. There was only one student in the room, who was bending over a distant table absorbed in his work. At the sound of our steps he glanced round and sprang to his feet with a cry of pleasure. " I've found it ! I've found it," he shouted to my companion, running towards us with a test-tube in his hand. " I have found a re-agent which is precipitated by haemoglobin, and by nothing else." Had he discovered a gold mine, greater delight could not have shone upon his features.

" Dr. Watson, Mr. Sherlock Holmes," said Stamford introducing us.

" How are you ? " he said cordially, gripping my hand with a strength for which I should hardly have given him credit. " You have been in Afghanistan, I perceive."

" How on earth did you know that ? " I asked in astonishment.

" Never mind," said he, chuckling to himself. " The question now is about haemoglobin. No doubt you see the significance of this discovery of mine ? "

" It is interesting, chemically, no doubt," I answered, " but practically——"

" Why, man, it is the most practical medico-legal discovery for years. Don't you see that it gives us an infallible test for blood stains. Come over here now ! " He seized me by the coat-sleeve in his eagerness, and drew me over to the table at which he had been working. " Let us have some fresh blood," he said, digging a long bodkin into his finger, and drawing off the resulting drop of blood in a chemical pipette. " Now, I add this small quantity of blood to a litre of water. You perceive that the resulting mixture has the appearance of pure water. The proportion of blood cannot be more than one in a million. I have no doubt, however, that we shall be able to obtain the characteristic reaction." As he spoke, he threw into the vessel a few white crystals, and then added some drops of a transparent fluid. In an instant the contents assumed a dull mahogany colour, and a brownish dust was precipitated to the bottom of the glass jar.

" Ha ! ha ! " he cried, clapping his hands, and looking as delighted as a child with a new toy. " What do you thing of that ? "

" It seems to be a very delicate test," I remarked.

" Beautiful ! beautiful ! The old guaia-cum test was very clumsy and uncertain. So is the microscopic examination for blood corpuscles. The latter is valueless if the stains are a few hours old. Now, this appears to act as well whether the blood is old or new. Had this test been invented, there are hundreds of men now walking the earth who would long ago have paid the penalty of their crimes."

" Indeed ! " I murmured.

" Criminal cases are continually hinging upon one point. A man is suspected of a crime months perhaps after it has been committed. His linen or clothes are examined and brownish stains discovered upon them. Are they blood stains, or mud stains, or rust stains, or fruit stains, or what are they ? That is a question which has puzzled many an expert, and why ? Because there was no reliable test. Now we have the Sherlock Holmes test, and there will no longer be any difficulty."

His eyes fairly glittered as he spoke, and he put his hand over his heart and bowed as if to some applauding crowd conjured up by his imagination.

" You are to be congratulated," I remarked, considerably surprised at his enthusiasm.

" There was the case of Von Bischoff at Frankfort last year. He would certainly have been hung had this test been in existence. Then there was Mason of Bradford, and the notorious Muller, and Lefevre of Montpellier, and Samson of New Orleans. I could name a score of cases in which it would have been decisive."

" You seem to be a walking calendar of crime," said Stamford with a laugh. " You might start a paper on those lines. Call it the 'Police News of the Past'."

" Very interesting reading it might be made, too," remarked Sherlock Holmes, sticking a small piece of plaster over the prick on his finger. " I have to be careful," he continued, turning to me with a smile, " for I dabble with poisons a good deal." He held out his hand as he spoke, and I noticed that it was mottled over with similar pieces of plaster, and discoloured with strong acids.

" We came here on business," said Stamford, sitting down on a high three-legged stool, and pushing another one in my direction with his foot. " My friend here wants to take diggings; and as you were complaining that you could get no one to go halves with you, I thought that I had better bring you together."

Sherlock Holmes seemed delighted at the

idea of sharing his rooms with me. " I have my eye on a suite in Baker Street," he said, " which would suit us down to the ground. You don't mind the smell of strong tobacco, I hope ? "

" I always smoke 'ship's' myself," I answered.

" That's good enough. I generally have chemicals about, and occasionally do experiments. Would that annoy you ? "

" By no means."

" Let me see—what are my other shortcomings. I get down in the dumps at times, and don't open my mouth for days on end. You must not think I am sulky when I do that. Just let me alone, and I'll soon be right. What have you to confess now ? It's just as well for two fellows to know the worst of one another before they begin to live together."

I laughed at this cross-examination. " I keep a bull pup," I said, " and I object to rows because my nerves are shaken, and I get up at all sorts of ungodly hours, and I am extremely lazy. I have another set of vices when I'm well, but those are the principal ones at present."

" Do you include violin playing in your category of rows ? " he asked, anxiously.

" It depends on the player," I answered. " A well-played violin is a treat for the gods—a badly-played one——"

" Oh, that's all right," he cried, with a merry laugh. " I think we may consider the thing as settled—that is, if the rooms are agreeable to you."

" When shall we see them ? "

" Call for me here at noon tomorrow, and we'll go together and settle everything," he answered.

" All right—noon exactly," said I, shaking his hand.

We left him working among his chemicals, and we walked together towards my hotel.

" By the way," I asked suddenly, stopping and turning upon Stamford, " how the deuce did he know that I had come from Afghanistan ? "

My companion smiled an enigmatical smile. " That's just his little peculiarity," he said. " A good many people have wanted to know how he finds things out."

" Oh ! a mystery is it ? " I cried, rubbing my hands. " This is very piquant. I am much obliged to you for bringing us together. ' The proper study of mankind is man ', you know." ' You must study him, then,' Stamford said, as he bade me good-bye. " You'll find him a knotty problem, though. I'll wager he

learns more about you than you about him. Good-bye."

" Goodbye," I answered, and strolled on to my hotel, considerably interested in my new acquaintance.

CHAPTER II

THE SCIENCE OF DEDUCTION

We met next day as he had arranged, and inspected the rooms at No. 221B, Baker Street, of which he had spoken at our meeting. They consisted of a couple of comfortable bedrooms and a single large airy sitting-room, cheerfully furnished, and illuminated by two broad windows. So desirable in every way were the apartments, and so moderate did the terms seem when divided between us, that the bargain was concluded upon the spot, and we at once entered into possession. That very evening I moved my things round from the hotel, and on the following morning Sherlock Holmes followed me with several boxes and portmanteaux. For a day or two we were busily employed in unpacking and laying out our property to the best advantage. That done, we gradually began to settle down and to accommodate ourselves to our new surroundings.

Holmes was certainly not a difficult man to live with. He was quiet in his ways, and his habits were regular. It was rare for him to be up after ten at night, and he had invariably breakfasted and gone out before I rose in the morning. Sometimes he spent his day at the chemical laboratory, sometimes in the dissecting-rooms, and occasionally in long walks, which appeared to take him into the lowest portions of the city. Nothing could exceed his energy when the working fit was upon him; but now and again a reaction would seize him, and for days on end he would lie upon the sofa in the sitting-room, hardly uttering a word or moving a muscle from morning to night. On these occasions I have noticed such a dreamy, vacant expression in his eyes, that I might have suspected him of being addicted to the use of some narcotic, had not the temperance and cleanliness of his whole life forbidden such a notion.

As the weeks went by, my interest in him and my curiosity as to his aims in life gradually deepened and increased. His very person and appearance were such as to strike the attention of the most casual observer. In height he was rather over six feet, and so excessively lean that he seemed to be considerably taller. His eyes were sharp and piercing, save during those intervals of torpor to which I have alluded; and his thin, hawk-like nose gave his whole expression an air of alertness and decision. His chin, too, had the prominence and squareness which mark the man of determination. His hands were invariably blotted with ink and stained with chemicals, yet he was possessed of extraordinary delicacy of touch, as I frequently had occasion to observe when I watched him manipulating his fragile philosophical instruments.

The reader may set me down as a hopeless busybody, when I confess how much this man stimulated my curiosity, and how often I endeavoured to break through the reticence which he showed on all that concerned himself. Before pronouncing judgment, however, be it remembered how objectless was my life, and how little there was to engage my attention. My health forbade me from venturing out unless the weather was exceptionally genial, and I had no friends who would call upon me and break the monotony of my daily existence. Under these circumstances I eagerly hailed the little mystery which hung around my companion, and spent much of my time in endeavouring to unravel it.

He was not studying medicine. He had himself, in reply to a question, confirmed Stamford's opinion upon that point. Neither did he appear to have pursued any course of reading which might fit him for a degree in science or any other recognized portal which would give him an entrance into the learned world. Yet this zeal for certain studies was remarkable, and within eccentric limits his knowledge was so extraordinarily ample and minute that his observations have fairly astounded me. Surely no man would work so hard or attain such precise information unless he had some definite end in view. Desultory readers are seldom remarkable for the exactness of their learning. No man burdens his mind with small matters unless he has some very good reason for doing so.

His ignorance was as remarkable as his knowledge. Of contemporary literature, philosophy and politics he appeared to know next to nothing. Upon my quoting Thomas Carlyle, he inquired in the naivest way who he might be and what he had done. My surprise reached a climax, however, when I found incidentally that he was ignorant of the Copernican Theory and of the composition of the Solar System. That any civilized human being in this nineteenth century should not be aware that the earth travelled round the sun appeared to be to me such an extraordinary fact that I could hardly realize it.

" You appear to be astonished," he said, smiling at my expression of surprise. " Now that I do know it I shall do my best to forget it."

" To forget it ! "

" You see," he explained, " I consider that a man's brain originally is like a little empty attic, and you have to stock it with such furniture as you choose. A fool takes in all the lumber of every sort that he comes across, so that the knowledge which might be useful to him gets crowded out, or at best is jumbled up with a lot of other things, so that he has a difficulty in laying his hands upon it. Now the skilful workman is very careful indeed as to what he takes into his brain-attic. He will have nothing but the tools which may help him in doing his work, but of these he has a large assortment, and all in the most perfect order. It is a mistake to think that that little room has elastic walls and can distend to any extent. Depend upon it there comes a time when for every addition of knowledge you forget something that you knew before. It is of the highest importance, therefore, not to have useless facts elbowing out the useful ones."

" But the Solar System ! " I protested.

" What the deuce is it to me ? " he interrupted impatiently; " you say that we go round the sun. If we went round the moon it would not make a pennyworth of difference to me or to my work."

I was on the point of asking him what that work might be, but something in his manner showed me that the question would be an unwelcome one. I pondered over our short conversation, however, and endeavoured to draw my deductions from it. He said that he would acquire no knowledge which did not bear upon his object. Therefore all the knowledge which he possessed was such as would be useful to him. I enumerated in my own mind all the various points upon which he had shown me that he was exceptionally well-informed. I even took a pencil and jotted them down. I could not help smiling at the document when I had completed it. It ran this way:—

SHERLOCK HOLMES—his limits

1. Knowledge of Literature.—Nil.
2.   „   „   Philosophy.—Nil.
3.   „   „   Astronomy.—Nil.

4.　　　„　　„　Politics.—Feeble.
5.　　　„　　„　Botany.—Variable.
Well up in belladonna, opium, and poisons generally. Knows nothing of practical gardening.
6. Knowledge of Geology.—Practical, but limited. Tells at a glance different soils from each other. After walks has shown me splashes upon his trousers, and told me by their colour and consistence in what part of London he had received them.
7. Knowledge of Chemistry.—Profound.
8.　　　„　　„　Anatomy.—Accurate, but un-systematic.
9.　　　„　　„　Sensational Literature.—Immense. He appears to know every detail of every horror perpetrated in the century.
10. Plays the violin well.
11. Is an expert singlestick player, boxer, and swordsman.
12. Has a good practical knowledge of British law.

When I had got so far in my list I threw it into the fire in despair. " If I can only find what the fellow is driving at by reconciling all these accomplishments, and discovering a calling which needs them all," I said to myself, " I may as well give up the attempt at once."

I see that I have alluded above to his powers upon the violin. These were very remarkable, but as eccentric as all his other accomplishments. That he could play pieces, and difficult pieces, I knew well, because at my request he has played me some of Mendelssohn's Lieder, and other favourites. When left to himself, however, he would seldom produce any music or attempt any recognizing air. Leaning back in his armchair of an evening, he would close his eyes and scrape carelessly at the fiddle which was thrown across his knee. Sometimes the chords were sonorous and melancholy. Occasionally they were fantastic and cheerful. Clearly they reflected the thoughts which possessed him, but whether the music aided those thoughts, or whether playing was simply the result of a whim or fancy, was more than I could determine. I might have rebelled against these exasperating solos had it not been that he usually terminated them by playing in quick succession a whole series of my favourite airs as a slight compensation for the trial upon my patience.

During the first week or so we had no callers, and I had begun to think that my companion was as friendless a man as I was myself. Presently, however, I found that he had many acquaintances, and those in the most different classes of society. There was one little sallow, rat-faced, dark eyed fellow, who was introduced to me as Mr. Lestrade, and who came three or four times in a single week. One morning a young girl called, fashionably dressed, and stayed for half an hour or more. The same afternoon brought a grey-headed, seedy visitor, looking like a Jew pedlar, who appeared to me to be much excited, and who was closely followed by a slip-shod elderly woman. On another occasion an old white-haired gentleman had an interview with my companion; and on another, a railway porter in his velveteen uniform. When any of these nodescript individuals put in an appearance, Sherlock Holmes used to beg for the use of the sitting-room, and I would retire to my bedroom. He always apologized to me for putting me to this inconvenience. " I have to use this room as a place of business," he said, " and these people are my clients." Again I had an opportunity of asking him a point-blank question, and yet again my delicacy prevented me from forcing another man to confide in me. I imagined at the time that he had some strong reason for not alluding to it, but he soon dispelled the idea by coming round to the subject of his own accord.

It was upon the 4th of March, as I have good reason to remember, that I rose somewhat earlier than usual, and found that Sherlock Holmes had not yet finished his breakfast. The landlady had become so accustomed to my late habits that my place had not been laid nor my coffee prepared. With the unreasonable petulance of mankind I rang the bell and gave a curt intimation that I was ready. Then I picked up a magazine from the table and attempted to while away the time with it, while my companion munched silently at his toast. One of the articles had a pencil mark at the heading, and I naturally began to run my eye thought it.

Its somewhat ambitious title was " The Book of Life," and it attempted to show how much an observant man might learn by an accurate and systematic examination of all that came in his way. It struck me as being a remarkable mixture of shrewdness and of absurdity. The reasoning was close and intense, but the deductions appeared to me to be far-fetched and exaggerated. The writer claimed by a momentary expression, a twitch of a muscle or a glance of an eye, to fathom a man's inmost thoughts. Deceit, according to him, was an impossibility in the case of one trained to observation and analysis. His conclusions were as infallible as so many propositions of Euclid. So startling would his results appear to the uninitiated that until they learned the processes by which he had arrived at them they might well consider him as a necro-mancer.

"From a drop of water," said the writer, "a logician could infer the possibility of an Atlantic or a Niagara without having seen or heard of one or the other. So all life is a great chain, the nature of which is known whenever we are shown a single link of it. Like all other arts, the Science of Deduction and Analysis is one which can only be acquired by long and patient study, nor is life long enough to allow any mortal to attain the highest possible perfection in it. Before turning to these moral and mental aspects of the matter which present the greatest difficulties, let the inquirer begin by mastering more elementary problems. Let him on meeting a fellow-mortal, learn at a glance to distinguish the history of the man, and the trade or profession to which he belongs. Puerile as such an exercise may seem, it sharpens the faculties of observation, and teaches one where to look and what to look for. By a man's finger-nails, by his coat-sleeve, by his boot, by his trouser-knees, by the callosities of his forefinger and thumb, by his expression, by his shirt-cuffs—by each of these things a man's calling is plainly revealed. That all united should fail to enlighten the competent inquirer in any case is almost inconceivable."

"What ineffable twaddle!" I cried, slapping the magazine down on the table; "I never read such rubbish in my life."

"What is it?" asked Sherlock Holmes.

"Why, this article," I said, pointing at it with my egg-spoon as I sat down to my breakfast. "I see that you have read it since you have marked it. I don't deny that it is smartly written. It irritates me, though. It is evidently the theory of some arm-chair lounger who evolves all these neat little paradoxes in the seclusion of his own study. It is not practical. I should like to see him clapped down in a third-class carriage on the Underground, and asked to give the trades of all his fellow-travellers. I would lay a thousand to one against him."

"You would lose your money," Holmes remarked calmly. "As for the article, I wrote it myself."

"You!"

"Yes; I have a turn both for observation and for deduction. The theories which I have expressed there and which appear to you to be so chimerical are really extremely practical—so practical that I depend upon them for my bread and cheese."

"And how?" I asked involuntarily.

"Well, I have a trade of my own. I suppose I am the only one in the world. I'm a consulting detective, if you can understand what that is. Here in London we have lots of Government detectives and lots of private ones. When these fellows are at fault, they come to me, and I manage to put them on the right scent. They lay all the evidence before me, and I am generally able, by the help of my knowledge of the history of crime, to set them straight. There is a strong family resemblance about misdeeds, and if you have all the details of a thousand at your finger ends, it is odd if you can't unravel the thousand and first. Lestrade is a well-known detective. He got himself into a fog recently over a forgery case, and that was what brought him here."

"And these other people?"

"They are mostly sent on by private inquiry agencies. They are all people who are in trouble about something and want a little enlightenment. I listen to their story, they listen to my comments, and then I pocket my fee."

"But do you mean to say," I said, "that without leaving your room you can unravel some knot which other men can make nothing of, although they have seen every detail for themselves?"

"Quite so. I have a kind of intuition that way. Now and again a case turns up which is a little more complex. Then I have to bustle about and see things with my own eyes. You see I have a lot of special knowledge which I apply to the problem, and which facilitates matters wonderfully. Those rules of deduction laid down in that article which aroused your scorn are invaluable to me in practical work. Observation with me is second nature. You appeared to be surprised when I told you, on our first meeting, that you had come from Afghanistan."

"You were told, no doubt."

"Nothing of the sort. I *knew* you came from Afghanistan. From long habit the train of thoughts ran so swiftly through my mind that I arrived at the conclusion without being conscious of intermediate steps. There were such steps, however. The train of reasoning ran: ' Here is a gentleman of a medical type, but with the air of a military man. Clearly an army doctor then. He has just come from the tropics, for his face is dark, and that is not the natural tint of his skin, for his wrists are fair. He has undergone hardship and sickness, as his haggard face says clearly. His left arm has been injured. He holds it in a still and unnatural manner. Where in the tropics could an English army doctor have seen much hardship and got his arm wounded ? Clearly in Afghanistan.' The whole train of thought did not occupy a second. I then remarked that you came from Afghanistan, and you were astonished."

" It is simple enough as you explain it," I said, smiling. " You remind me of Edgar Allan Poe's Dupin. I had no idea that such individuals did exist outside of stories."

Sherlock Holmes rose and lit his pipe. " No doubt you think that you are complimenting me in comparing me to Dupin," he observed. "Now, in my opinion, Dupin was a very inferior fellow. That trick of his of breaking in on his friends' thoughts with an apropos remark after a quarter of an hour's silence is really very showy and superficial. He had some analytical genius, no doubt; but he was by no means such a phenomenon as Poe appeared to imagine."

" Have you read Gaboriau's works ? " I asked. " Does Lecoq come up to your idea of a detective ? "

Sherlock Holmes sniffed sardonically. " Lecoq was a miserable bungler," he said, in an angry voice; " he had only one thing to recommend him, and that was his energy. That book made me positively ill. The question was how to identify an unknown prisoner. I could have done it in twenty-four hours. Lecoq took six months or so. It might be made a text-book for detectives to teach them what to avoid."

I felt rather indignant at having two characters whom I had admired treated in this cavalier style. I walked over to the window, and stood looking out into the busy street. " This fellow may be very clever," I said to myself, " but he is certainly very conceited."

" There are no crimes and no criminals in these days," he said, querulously. " What is the use of having brains in our profession ? I know well that I have it in me to make my name famous. No man lives or has ever lived who has brought the same amount of study and of natural talent to the detection of crime which I have done. And what is the result? There is no crime to detect, or, at most, some bungling villainly with a motive so transparent that even a Scotland Yard official can see through it."

I was still annoyed at his bumptious style of conversation. I thought it best to change the topic.

" I wonder what that fellow is looking for ? " I asked, pointing to a stalwart, plainly-dressed individual who was walking slowly down the other side of the street, looking anxiously at the numbers. He had a large blue envelope in his hand, and was evidently the bearer of a message.

" You mean the retired sergeant of Marines," said Sherlock Holmes.

" Brag and bounce ! " thought I to myself. " He knows that I cannot verify his guess."

The thought had hardly passed through my mind when the man whom we were watching caught sight of the number on our door, and ran rapidly across the roadway. We heard a loud knock, a deep voice below, and heavy steps ascending the stair.

" For Mr. Sherlock Holmes," he said, stepping into the room and handing my friend the letter.

Here was an opportunity of taking the conceit out of him. He little thought of this when he made that random shot. " May I ask, my lad," I said, in the blandest voice, " what your trade may be ? "

" Commissionaire, sir," he said, gruffly. " Uniform away for repairs."

" And you were ? " I asked, with a slightly malicious glance at my companion.

" A sergeant, sir, Royal Marine Light Infantry sir. No answer ? Right, sir."

He clicked his heels together, raised his hand in a salute, and was gone.

CHAPTER III

THE LAURISTON GARDENS MYSTERY

I confess that I was considerably startled by this fresh proof of the practical nature of my companion's theories. My respect for his powers of analysis increased wondrously. There still remained some lurking suspicion in my mind, however, that the whole thing was a prearranged episode, intended to dazzle me, though what earthly object he could have in taking me in was past my comprehension. When I looked at him, he had finshed reading the note, and his eyes had assumed the vacant, lack-lustre expression which showed mental abstraction.

"How in the world did you deduce that?" I asked.

"Deduce what?" said he, petulantly.

"Why, that he was a retired sergeant of Marines."

"I have no time for trifles," he answered brusquely. Then with a smile: "Excuse my rudeness. You broke the thread of my thoughts; but perhaps it is as well. So you actually were not able to see that that man was a sergeant of Marines?"

"No, indeed."

"It was easier to know it than to explain why I know it. If you were asked to prove that two and two made four, you might find some difficulty, and yet you are quite sure of the fact. Even across the street I could see a great blue anchor tattooed on the back of the fellow's hand. That smacked of the sea. He had a military carriage, however, and regulation side whiskers. There we have the marine. He was a man with some amount of self-importance and a certain air of command. You must have observed the way in which he held his head and swung his cane. A steady respectable, middle-aged man, too, on the face of him—all facts which led me to believe that he had been a sergeant."

"Wonderful!" I ejaculated.

"Commonplace," said Holmes, though I thought from his expression that he was pleased at my evident suprise and admiration. "I said just now that there were no criminals. It appears that I am wrong—look at this!" He threw me over the note which the commissionaire had brought.

"Why," I cried, as I cast my eye over it, "this is terrible!"

"It does seem to be a little out of the common," he remarked, calmly. "Would you mind reading it to me aloud?"

This is the letter which I read to him:—

"My dear Mr. Sherlock Holmes, There has been a bad business during the night at 3 Lauriston Gardens, off the Brixton Road. Our man on the beat saw a light there about two in the morning, and as the house was an empty one, suspected that something was amiss. He found the door open, and in the front room, which is bare of furniture, discovered the body of a gentleman, well dressed and having cards in his pocket bearing the name of 'Enoch J. Dreb-ber, Cleveland, Ohio, U.S.A.' There had been no robbery, nor is there any evidence as to how the man met his death. There are marks of blood in the room, but there is no wound upon his person. We are at a loss as to how he came into the empty house; indeed the whole affair is a puzzler. If you can come round to the house any time before twelve, you will find me there. I have left everything in *status quo* until I hear from you. If you are unable to come, I shall give you fuller details, and would esteem it a great kindness if you would favour me with your opinion. Yours faithfully, TOBIAS GREGSON."

"Gregson is the smartest of the Scotland Yarders," my friend remarked; "he and Lestrade are the pick of a bad lot. They are both quick and energetic, but conventional—shockingly so. They have their knives into one another, too. They are as jealous as a pair of professional beauties. There will be some fun over this case if they are both put upon the scent."

I was amazed at the calm way in which he rippled on. "Surely there is not a moment to be lost," I cried; "shall I go and order you a cab?"

"I'm not sure about whether I shall go. I am the most incurably lazy devil that ever stood in shoe leather—that is, when the fit is on me, for I can be spry enough at times."

"Why, it is just such a chance as you have been longing for."

"My dear fellow, what does it matter to me? Supposing I unravel the whole matter, you may be sure that Gregson, Lestrade, and Co. will pocket all the credit. That comes of being an unofficial personage."

"But he begs you to help him."

"Yes. He knows that I am his superior, and acknowledges it to me; but he would cut his tongue out before he would own it to any third person. However, we may as well go and have a look. I shall work it out on my own hook. I may have a laugh at them, if I have nothing else. Come on!"

He hustled on his overcoat, and bustled about in a way that showed that an energetic fit had superseded the apathetic one.

"Get your hat," he said.

"You wish me to come?"

"Yes, if you have nothing better to do." A minute later we were both in a hansom, driving furiously to the Brixton Road.

It was a foggy, cloudy morning, and a dun-coloured veil hung over the house-tops, looking like the reflection of the mud-coloured streets beneath. My companion was in the best of spirits, and prattled away about Cremona fiddles, and the difference between a Stradivarius and an Amati. As for myself, I was silent, for the dull weather and the melancholy business upon which we were engaged, depressed my spirits.

"You don't seem to give much thought to the matter in hand," I said at last, interrupting Holmes' musical disquisition.

"No data yet," he answered. "It is a capital mistake to theorize before you have all the evidence. It biases the judgment."

"You will have your data soon," I remarked, pointing with my finger; "this is the Brixton Road, and that is the house, if I am not very much mistaken."

"So it is. Stop, driver, stop!" We were still a hundred yards or so from it, but he insisted upon our alighting, and we finished our journey upon foot.

Number 3, Lauriston Gardens, wore an ill-omened and minatory look. It was one of four which stood back some little way from the street, two being occupied and two empty. The latter looked out with three tiers of vacant melancholy windows, which were black and dreary, save that here and there a "To Let" card had developed like a cataract upon the bleared panes. A small garden sprinkled over with a scattered eruption of sickly plants separated each of these houses from the street, and was traversed by a narrow pathway, yellowish in colour, and consisting apparently of a mixture of clay and gravel. The whole place was very sloppy from the rain which had fallen through the night. The garden was bounded by a three-foot brick wall with a fringe of wood rails upon the top, and against this wall was leaning a stalwart police constable, surrounded by a small knot of loafers, who craned their necks and strained their eyes in the vain hope of catching some glimpse of the proceedings within.

I had imagined that Sherlock Holmes would at once have hurried into the house and plunged into a study of the mystery. Nothing appeared to be further from his intention. With an air of nonchalance which, under the circumstances, seemed to me to border upon affectation, he lounged up and down the pavement, and gazed vacantly at the ground, the sky, the opposite houses and the line of railings. Having finished his scrutiny, he proceeded slowly down the path, or rather down the fringe of grass which flanked the path, keeping his eyes riveted upon the ground. Twice he stopped and once I saw him smile, and heard him utter an exclamation of satisfaction. There were many marks of footsteps upon the wet clayey soil; but since the police had been coming and going over it, I was unable to see how my companion could hope to learn anything from it. Still, I had had such extraordinary evidence of the quickness of his perceptive faculties, that I had no doubt that he could see a great deal which was hidden from me.

At the door of the house we were met by a tall, white-faced, flaxed-haired man, with a notebook in his hand, who rushed forward and wrung my companion's hand with effusion. "It is indeed kind of you to come," he said, "I have had everything left untouched."

"Except that!" my friend answered, pointing at the pathway. "If a herd of buffaloes had passed along there could not be a greater mess. No doubt, however, you had drawn your own conclusions, Gregson, before you permitted this."

"I have had so much to do inside the house," the detective said evasively. "My colleague, Mr. Lestrade, is here. I had relied upon him to look after this."

Holmes glanced at me and raised his eyebrows sardonically. "With two such men as yourself and Lestrade upon the ground, there will not be much for a third party to find out," he said.

Gregson rubbed his hands in a self-satisfied way: "I think we have done all that can be done," he answered; "it's a queer case though, and I knew your taste for such things."

"You did not come here in a cab?" asked Sherlock Holmes.

"No sir."

"Then let us go and look at the room." With which inconsequent remark he strode on into the house, followed by Gregson, whose features expressed his astonishment.

A short passage, bare-planked and dusty, led to the kitchen and offices. Two doors opened out of it to the left and to the right. One of these had obviously been closed for many weeks. The other belonged to the dining-room, which was the apartment in which the mysterious affair had occurred. Holmes walked in, and I followed him with that subdued feeling at my heart which the presence of death inspires.

It was a large square room, looking all the larger from the absence of furniture. A vulgar flaring paper adorned the walls, but it was blotched in places with mildew, and here and there great strips had become detached and hung down, exposing the yellow plaster beneath. Opposite the door was a showy fireplace, surmounted by a mantlepiece of imitation white marble. On one corner of this was stuck the stump of a red wax candle. The solitary window was so dirty that the light was hazy and uncertain, giving a dull grey tinge to everything, which was intensified by the thick layer of dust which coated the whole apartment.

All these details I observed afterwards. At present my attention was centered upon the single, grim, motionless figure which lay stretched upon the boards, with vacant, sightless eyes staring up at the discoloured ceiling. It was that of a man about forty-three or forty-four years of age, middle-sized, broad-shouldered, with crisp curling black hair, and a short, stubbly beard. He was dressed in a heavy broad-cloth frock coat and waistcoat, with light coloured trousers, and immaculate collar and cuffs. A top hat, well brushed and trim, was placed upon the floor beside him. His hands were clenched and his arms thrown abroad, while his lower limbs were interlocked, as though his death struggle had been a grievous one. On his rigid face there stood an expression of horror, and, as it seemed to me, of hatred, such as I have never seen upon human features. This malignant and terrible con-tortion, combined with the low forehead, blunt nose, and prognathous jaw, gave the dead man a singularly simious and ape-like appearance, which was increased by his writhing, unnatural posture. I have seen death in many forms, but never has it appeared to me in a more fearsome aspect than in that dark, grimy apartment, which looked out upon one of the main arteries of surburban London.

Lestrade, lean and ferret-like as ever, was standing by the doorway, and greeted my companion and myself.

" This case will make a stir, sir," he remarked. " It beats anything I have seen, and I am no chicken."

" There is no clue ? " said Gregson.

" None at all," chimed in Lestrade.

Sherlock Holmes approached the body, and, kneeling down, examined it intent-ly. " You are sure that there is no wound ? " he asked, pointing to numerous gouts and splashes of blood which lay all round.

" Positive ! " cried both detectives.

" Then, of course, this blood belongs to a second individual—presumably the murder-er, if murder has been committed. It re-minds me of the circumstances attendant on the death of Van Jansen, in Utrecht, in the year '34. Do you remember the case, Greg-son ? "

" No, sir."

" Read it up—you really should. There is nothing new under the sun. It has all been done before."

As he spoke, his nimble fingers were flying here, there, and everywhere, feeling, press-ing, unbuttoning, examining, while his eyes wore the same faraway expression which I have already remarked upon. So swiftly was the examination made, that one would hardly have guessed the minuteness with which it was conducted. Finally, he sniffed the dead man's lips, and then glanced at the soles of his patent leather boots.

" He has not been moved at all ? " he asked.

" No more than was necessary for the purposes of our examination."

" You can take him to the mortuary now," he said. " There is nothing more to be learned."

Gregson had a stretcher and four men at hand. At his call they entered the room, and the stranger was lifted and carried out. As they raised him, a ring tinkled down and rolled across the floor. Lestrade grabbed it up and stared at it with mystified eyes.

" There's been a woman here," he cried. " It's a woman's wedding-ring."

He held it out, as he spoke, upon the palm of his hand. We all gathered round him and gazed at it. There could be no doubt that the circlet of plain gold had once adorned the finger of a bride.

" This complicates matters," said Greg-son. " Heaven knows, they were compli-cated enough before."

" You're sure it doesn't simplify them ? " observed Holmes. " There's nothing to be learned by staring at it. What did you find in his pockets ? "

" We have it all here," said Gregson, pointing to a litter of objects upon one of the bottom steps of the stairs. " A gold watch, No. 97163, by Barraud of London. Gold Albert chain, very heavy and solid. Gold ring, with masonic device. Gold pin—bull-dog's head, with rubies as eyes. Russian leather card-case with cards of Enoch J. Drebber of Cleveland, corresponding with E.J.D. upon the linen. No purse, but loose money to the extent of seven pounds thir-teen. Pocket edition of Boccaccio's *De-cameron*, with name of Joseph Stangerson upon the fly-leaf. Two letters—one addres-sed to E. J. Drebber and one to Joseph Stangerson.

" At what address ? "

" American Exchange, Strand—to be left till called for. They are both from the Guion Steamship Company, and refer to the sailing of their boats from Liverpool. It is clear that this unfortunate man was about to return to New York."

" Have you made any inquiries as to this man Stangerson ? "

" I did it at once, sir," said Gregson. " I have had avertisements sent to all the newspapers, and one of my men has gone to the American Exchange, but he has not returned yet."

" Have you sent to Cleveland ? "

" We telegraphed this morning."

" How did you word your inquiries ? "

" We simply detailed the circumstances, and said that we should be glad of any information which could help us."

" You did not ask for particulars on any point which appeared to you to be crucial ? "

" I asked about Stangerson."

" Nothing else ? Is there no circumstance on which this whole case appears to hinge ? Will you not telegraph again ? "

" I have said all I have to say," said Gregson, in an offended voice.

Sherlock Holmes chuckled to himself, and appeared to be about to make some remark, when Lestrade, who had been in the front room while we were holding this conversation in the hall, reappeared upon the scene, rubbing his hands in a pompous and self-satisfied manner.

" Mr Gregson," he said, " I have just made a discovery of the highest importance, and one which would have been overlooked had I note made a careful examination of the walls."

The little man's eyes sparkled as he spoke, and he was evidently in a state of suppressed exultation of having scored a point against his colleague.

" Come here," he said, bustling back into the room, the atmosphere of which felt clearer since the removal of its ghastly inmate. " Now, stand there ! "

He struck a match on his boot and held it up against the wall.

" Look at that ! " he said, triumphantly.

I have remarked that the paper had fallen away in parts. In this particular corner of the room a large piece had peeled off, leaving a yellow square of coarse plastering. Across this bare space there was scrawled in blood-red letters a single word:—

RACHE

" What do you think of that ? " cried the detective, with the air of a showman exhibiting his show. " This was overlooked because it was in the darkest corner of the room, and no one thought of looking there. The murderer has written it with his or her own blood. See this smear where it has trickled down the wall ! That disposes of the idea of suicide anyhow. Why was that corner chosen to write it on ? I will tell you. See that candle on the mantelpiece. It was lit at the time, and if it was lit this corner would be the brightest instead of the darkest portion of the wall."

" And what does it mean now that you *have* found it ? " asked Gregson in a deprecatory voice.

" Mean ? Why, it means that the writer was going to put the female name Rachel, but was disturbed before he or she had time to finish. You mark my words, when this case comes to be cleared up you will find that a woman named Rachel has something to do with it. It's all very well for you to laugh, Mr. Sherlock Holmes. You may be very smart and clever, but the old hound is the best, when all is said and done."

" I really beg your pardon ! " said my companion, who had ruffled the little man's temper by bursting into an explosion of laughter. " You certainly have the credit of being the first of us to find this out and, as you say, it bears every mark of having been written by the other participant in last night's mystery. I have not had time to examine this room, yet, but with your permission I shall do so now."

As he spoke, he whipped a tape measure and a large round magnifying glass from his pocket. With these two implements he trotted noiselessly about the room, sometimes stopping, occasionally kneeling, and once lying flat upon his face. So engrossed was he with his occupation that he appeared to have forgotten our presence, for he chattered away to himself under his breath the whole time, keeping up a running fire of exclamations, groans, whistles, and little cries suggestive of encouragement and of hope. As I watched him I was irresistibly reminded of a pure-blooded, well-trained foxhound as it dashes backwards and forwards through the covert, whining in its eagerness, until it comes across the lost scent. For twenty minutes or more he continued his researches, measuring with the most exact care the distance between marks which were entirely invisible to me, and occasionally applying his tape to the walls in an equally incomprehensible manner. In one place he gathered up very carefully a little pile of grey dust from the floor, and packed it away in an envelope. Finally he examined with his glass the word upon the wall, going over every letter of it with the most minute exactness. This done, he appeared to be satisfied, for he replaced his tape and his glass in his pocket.

"They say that genius is an infinite capacity for taking pains," he remarked with a smile. "It's a very bad definition, but it does apply to detective work."

Gregson and Lestrade had watched the manoeuvres of their amateur companion with considerable curiosity and some contempt. They evidently failed to appreciate the fact, which I had begun to realize, that Sherlock Holmes' smallest actions were all directed towards some definite and practical end.

"What do you think of it, sir ? " they both asked.

"It would be robbing you of the credit of the case if I was to presume to help you," remarked my friend. "You are doing so well now that it would be a pity for anyone to interfere." There was a world of sarcasm in his voice as he spoke. "If you will let me know how your investigations go," he continued, "I shall be happy to give you any help I can. In the meantime I should like to speak to the constable who found the body. Can you give me his name and address ? "

Lestrade glanced at his notebook. "John Rance," he said. "He is off duty now. You will find him at 46, Audley Court, Kennington Park Gate."

Holmes took a note of the address.

"Come along, Doctor," he said, "we shall go and look him up. I'll tell you one thing which may help you in the case," he continued, turning to the two detectives. "There has been murder done, and the murderer was a man. He was more than six feet high, was in the prime of life, had small feet for his height, wore coarse, square-toed boots and smoked a Trichinopoly cigar. He came here with his victim in a four-wheeled cab, which was drawn by a horse with three old shoes and one new one on his off foreleg. In all probability the murderer had a florid face, and the fingernails of his right hand were remarkably long. These are only a few indications, but they may assist you."

Lestrade and Gregson, glanced at each other with an incredulous smile.

"If this man was murdered, how was it done ? " asked the former.

"Poison," said Sherlock Holmes curtly, and strode off. "One other thing, Lestrade," he added, turning round at the door, " 'Rache' is the German for 'revenge,' so don't lose your time by looking for Miss Rachel."

With which Parthian shot he walked away, leaving the two rivals open-mouthed behind him.

CHAPTER IV

WHAT JOHN RANCE HAD TO TELL

It was one o'clock when we left No. 3, Lauriston Gardens. Sherlock Holmes led me to the nearest telegraph office, whence he despatched a long telegram. He then hailed a cab, and ordered the driver to take us to the address give us by Lestrade.

"There is nothing like first-hand evidence," he remarked; "as a matter of fact, my mind is entirely made up upon the case, but still we may as well learn all that is to be learned."

"You amaze me, Holmes," said I. "Surely you are not as sure as you pretend to be of all those particulars which you gave."

"There's no room for mistake," he answered. "The very first thing which I observed on arriving there was that a cab had made two ruts with its wheels close to the kerb. Now, up to last night, we have had no rain for a week, so that those wheels which left such a deep impression must have been there during the night. There were the marks of the horse's hoof, too, the outline of one of which was far more clearly cut than that of the other three, showing that that was a new shoe. Since the cab was there after the rain began, and was not there at any time during the morning—I have Gregson's word for that— it follows that it must have been there during the night, and, therefore, that it brought those two individuals to the house."

"That seems simple enough," said I; "but how about the other man's height ? "

"Why, the height of a man, in nine cases out of ten, can be told from the length of his stride. It is a simple calculation enough, though there is no use my boring you with figures. I had this fellow's stride both on the clay outside and on the dust within. Then I had a way of checking my calculation. When a man writes on a wall, his instinct leads him to write about the level of his own eyes. Now that writing was just over six feet from the ground. It was child's play."

" And his age ? "

" Well, if a man can stride four and a half feet without the smallest effort, he can't be quite in the sere and yellow. That was the breadth of a puddle on the garden walk which he had evidently walked across. Patent-leather boots had gone round, and Square-toes had hopped over. There is no mystery about it at all. I am simply applying to ordinary life a few of those precepts of observation and deduction which I advocated in that article. Is there anything else that puzzles you ? "

" The finger-nails and the Trichinopoly," I suggested.

" The writing on the wall was done with a man's forefinger dipped in blood. My glass allowed me to observe that the plaster was slightly scratched in doing it, which would not have been the case if the man's nail had been trimmed. I gathered up some scattered ash from the floor. It was dark in colour and flakey—such an ash as is only made by a Trichinopoly. I have made a special study of cigar ashes—in fact, I have written a monograph upon the subject. I flatter myself that I can distinguish at a glance the ash of any known brand either of cigar or of tobacco. It is just in such details that the skilled detective differs from the Gregson and Lestrade type."

" And the florid face ? " I asked.

" Ah, that was a more daring shot, though I have no doubt that I was right. You must not ask me that at the present state of the affair."

I passed my hand over my brow. " My head is in a whirl," I remarked; " the more one thinks of it the more mysterious it grows. How came these two men—if there were two men—into an empty house ? What has become of the cabman who drove them ? How could one man compel another to take poison ? Where did the blood come from ? What was the object of the murderer, since robbery had no part in it ? How came the woman's ring there ? Above all, why should the second man write up the German word RACHE before decamping ? I confess that I cannot see any possible way of reconciling all these facts."

My companion smiled approvingly.

" You sum up the difficulties of the situation succinctly and well," he said. " There is much that is still obscure, though I have quite made up my mind on the main facts. As to poor Lestrade's discovery, it was simply a blind intended to put the police upon the wrong track, by suggesting Socialism and secret societies. It was not done by a German. The A, if you noticed, was printed somewhat after the German fashion. Now, a real German invariably prints in the Latin character, so that we may safely say that this was not written by one, but by a clumsy imitator who overdid his part. It was simply a ruse to divert inquiry into a wrong channel. I'm not going to tell you much more of the case, Doctor. You know a conjurer gets no credit once he has explained his trick; and if I show you too much of my method of working, you will come to the conclusion that I am a very ordinary individual after all."

" I shall never do that," I answered; " you have brought detection as near an exact science as it ever will be brought in this world."

My companion flushed up with pleasure at my words, and the earnest way in which I uttered them. I had already observed that he was as sensitive to flattery on the score of his art as any girl could be of her beauty.

" I'll tell you one other thing," he said. " Patent-leathers and Square-toes came in the same cab, and they walked down the pathway together as friendly as possible—arm-in-arm, in all probability. When they got inside, they walked up and down the room—or rather, Patent-leathers stood still while Square-toes walked up and down. I could read all that in the dust; and I could read that as he walked he grew more and more excited. That is shown by the increased length of his strides. He was talking all the while, and working himself up, no doubt, into a fury. Then the tragedy occured. I've told you all I know myself now, for the rest is mere surmise and conjecture. We have a good working basis, however, on which to start. We must hurry up, for I want to go to Hallé's concert to hear Norman-Neruda this afternoon."

The conversation had occured while our cab had been treading its way through a long succession of dingy streets and dreary byways. In the dingiest and dreariest of them our driver suddenly came to a stand. " That's Audley Court in there," he said, pointing to a narrow slit in the line of dead-coloured brick. " You'll find me here when you come back."

Audley Court was not an attractive locality. The narrow passage led us into a quadrangle paved with flags and lined by sordid dwellings. We picked our way through lines of discoloured linen, until we came to Number 46, the door of which was decorated with a small slip of brass on which the name Rance was engraved. On inquiry we found that the constable was in bed, and we were shown into a little front parlour to await his coming.

He appeared presently, looking a little irritable at being disturbed in his slumbers. "I made my report at the office," he said.

Holmes took a half-sovereign from his pocket and played with it pensively. "We thought that we should like to hear it all from your own lips," he said.

"I shall be most happy to tell you anything I can," the constable answered, with his eyes upon the little golden disc.

"Just let us hear it all in your own way as it occured."

"I'll tell it ye from the beginning," he said. "My time is from ten at night to six in the morning. At eleven there was a fight at the White Hart; but bar that it was quiet enough on the beat. At one o'clock it began to rain, and I met Harry Murcher—him who has the Holland Grove beat—and we stood together at the corner of Henrietta Street-a-talkin'. Presently—maybe about two or a little after—I thought I would take a look round and see that all was right down the Brixton Road. It was precious dirty and lonely. Not a soul did I meet all the way down, though a cab or two went past me. I was a-strollin' down, thinkin' between ourselves how uncommon handy a four of gin hot would be, when suddenly the glint of a light caught my eye in the window of that same house. Now, I knew that them two houses in Lauriston Gardens was empty on account of him that owns them who won't have the drains seen to, though the very last tenant what lived in one of them died o' typhoid fever. I was knocked all in a heap, therefore, at seeing a light in the window, and I suspected as something was wrong. When I got to the door——"

"You stopped, and then walked back to the garden gate," my companion interrupted. "What did you do that for?"

Rance gave a violent jump, and stared at Sherlock Holmes with the utmost amazement upon his features.

"Why, that's true, sir," he said; "though how you come to know it, Heaven only knows. Ye see when I got up to the door, it was so still and lonesome, that I thought I'd be none the worse for someone with me. I ain't afeard of anything on this side o' the grave; but I thought that maybe it was him that died o' the typhoid inspecting the drains

what killed him. The thought gave me a kind o' turn, and I walked back to the gate to see if I could see Murcher's lantern, but there wasn't no sign of him nor of anyone else."

"There was no one in the street?"

"Not a livin' soul, sir, nor as much as a dog. Then I pulled myself together and went back and pushed the door open. All was quiet inside, so I went into the room where the light was a-burnin'. There was a candle flickerin' on the mantelpiece—a red wax one—and by its light I saw——"

"Yes, I know all that you saw. You walked round the room several times, and you knelt down by the body, and then you walked through and tried the kitchen door, and then——"

John Rance sprang to his feet with a frightened face and suspicion in his eyes. "Where was you hid to see all that?" he cried. "It seems to me that you know a deal more than you should."

Holmes laughed and threw his card across the table to the constable. "Don't get arresting me for the murder," he said. "I am one of the hounds and not the wolf; Mr. Gregson or Mr. Lestrade will answer for that. Go on, though. What did you do next?"

Rance resumed his seat, without, however, losing his mystified expression. "I went back to the gate and sounded my whistle. That brought Murcher and two more to the spot."

"Was the street empty then?"

"Well, it was, as far as anybody that could be of any good goes."

"What do you mean?"

The constable's features broaded into a grin. "I've seen many a drunk chap in my time," he said, "but never anyone so cryin' drunk as that cove. He was at the gate when I came out a-leanin' up ag'in the railings, and a-singin' at the pitch o' his lungs about Columbine's New-fangled Banner, or such stuff. He couldn't stand, far less help."

"What sort of man was he?" asked Sherlock Holmes.

John Rance appeared to be somewhat irritated at this digression. "He was an uncommon drunk sort o'man," he said. "He'd ha' found hisself in the station if we hadn't been so took up."

"His face—his dress—didn't you notice them?" Holmes broke in impatiently.

"I should think I did notice them, seeing that I had to prop him up—me and Murcher between us. He was a long chap, with a red face, the lower part muffled round——"

" That will do," cried Holmes. "What became of him ? "

" We'd enough to do without lookin' after him," the policeman said, in an aggrieved voice "I'll wager he found his way home all right."

" How was he dressed ? "

" A brown overcoat."

" Had he a whip in his hand ? "

" A whip—no."

" He must have left it behind," muttered my companion.

" You didn't happen to see or hear a cab after that ? "

" No."

" There's a half-sovereign for you," my companion said, standing up and taking his hat. " I am afraid, Rance, that you will never rise in the force. That head of yours should be for use as well as ornament. You might have gained your sergeant's stripes last night. The man whom you held in your hands is the man who holds the clue of this mystery, and whom we are seeking. There is no use of arguing about it now; I tell you that it is so. Come along, Doctor."

We started off for the cab together, leaving our informant incredulous, but obviously uncomfortable.

" The blundering fool ! " Holmes said, bitterly, as we drove back to our lodgings. " Just to think of his having such an incomparable bit of luck, and not taking advantage of it."

" I am rather in the dark still. It is true that the description of this man tallies with your idea of the second party in this mystery. But why should he come back to the house after leaving it ? That is not the way of criminals."

" The ring, man, the ring: that was what he came back for. If we have no other way of catching him, we can always bait our line with the ring. I shall have him, Doctor—I'll lay you two to one that I have him. I must thank you for it all. I might not have gone but for you, and so have missed the finest study I ever came across: a study in scarlet, eh ? Why shouldn't we use a little art jargon ? There's the scarlet thread of murder running through the colourless skein of life, and our duty is to unravel it, and isolate it, and expose every inch of it. And now for lunch, and then Norman-Neruda. Her attack and her bowing are splendid. What's that little thing of Chopin's she plays so magnificently: Tra-la-la-lira-lira-lay."

Leaning back in the cab, this amateur bloodhound carolled away like a lark while I meditated upon the many-sidedness of the human mind.

CHAPTER V

OUR ADVERTISEMENT BRINGS A VISITOR

Our morning's exertions had been too much for my weak health, and I was tired out in the afternoon. After Holmes' departure for the concert, I lay down upon the sofa and endeavoured to get a couple of hours' sleep. It was a useless attempt. My mind had been too much excited by all that had occurred, and the strangest fancies and surmises crowded into it. Every time that I closed my eyes I saw before me the distorted, baboon-like countenance of the murdered man. So sinister was the impression which that face had produced upon me that I found it difficult to feel anything but gratitude for him who had removed its owner from the world. If ever human features bespoke vice of the most malignant type, they were certainly those of Enoch J. Drebber, of Cleveland. Still, I recognized that justice must be done, and that the depravity of the victim was no condonement in the eyes of the law.

The more I thought of it the more extraordinary did my companion's hypothesis that the man had been poisoned, appear. I remembered how he had sniffed his lips, and had no doubt that he had detected something which had given rise to the idea. Then, again, if not poison, what had caused the man's death, since there was neither wound nor marks of strangulation? But, on the other hand, whose blood was that which lay so thickly upon the floor? There were no signs of a struggle, nor had the victim any weapon with which he might have wounded an antagonist. As long as all these questions were unsolved, I felt that sleep would be no easy matter, either for Holmes or myself. His quiet, self-confident manner convinced me that he had already formed a theory which explained all the facts, though what it was I could not for an instant conjecture.

He was very late in returning—so late that I knew that the concert could not have detained him all the time. Dinner was on the table before he appeared.

" It was magnificent," he said, as he took his seat. " Do you remember what Darwin says about music ? He claims that the power of producing and appreciating it existed among the human race long before the power of speech was arrived at. Perhaps that is why we are so subtly influenced by it. There are vague memories in our souls of those misty centuries when the world was in its childhood."

" That's rather a broad idea," I remarked.

" One's ideas must be as broad as Nature if they are to interpret Nature," he answered. " What's the matter? You're not quite yourself. This Brixton Road affair has upset you."

" To tell the truth, it has," I said. " I ought to be more case-hardened after my Afghan experiences. I saw my own comrades hacked to pieces at Maiwand without losing my nerve."

" I can understand. There is a mystery about this which stimulates the imagination; where there is no imagination there is no horror. Have you seen the evening paper? "

" No."

" It gives a fairly good account of the affair. It does not mention the fact that when the man was raised up a woman's wedding-ring fell upon the floor. It is just as well it does not."

" Why? "

" Look at this advertisement," he answered. " I had one sent to every paper this morning immediately after the affair."

He threw the paper across to me and I glanced at the place indicated. It was the first announcement in the " Found " column. " In Brixton Road, this morning," it ran, " a plain gold wedding-ring, found in the roadway between the White Hart Tavern and Holland Grove. Apply Dr. Watson, 221B, Baker Street, between eight and nine this evening."

" Excuse me using your name," he said. " If I used my own, some of these dunderheads would recognize it and want to meddle in the affair."

" That is all right," I answered. " But supposing anyone applies, I have no ring."

" Oh yes, you have," said he, handing me one. " This will do very well. It is almost a fascimile."

" And who do you expect will answer this advertisement? "

" Why, the man in the brown coat—our florid friend with the square toes. If he does not come himself, he will send an accomplice."

" Would he not consider it as too dangerous? "

" Not at all. If my view of the case is

correct, and I have every reason to believe that it is, this man would rather risk anything than lose the ring. According to my notion he dropped it while stooping over Drebber's body, and did not miss it at the time. After leaving the house he discovered his loss and hurried back, but found the police already in possession, owing to his own folly in leaving the candle burning. He had to pretend to be drunk in order to allay the suspicions which might have been aroused by his appearance at the gate. Now put yourself in that man's place. On thinking the matter over, it must have occurred to him that it was possible that he had lost the ring in the road after leaving the house. What would he do then? He would eagerly look out for the evening papers in the hope of seeing it among the articles found. His eye, of course, would alight upon this. He would be overjoyed. Why should he fear a trap? There would be no reason in his eyes why the finding of the ring should be connected with the murder. He would come. He will come. You shall see him within an hour."

" And then? " I asked.

" Oh, you can leave me to deal with him then. Have you any arms? "

" I have my old service revolver and a few cartridges."

" You had better clean it and load it. He will be a desperate man; and though I shall take him unawares, it is as well to be ready for anything."

I went to my bedroom and followed his advice. When I returned with the pistol, the table had been cleared, and Holmes was engaged in his favourite occupation of scraping upon his violin.

" The plot thickens," he said, as I entered: " I have just had an answer to my American telegram. My view of the case is the correct one."

" And that is? " I asked eagerly.

" My fiddle would be the better for new strings," he remarked. " Put your pistol in your pocket. When the fellow comes, speak to him in an ordinary way. Leave the rest to me. Don't frighten him by looking at him too hard."

" It is eight o'clock now," I said, glancing at my watch.

" Yes. He will probably be here in a few minutes. Open the door slightly. That will do. Now put the key on the inside. Thank you! This is a queer old book I picked up at a stall yesterday—*De Jure inter Gentes*—published in Latin at Liège in the Lowlands, in 1642. Charles's head was still firm on his shoulders when this little brown-backed volume was struck off."

"Who is the printer?"

"Philippe de Croy, whoever he may have been. On the flyleaf, in very faded ink, is written 'Ex libris Gulielmi Whyte.' I wonder who William Whyte was. Some pragmatical seventeenth-century lawyer, I suppose. His writing has a legal twist about it. Here comes our man, I think."

As he spoke there was a sharp ring at the bell. Sherlock Holmes rose softly and moved his chair in the direction of the door. We heard the servant pass along the hall, and the sharp click of the latch as she opened it.

"Does Dr. Watson live here?" asked a clear but rather harsh voice. We could not hear the servant's reply, but the door closed, and someone began to ascend the stairs. The footfall was an uncertain and shuffling one. A look of surprise passed over the face of my companion as he listened to it. It came slowly along the passage, and there was a feeble tap at the door.

"Come in," I cried.

At my summons, instead of the man of violence whom we expected, a very old and wrinkled woman hobbled into the apartment. She appeared to be dazzled by the sudden blaze of light, and after dropping a curtsy, she stood blinking at us with her bleared eyes and fumbling in her pocket with nervous shaky fingers. I glanced at my companion, and his face had assumed such a disconsolate expression that it was all I could do to keep my countenance.

The old crone drew out an evening paper, and pointed at our advertisement. "It's this as has brought me, good gentlemen," she said, dropping another curtsy; "a gold wedding-ring in the Brixton Road. It belongs to my girl Sally, as was married only this time twelve-month, which her husband is steward aboard a Union boat, and what he'd say if he come 'ome and found her without her ring is more than I can think, he being short enough at the best o' times, but more especially when he has the drink. If it please you, she went to the circus last night along with——"

"Is that her ring?" I asked.

"The Lord be thanked!" cried the old woman; "Sally will be a glad woman this night. That's the ring."

"And what may your address be?" I inquired, taking up a pencil.

"13, Duncan Street, Houndsditch. A weary way from here."

"The Brixton Road does not lie between any circus and Houndsditch," said Sherlock Holmes sharply.

The old woman faced round and looked keenly at him from her little red-rimmed eyes. "The gentleman asked me for my address," she said. "Sally lives in lodgings at 3, Mayfield Place, Peckham."

"And your name is——?"

"My name is Sawyer—hers is Dennis, which Tom Dennis married her—and a smart, clean lad, too, as long as he's at sea, and no steward in the company more thought of; but when on shore, what with the women and what with liquor shops——"

"Here is your ring, Mrs. Sawyer," I interrupted, in obedience to a sign from my companion; "it clearly belongs to your daughter, and I am glad to be able to restore it to the rightful owner."

With many mumbled blessings and protestations of gratitude the old crone packed it away in her pocket, and shuffled off down the stairs. Sherlock Holmes sprang to his feet the moment she was gone and rushed into his room. He returned in a few seconds enveloped in an ulster and a cravat. "I'll follow her," he said hurriedly; "she must be an accomplice, and will lead me to him. Wait up for me." The hall door had hardly slammed behind our visitor before Holmes had descended the stair. Looking through the window I could see her walking feebly along the other side, while her pursuer dogged her some little distance behind. "Either his whole theory is incorrect," I though to myself, "or else he will be led now to the heart of the mystery." There was no need for him to ask me to wait up for him, for I felt that sleep was impossible until I heard the result of his adventure.

It was close upon nine when he set out. I had no idea how long he might be, but I sat stolidly puffing at my pipe and skipping over the pages of Henri Murger's *Vie de Bohème*. Ten o'clock passed, and I heard the footsteps of the maid as they pattered off to bed. Eleven, and the more stately tread of the landlady passed my door, bound for the same destination. It was close upon twelve before I heard the sharp sound of his latch-key. The instant he entered I saw by his face that he had not been successful. Amusement and chagrin seemed to be struggling for the mastery, until the former suddenly carried the day, and he burst into a hearty laugh.

"I wouldn't have the Scotland Yarders know it for the world," he cried, dropping into his chair: "I have chaffed them so much that they would never have let me hear the end of it. I can afford to laugh, because I know that I will be even with them in the long run."

" What is it then ? " I asked.

" Oh, I don't mind telling a story against myself. That creature had gone a little way when she began to limp and show every sign of being footsore. Presently she came to a halt, and hailed a four-wheeler which was passing. I managed to be close to her so as to hear the address, but I need not have been so anxious, for she sang it out loud enough to be heard the other side of the street: " Drive to 13, Duncan Street, Houndsditch," she cried. This begins to look genuine, I thought, and having seen her safely inside, I perched myself behind. That's an art which every detective should be an expert at. Well, away we rattled, and never drew rein until we reached the street in question. I hopped off before we came to the door, and strolled down the street in an easy lounging way. I saw the cab pull up. The driver jumped down, and I saw him open the door and stand expectantly. Nothing came out though. When I reached him, he was groping about frantically in the empty cab, and giving vent to the finest assorted collection of oaths that ever I listened to. There was no sign or trace of his passenger, and I fear it will be some time before he gets his fare. On inquiring at Number 13 we found the house belonged to a respectable paperhanger, named Keswick, and that no one of the name either of Sawyer or Dennis had ever been heard of there.

" You don't mean to say," I cried, in amazement, " that that tottering, feeble old woman was able to get out of the cab while it was in motion, without either you or the driver seeing her ? "

" Old woman be damned ! " said Sherlock Holmes, sharply. " We were the old women to be so taken in. It must have been a young man, and an active one, too, besides being an incomparable actor. The get-up was inimitable. He saw that he was followed, no doubt, and used this means of giving me the slip. It shows that the man we are after is not as lonely as I imagined he was, but has friends who are ready to risk something for him. Now, Doctor, you are looking done-up. Take my advice and turn in."

I was certainly feeling very weary, so I obeyed his injunction. I left Holmes seated in front of the smouldering fire, and long into the watches of the night I heard the low, melancholy wailings of his violin, and knew that he was still pondering over the strange problem which he had set himself to unravel.

CHAPTER VI

TOBIAS GREGSON SHOWS WHAT HE CAN DO

The papers next day were full of the " Brixton Mystery," as they termed it. Each had a long account of the affair, and some had leaders upon it in addition. There was some information in them which was new to me. I still retain in my scrap-book numerous clippings and extracts bearing upon the case. Here is a condensation of a few of them:—

The *Daily Telegraph* remarked that in the history of crime there had seldom been a tragedy which presented stranger features. The German name of the victim, the absence of all other motive, and the sinister inscription on the wall, all pointed to its perpetration by political refugees and revolutionists. The Socialists had many branches in America, and the deceased had, no doubt, infringed their unwritten laws, and been tracked down by them. After alluding airily to the Vehmgericht, aqua tofana, Carbonari, the Marchioness de Brinvilliers, the Darwinian theory, the principles of Malthus, and the Ratcliff Highway murders, the article concluded by admonishing the Government and advocating a closer watch over foreigners in England.

The *Standard* commented upon the fact that lawless outrages of the sort usually occurred under a Liberal Administration. They arose from the unsettling of the minds of the masses, and the consequent weakening of all authority. The deceased was an American gentleman who had been residing for some weeks in the Metropolis. He had stayed at the boarding-house of Madame Charpentier, in Torquay Terrace, Camberwell. He was accompanied in his travels by his private secretary, Mr. Joseph Stangerson. The two bade adieu to their landlady upon Tuesday, the 4th inst., and departed to Euston Station with the avowed intention of catching the Liverpool express. They were afterwards seen together upon the platform. Nothing more is known of them until Mr. Drebber's body was, as recorded, discovered in an empty house in the Brixton Road, many miles from Euston. How he came there, or how he met his fate, are questions which are still involved in mystery. Nothing is known of the whereabouts of Stangerson. We are glad to learn that Mr. Lestrade and Mr. Gregscn, of Scotland Yard, are both engaged upon the case, and it is confidently anticipated that these well-known officers will speedily throw light upon the matter.

The *Daily News* observed that there was no doubt as to the crime being a political one. The despotism and hatred of Liberalism which animated the Continental Governments had had the effect of driving to our shores a number of men who might have made excellent citizens were they not soured by the recollection of all that they had undergone. Among these men there was a stringent code of honour, any infringement of which was punished by death. Every effort should be made to find the secretary, Stangerson, and to ascertain some particulars of the habits of the deceased. A great step had been gained by the discovery of the address of the house at which he had boarded—a result which was entirely due to the acuteness and energy of Mr. Gregson of Scotland Yard.

Sherlock Holmes and I read these notices over together at breakfast, and they appeared to afford him considerable amusement.

" I told you that, whatever happened, Lestrade and Gregson would be sure to score."

" That depends on how it turns out."

" Oh, bless you, it doesn't matter in the least. If the man is caught, it will be *on account* of their exertions; if he escapes, it will be *in spite* of their exertions. It's heads I win and tails you lose. Whatever they do, they will have followers, 'Un sot trouve toujours un plus sot qui l'admire.' "

" What on earth is this ? " I cried, for at this moment there came the pattering of many steps in the hall and on the stairs, accompanied by audible expressions of disgust upon the part of our landlady.

" It's the Baker Street division of the detective police force," said my companion gravely; and as he spoke there rushed into the room half a dozen of the dirtiest and most ragged street Arabs that ever I clapped eyes on.

" 'Tention ! " cried Holmes, in a sharp tone, and the six dirty scoundrels stood in a line like so many disreputable statuettes. " In future you shall send up Wiggins alone to report, and the rest of you must wait in the street. Have you found it, Wiggins ? "

" No, sir, we hain't," said one of the youths.

" I hardly expected you would. You must keep on until you do. Here are your wages." He handed each of them a shilling. " Now off you go, and come back with a better report next time."

He waved his hand, and they scampered away downstairs like so many rats, and we heard their shrill voices next moment in the street.

" There's more work to be got out of one of those little beggars than half a dozen of the force," Holmes remarked. " The mere sight of an official-looking person seals men's lips. These youngsters, however, go everywhere, and hear everything. They are as sharp as needles, too; all they want is organization."

" Is it on this Brixton case that you are employing them ? " I asked.

" Yes; there is a point which I wish to ascertain. It is merely a matter of time. Hullo! we are going to hear some news now with a vengeance! Here is Gregson coming down the road with beatitude written upon every feature of his face. Bound for us, I know. Yes, he is stopping. There he is ! "

There was a violent peal at the bell, and in a few seconds the fair-haired detective came up the stairs, three steps at a time, and burst into our sitting-room.

" My dear fellow," he cried, wringing Holmes' unresponsive hand, " congratulate me! I have made the whole thing as clear as day."

A shade of anxiety seemed to me to cross my companion's expressive face.

" Do you mean that you are on the right track ? " he asked.

" The right track! Why, sir, we have the man under lock and key."

" And his name is ? "

" Arthur Charpentier, sub-lieutenant in Her Majesty's Navy," cried Gregson pompously, rubbing his fat hands and inflating his chest.

Sherlock Holmes gave a sigh of relief and relaxed into a smile.

" Take a seat, and try one of these cigars," he said. "We are anxious to know how you managed it. Will you have some whisky and water ? "

" I don't mind if I do," the detective answered. " The tremendous exertions which I have gone through during the last day or two have worn me out. Not so much bodily exertion, you understand, as the strain upon the mind. You will appreciate that, Mr. Sherlock Holmes, for we are both brainworkers."

" You do me too much honour," said Holmes gravely. " Let us hear how you arrived at this most gratifying result."

The detective seated himself in the armchair, and puffed complacently at his cigar. Then suddenly he slapped his thigh in a paroxysm of amusement.

"The fun of it is," he cried, "that the fool Lestrade, who thinks himself so smart, has gone off upon the wrong track altogether. He is after the secretary Stangerson, who had no more to do with the crime than the babe unborn. I have no doubt that he has caught him by this time."

The idea tickled Gregson so much that he laughed until he choked.

"And how did you get your clue?"

"Ah, I'll tell you all about it. Of course, Doctor Watson, this is strictly between ourselves. The first difficulty which we had to contend with was the finding of this American's antecedents. Some people would have waited until their advertisements were answered, or until parties came forward and volunteered information. That is not Tobias Gregson's way of going to work. You remember the hat beside the dead man?"

"Yes," said Holmes; "by John Underwood and Sons, 129, Camberwell Road."

Gregson looked quite crestfallen.

"I had no idea that you noticed that," he said. "Have you been there?"

"No."

"Ha!" cried Gregson in a relieved voice; "you should never neglect a chance, however small it may seem."

"To a great mind, nothing is little," remarked Holmes sententiously.

"Well, I went to Underwood, and asked him if he had sold a hat of that size and description. He looked over his books, and came on it at once. He had sent the hat to a Mr. Drebber, residing at Charpentier's Boarding Establishment, Torquay Terrace. Thus I got his address."

"Smart—very smart!" murmured Sherlock Holmes.

"I next called upon Madame Charpentier," continued the detective. "I found her very pale and distressed. Her daughter was in the room, too—an uncommonly fine girl she is, too; she was looking red about the eyes and her lips trembled as I spoke to her. That didn't escape my notice. I began to smell a rat. You know that feeling, Mr. Sherlock Holmes, when you come upon the right scent—a kind of thrill in your nerves. 'Have you heard of the mysterious death of your late boarder Mr. Enoch J. Drebber of Cleveland?' I asked.

"The mother nodded. She didn't seem able to get out a word. The daughter burst into tears. I felt more than ever that these people knew something of the matter.

"'At what o'clock did Mr. Drebber leave your house for the train?' I asked.

"'At eight o'clock,' she said, gulping in her throat to keep down her agitation. 'His secretary, Mr. Stangerson, said that there were two trains—one at 9.15 and one at 11. He was to catch the first.'

"'And was that the last which you saw of him?'

"A terrible change came over the woman's face as I asked the question. Her features turned perfectly livid. It was some seconds before she could get out the single word 'Yes'—and when it did come it was in a husky, unnatural tone.

"There was a silence for a moment, and then the daughter spoke in a calm, clear voice.

"'No good can ever come of falsehood, mother,' she said. 'Let us be frank with this gentleman. We did see Mr. Drebber again.'

"'God forgive you!' cried Madame Charpentier, throwing up her hands, and sinking back in her chair. 'You have murdered your brother.'

"'Arthur would rather that we spoke the truth,' the girl answered firmly.

"'You had best tell me all about it now,' I said. 'Half-confidences are worse than none. Besides, you do not know how much we know of it.'

"'On your head be it, Alice!' cried her mother; and then, turning to me: 'I will tell you all sir. Do not imagine that my agitation on behalf of my son arises from any fear lest he should have had a hand in this terrible affair. He is utterly innocent of it. My dread is, however, that in your eyes and in the eyes of others he may appear to be compromised. That, however, is surely impossible. His high character, his profession, his antecedents would all forbid it.'

"'Your best way is to make a clean breast of the facts,' I answered. 'Depend upon it, if your son is innocent he will be none the worse.'

"'Perhaps, Alice, you had better leave us together,' she said, and her daughter withdrew. 'Now, sir,' she continued, 'I had no intention of telling you all this, but since my poor daughter has disclosed it I have no alternative. Having once decided to speak, I will tell you all without omitting any particular.'

" 'It is your wisest course,' said I.

" 'Mr. Drebber has been with us nearly three weeks. He and his secretary, Mr. Stangerson, had been travelling on the Continent. I noticed a " Copenhagen " label upon each of their trunks, showing that that had been their last stopping place. Stangerson was a quiet, reserved man, but his employer, I am sorry to say, was far otherwise. He was coarse in his habits and brutish in his ways. The very night of his arrival he became very much the worse for drink, and, indeed, after twelve o'clock in the day he could hardly ever be said to be sober. His mannners towards the maid-servants were disgustingly free and familiar. Worst of all, he speedily assumed the same attitude towards my daughter Alice, and spoke to her more than once in a way which, fortunately, she is too innocent to understand. On one occasion he actually seized her in his arms and embraced her—an outrage which caused his own secretary to reproach him for his unmanly conduct.'

" 'But why did you stand all this ? ' I asked. 'I suppose that you can get rid of your boarders when you wish.'

" Madame Charpentier blushed at my pertinent questions. 'Would to God that I had given him notice on the very day that he came,' she said. 'But it was a sore temptation. They were paying a pound a day each—fourteen pounds a week, and this is the slack season. I am a widow, and my boy in the Navy has cost me much. I grudged to lose the money. I acted for the best. This last was too much, however, and I gave him notice to leave on account of it. That was the reason of his going.'

" 'Well ? '

" 'My heart grew light when I saw him drive away. My son is on leave just now, but I did not tell him anything of this, for his temper is violent, and he is passionately fond of his sister. When I closed the door behind them a load seemed to be lifted from my mind. Alas, in less than an hour there was a ring at the bell, and I learned that Mr. Drebber had returned. He was much excited, and evidently the worse for drink. He forced his way into the room, where I was sitting with my daughter, and made some incoherent remark about having missed the train. He then turned to Alice, and before my very face proposed to her that she should fly with him. " You are of age," he said, " and there is no law to stop you. I have money enough and to spare. Never mind the old girl here, but come along with me now

straight away. You shall live like a princess." Poor Alice was so frightened that she struck away from him, but he caught her by the wrist and endeavoured to draw her towards the door. I screamed, and at that moment my son Arthur came into the room. What happened then I do not know. I heard oaths and the confused sounds of a scuffle. I was too terrified to raise my head. When I did look up I saw Arthur standing in the doorway laughing, with a stick in his hand. " I don't think that fine fellow will trouble us again," he said. " I will just go after him and see what he does with himself." With those words he took his hat and started off down the street. The next morning we heard of Mr. Drebber's mysterious death.'

" This statement came from Madame Charpentier's lips with many gasps and pauses. At times she spoke so low that I could hardly catch the words. I made shorthand notes of all that she said, however, so that there should be no possibility of a mistake."

" It's quite exciting," said Sherlock Holmes, with a yawn. " What happened next ? "

" When Madame Charpentier paused," the detective continued, " I saw the whole case hung upon one point. Fixing her with my eye in a way which I always found effective with women, I asked her at what hour her son returned.

" 'I do not know,' she answered.

" 'Not know ? '

" 'No; he has a latch-key, and he let himself in.'

" 'After you went to bed ? '

" 'Yes.'

" 'When did you go to bed ? '

" 'About eleven.'

" 'So your son was gone at least two hours ? '

" 'Yes.'

" 'Possibly four or five ? '

" 'Yes.'

" 'What was he doing during that time ? '

" 'I do not know,' she answered, turning white to her very lips.

" Of course after that there was nothing more to be done. I found out where Lieutenant Charpentier was, took two officers with me, and arrested him. When I touched him on the shoulder and warned him to come quietly with us, he answered us as bold as brass: 'I suppose you are arresting me for being concerned in the death of the scoundrel Drebber,' he said. We had said nothing to him about it, so that his alluding to it had a most suspicious aspect."

" Very," said Holmes.

" He still carried the heavy stick which the mother described him as having with him when he followed Drebber. It was a stout oak cudgel."

" What is your theory, then ? "

" Well, my theory is that he followed Drebber as far as the Brixton Road. When there, a fresh altercation arose between them, in the course of which Drebber received a blow from the stick, in the pit of the stomach perhaps, which killed him without leaving any mark. The night was so wet that no one was about, so Charpentier dragged the body of his victim into the empty house. As to the candle, and the blood, and the writing on the wall, and the ring, they may all be so many tricks to throw the police on to the wrong scent."

" Well done ! " said Holmes in an encouraging voice. " Really, Gregson, you are getting along. We shall make something of you yet."

" I flatter myself that I have managed it rather neatly," the detective answered proudly. " The young man volunteered a statement, in which he said that after following Drebber some time, the latter perceived him, and took a cab in order to get away from him. On his way home he met an old shipmate, and took a long walk with him. On being asked where this old shipmate lived, he was unable to give any satisfactory reply. I think the whole case fits together uncommonly well. What amuses me is to think of Lestrade, who had started off upon the wrong scent. I am afraid he won't make much of it. Why, by Jove, here's the very man himself ! "

It was indeed Lestrade, who had ascended the stairs while we were talking, who now entered the room. The assurance and jauntiness which generally marked his demeanour and dress were, however, wanting. His face was disturbed and troubled, while his clothes were disarranged and untidy. He had evidently come with the intention of consulting with Sherlock Holmes, for on perceiving his colleague he appeared to be embarrassed and put out. He stood in the centre of the room, fumbling nervously with his hat and uncertain what to do. " This is a most extraordinary case," he said at last—" a most incomprehensible affair."

" Ah, you find it so, Mr. Lestrade ! " cried Gregson, triumphantly. " I thought you would come to that conclusion. Have you managed to find the secretary, Mr. Joseph Stangerson ? "

" The secretary, Mr. Joseph Stangerson," said Lestrade gravely, " was murdered at Halliday's Private Hotel about six o'clock this morning."

CHAPTER VII

LIGHT IN THE DARKNESS

The intelligence with which Lestrade greeted us was so momentous and so unexpected that we were all three fairly dumbfounded. Gregson sprang out of his chair and upset the remainder of his whisky and water. I stared in silence at Sherlock Holmes, whose lips were compressed and his brows drawn down over his eyes.

" Stangerson too ! " he muttered. " The plot thickens."

" It was quite thick enough before," grumbled Lestrade, taking a chair. " I seem to have dropped into a sort of council of war."

" Are you—are you sure of this piece of intelligence ? " stammered Gregson.

" I have just come from his room," said Lestrade. " I was the first to discover what had occurred."

" We have been hearing Gregson's view of the matter," Holmes observed. " Would you mind letting us know what you have seen and done ? "

" I have no objection," Lestrade answered, seating himself. " I freely confess that I was of the opinion that Stangerson was concerned in the death of Drebber. This fresh development has shown me that I was completely mistaken. Full of the one idea, I set myself to find out what had become of the secretary. They had been seen together at Euston Station about half past eight on the evening of the third. At two in the morning Drebber had been found in the Brixton Road. The question which confronted me was to find out how Stangerson had been employed between 8.30 and the time of the crime, and what had become of him afterwards. I telegraphed to Liverpool, giving a description of the man, and warning them to keep a watch upon the American boats. I then set to work calling upon all the hotels and lodging-houses in the vicinity of Euston. You see, I argued that if Drebber and his companion had become separated, the natural course for the latter would be to put up somewhere in the vicinity for the night, and then to hang about the station again next morning."

" They would be likely to agree on some meeting place beforehand," remarked Holmes.

"So it proved. I spent the whole of yesterday evening making inquiries entirely without avail. This morning I began very early, and at eight o'clock I reached Halliday's Private Hotel, in Little George Street. On my inquiry as to whether a Mr. Stangerson was living there, they at once answered me in the affirmative.

"'No doubt you are the gentleman whom he was expecting,' they said. 'He has been waiting for a gentleman for two days.'

"'Where is he now?' I asked.

"'He is upstairs in bed. He wished to be called at nine.'

"'I will go up and see him at once,' I said.

"It seemed to me that my sudden appearance might shake his nerves and lead him to say something unguarded. The Boots volunteered to show me the room; it was on the second floor, and there was a small corridor leading up to it. The Boots pointed out the door to me, and was about to go downstairs again when I saw something that made me feel sickish, in spite of my twenty years' experience. From under the door there curled a little red ribbon of blood, which had meandered across the passage and formed a little pool along the skirting at the other side. I gave a cry, which brought the Boots back. He nearly fainted when he saw it. The door was locked on the inside, but we put our shoulders to it, and knocked it in. The window of the room was open, and beside the window all huddled up, lay the body of a man in his nightdress. He was quite dead, and had been for some time, for his limbs were rigid and cold. When we turned him over, the Boots recognized him at once as being the same gentleman who had engaged the room under the name of Joseph Stangerson. The cause of death was a deep stab in the left side, which must have penetrated the heart. And now comes the strangest part of the affair. What do you suppose was above the murdered man?"

I felt a creeping of the flesh, and a presentiment of coming horror, even before Sherlock Holmes answered.

"The word RACHE, written in letters of blood," he said.

"That was it," said Lestrade, in an awe-struck voice; and we were all silent for a while.

There was something so methodical and so incomprehensible about the deeds of this unknown assassin, that it imparted a fresh ghastliness to his crimes. My nerves, which were steady enough on the field of battle, tingled as I thought of it.

"The man was seen," continued Lestrade. "A milk boy passing on his way to the dairy, happened to walk down the lane which leads from the mews at the back of the hotel. He noticed that a ladder, which usually lay there, was raised against one of the windows of the second floor, which was wide open. After passing, he looked back and saw a man descend the ladder. He came down so quietly and openly that the boy imagined him to be some carpenter or joiner at work in the hotel. He took no particular notice of him, beyond thinking in his own mind that it was early for him to be at work. He has an impression that the man was tall, had a reddish face, and was dressed in a long, brownish coat. He must have stayed in the room some little time after the murder, for we found blood-stained water in the basin, where he had washed his hands, and marks on the sheets where he had deliberately wiped his knife."

I glanced at Holmes on hearing the description of the murderer which tallied so exactly with his own. There was, however, no trace of exultation or satisfaction upon his face.

"Did you find nothing in the room which could furnish a clue to the murderer?" he asked.

"Nothing. Stangerson had Drebber's purse in his pocket, but it seems that this was usual, as he did all the paying. There was eighty-odd pounds in it, but nothing had been taken. Whatever the motives of these extraordinary crimes, robbery is certainly not one of them. There were no papers or memoranda in the murdered man's pocket, except a single telegram, dated from Cleveland about a month ago, and containing the words, 'J. H. is in Europe.' There was no name appended to this message."

"And there was nothing else?" Holmes asked.

"Nothing of any importance. The man's novel, with which he had read himself to sleep, was lying upon the bed, and his pipe was on a chair beside him. There was a glass of water on the table, and on the window-sill a small chip ointment box containing a couple of pills."

Sherlock Holmes sprang from his chair with an exclamation of delight.

"The last link," he cried, exultantly. "My case is complete."

The two detectives stared at him in amazement.

"I have now in my hands," my companion said, confidently, "all the threads which have formed such a tangle. There are, of course, details to be filled in, but I am as certain of all the main facts, from the time that Drebber parted from Stangerson at the station, up to the discovery of the body of the latter, as if I had seen them with my own eyes. I will give you proof of my knowledge. Could you lay your hand upon those pills ? "

" I have them," said Lestrade, producing a small white box: " I took them and the purse and the telegram, intending to have them put in a place of safety at the Police Station. It was the merest chance my taking these pills, for I am bound to say I do not attach any importance to them."

" Give them here," said Holmes. " Now, Doctor," turning to me, " are these ordinary pills ? "

They certainly were not. They were of a pearly grey colour, small, round, and almost transparent against the light. " From their lightness and transparency, I should imagine that they are soluble in water," I remarked.

" Precisely so," answered Holmes. " Now would you mind going down and fetching that poor little devil of a terrier which has been bad so long, and which the landlady wanted you to put out of its pain yesterday."

I went downstairs and carried the dog upstairs in my arms. Its laboured breathing and glazing eye showed that it was not far from its end. Indeed, its snow-white muzzle proclaimed that it had already exceeded the usual term of canine existence. I placed it upon a cushion on the rug.

" I will now cut one of these pills in two," said Holmes, and drawing his penknife he suited the action to the word. " One half I will place in this wine-glass, in which is a teaspoon of water. You perceive that our friend the doctor is right, and that it readily dissolves."

" This may be very interesting," said Lestrade, in the injured tone of one who suspects that he is being laughed at; " I cannot see, however, what it has to do with the death of Mr. Joseph Stangerson."

" Patience, my friend, patience ! You will find in time that it has everything to do with it. I shall now add a little milk to make the mixture palatable, and on presenting it to the dog we find that he laps it up readily enough."

As he spoke he turned the contents of the wine-glass into a saucer and placed it in front of the terrier, who speedily licked it dry. Sherlock Holmes' earnest demeanour had so far convinced us that we all sat in silence watching the animal intently, and expecting some startling effect. None such appeared, however. The dog continued to lie stretched upon the cushion, breathing in a laboured way but apparently neither the better nor the worse for its draught.

Holmes had taken out his watch, and as minute followed minute without result, an expression of the upmost chagrin and disappointment appeared upon his features. He gnawed his lip, drummed his fingers upon the table, and showed every other sympton of acute impatience. So great was his emotion that I felt sincerely sorry for him, while the two detectives smiled derisively, by no means displeased at this check which he had met.

" It can't be a coincidence," he cried, at last springing from his chair and pacing wildly up and down the room; " it is impossible that it should be a mere coincidence. The very pills which I suspected in the case of Drebber are actually found after the death of Stangerson. And yet they are inert. What can it mean ? Surely my whole chain of reasoning cannot have been false. It is impossible ! And yet this wretched dog is none the worse. Ah, I have it ! I have it it ! " With a perfect shriek of delight he rushed to the box, cut the other pill in two, dissolved it, added milk, and presented it to the terrier. The unfortunate creature's tongue seemed hardly to have moistened in it before it gave a convulsive shiver in every limb, and lay as rigid and lifeless as if it had been struck by lightning.

Sherlock Holmes drew a long breath, and wiped the perspiration from his forehead. " I should have more faith," he said: " I ought to know by this time that when a fact appears to be opposed to a long train of deductions, it invariably proves to be capable of bearing some other interpretation. Of the two pills in the box, one was of the most deadly poison, and the other was entirely harmless. I ought to have known that before ever I saw the box at all."

This last statement appeared to me to be so startling that I could hardly believe that he was in his sober senses. There was the dead dog, however, to prove that his conjecture had been correct. It seemed to me that the mists in my own mind were gradually clearing away, and I began to have a dim, vague perception of the truth.

" All this seems strange to you," continued Holmes, " because you failed at the beginning of the inquiry to grasp the importance of the single real clue which was presented to you. I had the good fortune to seize upon that, and everything which has occurred since then has served to confirm my original supposition, and, indeed, was the logical sequence of it. Hence things which have perplexed you and made the case more obscure have served to enlighten me and to strengthen my conclusions. It is a mistake to confound strangeness with mystery. The most commonplace crime is often the most mysterious, because it presents no new or special features from which deductions may be drawn. This murder would have been infinitely more difficult to unravel had the body of the victim been simply found lying in the roadway without any of those *outré* and sensational accompaniments which have rendered it remarkable. These strange details, far from making the case more difficult, have really had the effect of making it less so."

Mr Gregson, who had listened to this address with considerable impatience, could contain himself no longer. " Look here, Mr. Sherlock Holmes," he said, " we are all ready to acknowledge that you are a smart man, and that you have your own methods of working. We want something more than mere theory and preaching now, though. It is a case of taking the man. I have made my case out, and it seems I was wrong. Young Charpentier could not have been engaged in this second affair. Lestrade went after his man, Stangerson, and it appears that he was wrong too. You have thrown out hints here, and hints there, and seem to know more than we do, but the time has come when we feel that we have a right to ask you straight how much you do know of the business. Can you name the man who did it ? "

" I cannot help feeling that Gregson is right, sir," remarked Lestrade. " We have both tried, and we have both failed. You have remarked more than once since I have been in the room that you had all the evidence which you require. Surely you will not withhold it any longer ? "

" Any delay in arresting the assassin," I observed, " might give him time to perpetrate some fresh atrocity."

Thus pressed by us all, Holmes showed signs of irresolution. He continued to walk up and down the room with his head sunk on his chest and his brows drawn down, as was his habit when lost in thought.

" There will be no more murders," he said at last, stopping abruptly and facing us. " You can put that consideration out of the question. You have asked me if I know the name of the assassin. I do. The mere

knowing of his name is a small thing, however, compared with the power of laying our hands upon him. This I expect very shortly to do. I have good hopes of managing it through my own arrangments; but it is a thing which needs delicate handling, for we have a shrewd and desperate man to deal with, who is supported, as I have had occasion to prove, by another who is as clever as himself. As long as this man has no idea that anyone can have a clue there is some chance of securing him; but if he had the slightest suspicion, he would change his name, and vanish in an instant among the four million inhabitants of the great city. Without meaning to hurt either of your feelings, I am bound to say that I consider these men to be more than a match for the official force, and that is why I have not asked your assistance. If I fail, I shall, of course, incur the blame due to this omission; but that I am prepared for. At present I am ready to promise that the instant that I can communicate with you without endangering my own combinations, I shall do so."

Gregson and Lestrade seemed to be far from satisfied by this assurance, or by the depreciating allusion to the detective police. The former had flushed up to the roots of his flaxen hair, while the other's beady eyes glistened with curiosity and resentment. Neither of them had time to speak, however, before there was a tap at the door, and the spokesman of the street Arabs, young Wiggins, introduced his insignificant and unsavoury person.

" Please, sir," he said, touching his forelock, " I have the cab downstairs."

" Good boy," said Holmes, blandly. " Why don't you introduce this pattern at Scotland Yard ? " he continued, taking a pair of steel handcuffs from a drawer. " See how beautifully the spring works. They fasten in an instant."

" The old pattern is good enough," remarked Lestrade, " if we can only find the man to put them on."

" Very good, very good," said Holmes, smiling. " The cabman may as well help me with my boxes. Just ask him to step up, Wiggins."

I was surprised to find my companion speaking as though he were about to set out on a journey, since he had not said anything to me about it. There was a small portmanteau in the room, and this he pulled out and began to strap. He was busily engaged at it when the cabman entered the room.

" Just give me a help with this buckle,

cabman," he said, kneeling over his task, and never turning his head.

The fellow came forward with a somewhat sullen defiant air and put down his hands to assist. At that instant there was a sharp click, the jangling of metal, and Sherlock Holmes sprang to his feet again.

"Gentlemen," he cried, with flashing eyes, "let me introduce you to Mr. Jefferson Hope, the murderer of Enoch Drebber and of Joseph Stangerson.

The whole thing occurred in a moment—so quickly that I had no time to realize it. I have vivid recollection of that instant, of Holmes's triumphant expression and the ring of his voice, of the cabman's dazed, savage face, as he glared at the glittering handcuffs, which had appeared as if by magic upon his wrists. For a second or two we might have been a group of statues. Then with an inarticulate roar of fury, the prisoner wrenched himself free from Holmes's grasp, and hurled himself through the window. Woodwork and glass gave way before him; but before he got quite through, Gregson, Lestrade, and Holmes sprang upon him like so many staghounds. He was dragged back into the room, and then commenced a terrific conflict. So powerful and so fierce was he that the four of us were shaken off again and again. He appeared to have the convulsive strength of a man in an epileptic fit. His face and hands were terribly mangled by his passage through the glass, but loss of blood had no effect in diminishing his resistance. It was not until Lestrade succeeded in getting his hand inside his neckcloth and half-strangling him that we made him realize that his struggles were of no avail; and even then we felt no security until we had pinioned his feet as well as his hands. That done, we rose to our feet breathless and panting.

"We have his cab," said Sherlock Holmes. "It will serve to take him to Scotland Yard. And now, gentlemen," he continued, with a pleasant smile, "we have reached the end of our little mystery. You are very welcome to put any questions that you like to me now, and there is no danger that I will refuse to answer them."

PART II

The Country of the Saints

CHAPTER 1

ON THE GREAT ALKALI PLAIN

In the central portion of the great North American Continent there lies an arid and repulsive desert, which for many a long year served as a barrier against the advance of civilization. From the Sierra Nevada to Nebraska, and from the Yellowstone River in the north to the Colorado upon the south, is a region of desolation and silence. Nor is nature always in one mood throughout this grim district. It comprises snow-capped and lofty mountains, and dark and gloomy valleys. There are swift-flowing rivers which dash through jagged canyons; and there are enormous plains, which in winter are white with snow, and in summer are grey with the saline alkali dust. They all preserve, however, the common characteristics of barrenness, inhospitality, and misery.

There are no inhabitants of this land of despair. A band of Pawnees or of Blackfeet may occasionally traverse it in order to reach other hunting-grounds, but the hardiest of the braves are glad to lose sight of those awesome plains, and find themselves once more upon their prairies. The coyote skulks among the scrub, the buzzard flaps heavily through the air, and the clumsy grizzly bear lumbers through the dark ravines, and picks up such sustenance as it can amongst the rocks. These are the sole dwellers in the wilderness.

In the whole world there can be no more dreary view than that from the northern slope of the Sierra Blanco. As far as the eye can reach stretches the great flat plain-land, all dusted over with patches of alkali, and intersected by clumps of the dwarfish chaparral bushes. On the extreme verge of the horizon lies a long chain of mountain peaks, with their rugged summits flecked with snow. In this great stretch of country there is no sign of life, nor of anything appertaining to life. There is no bird in the steel-blue heaven, no movement upon the dull, grey earth—above all, there is absolute silence. Listen as one may, there is no shadow of a sound in all that mighty wilderness; nothing but silence—complete and heart-subduing silence.

It has been said there is nothing appertaining to life upon the broad plain. That is hardly true. Looking down from the Sierra Blanco, one sees a pathway traced out across the desert, which winds away and is lost in the extreme distance. It is rutted with wheels and trodden down by the feet of many adventurers. Here and there are scattered white objects which glisten in the sun, and stand out against the dull deposit of alkali. Approach, and examine them! They are bones: some large and coarse, others smaller and more delicate. The former have belonged to oxen, and the latter to men. For fifteen hundred miles one may trace this ghastly caravan route by these scattered remains of those who have fallen by the wayside.

Looking down on this very scene, there stood upon the fourth of May, eighteen hundred and forty-seven, a solitary traveller. His appearance was such that he might have been the very genius or demon of the region. An observer would have found it difficult to say whether he was nearer to forty or to sixty. His face was lean and haggard, and the brown parchment-like skin was drawn tightly over the projecting bones; his long, brown hair and beard were all flecked and dashed with white; his eyes were sunken in his head, and burned with an unnatural lustre; while the hand which grasped his rifle was hardly more fleshy than that of a skeleton. As he stood, he leaned upon his weapon for support, and yet his tall figure and the massive framework of his bones suggested a wiry and vigorous constitution. His gaunt face, however, and his clothes, which hung so baggily over his shrivelled limbs, proclaimed what it was that gave him that senile and decrepit appearance. The man was dying—dying from hunger and from thirst.

He had toiled painfully down the ravine, and on to this little elevation, in the vain hope of seeing some signs of water. Now the great salt plain stretched before his eyes, and the distant belt of savage mountains, without a sign anywhere of plant or tree which might indicate the presence of moisture. In all that broad landscape there was no gleam of hope. North, and east, and west he looked with wild, questioning eyes, and then he realized that his wanderings had come to an end, and that there, on that barren crag, he was about to die. " Why not here, as well as in a feather bed, twenty years hence," he muttered, as he seated himself in the shelter of a boulder.

Before sitting down, he had deposited upon the ground his useless rifle, and also a large bundle tied up in a grey shawl, which he had carried slung over his right shoulder. It appeared to be somewhat too heavy for his strength, for in lowering it, it came down on the ground with some little violence. Instantly there broke from the grey parcel a little moaning cry, and from it there protruded a small, scared face, with very bright brown eyes, and two little speckled dimpled fists.

" You've hurt me ! " said a childish voice, reproachfully.

" Have I though," the man answered penitently; " I didn't go for to do it." As he spoke he unwrapped the grey shawl and extricated a pretty little girl of about five years of age, whose dainty shoes and smart pink frock with its little linen apron all bespoke a mother's care. The child was pale and wan, but her healthy arms and legs showed that she had suffered less than her companion.

" How is it now ? " he answered anxiously, for she was still rubbing the towsy golden curls which covered the back of her head.

" Kiss it and make it well," she said, with perfect gravity, showing the injured part to him. " That's what mother used to do. Where's mother ? "

" Mother's gone. I guess you'll see her before long."

" Gone, eh ! " said the little girl. " Funny, she didn't say good-bye; she 'most always did if she was just goin' over to auntie's for tea, and now she's been away three days. Say, it's awful dry, ain't it ? Ain't there no water nor nothing to eat ? "

" No, there ain't nothing, dearie. You'll just need to be patient awhile, and then you'll be all right. Put your head up agin' me like that, and then you'll feel bullier. It ain't easy to talk when your lips is like leather, but I guess I'd best let you know how the cards lie. What's that you've got ? "

" Pretty things ! fine things ! " cried the little girl enthusiastically, holding up two glittering fragments of mica. " When we goes back to home I'll give them to brother Bob."

" You'll see prettier things than them soon," said the man confidently. " You just

wait a bit. I was going to tell you though— you remember when we left the river ? "

" Oh, yes."

" Well, we reckoned we'd strike another river soon, d'ye see. But there was somethin' wrong; compasses, or map, or somethin', and it didn't turn up. Water ran out. Just except a little drop for the likes of you and—and——"

" And you couldn't wash yourself," interrupted his companion gravely, staring up at his grimy visage.

" No, nor drink. And Mr. Bender, he was the fust to go, and then Indian Pete, and then Mrs. McGregor, and then Johnny Hones, and then dearie, your mother."

" Then mother's a deader too," cried the little girl, dropping her face in her pinafore and sobbing bitterly.

" Yes, they all went except you and me. Then I thought there was some chance of water in this direction, so I heaved you over my shoulder and we tramped it together. It don't seem as though we've improved matters. There's an almighty small chance for us now ! "

" Do you mean that we are going to die too ? " asked the child, checking her sobs, and raising a tear-stained face.

" I guess that's about the size of it."

" Why didn't you say so before ? " she said, laughing gleefully. " You gave me such a fright. Why, of course, now as long as we die we'll be with mother again."

" Yes, you will dearie."

" And you too. I'll tell her how awful good you've been. I'll bet she meets us at the door of heaven with a big pitcher of water, and a lot of buckwheat cakes, hot, and toasted on both sides, like Bob and me was fond of. How long will it be first ? "

" I don't know—not very long." The man's eyes were fixed upon the northern horizon. In the blue vault of the heaven there had appeared three little specks which increased in size ever moment, so rapidly did they approach. They speedily resolved themselves into three large brown birds, which circled over the heads of the two wanderers, and then settled upon some rocks which overlooked them. They were buzzards, the vultures of the west, whose coming in is the fore-runner of death.

" Cocks and hens," cried the little girl gleefully, pointing at their ill-omened forms, and clapping her hands to make them rise. " Say, did God make this country ? "

" In course He did," said her companion, rather startled by this unexpected question.

"He made the country down in Illinois, and He made the Missouri," the little girl continued. "I guess somebody else made the country in these parts. It's not nearly so well done. They forgot the water and the trees."

"What would ye think of offering up prayer?" the man asked diffidently.

"It ain't night yet," she answered.

"It don't matter. It ain't quite regular, but He won't mind that, you bet. You say over them ones that you used to say every night in the wagon when we was on the Plains."

"Why don't you say some yourself?" the child asked, with wondering eyes.

"I disremember them," he answered. "I hain't said none since I was half the height o' that gun. I guess it's never too late. You say them out, and I'll stand by you and come in on the choruses."

"Then you'll need to kneel down, and me too," she said, laying the shawl out for that purpose. "You've got to put your hands up like this. It makes you feel kind of good."

It was a strange sight, had there been anything but the buzzards to see it. Side by side on the narrow shawl knelt the two wanderers, the little prattling child and the reckless, hardened adventurer. Her chubby face and his haggard, angular visage were both turned up to the cloudless heaven in heartfelt entreaty to that dread Being with whom they were face to face, while the two voices—the one thin and clear, the other deep and harsh—united in the entreaty for mercy and forgiveness. The prayer finished, they resumed their seat in the shadow of the boulder until the child fell asleep, nestling upon the broad breast of her protector. He watched over her slumber for some time, but Nature proved to be too strong for him. For three days and three nights he had allowed himself neither rest nor repose. Slowly the eyelids drooped over the tired eyes, and the head sunk lower and lower upon the breast, until the man's grizzled beard was mixed with the gold tresses of his companion, and both slept the same deep and dreamless slumber.

Had the wanderer remained awake for another half-hour a strange sight would have met his eyes. Far away on the extreme verge of the alkali plain their rose up a little spray of dust, very slight at first, and hardly to be distinguished from the mists of the distance, but gradually growing higher and broader until it formed a solid, well-defined cloud. This cloud continued to increase in size until it became evident that it could only be raised by a great multitude of moving creatures. In more fertile spots the observer would have come to the conclusion that one of those great herds of bisons which graze upon the prairie land was approaching him. This was obviously impossible in these arid wilds. As the whirl of dust drew nearer to the solitary bluff upon which the two castaways were reposing, the canvas-covered tilts of wagons and the figures of armed horsemen began to show up through the haze, and the apparition revealed itself as being a great caravan upon its journey for the West. But what a caravan! When the head of it had reached the base of the mountains, the rear was not yet visible on the horizon. Right across the enormous plain stretched the straggling array, wagons and carts, men on horseback, and men on foot. Innumerable women who staggered along under burdens, and children who toddled beside the wagons or peeped out from under the white coverings. This was evidently no ordinary party of immigrants, but rather some nomad people who had been compelled from stress of circumstances to seek themselves a new country. There rose through the clear air a confused clattering and rumbling from this great mass of humanity, with the creaking of wheels and the neighing horses. Loud as it was, it was not sufficient to rouse the two tired wayfarers above them.

At the head of the column there rode a score or more of grave iron-faced men, clad in sombre homespun garments and armed with rifles. On reaching the base of the bluff they halted, and held a short council among themselves.

"The wells are to the right, my brothers," said one, hard-lipped, clean-shaven man with grizzly hair.

"To the right of the Sierra Blanco—so we shall reach the Rio Grande," said another.

"Fear not for water," cried a third. "He who could draw it from the rocks will not now abandon His chosen people."

"Amen! amen!" responded the whole party.

They were about to resume their journey when one of the youngest and keenest-eyed uttered an exclamation and pointed up at the rugged crag above them. From its summit there fluttered a little wisp of pink, showing up hard and bright against the grey rocks behind. At the sight there was a general reining up of horses and unslinging of guns, while fresh horsemen came galloping up to reinforce the vanguard. The word "Redskins" was on every lip.

"There can't be any number of Injuns here," said the elderly man who appeared to be in command. "We have passed the Pawnees, there are no other tribes until we cross the great mountains."

"Shall I go forward and see, Brother Stangerson," asked one of the band.

"And I," "And I," cried a dozen voices.

"Leave your horses below and we will await you here," the Elder answered. In a moment the young fellows had dismounted, fastened their horses, and were ascending the precipitous slope which led up to the object which had excited their curiosity. They advanced rapidly and noiselessly, with the confidence and dexterity of practised scouts. The watchers from the plain below could see them flit from rock to rock until their figures stood out against the skyline. The young man who had first given the alarm was leading them. Suddenly his followers saw him throw up his hands, as though overcome with astonishment, and on joining him they were affected in the same way by the sight which met their eyes.

On the little plateau which crowned the barren hill there stood a single giant boulder, and against this boulder there lay a tall man, long-bearded and hard-featured, but of an excessive thinness. His placid face and regular breathing showed that he was fast asleep. Beside him lay a little child, with her round white arms encircling his brown sinewy neck, and her golden-haired head resting upon the breast of his velveteen tunic. Her rosy lips were parted, showing the regular line of snow-white teeth within, and a playful smile played over her infantile features. Her plump little white legs, terminating in white socks and neat shoes with shining buckles, offered a strange contrast to the long shrivelled members of her companion. On the ledge of rock above this strange couple there stood three solemn buzzards, who, at the sight of the newcomers, uttered raucous screams of disappointment and flapped sullenly away.

The cries of the foul birds awoke the two sleepers, who stared about them in bewilderment. The man staggered to his feet and looked down upon the plain which had been so desolate when sleep had overtaken him, and which was now traversed by this enormous body of men and of beasts. His face assumed an expression of incredulity as he gazed, and he passed his bony hand over his eyes. "This is what they call delirium, I guess," he muttered. The child stood beside him, holding on to the skirt of his coat, and said nothing, but looked all around her with the wondering, questioning gaze of childhood.

The rescuing party were speedily able to convince the two castaways that their appearance was no delusion. One of them seized the little girl and hoisted her upon his shoulder, while two others supported her gaunt companion, and assisted him towards the wagons.

"My name is John Ferrier," the wanderer explained; "me and the little un are all that's left o' twenty-one people. The rest is all dead o' thirst and hunger away down in the south."

"Is she your child?" asked someone.

"I guess she is now," the other cried, defiantly; "she's mine 'cause I saved her. No man will take her from me. She's Lucy Ferrier from this day on. Who are you though?" he continued, glancing with curiosity at his stalwart, sunburned rescuers; "there seems to be a powerful lot of ye."

"Nigh upon ten thousand," said one of the young men; "we are the persecuted children of God—the chosen of the Angel Merona."

"I never heard tell on him," said the wanderer. "He appears to have chosen a fair crowd of ye,".

"Do not jest at that which is sacred," said the other sternly. "We are of those who believe in those sacred writings, drawn in Egyptian letters on plates of beaten gold, which were handed unto the holy Joseph Smith at Palmyra. We have come from Nauvoo, in the State of Illinois, where we had founded our temple. We have come to seek a refuge from the violent man and from the godless, even though it be the heart of the desert."

The name of Nauvoo evidently recalled recollections to John Ferrier. "I see," he said, "you are the Mormons."

"We are the Mormons," answered his companions with one voice.

"And where are you going?"

"We do not know. The hand of God is leading us under the person of our Prophet. You must come before him. He shall say what is to be done with you."

They had reached the base of the hill by this time, and were surrounded by crowds of pilgrims—pale-faced, meek-looking women; strong laughing children and anxious earnest-eyed men. Many were the cries of astonishment and of commiseration which arose from them when they perceived the youth of one of the strangers and the destitution of the other. Their escort did not halt, however, but pushed on, followed by a great crowd of Mormons, until they reached a wagon, which was conspicuous for its great size and for the gaudiness and smartness of its appearance. Six horses were yoked to it, whereas the others were furnished with two, or, at most four apiece. Beside the driver there sat a man who could not have been more than thirty years of age, but whose massive head and resolute expression marked him as leader. He was reading a brown-backed volume, but as the crowd approached he laid it aside, and listened attentively to an account of the episode. Then he turned to the castaways.

" If we take you with us," he said, in solemn words, " it can only be as believers in our own creed. We shall have no wolves in our fold. Better far that your bones should bleach in this wilderness than that you should prove to be that little speck of decay which in time corrupts the whole fruit. Will you come with us on these terms ? "

" Guess I'll come with you on any terms," said Ferrier, with such emphasis that the grave Elders could not restrain a smile. The leader alone retained his stern, impressive expression.

" Take him, Brother Stangerson," he said, " give him food and drink, and the child likewise. Let it be your task also to teach him our holy creed. We have delayed long enough ! Forward ! On, on to Zion ! "

" On, on to Zion ! " cried the crowd of Mormons, and the words rippled down the long caravan, passing from mouth to mouth until they died away in a dull murmur in the far distance. With a cracking of whips and a creaking of wheels the great wagons got into motion and soon the whole caravan was winding along once more. The Elder to whose care the two waifs had been committed led them to his wagon, where a meal was already awaiting them.

" You shall remain here," he said. " In a few days you will have recovered from your fatigues. In the meantime, remember that now and for ever you are of our religion. Brigham Young has said it, and he has spoken with the voice of Joseph Smith, which is the voice of God."

CHAPTER II

THE FLOWER OF UTAH

This is not the place to commemorate the trials and privations endured by the immigrant Mormons before they came to their final haven. From the shores of the Mississippi to the western slopes of the Rocky Mountains they had struggled on with a constancy almost unparelleled in history. The savage man, and the savage beast, hunger, thirst, fatigue, and disease—every impediment which Nature could place in the way—had all been overcome with Anglo-Saxon tenacity. Yet the long journey and the accumulated terrors had shaken the hearts of the stoutest among them. There was not one who did not sink upon his knees in heartfelt prayer when they saw the broad valley of Utah bathed in the sunlight beneath them, and learned from the lips of their leader that this was the promised land, and that these virgin acres were to be theirs for evermore.

Young speedily proved himself to be a skilful administrator as well as a resolute chief. Maps were drawn and charts prepared, in which the future city was sketched out. All around farms were apportioned and allotted in proportion to the standing of each individual. The tradesman was put to his trade and the artisan to his calling. In the town streets and squares sprang up as if by magic. In the country there was draining and hedging, planting and clearing, until the next summer saw the whole country golden with the wheat crop. Everything prospered in the strange settlement. Above all, the great temple which they had erected in the centre of the city grew ever taller and larger. From the first blush of dawn until the closing of the twilight, the clatter of the hammer and the rasp of the saw were never absent from the monument which the immigrants erected to Him who had led them safe through many dangers.

The two castaways, John Ferrier and the little girl, who had shared his fortunes and had been adopted as his daughter, accompanied the Mormons to the end of their great pilgrimage. Little Lucy Ferrier was borne along pleasantly enough in Elder Stangerson's wagon, a retreat which she shared with the Mormon's three wives and with his son, a headstrong, forward boy of twelve. Having rallied, with the elasticity of childhood, from the shock caused by her mother's death, she soon became a pet with the women, and reconciled herself to this new life in her moving canvas-covered home. In the meantime Ferrier having recovered from his privations, distinguished himself as a useful guide and an indefatigable hunter. So rapidly did he gain the esteem of his new companions, that when they reached the end of their wanderings, it was unanimously agreed that he should be provided with as large and as fertile a tract of land as any of the settlers, with the exception of Young himself, and of Stangerson, Kemball, Johnston and Drebber, who were the four principal Elders.

On the farm thus acquired John Ferrier built himself a substantial log-house, which received so many additions in succeeding years that it grew into a roomy villa. He was a man of a practical mind, keen in his dealings and skilful with his hands. His iron constitution enabled him to work morning and evening at improving and tilling his lands. Hence it came about that his farm and all that belonged to him prospered exceedingly. In three years he was better off than his neighbours, in six he was well-to-do, in nine he was rich, and in twelve there were not half a dozen men in the whole of Salt Lake City who could compare with him. From the great inland sea to the distant Wahsatch Mountains there was no name better known than that of John Ferrier.

There was one way and only one in which he offended the susceptibilities of his co-religionists. No argument or persuasion could ever induce him to set up a female establishment after the manner of his companions. He never gave reasons for this persistent refusal, but contented himself by resolutely and inflexibly adhering to his determination. There were some who accused him of lukewarmness in his adopted religion, and other who put it down to greed of wealth and reluctance to incur expense. Others, again spoke of some early love affair, and of a fair-haired girl who had pined away on the shores of the Atlantic. Whatever the reason, Ferrier remained strictly celibate. In every other respect he conformed to the religion of the young settlement, and gained the name of being an orthodox and straight-walking man.

Lucy Ferrier grew up within the log-house, and assisted her adopted father in all his undertakings. The keen air of the mountains and the balsamic odour of the pine trees took the place of nurse and mother to the young girl. As year succeeded to year she grew taller and stronger, her cheek more ruddy and her step more elastic. Many a wayfarer upon the high road which ran by Ferrier's farm felt long-forgotten thoughts revive in their minds as they watched her lithe, girlish figure tripping through the wheatfields, or met her mounted upon her father's mustang, and managing it with all the ease and grace of a true child of the West. So the bud blossomed into a flower, and the year which saw her father the richest of the farmers left her as fair a specimen of American girlhood as could be found in the whole Pacific slope.

It was not the father, however, who first discovered that the child had developed into the woman. It seldom is in such cases. That mysterious change is too subtle and too gradual to be measured by dates. Least of all does the maiden herself knew it until the tone of a voice or the touch of a hand sets her heart thrilling within her, and she learns, with a mixture of pride and of fear, that a new and a larger nature has awoke within her. There are few who cannot recall that day and remember the one little incident which heralded the dawn of a new life. In the case of Lucy Ferrier the occasion was serious enough in itself, apart from its future influence on her destiny and that of many besides.

It was a warm June morning, and the Latter Day Saints were as busy as the bees whose hive they have chosen for their emblem. In the fields and in the streets rose the same hum of human industry. Down the dusty high roads defiled long streams of heavily-laden mules, all heading to the west, for the gold fever had broken out in California, and the overland route lay through the city of the Elect. There, too, were droves of sheep and bullocks coming in from the outlying pasture lands, and trains of tired immigrants, men and horses equally weary of their interminable journey. Through all this motley assemblage, threading her way with the skill of an accomplished rider, there galloped Lucy Ferrier, her fair face flushed with the exercise and her long chestnut hair floating out behind her. She had a commission from her father in the city, and was dashing in as she had done many a time before, with all the fearlessness of youth, thinking only of her task and how it was to be performed. The travel-stained adventurers gazed after her in astonishment, and even the unemotional Indians, journeying in with their peltries, relaxed their accustomed stoicism as they marvelled at the beauty of the pale-faced maiden.

She had reached the outskirts of the city when she found the road blocked by a great drove of cattle, driven by a half-dozen wild-looking herdsmen from the plains. In her impatience she endeavoured to pass this obstacle by pushing her horse into what appeared to be a gap. Scarcely had she got fairly into it, however, before the beasts closed in behind her, and she found herself completely embedded in the moving stream of fierce-eyed long-horned bullocks. Accustomed as she was to deal with cattle, she was not alarmed at her situation, but took advantage of every opportunity to urge her horse on, in the hopes of pushing her way through the cavalcade. Unfortunately the horns of one of the creatures, either by accident or design, came in violent contact with the flank of the mustang, and excited it to madness. In an instant it reared up upon its hind legs with a snort of rage, and pranced and tossed in a way that would have unseated any but a skilful rider. The situation was full of peril. Every plunge of the excited horse brought it against the horns again, and goaded it to fresh madness. It was all that the girl could do to keep herself in the saddle, yet a slip would mean a terrible death under the hoofs of the unwieldy and terrified animals. Unaccustomed to sudden emergencies, her head began to swim, and her grip upon the bridle relax. Choked by the rising cloud of dust and by the steam from the struggling creatures, she might have abandoned her efforts in despair, but for a kindly voice at her elbow which assured her of assistance. At the same moment a sinewy brown hand caught the frightened horse by the curb, and forcing a way through the drove, soon brought her to the outskirts.

" You're not hurt, I hope, miss," said her preserver, respectfully.

She looked up at his dark, fierce face, and laughed saucily. " I'm awful frightened," she said, naïvely; " whoever would have thought that Poncho would have been so scared by a lot of cows ?"

" Thank God you kept your seat," the other said earnestly. He was a tall, savage-looking young fellow, mounted on a powerful roan horse, and clad in the rough dress of a hunter, with a long rifle slung over his shoulders. " I guess you are the daughter of John Ferrier," he remarked; " I saw you ride down from his house. When you see him, ask him if he remembers the Jefferson Hopes of St Louis. If he's the same Ferrier, my father and he were pretty thick."

" Hadn't you better come and ask yourself ? " she asked, demurely.

The young fellow seemed pleased at the suggestion, and his dark eyes sparkled with pleasure. " I'll do so," he said; " we've been in the mountains for two months, and are not over and above in visiting condition. He

must take us as he finds us."

" He has a good deal to thank you for, and so have I," she answered, " he's awful fond of me. If those cows had jumped on me he'd never got over it."

" Neither would I," said her companion.

" You ! Well, I don't see that it would make much matter to you, anyhow. You ain't even a friend of ours."

The young hunter's dark face grew so gloomy over this remark that Lucy Ferrier laughed aloud.

" There, I didn't mean that," she said; " of course, you are a friend now. You must come and see us. Now I must push along, or father won't trust me with his business any more. Good-bye ! "

Young Jefferson Hope rode on with his companions, gloomy and taciturn. He and they had been among the Nevada Mountains prospecting for silver, and were returning to Salt Lake City in the hope of raising capital enough to work some lodes which they had discovered. He had been as keen as any of them upon the business until this sudden incident had drawn his thoughts into another channel. The sight of the fair young girl, as frank and wholesome as the Sierra breezes, had stirred his volcanic, untamed heart to its depths. When she had vanished from his sight, he realized that a crisis had come in his life, and that neither silver speculations nor any other questions could ever be of such importance to him as this new and all-absorbing one. The love which had sprung up in his heart was not the sudden, changeable fancy of a boy, but rather that wild, fierce passion of a man of strong will and imperious temper. He had been accustomed to succeed in all that he undertook. He swore in his heart that he would not fail in this if human effort and human preserverance could render him successful.

He called on John Ferrier that night, and many times again, until his face was a familiar one at the farmhouse. John, cooped up in the valley, and absorbed in his work, had had little chance of learning the news of the outside world during the last twelve years. All this Jefferson Hope was able to tell him, and in a style which interested Lucy as well as her father. He had been a pioneer in California, and could narrate many a strange tale of fortunes made and fortunes lost in those wild, halcyon days. He had been a scout, too, and a trapper, a silver explorer, and a ranchman. Wherever stirring adventures were to be had, Jefferson Hope had been there in search of them. He soon become a favourite with the old farmer, who spoke eloquently of his virtues. On such occasions, Lucy was silent, but her blushing cheek and her bright, happy eyes showed only too clearly that her young heart was no longer her own. Her honest father may not have observed these symptoms, but they were assuredly not thrown away upon the man who had won her affections.

One summer evening he came galloping down the road and pulled up at the gate. She was at the doorway, and came down to meet him. He threw the bridle over the fence and strode up to the pathway.

" I am off, Lucy," he said, taking her two hands in his, and gazing tenderly down into her face; " I won't ask you to come with me now, but will you be ready to come when I am here again ? "

" And when will that be ? " she asked, blushing and laughing.

" A couple of months at the outside. I will come and claim you then, my darling. There's no one who can stand between us."

" And how about Father ? " she asked.

" He has given his consent, provided we get these mines working all right. I have no fear on that head."

" Oh, well; of course, if you and Father have arranged it all, there's no more to be said," she whispered, with her cheek against his broad breast.

" Thank God ! " he said, hoarsely, stopping and kissing her. " It is settled, then. The longer I stay, the harder it will be to go. They are waiting for me at the canyon. Goodbye, my own darling—goodbye. In two months you shall see me."

He tore himself from her as he spoke, and, flinging himself upon his horse, galloped furiously away, never even looking round, as though afraid that his resolution might fail him if he took one glance at what he was leaving. She stood at the gate, gazing after him until he vanished from her sight. Then she walked back into the house, the happiest girl in all Utah.

CHAPTER III

JOHN FERRIER TALKS WITH THE PROPHET

Three weeks had passed since Jefferson Hope and his comrades had departed from Salt Lake City. John Ferrier's heart was sore within him when he thought of the young man's return, and of the impending loss of his adopted child. Yet her bright and happy face reconciled him to the arrangement more than any argument could have done. He had always determined, deep down in his resolute heart, that nothing would ever induce him to allow his daughter to wed a Mormon. Such a marriage he regarded as no marriage at all, but as a shame and disgrace. Whatever he might think of the Mormon doctrines, upon that one point he was inflexible. He had to seal his mouth on the subject, however, for to express an unorthodox opinion was a dangerous matter in those days in the Land of the Saints.

Yes, a dangerous matter—so dangerous that even the most saintly dared only whisper their religious opinions with bated breath, lest something which fell from their lips might be misconstrued, and bring down a swift retribution upon them. The victims of persecution had now turned persecutors on their own account and persecutors of the most terrible description. Not the Inquisition of Seville, nor the German Vehmgericht, nor the Secret Societies of Italy, were ever able to put a more formidable machinery in motion than that which cast a cloud over the State of Utah.

Its invisibility, and the mystery which was attached to it, made this organisation doubly terrible. It appeared to be omniscient and omnipotent, and yet was neither seen nor heard. The man who held out against the Church vanished away, and none knew whither he had gone or what had befallen him. His wife and his children waited at home, but no father ever returned to tell them how he had fared at the hands of his secret judges. A rash word or a hasty act was followed by annihilation, and yet none knew what the nature might be of this terrible power, which was suspended over them. No wonder that men went about in fear and trembling, and that even in the heart of the wilderness they dared not whisper the doubts which oppressed them.

At first this vague and terrible power was exercised only upon the recalcitrants who, having embraced the Mormon faith, wished afterwards to pervert or to abandon it. Soon, however, it took a wider range. The supply of adult women was running short, and polygamy without a female population on which to draw was a barren doctrine indeed. Strange rumours began to be bandied about—rumours of murdered immigrants and rifled camps in regions where Indians had never been seen. Fresh women appeared in the harems of the

Elders—women who pined and wept, and bore upon their faces the traces of an unextinguishable horror. Belated wanderers upon the mountains spoke of gangs of armed men, masked, stealthy, and noiseless, who flitted by them in the darkness. These tales and rumours took substance and shape, and were corroborated and recorroborated, until they resolved themselves into a definite name. To this day, in the lonely ranches of the West, the name of the Danite Band, or the Avenging Angels, is a sinister and an ill-omened one.

Fuller knowledge of the organization which produced such terrible results served to increase rather than to lessen the horror which it inspired in the minds of men. None knew who belonged to this ruthless society. The names of the participators in the deeds of blood and violence done under the name of religion were kept profoundly secret. The very friend to whom you communicated your misgivings as to the Prophet and his mission might be one of those who would come forth at night with fire and sword to exact a terrible reparation. Hence every man feared his neighbour, and none spoke of things which were nearest his heart.

One fine morning John Ferrier was about to set out to his wheatfields, when he heard the click of the latch, and, looking through the window, saw a stout, sandy-haired middle-aged man coming up the pathway. His heart leapt to his mouth, for this was none other than the great Brigham Young himself. Full of trepidation—for he knew that such a visit boded him little good—Ferrier ran to the door to greet the Mormon chief. The latter, however, received his salutations coldly, and followed him with a stern face into the sitting-room.

"Brother Ferrier," he said, taking a seat, and eyeing the farmer keenly from under his light-coloured eyelashes, "the true believers have been good friends to you. We picked you up when you were starving in the desert, we shared our food with you, led you safe to the Chosen Valley, gave you a goodly share of land, and allowed you to wax rich under our protection. Is not this so?"

"It is so," answered John Ferrier.

"In return for all this we asked but one condition: that was, that you should embrace the true faith, and conform in every way to its usages. This you promised to do, and this, if common report says truly, you have neglected."

"And how have I neglected it?" asked Ferrier, throwing out his hands in expostulation. "Have I not given to the common fund? Have I not attended at the Temple? Have I not——?"

"Where are your wives?" asked Young, looking round him. "Call them in, that I may greet them."

"It is true that I have not married," Ferrier answered. "But women were few, and there were many who had better claims than I. I was not a lonely man: I had my daughter to attend to my wants."

"It is of that daughter that I would speak to you," said the leader of the Mormons. "She has grown to be the flower of Utah, and has found favour in the eyes of many who are high in the land."

John Ferrier groaned inwardly.

"There are stories of her which I would fain disbelieve—stories that she is sealed to some Gentile. This must be the gossip of idle tongues.

"What is the thirteenth rule in the code of the sainted Joseph Smith?" 'Let every maiden of the true faith marry one of the elect: for if she wed a Gentile, she commits a grievous sin.' This being so, it is impossible that you, who profess the holy creed, should suffer your daughter to violate it."

John Ferrier made no answer, but he played nervously with his riding-whip.

"Upon this one point your whole faith shall be tested—so it has been decided in the Sacred Council of Four. The girl is young, and we would not have her wed grey hairs, neither would we deprive her of all choice. We Elders have many heifers,* but our children must also be provided. Stangerson has a son, and Drebber has a son, and either of them would gladly welcome your daughter to their house. Let her choose between them. They are young and rich and of the true faith. What say you to that?"

Ferrier remained silent for some little time with his brows knitted.

"You will give us time," he said at last. "My daughter is very young—she is scarce of an age to marry."

"She shall have a month to chose," said Young, rising from his seat. "At the end of that time she shall give her answer."

He was passing through the door, when he turned, with flushed face and flashing eyes. "It were better for you, John Ferrier," he thundered, "that you and she were now lying blanched skeletons upon the

---

* Herbert C. Kemball, in one of his sermons, alludes to his hundred wives under this endearing epithet.

Sierra Blanco, than that you should put your weak wills against the orders of the Holy Four!"

With a threatening gesture of his hand, he turned from the door, and Ferrier heard his heavy steps scrunching along the shingly path.

He was still sitting with his elbow upon his knee considering how be should broach the matter to his daughter, when a soft hand was laid upon his, and looking up, he saw her standing beside him. One glance at her pale, frightened face showed him that she had heard what had passed.

"I could not help it," she said, in answer to his look. "His voice rang through the house. Oh, Father, Father, what shall we do?"

"Don't scare yourself," he answered, drawing her to him, and passing his broad, rough hand caressingly over her chestnut hair. "We'll fix it up somehow or another. You don't find your fancy kind o' lessening for this chap, do you?"

A sob and a squeeze of his hand was her only answer.

"No; of course not. I shouldn't care to hear you say you did. He's a likely lad, and he's a Christian, which is more than these folk here, in spite o' all their praying and preaching. There's a party starting for Nevada tomorrow, and I'll manage to send him a message letting him know the hole we are in. If I know anything o' that young man, he'll be back here with a speed that would whip electro-telegraphs."

Lucy laughed through her tears at her father's description.

"When he comes, he will advise us for the best. But it is for you that I am frightened, dear. One hears—one hears such dreadful stories about those who oppose the Prophet: something terrible always happens to them."

"But we haven't opposed him yet," her father answered. "It will be time to look out for squalls when we do. We have a clear month before us; at the end of that, I guess we had best shin out of Utah."

"Leave Utah!"

"That's about the size of it."

"But the farm?"

"We will raise as much as we can in money, and let the rest go. To tell the truth, Lucy, it isn't the first time I have thought of doing it. I don't care about knuckling under to any man, as these folk do to their darned Prophet. I'm a free-born American, and it's all new to me. Guess I'm too old to learn. If he comes browsing about this farm, he might chance to run up against a charge of buck-shot travelling in the opposite direction."

"But they won't let us leave," his daughter objected.

"Wait till Jefferson comes, and we'll soon manage that. In the meantime, don't you fret yourself, my dearie, and don't get your eyes swelled up, else he'll be walking into me when he sees you. There's nothing to be afeard about, and there's no danger at all."

John Ferrier uttered these consoling remarks in a very confident tone, but she could not help observing that he paid unusual care to the fastening of the doors that night, and that he carefully cleaned and loaded the rusty old shot-gun which hung upon the wall of his bedroom.

CHAPTER IV

A FLIGHT FOR LIFE

On the morning which followed his interview with the Mormon Prophet, John Ferrier went in to Salt Lake City, and having found his acquaintance, who was bound for the Nevada Mountains, he entrusted him with his message to Jefferson Hope. In it he told the young man of the imminent danger which threatened them, and how necessary it was that he should return. Having done thus he felt easier in his mind, and returned home with a light heart.

As he approached his farm, he was surprised to see a horse hitched to each of the posts of the gate. Still more surprised was he on entering to find two young men in possession of his sitting-room. One, with a long pale face, was leaning back in the rocking-chair, with his feet cocked up upon the stove. The other, a bull-necked youth with coarse, bloated features, was standing in front of the window with his hands in his pockets whistling a popular hymn. Both of them nodded to Ferrier as he entered, and the one on the rocking-chair commenced the conversation.

"Maybe you don't know us," he said. "This here is the son of Elder Drebber, and I'm Joseph Stangerson, who travelled with you in the desert when the Lord stretched out His hand and gathered you into the true fold."

"As He will all the nations in His own good time," said the other in a nasal voice; "He grindeth slowly but exceedingly small."

John Ferrier bowed coldly. He had guessed who his visitors were.

" We have come," continued Stangerson, " at the advice of our fathers to solicit the hand of your daughter for whichever of us may seem good to you and to her. As I have but four wives and brother Drebber here has seven, it appears to me that my claim is the stronger one."

" Nay, nay, Brother Stangerson," cried the other; " the question is not how many wives we have, but how many we can keep. My father has now given over his mills to me, and I am the richer man."

" But my prospects are better," said the other, warmly. " When the Lord removes my father, I shall have his tanning yard and his leather factory. Then I am your elder, and am higher in the Church."

" It will be for the maiden to decide," rejoined young Drebber, smirking at his own reflection in the glass. " We will leave it all to her decision."

During this dialogue John Ferrier had stood fuming in the doorway, hardly able to keep his riding-whip from the backs of his two visitors.

" Look here," he said at last, striding up to them, " when my daughter summons you, you can come, but until then I don't want to see your faces again."

The two young Mormons stared at him in amazement. In their eyes this competition between them for the maiden's hand was the highest of honours both to her and her father.

" There are two ways out of the room," cried Ferrier; " there is the door, and there is the window. Which do you care to use ? "

His brown face looked so savage, and his gaunt hands so threatening, that his visitors sprang to their feet and beat a hurried retreat. The old farmer followed them to the door.

" Let me know when you have settled which it is to be," he said, sardonically.

" You shall smart for this ! " Stangerson cried, white with rage. " You have defied the Prophet and the Council of Four. You shall rue it to the end of your days."

" The hand of the Lord shall be heavy upon you," cried young Drebber; " He will arise and smite you ! "

" Then I'll start the smiting," exclaimed Ferrier, furiously, and would have rushed upstairs for his gun had not Lucy seized him by the arm and restrained him. Before he could escape from her, the clatter of horses' hoofs told him that they were beyond his reach.

" The young canting rascals ! " he exclaimed, wiping the perspiration from his forehead; " I would sooner see you in your grave, my girl, than the wife of either of them."

" And so should I, Father," she answered, with spirit; " but Jefferson will soon be here."

" Yes. It will not be long before he comes. The sooner the better, for we do not know what their next move will be."

It was, indeed, high time that someone capable of giving advice and help should come to the aid of the sturdy old farmer and his adopted daughter. In the whole history of the settlement there had never been such a case of rank disobedience to the authority of the Elders. If minor errors were punished so sternly, what would be the fate of this arch rebel. Ferrier knew that his wealth and position would be of no avail to him. Others as well known and as rich as himself had been spirited away before now, and their goods given over to the Church. He was a brave man, but he trembled at the vague, shadowy terrors which hung over him. Any known danger he could face with a firm lip, but this suspense was unnerving. He concealed his fears from his daughter, however, and affected to make light of the whole matter, though she, with the keen eye of love, saw plainly that he was ill at ease.

He expected that he would receive some message or remonstrance from Young as to his conduct, and he was not mistaken, though it came in an unlooked-for manner. Upon rising next morning he found, to his surprise, a small square of paper pinned on to the coverlet of his bed just over his chest. On it was printed, in bold, straggling letters:—

" Twenty-nine days are given you for amendment, and then——"

The dash was more fear-inspiring than any threat could have been. How this warning came into his room puzzled John Ferrier sorely, for his servants slept in the outhouse, and the doors and windows had all be secured. He crumpled the paper up and said nothing to his daughter, but the incident struck a chill into his heart. The twenty-nine days were evidently the balance of the month which Young had promised. What strength or courage could avail against an enemy armed with such mysterious powers ? The hand which fastened the pin might have struck him to the heart, and he could never have known who had slain him.

Still more shaken was he next morning. They had sat down to their breakfast, when Lucy with a cry of surprise pointed upwards. In the centre of the ceiling was scrawled, with a burned stick apparently, the number 28. To his daughter it was unintelligible, and he did not enlighten her. That night he sat up with his gun and kept watch and ward. He saw and he heard nothing, and yet in the morning a great 27 had been painted upon the outside of his door.

Thus day followed day; and as sure as morning came he found that his unseen enemies had kept their register, and had marked up in some conspicuous position how many days were still left to him out of the month of grace. Sometimes the fatal numbers appeared upon the walls, sometimes upon the floors, occasionally they were on small placards stuck upon the garden gate or the railings. With all his vigilance John Ferrier could not discover whence these daily warnings proceeded. A horror which was almost superstitious came upon him at the sight of them. He became haggard and restless, and his eyes had the troubled look of some hunted creature. He had but one hope in life now, and that was for the arrival of the young hunter from Nevada.

Twenty had changed to fifteen, and fifteen to ten, but there was no news of the absentee. One by one the numbers dwindled down, and still there came no sign of him. Whenever a horseman clattered down the road, or a driver shouted at his team, the old farmer hurried to the gate, thinking that help had arrived at last. At last, when he saw five give way to four and that again to three, he lost heart, and abandoned all hope of escape. Single-handed, and with his limited knowledge of the mountains which surrounded the settlement, he knew that he was powerless. The more frequented roads were strictly watched and guarded, and none could pass along them without an order from the Council. Turn which way he would, there appeared to be no avoiding the blow which hung over him. Yet the old man never wavered in his resolution to part with life itself before he consented to what he regarded as his daughter's dishonour.

He was sitting alone one evening pondering deeply over his troubles, and searching vainly for some way out of them. That morning had shown the figure 2 upon the wall of his house, and the next day would be the last of the allotted time. What was to happen then ? All manner of vague and terrible fancies filled his imagination. And his daughter—what was to become of her after he was gone ? Was there no escape from the invisible network which was drawn all round them. He sank his head upon the table and sobbed at the thought of his own impotence.

What was that ? In the silence he heard a gentle scratching sound—low, but very distinct in the quiet of the night. It came from the door of the house. Ferrier crept into the hall and listened intently. There was a pause for a few moments, and then the low, insidious sound was repeated. Someone was evidently tapping very gently upon one of the panels of the door. Was it some midnight assassin who had come to carry out the murderous orders of the secret tribunal ? Or was it some agent who was marking up that the last day of grace had arrived. John Ferrier felt that instant death would be better than the suspense which shook his nerves and chilled his heart. Springing forward, he drew the bolt and threw the door open.

Outside all was calm and quiet. The night was fine, and the stars were twickling brightly overhead. The little front garden lay before the farmer's eyes bounded by the fence and gate, but neither there nor on the road was any human being to be seen. With a sigh of relief, Ferrier looked to right and to left, until, happening to glance straight down as his own feet, he saw to his astonishment a man lying flat on his face upon the ground, with arms and legs all asprawl.

So unnerved was he at the sight that he leaned up against the wall with his hand to his throat to stifle his inclination to call out. His first thought was that the prostrate figure was that of some wounded or dying man, but as he watched it he saw it writhe along the ground and into the hall with the rapidity and noiselessness of a serpent. Once within the house the man sprang to his feet, closed the door, and revealed to the astonished farmer the fierce face and resolute expression of Jefferson Hope.

" Good God ! " gasped John Ferrier, " How you scared me. Whatever made you come in like that ? "

" Give me food," the other said hoarsely. " I have had not time for bite or sup for eight-and-forty hours." He flung himself upon the cold meat and bread which were still lying upon the table from his host's supper, and devoured it voraciously. " Does Lucy bear up well ? he asked, when he had satisfied his hunger.

" Yes. She does not know the danger," her father answered.

" That is well. The house is watched on every side. That is why I crawled my way up to it. They may be darned sharp, but they're not quite sharp enough to catch a Washoe hunter."

John Ferrier felt a different man now that he realized that he had a devoted ally. He seized the young man's leathery hand and wrung it cordially. " You're a man to be proud of," he said. " There are not many who would come to share our danger and our troubles."

" You've hit it there, pard," the young hunter answered. " I have a respect for you, but if you were alone in this business I'd think twice before I put my head into such a hornet's nest. It's Lucy that brings me here, and before harm comes on her I guess there will be one less o' the Hope family in Utah."

" What are we to do ? "

" Tomorrow is your last day, and unless you act tonight you are lost. I have a mule and two horses waiting in the Eagle Ravine. How much money have you ? "

" Two thousand dollars in gold and five in notes."

" That will do. I have as much more to add to it. We must push for Carson City through the mountains. You had best wake Lucy. It is as well that the servants do not sleep in the house."

While Ferrier was absent, preparing his daughter for the approaching journey, Jefferson Hope packed all the eatables that he could find into a small parcel, and filled a stoneware jar with water, for he knew by experience that the mountain wells were few and far between. He had hardly completed his arrangements before the farmer returned with his daughter all dressed and ready for a start. The greeting between the lovers was warm, but brief for minutes were precious, and there was much to be done.

"We must make our start at once," said Jefferson Hope, speaking in a low but resolute voice, like one who realizes the greatness of the peril, but has steeled his heart to meet it. " The front and back entrances are watched, but with caution we may get away through the side window and across the fields. Once on the road we are only two miles from the Ravine where the horses are

waiting. By daybreak we should be halfway through the mountains."

" What if we are stopped ? " asked Ferrier.

Hope slapped the revolver butt which protruded from the front of his tunic. " If they are too many for us, we shall take two or three of them with us," he said with a sinister smile.

The lights inside the house had all been extinguished, and from the darkened window Ferrier peered over the fields which had been his own, and which he was now about to abandon forever. He had long nerved himself to the sacrifice, however, and the thought of the honour and happiness of his daughter outweighed any regret at his ruined fortunes. All looked so peaceful and happy, the rustling trees and the broad silent stretch of grainland, that it was difficult to realize that the spirit of murder lurked through it all. Yet the white face and set expression of the young hunter showed that in his approach to the house he had seen enough to satisfy him upon that head.

Ferrier carried the bag of gold and notes, Jefferson Hope had the scanty provisions and water, while Lucy had a small bundle containing a few of her more valued possessions. Opening the window very slowly and carefully, they waited until a dark cloud had somewhat obscured the night, and then one by one passed through into the little garden. With bated breath and crouching figures they stumbled across it, and gained the shelter of the hedge, which they skirted until they came to the gap which opened into the cornfield. They had just reached this point when the young man seized his two companions and dragged them down into the shadow, where they lay silent and trembling.

It was as well that his praire training had given Jefferson Hope the ears of a lynx. He and his friends had hardly crouched down before the melancholy hooting of a mountain owl was heard within a few yards of them, which was immediately answered by another hoot at a small distance. At the same moment a vague, shadowy figure emerged from the gap for which they had been making, and uttered the plaintive signal cry again, on which a second man appeared out of the obscurity.

" Tomorrow at midnight," said the first, who appeared to be in authority. " When the Whippoor-Will calls three times."

" It is well," returned the other. " Shall I tell Brother Drebber ? "

" Pass it on to him, and from him to the others. Nine to seven ! "

"Seven to five!" repeated the other; and the two figures flitted away in different directions. Their concluding words had evidently been some form of sign and countersign. The instant that their footsteps had died away in the distance, Jefferson Hope sprang to his feet, and helping his companions through the gap, led the way across the fields at the top of his speed, supporting and half-carrying the girl when her strength appeared to fail her.

"Hurry on! hurry on!" he gasped from time to time. "We are though the line of sentinels. Everything depends on speed. Hurry on!"

Once on the high road, they made rapid progress. Only once did they meet anyone, and then they managed to slip into a field, and so avoid recognition. Before reaching the town the hunter branched away into a rugged and narrow footpath which led to the mountains. Two dark, jagged peaks loomed above them through the darkness, and the defile which led between them was the Eagle Canyon in which the horses were awaiting them. With unerring instinct Jefferson Hope picked his way among the great boulders and along the bed of a dried-up watercourse, until he came to the retired corner screened with rocks, where the faithful animals had been picketed. The girl was placed upon the mule, and old Ferrier upon one of the horses, with his money-bag, while Jefferson Hope led the other along the precipitous and dangerous path.

It was a bewildering route for anyone who was not accustomed to face Nature in her wildest moods. On the one side a great crag towered up a thousand feet or more, black, stern, and menacing, with long basaltic columns upon its rugged surface like the ribs of some petrified monster. On the other hand a wild chaos of boulders and debris made all advance impossible. Between the two ran an irregular track, so narrow in places that they had to travel in Indian file, and so rough that only practised riders could have traversed it at all. Yet, in spite of all dangers and difficulties, the hearts of the fugitives were light within them, for every step increased the distance between them and the terrible despotism from which they were flying.

They soon had a proof, however, that they were still within the jurisdiction of the Saints. They had reached the very wildest and most desolate portion of the pass when the girl gave a startled cry, and pointed upwards. On a rock which overlooked the track, showing out dark and plain against the sky, there stood a solitary sentinel. He saw them as soon as they perceived him, and his military challenge of "Who goes there?" rang through the silent ravine.

"Travellers from Nevada," said Jefferson Hope, with his hand upon his rifle which hung by his saddle.

They could see the lonely watcher fingering his gun, and peering down at them as if dissatisfied at their reply.

"By whose permission?" he asked.

"The Holy Four," answered Ferrier. His Mormon experiences had taught him that that was the highest authority to which he could refer.

"Nine to seven," cried the sentinel.

"Seven to five," returned Jefferson Hope promptly, remembering the countersign which he had heard in the garden.

"Pass, and the Lord go with you," said the voice from above. Beyond his post the path broadened out, and the horses were able to break into a trot. Looking back, they could see the solitary watcher leaning upon his gun, and knew that they had passed the outlying post of the chosen people, and that freedom lay before them.

CHAPTER V

THE AVENGING ANGELS

All night their course lay through intricate defiles and over irregular and rock-strewn paths. More than once they lost their way, but Hope's intimate knowledge of the mountains enabled them to regain the track once more. When morning broke, a scene of marvellous though savage beauty lay before them. In every direction the great snow-capped peaks hemmed them in, peeping over each other's shoulders to the far horizon. So steep were the rocky banks on either side of them that the larch and the pine seemed to be suspended over their heads, and to need only a gust of wind to come hurtling down upon them. Nor was the fear entirely an illusion, for the barren valley was thickly strewn with trees and boulders which had fallen in a similar manner. Even as they passed, a great rock came thundering down with a hoarse rattle which woke the echoes in the silent gorges, and startled the weary horses into a gallop.

As the sun rose slowly above the eastern horizon, the caps of the great mountains lit up one after the other, like lamps at a festival, until they were all ruddy and glowing. The magnificent spectacle cheered the hearts of the three fugitives and gave them fresh energy. At a wild torrent which swept out of a ravine they called a halt and watered their horses, while they partook of a hasty breakfast. Lucy and her father would fain have rested longer, but Jefferson Hope was inexorable. "They will be upon our track by this time," he said. "Everything depends upon our speed. Once safe in Carson, we may rest for the remainder of our lives."

During the whole of that day they struggled on through the defiles, and by evening they calculated that they were more than thirty miles from their enemies. At night-time they chose the base of a beetling crag, where the rocks offered some protection from the chill wind, and there, huddled together for warmth, they enjoyed a few hours' sleep. Before daybreak, however, they were up and on their way once more. They had seen no signs of any pursuers, and Jefferson Hope began to think that they were fairly out of the reach of the terrible organization whose enmity they had incurred. He little knew how far that iron grasp could reach or how soon it was to close upon them and crush them.

About the middle of the second day of their flight their scanty store of provisions began to run out. This gave the hunter little uneasiness, however, for there was game to be had among the mountains, and he had frequently before had to depend upon his rifle for the needs of life. Choosing a sheltered nook, he piled together a few dried branches and made a blazing fire, at which his companions might warm themselves, for they were now nearly five thousand feet above the sea level, and the air was bitter and keen. Having tethered the horses, and bade Lucy adieu, he threw his gun over his shoulder, and set out in search of whatever chance might throw in his way. Looking back, he saw the old man and the young girl crouching over the blazing fire, while the three animals stood motionless in the background. Then the intervening rocks hid them from his view.

He walked for a couple of miles through one ravine after another without success, though, from the marks upon the bark of the trees, and other indications, he judged that there were numerous bears in the vicinity. At last, after two or three hours' fruitless search, he was thinking of turning back in despair, when casting his eyes upwards he saw a sight which sent a thrill of pleasure through his heart. On the edge of a jutting pinnacle, three or four hundred feet above him, there stood a creature somewhat resembling a sheep in appearance, but armed with a pair of gigantic horns. The big-horn—for so it is called—was acting, probably, as a guardian over a flock which were invisible to the hunter; but fortunately it was heading in the opposite direction, and had not perceived him. Lying on his face, he rested his rifle upon a rock, and took a long and steady aim before drawing the trigger. The animal sprang into the air, tottered for a moment upon the edge of the precipice, and then came crashing down into the valley beneath.

The creature was too unwieldy to lift, so the hunter contented himself with cutting away one haunch and part of the flank. With this trophy over his shoulder, he hastened to retrace his steps, for the evening was already drawing in. He had hardly started, however, before he realized the difficulty which faced him. In his eagerness he had wandered far past the ravines which were known to him, and it was no easy matter to pick out the path which he had taken. The valley in which he found himself divided and subdivided into many gorges, which were so like each other that it was impossible to distinguish one from the other. He followed one for a mile or more until he came to a mountain torrent which he was sure that he had never seen before. Convinced that he had taken the wrong turn, he tried another, but with the same result. Night was coming on rapidly, and it was almost dark before he at last found himself in a defile which was familiar to him. Even then it was no easy matter to keep to the right track, for the moon had not yet risen, and the high cliffs on either side made the obscurity more profound. Weighed down with his burden, and weary from his exertions, he stumbled along, keeping up his heart by the reflection that every step brought him nearer to Lucy, and that he carried with him enough to ensure them food for the remainder of their journey.

He had now come to the mouth of the very defile in which he had left them. Even in the darkness he could recognize the outline of the cliffs which bounded it. They must, he reflected, be awaiting him anxiously, for he had been absent nearly five hours. In the gladness of his heart he put his hands to his mouth and made the glen re-echo to a loud halloo as a signal that he was coming. He paused and listened for an answer. None came save his own cry, which clattered up the dreary, silent ravines, and was borne back to his ears in countless repetitions. Again he shouted, even louder than before, and again no whisper came back from the friends whom he had left such a short time ago. A vague, nameless dread came over him, and he hurried onwards frantically, dropping the precious food in his agitation.

When he turned the corner, he came full in sight of the spot where the fire had been lit. There was still a glowing pile of wood ashes there, but it had evidently not been tended since his departure. The same dead silence still reigned all round. With his fears all changed to convictions, he hurried on. There was no living creature near the remains of the fire; animals, man, maiden, all were gone. It was only too clear that some sudden and terrible disaster had occurred during his absence—a disaster which had embraced them all, and yet had left no traces behind it.

Bewildered and stunned by this blow, Jefferson Hope felt his head spin round, and had to lean upon his rifle to save himself from falling. He was essentially a man of action, however, and speedily recovered from his temporary impotence. Seizing a half-consumed piece of wood from the smouldering fire, he blew it into a flame, and proceeding with its help to examine the little camp. The ground was all stamped down by the feet of horses, showing that a large party of mounted men had overtaken the fugitives, and the direction of their tracks proved that they had afterwards turned back to Salt Lake City. Had they carried back both of his companions with them? Jefferson Hope had almost persuaded himself that they must have done so, when his eye fell upon an object which made every nerve of his body tingle within him. A little way on one side of the camp was a low-lying heap of reddish soil, which had not been there before. There was no mistaking it for anything but a newly-dug grave. As the young hunter approached it, he perceived that a stick had been planted on it, with a sheet of paper stuck in the cleft fork of it. The inscription upon the paper was brief, but to the point:

JOHN FERRIER

FORMERLY OF SALT LAKE CITY

Died August 4th, 1860

The sturdy old man, who he had left so short a time before, was gone, then, and this was all his epitaph. Jefferson Hope looked wildly round to see if there was a second grave, but there was no sign of one. Lucy had been carried back by their terrible pursuers to fulfil her original destiny, by becoming one of the harem of the Elder's son. As the young fellow realized the certainty of her fate, and his own powerlessness to prevent it, he wished that he, too, was lying with the old farmer in his last silent resting-place.

Again, however, his active spirit shook off the lethargy which springs from despair. If there was nothing else left to him, he could at least devote his life to revenge. With indomitable patience and perseverance, Jefferson Hope possessed also a power of sustained vindictiveness, which he may have learned from the Indians amongst whom he had lived. As he stood by the desolate fire, he felt that the only one thing which could assuage his grief would be thorough and complete retribution, brought by his own hand upon his enemies. His strong will and untiring energy should, he determined, be devoted to that one end. With a grim, white face, he retraced his steps to where he had dropped the food and having stirred up the smouldering fire, he cooked enough to last him for a few days. This he made up into a bundle, and, tired as he was, he set himself to walk back through the mountains upon the track of the Avenging Angels.

For five days he toiled footsore and weary through the defiles which he had already traversed on horseback. At night he flung himself down upon the rocks, and snatched a few hours of sleep; but before daybreak he was always well on his way. On the sixth day, he reached the Eagle Canyon, from which they had commenced their ill-fated flight. Thence he could look down upon the home of the Saints. Worn and exhausted, he leaned upon his rifle and shook his gaunt hand fiercely at the silent widespread city beneath him. As he looked at it, he observed that there were flags in the principal streets, and other signs of festivity. He was still speculating as to what this might mean when he heard the clatter of horse's hoofs, and saw a mounted man riding towards him. As he approached, he recognized him as a Mormon named Cowper, to whom he had rendered services at different times. He therefore accosted him when he got up to him, with the object of finding out what Lucy Ferrier's fate had been.

" I am Jefferson Hope," he said. " You remember me."

The Mormon looked at him with undisguised astonishment—indeed, it was difficult to recognize in this tattered, unkempt wanderer, with ghastly white face and fierce, wild eyes, the spruce young hunter of former days. Having, however, at last satisfied himself as to his identity, the man's surprise changed to consternation.

"You are mad to come here," he cried. " It is as much as my own life is worth to be seen talking with you. There is a warrant against you from the Holy Four for assisting the Ferriers away."

" I don't fear them, or their warrant," Hope said, earnestly. " You must know something of this matter, Cowper. I conjure you by everything you hold dear to answer a few questions. We have always been friends. For god's sake, don't refuse to answer me."

"What is it ? " the Mormon asked uneasily. " Be quick. The very rocks have ears and the trees eyes."

" What has become of Lucy Ferrier ? "

" She was married yesterday to young Drebber. Hold up, man, hold up; you have no life left in you."

" Don't mind me," said Hope faintly. He was white to the very lips, and had sunk down on the stone against which he had been leaning. " Married, you say ? "

" Married yesterday—that's what those flags are for on the Endowment House. There was some words between young Drebber and young Stangerson as to which was to have her. They'd both been in the party that followed them, and Stangerson had shot her father, which seemed to give him the best claim; but when they argued it out in council, Drebber's party was the stronger, so the Prophet gave her over to him. No one won't have her very long though, for I saw death in her face yesterday. She is more like a ghost than a woman. Are you off, then ? "

" Yes, I am off," said Jefferson Hope, who had risen from his seat. His face might have been chiselled out of marble, so hard and set was its expression, while its eyes flowed with a baleful light.

" Where are you going ? "

" Never mind," he answered; and, slinging his weapon over his shoulder, strode off down the gorge and so away into the heart of the mountains to the haunts of the wild beasts. Amongst them all there was none so fierce and so dangerous as himself.

The prediction of the Mormon was only too well fulfilled. Whether it was the terrible death of her father or the effects of her hateful marriage into which she had been forced, poor Lucy never held up her head again, but pined away and died within a month. Her sottish husband, who had married her principally for the sake of John Ferrier's property, did not affect any great grief at his bereavement; but his other wives mourned over her, and sat up with her the night before the burial, as is the Mormon custom. They were grouped round the bier in the early hours of the morning, when, to their inexpressible fear and astonishment, the door was flung open, and a savage-looking, weather-beaten man in tattered garments strode into the room. Without a glance or a word to the cowering women, he walked up to the white silent figure which had once contained the pure soul of Lucy Ferrier. Stooping over her, he pressed his lips reverently to her cold forehead, and then, snatching up her hand, he took the wedding-ring from her finger. " She shall not be buried in that," he cried with a fierce snarl, and before an alarm could be raised sprang down the stairs and was gone. So strange and so brief was the episode that the watchers might have found it hard to believe it themselves or persuade other people of it, had it not been for the undeniable fact that the circlet of gold which marked her as having been a bride had disappeared.

For some months Jefferson Hope lingered among the mountains, leading a strange wild life, and nursing in his heart the fierce desire for vengeance which possessed him. Tales were told in the city of the weird figure which was seen prowling about the suburbs, and which haunted the lonely mountain gorges. Once a bullet whistled through Stangerson's window and flattened itself upon the wall within a foot of him. On another occasion, as Drebber passed under a cliff a great boulder crashed down on him, and he only escaped a terrible death by throwing himself upon his face. The two young Mormons were not long in discovering the reason of these attempts upon their lives and led repeated expeditions into the mountains in the hope of capturing or killing their enemy, but always without success. Then they adopted the precaution of never going out alone or after nightfall, and of having their houses guarded. After a time they were able to relax these measures, for nothing was either heard or seen of their opponent, and they hoped that time had cooled his vindictiveness.

Far from doing so, it had, if anything augmented it. The hunter's mind was of a hard, unyielding nature, and the predominant idea of revenge had taken such complete possession of it that there was no room for any other emotion. He was, however, above all things, practical. He soon realized that even his iron constitution could not stand the incessant strain which he was putting upon it. Exposure and want of wholesome food were wearing him out. If he died like a dog among the mountains, what was to become of his revenge then? And yet such a death was sure to overtake him if he persisted. He felt that that was to play his enemy's game, so he reluctantly returned to the old Nevada mines, there to recruit his health and to amass money enough to allow him to pursue his object without privation.

His intention had been to be absent a year at the most but a combination of unforeseen circumstances prevented his leaving the mines for nearly five. At the end of that time, however, his memory of his wrongs and his craving for revenge were quite as keen as on that memorable night when he had stood by John Ferrier's grave. Disguised, and under an assumed name, he returned to Salt Lake City, careless what became of his own life, as long as he obtained what he knew to be justice. There he found evil tidings awaiting him. There had been a schism among the Chosen People a few months before, some of the younger members of the Church having rebelled against the authority of the Elders, and the result had been a secession of a certain number of the malcontents, who had left Utah and become Gentiles. Among these had been Drebber and Stangerson; and no one knew whither they had gone. Rumour reported that Drebber had managed to convert a large part of his property into money, and that he had departed a wealthy man, while his companion, Stangerson, was comparatively poor. There was no clue at all, however, as to their whereabouts.

Many a man, however vindictive, would have abandoned all thought of revenge in the face of such a difficulty, but Jefferson Hope never faltered for a moment. With the small competence he possessed, eked out by such employment as he could pick up, he travelled from town to town through the United States in quest of his enemies. Year passed into year, his black hair turned grizzled, but still he wandered on, a human bloodhound, with his mind wholly set upon the one object to which he had devoted his life. At last his perseverance was rewarded. It was but a glance of a face in a window, but that one glance told him that Cleveland in Ohio possessed the men whom he was in pursuit of. He returned to his miserable lodgings with his plan of vengeance all arranged. It chanced, however, that Drebber, looking from his window, had recognized the vagrant in the street, and had read murder in his eyes. He hurried before a justice of the peace, accompanied by Stangerson, who had become his private secretary, and represented to him that they were in danger of their lives from the jealousy and hatred of an old rival. That evening Jefferson Hope was taken into custody, and not being able to find sureties, was detained for some weeks. When at last he was liberated it was only to find that Drebber's house was deserted, and that he and his secretary had departed for Europe.

Again the avenger had been foiled, and again his concentrated hatred urged him to continue the pursuit. Funds were wanting, however, and for some time he had to return to work, saving every · dollar for his approaching journey. At last, having collected enough to keep life in him, he departed for Europe and tracked his enemies from city to city, working his way in any menial capacity, but never overtaking the fugitives. When he reached St. Petersburg, they had departed for Paris; and when he followed them there, he learned that they had just set off for Copenhagen. At the Danish capital he was again a few days late, for they had journeyed on to London, where at last he succeeded in running them to earth. As to what occured there, we cannot do better than quote the old hunter's own account, as duly recorded in Dr. Watson's Journal, to which we are already under such obligations.

CHAPTER VI

A CONTINUATION OF THE REMINISCENCES OF JOHN WATSON, M.D.

Our prisoner's furious resistance did not apparently indicate any ferocity in his disposition towards ourselves, for on finding himself powerless, he smiled in an affable manner, and expressed his hopes that he had not hurt any of us in the scuffle. "I guess you're going to take me to the police-station," he remarked to Sherlock Holmes. "My cab's at the door. If you'll loose my legs I'll walk down to it. I'm not so light to lift as I used to be."

Gregson and Lestrade exchanged glances, as if they thought this proposition rather a bold one; but Holmes at once took the prisoner at his word, and loosened the towel which he had bound round his ankles. He rose and stretched his legs, as though to assure himself that they were free once more. I remember that I thought to myself, as I eyed him, that I had seldom seen a more powerful man; and his dark, sunburned face bore an expression of determination and energy which was as formidable as his personal strength.

"If there's a vacant place for a chief of police, I reckon you are the man for it," he said, gazing with undisguised admiration at my fellow-lodger. "The way you kept on my trail was a caution."

"You had better come with me," said Holmes to the two detectives.

"I can drive you," said Lestrade.

"Good! and Gregson can come inside with me. You, too, Doctor. You have taken an interest in the case, and may as well stick to us."

I assented gladly, and we all descended together. Our prisoner made no attempt at escape, but stepped calmly into the cab which had been his, and we followed him. Lestrade mounted the box, whipped up the horse, and brought us in a very short time to our destination. We were ushered into a small chamber, where a police inspector noted down our prisoner's name and the names of the men with whose murder he had been charged. The official was a white-faced, unemotional man, who went through his duties in a dull, mechanical way. "The prisoner will be put before the magistrates in the course of the week," he said; "in the meantime, Mr Jefferson Hope, have you anything that you wish to say? I must warn you that your words will be taken down, and may be used against you."

"I've got a good deal to say," our prisoner said slowly: "I want to tell you gentleman all about it."

"Hadn't you better reserve that for your trial?" asked the inspector.

"I may never be tried," he answered. "You needn't look startled. It isn't suicide I am thinking of. Are you a doctor?" he turned his fierce dark eyes upon me as he asked this last question.

"Yes, I am," I answered.

"Then put your hand here," he said, with a smile, motioning with his manacled wrists towards his chest.

I did so; and became at once conscious of an extraordinary throbbing and commotion which was going on inside. The walls of his chest seemed to thrill and quiver as a frail building would do inside which some powerful engine was at work. In the silence of the room I could hear a dull humming and buzzing noise which proceeded from the same source.

"Why," I cried, "you have an aortic aneurism!"

"That's what they call it," he said, placidly. "I went to a doctor last week about it, and he told me that it is bound to burst before many days passed. It has been getting worse for years. I got it from over-exposure and under-feeding among the Salt Lake Mountains. I've done my work now, and I don't care how soon I go, but I should like to leave some account of the business behind me. I don't want to be remembered as a common cut-throat."

The inspector and the two detectives had a hurried discussion as to the advisability of allowing him to tell his story.

"Do you consider, Doctor, that there is immediate danger?" the former asked.

"Most certainly there is," I answered.

"In that case it is clearly our duty, in the interests of justice, to take his statement," said the inspector. "You are at liberty, sir, to give your account, which I again warn you will be taken down."

"I'll sit down, with your leave," the prisoner said, suiting the action to the word. "This aneurism of mine makes me easily tired, and the tussle we had half an hour ago has not mended matters. I'm on the brink of the grave, and I am not likely to lie to you. Every word I say is the absolute truth, and how you use it is a matter of no consequence to me."

With these words, Jefferson Hope leaned back in his chair and began the following remarkable statement. He spoke in a calm and methodical manner, as though the events which he narrated were commonplace enough. I can vouch for the accuracy of the subjoined account, for I have had access to Lestrade's notebook, in which the prisoner's words were taken down exactly as they were uttered.

"It don't much matter to you why I hated these men," he said; "it's enough that they were guilty of the death of two human beings—a father and a daughter—and that they had, therefore, forfeited their own lives. After the lapse of time that has passed since their crime, it was impossible for me to secure a conviction against them in any court. I knew of their guilt though, and I determined that I should be judge, jury and executioner all rolled into one. You'd have done the same, if you have any manhood in you, if you had been in my place.

" That girl that I spoke of was to have married me twenty years ago. She was forced into marrying that same Drebber, and broke her heart over it. I took the marriage ring from her dead finger, and I vowed that his dying eyes should rest upon that very ring, and that his last thoughts should be of the crime for which he was punished. I have carried it about with me, and have followed him and his accomplice over two continents until I caught them. They thought to tire me out, but they could not do it. If I die tomorrow, as is likely enough, I die knowing that my work in this world is done, and well done. They have perished, and by my hand. There is nothing left for me to hope for, or to desire.

" They were rich and I was poor, so that it was no easy matter for me to follow them. When I got to London my pocket was about empty, and I found that I must turn my hand to something for my living. Driving and riding are as natural to me as walking, so I applied at a cab-owner's office, and soon got employment. I was to bring a certain sum a week to the owner, and whatever was over that I might keep for myself. There was seldom much over, but I managed to scrape along somehow. The hardest job was to learn my way about, for I reckon that of all the mazes that ever were contrived, this city is the most confusing. I had a map beside me though, and when once I had spotted the principal hotels and stations, I got on pretty well.

" It was some time before I found out where my two gentlemen were living; but I inquired and inquired until at last I dropped across them. They were at a boarding-house in Camberwell, over the other side of the river. When once I found them out, I knew that I had them at my mercy. I had grown my beard, and there was no chance of their recognizing me. I would dog them and follow them until I saw my opportunity. I was determined that they should not escape me again.

" They were very near doing it for all that. Go where they would about London, I was always at their heels. Sometimes I followed them on my cab, and sometimes on foot, but the former was the best, for then they could not get away from me. It was only early in the morning or late at night

that I could earn anything, so that I began to get behindhand with my employer. I did not mind that, however, as long as I could lay my hand upon the men I wanted.

" They were very cunning, though. They must have thought that there was some chance of their being followed, for they would never go out alone, and never after nightfall. During two weeks I drove behind them every day, and never once saw them separate. Drebber himself was drunk half the time, but Stangerson was not to be caught napping. I watched them late and early, but never saw the ghost of a chance; but I was not discouraged, for something told me that the hour had almost come. My only fear was that this thing in my chest might burst a little too soon and leave my work undone.

" At last, one evening I was driving up and down Torquay Terrace, as the street was called in which they boarded, when I saw a cab drive up to their door. Presently some luggage was brought out and after a time Drebber and Stangerson followed it, and drove off. I whipped up my horse and kept within sight of them, feeling very ill at ease, for I feared that they were going to shift their quarters. At Euston Station they got out, and I left a boy to hold my horse and followed them on to the platform. I heard them ask for the Liverpool train, and the guard answered that one had just gone, and there would not be another for some hours. Stangerson seemed to be put out at that, but Drebber was rather pleased than otherwise. I got so close to them in the bustle that I could hear every word that passed between them. Drebber said that he had a little business of his own to do, and that if the other would wait for him he would soon rejoin him. His companion remonstrated with him, and reminded him that they had resolved to stick together. Drebber answered that the matter was a delicate one, and that he must go alone. I could not catch what Stangerson said to that, but the other burst out swearing, and reminded him that he was nothing more than his paid servant, and that he must not presume to dictate to him. On that the secretary gave it up as a bad job, and simply bargained with him that if he missed the last train he should rejoin him at Halliday's Private Hotel; to which Drebber answered that he would be back on the platform before eleven, and made his way out of the station.

" The moment for which I had waited so long had at last come. I had my enemies within my power. Together they could protect each other, but singly they were at my mercy. I did not act, however, with undue precipitation. My plans were already formed. There is no satisfaction in vengeance unless the offender has time to realize who it is that strikes him, and why retribution has come upon him. I had my plans arranged by which I should have the opportunity of making the man who had wronged me understand that his old sin had found him out. It chanced that some days before a gentleman who had been engaged in looking over some houses in the Brixton Road had dropped the key of one of them in my carriage. It was claimed that same evening, and returned; but in the interval I had taken a moulding of it, and had a duplicate constructed. By means of this I had access to at least one spot in this great city where I could rely upon being free from interruption. How to get Drebber to that house was the difficult problem which I had now to solve.

" He walked down the road and went into one or two liquor shops, staying for nearly half an hour in the last of them. When he came out, he staggered in his walk, and was evidently pretty well on. There was a hansom just in front of me, and he hailed it. I followed it so close that the nose of my horse was within a yard of his driver the whole way. We rattled across Waterloo Bridge and through miles of streets, until, to my astonishment, we found ourselves back in the terrace in which he had boarded. I could not imagine what his intention was in returning there; but I went on and pulled up my cab a hundred yards or so from the house. He entered it, and his hansom drove away. Give me a glass of water, if you please. My mouth gets dry with the talking."

I handed him the glass, and he drank it down.

" That's better," he said. " Well, I waited for a quarter of an hour, or more, when suddenly there came a noise like people struggling inside the house. Next moment the door was flung open and two men appeared, one of whom was Drebber, and the other was a young man whom I had never seen before. This fellow had Drebber by the collar, and when they came to the head of the steps he gave him a shove and a kick which sent him half across the road: ' You hound !' he cried, shaking his stick at him; ' I'll teach you to insult an honest girl !' He was so hot that I think he would have thrashed Drebber with his cudgel, only that the cur staggered away down the road as fast as his legs would carry him. He ran as far as the corner, and then seeing my cab he hailed me and jumped in. ' Drive me to Halliday's Private Hotel,' said he.

" When I had him fairly inside my cab, my heart jumped so with joy that I feared lest at this last moment my aneurism might go wrong. I drove along slowly, weighing in my own mind what it was best to do. I might take him right out into the country, and there in some deserted lane have my last interview with him. I had almost decided upon this when he solved the problem for me. The craze for drink had seized him again, and he ordered me to pull up outside a gin palace. He went in, leaving word that I should wait for him. There he remained until closing time, and when he came out he was so far gone that I knew the game was in my own hands.

" Don't imagine that I intended to kill him in cold blood. It would only have been rigid justice if I had done so, but I could not bring myself to do it. I had long determined that he should have a show for his life if he chose to take advantage of it. Among the many billets which I have filled in America during my wandering life, I was once janitor and sweeper-out of the laboratory at York College. One day the professor was lecturing on poisons, and he showed his students some alkaloid, as he called it, which he had extracted from some South American arrow poison, and which was so powerful that the least grain meant instant death. I spotted the bottle in which this preparation was kept, and when they were all gone, I helped myself to a little of it. I was a fairly good dispenser, so I worked this alkaloid into small soluble pills, and each pill I put in a box with a similar pill made without the poison. I determined at the time that when I had my chance my gentlemen should each have a draw out of one of these boxes, while I ate the pill that remained. It would be quite as deadly and a good deal less noisy than firing across a handkerchief. From that day I had always had my pill boxes about with me, and the time had now come when I was to use them.

" It was nearer one than twelve, and a wild bleak night, blowing hard and raining in torrents. Dismal as it was outside, I was glad within—so glad that I could have shouted out from pure exultation. If any of you gentlemen have ever pined for a thing, and longed for it during twenty long years, and then suddenly found it within your reach you would understand my feelings. I lit a cigar, and puffed at it to steady my nerves, but my hands were trembling and my temples throbbing with excitement. As I drove I could see old John Ferrier and sweet Lucy looking at me out of the darkness and smiling at me, just as plain as I see you all in this room. All the way they were ahead of me, one on each side of the horse, until I pulled up at the house in Brixton Road.

"There was not a soul to be seen, nor a sound to be heard, except the dripping of the rain. When I looked in at the window, I found Drebber all huddled together in a drunken sleep. I shook him by the arm. 'It's time to get out,' I said.

"'All right, cabby,' said he.

"I suppose he thought we had come to the hotel that he had mentioned, for he got out without another word, and followed me down the garden. I had to walk beside him to keep him steady, for he was still a little top-heavy. When we came to the door, I opened it, and led him into the front room. I give you my word that all the way, the father and the daughter were walking in front of us.

"'It's infernally dark,' said he, stamping about.

"'We'll soon have a light,' I said, striking a match and putting it to a wax candle which I had brought with me. 'Now, Enoch Drebber,' I continued, turning to him, and holding the light to my own face, 'who am I?'

"He gazed at me with bleared, drunken eyes for a moment, and then I saw the horror spring up in them, and convulse his whole features, which showed me that he knew me. He staggered back with a livid face, and I saw the perspiration break out upon his brow, while his teeth chattered in his head. At the sight I leaned my back against the door and laughed loud and long. I had always known that venegeance would be sweet, but I had never hoped for the contentment of soul which now possessed me."

"'You dog!' I said; 'I have hunted you from Salt Lake City to St. Petersburg, and you have always escaped me. Now, at last your wanderings have come to an end, for either you or I shall never see tomorrow's sun-rise.' He shrunk still farther away as I spoke, and I could see on his face that he thought I was mad. So I was for the time. The pulses in my temples beat like sledgehammers, and I believe I would have had a fit of some sort if the blood had not gushed from my nose and relieved me.

"'What do you think of Lucy Ferrier now?' I cried, locking the door, and shaking the key in his face. 'Punishment has been slow in coming, but it has overtaken you at last.' I saw his coward lips tremble as I spoke. He would have begged for his life, but he knew well that it was useless.

"'Would you murder me?' he stammered.

"'There is no murder,' I answered. 'Who talks of murdering a mad dog? What mercy had you upon my poor darling, when you dragged her from her slaughtered father, and bore her away to your accursed and shameless harem.'

"'It was not I who killed her father,' he cried.

"'But it was you who broke her innocent heart,' I shrieked, thrusting the box before him. 'Let the high God judge between us. Choose and eat. There is death in one and life in the other. I shall take what you leave. Let us see if there is justice upon the earth, or if we are ruled by chance.'

"He cowered away with wild cries and prayers for mercy, but I drew my knife and held it to his throat until he obeyed me. Then I swallowed the other, and we stood facing one another in silence for a minute of more, waiting to see which was to live and which was to die. Shall I ever forget the look which came over his face when the first warning pangs told that the poison was in his system? I laughed as I saw it, and held Lucy's marriage ring in front of his eyes. It was but for a moment, for the action of the alkaloid is rapid. A spasm of pain contorted his features; he threw his hands out in front of him, staggered, and then, with a hoarse cry, fell heavily upon the floor. I turned him over with my foot, and placed my hand upon his heart. There was no movement. He was dead!

"The blood had been streaming from my nose, but I had taken no notice of it. I don't know what it was that put it into my head to write upon the wall with it. Perhaps it was some mischievous idea of setting the police upon the wrong track, for I felt light-hearted and cheerful. I remembered a German being found in New York with RACHE written up above him, and it was argued at the time in the newspapers that the secret societies must have done it. I guessed that what puzzled the New Yorkers would puzzle the Londoners, so I dipped my finger in my own blood and printed it on a convenient place on the wall. Then I walked down to my cab and found that there was nobody about, and that the night was still very wild. I had driven some distance, when I put my hand into the pocket in which I usually kept Lucy's ring, and found that it was not there. I was thunderstruck at this, for it was the only memento that I had of her. Thinking that I might have dropped it when I stooped over Drebber's body, I drove back, and leaving my cab in a side street, I went boldly up to the house—for I was ready to dare anything rather than lose the ring. When I arrived there, I walked right into the arms of a police-officer who was coming out, and only managed to disarm his suspicions by pretending to be hopelessly drunk.

" That was how Enoch Drebber came to his end. All I had to do then was to do as much for Stangerson, and so pay off John Ferrier's debt. I knew that he was staying at Halliday's Private Hotel, and I hung about all day, but he never came out. I fancy that he suspected something when Drebber failed to put in an appearance. He was cunning, was Stangerson, and always on his guard. If he thought he could keep me off by staying indoors he was very much mistaken. I soon found out which was the window of his bedroom, and early next morning I took advantage of some of the ladders which were lying in the lane behind the hotel, and so made my way into his room in the grey of the dawn. I woke him up and told him that the hour had come when he was to answer for the life he had taken so long before. I described Drebber's death to him, and I gave him the same choice of the poisoned pills. Instead of grasping at the chance of safety which that offered him, he sprang from his bed and flew at my throat. In self-defence I stabbed him to the heart. It would have been the same in any case, for Providence would never have allowed his guilty hand to pick out anything but the poison.

" I have little more to say and it's as well, for I am about done up. I went on cabbing it for a day or so, intending to keep at it until I could save enough to take me back to America. I was standing in the yard when a ragged youngster asked if there was a cabby called Jefferson Hope, and said that his cab was wanted by a gentleman at 221B, Baker Street. I went round, suspecting no harm, and the next thing I knew, this young man here had the bracelets on my wrists, and as neatly shackled as ever I saw in my life. That's the whole of my story, gentlemen. You may consider me to be a murderer; but I hold that I am just as much an officer of justice as you are."

So thrilling had the man's narrative been and his manner was so impressive that we had sat silent and absorbed. Even the professional detectives, blasé as they were in every detail of crime, appeared to be keenly interested in the man's story. When he finished, we sat for some minutes in a stillness which was only broken by the scratching of Lestrade's pencil as he gave the finishing touches to his shorthand account.

" There is only one point on which I should like a little more information," Sherlock Holmes said at last. " Who was your accomplice who came for the ring which I advertised ? "

The prisoner winked at my friend jocosely. " I can tell my own secrets," he said, " but I don't get other people into trouble. I saw your advertisement, and I thought it might be a plant, or it might be the ring which I wanted. My friend volunteered to go and see. I think you'll own he did it smartly."

" Not a doubt of that," said Holmes heartily.

" Now, gentlemen," the inspector remarked, gravely, " the forms of the law must be complied with. On Thursday the prisoner will be brought before the magistrates, and your attendance will be required. Until then I will be repsonsible for him." He rang the bell as he spoke, and Jefferson Hope was led off by a couple of warders, while my friend and I made our way out of the station and took a cab back to Baker Street.

CHAPTER VII

THE CONCLUSION

We had all been warned to appear before the magistrates upon the Thursday; but when the Thursday came there was no occasion for our testimony. A higher Judge had taken the matter before a tribunal where strict justice would be meted out to him. On the very night after his capture the aneurism burst, and he was found in the morning stretched upon the floor of the cell, with a placid smile upon his face, as though he had been able in his dying moments to look back upon a useful life, and on work well done.

" Gregson and Lestrade will be wild about his death," Holmes remarked, as we chatted it over next evening. " Where will their grand advertisement be now ? "

" I don't see that they had very much to do with his capture," I answered.

" What you do in this world is a matter of no conseqeunce," returned my companion, bitterly. " The question is, what can you make people believe that you have done. Never mind," he continued, more brightly, after a pause. " I would not have missed the investigation for anything. There has been no better case within my recollection. Simple as it was, there were several most instructive points about it."

" Simple ! " I ejaculated.

" Well, really, it can hardly be described as otherwise," said Sherlock Holmes, smiling at my surprise. " The proof of its intrinsic simplicity is, that without any help save a few very ordinary deductions I was able to lay my hands upon the criminal within three days."

" That is true," said I.

" I have already explained to you that what is out of the common is usually a guide rather than a hindrance. In solving a problem of this sort, the grand thing is to be able to reason backwards. That is a very useful accomplishment, and a very easy one, but people do not practice it much. In the every-day affairs of life it is more useful to reason forwards, and so the other comes to be neglected. There are fifty who can reason synthetically for one who can reason analytically."

" I confess," said I " that I do not quite follow you."

" I hardly expected that you would. Let me see if I can make it clearer. Most people, if you describe a train of events to them, will tell you what the result would be. They can put those events together in their minds, and argue from them that something will come to pass. There are a few people, however, who, if you told them a result, would be able to evolve from their own inner consciousness what the steps were which led up to that result. This power is what I mean which I talk of reasoning backwards, or analytically."

" I understand," said I.

" Now this was a case in which you were given the result and had to find everything else for yourself. Now let me endeavour to show you the different steps in my reasoning. To begin at the beginning. I approached the house, as you know, on foot, and with my mind entirely free from all impressions. I naturally began by examining the roadway, and there, as I have already explained to you, I saw clearly the marks of a cab, which I ascertained by inquiry, must have been there during the night. I satisfied myself that it was a cab and not a private carriage by the narrow gauge of the wheels. The ordinary London growler is considerably less wide than a gentleman's brougham.

" This was the first point gained. I then walked slowly down the garden path, which happened to be composed of a clay soil, peculiarly suitable for taking impressions. No doubt it appeared to you to be a mere trampled line of slush, but to my trained eyes every mark upon its surface had a meaning. There is no branch of detective science which is so important and so much neglected as the art of tracing footsteps. Happily, I have always laid great stress upon it, and much practice has made it second nature to me. I saw the heavy footmarks of the constable, but I saw also the track of the two men who had first passed through the garden. It was easy to tell that they had been before the others, because in places their marks had been entirely obliterated by the others coming upon the top of them. In this way my second link was formed, which told me that the nocturnal visitors were two in number, one remarkable for his height (as I calculated from the length of his stride) and the other fashionably dressed, to judge from the small and elegant impression left by his boots.

" On entering the house this last inference was confirmed. My well-booted man lay before me. The tall one, then, had done the murder, if murder there was. There was no wound upon the dead man's person, but the agitated expression upon his face assured me that he had foreseen his fate before it came upon him. Men who die from heart disease, or any sudden natural cause, never by any chance exhibit agitation upon their features. Having sniffed the dead man's lips, I detected a slightly sour smell, and I came to the conclusion that he had had poison forced upon him. Again, I argued that it had been forced upon him from the hatred and fear expressed upon his face. By the method of exclusion, I had arrived at this result, for no other hypothesis would meet the facts. Do not imagine that it was a very unheard-of-idea. The forcible adminstration of poisons is by no means a new thing in criminal annals. The cases of Dolsky in Odessa, and of Leturier in Montpellier, will occur at once to any toxicologist.

" And now came the great question as to the reason why. Robbery had not been the object of the murder, for nothing was taken. Was is politics, then, or was it a woman ? That was the question which confronted me. I was inclined from the first to the latter supposition. Political assassins are only too glad to do their work and fly. This murder had, on the contrary, been done most deliberately, and the perpetrator had left his tracks all over the room, showing that he had been there all the time. It must have been a private wrong, and not a political one, which called for such a methodical revenge. When the inscription was discovered upon the wall, I was more inclined than ever to my opinion. The thing was too evidently a blind. When the ring was found, however, it settled the question. Clearly the murderer had used it to remind his victim of some dead or absent woman. It was at this point that I asked Gregson whether he had inquired in his telegram to Cleveland as to any particular point in Mr. Drebber's former career. He answered, you remember, in the negative.

"I then proceeded to make a careful examination of the room, which confirmed me in my opinion as to the murderer's height, and furnished me with the additional details as to the Trichinopoly cigar and the length of his nails. I had already come to the conclusion, since there were no signs of a struggle, that the blood which covered the floor had burst from the murderer's nose in his excitement. I could perceive that the track of blood coincided with the track of his feet. It is seldom that any man, unless he is very full-blooded, breaks out in this way through emotion, so I hazarded the opinion that the criminal was probably a robust and ruddy-faced man. Events proved that I had judged correctly.

"Having left the house, I proceeded to do what Gregson had neglected. I telegraphed to the head of the police at Cleveland, limiting my inquiry to the circumstances connected with the marriage of Enoch Drebber. The answer was conclusive. It told me that Drebber had already applied for the protection of the law against an old rival in love, named Jefferson Hope, and that this same Hope was at present in Europe. I knew now that I held the clue to the mystery in my hand, and all that remained was to secure the murderer.

"I had already determined in my own mind that the man who had walked into the house with Drebber was none other than the man who had driven the cab. The marks on the road showed me that the horse had wandered on in a way which would have been impossible had there been anyone in charge of it. Where, then, could the driver be, unless he were inside the house? Again, it is absurd to suppose that any sane man would carry out a deliberate crime under the very eyes, as it were, of a third person, who was sure to betray him. Lastly, supposing one man wished to dog another through

London, what better means could he adopt than to turn cab driver. All these considerations led me to the irresistible conclusion that Jefferson Hope was to be found among the jarveys of the Metropolis.

"If he had been one, there was no reason to believe that he had ceased to be. On the contrary from his point of view, any sudden change would be likely to draw attention to himself. He would probably, for a time at least, continue to perform his duties. There was no reason to suppose that he was going under an assumed name. Why should he change his name in a country where no one knew his original one? I therefore organized my Street Arab detective corps, and sent them systematically to every cab proprietor in London until they ferreted out the man that I wanted. How well they succeeded, and how quickly I took advantage of it, are still fresh in your recollection. The murder of Stangerson was an incident which was entirely unexpected, but which could hardly in any case have been prevented. Through it, as you know, I came into possession of the pills, the existence of which I had already surmised. You see, the whole thing is a chain of logical sequences without a break or flaw."

"It is wonderful!" I cried. "Your merits should be publicly recognized. You should publish an account of the case. If you won't, I will for you."

"You may do what you like, Doctor," he answered. "See here!" he continued, handing a paper over to me, "look at this!"

It was the *Echo* for the day, and the paragraph to which he pointed was devoted to the case in question.

"The public," it said, "have lost a sensational treat through the sudden death of the man Hope, who was suspected of the murder of Mr. Enoch Drebber and of Mr. Joseph Stangerson. The details of the case will probably be never known now, though we are informed upon good authority that the crime was the result of an old-standing and romantic feud, in which love and Mormonism bore a part. It seems that both the victims belonged, in their younger days, to the Latter Day Saints, and Hope, the deceased prisoner, hails also from Salt Lake City. If the case has had no other effect, it, at least, brings out in the most striking manner the efficiency of our detective police force, and will serve as a lesson to all foreigners that they will do wisely to settle their feuds at home, and not to carry them on to British soil. It is an open secret that the credit of this smart capture belongs entirely to the well-known Scotland Yard officials, Messrs. Lestrade and Gregson. The man was apprehended, it appears, in the rooms of a certain Mr. Sherlock Holmes, who has himself, as an amateur, shown some talent in the detective line, and who, with such instructors may hope in time to attain to some degree of their skill. It is expected a testimonial of some sort will be presented to the two officers as a fitting recognition of their services."

" Didn't I tell you when we started ? " cried Sherlock Holmes, with a laugh. " That's the result of all our Study in Scarlet; to get them a testimonial ! "

" Never mind," I answered; " I have all the facts in my journal, and the public shall know them. In the meantime you must make yourself contented by the consciousness of success, like the Roman miser:—

" Populus me sibilat, at mihi plaudo
Ipse domi simul ac nummos contemplar in
arca ' "

The Sign of Four

CHAPTER 1

THE SCIENCE OF DEDUCTION

Sherlock Holmes took his bottle from the corner of the mantelpiece, and his hypodermic syringe from its neat morocco case. With his long, white nervous fingers he adjusted the delicate needle, and rolled back his left shirt-cuff. For some little time his eyes rested thoughtfully upon the sinewy forearm and wrist, all dotted and scarred with innumerable puncture-marks. Finally, he thrust the sharp point home, pressed down the tiny piston and sank back into the velvet-lined armchair with a long sigh of satisfaction.

Three times a day for many months I had witnessed this performance, but the custom had not reconciled my mind to it. On the contrary, from day to day I had become more irritable at the sight, and my conscience swelled nightly within me at the thought that I had lacked the courage to protest. Again and again I had registered a vow that I should deliver my soul upon the subject; but there was that in the cool, nonchalant air of my companion which made him the last man with whom one would care to take anything approaching to a liberty. His great powers, his masterly manner, and the experience which I had had of his many extraordinary qualities, all made me diffident and backward in crossing him.

Yet upon that afternoon, whether it was the Beaune which I had taken with my lunch, or the additional exasperation produced by the extreme deliberation of his manner, I suddenly felt that I could hold out no longer.

"Which is it today," I asked "morphine or cocaine?"

He raised his eyes languidly from the old black-letter volume which he had opened.

"It is cocaine," he said, "a seven-per-cent solution. Would you care to try it?"

"No, indeed," I answered, brusquely. "My constitution has not got over the Afghan campaign yet. I cannot afford to throw any extra strain upon it."

He smiled at my vehemence. "Perhaps you are right, Watson," he said. "I suppose that its influence is physically a bad one. I find it, however, so transcendingly stimulating and clarifying to the mind that its second action is a matter of small moment."

"But consider!" I said, earnestly. "Count the cost! Your brain may, as you say, be roused and excited, but it is a pathological and morbid process, which involves increased tissue-change, and may at last leave a permanent weakness. You know, too, what a black reaction comes upon you. Surely the game is hardly worth the candle. Why should you, for a mere passing pleasure, risk the loss of those great powers with which you have been endowed? Remember that I speak not only as one comrade to another, but as a medical man to one for whose constitution he is to some extent answerable."

He did not seem offended. On the contrary, he put his finger-tips together, and leaned his elbows on the arms of his chair, like one who has a relish for conversation.

"My mind," he said, "rebels at stagnation. Give me problems, give me work, give me the most abstruse cryptogram, or the most intricate analysis, and I am in my own proper atmosphere. I can dispense then with artificial stimulants. But I abhor the dull routine of existence. I crave for mental exaltation. That is why I have chosen my own particular profession, or rather created it for I am the only one in the world."

"The only unofficial detective?" I said, raising my eyebrows.

"The only unofficial consulting detective," he answered. "I am the last and highest court of appeal in detection. When Gregson, or Lestrade, or Athelney Jones are out of their depths—which, by the way, is their normal state—the matter is laid before me. I examine the data, as an expert, and pronounce a specialist's opinion. I claim no credit in such cases. My name figures in no newspaper. The work itself, the pleasure of finding a field for my peculiar powers, is my highest reward. But you have yourself had some experience of my methods of work in the Jefferson Hope case."

"Yes indeed," said I, cordially. "I was

never so struck by anything in my life. I even embodied it in a small brochure, with the somewhat fantastic title of 'A Study in Scarlet.' "

He shook his head sadly.

"I glanced over it," said he. "Honestly, I cannot congratulate you upon it. Detection is, or ought to be, an exact science, and should be treated in the same cold and unemotional manner. You have attempted to tinge it with romanticism, which produces much the same effect as if you worked a love-story or an elopement into the fifth proposition of Euclid."

"But the romance was there," I remonstrated. "I could not tamper with the facts."

"Some facts should be suppressed, or, at least, a just sense of proportion should be observed in treating them. The only point in the case which deserved mention was the curious analytical reasoning from effects to causes, by which I succeeded in unravelling it."

I was annoyed at this criticism of a work which had been specially designed to please him. I confess, too, that I was irritated by the egotism which seemed to demand that every line of my pamphlet should be devoted to his own special doings. More than once during the years that I had lived with him in Baker Street I had observed that a small vanity underlay my companion's quiet and didactic manner. I made no remark, however, but sat nursing my wounded leg. I had had a Jezail bullet through it some time before, and, though it did not prevent me from walking, it ached wearily at every change of the weather.

"My practice has extended recently to the Continent," said Holmes, after a while, filling up his old briar-root pipe. "I was consulted last week by François le Villard, who, as you probably know, has come rather to the front lately in the French detective service. He has all the Celtic power of quick intuition, but he is deficient in the wide range of exact knowledge which is essential to the higher developments of his art. The case was concerned with a will, and possessed some features of interest. I was able to refer him to two parellel cases, the one at Riga in 1857, and the other at St Louis in 1871, which have suggested to him the true solution. Here is the letter which I had this morning acknowledging my assistance."

He tossed over, as he spoke, a crumpled sheet of foreign notepaper. I glanced my eyes down it, catching a profusion of notes of admiration, with stray ' magnifiques ',' coup-de-maitres ', and ' tours de force ', all testifying to the ardent admiration of the Frenchman.

"He speaks as a pupil to his master," said I.

"Oh, he rates my assistance too highly," said Sherlock Holmes lightly. "He has considerable gifts himself. He possesses two out of the three qualities necessary for the ideal detective. He has the power of observation and that of deduction. He is only wanting in knowledge, and that may come in time. He is now translating my small works into French."

"Your works?"

"Oh, didn't you know?" he cried, laughing. "Yes, I have been guilty of several monographs. They are all upon technical subjects. Here, for example, is one 'Upon the Distinction between the Ashes of the Various Tobaccos.' In it I enumerate a hundred and forty forms of cigar, cigarette, and pipe tobacco, with coloured plates illustrating the difference in the ash. It is a point which is continually turning up in criminal trials, and which is sometimes of supreme importance as a clue. If you can say definitely, for example, that some murder had been done by a man who was smoking an Indian lunkah, it obviously narrows your field of search. To the trained eye there is as much difference between the black ash of a Trichinopoly and the white fluff of bird's-eye as there is between a cabbage and a potato."

"You, have an extraordinary genius for minutiae," I remarked.

"I appreciate their importance. Here is my monograph upon the tracing of footsteps, with some remarks upon the uses of plaster of Paris as a preserver of impresses. Here, too, is a curious little work upon the influence of a trade upon the form of the hand, with lithotypes of the hands of slaters, sailors, cork-cutters, compositors, weavers, and diamond-polishers. That is a matter of great practical interest to the scientific detective—especially in cases of unclaimed bodies, or discovering the antecedents of criminals. But I weary you with my hobby."

"Not at all," I answered, earnestly. "It is of the greatest interest to me especially since I have had the opportunity of observing your practical application of it. But you spoke just now of observation and deduction. Surely the one to some extent implies the other."

"Why hardly," he answered, leaning back luxuriously in his armchair, and sending up thick blue wreaths from his pipe. " For example, observation shows me that you have been to the Wigmore Street Post Office this morning, but deduction lets me know that when there you dispatched a telegram."

" Right ! " said I. " Right on both points ! But I confess that I don't see how you arrived at it. It was a sudden impulse upon my part, and I have mentioned it to no one."

" It is simplicity itself," he remarked, chuckling at my surprise—" so absurdly simple that an explanation is superfluous; and yet it may serve to define the limits of observation and of deduction. Observation tells me that you have a little reddish mould adhering to your instep. Just opposite the Wigmore Street office they have taken up the pavement and thrown up some earth, which lies in such a way that it is difficult to avoid treading in it in entering. The earth is of the peculiar reddish tint which is found, as far as I know, nowhere else in the neighbourhood. So much is observation. The rest is deduction."

" How, then, did you deduce the telegram ? "

" Why, of course I knew that you had not written a letter, since I sat opposite to you all morning. I see also in your open desk there that you have a sheet of stamps and a thick bundle of postcards. What could you go into the post-office for, then, but to send a wire ? Eliminate all other factors, and the one which remains must be the truth."

" In this case it certainly is so," I replied, after a little thought. The thing, however, is, as you say, of the simplest. Would you think me impertinent if I were to put your theories to a more severe test ? "

" On the contrary," he answered; " it would prevent me from taking a second dose of cocaine. I should be delighted to look into any problem which you might submit to me."

" I have heard you say that it is difficult for a man to have any object in daily use without leaving the impress of his individuality upon it in such a way that a trained observer might read it. Now, I have here a watch which has recently come into my possession. Would you have the kindness to let me have an opinion upon the character or habits of the late owner ? "

I handed him over the watch with some slight feeling of amusement in my heart, for the test was, as I thought, an impossible one, and I intended it as a lesson against the somewhat dogmatic tone which he occasionally assumed. He balanced the watch in his hand, gazed hard at the dial, opened the back, and examined the works, first with his naked eyes and then with a powerful convex lens. I could hardly keep from smiling at his crestfallen face when he finally snapped the case to and handed it back.

" There are hardly any data," he remarked. " The watch has been recently cleaned, which robs me of my most suggestive facts."

" You are right," I answered. " It was cleaned before being sent to me."

In my heart I accused my companion of putting forward a most lame and impotent excuse to cover his failure. What data could he expect from an uncleaned watch ?

" Though unsatisfactory, my research has not been entirely barren," he observed, staring up at the ceiling with dreamy, lack-lustre eyes. " Subject to your correction, I should judge that the watch belonged to your elder brother who inherited it from your father."

" That you gather, no doubt, from the H.W. on the back ? "

" Quite so. The W. suggests your own name. The date of the watch is nearly fifty years back, and the initials are as old as the watch; so it was made for the last generation. Jewellery usually descends to the eldest son, and he is most likely to have the same name as the father. Your father has, if I remember right, been dead for many years. It has, therefore, been in the hands of your eldest brother."

" Right, so far," said I. " Anything else ? "

" He was a man of untidy habits—very untidy and careless. He was left with good prospects, but threw away his chances, lived for some time in poverty with occasional short intervals of prosperity, and, finally, taking to drink, he died. That is all I can gather."

I sprang from my chair and limped impatiently about the room with considerably bitterness in my heart.

" This is unworthy of you, Holmes," I said. " I could not have believed that you would have descended to this. You have made inquiries into the history of my unhappy brother, and you now pretend to deduce this knowledge in some fanciful way. You cannot expect me to believe that you have read all this from his old watch ! It is so unkind, and to speak plainly, has a touch of charlatanism in it."

" My dear Doctor," said he, kindly, " pray accept my apologies. Viewing the matter as an abstract problem, I had forgotten how personal and painful a thing it might be to you. I assure you, however, that I never even knew that you had a brother until you handed me the watch."

"Then how in the name of all that is wonderful did you get these facts? They are absolutely correct in every particular."

"Ah, that is good luck. I could only say what was the balance of probability. I didn't at all expect to be so accurate."

"But it was not mere guess-work?"

"No, no; I never guess. It is a shocking habit—destructive to the logical faculty. What seems strange to you is only because you do not follow my train of thought or observe the small facts upon which large inferences may depend. For example, I began by stating that your brother was careless. When you observe the lower part of that watch-case you will notice that it is not only dinted in two places, but it is cut and marked all over from the habit of keeping other hard objects, such as coins or keys, in the same pocket. Surely, it is no great feat to assume that a man who treats a fifty-guinea watch so cavalierly must be a careless man. Neither is it a very far-fetched inference that a man who inherits one article of such value is pretty well provided for in other respects."

I nodded, to show that I followed his reasoning.

"It is very customary for pawnbrokers in England, when they take a watch, to scratch the number of the ticket with a pin-point upon the inside of the case. It is more handy than a label, as there is no risk of the number being lost or transposed. There are no less than four such numbers visible to my lens on the inside of this case. Inference—that your brother was often at low water. Second inference—that he had occasional bursts of prosperity, or he could not have redeemed the pledge. Finally, I ask you to look at the inner plate which contains the keyhole. What sober man's key could have scored those grooves? But you will never see a drunkard's watch without them. He winds it at night, and he leaves these traces of his unsteady hand. Where is the mystery to all this?"

"It is as clear as daylight," I answered. "I regret the injustice which I did you. I should have had more faith in your marvellous faculty. May I ask whether you have any professional inquiry on foot at present?"

"None. Hence the cocaine. I cannot live without brain-work. What else is there to live for? Stand at the window here. Was there ever such a dreary, dismal, unprofit-able world? See how the yellow fog swirls down the street and drifts across the dun-coloured houses. What could be more hopelessly prosaic and material? What is the use of having powers, Doctor, when one has no field upon which to exert them? Crime is commonplace, existence is commonplace, and no qualities save those which are commonplace have any function upon earth."

I had opened my mouth to reply to this tirade, when, with a crisp knock, our landlady entered, bearing a card upon the brass salver.

"A young lady for you, sir," she said, addressing my companion.

"Miss Mary Morstan," he read. "Hum! I have no recollection of her name. Ask the young lady to step up, Mrs. Hudson. Don't go, Doctor. I should prefer that you remain."

CHAPTER II

THE STATEMENT OF THE CASE

Miss Morstan entered the room with a firm step and an outward composure of manner. She was a blonde young lady, small, dainty, well-gloved, and dressed in the most perfect taste. There was, however, a plainness and simplicity about her costume which bore with it a suggestion of limited means. The dress was a sombre greyish beige, untrimmed and unbraided, and she wore a small turban of the same dull hue, relieved only by a suspicion of white feather in the side. Her face had neither regularity of feature nor beauty of complexion, but her expression was sweet and amiable, and her large blue eyes were singularly spiritual and sympathetic. In an experience of women which extends over many nations and three separate continents, I have never looked upon a face which gave a clearer promise of a refined and sensitive nature. I could not but observe that, as she took the seat which Sherlock Holmes placed for her, her lip trembled, her hand quivered, and she showed every sign of intense upward agitation.

"I have come to you Mr. Holmes," she said, "because you once enabled my employer, Mrs. Cecil Forrester, to unravel a little domestic complication. She was much impressed by your kindness and skill."

"Mrs. Cecil Forrester," he repeated, thoughtfully. "I believe that I was of some slight service to her. The case, however, as I remember it, was a very simple one."

"She did not think so. But at least you cannot say the same of mine. I can hardly imagine anything more strange, more utterly inexplicable, than the situation in which I find myself."

Holmes rubbed his hands, and his eyes glistened. He leaned forward in his chair with an expression of extraordinary concentration upon his clear-cut, hawk-like features.

"State your case," said he, in brisk, business tones.

I felt that my position was an embarrassing one.

"You will, I am sure, excuse me," I said, rising from my chair.

To my surprise, the young lady held up her gloved hand to detain me.

"If your friend," she said, "would be good enough to stop, he might be of inestimable service to me."

I relapsed into my chair.

"Briefly," she continued, "the facts are these. My father was an officer in an Indian regiment, who sent me home when I was quite a child. My mother was dead, and I had no relative in England. I was placed, however, in a comfortable boarding establishment at Edinburgh, and there I remained until I was seventeen years of age. In the year 1878 my father, who was senior captain of his regiment, obtained twelve months' leave and came home. He telegraphed to me from London that he had arrived all safe, and directed me to come down at once, giving the Langham Hotel as his address. His message, as I remember, was full of kindness and love. On reaching London I drove to the Langham, and was informed that Captain Morstan was staying there, but that he had gone out the night before and had not returned. I waited all day without news of him. That night, on the advice of the manager of the hotel, I communicated with the police, and next morning we advertised in all the papers. Our inquiries led to no result; and from that day to this no word has ever been heard of my unfortunate father. He came home with his heart full of hope to find some peace, some comfort, and instead——"

She put her hand to her throat, and a choking sob cut short the sentence.

"The date?" asked Holmes, opening his notebook.

"He disappeared upon the 3rd of December, 1878—nearly ten years ago."

"His luggage?"

"Remained at the hotel. There was nothing in it to suggest a clue—some clothes, some books, and a considerable number of curiosities from the Andaman Islands. He had been one of the officers in charge of the convict guard there."

"Has he any friends in town?"

"Only one that we know of—Major Sholto, of his own regiment, the 34th Bombay Infantry. The major had retired some little time before, and lived at Upper Norwood. We communicated with him, of course, but he did not know that his brother officer was in England."

"A singular case," remarked Holmes.

"I have not yet described to you the most singular part. About six years ago—to be exact, upon the 4th of May, 1882—an advertisement appeared in the *The Times* asking for the address of Miss Mary Morstan, and stating that it would be to her advantage to come forward. There was no name and address appended. I had at the time just entered the family of Mrs. Cecil Forrester in the capacity of governess. By her advice I published my address in the advertisement column. The same day there arrived through the post a small cardboard box addressed to me, which I found to contain a very large and lustrous pearl. No word of writing was enclosed. Since then every year upon the same date there has always appeared a similar box, containing a similar pearl, without any clue as to the sender. They have been pronounced by an expert to be of a rare variety and of considerable value. You can see for yourselves that they are very handsome."

She opened a flat box as she spoke, and showed me six of the finest pearls that I had ever seen.

"Your statement is most interesting," said Sherlock Holmes. "Has anything else occurred to you?"

"Yes, and no later than today. That is why I have come to you. This morning I received this letter, which you will perhaps read for yourself."

"Thank you," said Holmes. "The envelope, too, please. Postmark, London, S.W. Date, July 7. Hum! Man's thumbmark on corner—probably postman. Best quality paper. Envelopes at sixpence a packet. Particular man in his stationery. No address. "Be at the third pillar from the left outside the Lyceum Theatre tonight at seven o'clock. If you are distrustful bring two friends. You are a wronged woman, and shall have justice. Do not bring police. If you do, all will be in vain. Your unknown friend." Well, really, this is a pretty little mystery! What do you intend to do, Miss Morstan?"

" That is exactly what I want to ask you."

" Then we shall most certainly go—you and I and—yes, why, Dr. Watson is the very man. Your correspondent says two friends. He and I have worked together before."

" But would he come ? " she asked, with something appealing in her voice and expression.

" I shall be proud and happy," said I, fervently, " if I can be of any service."

" You are both very kind," she answered. " I have led a retired life, and have no friends whom I could appeal to. If I am here at six it will do, I suppose ? "

" You must not be later," said Holmes. " There is one other point, however. Is this handwriting the same as that upon the pearl-box addresses ? "

" I have them here," she answered, producing half-a-dozen pieces of paper.

" You are certainly a model client. You have the correct intuition. Let us see, now." He spread out the papers upon the table, and gave little, darting glances from one to the other. " They are disguised hands, except the letter," he said, presently; " but there can be no question as to the authorship. See how the irrepressible Greek *e* will break out, and see the twirl of the final *s*. They are undoubtedly by the same person. I should not like to suggest false hopes, Miss Morstan, but is there any resemblance between this hand and that of your father ? "

" Nothing could be more unlike."

" I expected to hear you say so. We shall look out for you, then, at six. Pray allow me to keep the papers. I may look into the matter before then. It is only half-past three. *Au revoir*, then."

" *Au revoir*," said our visitor; and with a bright, kindly glance from one to the other of us, she replaced her pearl-box in her bosom and hurried away.

Standing at the window, I watched her walking briskly down the street, until the grey turban and white feather were but a speck in the sombre crowd.

" What a very attractive woman ! " I exclaimed, turning to my companion.

He had lit his pipe again, and was leaning back with drooping eyelids. " Is she ? " he said, languidly; " I did not observe."

" You really are an automaton—a calculating machine," I cried. " There is something positively inhuman about you at times."

He smiled gently.

" It is of the first importance," he said, " not to allow your judgment to be biased by personal qualities. A client is to me a mere unit, a factor in a problem. The emotional qualities are antagonistic to clear reasoning. I assure you that the most winning woman I ever knew was hanged for poisoning three little children for their insurance money, and the most repellent man of my acquaintance is a philanthropist who has spent nearly a quarter of a million upon the London poor."

" In this case, however——"

" I never make exceptions. An exception disproves the rule. Have you ever had occasion to study character in handwriting ? What do you make of this fellow's scribble ? "

" It is legible and regular," I answered. " A man of business habits and some force of character."

Holmes shook his head.

" Look at his long letters," he said. " They hardly rise above the common herd. That *d* might be an *a*, and that *l* an *e*. Men of character always differentiate their long letters, however illegibly they may write. There is vacillation in his *k*'s and self-esteem in his capitals. I am going out now. I have some few references to make. Let me recommend this book—one of the most remarkable ever penned. It is Winwood Reade's *Martyrdom of Man*. I shall be back in an hour."

I sat in the window with the volume in my hand but my thoughts were far from the daring speculations of the writer. My mind ran upon our late visitor—her smiles, the deep, rich tones of her voice, the strange mystery which overhung her life. If she were seventeen at the time of her father's disappearance she must be seven-and-twenty now—a sweet age, when youth has lost its self-consciousness and become a little sobered by experience. So I sat and mused, until such dangerous thoughts came into my head that I hurried away to my desk and plunged furiously into the latest treatise upon pathology. What was I, an Army surgeon with a weak leg and a weaker bank account, that I should dare to think of such thing ? She was a unit, a factor—nothing more. If my future were black, it was better surely to face it like a man than to attempt to brighten it more by mere will-o'-the-wisps of the imagination.

CHAPTER III

IN QUEST OF A SOLUTION

It was half-past five before Holmes returned. He was bright, eager, and in excellent spirits, a mood which in his case alternated with fits of the blackest depression.

"There is no great mystery in this matter," he said, taking the cup of tea which I had poured out for him; "the facts appear to admit of only one explanation."

"What! you have solved it already?"

"Well, that would be too much to say. I have discovered a suggestive fact, that is all. It is, however, *very* suggestive. The details are still to be added. I have just found, on consulting the back files of *The Times*, that Major Sholto, of Upper Norwood, late of the 34th Bombay Infantry, died upon the 28th of April, 1882."

"I may be very obtuse, Holmes, but I fail to see what this suggests."

"No? You surprise me. Look at it in this way, then. Captain Morstan disappears. The only person in London whom he could have visited is Major Sholto. Major Sholto denies having heard that he was in London. Four years later Sholto dies. Within a week of his death Captain Morstan's daughter receives a valuable present, which is repeated from year to year, and now culminates in a letter which describes her as a wronged woman. What wrong can it refer to except deprivation of her father? And why should the presents begin immediately after Sholto's death, unless it is that Sholto's heir knows something of the mystery and desires to make compensation? Have you any alternative theory which will meet the facts?

"But what a strange compensation! And how strangely made! Why, too, should he write a letter now, rather than six years ago? Again, the letter speaks of giving justice. What justice can she have? It is too much to suppose that her father is still alive. There is no other injustice in her case that you know of."

"There are difficulties; there are certainly difficulties," said Sherlock Holmes, pensively; "but our expedition of tonight will solve them all. Ah, here is a four-wheeler, and Miss Morstan inside. Are you ready? Then we had better go down for it is a little past the hour."

I picked up my hat and my heaviest stick, but I observed that Holmes took his revolver from his drawer and slipped it into his pocket. It was clear that he thought that our night's work might be a serious one.

Miss Morstan was muffled in a dark cloak, and her sensitive face was composed, but pale. She must have been more than woman if she did not feel some uneasiness at the strange enterprise upon which we were embarking, yet her self-control was perfect, and she readily answered the few additional questions which Sherlock Holmes put to her.

"Major Sholto was a very particular friend of Papa's," she said. "His letters were full of allusions to the Major. He and Papa were in command of the troops at the Andaman Islands, so they were thrown a great deal together. By the way, a curious paper was found in Papa's desk which no one could understand. I don't suppose that it is of the slightest importance, but I thought you might care to see it, so I brought it with me. It is here."

Holmes unfolded the paper carefully and smoothed it out upon his knee. He then very methodically examined it all over with his double lens.

"It is a paper of native Indian manufacture," he remarked. "It has at some time been pinned to a board. The diagram upon it appears to be a plan of part of a large building with numerous halls, corridors and passages. At one point is a small cross done in red ink, and above it is '3.37 from left' in added pencil writing. In the left hand corner is a curious hieroglyphic like four crosses in a line with their arms touching. Beside it is written, in very rough and coarse characters, 'The sign of the four—Jonathan Small, Mahomet Singh, Abdullah Khan, Dost Akbar.' No, I confess that I do not see how this bears upon the matter. Yet it is evidently a document of importance. It has been kept very carefully in a pocket-book; for the one side is as clean as the other."

"It was in his pocket-book that we found it."

"Preserve it carefully, then, Miss Morstan, for it may prove to be of use to us. I begin to suspect that this matter may turn out to be much deeper and more subtle than I at first supposed. I must reconsider my ideas."

He leaned back in the cab, and I could see by his drawn brow and his vacant eye that he was thinking intently. Miss Morstan and I chatted in an undertone about our present expedition and its possible outcome, but our companion maintained his impenetrable reserve until the end of our journey.

It was a September evening, and not yet seven o'clock, but the day had been a dreary one, and a dense drizzly fog lay low upon the great city. Mud-coloured clouds drooped sadly over the muddy streets. Down the Strand the lamps were but misty splotches of diffused light, which threw a feeble circular glimmer upon the slimy pavement. The yellow glare from the shop-windows streamed out into the steamy, vaporous air, and threw a murky, shifting radiance across the crowded thoroughfare. There was, to my mind, something eerie and ghost-like in the endless procession of faces which flitted across these narrow bars of light—sad faces and glad, haggard and merry. Like all human kind, they flitted from the gloom into the light, and so back into the gloom once more. I am not subject to impressions, but the dull, heavy evening, with the strange business upon which we were engaged, combined to make me nervous and depressed. I could see from Miss Morstan's manner that she was suffering from the same feeling. Holmes alone could rise superior to petty influences. He held his open note-book upon his knee, and from time to time he jotted down figures and memoranda in the light of his pocket-lantern.

At the Lyceum Theatre the crowds were already thick at the side-entrances. In front a continuous stream of hansoms and four-wheelers were rattling up, discharging their cargoes of shirt-fronted men and beshawled and bediamonded women. We had hardly reached the third pillar, which was our rendezvous, before a small, dark, brisk man in the dress of a coachman accosted us.

" Are you the parties who come with Miss Morstan ? " he asked

" I am Miss Morstan, and these two gentlemen are my friends," said she.

He bent a pair of wonderfully penetrating and questioning eyes upon us.

" You will excuse me, miss," he said, with a certain dogged manner, " but I was to ask you to give me your word that neither of your companions is a police-officer."

" I give you my word on that," she answered.

He gave a shrill whistle, on which a street arab led across a four-wheeler and opened the door. The man who had addressed us mounted to the box, while we took our places inside. We had hardly done so before the driver whipped up his horse, and we plunged away at a furious pace through the foggy streets.

The situation was a curious one. We were driving to an unknown place on an unknown errand. Yet our invitation was either a complete hoax—which was an inconceivable hypothesis—or else we had good reason to think that important issues might hang upon our journey. Miss Morstan's demeanour was as resolute and collected as ever. I endeavoured to cheer and amuse her by reminiscences of my adventures in Afghanistan; but, to tell the truth, I was myself so excited at our situation, and so curious as to our destination, that my stories were slightly involved. To this day she declares that I told her one moving anecdote as to how a musket looked into my tent at the dead of night, and how I fired a double-barrelled tiger cub at it. At first I had some idea as to the direction in which we were driving; but soon, what with our pace, the fog, and my own limited knowledge of London, I lost my bearings, and knew nothing, save that we seemed to be going a very long way. Sherlock Holmes was never at fault, however, and he muttered the names as the cab rattled through squares and in and out by tortuous by-streets.

" Rochester Row," said he. " Now Vincent Square. Now we come out on the Vauxhall Bridge Road. We are making for the Surrey side, apparently. Yes I thought so. Now we are on the bridge. You can catch glimpses of the river."

We did indeed get a fleeting view of a stretch of the Thames, with the lamps shining upon the broad, silent water; but our cab dashed on, and was soon involved in a labyrinth of streets upon the other side.

" Wandsworth Road," said my companion. " Priory Road. Larkhall Lane. Stockwell Place. Robert Street. Coldharbour Lane. Our quest does not appear to take us to very fashionable regions."

We had indeed reached a questionable and forbidding neighbourhood. Long lines of dull brick houses were only relieved by the coarse glare and tawdry brilliancy of public-houses at the corners. Then came rows of two-storied villas, each with a frontage of miniature garden, and then again interminable lines of new, staring brick building—the monster tentacles which the giant city was throwing out into the country. At last the cab drew up at the third house in a new terrace. None of the other houses were inhabited, and that at which we stopped was as dark as its neighbours, save for a single glimmer in the kitchen-window. On our knocking, however, the door was instantly thrown open by a Hindu servant, clad in a yellow turban, white loose-fitting clothes, and a yellow sash. There was something strangely incongruous in this Oriental figure framed in the commonplace doorway of a third-rate suburban dwelling-house.

" The sahib awaits you," said he, and even as he spoke there came a high piping voice from some inner room.

" Show them in to me, khidmutgar," it cried. " Show them straight in to me."

CHAPTER IV

THE STORY OF THE BALD-HEADED MAN

We followed the Indian down a sordid and common passage, ill-lit and worse furnished, until he came to a door upon the right, which he threw open. A blaze of yellow light streamed out upon us, and in the centre of the glare there stood a small man with a very high head, a bristle of red hair all round the fringe of it, and a bald, shining scalp which shot out from among it like a mountain-peak from fir-trees. He writhed his hands together as he stood, and his features were in a perpetual jerk—now smiling, now scowling, but never for an instant in repose. Nature had given him a pendulous lip, and a too visible line of yellow and irregular teeth, which he strove feebly to conceal by constantly passing his hand over the lower part of his face. In spite of his obtrusive baldness, he gave the impression of youth. In point of fact, he had just turned his thirtieth year.

" Your servant, Miss Morstan," he kept repeating, in a thin, high voice. " Your servant, gentlemen. Pray step into my little sanctum. A small place, miss, but furnished to my own liking. An oasis of art in the howling desert of South London."

We were astonished by the appearance of the apartment into which he invited us. In that sorry house it looked as out-of-place as a diamond of the first water in the setting of brass. The richest and glossiest of curtains and tapestries draped the walls, looped back here and there to expose some richly-mounted painting or Oriental vase. The carpet was of amber and black, so soft and so thick that the foot sank pleasantly into it, as into a bed of moss. Two great tiger-skins thrown athwart it increased the suggestion of Eastern luxury, as did a huge hookah which stood upon a mat in the corner. A lamp in the fashion of a silver dove was hung from an almost invisible golden wire in the centre of the room. As it burned it filled the air with a subtle and aromatic odour.

" Mr Thaddeus Sholto," said the little man, still jerking and smiling. " That is my name. You are Miss Morstan of course. And these gentlemen——"

" This is Mr. Sherlock Holmes, and this Dr. Watson."

" A doctor, eh ? " cried he, much ex-cited. " Have you your stethoscope ? I might ask you—would you have the kindness ? I have grave doubts as to my mitral valve, if you would be so good. The aortic I may rely on, but I should value your opinon upon the mitral."

I listened to his heart, as requested, but was unable to find anything amiss, save, indeed, that he was in an ecstasy of fear, for he shivered from head to foot.

" It appears to be normal," I said. " You have no cause for uneasiness."

" You will excuse my anxiety, Miss Morstan," he remarked airily. " I am a great sufferer, and I have long had suspicions as to that valve. I am delighted to hear that they are unwarranted. Had your father, Miss Morstan, refrained from throwing a strain upon his heart, he might have been alive now."

I could have struck the man across the face, so hot was I at this callous and off-hand reference to so delicate a matter. Miss Morstan sat down, and her face grew white to the lips.

" I knew in my heart that he was dead," said she.

" I can give you every information," said he, " and what is more, I can do you justice; and I will, too, whatever Brother Bartholomew may say. I am so glad to have your friends here, not only as an escort to you, but also as witnesses to what I am about to do and say. The three of us can show a bold front to brother Bartholomew. But let us have no outsiders—no police or officials. We can settle everything satisfactorily among ourselves, without any interference. Nothing would annoy Brother Bartholomew more than any publicity."

He sat down upon a low settee, and blinked at us inquiringly with his weak, watery blue eyes.

" For my part," said Holmes, " whatever you may choose to say will go no farther."

I nodded to show my agreement.

" That is well ! " said he. " May I offer you a glass of Chianti, Miss Morstan ? Or of Tokay ? I keep no other wines. Shall I open a flask ? No ? Well, then, I trust that you have no objection to tobacco smoke, to the balsamic odour of the Eastern tobacco. I am a little nervous, and I find my hookah an invaluable sedative."

He applied a taper to the great bowl, and the smoke bubbled merrily through the rosewater. We sat all three in a semi-circle, with our heads advanced and our chins upon our hands, while the strange, jerky little fellow, with his high, shining head, puffed uneasily in the centre.

"When I first determined to make this communication to you," said he, "I might have given you my address; but I feared that you might disregard my request and bring unpleasant people with you. I took the liberty, therefore, of making an appointment in such a way that my man Williams might be able to see you first. I have complete confidence in his discretion, and he had orders, if he were dissatisfied, to proceed no further in the matter. You will excuse these precautions but I am a man of somewhat retiring, and I might even say refined, tastes, and there is nothing more unaesthetic than a policeman. I have a natural shrinking from all forms of rough materialism. I seldom come in contact with the rough crowd. I live, as you see, with some little atmosphere of elegance around me. I may call myself a patron of the arts. It is my weakness. The landscape is a genuine Corot, and, though a connoisseur might perhaps throw a doubt upon that Salvator Rosa, there cannot be the least question about the Bouguereau. I am partial to the modern French school."

"You will excuse me, Mr. Sholto," said Miss Morstan, "but I am here at your request to learn something which you desire to tell me. It is very late, and I should desire the interview to be as short as possible."

"At the best, it must take some time," he answered; "for we shall certainly have to go to Norwood to see Brother Bartholomew. We shall all go and try if we can get the better of Brother Bartholomew. He is very angry with me for taking the course which has seemed right to me. I had quite high words with him last night. You cannot imagine what a terrible fellow he is when he is angry."

"If we are to go to Norwood, it would perhaps be as well to start at once," I ventured to remark.

He laughed until his ears were quite red.

"That would hardly do," he cried. "I don't know what he would say if I brought you in that sudden way. No, I must prepare you by showing you how we all stand to each other. In the first place, I must tell you that there are several points in the story of which I am myself ignorant. I can only lay the facts before you as far as I know them myself.

"My father was, as you may have guessed Major John Sholto, once of the Indian Army. He retired some eleven years ago, and came to live at Pondicherry Lodge, in Upper Norwood. He had prospered in India,

and brought back with him a considerable sum of money, a large collection of valuable curiosities, and a staff of native servants. With these advantages he bought himself a house, and lived in great luxury. My twin brother Bartholomew and I were the only children.

"I very well remember the sensation which was caused by the disappearance of Captain Morstan. We read the details in the papers, and knowing that he had been a friend of our father's, we discussed the case freely in his presence. He used to join in our speculations as to what could have happened. Never for instant did we suspect that he had the whole secret hidden in his own breast, that of all men he alone knew the fate of Arthur Morstan.

"We did know, however, that some mystery, some positive danger, overhung our father. He was very fearful of going out alone, and he always employed two prizefighters to act as porters at Pondicherry Lodge. William, who drove you tonight, was one of them. He was once light-weight champion of England. Our father would never tell us what it was he feared, but he had a most marked aversion to men with wooden legs. On one occasion he actually fired his revolver at a wooden-legged man who proved to be a harmless tradesman canvassing for orders. We had to pay a large sum to hush the matter up. My brother and I used to think this a mere whim of my father's; but events have since led us to change our opinion.

"Early in 1882 my father received a letter from India which was a great shock to him. He nearly fainted at the breakfast-table when he opened it, and from that day he sickened to his death. What was in the letter we could never discover but I could see as he held it that it was short and written in a scrawling hand. He had suffered from an enlarged spleen, but he now became rapidly worse, and towards the end of April we were informed that he was beyond all hope, and that he wished to make a last communication to us.

"When we entered his room he was propped up with pillows and breathing heavily. He besought us to lock the door and come on either side of the bed. Then, grasping our hands, he made a remarkable statement to us, in a voice which was broken as much by emotion as by pain. I shall try and give it you in his very own words.

"'I have only one thing,' he said, 'which weighs upon my mind at this supreme moment. It is my treatment of poor Morstan's orphan. The cursed greed which has been my besetting sin through life has withheld from her the treasure, half at least of which should have been hers. And yet I have made no use of it myself, so blind and foolish a thing is avarice. The mere feeling of possession has been so dear to me that I could not bear to share it with another. See that chaplet tipped with pearls beside the quinine-bottle? Even that I could not bear to part with, although I had got it out with the design of sending it to her. You, my sons will give her a fair share of the Agra treasure. But send her nothing—not even the chaplet—until I am gone. After all, men have been as bad as this and have recovered.

" 'I will tell you how Morstan died,' he continued. 'He had suffered for years from a weak heart, but concealed it from everyone. I alone knew it. When in India, he and I, through a remarkable chain of circumstances, came into possession of a considerable treasure. I brought it over to England, and on the night of Morstan's arrival he came straight over here to claim his share. He walked over from the station and was admitted by my faithful old Lal Chowdar, who is now dead. Morstan and I had a different opinion as to the division of the treasure, and we came to heated words. Morstan had sprung out of his chair in a paroxysm of anger, when he suddenly pressed his hand to his side, his faced turned a sickly hue, and he fell backwards, cutting his head against the corner of the treasure-chest. When I stooped over him I found, to my horror, that he was dead.

" 'For a long time I sat half distracted wondering what I should do. My first impulse was, of course to call for assistance; but I could not but recognize that there was every chance that I would be accused of his murder. His death at the moment of a quarrel, and the gash in his head, would be black against me. Again, an official inquiry could not be made without bringing out some facts about the treasure, which I was particularly anxious to keep secret. He had told me that no soul upon earth knew where he had gone. There seemed to be no necessity why any soul ever should know.

" 'I was still pondering over the matter, when, looking up, I saw my servant, Lal Chowdar, in the doorway. He stole in and bolted the door behind him. ' Do not fear, sahib," he said, " no one need know that you have killed him. Let us hide him away, and who is the wiser? " " I did not kill him,"

said I. Lal Chowdar shook his head and smiled. " I heard it all sahib," said he; " I heard you quarrel, and I heard the blow. But my lips are sealed. All are asleep in the house. Let us put him away together." That was enough to decide me. If my own servant could not believe my innocence, how could I hope to make it good before twelve foolish tradesmen in a jury-box? Lal Chowdar and I disposed of the body that night and within a few days the London papers were full of the mysterious disappearance of Captain Morstan. You will see from what I say that I can hardly be blamed in the matter. My fault lies in the fact that we concealed not only the body, but also the treasure, and that I have clung to Morstan's share as well as my own. I wish you, therefore, to make restitution. Put your ears to my mouth. The treasure is hidden in——"

" At this instant a horrible change came over his expression; his eyes stared wildly, his jaw dropped and he yelled, in a voice which I can never forget, " Keep him out! For Christ's sake, keep him out! " We both stared round at the window behind us upon which his gaze was fixed. A face was looking in at us out of the darkness. We could see the whitening of the nose where it was pressed against the glass. It was a bearded, hairy face, with wild, cruel eyes and an expression of concentrated malevolence. My brother and I rushed towards the window, but the man was gone. When we returned to my father, his head had dropped and his pulse had ceased to beat.

" We searched the garden that night, but found no sign of the intruder, save that just under the window a single footmark was visible in the flower bed. But for that one trace, we might have thought that our imaginations had conjured up that wild, fierce face. We soon, however, had another and more striking proof that there were secret agencies at work all round us. The window of my father's room was found open in the morning, his cupboards and boxes had been rifled, and upon his chest was fixed a torn piece of paper, with the words, ' The sign of four,' scrawled across it. What the phrase meant, or who our secret visitor may have been, we never knew. As far as we can judge, none of my father's property had been actually stolen, though everything had been turned out. My brother and I naturally associated this peculiar incident with the fear which haunted my father during his life; but it is still a complete mystery to us."

The little man stopped to relight his

hookah, and puffed thoughtfully for a few moments. We had all sat absorbed, listening to his extraordinary narrative. At the short account of her father's death Miss Morstan had turned deadly white, and for a moment I feared that she was about to faint. She rallied, however, on drinking a glass of water which I quietly poured out for her from a Venetian carafe upon the side-table. Sherlock Holmes leaned back in his chair with an abstracted expression and the lids drawn low over his glittering eyes. As I glanced at him I could not think how, on that very day, he had complained bitterly of the commonplaceness of life. Here at least was a problem which would tax his sagacity to the utmost. Mr. Thaddeus Sholto looked from one to the other of us with an obvious pride at the effect which his story had produced, and then continued, between the puffs of his overgrown pipe.

" My brother and I," said he, " were, as you may imagine, much excited as to the treasure which my father had spoken of. For weeks and for months we dug and delved in every part of the garden without discovering its whereabouts. It was maddening to think that the hiding-place was on his very lips at the moment he died. We could judge the splendour of the missing riches by the chaplet which he had taken out. Over this chaplet my brother Bartholomew and I had some little discussion. The pearls were evidently of great value, and he was averse to part with them, for, between friends, my brother was himself a little inclined to my father's fault. He thought, too, that if we parted with the chaplet it might give rise to gossip, and finally bring us into trouble. It was all that I could do to persuade him to let me find out Miss Morstan's address and send her a detached pearl at fixed intervals, so that at least she might never feel destitute."

" It was a kindly thought," said our companion, earnestly; " it was extremely good of you."

The little man waved his hand deprecatingly.

" We were your trustees of it, he said. " That was the view which I took, though Brother Bartholomew could not altogether see it in that light. We had plenty of money ourselves. I desired no more. Besides, it would have been such bad taste to have treated a young lady in so scurvy a fashion. ' *Le mauvais goût mène au crime.*' The French have a very neat way of putting these things. Our difference of opinion on this subject went so far that I thought

it best to set up rooms for myself; so I left Pondicherry Lodge, taking the old khidmutgar and Williams with me. Yesterday, however, I learnt that an event of extreme importance has occurred. The treasure has been discovered. I instantly communicated with Miss Morstan, and it only remains for us to drive out to Norwood and demand our share. I explained my views last night to Brother Bartholomew so we shall be expected, if not welcome, visitors."

Mr. Thaddeus Sholto ceased, and sat twitching on his luxurious settee. We all remained silent. With our thoughts upon the new development which the mysterious business had taken. Holmes was the first to spring to his feet.

" You have done well, sir, from first to last," said he. " It is possible that we may be able to make you some small return by throwing some light upon that which is still dark to you. But, as Miss Morstan remarked just now, it is late, and we had best put the matter through without delay."

Our new acquaintance very deliberately coiled up the tube of his hookah, and produced from behind a curtain a very long, befrogged top-coat with astrakhan collar and cuffs. This he buttoned tightly up in spite of the extreme closeness of the night, and finished his attire by putting on a rabbit-skin cap with hanging lappets which covered the ears, so that no part of him was visible save his mobile and peaky face.

" My health is somewhat fragile," he remarked, as he led the way down the passage. " I am compelled to be a valetudinarian."

Our cab was awaiting us outside, and our programme was evidently prearranged, for the driver started off at once at a rapid pace. Thaddeus Sholto talked incessantly, in a voice which rose high above the rattle of the wheels.

" Bartholomew is a clever fellow," said he. " How do you think he found out where the treasure was ? He had come to the conclusion that it was somewhere indoors: so he worked out all the cubic space of the house, and made measurements everywhere, so that not one inch should be unaccounted for. Among other things, he found that the height of the building was seventy-four feet, but on adding together the heights of all the separate rooms, and making every allowance for the space between, which he ascertained by borings, he could not bring the total to more than seventy feet. There were four feet unaccounted for. These could only be at the top of the building. He knocked a hole, therefore, in the lath and plaster ceiling of the highest room, and there, sure enough, he came upon another little garret above it, which had been sealed up and was known to no one. In the centre stood the treasure-chest, resting upon two rafters. He lowered it through the hole and there it lies. He computes the value of the jewels at not less than half a million sterling."

At the mention of this gigantic sum we all stared at one another open-eyed. Miss Morstan, could we secure her rights, would change from a needy governess to the richest heiress in England. Surely it was the place of a loyal friend to rejoice at such news; yet I am ashamed to say that selfishness took me by the soul, and that my heart turned as heavy as lead within me. I stammered out some few halting words of congratulation, and then sat downcast, with my head drooped, deaf to the babble of our new acquaintance. He was clearly a confirmed hypochondriac, and I was dreamily conscious that he was pouring forth interminable trains of symptoms, and imploring information as to the composition and action of innumerable quack nostrums, some of which he bore about in a leather case in his pocket. I trust that he may not remember any of the answers which I gave him that night. Holmes declares that he overheard me caution him against the great danger of taking more than two drops of castor-oil, while I recommended strychnine in large doses as a sedative. However that may be, I was certainly relieved when our cab pulled up with a jerk and the coachman sprang down to open the door.

"This, Miss Morstan, is Pondicherry Lodge," said Mr Thaddeus Sholto, as he handed her out.

CHAPTER V

THE TRAGEDY OF PONDICHERRY LODGE

It was nearly eleven o'clock when we reached this final stage of our night's adventures. We had left the damp fog of the great city behind us, and the night was fairly fine. A warm wind blew from the westward and heavy clouds moved slowly across the sky with half a moon peeping occasionally through the rifts. It was clear enough to see for some distance, but Thaddeus Sholto took down one of the sidelamps from the carriage to give us a better light upon our way.

Pondicherry Lodge stood in its own grounds, and was girt round with a very high stone wall topped with broken glass. A single narrow iron-clamped door formed the only means of entrance. On this our guide knocked with a peculiar postman-like rat-tat.

"Who is there?" cried a gruff voice from within. "It is I, McMurdo. You surely know my knock by this time."

There was a grumbling sound and a clanking and jarring of keys. The door swung heavily back, and a short, deep-chested man stood in the opening, with the yellow light of the lantern shining upon his protruded face and twinkling, distrustful eyes.

"That you, Mr. Thaddeus? But who are the others? I had no orders about them from the master."

"No, McMurdo? You surprise me! I told my brother last night that I should bring some friends."

"He hain't been out o' his room today, Mr. Thaddeus, and I have no orders. You know very well that I must stick to regulations. I can let you in, but your friends must just stop where they are."

This was an unexpected obstacle. Thaddeus Sholto looked about him in a perplexed and helpless manner.

"This is too bad of you, McMurdo!" he said. "If I guarantee them, that is enough for you. There is the young lady, too. She cannot wait on the public road at this hour."

"Very sorry, Mr. Thaddeus," said the porter, inexorably. "Folk may be friends o' yours, and yet no friends o' the master's. He pays me well to do my duty, and my duty I'll do. I don't know none o' your friends."

"Oh, yes, you do, McMurdo," cried Sherlock Holmes, genially. "I don't think you have forgotten me. Don't you remember the amateur who fought three rounds with you at Alison's rooms on the night of your benefit four years back?"

"Not Mr. Sherlock Holmes!" roared the prizefighter. "God's truth! how could I have mistook you? If instead of o' standing there so quiet you had just stepped up and given me that cross-hit of yours under the jaw, I'd ha' known you without a question. Ah, you're the one that has wasted your gifts, you have! You might have aimed high, if you had joined the fancy."

"You see, Watson, if all else fails me, I have still one of the scientific professions open to me," said Holmes laughing. "Our friend won't keep us out in the cold now, I am sure."

"In you come, sir, in you come—you and your friends," he answered. "Very sorry, Mr Thaddeus, but orders are very strict. Had to be certain of your friends before I let them in."

Inside, a gravel path wound through desolate grounds to a huge clump of a house, square and prosaic, all plunged in shadow save where a moonbeam struck one corner and glimmered in a garret window. The vast size of the building, with its gloom and its deathly silence, struck a chill to the heart. Even Thaddeus Sholto seemed ill at ease, and the lantern quivered and rattled in his hand.

"I cannot understand it," he said. "There must be some mistake. I distinctly told Bartholomew that we should be here, and yet there is no light in his window. I do not know what to make of it."

"Does he always guard the premises in this way?" asked Holmes.

"Yes, he has followed my father's custom. He was the favourite son, you know, and I sometimes think that my father may have told him more than he ever told me. That is Bartholomew's window up there where the moonshine strikes. It is quite bright, but there is no light from within, I think."

"None," said Holmes. "But I see the glint of a light in that little window beside the door."

"Ah, that is the housekeeper's room. That is where old Mrs. Bernstone sits. She can tell us all about it. But perhaps you would not mind waiting here for a minute or two, for if we all go in together, and she has not word of our coming, she may be alarmed. But, hush, what is that?"

He held up the lantern, and his hand shook until the circles of light flickered and wavered all round us. Miss Morstan seized my wrist, and we all stood, with thumping hearts, straining our ears. From the great black house there sounded through the silent night the saddest and most pitiful sounds, the shrill, broken whimpering of a frightened woman.

"It is Mrs. Bernstone," said Sholto. "She is the only woman in the house. Wait here. I shall be back in a moment."

He hurried for the door, and knocked in his peculiar way. We could see a tall old woman admit him, and sway with pleasure at the very sight of him.

"Oh Mr. Thaddeus, sir, I am so glad you have come! I am so glad you have come, Mr. Thaddeus, sir!"

We heard her reiterate her rejoicings until the door was closed and her voice died away into a muffled monotone.

Our guide had left us the lantern. Holmes swung it slowly round, peered keenly at the house, and at the great rubbish-heaps which cumbered the grounds. Miss Morstan and I stood together, and her hand was in mine. A wondrous subtle thing is love, for here were we two, who had never seen each other before that day, between whom no word or even look of affection had ever passed, and yet now in an hour of trouble our hands instinctively sought for each other. I have marvelled at it since, but at the time it seemed the most natural thing that I should go out to her so, and, as she has often told me, there was in her also the instinct to turn to me for comfort and protection. So we stood hand in hand, like two children, and there was peace in our hearts for all the dark things that surrounded us.

"What a strange place!" she said, looking round.

"It looks as though all the moles in England had been let loose in it. I have seen something of the sort on the side of a hill near Ballarat, where the prospectors had been at work."

"And from the same cause," said Holmes. "These are the traces of the treasure-seekers. You must remember that they were six years looking for it. No wonder that the grounds look like a gravel-pit."

At that moment the door of the house burst open, and Thaddeus Sholto came running out, with his hands thrown forward and terror in his eyes.

"There is something amiss with Bartholomew!" he cried. "I am frightened! My nerves cannot stand it."

He was indeed, half blubbering with fear, and his twitching, feeble face peeping out from the great astrakhan collar and the helpless, appealing expression of a terrified child.

"Come into the house," said Holmes, in his crisp, firm way.

"Yes, do!" pleaded Thaddeus Sholto. "I really do not feel equal to giving directions."

We all followed him into the housekeeper's room, which stood upon the left-hand side of the passage. The old woman was pacing up and down with a scared look and restless, picking fingers, but the sight of Miss Morstan appeared to have a soothing effect upon her.

"God bless your sweet, calm face!" she cried, with an hysterical sob. "It does me good to see you. Oh, but I have been sorely tried this day ! "

Our companion patted the thin, work-worn hand, and murmured some few words of kindly, womanly comfort, which brought the colour back into the other's bloodless cheeks.

" Master has locked himself in, and will not answer me," she explained. " All day I have waited to hear from him, for he often likes to be alone; but an hour ago I feared something was amiss, so I went up and peeped through the keyhole. You must go up and look for yourself. I have seen Mr. Bartholomew Sholto in joy and in sorrow for ten long years, but I never saw him with such a face on him as that."

Sherlock Holmes took the lamp and led the way, for Thaddeus Sholto's teeth were chattering in his head. So shaken was he that I had to pass my hand under his arm as we went up the stairs, for his knees were trembling under him. Twice as we ascended Holmes whipped his lens out of his pocket and carefully examined marks which appeared to me to be mere shapeless smudges of dust upon the coconut-matting which served as a stair-carpet. He walked slowly from step to step, holding the lamp low, and shooting keen glances to right and left. Miss Morstan had remained behind with the frightened housekeeper.

The third fight of stairs ended in a straight passage of some length with a great picture in Indian tapestry upon the right of it and three doors on the left. Holmes advanced along it in the same slow and methodical way, while we kept close at heels with our long black shadows streaming backwards down the corridor. The third door was that which we were seeking. Holmes knocked without receiving any answer, and then tried to turn the handle and force it open. It was locked on the inside, however, and by a broad and powerful bolt, as we could see as we set our lamp up against it. The key being turned, however, the hole was not entirely closed. Sherlock Holmes bent down to it, and instantly rose again with a sharp intaking of the breath.

" There is something devilish in this, Watson," said he, more moved than I have ever before seen him. " What do you make of it ? "

I stooped to the hole, and recoiled in horror. Moonlight was streaming into the room, and it was bright with a vague and shifty radiance. Looking straight at me, and suspended, as it were, in the air, for all beneath was in shadow, there hung a face—

the very face of our companion Thaddeus. There was the same high, shining head, the same circular bristle of red hair, the same bloodless countenance. The features were set, however, in a horrible smile, a fixed and unnatural grin, which in that still and moonlit room was more jarring to the nerves than any scowl or contortion. So like was the face to that of our little friend that I looked round at him to make sure that he was indeed with us. Then I recalled to mind that he had mentioned to us that his brother and he were twins.

" This is terrible ! " I said to Holmes. " What is to be done ? "

" The door must come down," he answered, and, springing against it, he put all his weight upon the lock.

It creaked and groaned, but did not yield. Together we flung ourselves upon it once more, and this time it gave way with a sudden snap, and we found ourselves within Bartholomew Sholto's chamber.

It appeared to have been fitted up as a chemical laboratory. A double line of glass-stoppered bottles was drawn up upon the wall opposite the door, and the table was littered over with Bunsen burners, test-tubes, and retorts. In the corners stood carboys of acid in wicker baskets. One of these appeared to leak or to have been broken, for a stream of dark-coloured liquid had trickled out from it, and the air was heavy with a peculiarly pungent, tar-like odour. A set of steps stood at one side of the room, in the midst of a litter of lath and plaster, and above them there was an opening in the ceiling large enough for a man to pass through. At the foot of the steps a long coil of rope was thrown carelessly together.

By the table, in a wooden arm-chair, the master of the house was seated all in a heap, with his head sunk upon his left shoulder, and that ghastly, inscrutable smile upon his face. He was still and cold, and had clearly been dead for many hours. It seemed to me that not only his features, but all his limbs were twisted and turned in the most fantastic fashion. By his hand on the table there lay a peculiar instrument—a brown, close-grained stick, with a stone head like a hammer, rudely lashed on with coarse twine. Beside it was a torn sheet of note-paper with some words scrawled upon it. Holmes glanced at it, then handed it to me.

" You see," he said, with a significant raising of the eyebrows.

In the light of the lantern I read, with a

thrill of horror, "The sign of the four."

"In God's name, what does it all mean?" I asked.

"It means murder," said he, stooping over the dead man. "Ah! I expected it. Look here!"

He pointed to what looked like a long, dark thorn stuck in the skin just above the ear.

"It looks like a thorn," said I.

"It is a thorn. You may pick it out. But be careful for it is poisoned."

I took it up between my finger and thumb. It came away from the skin so readily that hardly any mark was left behind. One tiny speck of blood showed where the puncture had been.

"This is an insoluble mystery to me," said I. "It grows darker instead of clearer."

"On the contrary," he answered, "it clears every instant. I only require a few missing links to have an entirely connected case."

We had almost forgotten our companion's presence since we entered the chamber. He was still standing in the doorway, the very picture of terror, wringing his hands and moaning to himself. Suddenly, however, he broke out into a sharp, querulous cry.

"The treasure is gone!" he said. "They have robbed him of the treasure! There is the hole through which we lowered it. I helped him to do it! I was the last person who saw him! I left him here last night, and I heard him lock the door as I came downstairs."

"What time was that?"

"It was ten o'clock. And now he is dead, and the police will be called in, and I shall be suspected of having had a hand in it. Oh, yes, I am sure I shall. But you don't think so, gentlemen? Surely you don't think that it was I? Oh, dear! oh, dear! I know that I shall go mad!"

He jerked his arms and stamped his feet in a kind of convulsive frenzy.

"You have no reason to fear, Mr. Sholto," said Holmes, kindly, putting his hand upon his shoulder; "take my advice, and drive down to the station and report the matter to the police. Offer to assist them in every way. We shall wait here until your return."

The little man obeyed in a half-stupefied fashion and we heard him stumbling down the stairs in the dark.

CHAPTER VI

SHERLOCK HOLMES GIVES A DEMONSTRATION

"Now, Watson," said Holmes, rubbing his hands, "we have half an hour to ourselves. Let us make good use of it. My case is, as I have told you, almost complete; but we must not err on the side of over-confidence. Simple as the case seems now, there may be something deeper underlying it."

"Simple!" I ejaculated.

"Surely," said he, with something of the air of a clinical professor expounding to his class. "Just sit in the corner there, that your footprints may not complicate matters. Now to work! In the first place, how did these folk come, and how did they go? The door has not been opened since last night. How about the window?" He carried the lamp across to it, muttering his observations aloud the while, but addressing them to himself rather than to me. "Window is snibbed on the inner side. Framework is solid. No hinges at the side. Let us open it. No water-pipe near. Roof quite out of reach. Yet a man has mounted by the window. It rained a little last night. Here is the print of a foot in mould upon the sill. And here is a circular muddy mark, and here again upon the floor and here again by the table. See here, Watson! This is really a very pretty demonstration."

I looked at the round, well-defined muddy discs.

"That is not a footmark," said I.

"It is something much more valuable to us. It is the impression of a wooden stump. You see here on the sill is the boot-mark, a heavy boot with a broad metal heel and beside it is the mark of the timber-toe."

"It is the wooden-legged man."

"Quite so. But there has been someone else—a very able and efficient ally. Could you scale that wall, Doctor?"

I looked out of the open window. The moon still shone brightly on that angle of the house. We were a good sixty feet from the ground, and look where I would, I could see no foothold, not as much as a crevice in the brickwork.

"It is absolutely impossible," I answered.

"Without aid it is so. But suppose you had a friend up here who lowered you this good stout rope which I see in the corner, securing one end of it to this great hook in the wall. Then, I think, if you were an active man, you might swarm up, wooden leg and all. You would depart, of course, in the same fashion, and your ally would draw up the rope, untie it from the hook, shut the window, snib it on the inside, and get away in the way that he originally came. As a minor point, it may be noted," he continued, fingering the rope, " that our wooden-legged friend, though a fair climber, was not a professional sailor. His hands were far from horny. My lens discloses more than one blood-mark, especially towards the end of the rope, from which I gather that he slipped down with such velocity that he took the skin off his hand."

" This is all very well," said I; " but the thing becomes more unintelligible than ever. How about this mysterious ally? How came he into the room?"

" Yes, the ally!" repeated Holmes, pensively. " There are features of interest about this ally. He lifts the case from the regions of the commonplace. I fancy that this ally breaks fresh ground in the annals of crime in this country—though parallel cases suggest themselves from India, and, if my memory serves me, from Senegambia."

" How came he, then?" I reiterated. " The door is locked; the window inaccessible. Was it through the chimney?"

" The grate is much too small," he answered. "I had already considered that possibility."

" How then?" I persisted.

" You will not apply my precept," he said, shaking his head. " How often have I said to you that when you have eliminated the impossible, whatever remains, *however improbable*, must be the truth? We know that he did not come through the door, the window, or the chimney. We also know that he could not have been concealed in the room, as there is no concealment possible. Whence, then, did he come?"

" He came through the hole in the roof?" I cried.

" Of course he did. He must have done so. If you will have the kindness to hold the lamp for me, we shall now extend our researches to the room above—the secret room in which the treasure was found."

He mounted the steps, and seizing a rafter with either hand, he swung himself up into the garret. Then, lying on his face, he reached down for the lamp, and held it while I followed him.

The chamber in which we found ourselves was about ten feet one way and six the other. The floor was formed by the rafters with thin lath-and-plaster between, so that in walking one had to step from beam to beam. The roof ran up to an apex, and was evidently the inner shell of the true roof of the house. There was no furniture of any sort, and the accumulated dust of years lay thick upon the floor.

" Here you are, you see," said Sherlock Homes, putting his hand against the sloping wall. " This is a trap-door which leads out on to the roof. I can press it back, and here is the roof itself, sloping at a gentle angle. This then, is the way by which Number One entered. Let us see if we can find some other traces of his individuality."

He held down the lamp to the floor, and as he did so I saw for the second time that night a startled, surprised look come over his face. For myself, as I followed his gaze, my skin was cold under my clothes. The floor was covered thickly with the prints of a naked foot—clear, well defined, perfectly formed, but scarce half the size of those of an ordinary man.

" Holmes," I said in a whisper, " a child has done this horrid thing."

He had recovered his self-possession in an instant.

" I was staggered for the moment," he said, " but the thing is quite natural. My memory failed me, or I should have been able to foretell it. There is nothing more to be learned here. Let us go down."

" What is your theory, then, as to those footmarks?" I asked eagerly, when we had regained the lower room once more.

" My dear Watson, try a little analysis yourself," said he, with a touch of impatience. " You know my methods. Apply them, and it will be instructive to compare results."

" I cannot conceive anything which will cover the facts," I answered.

" It will be clear enough to you soon," he said, in an off-hand way. " I think that there is nothing else of importance here, but I will look."

He whipped out his lens and a tape measure, and hurried about the room on his knees, measuring, comparing, examining, with his long, thin nose only a few inches from the planks, and his beady eyes gleaming and deep-set like those of a bird. So swift, silent, and furtive were his movements, like those of a trained bloodhound picking out a scent, that I could not but think what a terrible criminal he would have made had he turned his energy and sagacity against the law instead of exerting them in its defence. As he hunted about he kept muttering to himself, and finally he broke out into a loud crow of delight.

" We are certainly in luck," said he. " We ought to have very little trouble now. Number One has had the misfortune to tread in the creosote. You can see the outline of the edge of his small foot here at the side of this evil-smelling mess. The carboy has been cracked, you see, and the stuff has leaked out."

" What then ? " I asked.

" Why, we have got him, that's all," said he. " I know a dog that would follow that scent to the world's end. If a pack can track a trailed herring across a shire, how far can a specially-trained hound follow so pungent a smell as this ? It sounds like a sum in the rule of three. The answer should give us the—— But, halloa ! here are the accredited representatives of the law."

Heavy steps and the clamour of loud voices were audible from below, and the hall door shut with a loud crash.

" Before they come," said Holmes, " just put your hand here on this poor fellow's arm, and here on his leg. What do you feel ?"

" The muscles are as hard as a board," I answered.

" Quite so. They are in a state of extreme contraction, far exceeding the usual *rigor mortis*. Coupled with this disortion of the face, this Hippocratic smile, or *'risus sardonicus'*, as the old writers called it, what conclusion would it suggest to your mind ?"

" Death from some powerful vegetable alkaloid," I answered, " some strychnine-like substance which would produce tetanus."

" That was the idea which occurred to me the instant I saw the drawn muscles of the face. On getting into the room I at once looked for means by which the poison had entered the system. As you saw, I discovered a thorn which had been driven or shot with no great force into the scalp. You observe that the part struck was that which would be turned towards the hole in the ceiling if the man were erect in his chair. Now examine this thorn."

I took it up gingerly and held it in the light of the lantern. It was long, sharp, and black, with a glazed look near the point as though some gummy substance had dried upon it. The blunt end had been trimmed and rounded off with a knife.

" Is that an English thorn ? " he asked.

" No it certainly is not."

" With all these data you should be able to draw some just inference. But here are the regulars; so the auxiliary forces may beat a retreat."

As he spoke, the steps which had been coming nearer sounded loudly on the passage, and a very stout, portly man in a grey suit strode heavily into the room. He was red-faced, burly, and plethoric, with a pair of very small, twinkling eyes, which looked keenly out from between swollen and puffy pouches. He was closely followed by an inspector in uniform, and by the still palpitating Thaddeus Sholto.

" Here's a business ! " he cried, in a muffled, husky voice. " Here's a pretty business ! But who are all these ? Why, the house seems to be as full as a rabbit-warren ! "

" I think you must recollect me, Mr. Athelney Jones," said Homes, quietly.

" Why, of course I do ! " he wheezed. " It's Mr. Sherlock Holmes, the theorist. Remember you ! I'll never forget how you lectured us all on causes and inferences and effects in the Bishopsgate jewel case. It's true you set us on the right track; but you'll own now that it was more by good luck than good guidance."

" It was a piece of very simple reasoning."

" Oh, come, now, come ! never be ashamed to own up. But what is all this ? Bad business ! Bad business ! Stern facts here—no room for theories. How lucky that I happened to be out in Norwood over another case ! I was at the station when the message arrived. What d'you think the man died of ? "

" Oh, this is hardly a case for me to theorize over," said Holmes, drily.

" No, no. Still, we can't deny that you hit the nail on the head sometimes. Dear me ! Door locked, I understand. Jewels worth half a million missing. How was the window ? "

" Fastened; but there are steps on the sill."

" Well, well, if it was fastened the steps could have nothing to do with the matter. That's common sense. Man might have died in a fit; but then the jewels are missing. Ha! I have a theory. These flashes come upon me at times. Just step outside, sergeant, and you, Mr. Sholto. Your friend can remain. What do you think of this Holmes ? Sholto was, on his own confession, with his brother last night. The brother died in a fit, on which Sholto walked off with the treasure ! How's that ? "

" On which the dead man very considerately got up and locked the door on the inside."

" Hum ! There's a flaw there. Let us apply commonsense to the matter. This Thaddeus Sholto *was* with his brother; there *was* a quarrel: so much we know. The brother is dead and the jewels are gone. So much also we know. No one saw the brother from the time Thaddeus left him. His bed had not been slept in. Thaddeus is evidently in a most disturbed state of mind. His appearance is—well, not attractive. You see that I am weaving my web round Thaddeus. The net begins to close up on him."

"You are not quite in possession of the facts yet," said Holmes. "This splinter of wood, which I have every reason to believe to be poisoned, was in the man's scalp where you still see the mark; this card, inscribed as you see it, was on the table, and beside it lay this rather curious stone-headed instrument. How does all that fit into your theory?"

"Confirms it in every respect," said the fat detective, pompously. "House full of Indian curiosities. Thaddeus brought this up, and if this splinter be poisonous, Thaddeus may as well have made murderous use of it as any other man. The card is some hocus-pocus—a blind, as like as not. The only question is, how did he depart? Ah, of course, there is a hole in the roof."

With great activity, considering his bulk, he sprang up the steps and squeezed through into the garret, and immediately afterwards we heard his exulting voice proclaiming that he had found the trap-door.

"He can find something," remarked Holmes, shrugging his shoulders; "he has occasional glimmerings of reason. *Il n'y a pas des sots si incommodes que ceux qui ont de l'esprit!*"

"You see!" said Athelney Jones, reappearing down the steps again; "facts are better than theories, after all. My view of the case is confirmed. There is a trap-door communicating with the roof, and it is partly open."

"It was I who opened it."

"Oh, indeed! You did notice it, then?" He seemed a little crestfallen at the discovery. "Well, whoever noticed it, it shows our gentleman got away. Inspector!"

"Yes, sir," from the passage.

"Ask Mr. Sholto to step this way. Mr. Sholto, it is my duty to inform you that anything which you may say will be used against you. I arrest you in the Queen's name as being concerned in the death of your brother."

"There, now! Didn't I tell you?" cried the poor little man, throwing out his hands, and looking from one to the other of us.

"Don't trouble yourself about it, Mr. Sholto," said Holmes; "I think that I can engage to clear you of the charge."

"Don't promise too much, Mr. Theorist, don't promise too much!" snapped the detective. "You may find it a harder matter than you think."

"Not only will I clear him, Mr. Jones, but I will make you a free present of the name and description of one of the two people who were in this room last night. His name, I have reason to believe, is Jonathan Small. He is a poorly educated man, small, active, with his right leg off, and wearing a wooden stump which is worn away on the inner side. His left boot had a coarse, square-toed sole, with a band round the heel. He is a middle-aged man much sunburned, and has been a convict. These few indications may be of some assistance to you, coupled with the fact that there is a good deal of skin missing from the palm of his hand. The other man——"

"Ah, the other man?" asked Athelney Jones, in a sneering voice, but impressed none the less, as I could easily see, by the precision of the other's manner.

"Is a rather curious person," said Sherlock Holmes, turning upon his heel. "I hope before very long to be able to introduce you to the pair of them. A word with you, Watson."

He led me out to the head of the stair.

"This unexpected occurrence," he said, "has caused us rather to lose sight of the original purpose of our journey."

"I have just been thinking so," I answered; "it is not right that Miss Morstan should remain in this stricken house."

"No. You must escort her home. She lives with Mrs. Cecil Forrester, in Lower Camberwell, so it is not very far. I will wait for you here if you will drive out again. Or perhaps you are too tired?"

"By no means. I don't think I could rest until I know more of this fantastic business. I have seen something of the rough side of life, but I give you my word that this quick succession of strange surprises tonight has shaken my nerve completely. I should like, however, to see the matter through with you, now that I have got so far."

"Your presence will be of great service to me," he answered. "We shall work the case out independently, and leave this fellow Jones to exult over any mare's-nest which he may choose to construct. When you have dropped Miss Morstan, I wish you to go to No. 3, Pinchin Lane, down near the water's edge at Lambeth. The third house on the right-hand side is a bird stuffer's; Sherman is the name. You will see a weasel holding a young rabbit in the window. Knock old Sherman up, and tell him with my compliments, that I want Toby at once. You will bring Toby back in the cab with you."

" A dog, I suppose ? "

" Yes, a queer mongrel, with a most amazing power of scent. I would rather have Toby's help than that of the whole detective force of London."

" I shall bring him then," said I. " It is one now. I ought to get back before three, if I get can a fresh horse."

" And I," said Holmes, " shall see what I can learn from Mrs. Bernstone, and from the Indian servant, who, Mr. Thaddeus tells me, sleeps in the next garret. Then I shall study the great Jones's methods and listen to his not too delicate sarcasms. *Wir sind gewohnt dass die Menschen verhöhnen was sie nicht verstehen.* Goethe is always pithy."

CHAPTER VII

THE EPISODE OF THE BARREL

The police had brought a cab with them, and in this I escorted Miss Morstan back to her home. After the angelic fashion of women, she had borne trouble with a calm face as long as there was someone weaker than herself to support, and I had found her bright and placid by the side of the frightened housekeeper. In the cab, however, she first turned faint, and then burst into a passion of weeping—so sorely had she been tried by the adventures of the night. She has told me since that she thought me cold and distant upon that journey. She little guessed the struggle within my breast, or the effort of self-restraint which held me back. My sympathies and my love went out to her, even as my hand had in the garden. I felt that years of the conventionalities of life could not teach me to know her sweet, brave nature as had this one day of strange experiences. Yet there were two thoughts which sealed the words of affection upon my lips. She was weak and helpless, shaken in mind and nerve. It was to take her at a disadvantage to obtrude love upon her at such a time. Worse still, she was rich. If Holmes's researches were successful, she would be an heiress. Was it fair, was it honourable, that a half-pay surgeon should take such advantage of an intimacy which chance had brought about ? Might she not look upon me as a mere vulgar fortune-seeker ? I could not bear to risk that such a thought should cross her mind. This Agra treasure intervened like an impassable barrier between us.

It was nearly two o'clock when we reached Mrs. Cecil Forrester's. The servants had retired hours ago, but Mrs. Forrester had been so interested by the strange message which Miss Morstan had received that she had sat up in the hope of her return. She opened the door herself, a middle-aged, graceful woman, and it gave me joy to see how tenderly her arm stole round the other's waist, and how motherly was the voice in which she greeted her. She was clearly no mere paid dependent, but an honoured friend. I was introduced, and Mrs. Forrester earnestly begged me to step in and to tell her our adventures. I had explained, however, the importance of my errand, and promised faithfully to call and report any progress which we might make with the case. As we drove away I stole a glance back, and I still seem to see that little group on the step—the two graceful, clinging figures, the half-opened door, the hall-light shining through stained glass, the barometer and the bright stair-rods. It was soothing to catch even that passing glimpse of a tranquil English home in the midst of the wild, dark business which had absorbed us.

And the more I thought of what had happened, the wilder and darker it grew. I reviewed the whole extraordinary sequence of events as I rattled on through the silent gaslit streets. There was the original problem: that, at least, was pretty clear now. The death of Captain Morstan, the sending of the pearls, the advertisement, the letter—we had had light upon all those events. They had only led us, however, to a deeper and far more tragic mystery. The Indian treasure, the curious plan found among Morstan's baggage, the strange scene at Major Sholto's death, the re-discovery of the treasure immediately followed by the murder of the discoverer, the very singular accompaniments to the crime, the footsteps, the remarkable weapons, the words upon the card, corresponding with those upon Captain Morstan's chart—here was, indeed, a labryinth in which a man less singularly endowed than my fellow-lodger might well despair of ever finding the clue.

Pinchin Lane was a row of shabby, two-storied brick houses in the lower quarter of Lambeth. I had to knock for some time at No. 3 before I could make any impression. At last, however, there was the glint of a candle behind the blind, and a face looked out at the upper window.

" Go on you drunken vagabond," said the

face. " If you kick up any more row, I'll open the kennels and let our forty-three dogs upon you."

" If you'll let one out, it's just what I have come for," said I.

"Go on ! " yelled the voice. " So help me gracious, I have a wiper in this bag, an' I'll drop it on your 'ead if you don't hook it ! "

" But I want a dog," I cried.

" I won't be argued with ! " shouted Mr. Sherman. " Now, stand clear; for when I say 'Three,' down goes the wiper."

" Mr. Sherlock Holmes——" I began; but the words had a most magical effect, for the window instantly slammed down, and within a minute the door was unbarred and open. Mr. Sherman was a lanky, lean old man, with stooping shoulders, a stringy neck, and blue-tinted glasses.

" A friend of Mr. Sherlock is always welcome," said he. " Step in, sir. Keep clear of the badger, for he bites. Ah, naughty, naughty ! would you take a nip at the gentleman ! " This to a stoat, which thrust its wicked head and red eyes between the bars of its cage. "Don't mind that, sir; it's only a slow-worm. It hain't got no fangs, so I gives it the run o' the room, for it keeps the beetles down. You must not mind my bein' just a little short wi' you at first, for I'm guyed at by the children, and there's many a one just comes down this lane to knock me up. What was it that Mr. Sherlock Holmes wanted, sir ? "

" He wanted a dog of yours."

" Ah ! that would be Toby."

" Yes, 'Toby' was the name."

" Toby lives at No. 7 on the left here."

He moved slowly forward with his candle among the queer animal family which he had gathered around him. In the uncertain, shadowy light I could see dimly that there were glancing, glimmering eyes peeping down at us from every cranny and corner. Even the rafters above our heads were lined by solemn fowls, who lazily shifted their weight from one leg to the other as our voices disturbed their slumbers.

Toby proved to be an ugly, long-haired, lop-eared creature, half spaniel and half lurcher, brown and white in colour, with a very clumsy, waddling gait. It accepted, after some hesitation, a lump of sugar which the old naturalist handed to me, and, having thus sealed an alliance, it followed me to the cab, and made no difficulties about accompanying me. It had just struck three on the Palace clock when I found myself back once more at Pondicherry Lodge. The ex-prizefighter McMurdo had, I found, been arrested as an accessory, and both he and Mr. Sholto had been marched off to the station. Two constables guarded the narrow gate, but they allowed me to pass with the dog on mentioning the detective's name.

Holmes was standing on the doorstep, with his hands in his pockets, smoking his pipe.

" Ah, you have him there ! " said he. " Good dog, then ! Athelney Jones has gone. We have had an immense display of energy since you left. He has arrested not only friend Thaddeus, but the gate-keeper, the housekeeper, and the Indian servant. We have the place to ourselves, but for a sergeant upstairs. Leave the dog here and come up."

We tied Toby to the hall table, and reascended the stairs. The room was as we had left it, save that a sheet had been draped over the central figure. A weary-looking sergeant reclined in the corner.

" Lend me your bull's-eye sergeant," said my companion. " Now tie this bit of card round my neck, so as to hang in front of me. Thank you. Now I must kick off my boots and stockings. Just you carry them down with you, Watson. I am going to do a little climbing. And dip my handkerchief into the creosote. That will do. Now come up into the garret with me for a moment."

We clambered up through the hole. Holmes turned his light once more upon the footsteps in the dust.

" I wish you particularly to notice these footmarks," he said. " Do you observe anything noteworthy about them ? "

" They belong," I said, " to a child or small woman."

" Apart from their size, though. There is nothing else ? "

" They appear to be much as other footmarks."

" Not at all ! Look here ! This is the print of a right foot in the dust. Now I make one with my naked foot beside it. What is the chief difference ? "

" Your toes are all cramped together. The other print has each toe distinctly divided."

" Quite so. That is the point. Bear that in mind. Now, would you kindly step over to that flap-window and smell the edge of the woodwork ? I shall stay over here, as I have this handkerchief in my hand."

I did as he directed, and was instantly conscious of a strong tarry smell.

" That is where he put his foot in getting out. If you can trace him, I should think that Toby will have no difficulty. Now run downstairs, loose the dog, and look out for Blondin."

By the time that I had got out into the grounds Sherlock Holmes was on the roof, and I could see him like an enormous glow-worm crawling very slowly along the ridge. I lost sight of him behind a stack of chimneys, but he presently reappeared, and then vanished once more upon the opposite side. When I made my way round there I found him seated at one of the corner eaves.

" That you, Watson ? " he cried.

" Yes."

" This is the place. What is that black thing down there ? "

" A water-barrel."

" Top on it ? "

" Yes."

" No sign of a ladder ? "

" No."

" Confound the fellow ! It's a most break-neck place. I ought to be able to come down where he could climb up. The water-pipe feels pretty firm. Here goes anyhow."

There was a scuffling of feet, and the lantern began to come steadily down the side of the wall. Then with a light spring he came on to the barrel and from there to the earth.

" It was easy to follow him," he said, drawing on his stockings and boots. " Tiles were loosened the whole way along, and in his hurry he dropped this. It confirms my diagnosis, as you doctors express it."

The object which he held up to me was a small pocket or pouch woven out of coloured grasses and with a few tawdry beads strung round it. In shape and size it was not unlike a cigarette-case. Inside were half-a-dozen spines of dark wood, sharp at one end and rounded at the other, like that which had struck Bartholomew Sholto.

" They are hellish things," said he. " Look out that you don't prick yourself. I'm delighted to have them, for the chances are that they are all he has. There is the less fear of you or me finding one in our skin before too long. I would sooner face a Martini bullet myself. Are you game for a six-mile trudge, Watson ? "

" Certainly," I answered.

" Your leg will stand it ? "

" Oh, yes."

" Here you are doggy ! Good old Toby ! Smell it, Toby, smell it ! " he pushed the creosote handkerchief under the dog's nose, while the creature stood with its fluffy legs separated, and with a most comical cock to its head, like a connoisseur sniffing the *bouquet* of a famous vintage. Holmes then threw the handkerchief to a distance, fastened a stout cord to the mongrel's collar, and led him to the foot of the water-barrel. The creature instantly broke into a succession of high, tremulous yelps, and, with his nose on the ground, and his tail in the air, pattered off upon the trail at a pace which strained his leash and kept us at the top of our speed.

The east had been gradually whitening, and we could now see some distance in the cold, grey light. The square, massive, house, with its black, empty windows and high, bare walls, towered up, sad and forlorn, behind us. Our course led right across the grounds, in and out among the trenches and pits with which they were scarred and intersected. The whole place, with its scattered dirt-heaps and ill-grown shrubs, had a blighted, ill-omened look which harmonized with the black tragedy which hung over it.

On reaching the boundary wall Toby ran along, whining eagerly, underneath its shadow, and stopped finally in a corner screened by a young beech. Where the two walls joined, several bricks had been loosened, and the crevices left were worn down and rounded upon the lower side, as though they had frequently been used as a ladder. Holmes clambered up, and, taking the dog from me, he dropped it over upon the other side.

" There's the print of wooden leg's hand," he remarked, as I mounted up beside him. " You see the slight smudge of blood upon the white plaster. What a lucky thing it is that we have had no very heavy rain since yesterday ! The scent will lie upon the road in spite of their eight-and-twenty hours' start."

I confess that I had my doubts myself when I reflected upon the great traffic which had passed along the London road in the interval. My fears were soon appeased, however. Toby never hesitated or swerved, but waddled on in his peculiar rolling fashion. Clearly, the pungent smell of the creosote rose high above all other contending scents.

" Do not imagine," said Holmes, " that I depend for my success in this case upon the mere chance of one of these fellows having put his foot in the chemical. I have knowledge now which would enable me to trace them in many different ways. This, however, is the readiest, and, since fortune has put it into our hands, I should be culpable if I neglected it. It has, however, prevented the case from becoming the pretty little intellectual problem which it at one time promised to be. There might have been some credit to be gained out of it, but for this too palpable clue."

"There is credit, and to spare," said I. "I assure you, Holmes, that I marvel at the means by which you obtain your results in this case, even more than I did in the Jefferson Hope murder. The thing seems to me to be deeper and more inexplicable. How, for example, could you describe with such confidence the wooden-legged man?"

"Pshaw, my dear boy! it was simplicity itself. I don't wish to be theatrical. It is all patent and above-board. Two officers who are in command of a convict guard learn an important secret as to buried treasure. A map is drawn for them by an Englishman named Jonathan Small. You remember that we saw the the name upon the chart in Captain Morstan's possession. He had signed it on behalf of himself and his associates—the sign of the four, as he somewhat dramatically called it. Aided by this chart, the officers—or one of them—gets the treasure and brings it to England, leaving, we will suppose, some condition under which he received it unfulfilled. Now, then, why did not Jonathan Small get the treasure himself?

The answer is obvious. The chart is dated at a time when Morstan was brought into close association with convicts. Jonathan Small did not get the treasure because he and his associates were themselves convicts and could not get away."

"But this is mere speculation," said I.

"It is more than that. It is the only hypothesis which covers the facts. Let us see how it fits in with the sequel. Major Sholto remains at peace for some years, happy in the possession of his treasure. Then he receives a letter from India which gives him a great fright. What was that?"

"A letter to say that the men whom he had wronged had been set free."

"Or had escaped. That is much more likely, for he would have known what their term of imprisonment was. It would not have been a surprise to him. What does he do then? He guards himself against a wooden-legged man—a white man, mark you, for he mistakes a white tradesman for him, and actually fires a pistol at him. Now, only one white man's name is on the chart. The others are Hindus or Mohammedans. There is no other white man. Therefore we may say with confidence that the wooden-legged man is identical with Jonathan Small.

Does the reasoning strike you as being faulty?"

"No: it is clear and concise."

"Well, now, let us put ourselves in the place of Jonathan Small. Let us look at it from his point of view. He comes to England with the double idea of regaining what he would consider to be his rights, and of having his revenge upon the man who had wronged him. He found out where Sholto lived, and very possibly he established communications with someone inside the house. There is the butler, Lal Rao, whom we have not seen. Mrs. Bernstone gives him far from a good character. Small could not find out, however, where the treasure was hid, for no one ever knew, save the major and one faithful servant who had died. Suddenly, Small learns that the major is on his death bed. In a frenzy lest the secret of the treasure die with him, he runs the gauntlet of the guards, makes his way to the dying man's window, and is only deterred from entering by the presence of his two sons. Mad with hate, however, against the dead man, he enters the room that night, searches his private papers in the hope of discovering some memorandum relating to the treasure, and finally leaves a memento of his visit in the short inscription upon the card. He had doubtless planned beforehand that, should he slay the major, he would leave some such record upon the body as a sign that it was not a common murder, but, from the point of view of the four associates, something in the nature of an act of justice. Whimsical and bizarre conceits of this kind are common enough to the annals of crime, and usually afford valuable indications as to the criminal. Do you follow all this?"

"Very clearly."

"Now, what could Jonathan Small do? He could only continue to keep a secret watch upon the efforts to find the treasure. Possibly he leaves England and only comes back at intervals. Then comes the discovery of the garret, and he is instantly informed of it. We again trace the presence of some confederate in the household. Jonathan, with his wooden leg, is utterly unable to reach the lofty room of Bartholomew Sholto. He takes with him, however, a rather curious associate, who gets over this difficulty, but dips his naked foot into creosote, whence come Toby, and a six-mile limp for a half-pay officer with a damaged *tendo Achillis.*"

"But it was the associate, and not Jonathan, who committed the crime."

" Quite so. And rather to Jonathan's disgust, to judge by the way he stamped about when he got into the room. He bore no grudge against Bartholomew Sholto, and would have preferred if he could have been simply bound and gagged. He did not wish to put his head into a halter. There was no help for it, however: the savage instincts of his companion had broken out, and the poison had done its work: so Jonathan Small left his record, lowered the treasure-box to the ground, and followed it himself. That was the train of events as far as I can decipher them. Of course, as to his personal appearance he must be middle-aged, and must be sunburned after serving his time in such an oven as the Andamans. His height is readily calculated from the length of his stride, and we know that he was bearded. His hairiness was the one point which impressed itself upon Thaddeus Sholto when he saw him at the window. I don't know that there is anything else."

" The associate ? "

" Ah, well, there is no great mystery in that. But you will know all about it soon enough. How sweet the morning air is ! See how that one little cloud floats like a pink feather from some gigantic flamingo. Now the red rim of the sun pushes itself over the London cloud-bank. It shines on a good many folk, but on none, I dare bet, who are on a stranger errand than you and I. How small we feel, with our petty ambitions and strivings, in the presence of the great elemental forces of Nature ! Are you well up in your Jean Paul ? "

" Fairly so. I worked back to him through Carlyle."

" That was like following the brook to the parent lake. He makes one curious but profound remark. It is that the chief proof of man's real greatness lies in his perception of his own smallness. It argues, you see, a power of comparison and of appreciation which is in itself a proof of nobility. There is much food for thought in Richter. You have not a pistol, have you ? "

" I have my stick."

" It is just possible that we may need something of the sort if we get to their lair. Jonathan I shall leave to you, but if the other turns nasty I shall shoot him dead."

He took out his revolver as he spoke, and, having loaded two of the chambers, he put it back into the right-hand pocket of his jacket.

We had during this time been following the guidance of Toby down the half rural villa-lined roads which lead to the Metropolis.

Now, however, we were beginning to come among continuous streets, where labourers and dockmen were already astir, and slatternly women were taking down shutters and brushing doorsteps. At the square-topped corner public-houses business was just beginning, and rough-looking men were emerging, rubbing their sleeves across their beards after their morning wet. Strange dogs sauntered up and stared wonderingly at us as we passed, but our inimitable Toby looked neither to the right nor to the left, but trotted onwards with his nose to the ground and an occasional eager whine which spoke of a hot scent.

We had traversed Streatham, Brixton, Camberwell, and now found ourselves in Kennington Lane, having borne away through the side streets to the east of the Oval. The men whom we pursued seemed to have taken a curiously zig-zag road, with the idea probably of escaping observation. They had never kept to the main road if a parallel side-street would serve their turn. At the foot of Kennington Lane they had edged away to the left through Bond Street and Miles Street. Where the latter street turns into Knight's Place, Toby ceased to advance, but began to run backwards and forwards with one ear cocked and the other drooping, the very picture of canine indecision. Then he waddled round in circles, looking up to us from time to time, as if to ask sympathy in his embarrassment.

" What the deuce is the matter with the dog ? " growled Holmes. " They surely would not take a cab, or go off in a balloon."

" Perhaps they stood here for some time," I suggested.

" Ah! it's all right. He's off again," said my companion, in a tone of relief.

He was indeed off, for after sniffing round again he suddenly made up his mind, and darted away with an energy and determination such as he had not yet shown. The scent appeared to be much hotter than before, for he had not even put his nose to the ground, but tugged at his leash and tried to break into a run. I could see by the gleam in Holmes's eyes that he thought we were nearing the end of our journey.

Our course now ran down Nine Elms until we came to Broderick and Nelson's large timberyard, just past the White Eagle tavern. Here the dog, frantic with excitement, turned down through the side gate into the enclosure, where the sawyers were already at work. On the dog raced through sawdust and shavings, down an alley, round a passage, between two wood-piles, and finally, with a triumphant yelp, sprang upon a large barrel which still stood upon the hand-trolley on which it had been brought. With lolling tongue and blinking eyes, Toby stood upon the cask, looking from one to the other of us for some sign of appreciation. The staves of the barrel and the wheels of the trolley were smeared with a dark liquid, and the whole air was heavy with the smell of creosote.

Sherlock Holmes and I looked blankly at each other, and then burst simultaneously into an uncontrollable fit of laughter.

CHAPTER VIII

THE BAKER STREET IRREGULARS

" What now ? " I asked. " Toby has lost his character for infallibility."

" He acted according to his lights," said Holmes, lifting him down from the barrel and walking him out of the timber-yard. " If you consider how much creosote is carted about London in one day, it is no great wonder that our trail should have been crossed. It is much used now, especially for the seasoning of wood. Poor Toby is not to blame."

" We must get on the main scent again, I suppose."

" Yes. And, fortunately, we have no distance to go. Evidently what puzzled the dog at the corner of Knight's Place was that there were two different trails running in opposite directions. We took the wrong one. It only remains to follow the other."

There was no difficulty about this. On leading Toby to the place where he had commited his fault, he cast about in a wide circle and finally dashed off in a fresh direction.

" We must now take care that he does not now bring us to the place where the creosote-barrel came from," I observed.

" I had thought of that. But you notice that he keeps on the pavement, whereas the barrel passed down the roadway. No, we are on the true scent now."

It tended down towards the river-side, running through Belmont Place and Prince's Street. At the end of Broad Street it ran right down to the water's edge, where there was a small wooden wharf. Toby led us to the very edge of this, and there stood whining, looking out on the dark current beyond.

" We are out of luck," said Holmes. " They have taken to a boat here."

Several small punts and skiffs were lying about in the water and on the edge of the wharf. We took Toby round to each in turn, but, though he sniffed earnestly, he made no sign.

Close to the rude landing-stage was a small brick house, with a wooden placard slung out through the second window. "Mordecai Smith" was printed across it in large letters, and underneath, "Boats to hire by the hour or day." A second inscription above the door informed us that a steam-launch was kept—a statement which was confirmed by a great pile of coke upon the jetty. Sherlock Holmes looked slowly round, and his face assumed an ominous expression.

" This looks bad," said he. " These fellows are sharper than I expected. They seem to have covered their tracks. There has, I fear, been preconcerted management here."

He was approaching the door of the house, when it opened, and a little curly-headed lad of six came running out, followed by a stoutish, red-faced woman with a large sponge in her hand.

" You come back and be washed, Jack," she shouted. " Come back, you young imp ; for if your father comes home and finds you like that, he'll let us hear of it."

" Dear little chap ! " cried Holmes, strategically. "What a rosy-cheeked young rascal! Now, Jack is there anything you would like?"

The youth pondered for a moment.

" I'd like a shillin'," said he.

" Nothing you would like better ? "

" I'd like two shillin' better," the prodigy answered after some thought.

" Here you are, then ! Catch !—A fine child, Mrs. Smith!"

" Lor' bless you, sir, he is that, and forward. He gets a'most too much for me to manage, 'specially when my man is away days at a time."

" Away, is he ? " said Holmes, in a disappointed voice. " I am sorry for that, for I wanted to speak with Mr. Smith."

" He's been away since yesterday mornin', sir, and truth to tell I am beginning to feel frightened about him. But if it was about a boat, sir, maybe I could serve as well."

" I wanted to hire his steam launch."

" Why, bless you, sir, it is in the steam launch that he has gone. That's what puzzles me; for I know there ain't no more coals in her than would take her to about Woolwich and back. If he'd been away in the barge I'd ha' thought nothing'; for many a time a job has taken him as far as

Gravesend, and then if there was much doin' there he might ha' stayed over. But what good is a steam launch without coals?"

"He might have bought some at a wharf down the river."

"He might, sir, but it weren't his way. Many a time I've heard him call out at the prices they charge for a few odd bags. Besides, I don't like that wooden-legged man, wi' his ugly face and outlandish talk. What did he want always knockin' about here for?"

"A wooden-legged man?" said Holmes, with bland surprise.

"Yes, sir, a brown, monkey-faced chap that's called more'n once for my old man. It was him that roused him up yesternight and, what's more, my man knew he was comin', for he had steam up in the launch. I tell you straight, sir, I don't feel easy in my mind about it."

"But my dear Mrs. Smith," said Holmes, shrugging his shoulders, "you are frightening yourself about nothing. How could you possibly tell that it was the wooden-legged man who came in the night? I don't understand how you can be so sure."

"His voice, sir. I know his voice, which is kind o' thick and foggy. He tapped at the winder—about three it would be. 'Show a leg matey,' said he: 'time to turn out guard.' My old man woke up Jim—that's my eldest—and away they went, without so much as a word to me. I could hear the wooden leg clackin' on the stones."

"And was this wooden-legged man alone?"

"Couldn't say, I am sure, sir. I didn't hear no one else."

"I am sorry, Mrs. Smith, for I wanted a steam launch, and I have heard good reports of the—— Let me see, what is her name?"

"The *Aurora*, sir."

"Ah! She's not that old green launch with a yellow line, very broad in the beam?"

"No indeed. She's as trim a little thing as any on the river. She's been fresh painted, black with two red streaks."

"Thanks. I hope that you will hear soon from Mr. Smith. I am going down the river, and if I should see anything of the *Aurora* I shall let him know that you are uneasy. A black funnel, you say?"

"No, sir. Black with a white band."

"Ah, of course. It was the sides which were black. Good morning, Mrs. Smith. There is a boatman here with a wherry, Watson. We shall take it and cross the river."

"The main thing with people of that sort," said Holmes, as we sat in the sheets of the wherry, "is never to let them think that their information can be of the slightest importance to you. If you do, they will instantly shut up like an oyster. If you listen to them under protest, as it were, you are very likely to get what you want."

"Our course now seems pretty clear," said I.

"What would you do, then?"

"I would engage a launch and go down the river on the track of the *Aurora*."

"My dear fellow, it would be a colossal task. She may have touched at any wharf on either side of the stream between here an Greenwich. Below the bridge there is a perfect labyrinth of landing-places for miles. It would take you days and days to exhaust them, if you set about it alone."

"Employ the police, then."

"No. I shall probably call Athelney Jones in at the last moment. He is not a bad fellow, and I should not like to do anything which would injure him professionally. But I have a fancy for working it out for myself, now that we have gone so far."

"Could we advertise, then, asking for information from wharfingers?"

"Worse and worse! Our men would know that the chase was hot at their heels, and they would be off out of the country. As it is, they are likely enough to leave, but as long as they think they are perfectly safe they will be in no hurry. Jones's energy will be of use to us there, for his view of the case is sure to push itself to the daily Press, and the runaways will think that everyone is off on the wrong scent."

"What are we to do, then?" I asked, as we landed near Millbank Penitentiary.

"Take this hansom, drive home, have some breakfast, and get an hour's sleep. It is quite on the cards that we may be afoot tonight again. Stop at the telegraph office, cabby! We will keep Toby, for he may be of use to us."

We pulled up at the Great Peter Street Post Office, and Holmes dispatched his wire.

"Whom do you think that is to?" he asked, as we resumed our journey.

"I am sure I don't know."

"You remember the Baker Street division of the detective police force whom I employed in the Jefferson Hope case?"

"Well?" said I, laughingly.

"This is just the case where they might be invaluable. If they fail, I have other resources; but I shall try them first. That wire was to my dirty little lieutenant, Wiggins, and I expect that he and his gang will be with us before we have finished our breakfast."

It was between eight and nine o'clock now and I was conscious of a strong reaction after the successive excitements of the night. I was limp and weary, befogged in mind and fatigued in body. I had not the professional enthusiasm which carried my companion on, nor could I look at the matter as a mere abstract intellectual problem. As far as the death of Bartholomew Sholto went, I had heard little good of him, and could feel no intense antipathy to his murderers. The treasure, however, was a different matter. That, or part of it, belonged rightfully to Miss Morstan. While there was a chance of recovering it I was ready to devote my life to the one object. True, if I found it, it would probably put her for ever beyond my reach. Yet it would be a petty and selfish love which would be influenced by such a thought as that. If Holmes could work to find the criminals, I had a tenfold stronger reason to urge me on to find the treasure.

A bath at Baker Street and a complete change freshened me up wonderfully. When I came down to our room I found the breakfast laid and Holmes pouring the coffee.

" Here it is," said he, laughing, and pointing to an open newspaper. " The energetic Jones and the ubiquitous reporter have fixed it up between them. But you have had enough of the case. Better have your ham and eggs first."

I took the paper from him and read the short notice, which was headed, " Mysterious Business at Upper Norwood."

About twelve o'clock last night, [said the *Standard*] Mr. Bartholomew Sholto, of Pondicherry Lodge, Upper Norwood, was found dead in his room under circumstances which point to foul play. As far as we can learn, no actual traces of violence were found upon Mr. Sholto's person, but a valuable collection of Indian gems which the deceased gentleman had inherited from his father had been carried off. The discovery was first made by Mr. Sherlock Holmes and Dr. Watson, who had called at the house with Mr. Thaddeus Sholto, brother of the deceased. By a singular piece of good fortune, Mr. Athelney Jones, the well-known member of the detective police force, happened to be at the Norwood Police Station, and was on the ground within half an hour of the first alarm. His trained and experienced faculties were at once directed towards the detection of the criminals, with the gratifying result that the brother, Thaddeus Sholto, has already been arrested, together with the housekeeper, Mrs. Bernstone, and Indian butler name Lal Rao, and a porter, or gatekeeper, named McMurdo. It is quite certain that the thief or thieves were well acquainted with the house, for Mr. Jones's well-known technical knowledge and his powers of minute observation have enabled him to prove conclusively that the miscreants could not have entered by the door or by the window but must have made their way across the roof of the building, and so through a trap-door into a room which communicated with that in which the body was found. This fact, which has been very clearly made out, proves conclusively that it was no mere haphazard burglary. The prompt and energetic action of the officers of the law shows the great advantage of the presence on such occasions of a single vigorous and masterful mind. We cannot but think that it supplied an argument to those who would wish to see our detectives more decentralized, and so brought into closer and more effective touch with the cases which it is their duty to investigate.

" Isn't it gorgeous ? " said Holmes, grinning over his coffee cup. " What do you think of it ? "

" I think that we have had a close shave ourselves of being arrested for the crime."

At this moment there was a loud ring at the bell and I could here Mrs. Hudson, our landlady, raising her voice in a wail of expostulation and dismay.

" By heavens, Holmes," said I, half rising, " I believe that they are really after us."

" No, it's not quite so bad as that. It is the unofficial force—the Baker Street irregulars."

As he spoke, there came a swift pattering of naked feet upon the stairs, a clatter of high voices, and in rushed a dozen dirty and ragged little street arabs. There was some show of discipline among them, despite their tumultuous entry, for they instantly drew up in line and stood facing us with expectant faces. One of their number, taller and older than the others, stood forward with an air of lounging superiority which was very funny in such a disreputable little scarecrow.

" Got your message, sir," said he, "and brought 'em on sharp. Three bob and a tanner for tickets."

" Here you are," said Holmes, producing some silver. " In future they can report to you, Wiggins and you to me. I cannot have a house invaded in this way. However, it is just as well that you should all hear the instructions. I want to find the where-abouts of a steam launch called the *Aurora*, owner Mordecai Smith, black with two red streaks, funnel black with a white band. She is down the river somewhere. I want one boy to be at Mordecai Smith's landing-stage opposite Millbank to say if the boat comes back. You must divide it out among yourselves, and do both banks thorough-ly. Let me know the moment you have news. It that all clear ? "

" Yes, guv'nor," said Wiggins.

" The old scale of pay, and a guinea to the boy who finds the boat. Here's a day in advance. Now, off you go ! "

He handed them a shilling each, and away they buzzed down the stairs, and I saw them a moment later streaming down the street.

" If the launch is above water they will find her," said Holmes, as he rose from the table and lit his pipe. " They can go everywhere, see everything, overhear everyone. I expect to hear before evening that they have spotted her. In the meanwhile, we can do nothing but await results. We cannot pick up the broken trail until we find either the *Aurora* or Mr. Mordecai Smith.

" Toby could eat these scraps, I dare say. Are you going to bed, Holmes ? "

" No; I am not tired. I have a curious constitution. I never remember feeling tired by work, though idleness exhausts me completely. I am going to smoke and to think over this queer business to which my fair client has introduced us. If ever man had an easy task, this of ours ought to be. Wooden-legged men are not so common, but the other man must, I should think, be absolutely unique."

" That other man again ! "

" I have no wish to make a mystery of him to you, anyway. But you must have formed your own opinion. Now, do consider the data. Diminutive footmarks, toes never fet-tered by boots, naked feet, stone-headed wooden mace, great agility, small poisoned darts. What do you make of all this ? "

" A savage ! " I exclaimed. " Perhaps one of those Indians who were the associates of Jonathan Small."

" Hardly that," said he. " When first I saw signs of strange weapons, I was inclined to think so; but the remarkable character of the footmarks caused me to reconsider my views. Some of the inhabitants of the Indi-an Peninsular are small men, but none could have left such marks as that. The Hindu proper has long and thin feet. The sandal-wearing Mohammedan has the great toe well separated from the others, because the thong is commonly passed between. These little darts, too, could only be shot in one way. They are from a blow-pipe. Now, then, where are we to find our savage ? "

" South American," I hazarded.

He stretched his hand up, and took down a bulky volume from the shelf.

" This is the first volume of a gazetteer which is now being published. It may be looked upon as the very latest authority. What have we here ? ' Andaman Islands, situated 340 miles to the north of Sumatra, in the Bay of Bengal.' Hum, Hum ! What's all this ? Moist climate, coral reefs, sharks, Port Blair, convict barracks, Rutland Island, cottonwoods—— Ah, here we are ! The aborigines of the Andaman Is-lands may perhaps claim the distinction of being the smallest race upon this earth, though some anthropologists prefer the Bushmen of Africa, the Diggers of America, and the Terra del Fuegians. The average height is rather below four feet, although many full-grown adults may be found who are very much smaller than this. They are a fierce, morose, and intractable people, though capable of forming most devoted friendships when their confidence has once been gained.' Mark that, Watson. Now then, listen to this. ' They are naturally hideous, having large, misshapen heads, small, fierce eyes, and distorted features. Their feet and hands, however, are remarkably small. So intractable and fierce are they, that all the efforts of the British officials have failed to win them over in any degree. They have always been a terror to shipwrecked crews, braining the survivors with their stone-headed clubs, or shooting them with their poisoned arrows. These massacres are invariably concluded by a cannibal feast.' Nice, amiable people, Wat-son ! If this fellow had been left to his own unaided devices, this affair might have taken an even more ghastly turn. I fancy that even as it is, Jonathan Small would give a good deal not to have employed him."

" But how came he to have so singular a companion ? "

" Ah, that is more than I can tell. Since, however, we had already determined that Small had come from the Andamans, it is not so very wonderful that this islander should be with him. No doubt we shall know all about it in time. Look here, Watson; you look regularly done. Lie down there on the sofa, and see if I can put you to sleep."

He took up his violin from the corner, and as I stretched myself out he began to play some low, dreamy, melodious air—his own, no doubt, for he had a remarkable gift for improvisation. I have a vague remembrance of his gaunt limbs, his earnest face, and the rise and fall of his bow. Then I seemed to be floated peacefully away upon a soft sea of sound, until I found myself in dreamland, with the sweet face of Mary Morstan looking down upon me.

CHAPTER IX

A BREAK IN THE CHAIN

It was late in the afternoon before I woke, strengthened and refreshed. Sherlock Holmes still sat exactly as I had left him save that he had laid aside his violin and was deep in a book. He looked across at me as I stirred, and I noticed that his face was dark and troubled.

"You have slept soundly," he said. "I feared that our talk would wake you."

"I heard nothing," I answered. "Have you had fresh news, then?"

"Unfortunately, no. I confess that I am surprised and disappointed. I expected something definite by this time. Wiggins has just been up to report. He says that no trace can be found of the launch. It is a provoking check, for every hour is of importance."

"Can I do anything?" I am perfectly fresh now, and quite ready for another night's outing."

"No; we can do nothing. We can only wait. If we go ourselves, the message might come in our absence, and delay be caused. You can do what you will, but I must remain on guard."

"Then I shall run over to Camberwell and call upon Mrs. Cecil Forrester. She asked me to, yesterday."

"On Mrs. Cecil Forrester?" asked Holmes, with the twinkle of a smile in his eyes.

"Well, of course, on Miss Morstan too. They were anxious to hear what happened."

"I would not tell them too much," said Holmes. "Women are never to be entirely trusted—not the best of them."

I did not pause to argue over this atrocious sentiment.

"I shall be back in an hour or two," I remarked.

"All right! Good luck! But, I say, if you are crossing the water you may as well return Toby, for I don't think it is at all likely that we shall have any use for him now."

I took our mongrel accordingly, and left him, together with a half-sovereign, at the old naturalist's in Pinchin Lane. At Camberwell I found Miss Morstan a little weary after her night's adventures, but very eager to hear the news. Mrs. Forrester, too, was full of curiosity. I told them all that we had done, suppressing, however, the more dreadful parts of the tragedy. Thus, although I spoke of Mr. Sholto's death, I said nothing of the exact manner and method of it. With all my omissions, however, there was enough to startle and amaze them.

"It is a romance!" cried Mrs. Forrester. "An injured lady, half a million in treasure, a black cannibal, and a wooden-legged ruffian. They take the place of the conventional dragon or wicked earl."

"And two knights-errant to the rescue," added Miss Morstan, with a bright glance at me.

"Why, Mary, your fortune depends upon the issue of this search. I don't think that you are nearly excited enough. Just imagine what it must be to be so rich, and to have the world at your feet!"

It sent a little thrill of joy to my heart to notice that she showed no sign of elation at the prospect. On the contrary, she gave a toss of her proud head, as though the matter were one in which she took small interest.

"It is for Mr. Thaddeus Sholto that I am anxious, she said. "Nothing else is of any consequence; but I think that he has behaved most kindly and honourably throughout. It is our duty to clear him of this dreadful and unfounded charge."

It was evening before I left Camberwell, and quite dark by the time I reached home. My companion's book and pipe lay by his chair, but he had disappeared. I looked about in the hope of seeing a note, but there was none.

"I suppose that Mr. Sherlock Holmes has gone out?" I said to Mrs. Hudson as she came up to lower the blinds.

"No sir. He has gone to his room, sir. Do you know, sir," sinking her voice into an impressive whisper, "I am afraid for his health?"

"Why so, Mrs. Hudson?"

"Well, he's that strange, sir. After you was gone he walked and he walked, up and down, and up and down, until I was weary of the sound of his footstep. Then I heard him talking to himself and muttering, and every time the bell rang out he came on the stairhead, with 'What is that, Mrs. Hudson?' And now he has slammed off to his room, but I can hear him walking away the same as ever. I hope he's not going to be ill, sir. I ventured to say something to him about cooling medicine, but he turned on me, sir, with such a look that I don't know how ever I got out of the room."

" I don't think that you have any cause to be uneasy, Mrs. Hudson," I answered. " I have seen him like this before. He has some small matter upon his mind which makes him restless."

I tried to speak lightly to our worthy landlady, but I was myself uneasy when through the long night I still from time to time heard the dull sound of his tread and I knew how his keen spirit was chafing against this involuntary inaction.

At breakfast-time he looked worn and haggard, with a little fleck of feverish colour upon either cheek.

" You are knocking yourself up, old man," I remarked. " I heard you marching about in the night."

"No, I could not sleep," he answered. " This infernal problem is consuming me. It is too much to be baulked by so petty an obstacle, when all else has been overcome. I know the men, the launch, everything; and yet I can get no news. I have set other agencies at work, and used every means at my disposal. The whole river has now been searched on either side, but there is no news, nor has Mrs. Smith heard of her husband. I shall come to the conclusion soon that they have scuttled the craft. But there are objections to that."

" Or that Mrs. Smith has put us on a wrong scent."

" No, I think that may be dismissed. I had inquiries made, and there is a launch of that description."

" Could it have gone up the river?"

" I have considered that possibility too, and there is a search party who will work up as far as Richmond. If no news comes today, I shall start off myself tomorrow, and go for the men rather than the boat. But surely, surely, we shall hear something."

We did not, however. Not a word came to us either from Wiggins or from the other agencies. There were articles in most of the papers upon the Norwood tragedy. They all appeared to be rather hostile to the unfortun-

ate Thaddeus Sholto. No fresh details were to be found, however, in any of them save that an inquest was to be held upon the following day. I walked over to Camberwell in the evening to report our ill-success to the ladies, and on my return I found Holmes dejected and somewhat morose. He would hardly reply to my questions, and busied himself all the evening in an abstruse chemical analysis which involved much heating of retorts and distilling of vapours, ending at last in a smell which fairly drove me out of the apartment. Up to the small hours of the morning I could hear the clinking of his test-tubes, which told me that he was still engaged in his malodorous experiment.

In the early dawn I woke with a start, and was surprised to find him standing by my bedside, clad in a rude sailor dress with a pea-jacket, and a coarse red scarf round his neck.

" I am off down the river, Watson," said he. " I have been turning it over in my mind, and I can see only one way out of it. It is worth trying, at all events."

" Surely I can come with you, then? " said I.

" No; you can be much more useful if you will remain here as my representative. I am loth to go, for it is quite on the cards that some message may come during the day, though Wiggins was despondent about it last night. I want you to open all notes and telegrams, and to act on your own judgment if any news should come. Can I rely upon you? "

" Most certainly."

" I am afraid that you will not be able to wire to me, for I can hardly tell yet where I may find myself. If I am in luck, however, I may not be gone so very long. I shall have news of some sort or other before I get back."

I heard nothing of him by breakfast-time. On opening the *Standard*, however, I found that there was a fresh allusion to the business.

With reference to the Upper Norwood tragedy, [it remarked] we have reason to believe that the matter promises to be even more complex and mysterious than was originally supposed. Fresh evidence has shown that it is quite impossible that Mr. Thaddeus Sholto could have been in any way concerned in the matter. He and the housekeeper, Mrs. Bernstone, were both released yesterday evening. It is believed, however, that the police have a clue as to the real culprits, and that is being prosecuted by Mr. Athelney Jones, of Scotland Yard, with all his well-known energy and sagacity. Further arrests may be expected at any moment.

"That is satisfactory so far as it goes," thought I. "Friend Sholto is safe, at any rate. I wondered what the fresh clue may be, though it seems a stereotyped form whenever the police have made a blunder."

I tossed the paper down upon the table, but at that moment my eye caught an advertisement in the agony column. It ran this away:—

LOST.—Whereas Mordecai Smith, boatman, and his son Jim, left Smith's Wharf at or about three o'clock last Tuesday morning in the steam launch *Aurora*, black with two red stripes, funnel black with white band, the sum of five pounds will be paid to anyone who can give information to Mrs. Smith at Smith's Wharf, or at 221B Baker Street, as to the whereabouts of the said Mordecai Smith and the launch *Aurora*.

This was clearly Holmes's doing. The Baker Street address was enough to prove that. It struck me as rather ingenious, because it might be read by the fugitives without their seeing in it more than the natural anxiety of a wife for her missing husband.

It was a long day. Every time that a knock came to the door, or a sharp step passed in the street, I imagined that it was either Holmes returning or an answer to his advertisement. I tried to read but my thoughts would wander off to our strange quest and to the ill-assorted and villainous pair whom we were pursuing. Could there be, I wondered, some radical flaw in my companion's reasoning? Might he not be suffering from some large self-deception? Was it not possible that his nimble and speculative mind had built up this wild theory upon faulty premises? I had never known him to be wrong and yet the keenest reasoner may occasionally be deceived. He was likely, I thought, to fall into error through the over-refinement of his logic—his preference of a subtle and bizarre explanation when a plainer and more commonplace one lay ready to his hand. Yet on the other hand, I had myself seen the evidence, and I had heard the reasons for his deductions. When I looked back on the long chain of

curious circumstances, many of them trivial in themselves, but all tending in the same direction, I could not disguise from myself that even if Holmes's explanation were incorrect the true theory must be equally *outré* and startling.

At three o'clock in the afternoon there was a loud peal at the bell, an authoritative voice in the hall, and, to my surprise, no less a person than Mr. Athelney Jones was shown up to me. Very different was he, however, from the brusque and masterful professor of commonsense who had taken over the case so confidently at Upper Norwood. His expression was downcast, and his bearing meek and even apologetic.

"Good-day, sir; good-day," said he. "Mr Sherlock Holmes is out, I understand?"

"Yes, I cannot be sure when he will be back. But perhaps you would care to wait. Take that chair and try one of these cigars."

"Thank you; I don't mind if I do," said he, mopping his face with a red bandanna handkerchief.

"And a whisky and soda?"

"Well, half a glass. It is very hot for the time of year; and I have had a good deal to worry and try me. You know my theory about this Norwood case?"

"I remember that you expressed one."

"Well, I have been obliged to reconsider it. I had my net tightly round Mr. Sholto, sir, when pop he went though a hole in the middle of it. He was able to prove an alibi which could not be shaken. From the time he left his brother's room he was never out of sight of someone or other. So it could not be he who climbed over roofs and through trap-doors. It's a very dark case, and my professional credit is at stake. I should be very glad of a little assistance."

"We all need help sometimes," said I.

"Your friend Mr. Sherlock Holmes is a wonderful man, sir," said he, in a husky and confidential voice. "He's a man who is not to be beat. I have known that young man go into a good many cases, but I never saw the case yet that he could not throw a little light upon. He is irregular in his methods, and a little quick perhaps in jumping at theories; but, on the whole, I think he would have made a most promising officer, and I don't care who knows it. I have had a wire from him this morning, by which I understand that he has got some clue to this Sholto business. Here is his message."

He took the telegram out of his pocket, and handed it to me. It was dated from Poplar at twelve o'clock. "Go to Baker Street at once," it said. "If I have not returned, wait for me. I am close on the track of the Sholto gang. You can come with us tonight if you want to be in at the finish."

"This sounds well. He has evidently picked up the scent again," said I.

"Ah, then he has been at fault too," exclaimed Jones, with evident satisfaction. "Even the best of us are thrown off sometimes. Of course this may prove to be a false alarm; but it is my duty as an officer of the law to allow no chance to slip. But there is someone at the door. Perhaps this is he."

A heavy step was heard ascending the stair, with a great wheezing and rattling as from a man who was sorely put to it for breath. Once or twice he stopped, as though the climb were too much for him, but at last he made his way to our door and entered. His appearance corresponded to the sounds which we had heard. He was an aged man, clad in seafaring garb, with an old pea-jacket buttoned up to his throat. His back was bowed, his knees were shaky, and his breathing was painfully asthmatic. As he leaned upon a thick oaken cudgel his shoulders heaved in the effort to draw the air into his lungs. He had a coloured scarf round his chin, and I could see little of his face save a pair of keen dark eyes, overhung by bushy white brows, and long grey side-whiskers. Altogether he gave me the impression of a respectable master mariner who had fallen into years and poverty.

"What is it, my man?" I asked.

He looked about him in the slow methodical fashion of old age.

"Is Mr. Sherlock Holmes here?" said he.

"No; but I am acting for him. You can tell me any message you have for him."

"It was to him himself I was to tell it," said he.

"But I tell you I am acting for him. Was it about Mordecai Smith's boat?"

"Yes. I knows well where it is. An' I know where the men he is after are. An' I knows where the treasure is. I knows all about it."

"Then tell me, and I shall let him know."

"It was to him I was to tell it," he repeated, with the petulant obstinacy of a very old man.

"Well you must wait for him."

"No, no; I ain't goin' to lose a whole day to please no one. If Mr. Holmes ain't here, then Mr. Holmes must find it all out for himself. I don't care about the look of either of you, and I won't tell a word."

He shuffled towards the door, but Athelney Jones got in front of him.

"Wait a bit, my friend," said he. "You must have important information, and you must not walk off. We shall keep you, whether you like or not, until our friend returns."

The old man made a little run towards the door, but as Athelney Jones put his broad back up against it, he recognized the uselessness of resistance.

"Pretty sort o' treatment this!" he cried, stamping his stick. "I come here to see a gentleman, and you two, who I never saw in my life, seize me and treat me in this fashion!"

"You will be none the worse," I said. "We shall recompense you for the loss of your time. Sit over here on the sofa, and you will not have long to wait."

He came across sullenly enough, and seated himself with his face resting on his hands. Jones and I resumed our cigars and our talk. Suddenly, however, Holmes's voice broke upon us.

"I think that you might offer me a cigar too," he said.

We both started in our chairs. There was Holmes sitting close to us with an air of quiet amusement.

"Holmes!" I exclaimed. "You here! But where is the old man?"

"Here is the old man," said he, holding out a heap of white hair. "Here he is—wig, whiskers, eyebrows, and all. I thought my disguise was pretty good, but I hardly expected that it would stand the test."

"Ah, you rogue!" cried Jones, highly delighted. "You would have made an actor, and a rare one. You had the proper workhouse cough, and those weak legs of yours are worth ten pound a week. I thought I knew the glint of your eye, though. You didn't get away from us so easily, you see."

"I have been working in all that get-up all day," said he, lighting a cigar. "You see, a good many of the criminal classes begin to know me—especially since our friend here took to publishing some of my cases: so I can only go on the warpath under some simple disguise like this. You got my wire?"

"Yes; that was what brought me here."

"How has your case prospered?"

"It has all come to nothing. I have had to release two of my prisoners, and there is no evidence against the other two."

"Never mind. We shall give you two others in place of them. But you must put yourself under my orders. You are welcome to all the official credit, but you must act on the lines that I point out. Is that agreed?"

"Entirely, if you will help me to the men."

" Well, then, in the first place I shall want a fast police-boat—a steam-launch—to be at the Westminster Stairs at seven o'clock.

" That is easily managed. There is always one about there; but I can step across the road and telephone to make sure."

" Then I shall want two staunch men, in case of resistance."

" There will be two or three in the boat. What else ? "

" When we secure the men we shall get the treasure. I think that it would be a pleasure to my friend here to take the box round to the young lady to whom half of it rightfully belongs. Let her be the first to open it. Eh, Watson ? "

" It would be a great pleasure to me."

" Rather an irregular ' proceeding," said Jones, shaking his head. " However, the whole thing is irregular, and I suppose we must wink at it. The treasure must afterwards be handed over to the authorities until after the official investigation."

" Certainly. That is easily managed. One other point. I should much like to have a few details about this matter from the lips of Jonathan Small himself. You know I like to work the details of my cases out. There is no objection to my having an unofficial interview with him either in my rooms or elsewhere, as long as he is efficiently guarded ? "

" Well, you are master of the situation. I have had no proof yet of the existence of this Jonathan Small. However, if you can catch him, I don't see how I can refuse you an interview with him."

" That is understood, then ? "

" Perfectly. Is there anything else ? "

" Only that I insist upon your dining with us. It will be ready in half an hour. I have oysters and a brace of grouse, with something a little choice in white wines. Watson, you have never yet recognized my merits as a housekeeper."

CHAPTER X

THE END OF THE ISLANDER

Our meal was a merry one. Holmes could talk exceedingly well when he chose, and that night he did choose. He appeared to be in a state of nervous exaltation. I have never known him so brilliant. He spoke on a quick succession of subjects—miracle plays, on medieval pottery, on Stradivarius violins, on the Buddhism of Ceylon, and on the warships of the future—handling each as though he had made a special study of it. His bright humour marked the reaction from his black depression of the preceding

days. Athelney Jones proved to be a sociable soul in his hours of relaxation, and faced his dinner with the air of a *bon vivant*. For myself, I felt elated at the thought that we were nearing the end of our task, and I caught something of Holmes's gaiety. None of us alluded during dinner to the cause which had brought us together.

When the cloth was cleared, Holmes glanced at his watch, and filled up three glasses of port.

" One bumper," said he, " to the success of our little expedition. And now it is high time we were off. Have you a pistol, Watson ? "

" I have my old service-revolver in my desk."

" You had best take it, then. It is well to be prepared. I see that the cab is at the door. I ordered it for half-past six."

It was a little past seven before we reached the Westminster Wharf, and found our launch awaiting us. Holmes eyed it critically.

" Is there anything to mark it as a police-boat ? "

" Yes; that green lamp to the side."

" Then take it off."

The small change was made, we stepped on board, and the ropes were cast. Jones, Holmes, and I sat in the stern. There was one man at the rudder, one to tend the engines, and two burly police-inspectors forward.

" Where to ? " asked Jones.

" To the Tower. Tell them to stop opposite to Jacobson's Yard."

Our craft was evidently a very fast one. We shot past the long lines of loaded barges as though they were stationary. Holmes smiled with satisfaction as we overhauled a river steamer and left her behind us.

" We ought to be able to catch anything on the river," he said.

" Well, hardly that. But there are not many launches to beat us."

"We shall have to catch the *Aurora*, and she has a name for being a clipper. I will tell you how the land lies, Watson. You recollect how annoyed I was at being baulked by so small a thing ? "

" Yes."

" Well, I gave my mind a thorough rest by plunging into a chemical analysis. One of our greatest statesmen has said that a change of work is the best rest. So it is. When I had succeeded in dissolving the hydrocarbon which I was at work at, I came back to the problem of the Sholtos, and I thought the whole matter out again. My boys had been up the river and down the river without result. The launch was not at any landing-stage or wharf, nor had it returned. Yet it could hardly have been scuttled to hide their traces, though that always remained as a possible hypothesis if all failed. I knew that this man Small had a certain degree of low cunning, but I did not think him capable of anything in the nature of delicate finesse. I then reflected that since he had certainly been in London some time—as we had evidence that he maintained a continual watch over Pondicherry Lodge—he could hardly leave at a moment's notice, but would need some little time, if it were only a day, to arrange his affairs. That was the balance of probability, at any rate."

" It seems to me to be a little weak," said I: " it is more probable that he had arranged his affairs before ever he set out upon his expedition."

" No, I hardly think so. This lair of his would be too valuable a retreat in case of need for him to give it up until he was sure that he could do without it. But a second consideration struck me. Jonathan Small must have felt that the peculiar appearance of his companion, however much he may have top-coated him, would give rise to gossip, and possibly be associated with this Norwood tragedy. He was quite sharp enough to see that. They had started from their head-quarters under cover of darkness, and he would wish to get back before it was broad light. Now, it was past three o'clock, according to Mrs. Smith, when they got the boat. It would be quite bright, and people would be about in an hour or so. Therefore, I argued, they did not go very far. They paid Smith well to hold his tongue, reserved his launch for the final escape, and hurried to their lodgings with the treasure-box. In a couple of nights, when they had time to see what view the papers took, and whether there was any suspicion, they would make their way under cover of darkness to some ship at Gravesend or in the Downs, where no doubt they had already arranged for passages to America or the Colonies."

" But the launch ? They could not have taken that to their lodgings."

" Quite so. I argued that the launch must be no great way off, in spite of its invisibility. I then put myself in the place of Small, and looked at it as a man of his capacity would. He would probably consider that to send back the launch or to keep it at a wharf would make pursuit easy if the police did happen to get on his track. How, then, could he conceal the launch and yet have her at hand when he wanted ? I wondered what I should do myself if I were in his shoes. I could only think of one way of doing it. I might hand the launch over to some boat-builder or repairer, with directions to make a trifling change in her. She would then be removed to his shed or yard, and so be effectually concealed, while at the same time I could have her at a few hours' notice."

" That seems simple enough."

" It is just these very simple things which are extremely liable to be overlooked. However, I determined to act on the idea. I started at once in this harmless seaman's rig, and inquired at all the yards down the river. I drew blank at fifteen, but at the sixteenth—Jacobson's—I learned that the *Aurora* had been handed over to them two days ago by a wooden-legged man, with some trivial directions as to her rudder. ' There ain't naught amiss with her rudder,' said the foreman. ' There she lies, with the red streaks.' At that moment who should come down but Mordecai Smith, the missing owner ? He was rather the worse for liquor. I should not, of course, have known him, but he bellowed out his name and the name of his launch. ' I want her tonight at eight o'clock,' said he, ' eight o'clock sharp, mind, for I have two gentlemen who won't be kept waiting.' They had evidently paid him well for he was very flush of money, chucking shillings about to the men. I followed him some distance, but he subsided into an ale-house; so I went back to the yard, and, happening to pick up one of my boys on the way, I stationed him as a sentry over the launch. He is to stand at the water's edge and wave his handkerchief to us when they start. We shall be lying off in the stream, and it will be a strange thing if we do not take men, treasure and all."

" You have planned it all very neatly, whether they are the right men or not," said Jones; " but if the affair were in my hands I should have had a body of police in Jacobson's Yard, and arrested them when they came down."

" Which would have been never. This man Small is a pretty shrewd fellow. He would send a scout on ahead, and if anything made him suspicious he would lie snug for another week."

" But you might have stuck to Mordecai Smith, and so been led to their hiding-place," said I.

" In that case I should have wasted my day. I think that it is a hundred to one against Smith knowing where they live. As long as he has liquor and good pay, why should he ask questions ? They send him messages what to do. No, I thought over every possible course, and this is the best."

While this conversation had been proceeding, we had been shooting the long series of bridges which span the Thames. As we passed the City, the last rays of the sun were gilding the cross upon the summit of St. Paul's. It was twilight before we reached the Tower.

" That is Jacobson's Yard," said Holmes, pointing to a bristle of masts and rigging on the Surrey side. " Cruise gently up and down here under cover of this string of lighters." He took a pair of night-glasses from his pocket and gazed some time at the shore. " I can see my sentry at his post," he remarked, " but no sign of a handkerchief."

" Suppose we go down stream a short way and lie in wait for them," said Jones eagerly.

We were all eager by this time, even the policemen and stokers, who had a very vague idea of what was going forward.

" We have no right to take anything for granted," Holmes answered. " It is certainly ten to one that they go down stream, but we cannot be certain. From this point we can see the entrance of the yard, and they can hardly see us. It will be a clear night and plenty of light. We must stay where we are. See how the folk swarm over yonder in the gaslight."

They are coming from work in the yard."

" Dirty-looking rascals, but I suppose every one has some little immortal spark concealed about him. You would not think it, to look at them. There is no *a priori* probability about it. A strange enigma is man ! "

" Somone calls him a soul concealed in an animal," I suggested.

" Winwood Reade is good upon the subject," said Holmes. " He remarks that, while the individual man is an insoluble puzzle, in the aggregate he becomes a mathematical certainty. You can, for example, never foretell what any one man will do, but you can say with precision what an average number will be up to. Individuals vary, but percentages remain constant. So says the statistician. But do I see a handkerchief? Surely there is a white flutter over yonder."

" Yes, it is your boy," I cried. " I can see him plainly."

" And there is the *Aurora*," exclaimed Holmes, " and going like the devil ! Full speed ahead, engineer. Make after that launch with the yellow light. By Heaven, I shall never forgive myself if she proves to have the heels of us ! "

She had slipped unseen through the yard-entrance and passed behind two or three small craft, so that she had fairly got her speed up before we saw her. Now she was flying down the steam, near in to the shore, going at a tremendous rate. Jones looked gravely at her and shook his head.

" She is very fast," he said. " I doubt if we shall catch her."

" We *must* catch her ! " cried Holmes, between his teeth. " Heap it on stokers ! Make her do all she can ! If we burn the boat we must have them ! "

We were fairly after her now. The furnaces roared, and the powerful engines whizzed and clanked, like a great metallic heart. Her sharp, steep prow cut through the still river-water and sent two rolling waves to right and to left of us. With every throb of the engines we sprang and quivered like a living thing. One great yellow lantern in our bows threw a long, flickering funnel of light in front of us. Right ahead a dark blur upon the water showed where the *Aurora* lay and the swirl of white foam behind her spoke of the pace at which she was going. We flashed past barges, steamers, merchant-vessels, in and out, behind this one and round the other. Voices hailed us out of the darkness, but still the *Aurora* thundered on, and still we followed close upon her track.

" Pile it on, men, pile it on ! " said Holmes, looking down into the engine-room, while the fierce glow from below beat upon his eager, aquiline face. " Get every pound of steam you can."

" I think we gain a little," said Jones, with his eyes on the *Aurora*.

" I am sure of it," said I. " We shall be up with her in a very few minutes."

At that moment, however, as our evil fate would have it, a tug with three barges in tow blundered in between us. It was only by putting our helm hard down that we avoided a collision, and before we could round them and recover our way the *Aurora* had gained a good two hundred yards. She was still, however, well in view, and the murky, uncertain twilight was settling into a clear, starlit night. Our boilers were strained to their utmost and the frail shell vibrated and creaked with the fierce energy which was driving us along. We had shot through the Pool, past the West India Docks, down the long Deptford Reach, and up again after rounding the Isle of Dogs. The dull blur in front of us revolved itself now clearly enough into the dainty *Aurora*. Jones turned our searchlight upon her, so that we could plainly see the figures upon her deck. One man sat by the stern, with something black between his knees, over which he stooped. Beside him lay a dark mass, which looked like a Newfoundland dog. The boy held the tiller, while against the red glare of the furnace I could see old Smith, stripped to the waist, and shovelling coals for dear life. They may have had some doubt at first as to whether we were really pursuing them, but now as we followed every winding and turning which they took there could no longer be any question about it. At Greenwich we were about three hundred paces behind them. At Blackwall we couldn't have been more than two hundred and fifty. I have coursed many creatures in many countries during my chequered career, but never did sport give me such a wild thrill as this mad, flying man-hunt down the Thames. Steadily we drew in upon them, yard by yard. In the silence of the night we could hear the panting and clanking of their machinery. The man in the stern still crouched upon the deck, and his arms were moving as though he were busy, while every now and then he would look up and measure with a glance the distance which still separated us. Nearer we came and nearer. Jones yelled to them to stop. We were not more than four boats' lengths behind them, both boats flying at a tremendous pace. It was a clear reach of the river, with Barking Level upon one side and melancholy Plumstead Marshes upon the other. At our hail the man in the stern sprang up from the deck and shook his two clenched fists at us, cursing the while in a high, cracked voice. He was a good-sized, powerful man, and as he stood poising himself with legs astride, I could see that, from the thigh downwards, there was but a wooden stump upon the right side. At the sound of his strident, angry cries, there was a movement of the huddled bundle on the deck. It straightened itself into a little back man—the smallest I have ever seen—with a great, misshapen head and a shock of tangled, dishevelled hair. Holmes had already drawn his revolver, and I whipped out mine at the sight of this savage, distorted creature. He was wrapped in some sort of a dark ulster or blanket, which left only his face exposed; but that face was enough to give a man a sleepless night. Never have I seen features so deeply marked with all

bestiality and cruelty. His small eyes glowed and burned with a sombre light, and his thick lips were writhed back from his teeth, which grinned and chattered at us with half-animal fury.

" Fire if he raises his hand," said Holmes, quietly.

We were within a boat's-length by this time, and almost within touch of our quarry. I can see the two men now as they stood: the white man with his legs far apart, shrieking out curses, and the unhallowed dwarf with his hideous face, and his strong, yellow teeth gnashing at us in the light of our lantern.

It was well that we had to so clear a view of him. Even as we looked he plucked out from under his covering a short round piece of wood like a school-ruler, and clapped it to his lips. Our pistols rang out together. He whirled round, threw his arms in the air, and, with a kind of choking cough, fell sideways into the stream. I caught one glimpse of his venomous, menacing eyes amid the white swirl of the waters. At the same moment the wooden-legged man threw himself upon the rudder and put it hard down so that his boat made straight in for the southern bank, while we shot past her stern, only clearing her by a few feet. We were round after her in an instant, but she was already nearly at the bank. It was a wild and desolate place, where the moon glimmered upon a wide expanse of marshland, with pools of stagnant water and beds of decaying vegetation. The launch, with a dull thud, ran up upon the mud-bank with her bow in the air and her stern flush with the water. The fugitive sprang out, but his stump instantly sank its whole length into the sodden soil. In vain he struggled and writhed. Not one step could he possibly take either forwards or backwards. He yelled in impotent rage, and kicked frantically into the mud with his other foot; but his struggles only bored his wooden pin the deeper into the sticky bank. When we brought our launch alongside he was so firmly anchored that it was only by throwing the end of a rope over his shoulders that we were able to haul him out, and to drag him, like some evil fish, over our side. The two Smiths, father and son, sat sullenly in their launch, but came aboard meekly enough when commanded. The *Aurora* herself we hauled off and made fast to our stern. A solid iron chest of Indian workmanship stood upon the deck. This, there could be no question, was the same that had contained the ill-omened treasure of the Sholtos.

There was no key, but it was of considerable weight, so we transferred it carefully to our own little cabin. As we steamed slowly up-stream again, we flashed our searchlight in every direction, but there was no sign of the Islander. Somewhere in the dark ooze at the bottom of the Thames lie the bones of that strange visitor to our shores.

"See here," said Holmes, pointing to the wooden hatchway. "We were hardly quick enough with our pistols." There, sure enough, just behind where we had been standing, stuck one of those murderous darts which we knew so well. It must have whizzed between just at the instant we fired. Holmes smiled at it and shrugged his shoulders in his easy fashion, but I confess it turned me sick to think of the horrible death which had passed so close to us that night.

CHAPTER XI

THE GREAT AGRA TREASURE

Our captive sat in the cabin opposite to the iron box which he had done so much and waited so long to gain. He was a sun-burned, reckless-eyed fellow, with a network of lines and wrinkles all over his mahogany features, which told of a hard, open-air life. There was a singular prominence about his bearded chin which marked a man who was not to be easily turned from his purpose. His age may have been fifty or thereabouts, for his black, curly hair was thickly shot with grey. His face in repose was not an unpleasing one, though his heavy brows and aggressive chin gave him, as I had lately seen, a terrible expression when moved to anger. He now sat with his handcuffed hands upon his lap, and his head sunk upon his breast, while he looked with his keen, twinkling eyes at the box which had been the cause of his ill-doings. It seemed to me that there was more sorrow than anger in his rigid and contained countenance. Once he looked up at me with a gleam of something like humour in his eyes.

"Well, Jonathan Small," said Holmes, lighting a cigar, "I am sorry that it has come to this."

"And so am I, sir," he answered, frankly. "I don't believe that I can swing over the job. I give you my word on the Book that I never raised a hand against Mr. Sholto. It was that little hell-hound Tonga who shot one of his cursed darts into him. I had no part in it, sir. I was as grieved as if it had been my blood-relation. I welted the

little devil with the slack end of the rope for it, but it was done, and I could not undo it again."

"Have a cigar," said Holmes; "and you had best take a pull out of my flask, for you are very wet. How could you expect so small and weak a man as this black fellow to overpower Mr. Sholto and hold him while you were climbing the rope?"

"You seem to know as much about it as if you were there, sir. The truth is that I hoped to find the room clear. I knew the habits of the house pretty well, and it was the time when Mr. Sholto usually went down to his supper. I shall make no secret of the business. The best defence that I can make is just the simple truth. Now, if it had been the old major I would have swung for him with a light heart. I would have thought no more of knifing him than of smoking this cigar. But it's cursed hard that I should be lagged over this young Sholto, with whom I had no quarrel whatever."

"You are under the charge of Mr. Athelney Jones, of Scotland Yard. He is going to bring you up to my rooms, and I shall ask you for a true account of the matter. You must make a clean breast of it, for if you do I hope that I may be of use to you. I think I can prove that the poison acts so quickly that the man was dead before ever you reached the room."

"That he was, sir. I never got such a turn in my life as when I saw him grinning at me with his head on his shoulder as I climbed through the window. It fairly shook me, sir. I'd have half killed Tonga for it if he had not scrambled off. That was how he came to leave his club, and some of his darts too, as he tells me, which I dare say helped to put you on our track; though how you kept on it is more than I can tell. I don't feel any malice against you for it. But it does seem a queer thing," he added, with a bitter smile, "that I, who have a fair claim to half a million of money should spend the first half of my life building a breakwater in the Andamans, and am like to spend the other half digging drains at Dartmoor. It was an evil day for me when first I clapped eyes upon the merchant Achmet and had to do with the Agra treasure, which never brought anything but a curse yet upon the man who owned it. To him it brought murder, to Major Sholto it brought fear and guilt, to me it has meant slavery for life."

At this moment Athelney Jones thrust his face and shoulders into the tiny cabin.

"Quite a family party," he remarked. "I

think I shall have a pull at that flask, Holmes. Well, I think we may congratulate each other. Pity we didn't take the other alive; but there was no choice. I say, Holmes, you must confess that you cut it rather fine. It was all we could do to over-haul her."

"All is well that ends well," said Holmes. "But I certainly did not know that the *Aurora* was such a clipper."

"Smith says she is one of the fastest launches on the river, and that if he had had another man to help him with the engines we should never have caught her. He swears he knew nothing of this Norwood business."

"Neither he did," cried our prisoner— "not a word. I chose his launch because I heard that she was a flier. We told him nothing; but we paid him well, and he was to get something handsome if we reached our vessel, the *Esmeralda*, at Gravesend, outward bound for the Brazils."

"Well, if he has done no wrong we shall see that no wrong comes to him. If we are pretty quick in catching our men, we are not so quick in condemning them." It was amusing to notice how the consequential Jones was already beginning to give himself airs on the strength of the capture. From the slight smile which played over Sherlock Holmes's face, I could see that the speech had not been lost on him.

"We will be at the Vauxhall Bridge presently," said Jones, " and shall land you, Dr. Watson, with the treasure-box. I need hardly tell you that I am taking a very grave responsibility upon myself in doing this. It is most irregular; but of course an agreement is an agreement. I must, however, as a matter of duty, send an inspector with you, since you have so valuable a charge. You will drive, no doubt ? "

"Yes, I shall drive."

"It is a pity there is no key, that we may make an inventory first. You will have to break it open. Where is the key, my man ? "

"At the bottom of the river," said Small, shortly.

"Hum ! There was no use your giving this unnecessary trouble. We have had work enough through you. However, doctor, I need not warn you to be careful. Bring the box back with you to the Baker Street rooms. You will find us there, on our way to the station."

They landed me at Vauxhall, with my heavy iron box, and with a bluff, genial inspector as my companion. A quarter of an hour's drive brought us to Mrs. Cecil Forrester's. The servant seemed surprised at so late a visitor. Mrs. Cecil Forrester was out for the evening, she explained, and likely to be very late. Miss Morstan, however, was in the drawing-room; so to the drawing-room I went, box in hand, leaving the obliging inspector in the cab.

She was seated by the open window, dressed in some sort of white, diaphanous material, with a little touch of scarlet at the neck and waist. The soft light of a shaded lamp fell upon her as she leaned back in the basket chair, playing over her sweet grave face, and tinting with a dull, metallic sparkle the rich coils of her luxuriant hair. One white arm and hand drooped over the side of the chair, and her whole pose and figure spoke of an absorbing melancholy. At the sound of my footfall she sprang to her feet, however, and a bright flush of surprise and of pleasure coloured her pale cheeks.

"I heard a cab drive up," she said. "I thought that Mrs. Forrester had come back very early, but I never dreamed that it might be you. What news have you brought me ? "

"I have brought something better than news," said I, putting down the box upon the table and speaking jovially and boisterously, though my heart was heavy within me. "I have brought you something which is worth all the news in the world. I have brought you a fortune."

She glanced at the iron box.

"Is that the treasure, then ? " she asked, coolly enough.

"Yes, this is the great Agra treasure. Half of it is yours and half is Thaddeus Sholto's. You will have a couple of hundred thousand each. Think of that ! There will be few richer young ladies in England. Is it not glorious ? "

I think that I must have been rather over acting my delight, and that she detected a hollow ring in my congratuations, for I saw her eyebrows rise a little, and she glanced at me curiously.

"If I have it," said she, " I owe it to you."

"No, no," I answered, " not to me, but to my friend Sherlock Holmes. With all the will in the world, I could never have followed up a clue which has taxed even his analytical genius. As it was, we very nearly lost it at the last moment."

"Pray sit down and tell me all about it, Dr. Watson," said she.

I narrated briefly what had occurred since I had seen her last. Holmes's new method of search, the discovery of the *Aurora*, the appearance of Athelney Jones, our expedition in the evening, and the wild chase down the Thames. She listened with parted lips and shining eyes to my recital of our adventures. When I spoke of the dart which had so narrowly missed us, she turned so white that I feared that she was about to faint.

"It is nothing," she said, as I hastened to pour her out some water. "I am all right again. It was a shock to me to hear that I had placed my friends in such horrible peril."

"That is all over," I answered. "It was nothing. I will tell you no more gloomy details. Let us turn to something brighter. There is the treasure. What could be brighter than that? I got leave to bring it with me, thinking it would interest you to be the first to see it."

"It would be of the greatest interest to me," she said. There was no eagerness in her voice, however. It had struck her, doubtless, that it might seem ungracious upon her part to be indifferent to a prize which had cost so much to win.

"What a pretty box!" she said, stooping over it. "This is Indian work, I suppose?"

"Yes: it is Benares metalwork."

"And so heavy!" she exclaimed, trying to raise it. "The box alone must be of some value. Where is the key?"

"Small threw it into the Thames," I answered. "I must borrow Mrs. Forresters poker."

There was in the front a thick and broad hasp, wrought in the image of a sitting Buddha. Under this I thrust the end of the poker and twisted it outward as a lever. The hasp sprang open with a loud snap. With trembling fingers I flung back the lid. We both stood gazing in astonishment. The box was empty!

No wonder it was heavy. The ironwork was two-thirds of an inch thick, all round. It was massive, well-made, and solid, like a chest constructed to carry things of great price, but not one shred or crumb of metal or jewellery lay within it. It was absolutely and completely empty.

"The treasure is lost," said Miss Morstan, calmly.

As I listened to the words and realized what they meant, a great shadow seemed to pass from my soul. I did not know how this Agra treasure had weighed me down, until now that it was finally removed. It was selfish, no doubt, disloyal, wrong, but I could realize nothing save that the golden barrier was gone from between us.

"Thank God!" I ejaculated from my very heart.

She looked at me with a quick, questioning smile.

"Why do you say that?"

"Because you are within my reach again," I said, taking her hand. She did not withdraw it. "Because I love you, Mary, as truly as ever a man loved a woman. Because this treasure, these riches, sealed my lips. Now that they are gone I can tell you how I love you. That is why I said, 'Thank God'."

"Then I say 'Thank God', too," she whispered, as I drew her to my side.

Whoever had lost a treasure, I knew that night that I had gained one.

CHAPTER XII

THE STRANGE STORY OF JONATHAN SMALL

A very patient man was that inspector in the cab, for it was a weary time before I rejoined him. His face clouded over when I showed him the empty box.

"There goes the reward!" said he, gloomily. "Where there is no money there is no pay. This night's work would have been worth a tenner each to Sam Brown and me if the treasure had been there."

"Mr. Thaddeus Sholto is a rich man," I said; "he will see that you are rewarded, treasure or no."

The inspector shook his head despondently, however,

"It's a bad job," he repeated; "and so Mr. Athelney Jones will think."

His forecast proved to be correct, for the detective looked blank enough when I got to Baker Street and showed him the empty box. They had only just arrived, Holmes, the prisoner, and he, for they had changed their plans so far as to report themselves at a station upon the way. My companion lounged in his armchair with his usual listless expression, while Small sat stolidly opposite to him with his wooden leg cocked over his sound one. As I exhibited the empty box he leaned back in his chair and laughed aloud.

"This is your doing, Small," said Athelney Jones, angrily.

"Yes, I have put it where you shall never lay hand on it," he cried, exultantly. "It is my treasure, and if I can't have the loot I'll take darned good care that no one else does. I tell you that no living man has any right to it, unless it is three men who are in the Andaman convict-barracks and myself. I know now that I cannot have the use of it, and I know that they cannot. I have acted all through for them as much as for myself. It's been the sign of four with us always. Well, I know that they would have had me do just what I have done, and throw the treasure into the Thames rather than let it go to kith or kin of Sholto or Morstan. It was not to make them rich that we did for Achmet. You'll find the treasure where the key is, and where little Tonga is. When I saw that your launch must catch us, I put the loot away in a safe place. There are no rupees for you this journey."

" You are deceiving us, Small," said Athelney Jones, sternly. "If you had wished to throw the treasure into the Thames, it would have been easier for you to have thrown box and all."

" Easier for me to throw, and easier for you to recover," he answered, with a shrewd, side-long look. " The man that was clever enough to hunt me down is clever enough to pick an iron box from the bottom of a river. Now that they are scattered over five miles or so, it may be a harder job. It went to my heart to do it, though. I was half mad when you came up with us. However, there's no good grieving over it. I've had ups in my life, and I've had downs, but I've learned not to cry over spilled milk."

" This is a very serious matter, Small," said the detective. " If you had helped justice, instead of thwarting it in this way, you would have had a better chance at your trial."

"Justice!" snarled the ex-convict. "A pretty justice! Whose loot is this, if it is not ours? Where is the justice that I should give it up to those who have never earned it? Look how I have earned it! Twenty long years in that fever-ridden swamp, all day at work under the mangrove-tree, all night chained up in the filthy convict-huts, bitten by mosquitoes, racked with ague, bullied by every cursed black-faced policeman who loved to take it out of a white man. That was how I earned the Agra treasure, and you talk to me of justice because I cannot bear to feel that I have paid this price only that another may enjoy it! I would rather swing a score of times, or have one of Tonga's darts in my hide, than live in a convict's cell and feel that another man is at ease in a palace with the money that should be mine."

Small had dropped his mask of stoicism,

and all this came out in a wild whirl of words while his eyes blazed and the handcuffs clanked together with the impassioned movement of his hands. I could understand, as I saw the fury and the passion of the man, that it was no groundless or unnatural terror which had possessed Major Sholto when he first learned that the injured convict was upon his track.

" You forget that we know nothing of all this," said Holmes, quietly. " We have not heard your story, and we cannot tell how far justice may originally have been on your side."

" Well, sir, you have been fair-spoken to me, though I can see that I have you to thank that I have these bracelets upon my wrists. Still, I bear no grudge for that. It is all fair and above-board. If you want to hear my story, I have no wish to hold it back. What I say to you is God's truth, every word of it. Thank you, you can put the glass beside me here, and I'll put my lips to it if I am dry.

" I am a Worcestershire man myself, born near Pershore. I dare say you would find a heap of Smalls living there now if you were to look. I have often thought of taking a look round there, but the truth is that I was never much of a credit to the family, and I doubt if they would be so very glad to see me. They are all steady, chapel-going folk, small farmers, well-known and respected over the countryside, while I was always a bit of a rover. At last, however, when I was about eighteen, I gave them no more trouble, for I got into a mess over a girl, and could only get out of it by taking the Queen's shilling and joining the 3rd Buffs, which was just starting for India.

" I wasn't destined to do much soldiering, however. I had just got past the goose-step, and learned to handle my musket, when I was fool enough to go swimming in the Ganges. Luckily for me, my company sergeant, John Holder, was in the water at the same time, and he was one of the finest swimmers in the Service. A crocodile took me, just as I was half-way across, and nipped off my right leg as clean as a surgeon could have done it, just above the knee. What with the shock and the loss of blood, I fainted, and should have been drowned if Holder had not caught hold of me and paddled for the bank. I was five months in hospital over it, and when at last I was able to limp out of it with this timber toe strapped to my stump, I found myself invalided out of the army and unfitted for any active occupation.

" I was, as you can imagine, pretty down on my luck at this time, for I was a useless cripple, though not yet in my twentieth year. However, my misfortune soon proved to be a blessing in disguise. A man named Abel White, who had come out there as an indigo-planter, wanted an overseer to look after his coolies and keep them up to their work. He happened to be a friend of our colonel's, who had taken an interest in me since the accident. To make a long story short, the colonel recommended me strongly for the post, and, as the work was mostly to be done on horseback, my leg was no great obstacle, for I had enough knee left to keep a good grip on the saddle. What I had to do was ride over the plantation, to keep an eye on the men as they worked, and to report the idlers. The pay was fair, I had comfortable quarters, and altogether I was content to spend the remainder of my life in indigo-planting. Mr. Abel White was a kind man, and he would often drop into my little shanty and smoke a pipe with me, for white folk out there feel their hearts warm to each other as they never do here at home.

" Well, I was never in luck's way long. Suddenly, without a note of warning, the great mutiny broke upon us. One month India lay as still and peaceful, to all appearance, as Surrey or Kent; the next there were two hundred thousand black devils let loose, and the country was a perfect hell. Of course you know all about it, gentlemen—a deal more than I do, very like, since reading is not in my line. I only know what I saw with my own eyes. Our plantation was at a place called Muttra, near the border of the North-west Provinces. Night after night the whole sky was alight with the burning bungalows and day after day we had small companies of Europeans passing through our estate with their wives and children, on their way to Agra, where were the nearest troops. Mr. Abel White was an obstinate man. He had it in his head that the affair had been exaggerated, and that it would blow over as suddenly as it had sprung up. There he sat on his veranda, drinking whisky-pegs and smoking cheroots, while the country was in a blaze about him. Of course, we stuck by him, I and Dawson, who, with his wife, used to do the book-work and the managing. Well, one fine day the crash came. I had been away on a distant plantation, and was riding slowly home in the evening, when my eye fell upon something all huddled together at the bottom of a steep nullah. I rode down to see what it was, and the cold struck through my heart when I found it was Dawson's wife, all cut into ribbons and half-eaten by jackals and native dogs. A little farther up the road Dawson himself was lying on his face, quite dead, with an empty revolver in his hand, and four Sepoys lying across each other in front of him. I reined up my horse, wondering which way I should turn but at that moment I saw thick smoke curling up from Abel White's bungalow, and the flames beginning to burst through the roof. I knew then that I could do my employer no good, but would only throw my own life away if I meddled in the matter. From where I stood I could see hundreds of the black fiends, with their red coats still on their backs, dancing and howling round the burning house. Some of them pointed at me, and a couple of bullets sang past my head; so I broke away across the paddy-fields, and found myself late at night safe within the walls at Agra.

" As it proved, however, there was no great safety here either. The whole country was up like a swarm of bees. Whenever the English could collect in little bands, they held just the ground that their guns commanded. Everywhere else they were helpless fugitives. It was a fight of the millions against the hundreds; and the cruellest part of it was that these men that we fought against, foot, horse, and gunners, were our own picked troops, whom we had taught and trained, handling our own weapons and blowing our own bugle-calls. At Agra there were the 3rd Bengal Fusiliers, some Sikhs, two troops of horse, and a battery of artillery. A volunteer corps of clerks and merchants had been formed, and this I joined, wooden leg and all. We went out to meet the rebels at Shahgunge early in July, and we beat them back for a time, but our powder gave out and we had to fall back upon the city.

" Nothing but the worst news come to us from every side—which is not to be wondered at, for if you look at the map you will see that we were right in the heart of it. Lucknow is rather better than a hundred miles to the east, and Cawnpore about as far to the south. From every point on the compass there was nothing but torture and murder and outrage.

" The city of Agra is a great place, swarming with fanatics and fierce devil worshippers of all sorts. Our handful of men were lost among the narrow, winding streets. Our leader moved across the river, therefore, and took up his position in the old fort of Agra. I don't know if any of you gentlemen have ever read or heard anything of that old fort. It was a very queer place—the queerest that ever I was in, and I have been in some rum corners too. First, of all, it is enormous in size. I should think that the enclosure must be acres and acres. There is a modern part, which took all our garrison, women, children, stores, and everything else, with plenty of room over. But the modern part is nothing like the size of the old quarter, where nobody goes, and which is given over to the scorpions and the centipedes. It is all full of great, deserted halls, and winding passages, and long corridors twisting in and out, so that it is easy enough for folk to get lost in it. For this reason it was seldom that anyone went into it, though now and again a party with torches might go exploring.

"The river washes along the front of the old fort, and so protects it, but on the sides and behind there are many doors, and these had to be guarded, of course, in the old quarter as well as in that which was actually held by our troops. We were short-handed, with hardly men enough to man the angles of the building and to serve the guns. It was impossible for us, therefore, to station a strong guard at every one of the innumerable gates. What we did was to organize a central guard-house in the middle of the fort, and to leave each gate under the charge of one white man and two or three natives. I was selected to take charge during certain hours of the night of a small isolated door upon the south-west side of the building. Two Sikh troopers were placed under my command, and I was instructed if anything went wrong to fire my musket, when I might rely upon help coming at once from the central guard. As the guard was a good two hundred paces away, however, and as the space between was cut up into a labyrinth of passages and corridors, I had great doubts as to whether they could arrive in time to be of any use in case of an actual attack.

"Well, I was pretty proud at having this small command given me, since I was a raw recruit, and a game-legged one at that. For two nights I kept the watch with my Punjaubees. They were tall, fierce-looking chaps, Mahomet Singh and Abdullah Khan by name, both old fighting-men, who had borne arms against us at Chilian Wallah. They could talk English pretty well, but I could get little out of them. They preferred to stand together and jabber all night in their queer Sikh lingo. For myself, I used to stand outside the gateway, looking down on the broad, winding river and on the twinkling lights of the great city. The beating of drums, the rattle of tom-toms, and the yells and howls of the rebels, drunk with opium and with bang, were enough to remind us all night of our dangerous neighbours across the stream. Every two hours the officer of the night used to come round to all the posts, to make sure that all was well.

"The third night of my watch was dark and dirty, with a small, driving rain. It was dreary work standing in the gateway hour after hour in such weather. I tried again and again to make my Sikhs talk, but without much success. At two in the morning the rounds passed, and broke for a moment the weariness of the night. Finding that my companions would not be led into conversation, I took out my pipe, and laid down my musket to strike a match. In an instant the two Sikhs were upon me. One of them snatched my firelock up and levelled it at my head, while the other held a great knife to my throat and swore between his teeth that he would plunge it into me if I moved a step.

"My first thought was that these fellows were in league with the rebels, and that this was the beginning of an assault. If our door were in the hands of the Sepoys the place must fall, and the women and children be treated as they were in Cawnpore. Maybe you gentlemen think that I am just making a case out for myself, but I give you my word that when I thought of that, though I felt the point of the knife at my throat, I opened my mouth with the intention of giving a scream, if it was my last one, which might alarm the main guard. The man who held me seemed to know my thoughts; for, even as I braced myself to it, he whispered: 'Don't make a noise. The fort is safe enough. There are no rebel dogs on this side of the river.' There was the ring of truth in what he said, and I knew that if I raised my voice I was a dead man. I could read it in the fellow's brown eyes. I waited, therefore, in silence to see what it was that they wanted from me.

"'Listen to me sahib,' said the taller and fiercer of the pair, the one whom they called Abdullah Kahn. 'You must either be with us for now, or you must be silenced for ever. The thing is too great a one for us to hesitate. Either you are heart and soul with us or on your oath on the cross of the Christians, or your body this night shall be thrown into the ditch, and we shall pass over to our brothers in the rebel army. There is no middle way. Which is it to be—death or life? We can only give you three minutes to decide, for the time is passing and all must be done before the rounds come again.'

" ' How can I decide? ' I said. ' You have not told me what you want of me. But I tell you now that if it is anything against the safety of the fort I will have no truck with it, so you can drive home your knife, and welcome.'

" ' It is nothing against the fort,' said he. ' We only ask you to do that which your countrymen come to this land for. We ask you to be rich. If you will be one of us this night, we will swear to you upon the naked knife, and by the threefold oath, which no Sikh was ever known to break, that you shall have your fair share of the loot. A quarter of the treasure shall be yours. We can say no fairer.'

" ' But what is the treasure, then? ' I asked. ' I am as ready to be rich as you can be, if you will but show me how it can be done.'

" ' You will swear, then? ' said he, ' by the bones of. your father, by the honour of your mother, by the cross of your faith, to raise no hand and speak no word against us, either now or afterwards? '

" ' I will swear it,' I answered, ' provided that the fort is not endangered.'

" ' Then, my comrade and I will swear that you shall have a quarter of the treasure, which shall be equally divided among the four of us.'

" ' There are but three,' said I.

" ' No; Dost Akbar must have his share. We can tell the tale to you while we await them. Do you stand at the gate, Mahomet Singh, and give notice of their coming. The thing stands thus, sahib, and I tell it to you because I know that an oath is binding upon a Feringhee, and that we may trust you. Had you been a lying Hindoo, though you had sworn by all the gods in their false temples, your blood would have been upon the knife and your body in the water. But the Sikh knows the Englishman, and the Englishman knows the Sikh. Hearken, then, to what I have to say.

" ' There is a rajah in the northern provinces who has much wealth, though his lands are small. Much has come to him from his father, and more still he has set by himself, for he is of a low nature, and hoards his gold rather than spend it. When the troubles broke out he would be friends both with the lion and the tiger—with the Sepoy and with the Company's Raj. Soon, however, it seemed to him that the white men's day was come, for through all the land he could hear of nothing but of their death and their overthrow. Yet, being a careful man, he made such plans that, come what might, half at least of his treasure should be left to him. That which was in gold and silver he kept by him in the vaults of his palace; but the most precious stones and the holiest pearls that he had he put in an iron box, and sent it by a trusty servant, who, under the guise of a merchant, should take it to the fort at Agra, there to lie until the land is at peace. Thus, if the rebels won he would have his money; but if the Company conquered, his jewels would be saved to him. Having thus divided his hoard, he threw himself into the cause of the Sepoys, since they were strong upon his borders. By doing this, mark you, sahib, his property becomes the due of those who have been true to their salt.

" ' This pretended merchant, who travels under the name of Achmet, is now in the city of Agra, and desires to gain his way into the fort. He has with him as travelling companion my foster-brother, Dost Akbar, who knows his secret. Dost Akbar has promised this night to lead him to a side-postern of the fort, and has chosen this one for his purpose. Here he will come presently, and here he will find Mahomet Singh and myself awaiting him. The place is lonely, and none shall know of his coming. The world shall know of the merchant, Achmet, no more, but the great treasure of the rajah shall be divided among us. What say you to it, sahib? '

" In Worcestershire the life of a man seems a great and sacred thing; but it is very different when there is fire ' and blood all round you, and you have been used to meeting death at every turn. Whether Achmet the merchant lived or died was a thing as light as air to me, but at the talk about the treasure my heart turned to it, and I thought of what I might do in the old country with it, and how my folks would stare when they saw their ne'er-do-well coming back with his pockets full of gold moidores. I had, therefore, already made up my mind. Abdullah Kahn, however, thinking that I hesitated, pressed the matter more closely.

" ' Consider, sahib,' said he, ' that if this man is taken by the commandant he will be hung or shot, and his jewels taken by the

Government, so that no man will be a rupee the better for them. Now, since we do the taking of him, why should we not do the rest as well ? The jewels will be as well with us as in the Company's coffers. There will be enough to make every one of us rich men and great chiefs. No one can know about the matter, for here we are cut off from all men. What could be better for the purpose ? Say again, sahib, whether you are with us, or we must look upon you as an enemy.'

" 'I am with you heart and soul,' said I.

" 'It is well,' he answered, handing back my firelock. ' You see that we trust you, for your word, like ours, is not to be broken. We have now only to wait for my brother and the merchant.'

" 'Does you brother know, then, of what you will do ? ' I asked.

" 'The plan is his. He has devised it. We will go to the gate and share the watch with Mahomet Singh.'

" The rain was still falling steadily, for it was just the beginning of the wet season. Brown, heavy clouds were drifting across the sky, and it was hard to see more than a stone-cast. A deep moat lay in front of our door, but the water was in places nearly dried up, and it could easily be crossed. It was strange to see me standing there with those two wild Punjaubees waiting for the man who was coming to his death.

" Suddenly my eye caught the glint of a shaded lantern at the other side of the moat. It vanished among the mound-heaps, and then appeared again coming slowly in our direction.

" 'Here they are !' I exclaimed.

" 'You will challenge him, sahib, as usual,' whispered Abdullah. ' Give him no cause for fear. Send us in with him, and we shall do the rest while you stay here on guard. Have the lantern ready to uncover, that we many be sure that it is indeed the man.'

" The light flickered onwards, now stopping and now advancing, until I could see two dark figures upon the other side of the moat. I let them scramble down the sloping bank, splash through the mire, and climb half-way up to the gate, before I challenged them.

" 'Who goes there ? ' said I, in a subdued voice.

" 'Friends,' came the answer. I uncovered my lantern and threw a flood of light upon them. The first was an enormous Sikh, with a black beard which swept nearly down to his cummerbund. Outside of a show I have never seen so tall a man. The other was a little, fat, round fellow, with a great yellow turban, and a bundle in his hand, done up in a shawl. He seemed to be all in a quiver with fear, for his hands twitched as if he had the ague, and his head kept turning to left and right with two bright little twinkling eyes, like a mouse when he ventures out from his hole. It gave me chills to think of killing him, but I thought of the treasure, and my heart set as hard as a flint within me. When he saw my white face he gave a little chirrup of joy, and came running up towards me.

" 'You're protection, sahib,' he panted; ' your protection for the unhappy merchant Achmet. I have travelled across Rajpootana that I might seek the shelter of the fort at Agra. I have been robbed and beaten and abused because I have been the friend of the Company. It is a blessed night this when I am once more in safety—I and my poor possessions.'

" 'What have you in the bundle ? ' I asked.

" 'An iron box,' he answered, ' which contains one or two little family matters which are of no value to others, but which I should be sorry to lose. Yet I am not a beggar; and I shall reward you, young sahib, and your governor also, if he will give me the shelter I ask.'

" I could not trust myself to speak longer with the man. The more I looked at his fat, frightened face, the harder did it seem that we should slay him in cold blood. It was best to get it over.

" 'Take him to the main guard,' said I. The two Sikhs closed in upon him on each side, and the giant walked behind, while they marched in through the gateway. Never was a man so compassed round with death. I remained at the gateway with the lantern.

" I could hear the measured tramp of their footsteps sounding through the lonely corridors. Suddenly it ceased, and I heard voices, and a scuffle, with the sound of blows. A moment later there came, to my horror, a rush of footsteps coming in my direction, with a loud breathing of a running man. I turned my lantern down the long, straight passage, and there was the fat man, running like the wind, with a smear of blood across his face, and close at heels, bounding like a tiger, the great, black-bearded Sikh, with a knife flashing in his hand. I have never seen a man run so fast as that little merchant. He was gaining on the Sikh, and I could see that if he once passed me and got to the open air he would save himself yet. My heart softened to him but again the thought of his treasure turned me hard and bitter. I cast my firelock between his legs as he raced past, and he rolled twice over like a shot rabbit. Ere he could stagger to his feet the Sikh was upon him, and buried his knife twice in his side. The man never uttered moan nor moved muscle, but lay where he had fallen. I think myself that he may have broken his neck with the fall. You see, gentlemen, that I am keeping my promise. I am just telling you every word of the business just exactly as it happened, whether it is in my favour or not."

He stopped and held out his manacled hands for the whisky-and-water which Holmes had brewed for him. For myself, I confess that I had now conceived the utmost horror of the man, not only for this cold-blooded business in which he had been concerned, but even more for the somewhat flippant and careless way in which he narrated it. Whatever punishment was in store for him, I felt that he might expect no sympathy from me. Sherlock Holmes and Jones sat with their hands upon their knees, deeply interested in the story, but with the same disgust written upon their faces. He may have observed it, for there was a touch of defiance in his voice and manner as he proceeded.

"It was all very bad, no doubt," said he. "I should like to know how many fellows in my shoes would have refused to share in this loot when they knew that they would have their throats cut for their pains. Besides, it was my life or his when once he was in the fort. If he had got out, the whole business would come to light, and I should have been court-martialled and shot as likely as not; for people were not very lenient at a time like that."

"Go on with your story," said Holmes, shortly.

"Well, we carried him in, Abdullah, Akbar, and I. A fine weight he was, too, for all that he was so short. Mahomet Singh was left to guard the door. We took him to a place which the Sikhs had already prepared. It was some distance off, where a winding passage leads to a great empty hall, the brick walls of which were all crumbling to pieces. The earth floor had sunk in at one place, making a natural grave, so we left Achmet the merchant there, having first covered him over with loose bricks. This done, we all went back to the treasure.

"It lay where he had dropped it when he was first attacked. The box was the same which now lies open upon your table. A key was hung by a silken cord to that carved handle upon the top. We opened it, and the light of the lantern gleamed upon a collection of gems such as I have read and thought about when I was a little lad at Pershore. It was blinding to look upon them. When we had feasted our eyes we took them all out and made a list of them. There were one hundred and forty-three diamonds of the first water, including one which has been called, I believe, ' the Great Mogul,' and is said to be the second largest stone in existence. Then there were ninety-seven very fine emeralds, and one hundred and seventy rubies, some of which, however, were small. There were forty carbuncles, two hundred and ten saphires, sixty-one agates, and a great quantity of beryls, onyxes, cats'-eyes, turquoises, and other stones, the very names of which I did not know at the time, though I have become familiar with them since. Besides this, there were nearly three hundred very fine pearls, twelve of which were set in a gold coronet. By the way, these last had been taken out of the chest, and were not there when I recovered it.

"After we had counted our treasures we put them back into the chest and carried them to the gateway to show them to Mahomet Singh. Then we solemnly renewed our oath to stand by each other and be true to our secret. We agreed to conceal our loot in a safe place until the country should be at peace again, and then divide it equally among ourselves. There was no such use dividing it at present, for if gems of such value were found upon us it would cause suspicion, and there was no privacy in the fort nor any place where we could keep them. We carried the box, therefore, into the same hall where we had buried the body, and there, under certain bricks in the best-preserved wall, we made a hollow and put our treasure. We made careful note of the place, and next day I drew four plans, one for each of us, and put the sign of the four of us at the bottom, for we had sworn that we should each always act for all, so that none might take any advantage. That is an oath that I can put my hand to my heart and swear that I have never broken.

"Well, there's no use my telling you gentlemen what came of the Indian Mutiny. After Wilson took Delhi and Sir Colin relieved Lucknow the back of the business was broken. Fresh troops came pouring in, and Nana Sahib made himself scarce over the frontier. A flying column under Colonel Greathead came round to Agra and cleared the Pandies away from it. Peace seemed to be settling upon the country, and we four were beginning to hope that the time was at hand when we might safely go off with our share of the plunder. In a moment, however, our hopes were shattered by our being arrested as the murderers of Achmet.

"It came about in this way. When the rajah put his jewels into the hands of Achmet, he did it because he knew that he was a trusty man. They are suspicious folk in the East, however; so what does this rajah do but take a second even more trusty servant and set him to play the spy upon the first ? The second man was ordered never to let Achmet out of his sight, and he followed him like his shadow. He went after him that night, and saw him pass through the doorway. Of course, he thought he had taken refuge in the fort, and applied for admission there himself next day, but could find no trace of Achmet. This seemed to him so strange that he spoke about it to a sergeant of guides, who brought it to the ears of the commandant. A thorough search was quickly made and the body was discovered. Thus at the very moment that we thought that all was safe we were all four seized and brought to trial on a charge of murder—three of us because we had held the gate that night, and the fourth because he was known to have been in the company of the murdered man. Not a word about the jewels came out at the trial, for the rajah had been deposed and driven out of India; so no one had any particular interest in them. The murder, however, was clearly made out, and it was certain that we must all have been concerned in it. The three Sikhs got penal servitude for life, and I was condemned to death, though my sentence was afterwards commuted into the same as the others.

"It was a rather queer position that we found ourselves in then. There we were all four tied by the leg and with precious little chance of ever getting out again, while we each held a secret which might have put each of us in a palace if we could only have made use of it. It was enough to make a man eat his heart out to have to stand the kick and the cuff of every petty jack-in-office, to have rice to eat and water to drink, when that gorgeous fortune was ready for him outside, just waiting to be picked up. It might have driven me mad; but I was always a pretty stubborn one, so I just held on and bided my time.

"At last it seemed to me to have come. I was changed from Agra to Madras, and from there to Blair Island in the Andamans. There are very few white convicts at this settlement, and, as I had behaved well from the first, I soon found myself a sort of privileged person. I was given a hut in Hope Town, which is a small place on the slopes of Mount Harriet, and I was left pretty much to myself. It is a dreary, fever-stricken place, and all beyond our little clearings was infested with wild cannibal natives, who were ready enough to blow a poisoned dart at us if they saw a chance. There was digging and ditching and yam-planting, and a dozen other things to be done, so we were busy enough all day; though in the evening we had a little time to ourselves. Among other things, I learned to dispense drugs for the surgeon, and picked up a smattering of his knowledge. All the time I was on the lookout for a chance to escape; but it is hundreds of miles from any other land, and there is little or no wind in those seas; so it was a terribly difficult job to get away.

"The surgeon, Dr. Somerton, was a fast, sporting young chap, and the other young officers would meet in his rooms of an evening and play cards. The surgery, where I used to make up my drugs, was next to his sitting-room, with a small window between us. Often, if I felt lonesome, I used to turn out the lamp in the surgery, and then, standing there, I could hear their talk and watch their play. I am fond of a hand at cards myself, and it was almost as good as having one to watch the others. There was Major Sholto, Captain Morstan, and Lieutenant Bromley Brown, who were in command of the native troops, and there was the surgeon himself, and two or three prison-officials, crafty old hands who played a nice, sly, safe game. A very snug little party they used to make.

"Well, there was one thing which very soon struck me, and that was that the soldiers used always to lose and the civilians to win. Mind, I don't say there was anything unfair, but so it was. These prison-chaps had done little else than play cards ever since they had been at the Andamans, and they knew each other's game to a point, while the others just played to pass the time and threw their cards down anyhow. Night after night the soldiers got up poorer men, and the poorer they got the more keen they were to play. Major Sholto was the hardest hit. He used to to pay in notes and gold at first, but soon it came to notes of hand and for big sums. He sometimes would win for a few deals, just to give him heart, and then the luck would set in against him worse than ever. All day he would wander about as black as thunder, and he took to drinking a deal more than was good for him.

"One night he lost even more heavily than usual. I was sitting in my hut when he and Captain Morstan came stumbling along on the way to their quarters. They were bosom friends, those two, and never far apart. The Major was raving about his losses.

"'It's all up, Morstan,' he was saying as they passed my hut. 'I shall have to send in my papers. I am a ruined man.'

"'Nonsense, old chap!' said the other, slapping him upon the shoulder. 'I've had a nasty facer myself, but——' That was all I could hear, but it was enough to set me thinking.

"A couple of days later Major Sholto was strolling on the beach: so I took the chance of speaking to him.

"'I wish to have your advice, Major,' said I.

"'Well, Small, what is it?' he asked, taking his cheroot from his lips.

"'I wanted to ask you, sir,' said I, 'who is the proper person to whom hidden treasure should be handed over. I know where half a million lies, and, as I cannot use it myself, I thought perhaps the best thing that I could do would be to hand it over to the proper authorities, and then perhaps they would get my sentence shortened for me.'

"'Half a million, Small?' he gasped, looking hard at me to see if I was in earnest.

"'Quite that, sir—in jewels and pearls. It lies there ready for anyone. And the queer thing about it is that the real owner is outlawed and cannot hold property, so that it belongs to the first comer.'

"'To Government, Small,' he stammered, 'to Government.' But he said it in a halting fashion and I knew in my heart that I had got him.

"'You think, then, sir, that I should give the information to the Governor-General?' said I, quietly.

"'Well, well, you must not do anything rash, or that you might repent. Let me hear all about it, Small. Give me the facts.'

"I told him the whole story, with small changes, so that he could not identify the places. When I had finished he stood stock still and full of thought. I could see by the twitch of his lip that there was a struggle going on within him.

"'This is a very important matter, Small,' he said at last. 'You must not say a word to anyone about it, and I shall see you again soon.'

"Two nights later he and his friend, Captain Morstan, came to my hut in the dead of night with a lantern.

"'I want you just to let Captain Morstan hear the story from your own lips, Small,' said he.

"I repeated it as I had told it before.

"'It rings true, eh?' said he. 'It's good enough to act upon?'

"Captain Morstan nodded.

"'Look here, Small,' said the Major, 'we have been talking it over, my friend here and I, and we have come to the conclusion that this secret of yours is hardly a Government matter, after all, but is a private concern of your own, which, of course, you have the power of disposing of as you think best. Now the question is, What price would you ask for it? We might be inclined to take it up, and at least look into it, if we could agree as to terms.' He tried to speak in a cool, careless way, but his eyes were shining with excitement and greed.

"'Why, as to that, gentlemen,' I answered, trying also to be cool, but feeling as excited as he did, 'there is only one bargain which a man in my position can make. I shall want you to help me to my freedom, and to help my three companions to theirs. We shall then take you into partnership, and give you a fifth share to divide between you.'

"'Hum!' said he. 'A fifth share! That is not very tempting.'

"'It would come to fifty thousand apiece,' said I.

"'But how can we gain your freedom? You know very well that you ask an impossibility.'

"'Nothing of the sort,' I answered. 'I have thought it all out to the last detail. The only bar to our escape is that we can get no boat fit for the voyage, and no provisions to last us for so long a time. There are plenty of little yachts and yawls at Calcutta or Madras which would serve our turn well. Do you bring one over. We shall engage to get aboard her by night, and if you will drop us on any part of the Indian coast you will have done your part of the bargain.'

"'If there were only one,' he said.

"'None or all,' I answered. 'We have sworn it. The four of us must always act together.

"'You see, Morstan,' said he, 'Small is a

man of his word. He does not flinch from his friends. I think we may very well trust him.'

" ' It's a dirty business,' the other answered. ' Yet, as you say, the money will save our commissions handsomely.'

" ' Well, Small,' said the Major, ' we must, I suppose try and meet you. We must first, of course, test the truth of your story. Tell me where the box is hid and I shall get leave of absence and go back to India in the monthly relief-boat to inquire into the affair.'

" ' Not so fast,' said I, growing bolder as he got hot. ' I must have the consent of my three comrades. I tell you that it is four or none with us.'

" ' Nonsense ! " he broke in, " ' What have three black fellows to do with our agreement ? '

' Black or blue,' said I, ' they are in with me, and we all go together.'

" Well, the matter ended by a second meeting, at which Mahomet Singh, Abdullah Khan, and Dost Akbar were all present. We talked the matter over again, and at last we came to an arrangement. We were to provide both the officers with charts of the part of the Agra fort, and mark the place in the wall where the treasure was hid. Major Sholto was to go to India to test our story. If he found the box he was to leave it there, to send out a small yacht provisioned for a voyage, which was to lie off Rutland Island, and to which we were to make our way, and finally to return to his duties. Captain Morstan was then to apply for leave of absence, to meet us at Agra, and there we were to have a final division of the treasure, he taking the Major's share as well as his own. All this we sealed by the most solemn oaths that the mind could think or the lips utter. I sat up all night with paper and ink, and by the morning I had the two charts all ready, signed with the sign of four—that is, Abdullah, Akbar, Mahomet, and myself.

" Well, gentleman, I weary you with my long story, and I know that my friend Mr. Jones is impatient to get me safely stowed in chokey. I'll make it as short as I can. The villain Sholto went off to India, but he never came back again. Captain Morstan showed me his name among a list of passengers in one of the mailboats very shortly afterwards. His uncle had died, leaving him a fortune, and he had left the army; yet he could stoop to treat five men as he had treated us. Morstan went over to Agra shortly afterwards, and found, as we expected, that the treasure was indeed gone. The scoundrel had stolen it all, without carrying out one of the conditions on which we had sold him the secret. From that day I lived only for vengeance. I thought of it by day and I nursed it by night. It became an overpowering, absorbing passion with me. I cared nothing for the law—nothing for the gallows. To escape, to track down Sholto, to have my hand upon his throat—that was my one thought. Even the Agra treasure had come to be a smaller thing in my mind than the slaying of Sholto.

" Well, I have set my mind on many things in this life, and never one which I did not carry out. But it was weary years before my time came. I have told you that I had picked up something of medicine. One day when Dr. Somerton was down with a fever a little Andaman Islander was picked up by a convict-gang in the woods. He was sick to death, and had gone to a lonely place to die. I took him in hand, though he was as venomous as a young snake, and after a couple of months I got him all right and able to walk. He took a kind of fancy to me then, and would hardly go back to his woods, but was always hanging about my hut. I learned a little of his lingo from him, and this made him all the fonder of me.

" Tonga—for that was his name—was a fine boatman, and owned a big, roomy canoe of his own. When I found that he was devoted to me and would do anything to serve me, I saw my chance of escape. I talked it over with him. He was to bring his boat round on a certain night to an old wharf which was never guarded, and there he was to pick me up. I gave him directions to have several gourds of water and a lot of yams, coconuts, and sweet potatoes.

" He was staunch and true, was little Tonga. No man ever had a more faithful mate. On the night named he had his boat at the wharf. As it chanced, however, there was one of the convict-guard down there—a vile Pathan who had never missed a chance of insulting and injuring me. I had always vowed vengeance, and now I had my chance. It was as if fate had placed him in my way that I might pay my debt before I left the island. He stood on the bank with his back to me, and his carbine on his shoulder. I look about for a stone to beat out his brains with, but none could I see.

" Then a queer thought came into my head, and showed me where I could lay my hand on a weapon. I sat down in the darkness and unstrapped my wooden leg. With three long hops I was on him. He pulled his carbine to his shoulder, but I struck him full, and knocked the whole front of his skull in. You can see the split in the wood now where I hit him. We both went down together, for I could not keep my balance; but when I got up I found him lying quiet enough. I made for the boat, and in an hour we were well out at sea. Tonga had brought all his earthly possessions with him, his arms and his gods. Among other things, he had a long bamboo spear, and some Andaman coconut-matting, with which I made a sort of sail. For ten days we were beating about, trusting to luck, and on the eleventh we were picked up by a trader which was going from Singapore to Jiddah with a cargo of Malay pilgrims. They were a rum crowd, and Tonga and I soon managed to settle down among them. They had one very good quality; they let you alone and asked no questions.

" Well, if I were to tell you all the adventures that my little chum and I went through, you would not thank me, for I would have you here until the sun was shining. Here and there we drifted about the world, something always turning up to keep us from London. All the time, however, I never lost sight of my purpose. I would dream of Sholto at night. At last, however, some three or four years ago, we found ourselves in England. I had no great difficulty in finding where Sholto lived, and I set to work to discover whether he had realized the treasure, or if he still had it. I made friends with someone who could help me—I name no names, for I don't want to get anyone else in a hole—and I soon found that he still had the jewels. Then I tried to get at him in many ways; but he was pretty sly, and had always two prize-fighters, besides his sons and his khidmutgar, on guard over him.

" One day, however, I got word that he was dying. I hurried at once to the garden, mad that he should slip out of my clutches like that, and, looking through the window, I saw him lying in bed, with his sons on each side of him. I'd have come through and taken my chance with the three of them, only even as I looked at him his jaw dropped, and I knew that he was gone. I got into his room the same night, though, and I searched his papers to see if there was any record of where he had hidden the jewels. There was not a line, however, so I came away, bitter and savage as a man might be. Before I left I bethought me that if I ever met my Sikh friends again it would be a satisfaction to know that I had left some mark of our hatred; so I scrawled down the sign of the

four of us, as it had been on the chart, and I pinned in on his bosom. It was too much that he should be taken to the grave without some token from the men whom he had robbed and befooled.

" We earned a living at this time by my exhibiting poor Tonga at fairs and other such places as the black cannibal. He would eat raw meat and dance his war-dance; so we always had a hatful of pennies after a day's work. I still heard all the news from Pondicherry Lodge, and for some years there was no news to hear, except that they were hunting for the treasure. At last, however, came what we had waited for so long. The treasure had been found. It was up at the top of the house, in Mr. Bartholomew Sholto's chemical laboratory. I came at once and had a look at the place, but I could not see how, with my wooden leg, I was to make my way up to it. I learned, however, about a trap-door in the roof, and also about Mr. Sholto's supper-hour. It seemed to me that I could manage the thing easily through Tonga. I brought him out with me with a long rope wound round his waist. He could climb like a cat, and he soon made his way through the roof, but as ill-luck would have it, Bartholomew Sholto was still in the room, to his cost. Tonga thought he had done something very clever in killing him, for when I came up the rope I found him strutting about as proud as a peacock. Very much surprised was he when I made at him with the rope's end and cursed him for a little bloodthirsty imp. I took the treasure box and let it down, and then slid down myself, having first left the sign of the four upon the table, to show that the jewels had come back at last to those who had most right to them. Tonga then pulled up the rope, closed the window, and made off the way that he had come.

" I don't know that I have anything else to tell you. I had heard a waterman speak of the speed of Smith's launch, the *Aurora*, so I thought she would be a handy craft for our escape. I engaged with old Smith, and was to give him a big sum if he got us safe to our ship. He knew, no doubt, that there was some screw loose, but he was not in our secrets. All this is the truth, and if I tell it to you, gentlemen, it is not to amuse you—for you have not done me a very good turn—but it is because I believe the best defence I can make is just to hold back nothing, but let all the world know how badly I have myself been served by Major Sholto and how innocent I am of the death of his son."

" A very remarkable account," said Sherlock Holmes. "A fitting wind-up to an extremely interesting case. There is nothing at all new to me in the latter part of your narrative, except that you brought your own rope. That I did not know. By the way, I had hoped that Tonga had lost all his darts; yet he managed to shoot one at us in the boat."

"He had lost them all, sir, except the one which was in his blow-pipe at the time."

"Ah, of course," said Holmes. "I had not thought of that."

"Is there any other point which you would like to ask about?" asked the convict, affably.

"I think not, thank you," my companion answered.

"Well, Holmes," said Athelney Jones, "you are a man to be humoured, and we all know that you are a connoisseur of crime; but duty is duty, and I have gone rather far in doing what you and your friend asked me. I shall feel more at ease when we have our story-teller here safe under lock and key. The cab still awaits, and there are two inspectors downstairs. I am much obliged to you both for your assistance. Of course, you will be wanted for the trial. Good-night to you."

"Goodnight, gentlemen both," said Jonathan Small.

"You first, Small," remarked the wary Jones as they left the room. "I'll take particular care that you don't club me with your wooden leg, whatever you may have done to the gentleman at the Andaman Isles."

"Well, and there is the end of our little drama," I remarked, after we had sat some time smoking in silence. "I fear that it may be the last investigation in which I shall have the chance of studying your methods. Miss Morstan has done me the honour to accept me as a husband in prospective."

He gave a most dismal groan.

"I feared as much," said he. "I really cannot congratulate you."

I was a little hurt.

"Have you any reason to be dissatisfied with my choice?" I asked.

"Not at all. I think she is one of the most charming young ladies I ever met, and might have been most useful in such work as we have been doing. She had a decided genius that way; witness the way in which she preserved that Agra plan from all the other papers of her father. But love is an emotional thing, and whatever is emotional is opposed to that true cold reason which I place above all things. I should never marry myself, lest I bias my judgment."

"I trust," said I, laughing, "that my judgment may survive the ordeal. But you look weary."

"Yes, the reaction is already upon me. I shall be as limp as a rag for a week."

"Strange," said I, "how terms of what in another man I should call laziness alternate with your fits of splendid energy and vigour."

"Yes," he answered, "there are in me the makings of a very fine loafer, and also of a pretty spry sort of fellow. I often think of those lines of old Goethe:— *Schade dass die Natur nur einen Mensch aus dir schuf, Den zum würdigen Mann war und zum Schelmen der Stoff.* By the way, apropos of this Norwood business, you see that they had, as I surmised, a confederate in the house, who could be none other than Lal Rao, the butler: so Jones actually has the undivided honour of having caught one fish in his great haul."

"The division seems rather unfair," I remarked. "You have done all the work in this business. I get a wife out of it, Jones gets the credit; pray what remains for you?"

"For me," said Sherlock Holmes, "there still remains the cocaine-bottle." And he stretched his long, white hand up for it.

THE ADVENTURES
OF SHERLOCK HOLMES

*Facsimile from the Strand Magazine, Volumes II and III,
July 1891 – June 1892.*

Adventures of Sherlock Holmes.

ADVENTURE I.—A SCANDAL IN BOHEMIA.

By A. Conan Doyle.

O, Sherlock Holmes she is always *the* woman. I have seldom heard him mention her under any other name. In his eyes she eclipses and predominates the whole of her sex. It was not that he felt any emotion akin to love for Irene Adler. All emotions, and that one particularly, were abhorrent to his cold, precise, but admirably balanced mind. He was, I take it, the most perfect reasoning and observing machine that the world has seen ; but, as a lover, he would have placed himself in a false position. He never spoke of the softer passions, save with a gibe and a sneer. They were admirable things for the observer —excellent for drawing the veil from men's motives and actions. But for the trained reasoner to admit such intrusions into his own delicate and finely adjusted temperament was to introduce a distracting factor which might throw a doubt upon all his mental results. Grit in a sensitive instrument, or a crack in one of his own high-power lenses, would not be more disturbing than a strong emotion in a nature such as his. And yet there was but one woman to him, and that woman was the late Irene Adler, of dubious and questionable memory.

I had seen little of Holmes lately. My marriage had drifted us away from each other. My own complete happiness, and the home-centred interests which rise up around the man who first finds himself master of his own establishment, were sufficient to absorb all my attention ; while Holmes, who loathed every form of society with his whole Bohemian soul, remained in our lodgings in Baker-street, buried among his old books, and alternating from week to week between cocaine and ambition, the drowsiness of the drug, and the fierce energy of his own keen nature. He was still, as ever, deeply attracted by the study of crime, and occupied his immense faculties and extraordinary powers of observation in following out those clues, and clearing up those mysteries, which had been abandoned as hopeless by the official police. From time to time I heard some vague account of his doings : of his summons to Odessa in the case of the Trepoff murder, of his clearing up of the singular tragedy of the Atkinson brothers at Trincomalee, and finally of the mission which he had accomplished so delicately and successfully for the reigning family of Holland. Beyond these signs of his activity, however, which I merely shared with all the readers of the daily press, I knew little of my former friend and companion.

One night—it was on the 20th of March, 1888—I was returning from a journey to a patient (for I had now returned to civil practice), when my way led me through Baker-street. As I passed the well-remembered door, which must always be associated in my mind with my wooing, and with the dark incidents of the Study in Scarlet, I was seized with a keen desire to see Holmes again, and to know how he was employing his extraordinary powers. His rooms were brilliantly lit, and, even as I looked up, I saw his tall spare figure pass twice in a dark silhouette against the blind. He was pacing the room swiftly, eagerly, with his head sunk upon his chest, and his hands clasped behind him. To me, who knew his every mood and habit, his attitude and manner told their own story. He was at work again. He had arisen out of his drug-created dreams, and was hot upon the scent of some new problem. I rang the bell, and was shown up to the chamber which had formerly been in part my own.

His manner was not effusive. It seldom was ; but he was glad, I think, to see me. With hardly a word spoken, but with a kindly eye, he waved me to an armchair, threw across his case of cigars, and indicated a spirit case and a gasogene in the corner. Then he stood before the fire, and looked me over in his singular introspective fashion.

"Wedlock suits you," he remarked. "I think, Watson, that you have put on seven and a half pounds since I saw you."

"Seven," I answered.

"Indeed, I should have thought a little more. Just a trifle more, I fancy, Watson. And in practice again, I observe. You did not tell me that you intended to go into harness."

"Then, how do you know ? "

"I see it, I deduce it. How do I know

that you have been getting yourself very wet lately, and that you have a most clumsy and careless servant girl?"

"My dear Holmes," said I, "this is too much. You would certainly have been burned, had you lived a few centuries ago. It is true that I had a country walk on Thursday and came home in a dreadful mess; but, as I have changed my clothes, I can't imagine how you deduce it. As to Mary Jane, she is incorrigible, and my wife has given her notice; but there again I fail to see how you work it out."

He chuckled to himself and rubbed his long nervous hands together. "It is simplicity itself," said he; "my eyes tell me that on the inside of your left shoe, just where the firelight strikes it, the leather is scored by six almost parallel cuts. Obviously they have been caused by someone who has very carelessly scraped round the edges of the sole in order to remove crusted mud from it. Hence, you see, my double deduction that you had been out in vile

"THEN HE STOOD BEFORE THE FIRE."

weather, and that you had a particularly malignant boot-slitting specimen of the London slavey. As to your practice, if a gentleman walks into my rooms smelling of iodoform, with a black mark of nitrate of silver upon his right fore-finger, and a bulge on the side of his top-hat to show where he has secreted his stethoscope, I must be dull indeed, if I do not pronounce him to be an active member of the medical profession."

I could not help laughing at the ease with which he explained his process of deduction. "When I hear you give your reasons," I remarked, "the thing always appears to me to be so ridiculously simple that I could easily do it myself, though at

each successive instance of your reasoning I am baffled, until you explain your process. And yet I believe that my eyes are as good as yours."

"Quite so," he answered, lighting a cigarette, and throwing himself down into an armchair. "You see, but you do not observe. The distinction is clear. For example, you have frequently seen the steps which lead up from the hall to this room."

"Frequently."

"How often?"

"Well, some hundreds of times."

"Then how many are there?"

"How many! I don't know."

"Quite so! You have not observed.

And yet you have seen. That is just my point. Now, I· know that there are seventeen steps, because I have both seen and observed. By the way, since you are interested in these little problems, and since you are good enough to chronicle one or two of my trifling experiences, you may be interested in this." He threw over a sheet of thick pink-tinted notepaper which had been lying open upon the table. " It came by the last post," said he. " Read it aloud."

The note was undated, and without either signature or address.

" There will call upon you to-night, at a quarter to eight o'clock," it said, " a gentleman who desires to consult you upon a matter of the very deepest moment. Your recent services to one of the Royal Houses of Europe have shown that you are one who may safely be trusted with matters which are of an importance which can hardly be exaggerated. This account of you we have from all quarters received. Be in your chamber then at that hour, and do not take it amiss if your visitor wear a mask."

" This is indeed a

mystery," I remarked. "What do you imagine that it means ? "

" I have no data yet. It is a capital mistake to theorise before one has data. Insensibly one begins to twist facts to suit theories, instead of theories to suit

facts. But the note itself. What do you deduce from it ? "

I carefully examined the writing, and the paper upon which it was written.

" The man who wrote it was presumably well to do," I remarked, endeavouring to imitate my companion's processes. " Such paper could not be bought under half a crown a packet. It is peculiarly strong and stiff."

" Peculiar—that is the very word," said Holmes. " It is not an English paper at all. Hold it up to the light."

I did so, and saw a large *E* with a small *g*, a *P*, and a large *G* with a small *t* woven into the texture of the paper.

" What do you make of that ? " asked Holmes.

" The name of the maker, no doubt ; or his monogram, rather."

" Not at all. The *G* with the small *t* stands for " Gesellschaft," which is the German for " Company." It is a customary contraction like our " Co." *P,* of course, stands for " Papier." Now for the *Eg.* Let us glance at our Continental Gazetteer." He took down a heavy brown volume from his shelves. " Eglow, Eglonitz—here we are, Egria. It is in a German - speaking country—in Bohemia, not far from Carlsbad. 'Remarkable as being the scene of the death of Wallenstein, and for its numerous glass factories and paper mills.' Ha, ha, my boy, what do you make of that ? " His eyes sparkled, and he sent up a great blue triumphant cloud from his cigarette.

" The paper was made in Bohemia," I said.

" Precisely. And the man who wrote the note is a German. Do you note the peculiar construction of the sentence—'This account of you we have from all quarters received.' A Frenchman or Russian could not have written that. It is the German who is so uncourteous to his verbs. It only remains, therefore, to discover what is wanted by this German who writes upon Bohemian paper, and prefers wearing a mask to showing his face. And here he comes, if I am not mistaken, to resolve all our doubts."

As he spoke there was the sharp sound of horses' hoofs and grating wheels against the curb, followed by a sharp pull at the bell. Holmes whistled.

"A pair, by the sound," said he. "Yes," he continued, glancing out of the window. "A nice little brougham and a pair of beauties. A hundred and fifty guineas apiece. There's money in this case, Watson, if there is nothing else."

"I think that I had better go, Holmes."

"Not a bit, Doctor. Stay where you are. I am lost without my Boswell. And this promises to be interesting. It would be a pity to miss it."

"But your client——"

"Never mind him. I may want your help, and so may he. Here he comes. Sit down in that armchair, Doctor, and give us your best attention."

A slow and heavy step, which had been heard upon the stairs and in the passage, paused immediately outside the door. Then there was a loud and authoritative tap.

"Come in !" said Holmes.

A man entered who could hardly have been less than six feet six inches in height, with the chest and limbs of a Hercules. His dress was rich with a richness which would, in England, be looked upon as akin to bad taste. Heavy bands of Astrakhan were slashed across the sleeves and fronts of his double-breasted coat, while the deep blue cloak which was thrown over his shoulders

"A MAN ENTERED."

was lined with flame-coloured silk, and secured at the neck with a brooch which consisted of a single flaming beryl. Boots which extended half way up his calves, and which were trimmed at the tops with rich brown fur, completed the impression of barbaric opulence which was suggested by his whole appearance. He carried a broad-brimmed hat in his hand, while he wore across the upper part of his face, extending down past the cheek-bones, a black vizard mask, which he had apparently adjusted that very moment, for his hand was still raised to it as he entered. From the lower part of the face he appeared to be a man of strong character, with a thick, hanging lip, and a long straight chin, suggestive of resolution pushed to the length of obstinacy.

"You had my note ? " he asked, with a deep harsh voice and a strongly marked German accent. "I told you that I would call." He looked from one to the other of us, as if uncertain which to address.

"Pray take a seat," said Holmes. "This is my friend and colleague, Dr. Watson, who is occasionally good enough to help me in my cases. Whom have I the honour to address ?"

"You may address me as the Count Von Kramm, a Bohemian nobleman. I understand that this gentleman, your friend, is a man of honour and discretion, whom I may trust with a matter of the most extreme importance. If not, I should much prefer to communicate with you alone."

I rose to go, but Holmes caught me by

the wrist and pushed me back into my chair. "It is both, or none," said he. "You may say before this gentleman anything which you may say to me."

The Count shrugged his broad shoulders. "Then I must begin," said he, " by binding you both to absolute secrecy for two years, at the end of that time the matter will be of no importance. At present it is not too much to say that it is of such weight that it may have an influence upon European history."

"I promise," said Holmes.

"And I."

"You will excuse this mask," continued our strange visitor. "The august person who employs me wishes his agent to be unknown to you, and I may confess at once that the title by which I have just called myself is not exactly my own."

"I was aware of it," said Holmes dryly.

"The circumstances are of great delicacy, and every precaution has to be taken to quench what might grow to be an immense scandal and seriously compromise one of the reigning families of Europe. To speak plainly, the matter implicates the great House of Ormstein, hereditary kings of Bohemia."

"I was also aware of that," murmured Holmes, settling himself down in his armchair, and closing his eyes.

Our visitor glanced with some apparent surprise at the languid, lounging figure of the man who had been no doubt depicted to him as the most incisive reasoner, and most energetic agent in Europe. Holmes slowly reopened his eyes, and looked impatiently at his gigantic client.

"If your Majesty would condescend to state your case," he remarked, "I should be better able to advise you."

The man sprang from his chair, and paced up and down the room in uncontrollable agitation. Then, with a gesture of desperation, he tore the mask from his face and hurled it upon the ground. "You are right," he cried, "I am the King. Why should I attempt to conceal it ? "

"Why, indeed?" murmured Holmes.

"HE TORE THE MASK FROM HIS FACE."

"Your Majesty had not spoken before I was aware that I was addressing Wilhelm Gottsreich Sigismond von Ormstein, Grand Duke of Cassel-Felstein, and hereditary King of Bohemia."

"But you can understand," said our strange visitor, sitting down once more and passing his hand over his high, white forehead, " you can understand that I am not accustomed to doing such business in my own person. Yet the matter was so delicate that I could not confide it to an agent without putting myself in his power. I have come *incognito* from Prague for the purpose of consulting you."

"Then, pray consult," said Holmes, shutting his eyes once more.

"The facts are briefly these : Some five years ago, during a lengthy visit to Warsaw, I made the acquaintance of the well-known adventuress Irene Adler. The name is no doubt familiar to you."

"Kindly look her up in my index, Doctor," murmured Holmes, without opening his eyes. For many years he had adopted a system of docketing all paragraphs concerning men and things; so that it was difficult to name a subject or a person on which he could not at once furnish information. In this case I found her biography sandwiched in between that of a Hebrew Rabbi and that of a staff-commander who had written a monograph upon the deep sea fishes.

"Let me see?" said Holmes. "Hum! Born in New Jersey in the year 1858. Contralto—hum! La Scala, hum! Prima donna Imperial Opera of Warsaw—Yes! Retired from operatic stage—ha! Living in London—quite so! Your Majesty, as I understand, became entangled with this young person, wrote her some compromising letters, and is now desirous of getting those letters back."

"Precisely so. But how——"

"Was there a secret marriage?"

"None."

"No legal papers or certificates?"

"None."

"Then I fail to follow your Majesty. If this young person should produce her letters for blackmailing or other purposes, how is she to prove their authenticity?"

"There is the writing."

"Pooh, pooh! Forgery."

"My private notepaper."

"Stolen."

"My own seal."

"Imitated."

"My photograph."

"Bought."

"We were both in the photograph."

"Oh dear! That is very bad! Your Majesty has indeed committed an indiscretion."

"I was mad—insane."

"You have compromised yourself seriously."

"I was only Crown Prince then. I was young. I am but thirty now."

"It must be recovered."

"We have tried and failed."

"Your Majesty must pay. It must be bought."

"She will not sell."

"Stolen, then."

"Five attempts have been made. Twice burglars in my pay ransacked her house. Once we diverted her luggage when she travelled. Twice she has been waylaid. There has been no result."

"No sign of it?"

"Absolutely none."

Holmes laughed. "It is quite a pretty little problem," said he.

"But a very serious one to me," returned the King, reproachfully.

"Very, indeed. And what does she propose to do with the photograph?"

"To ruin me."

"But how?"

"I am about to be married."

"So I have heard."

"To Clotilde Lothman von Saxe-Meningen, second daughter of the King of Scandinavia. You may know the strict principles of her family. She is herself the very soul of delicacy. A shadow of a doubt as to my conduct would bring the matter to an end."

"And Irene Adler?"

"Threatens to send them the photograph. And she will do it. I know that she will do it. You do not know her, but she has a soul of steel. She has the face of the most beautiful of women, and the mind of the most resolute of men. Rather than I should marry another woman, there are no lengths to which she would not go—none."

"You are sure that she has not sent it yet?"

"I am sure."

"And why?"

"Because she has said that she would send it on the day when the betrothal was publicly proclaimed. That will be next Monday."

"Oh, then, we have three days yet," said Holmes, with a yawn. "That is very fortunate, as I have one or two matters of importance to look into just at present. Your Majesty will, of course, stay in London for the present?"

"Certainly. You will find me at the Langham, under the name of the Count Von Kramm."

"Then I shall drop you a line to let you know how we progress."

"Pray do so. I shall be all anxiety."

"Then, as to money?"

"You have *carte blanche.*"

"Absolutely?"

"I tell you that I would give one of the provinces of my kingdom to have that photograph."

"And for present expenses?"

The king took a heavy chamois leather bag from under his cloak, and laid it on the table.

"There are three hundred pounds in gold, and seven hundred in notes," he said.

Holmes scribbled a receipt upon a sheet of his note-book, and handed it to him.

"And mademoiselle's address?" he asked.

"Is Briony Lodge, Serpentine-avenue, St. John's Wood."

Holmes took a note of it. "One other question," said he. "Was the photograph a cabinet?"

"It was."

"Then, good night, your Majesty, and I trust that we shall soon have some good news for you. And good night, Watson," he added, as the wheels of the Royal brougham rolled down the street. "If you will be good enough to call to-morrow afternoon, at three o'clock, I should like to chat this little matter over with you."

II.

At three o'clock precisely I was at Baker-street, but Holmes had not yet returned. The landlady informed me that he had left the house shortly after eight o'clock in the morning. I sat down beside the fire, however, with the intention of awaiting him, however long he might be. I was already deeply interested in his inquiry, for, though it was surrounded by none of the grim and strange features which were associated with the two crimes which I

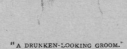

"A DRUNKEN-LOOKING GROOM."

have already recorded, still, the nature of the case and the exalted station of his client gave it a character of its own. Indeed, apart from the nature of the investigation which my friend had on hand, there was something in his masterly grasp of a situation, and his keen, incisive reasoning, which made it a pleasure to me to study his system of work, and to follow the quick, subtle methods by which he disentangled the most inextricable mysteries. So accustomed was I to his in-

variable success that the very possibility of his failing had ceased to enter into my head.

It was close upon four before the door opened, and a drunken-looking groom, ill-kempt and side-whiskered, with an inflamed face and disreputable clothes, walked into the room. Accustomed as I was to my friend's amazing powers in the use of disguises, I had to look three times before I was certain that it was indeed he. With a nod he vanished into the bedroom, whence he emerged in five minutes tweed-suited and respectable, as of old. Putting his hands into his pockets, he stretched out his legs in front of the fire, and laughed heartily for some minutes.

"Well, really!" he cried, and then he choked; and laughed again until he was obliged to lie back, limp and helpless, in the chair.

"What is it?"

"It's quite too funny. I am sure you could never guess how I employed my morning, or what I ended by doing."

"I can't imagine. I suppose that you have been watching the habits, and perhaps the house, of Miss Irene Adler."

"Quite so, but the sequel was rather unusual. I will tell you, however. I left the house a little after eight o'clock this morning, in the character of a groom out of work. There is a wonderful sympathy and freemasonry among horsey men. Be one of them, and you will know all that there is to know. I soon found Briony Lodge. It is a *bijou* villa, with a garden at the back, but built out in front right up to the road, two stories. Chubb lock to the door. Large sitting-room on the right side, well furnished, with long windows almost to the floor, and those preposterous

English window fasteners which a child could open. Behind there was nothing remarkable, save that the passage window could be reached from the top of the coach-house. I walked round it and examined it closely from every point of view, but without noting anything else of interest.

"I then lounged down the street, and found, as I expected, that there was a mews in a lane which runs down by one wall of the garden. I lent the ostlers a hand in rubbing down their horses, and I received in exchange twopence, a glass of half-and-half, two fills of shag tobacco, and as much information as I could desire about Miss Adler, to say nothing of half a dozen other people in the neighbourhood in whom I was not in the least interested, but whose biographies I was compelled to listen to."

"And what of Irene Adler?" I asked.

"Oh, she has turned all the men's heads down in that part. She is the daintiest thing under a bonnet on this planet. So say the Serpentine-mews, to a man. She lives quietly, sings at concerts, drives out at five every day, and returns at seven sharp for dinner. Seldom goes out at other times, except when she sings. Has only one male visitor, but a good deal of him. He is dark, handsome, and dashing; never calls less than once a day, and often twice. He is a Mr. Godfrey Norton, of the Inner Temple. See the advantages of a cabman as a confidant. They had driven him home a dozen times from Serpentine-mews, and knew all about him. When I had listened to all that they had to tell, I began to walk up and down near Briony Lodge once more, and to think over my plan of campaign.

"This Godfrey Norton was evidently an important factor in the matter. He was a lawyer. That sounded ominous. What was the relation between them, and what the object of his repeated visits? Was she his client, his friend, or his mistress? If the former, she had probably transferred the photograph to his keeping. If the latter, it was less likely. On the issue of this question depended whether I should continue my work at Briony Lodge, or turn my attention to the gentleman's chambers in the Temple. It was a delicate point, and it widened the field of my inquiry. I fear that I bore you with these details, but I have to let you see my little difficulties, if you are to understand the situation."

"I am following you closely," I answered.

"I was still balancing the matter in my mind, when a hansom cab drove up to Briony Lodge, and a gentleman sprang out. He was a remarkably handsome man, dark, aquiline, and moustached—evidently the man of whom I had heard. He appeared to be in a great hurry, shouted to the cabman to wait, and brushed past the maid who opened the door with the air of a man who was thoroughly at home.

"He was in the house about half an hour, and I could catch glimpses of him, in the windows of the sitting-room, pacing up and down, talking excitedly and waving his arms. Of her I could see nothing. Presently he emerged, looking even more flurried than before. As he stepped up to the cab, he pulled a gold watch from his pocket and looked at it earnestly. "Drive like the devil,' he shouted, 'first to Gross & Hankey's in Regent-street, and then to the church of St. Monica in the Edgware-road. Half a guinea if you do it in twenty minutes!'

"Away they went, and I was just wondering whether I should not do well to follow them, when up the lane came a neat little landau, the coachman with his coat only half buttoned, and his tie under his ear, while all the tags of his harness were sticking out of the buckles. It hadn't pulled up before she shot out of the hall door and into it. I only caught a glimpse of her at the moment, but she was a lovely woman, with a face that a man might die for.

"'The Church of St. Monica, John,' she cried, 'and half a sovereign if you reach it in twenty minutes.'

"This was quite too good to lose, Watson. I was just balancing whether I should run for it, or whether I should perch behind her landau, when a cab came through the street. The driver looked twice at such a shabby fare; but I jumped in before he could object. 'The Church of St. Monica,' said I, 'and half a sovereign if you reach it in twenty minutes.' It was twenty-five minutes to twelve, and of course it was clear enough what was in the wind.

"My cabby drove fast. I don't think I ever drove faster, but the others were there before us. The cab and the landau with their steaming horses were in front of the door when I arrived. I paid the man, and hurried into the church. There was not a soul there save the two whom I had followed and a surpliced clergyman, who seemed to be expostulating with them. They were all three standing in a knot in front of the altar. I lounged up the side aisle like any other idler who has dropped into a church. Suddenly, to my surprise, the three at the altar faced round to me, and Godfrey Norton came running as hard as he could towards me."

"Thank God!" he cried. "You'll do. Come! Come!"

"What then?" I asked.

"Come man, come, only three minutes, or it won't be legal."

"I FOUND MYSELF MUMBLING RESPONSES."

I was half dragged up to the altar, and, before I knew where I was, I found myself mumbling responses which were whispered in my ear, and vouching for things of which I knew nothing, and generally assisting in the secure tying up of Irene Adler, spinster, to Godfrey Norton, bachelor. It was all done in an instant, and there was the gentleman thanking me on the one side and the lady on the other, while the clergyman beamed on me in front. It was the most preposterous position in which I ever found myself in my life, and it was the thought of it that started me laughing just now. It seems that there had been some informality about their licence, that the clergyman absolutely refused to marry them without a witness of some sort, and that my lucky appearance saved the bridegroom from having to sally out into the streets in search of a best man. The bride gave me a sovereign, and I mean to wear it on my watch chain in memory of the occasion."

"This is a very unexpected turn of affairs," said I ; "and what then?"

"Well, I found my plans very seriously menaced. It looked as if the pair might take an immediate departure, and so necessitate very prompt and energetic measures on my part. At the church door, however, they separated, he driving back to the Temple, and she to her own house. 'I shall drive out in the Park at five as usual,' she said as she left him. I heard no more. They drove away in different directions, and I went off to make my own arrangements."

"Which are?"

"Some cold beef and a glass of beer," he answered, ringing the bell. "I have been too busy to think of food, and I am likely to be busier still this evening. By the way, Doctor, I shall want your co-operation."

"I shall be delighted."

"You don't mind breaking the law?"

"Not in the least."

"Nor running a chance of arrest?"

"Not in a good cause."

"Oh, the cause is excellent!"

"Then I am your man."

"I was sure that I might rely on you."

"But what is it you wish?"

"When Mrs. Turner has brought in the tray I will make it clear to you. Now," he said, as he turned hungrily on the simple fare that our landlady had provided, "I must discuss it while I eat, for I have not much time. It is nearly five now. In two hours we must be on the scene of action. Miss Irene, or Madame, rather, returns from her drive at seven. We must be at Briony Lodge to meet her."

"And what then?"

"You must leave that to me. I have already arranged what is to occur. There is only one point on which I must insist. You must not interfere, come what may. You understand?"

"I am to be neutral?"

"To do nothing whatever. There will probably be some small unpleasantness.

Do not join in it. It will end in my being conveyed into the house. Four or five minutes afterwards the sitting-room window will open. You are to station yourself close to that open window."

"Yes."

"You are to watch me, for I will be visible to you."

"Yes."

"And when I raise my hand—so—you will throw into the room what I give you to throw, and will, at the same time, raise the cry of fire. You quite follow me?"

"Entirely."

"It is nothing very formidable," he said, taking a long cigar-shaped roll from his pocket. "It is an ordinary plumber's smoke rocket, fitted with a cap at either end to make it self-lighting. Your task is confined to that. When you raise your cry of fire, it will be taken up by quite a number of people. You may then walk to the end of the street, and I will rejoin you in ten minutes. I hope that I have made myself clear?"

"I am to remain neutral, to get near the window, to watch you, and, at the signal, to throw in this object, then to raise the cry of fire, and to wait you at the corner of the street."

"Precisely."

"Then you may entirely rely on me."

"That is excellent. I think perhaps it is almost time that I prepared for the new *rôle* I have to play."

"A SIMPLE MINDED CLERGYMAN.

He disappeared into his bedroom, and returned in a few minutes in the character of an amiable and simple-minded Nonconformist clergyman. His broad black hat, his baggy trousers, his white tie, his sympathetic smile, and general look of peering and benevolent curiosity were such as Mr. John Hare alone could have equalled. It was not merely that Holmes changed his costume. His expression, his manner, his very soul seemed to vary with every fresh part that he assumed. The stage lost a fine actor, even as science lost an acute

reasoner, when he became a specialist in crime.

It was a quarter past six when we left Baker-street, and it still wanted ten minutes to the hour when we found ourselves in Serpentine-avenue. It was already dusk, and the lamps were just being lighted as we paced up and down in front of Briony Lodge, waiting for the coming of its occupant. The house was just such as I had pictured it from Sherlock Holmes' succinct description, but the locality appeared to be less private than I expected. On the contrary, for a small street in a quiet neighbourhood, it was remarkably animated. There was a group of shabbily-dressed men smoking and laughing in a corner, a scissors grinder with his wheel, two guardsmen who were flirting with a nurse-girl, and several well-dressed young men who were lounging up and down with cigars in their mouths.

"You see," remarked Holmes, as we paced to and fro in front of the house, "this marriage rather simplifies matters. The photograph becomes a double-edged weapon now. The chances are that she would be as averse to its being seen by Mr. Godfrey Norton, as our client is to its coming to the eyes of his Princess. Now the question is—Where are we to find the photograph?"

"Where, indeed?"

"It is most unlikely that she carries it about with her. It is cabinet size. Too large for easy concealment about a woman's dress. She knows that the King is capable of having her waylaid and searched. Two attempts of the sort have already been made. We may take it then that she does not carry it about with her."

"Where, then?"

"Her banker or her lawyer. There is that double possibility. But I am inclined to think neither. Women are naturally secretive, and they like to do their own secreting. Why should she hand it over to anyone else ? She could trust her own guardianship, but she could not tell what indirect or political influence might be brought to bear upon a business man. Besides, remember that she had resolved to use it within a few days. It must be where she can lay her hands upon it. It must be in her own house."

"But it has twice been burgled."

"Pshaw ! They did not know how to look."

"But how will you look ? "

"I will not look."

"What then ?"

"I will get her to show me."

"But she will refuse."

"She will not be able to. But I hear the rumble of wheels. It is her carriage. Now carry out my orders to the letter."

As he spoke the gleam of the sidelights of a carriage came round the curve of the avenue. It was a smart little landau which rattled up to the door of Briony Lodge. As it pulled up one of the loafing men at the corner dashed forward to open the door in the hope of earning a copper, but was elbowed away by another loafer who had rushed up with the same intention. A fierce quarrel broke out, which was increased by the two guardsmen, who took sides with one of the loungers, and by the scissors grinder, who was equally hot upon the other side. A blow was struck, and in an instant the lady, who had stepped from her carriage, was the centre of a little knot of flushed and struggling men who struck savagely at each other with their fists and sticks. Holmes dashed into the crowd to protect the lady ; but, just as he reached her, he gave a cry and dropped to the ground, with the blood running freely down his face. At his fall the guardsmen took to their heels in one direction and the loungers in the other, while a number of better dressed people who had watched the scuffle without taking part in it, crowded in to help the lady and to attend to the injured man. Irene Adler, as I will still call her, had hurried up the steps; but she stood at the top with her superb figure outlined against the lights of the hall, looking back into the street.

"Is the poor gentleman much hurt ? " she asked.

"He is dead," cried several voices.

"No, no, there's life in him," shouted another. "But he'll be gone before you can get him to hospital."

"He's a brave fellow," said a woman. "They would have had the lady's purse and watch if it hadn't been for him. They were a gang, and a rough one too. Ah, he's breathing now."

"He can't lie in the street. May we bring him in, marm ? "

"Surely. Bring him into the sitting-

"HE GAVE A CRY AND DROPPED."

room. There is a comfortable sofa. This way, please ! "

Slowly and solemnly he was borne into Briony Lodge, and laid out in the principal room, while I still observed the proceedings from my post by the window. The lamps had been lit, but the blinds had not been drawn, so that I could see Holmes as he lay upon the couch. I do not know whether he was seized with compunction at that moment for the part he was playing, but I know that I never felt more heartily ashamed of myself in my life than when I saw the beautiful creature against whom I was conspiring, or the grace and kindliness with which she waited upon the injured man. And yet it would be the blackest treachery to Holmes to draw back now from the part which he had entrusted to me. I hardened my heart, and took the smoke-rocket from under my ulster. After all, I thought, we are not injuring her. We are but preventing her from injuring another.

Holmes had sat up upon the couch, and I saw him motion like a man who is in need of air. A maid rushed across and threw open the window. At the same instant I saw him raise his hand, and at the signal I tossed my rocket into the room with a cry of " Fire." The word was no sooner out of my mouth than the whole crowd of spectators, well dressed and ill — gentlemen, ostlers, and servant maids — joined in a general shriek of " Fire." Thick clouds of smoke curled through the room, and out at the open window. I caught a glimpse of rushing figures, and a moment later the voice of Holmes from within, assuring them that it was a false alarm. Slipping through the shouting crowd I made my way to the corner of the street, and in ten minutes was rejoiced to find my friend's arm in mine, and to get away from the scene of uproar. He walked swiftly and in silence for some few minutes, until we had turned down one of the quiet streets which lead towards the Edgware-road.

" You did it very nicely, Doctor," he remarked. " Nothing could have been better. It is all right."

" You have the photograph ! "

" I know where it is."

" And how did you find out ? "

" She showed me, as I told you that she would."

" I am still in the dark."

" I do not wish to make a mystery," said he laughing. " The matter was perfectly simple. You, of course, saw that everyone in the street was an accomplice. They were all engaged for the evening."

" I guessed as much."

" Then, when the row broke out, I had a little moist red paint in the palm of my hand. I rushed forward, fell down, clapped my hand to my face, and became a piteous spectacle. It is an old trick."

" That also I could fathom."

" Then they carried me in. She was bound to have me in. What else could she do ? And into her sitting-room, which was the very room which I suspected. It lay between that and her bedroom, and I was determined to see which. They laid me on a couch, I motioned for air, they were compelled to open the window, and you had your chance."

" How did that help you ? "

" It was all-important. When a woman thinks that her house is on fire, her instinct is at once to rush to the thing which she values most. It is a perfectly overpowering impulse, and I have more than once taken advantage of it. In the case of the Darlington Substitution Scandal it was of use to me, and also in the Arnsworth Castle business. A married woman grabs at her baby—an unmarried one reaches for her jewel box. Now it was clear to me that our lady of to-day had nothing in the house more precious to her than what we are in quest of. She would rush to secure it. The alarm of fire was admirably done. The smoke and shouting were enough to shake nerves of steel. She responded beautifully. The photograph is in a recess behind a sliding panel just above the right bell pull. She was there in an instant, and I caught a glimpse of it as she half drew it out. When I cried out that it was a false alarm, she replaced it, glanced at the rocket, rushed from the room, and I have not seen her since. I rose, and, making my excuses, escaped from the house. I hesitated whether to attempt to secure the photograph at once ; but the coachman had come in, and, as he was watching me narrowly, it seemed safer to wait. A little over-precipitance may ruin all."

" And now ? " I asked.

" Our quest is practically finished. I shall call with the King to-morrow, and with you, if you care to come with us. We will be shown into the sitting-room to wait for the lady, but it is probable that when she comes she may find neither us nor the photograph. It might be a satisfaction to

His Majesty to regain it with his own hands."

"And when will you call?"

"At eight in the morning. She will not be up, so that we shall have a clear field. Besides, we must be prompt, for this marriage may mean a complete change in her life and habits. I must wire to the King without delay."

We had reached Baker-street, and had stopped at the door. He was searching his pockets for the key, when someone passing said:—

"Good-night, Mister Sherlock Holmes."

There were several people on the pavement at the time, but the greeting appeared to come from a slim youth in an ulster who had hurried by.

"I've heard that voice before," said Holmes, staring down the dimly lit street. "Now, I wonder who the deuce that could have been."

III.

I slept at Baker-street that night, and we were engaged upon our toast and coffee in the morning when the King of Bohemia rushed into the room.

"You have really got it!" he cried, grasping Sherlock Holmes by either shoulder, and looking eagerly into his face.

"Not yet."

"But you have hopes?"

"I have hopes."

"Then, come. I am all impatience to be gone."

"We must have a cab."

"No, my brougham is waiting."

"Then that will simplify matters." We descended, and started off once more for Briony Lodge.

"GOOD-NIGHT, MR. SHERLOCK HOLMES."

"Irene Adler is married," remarked Holmes.

"Married! When?"

"Yesterday."

"But to whom?"

"To an English lawyer named Norton."

"But she could not love him?"

"I am in hopes that she does."

"And why in hopes?"

"Because it would spare your Majesty all fear of future annoyance. If the lady loves her husband, she does not love your Majesty. If she does not love your Majesty, there is no reason why she should interfere with your Majesty's plan."

"It is true. And yet—! Well! I wish she had been of my own station! What a queen she would have made!" He relapsed into a moody silence which was not broken, until we drew up in Serpentine-avenue.

The door of Briony Lodge was open, and an elderly woman stood upon the steps. She watched us with a sardonic eye as we stepped from the brougham.

"Mr. Sherlock Holmes, I believe?" said she.

"I am Mr. Holmes," answered my companion, looking at her with a questioning and rather startled gaze.

"Indeed! My mistress told me that you were likely to call. She left this morning with her husband, by the 5.15 train from Charing-cross, for the Continent."

"What!" Sherlock Holmes staggered back, white with chagrin and surprise. "Do you mean that she has left England?"

"Never to return."

"And the papers?" asked the King, hoarsely. "All is lost."

"We shall see." He pushed past the servant, and rushed into the drawing-room, followed by the King and myself. The furniture was scattered about in every direction, with dismantled shelves, and open drawers, as if the lady had hurriedly ransacked them before her flight. Holmes rushed at the bell-pull, tore back a small sliding shutter, and, plunging in his hand, pulled out a photograph and a letter. The photograph was of Irene Adler herself in evening dress, the letter was superscribed to "Sherlock Holmes, Esq. To be left till called for." My friend tore it open, and we all three read it together. It was dated at midnight of the preceding night, and ran in this way:—

"MY DEAR MR. SHERLOCK HOLMES,— You really did it very well. You took me in completely. Until after the alarm of fire, I had not a suspicion. But then, when I found how I had betrayed myself, I began to think. I had been warned against you months ago. I had been told that, if the King employed an agent, it would certainly be you. And your address had been given me. Yet, with all this, you made me reveal what you wanted to know. Even after I became suspicious, I found it hard to think evil of such a dear, kind old clergyman. But, you know, I have been trained as an actress myself. Male costume is nothing new to me. I often take advantage of the freedom which it gives. I sent John, the coachman, to watch you, ran upstairs, got into my walking clothes, as I call them, and came down just as you departed.

"Well, I followed you to your door, and so made sure that I was really an object of interest to the celebrated Mr. Sherlock Holmes. Then I, rather imprudently, wished you good night, and started for the Temple to see my husband.

"We both thought the best resource was flight, when pursued by so formidable an antagonist; so you will find the nest empty when you call to-morrow. As to the photograph, your client may rest in peace. I love and am loved by a better man than he. The King may do what he will without hindrance from one whom he has cruelly wronged. I keep it only to safeguard myself, and to preserve a weapon which will always secure me from any steps which he might take in the future. I leave a photograph which he might care to possess; and I remain, dear Mr. Sherlock Holmes, very truly yours,

"IRENE NORTON, *née* ADLER."

"What a woman—oh, what a woman!" cried the King of Bohemia, when we had all three read this epistle. "Did I not tell you how quick and resolute she was? Would she not have made an admirable queen? Is it not a pity that she was not on my level?"

"From what I have seen of the lady, she seems, indeed, to be on a very different level to your Majesty," said Holmes, coldly. "I am sorry that I have not been able to

"THIS PHOTOGRAPH!"

bring your Majesty's business to a more successful conclusion."

"On the contrary, my dear sir," cried the King. "Nothing could be more successful. I know that her word is inviolate. The photograph is now as safe as if it were in the fire."

"I am glad to hear your Majesty say so."

"I am immensely indebted to you. Pray tell me in what way I can reward you. This ring——." He slipped an emerald snake ring from his finger, and held it out upon the palm of his hand.

"Your Majesty has something which I should value even more highly," said Holmes.

"You have but to name it."

"This photograph!"

The King stared at him in amazement.

"Irene's photograph!" he cried. "Certainly, if you wish it."

"I thank your Majesty. Then there is no more to be done in the matter. I have the honour to wish you a very good morning." He bowed, and, turning away without observing the hand which the King had stretched out to him, he set off in my company for his chambers.

And that was how a great scandal threatened to affect the kingdom of Bohemia, and how the best plans of Mr. Sherlock Holmes were beaten by a woman's wit. He used to make merry over the cleverness of women, but I have not heard him do it of late. And when he speaks of Irene Adler, or when he refers to her photograph, it is always under the honourable title of *the* woman.

Adventures of Sherlock Holmes.

ADVENTURE II.—THE RED-HEADED LEAGUE.

By A. Conan Doyle.

I HAD called upon my friend, Mr. Sherlock Holmes, one day in the autumn of last year, and found him in deep conversation with a very stout, florid-faced, elderly gentleman, with fiery red hair. With an apology for my intrusion, I was about to withdraw, when Holmes pulled me abruptly into the room, and closed the door behind me.

"You could not possibly have come at a better time, my dear Watson," he said cordially.

"I was afraid that you were engaged."

"So I am. Very much so."

"Then I can wait in the next room."

"Not at all. This gentleman, Mr. Wilson, has been my partner and helper in many of my most successful cases, and I have no doubt that he will be of the utmost use to me in yours also."

The stout gentleman half rose from his chair, and gave a bob of greeting, with a quick little questioning glance from his small, fat-encircled eyes.

"Try the settee," said Holmes, relapsing into his armchair, and putting his finger-tips together, as was his custom when in judicial moods. "I know, my dear Watson, that you share my love of all that is bizarre and outside the conventions and humdrum routine of every-day life. You have shown your relish for it by the enthusiasm which has prompted you to chronicle, and, if you will excuse my saying so, somewhat to embellish so many of my own little adventures."

"Your cases have indeed been of the greatest interest to me," I observed.

"You will remember that I remarked the other day, just before we went into the very simple problem presented by Miss Mary Sutherland, that for strange effects and extraordinary combinations we must go to life itself, which is always far more daring than any effort of the imagination."

"A proposition which I took the liberty of doubting."

"You did, Doctor, but none the less you must come round to my view, for otherwise I shall keep on piling fact upon fact on you, until your reason breaks down under them and acknowledges me to be right. Now, Mr. Jabez Wilson here has been good enough to call upon me this morning, and to begin a narrative which promises to be one of the most singular which I have listened to for some time. You have heard me remark that the strangest and most unique things are very often connected not with

MR. JABEZ WILSON.

the larger but with the smaller crimes, and occasionally, indeed, where there is room for doubt whether any positive crime has been committed. As far as I have heard, it is impossible for me to say whether the present case is an instance of crime or not, but the course of events is certainly among the most singular that I have ever listened to. Perhaps, Mr. Wilson, you would have the great kindness to recommence your narrative. I ask you, not merely because my friend Dr. Watson has not heard the opening part, but also because the peculiar nature of the story makes me anxious to have every possible detail from your lips. As a rule, when I have heard some slight indication of the course of events I am able to guide myself by the thousands of other similar cases which occur to my memory. In the present instance I am forced to admit that the facts are, to the best of my belief, unique."

The portly client puffed out his chest with an appearance of some little pride, and pulled a dirty and wrinkled newspaper from the inside pocket of his greatcoat. As he glanced down the advertisement column, with his head thrust forward, and the paper flattened out upon his knee, I took a good look at the man, and endeavoured after the fashion of my companion to read the indications which might be presented by his dress or appearance.

I did not gain very much, however, by my inspection. Our visitor bore every mark of being an average commonplace British tradesman, obese, pompous, and slow. He wore rather baggy grey shepherd's check trousers, a not overclean black frockcoat, unbuttoned in the front, and a drab waistcoat with a heavy brassy Albert chain, and a square pierced bit of metal dangling down as an ornament. A frayed top hat and a faded brown overcoat with a wrinkled velvet collar lay upon a chair beside him. Altogether, look as I would, there was nothing remarkable about the man save his blazing red head, and the expression of extreme chagrin and discontent upon his features.

Sherlock Holmes' quick eye took in my occupation, and he shook his head with a smile as he noticed my questioning glances. "Beyond the obvious facts that he has at some time done manual labour, that he takes snuff, that he is a Freemason, that he has been in China, and that he has done a considerable amount of writing lately, I can deduce nothing else."

Mr. Jabez Wilson started up in his chair, with his forefinger upon the paper, but his eyes upon my companion.

"How, in the name of good fortune, did you know all that, Mr. Holmes?" he asked. "How did you know, for example, that I did manual labour. It's as true as gospel, for I began as a ship's carpenter."

"Your hands, my dear sir. Your right hand is quite a size larger than your left. You have worked with it, and the muscles are more developed."

"Well, the snuff, then, and the Freemasonry?"

"I won't insult your intelligence by telling you how I read that, especially as, rather against the strict rules of your order, you use an arc and compass breastpin."

"Ah, of course, I forgot that. But the writing?"

"What else can be indicated by that right cuff so very shiney for five inches, and the left one with the smooth patch near the elbow where you rest it upon the desk."

"Well, but China?"

"The fish which you have tattooed immediately above your right wrist could only have been done in China. I have made a small study of tattoo marks, and have even contributed to the literature of the subject. That trick of staining the fishes' scales of a delicate pink is quite peculiar to China. When, in addition, I see a Chinese coin hanging from your watch-chain, the matter becomes even more simple."

Mr. Jabez Wilson laughed heavily. "Well, I never!" said he. "I thought at first that you had done something clever, but I see that there was nothing in it after all."

"I begin to think, Watson," said Holmes, "that I make a mistake in explaining. 'Omne ignotum pro magnifico,' you know, and my poor little reputation, such as it is, will suffer shipwreck if I am so candid. Can you not find the advertisement, Mr. Wilson?"

"Yes, I have got it now," he answered, with his thick, red finger planted half-way down the column. "Here it is. This is what began it all. You just read it for yourself, sir."

I took the paper from him, and read as follows:—

"To THE RED-HEADED LEAGUE. On account of the bequest of the late Ezekiah Hopkins, of Lebanon, Penn., U.S.A., there is now another vacancy open which entitles a member of the League to a salary of four pounds a week for purely nominal services.

All red-headed men who are sound in body and mind, and above the age of twenty-one years, are eligible. Apply in person on Monday, at eleven o'clock, to Duncan Ross, at the offices of the League, 7, Pope's-court, Fleet-street."

"What on earth does this mean?" I ejaculated, after I had twice read over the extraordinary announcement.

"WHAT ON EARTH DOES THIS MEAN?"

Holmes chuckled, and wriggled in his chair, as was his habit when in high spirits. "It is a little off the beaten track, isn't it?" said he. "And now, Mr. Wilson, off you go at scratch, and tell us all about yourself, your household, and the effect which this advertisement had upon your fortunes. You will first make a note, Doctor, of the paper and the date."

"It is *The Morning Chronicle*, of April 27, 1890. Just two months ago."

"Very good. Now, Mr. Wilson?"

"Well, it is just as I have been telling you, Mr. Sherlock Holmes," said Jabez Wilson, mopping his forehead, "I have a small pawnbroker's business at Coburg-square, near the City. It's not a very large affair, and of late years it has not done more than just give me a living. I used to be able to keep two assistants, but now I only keep one; and I would have a job to pay him, but that he is willing to come

for half wages, so as to learn the business."

"What is the name of this obliging youth?" asked Sherlock Holmes.

"His name is Vincent Spaulding, and he's not such a youth either. It's hard to say his age. I should not wish a smarter assistant, Mr. Holmes; and I know very well that he could better himself, and earn twice what I am able to give him. But after all, if he is satisfied, why should I put ideas in his head?"

"Why, indeed? You seem most fortunate in having an *employé* who comes under the full market price. It is not a common experience among employers in this age. I don't know that your assistant is not as remarkable as your advertisement."

"Oh, he has his faults, too," said Mr. Wilson. "Never was such a fellow for photography. Snapping away with a camera when he ought to be improving his mind, and then diving down into the cellar like a rabbit into its hole to develop his pictures. That is his main fault; but, on the whole, he's a good worker. There's no vice in him."

"He is still with you, I presume?"

"Yes, sir. He and a girl of fourteen, who does a bit of simple cooking, and keeps the place clean—that's all I have in the house, for I am a widower, and never had any family. We live very quietly, sir, the three of us; and we keep a roof over our heads, and pay our debts, if we do nothing more.

"The first thing that put us out was that advertisement. Spaulding, he came down into the office just this day eight weeks with this very paper in his hand, and he says :—

"'I wish to the Lord, Mr. Wilson, that I was a red-headed man.'

"'Why that?' I asks.

"'Why,' says he, 'here's another vacancy on the League of the Red-headed

Men. It's worth quite a little fortune to any man who gets it, and I understand that there are more vacancies than there are men, so that the trustees are at their wits' end what to do with the money. If my hair would only change colour, here's a nice little crib all ready for me to step into.'

"'Why, what is it, then?' I asked. You see, Mr. Holmes, I am a very stay-at-home man, and, as my business came to me instead of my having to go to it, I was often weeks on end without putting my foot over the door-mat. In that way I didn't know much of what was going on outside, and I was always glad of a bit of news.

"'Have you never heard of the League of the Red-headed Men?' he asked, with his eyes open.

"'Never.'

"'Why, I wonder at that, for you are eligible yourself for one of the vacancies.'

"'And what are they worth?' I asked.

"'Oh, merely a couple of hundred a year, but the work is slight, and it need not interfere very much with one's other occupations.'

"Well, you can easily think that that made me prick up my ears, for the business has not been over good for some years, and an extra couple of hundred would have been very handy.

"'Tell me all about it,' said I.

"'Well,' said he, showing me the advertisement, 'you can see for yourself that the League has a vacancy, and there is the address where you should apply for particulars. As far as I can make out, the League was founded by an American millionaire, Ezekiah Hopkins, who was very peculiar in his ways. He was himself red-headed, and he had a great sympathy for all red-headed men; so, when he died, it was found that he had left his enormous fortune in the hands of trustees, with instructions to apply the interest to the providing of easy berths to men whose hair is of that colour. From all I hear it is splendid pay, and very little to do.'

"'But,' said I, 'there would be millions of red-headed men who would apply.'

"'Not so many as you might think,' he answered. 'You see it is really confined to Londoners, and to grown men. This American had started from London when he was young, and he wanted to do the old town a good turn. Then, again, I have heard it is no use your applying if your hair is light red, or dark red, or anything but real, bright, blazing, fiery red. Now, if you cared to apply, Mr. Wilson, you would just walk in; but perhaps it would hardly be worth your while to put yourself out of the

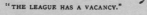

"THE LEAGUE HAS A VACANCY."

way for the sake of a few hundred pounds."

"Now, it is a fact, gentlemen, as you may see for yourselves, that my hair is of a very full and rich tint, so that it seemed to me that, if there was to be any competition in the matter, I stood as good a chance as any man that I had ever met. Vincent Spaulding seemed to know so much about it that I thought he might prove useful, so I just ordered him to put up the shutters for the day, and to come right away with me. He was very willing to have a holiday, so we shut the business up, and started off for the address that was given us in the advertisement.

" I never hope to see such a sight as that again, Mr. Holmes. From north, south, east, and west every man who had a shade of red in his hair had tramped into the City to answer the advertisement. Fleet-street was choked with red-headed folk, and Pope's-court looked like a coster's orange barrow. I should not have thought there were so many in the whole country as were brought together by that single advertisement. Every shade of colour they were—straw, lemon, orange, brick, Irish-setter, liver, clay ; but, as Spaulding said, there were not many who had the real vivid flame-coloured tint. When I saw how many were waiting, I would have given it up in despair ; but Spaulding would not hear of it. How he did it I could not imagine, but he pushed and pulled and butted until he got me through the crowd, and right up to the steps which led to the office. There was a double stream upon the stair, some going up in hope, and some coming back dejected ; but we wedged in as well as we could, and soon found ourselves in the office."

" Your experience has been a most entertaining one," remarked Holmes, as his client paused and refreshed his memory with a huge pinch of snuff. " Pray continue your very interesting statement."

" There was nothing in the office but a couple of wooden chairs and a deal table, behind which sat a small man, with a head that was even redder than mine. He said a few words to each candidate as he came up, and then he always managed to find some fault in them which would disqualify them. Getting a vacancy did not seem to be such a very easy matter after all. However, when our turn came, the little man was much more favourable to me than to any of the others, and he closed the door as we entered, so that he might have a private word with us.

" ' This is Mr. Jabez Wilson,' said my assistant, ' and he is willing to fill a vacancy in the League.'

" ' And he is admirably suited for it,' the other answered. ' He has every requirement. I cannot recall when I have seen anything so fine.' He took a step backwards, cocked his head on one side, and gazed at my hair until I felt quite bashful. Then suddenly he plunged forward, wrung my hand, and congratulated me warmly on my success.

" ' It would be injustice to hesitate,' said he. ' You will, however, I am sure, excuse me for taking an obvious precaution.' With that he seized my hair in both his hands, and tugged until I yelled with the pain. ' There is water in your eyes,' said he, as he released me. ' I perceive that all is as it should be. But we have to be careful, for we have twice been deceived by wigs and once by paint. I could tell you tales of cobbler's wax which would disgust you with human nature.' He stepped over to the window, and shouted through it at the top of his voice that the vacancy was filled. A groan of disappointment came up from below, and the folk all trooped away in different directions, until there was not a red head to be seen except my own and that of the manager.

" HE CONGRATULATED ME WARMLY.'

" ' My name,' said he, ' is Mr. Duncan Ross, and I am myself one of the pensioners upon the fund left by our noble benefactor. Are you a married man, Mr. Wilson ? Have you a family ? '

" I answered that I had not.

" His face fell immediately.

" ' Dear me ! ' he said, gravely, ' that is very serious indeed ! I am sorry to hear you say that. The fund was, of course, for the propagation and spread of the red-heads as well as for their maintenance. It is exceedingly unfortunate that you should be a bachelor.'

"My face lengthened at this, Mr. Holmes, for I thought that I was not to have the vacancy after all ; but, after thinking it over for a few minutes, he said that it would be all right.

"'In the case of another,' said he, 'the objection might be fatal, but we must stretch a point in favour of a man with such a head of hair as yours. When shall you be able to enter upon your new duties ? '

"'Well, it is a little awkward, for I have a business already,' said I.

"'Oh, never mind about that, Mr. Wilson!' said Vincent Spaulding. 'I shall be able to look after that for you.'

"'What would be the hours?' I asked.

"'Ten to two.'

"Now a pawnbroker's business is mostly done of an evening, Mr. Holmes, especially Thursday and Friday evening, which is just before pay-day ; so it would suit me very well to earn a little in the mornings. Besides, I knew that my assistant was a good man, and that he would see· to anything that turned up.

"'That would suit me very well,' said I. 'And the pay?'

"'Is four pounds a week.'

"'And the work?'

"'Is purely nominal.'

"'What do you call purely nominal?'

"'Well, you have to be in the office, or at least in the building, the whole time. If you leave, you forfeit your whole position for ever. The will is very clear upon that point. You don't comply with the conditions if you budge from the office during that time.'

"'It's only four hours a day, and I should not think of leaving,' said I.

"'No excuse will avail,' said Mr. Duncan Ross, 'neither sickness, nor business, nor anything else. There you must stay, or you lose your billet.'

"'And the work?'

"'Is to copy out the "Encyclopædia Britannica." There is the first volume of it in that press. You must find your own ink, pens, and blotting-paper, but we provide this table and chair. Will you be ready to-morrow?'

"'Certainly,' I answered.

"'Then, good-bye, Mr. Jabez Wilson, and let me congratulate you once more on the important position which you have been fortunate enough to gain.' He bowed me out of the room, and I went home with my assistant, hardly knowing what to say or do, I was so pleased at my own good fortune.

"Well, I thought over the matter all day, and by evening I was in low spirits again ; for I had quite persuaded myself that the whole affair must be some great hoax or fraud, though what its object might be I could not imagine. It seemed altogether past belief that anyone could make such a will, or that they would pay such a sum for doing anything so simple as copying out the 'Encyclopædia Britannica.' Vincent Spaulding did what he could to cheer me up, but by bedtime I had reasoned myself out of the whole thing. However, in the morning I determined to have a look at it anyhow, so I bought a penny bottle of ink, and with a quill pen, and seven sheets of foolscap paper, I started off for Pope's-court.

"Well, to my surprise and delight everything was as right as possible. The table was set out ready for me, and Mr. Duncan Ross was there to see that I got fairly to work. He started me off upon the letter A, and then he left me ; but he would drop in from time to time to see that all was right with me. At two o'clock he bade me good-day, complimented me upon the amount that I had written, and locked the door of the office after me.

"This went on day after day, Mr. Holmes, and on Saturday the manager came in and planked down four golden sovereigns for my week's work. It was the same next week, and the same the week after. Every morning I was there at ten, and every afternoon I left at two. By degrees Mr. Duncan Ross took to coming in only once of a morning, and then, after a time, he did not come in at all. Still, of course, I never dared to leave the room for an instant, for I was not sure when he might come, and the billet was such a good one, and suited me so well, that I would not risk the loss of it.

"Eight weeks passed away like this, and I had written about Abbots, and Archery, and Armour, and Architecture, and Attica, and hoped with diligence that I might get on to the Bs before very long. It cost me something in foolscap, and I had pretty nearly filled a shelf with my writings. And then suddenly the whole business came to an end."

" To an end ? "

" Yes, sir. And no later than this morning. I went to my work as usual at ten o'clock, but the door was shut and locked, with a little square of cardboard hammered on to the middle of the panel with a tack. Here it is, and you can read for yourself."

He held up a piece of white cardboard, about the size of a sheet of notepaper. It read in this fashion :—

" THE RED-HEADED LEAGUE
IS
DISSOLVED.
Oct. 9, 1890."

Sherlock Holmes and I surveyed this curt announcement and the rueful face behind it, until the comical side of the affair so completely over-topped every other consideration that we both burst out into a roar of laughter.

" THE DOOR WAS SHUT AND LOCKED."

" I cannot see that there is anything very funny," cried our client, flushing up to the roots of his flaming head. " If you can do nothing better than laugh at me, I can go elsewhere."

" No, no," cried Holmes, shoving him back into the chair from which he had half risen. " I really wouldn't miss your case for the world. It is most refreshingly unusual. But there is, if you will excuse my saying so, something just a little funny about it. Pray what steps did you take when you found the card upon the door ? "

" I was staggered, sir. I did not know what to do. Then I called at the offices round, but none of them seemed to know anything about it. Finally, I went to the landlord, who is an accountant living on the ground floor, and I asked him if he could tell me what had become of the Red-headed League. He said that he had never heard of any such body. Then I asked him who Mr. Duncan Ross was. He answered that the name was new to him."

" ' Well,' said I, ' the gentleman at No. 4.'

" ' What, the red-headed man ? '

" ' Yes.'

" ' Oh,' said he, ' his name was William Morris. He was a solicitor, and was using my room as a temporary convenience until his new premises were ready. He moved out yesterday.'

" ' Where could I find him ? '

" ' Oh, at his new offices. He did tell me the address. Yes, 17, King Edward-street, near St. Paul's.' "

" I started off, Mr. Holmes, but when I got to that address it was a manufactory of artificial knee-caps, and no one in it had ever heard of either Mr. William Morris, or Mr. Duncan Ross."

" And what did you do then ? " asked Holmes.

" I went home to Saxe-Coburg-square, and I took the advice of my assistant. But he could not help me in any way. He could only say that if I waited I should hear by post. But that was not quite good enough, Mr. Holmes. I did not wish to lose such a place without a struggle, so, as I had heard that you were good enough to give advice to poor folk who were in need of it, I came right away to you."

" And you did very wisely," said Holmes. " Your case is an exceedingly remarkable one, and I shall be happy to look into it. From what you have told me I think that it is possible that graver issues hang from it than might at first sight appear."

"Grave enough ! " said Mr. Jabez Wilson. "Why, I have lost four pound a week."

"As far as you are personally concerned," remarked Holmes, " I do not see that you have any grievance against this extraordinary league. On the contrary, you are, as I understand, richer by some thirty pounds, to say nothing of the minute knowledge which you have gained on every subject which comes under the letter A. You have lost nothing by them."

"No, sir. But I want to find out about them, and who they are, and what their object was in playing this prank—if it was a prank—upon me. It was a pretty expensive joke for them, for it cost them two and thirty pounds."

"We shall endeavour to clear up these points for you. And, first, one or two questions, Mr. Wilson. This assistant of yours who first called your attention to the advertisement—how long had he been with you ? "

"About a month then."

"How did he come ? "

"In answer to an advertisement."

"Was he the only applicant ? "

"No, I had a dozen."

"Why did you pick him ? "

"Because he was handy, and would come cheap."

"At half wages, in fact."

"Yes."

"What is he like, this Vincent Spaulding ? "

"Small, stout-built, very quick in his ways, no hair on his face, though he's not short of thirty. Has a white splash of acid upon his forehead."

Holmes sat up in his chair in considerable excitement. "I thought as much," said he. "Have you ever observed that his ears are pierced for earrings ? "

"Yes, sir. He told me that a gipsy had done it for him when he was a lad."

"Hum ! " said Holmes, sinking back in deep thought. "He is still with you ? "

"Oh yes, sir ; I have only just left him."

"And has your business been attended to in your absence ? "

"Nothing to complain of, sir. There's never very much to do of a morning."

"That will do, Mr. Wilson. I shall be happy to give you an opinion upon the subject in the course of a day or two. To-day is Saturday, and I hope that by Monday we may come to a conclusion."

"Well, Watson," said Holmes, when our visitor had left us, "what do you make of it all ? "

"I make nothing of it," I answered, frankly. "It is a most mysterious business.'

"As a rule," said Holmes, "the more bizarre a thing is the less mysterious it proves to be. It is your commonplace, featureless crimes which are really puzzling, just as a commonplace face is the most difficult to identify. But I must be prompt over this matter."

"What are you going to do then ? " I asked.

"To smoke," he answered. "It is quite a three pipe problem, and I beg that you won't speak to me for fifty minutes." He curled himself up in his chair, with his thin knees drawn up to his hawk-like nose, and there he sat with his eyes closed and his black clay pipe thrusting out like the bill of some strange bird. I had come to the conclusion that he had dropped asleep, and indeed was nodding myself, when he suddenly sprang out of his chair with the gesture of a man who has made up his mind, and put his pipe down upon the mantelpiece.

"Sarasate plays at the St. James's Hall this afternoon," he remarked. "What do you think, Watson? Could your patients spare you for a few hours ? "

"I have nothing to do

"HE CURLED HIMSELF UP IN HIS CHAIR."

to-day. My practice is never very absorbing."

"Then, put on your hat, and come. I am going through the City first, and we can have some lunch on the way. I observe that there is a good deal of German music on the programme, which is rather more to my taste than Italian or French. It is introspective, and I want to introspect. Come along!"

We travelled by the Underground as far as Aldersgate; and a short walk took us to Saxe-Coburg-square, the scene of the singular story which we had listened to in the morning. It was a pokey, little, shabby-genteel place, where four lines of dingy two-storied brick houses looked out into a small railed-in enclosure, where a lawn of weedy grass, and a few clumps of faded laurel bushes made a hard fight against a smoke-laden and uncongenial atmosphere. Three gilt balls and a brown board with "JABEZ WILSON" in white letters, upon a corner house, announced the place where our red-headed client carried on his business. Sherlock Holmes stopped in front of it with his head on one side, and looked it all over, with his eyes shining brightly between puckered lids. Then he walked slowly up the street, and then down again to the corner, still looking keenly at the houses. Finally he returned to the pawnbroker's, and, having thumped vigorously upon the pavement with his stick two or three times, he went up to the door and knocked. It was instantly opened by a bright-looking, clean-shaven young fellow, who asked him to step in.

"THE DOOR WAS INSTANTLY OPENED."

"Thank you," said Holmes, "I only wished to ask you how you would go from here to the Strand."

"Third right, fourth left," answered the assistant promptly, closing the door.

"Smart fellow, that," observed Holmes as we walked away. "He is, in my judgment, the fourth smartest man in London, and for daring I am not sure that he has not a claim to be third. I have known something of him before."

"Evidently," said I, "Mr. Wilson's assistant counts for a good deal in this mystery of the Red-headed League. I am sure that you inquired your way merely in order that you might see him."

"Not him."

"What then?"

"The knees of his trousers."

"And what did you see?"

"What I expected to see."

"Why did you beat the pavement?"

"My dear Doctor, this is a time for observation, not for talk. We are spies in an enemy's country. We know something of Saxe-Coburg-square. Let us now explore the parts which lie behind it."

The road in which we found ourselves as we turned round the corner from the retired Saxe-Coburg-square presented as great a contrast to it as the front of a picture does to the back. It was one of the main arteries which convey the traffic of the City to the north and west. The roadway was blocked with the immense stream of commerce flowing in a double tide inwards and outwards, while the footpaths were black with the hurrying swarm of pedestrians. It was difficult to realise as we looked at the line of fine shops and stately business premises that they really abutted on the other side upon the faded and stagnant square which we had just quitted.

"Let me see," said Holmes, standing at the corner, and glancing along the line, "I should like just to remember the order of the houses here. It is a hobby of mine to have an exact knowledge of London. There is Mortimer's, the tobacconist, the little newspaper shop, the Coburg branch of the City and Suburban Bank, the Vegetarian Restaurant, and McFarlane's carriage-building depôt. That carries us right on to the other block. And now, Doctor, we've done our work, so it's time we had some play. A sandwich, and a cup of coffee, and then off to violin-land, where all is sweetness, and delicacy, and harmony, and there are no red-headed clients to vex us with their conundrums."

My friend was an enthusiastic musician, being himself not only a very capable performer, but a composer of no ordinary merit. All the afternoon he sat in the stalls wrapped in the most perfect happiness, gently waving his long thin fingers in time to the music, while his gently smiling face and his languid dreamy eyes were as unlike those of Holmes the sleuth-hound; Holmes the relentless, keen-witted, ready-handed criminal agent, as it was possible to conceive. In his singular character the dual nature alternately asserted itself, and his extreme exactness and astuteness represented, as I have often thought, the reaction against the poetic and contemplative mood which occasionally predominated in him. The swing of his nature took him from extreme languor to devouring energy; and, as I knew well, he was never so truly formidable as when, for days on end, he had been lounging in his armchair amid his improvisations and his black-letter editions. Then it was that the lust of the chase would

"ALL AFTERNOON HE SAT IN THE STALLS."

suddenly come upon him, and that his brilliant reasoning power would rise to the level of intuition, until those who were unacquainted with his methods would look askance at him as on a man whose knowledge was not that of other mortals. When I saw him that afternoon so enwrapped in the music at St. James's Hall I felt that an evil time might be coming upon those whom he had set himself to hunt down.

"You want to go home, no doubt, Doctor," he remarked, as we emerged.

"Yes, it would be as well."

"And I have some business to do which will take some hours. This business at Coburg-square is serious."

"Why serious?"

"A considerable crime is in contemplation. I have every reason to believe that we shall be in time to stop it. But to-day being Saturday rather complicates matters. I shall want your help to-night."

"At what time?"

"Ten will be early enough."

"I shall be at Baker-street at ten."

"Very well. And, I say, Doctor! there may be some little danger, so kindly put your army revolver in your pocket." He waved his hand, turned on his heel, and disappeared in an instant among the crowd.

I trust that I am not more dense than my neighbours, but I was always oppressed with a sense of my own stupidity in my dealings with Sherlock Holmes. Here I had heard what he had heard, I had seen what he had seen, and yet from his words it was evident that he saw clearly not only what had happened, but what was about to happen, while to me the whole business was still confused and grotesque. As I drove home to my house in Kensington I thought over it all, from the extraordinary story of the red-headed copier of the "Encyclopædia" down to the visit to Saxe-Coburg-square, and the ominous words with which he had parted from me. What was this nocturnal expedition, and why should I go armed? Where were we going, and what were we to do? I had the hint from Holmes that this smooth-faced pawnbroker's assistant was a formidable man—a man who might play a deep game. I tried to puzzle it out, but gave it up in despair, and set the matter aside until night should bring an explanation.

It was a quarter past nine when I started from home and made my way across the Park, and so through Oxford-street to Baker-street. Two hansoms were standing at the door, and, as I entered the passage, I heard the sound of voices from above. On entering his room, I found Holmes in animated conversation with two men, one of whom I recognised as Peter Jones, the official police agent; while the other was a long, thin, sad-faced man, with a very shiny hat and oppressively respectable frock-coat.

"Ha! our party is complete," said Holmes, buttoning up his pea-jacket, and taking his heavy hunting crop from the rack. "Watson, I think you know Mr. Jones, of Scotland-yard? Let me introduce you to Mr. Merryweather, who is to be our companion in to-night's adventure."

"We're hunting in couples again, Doctor, you see," said Jones, in his consequential way. "Our friend here is a wonderful man for starting a chase. All he wants is an old dog to help him to do the running down."

"I hope a wild goose may not prove to be the end of our chase," observed Mr. Merryweather, gloomily.

"You may place considerable confidence in Mr. Holmes, sir," said the police agent, loftily. "He has his own little methods, which are, if he won't mind my saying so, just a little too theoretical and fantastic, but he has the makings of a detective in him. It is not too much to say that once or twice, as in that business of the Sholto murder and the Agra treasure, he has been more nearly correct than the official force."

"Oh, if you say so, Mr. Jones, it is all right!" said the stranger, with deference. "Still, I confess that I miss my rubber. It is the first Saturday night for seven-and-twenty years that I have not had my rubber."

"I think you will find," said Sherlock Holmes, "that you will play for a higher stake to-night than you have ever done yet, and that the play will be more exciting. For you, Mr. Merryweather, the stake will be some thirty thousand pounds; and for you, Jones, it will be the man upon whom you wish to lay your hands."

"John Clay, the murderer, thief, smasher and forger. He's a young man, Mr. Merryweather, but he is at the head of his profession, and I would rather have my bracelets on him than on any criminal in London. He's a remarkable man, is young John Clay. His grandfather was a Royal Duke, and he himself has been to Eton and Oxford. His brain is as cunning as his fingers, and though we meet signs of him at every turn, we never know where to find the man himself. He'll crack a crib in Scotland one week, and be raising money to build an orphanage in Cornwall the next. I've been on his track for years, and have never set eyes on him yet."

"I hope that I may have the pleasure of introducing you to-night. I've had one or two little turns also with Mr. John Clay, and I agree with you that he is at the head of his profession. It is past ten, however, and quite time that we started. If you two will take the first hansom, Watson and I will follow in the second."

Sherlock Holmes was not very communicative during the long drive, and lay back in the cab humming the tunes which he had heard in the afternoon. We rattled through an endless labyrinth of gas-lit streets until we emerged into Farringdon-street.

"We are close there now," my friend remarked. "This fellow Merryweather is a bank director and personally interested in the matter. I thought it as well to have Jones with us also. He is not a bad fellow, though an absolute imbecile in his profession. He has one positive virtue. He is as brave as a bulldog, and as tenacious as a lobster if he gets his claws upon anyone. Here we are, and they are waiting for us."

We had reached the same crowded thoroughfare in which we had found ourselves in the morning. Our cabs were dismissed, and, following the guidance of Mr. Merryweather, we passed down a narrow passage, and through a side door, which he opened for us. Within there was a small corridor, which ended in a very massive iron gate. This also was opened, and led down a flight of winding stone steps, which terminated at another formidable gate. Mr. Merryweather stopped to light a lantern, and then conducted us down a dark, earth-smelling passage, and so, after opening a third door, into a huge vault or cellar, which was piled all round with crates and massive boxes.

"You are not very vulnerable from above," Holmes remarked, as he held up the lantern, and gazed about him.

"Nor from below," said Mr. Merryweather, striking his stick upon the flags which lined the floor. "Why, dear me, it sounds quite hollow!" he remarked, looking up in surprise.

"I must really ask you to be a little more quiet," said Holmes, severely. "You have already imperilled the whole success of our expedition. Might I beg that you would have the goodness to sit down upon one of those boxes, and not to interfere?"

The solemn Mr.

"MR. MERRYWEATHER STOPPED TO LIGHT A LANTERN."

Merryweather perched himself upon a crate, with a very injured expression upon his face, while Holmes fell upon his knees upon the floor, and, with the lantern and a magnifying lens, began to examine minutely the cracks between the stones. A few seconds sufficed to satisfy him, for he sprang to his feet again, and put his glass in his pocket.

"We have at least an hour before us," he remarked, "for they can hardly take any steps until the good pawnbroker is safely in bed. Then they will not lose a minute, for the sooner they do their work the longer time they will have for their escape. We are at present, Doctor—as no doubt you have divined—in the cellar of the City branch of one of the principal London banks. Mr. Merryweather is the chairman of directors, and he will explain to you that there are reasons why the more daring criminals of London should take a considerable interest in this cellar at present."

"It is our French gold," whispered the director. "We have had several warnings that an attempt might be made upon it."

"Your French gold?"

"Yes. We had occasion some months ago to strengthen our resources, and borrowed, for that purpose, thirty thousand napoleons from the Bank of France. It has become known that we have never had occasion to unpack the money, and that it is still lying in our cellar. The crate upon which I sit contains two thousand napoleons packed between layers of lead foil. Our reserve of bullion is much larger at present than is usually kept in a single branch office, and the directors have had misgivings upon the subject."

"Which were very well justified," observed Holmes. "And now it is time that we arranged our little plans. I expect that within an hour matters will come to a head. In the meantime, Mr. Merryweather, we must put the screen over that dark lantern."

"And sit in the dark?"

"I am afraid so. I had brought a pack of cards in my pocket, and I thought that, as we were a *partie carrée*, you might have your rubber after all. But I see that the enemy's preparations have gone so far that we cannot risk the presence of a light.

And, first of all, we must choose our positions. These are daring men, and, though we shall take them at a disadvantage they may do us some harm, unless we are careful. I shall stand behind this crate, and do you conceal yourselves behind those. Then, when I flash a light upon them, close in swiftly. If they fire, Watson, have no compunction about shooting them down."

I placed my revolver, cocked, upon the top of the wooden case behind which I crouched. Holmes shot the slide across the front of his lantern, and left us in pitch darkness—such an absolute darkness as I have never before experienced. The smell of hot metal remained to assure us that the light was still there, ready to flash out at a moment's notice. To me, with my nerves worked up to a pitch of expectancy, there was something depressing and subduing in the sudden gloom, and in the cold, dank air of the vault.

"They have but one retreat," whispered Holmes. "That is back through the house into Saxe-Coburg-square. I hope that you have done what I asked you, Jones?"

"I have an inspector and two officers waiting at the front door."

"Then we have stopped all the holes. And now we must be silent and wait."

What a time it seemed! From comparing notes afterwards it was but an hour and a quarter, yet it appeared to me that the night must have almost gone, and the dawn be breaking above us. My limbs were weary and stiff, for I feared to change my position, yet my nerves were worked up to the highest pitch of tension, and my hearing was so acute that I could not only hear the gentle breathing of my companions, but I could distinguish the deeper, heavier in-breath of the bulky Jones from the thin sighing note of the bank director. From my position I could look over the case in the direction of the floor. Suddenly my eyes caught the glint of a light.

At first it was but a lurid spark upon the stone pavement. Then it lengthened out until it became a yellow line, and then, without any warning or sound, a gash seemed to open and a hand appeared, a white, almost womanly hand, which felt about in the centre of the little area of light. For a minute or more the hand, with its writhing fingers, protruded out of the floor. Then it was withdrawn as suddenly as it appeared, and all was dark again save the single lurid spark, which marked a chink between the stones.

Its disappearance, however, was but momentary. With a rending, tearing sound, one of the broad, white stones turned over upon its side, and left a square, gaping hole, through which streamed the light of a lantern. Over the edge there peeped a clean-cut, boyish face, which looked keenly about it, and then, with a hand on either side of the aperture, drew itself shoulder high and waist high, until one knee rested upon the edge. In another instant he stood at the side of the hole, and was hauling after him a companion, lithe and small like himself, with a pale face and a shock of very red hair.

"It's all clear," he whispered. "Have you the chisel and the bags. Great Scott! Jump, Archie, jump, and I'll swing for it!"

Sherlock Holmes had sprung out and seized the intruder by the collar. The other dived down the hole, and I heard the sound of rending cloth as Jones clutched at his skirts. The light flashed upon the barrel of a revolver, but Holmes' hunting crop came down on the man's wrist, and the pistol clinked upon the stone floor.

"It's no use, John Clay," said Holmes blandly, "You have no chance at all."

"So I see," the other answered, with the utmost coolness. "I fancy that my pal is all right, though I see you have got his coat-tails."

"There are three men waiting for him at the door," said Holmes.

"Oh, indeed. You seem to have done the thing very completely. I must compliment you."

"And I you," Holmes answered. "Your red-headed idea was very new and effective."

"You'll see your pal again presently," said Jones. "He's quicker at climbing down holes than I am. Just hold out while I fix the derbies."

"I beg that you will not touch me with your filthy hands," remarked our prisoner, as the handcuffs clattered upon his wrists. "You may not be aware that I have royal blood in my veins. Have the goodness also when you address me always to say 'sir' and 'please.'"

"All right," said Jones, with a stare and a snigger. "Well, would you please, sir, march upstairs, where we can get a cab to carry your highness to the police-station."

"That is better," said John Clay, serenely. He made a sweeping bow to the three of us, and walked quietly off in the custody of the detective.

"Really, Mr. Holmes," said Mr. Merry-

"IT'S NO USE, JOHN CLAY."

the League, and the copying of the 'Encyclopædia,' must be to get this not over-bright pawnbroker out of the way for a number of hours every day. It was a curious way of managing it, but really it would be difficult to suggest a better. The method was no doubt suggested to Clay's ingenious mind by the colour of his accomplice's hair. The four pounds a week was a lure which must draw him, and what was it to them, who were playing for thousands? They put in the advertisement, one rogue has the temporary office, the other rogue incites the man to apply for it, and together they manage to secure his absence every morning in the week. From the time that I heard of the assistant having come for half wages, it was obvious to me that he had some strong motive for securing the situation."

"But how could you guess what the motive was?"

"Had there been women in the house, I should have suspected a mere vulgar intrigue. That, however, was out of the question. The man's business was a small one, and there was nothing in his house which could account for such elaborate preparations, and such an expenditure as they were at. It must then be something out of the house. What could it be? I thought of the assistant's fondness for photography, and his trick of vanishing into the cellar. The cellar! There was the end of this tangled clue. Then I made inquiries as to this mysterious assistant, and found that I had to deal with one of the coolest and most daring criminals in London. He was doing something in the cellar—something which took many hours a day for months on end. What could it be, once more? I could think of nothing save that he was running a tunnel to some other building.

"So far I had got when we went to visit the scene of action. I surprised you by beating upon the pavement with my stick. I was ascertaining whether the cellar stretched out in front or behind. It was

weather, as we followed them from the cellar, "I do not know how the bank can thank you or repay you. There is no doubt that you have detected and defeated in the most complete manner one of the most determined attempts at bank robbery that have ever come within my experience."

"I have had one or two little scores of my own to settle with Mr. John Clay," said Holmes, "I have been at some small expense over this matter, which I shall expect the bank to refund, but beyond that I am amply repaid by having had an experience which is in many ways unique, and by hearing the very remarkable narrative of the Red-headed League."

"You see, Watson," he explained, in the early hours of the morning, as we sat over a glass of whisky and soda in Baker-street, "it was perfectly obvious from the first that the only possible object of this rather fantastic business of the advertisement of not in front. Then I rang the bell, and, as I hoped, the assistant answered it. We have had some skirmishes, but we had never set eyes upon each other before. I hardly looked at his face. His knees were what I wished to see. You must yourself have remarked how worn, wrinkled, and stained they were. They spoke of those hours of burrowing. The only remaining point was what they were burrowing for. I walked round the corner, saw that the City and Suburban Bank abutted on our friend's premises, and felt that I had solved my problem. When you drove home after the concert I called upon Scotland Yard, and upon the chairman of the bank directors, with the result that you have seen."

" And how could you tell that they would make their attempt to-night ? " I asked.

"Well, when they closed their League offices that was a sign that they cared no longer about Mr. Jabez Wilson's presence, in other words, that they had completed their tunnel. But it was essential that they should use it soon as it might be discovered, or the bullion might be removed. Saturday would suit them better than any other day, as it would give them two days for their escape. For all these reasons I expected them to come to-night."

" You reasoned it out beautifully," I exclaimed in unfeigned admiration. "It is so long a chain, and yet every link rings true."

" It saved me from ennui," he answered, yawning. " Alas ! I already feel it closing in upon me. My life is spent in one long effort to escape from the commonplaces of existence. These little problems help me to do so."

" And you are a benefactor of the race," said I.

He shrugged his shoulders. " Well, perhaps, after all, it is of some little use," he remarked. " ' L'homme c'est rien— l'œuvre c'est tout,' as Gustave Flaubert wrote to Georges Sand."

Adventures of Sherlock Holmes.

ADVENTURE III.—A CASE OF IDENTITY.

By A. Conan Doyle.

"MY dear fellow," said Sherlock Holmes, as we sat on either side of the fire in his lodgings at Baker-street, "life is infinitely stranger than anything which the mind of man could invent. We would not dare to conceive the things which are really mere commonplaces of existence. If we could fly out of that window hand in hand, hover over this great city, gently remove the roofs, and peep in at the queer things which are going on, the strange coincidences, the plannings, the cross-purposes, the wonderful chains of events, working through generations, and leading to the most *outré* results, it would make all fiction with its conventionalities and foreseen conclusions most stale and unprofitable."

"And yet I am not convinced of it," I answered. "The cases which come to light in the papers are, as a rule, bald enough, and vulgar enough. We have in our police reports realism pushed to its extreme limits, and yet the result is, it must be confessed, neither fascinating nor artistic."

"A certain selection and discretion must be used in producing a realistic effect," remarked Holmes. "This is wanting in the police report, where more stress is laid perhaps upon the platitudes of the magistrate than upon the details, which to an observer contain the vital essence of the whole matter. Depend upon it there is nothing so unnatural as the commonplace."

I smiled and shook my head. "I can quite understand your thinking so," I said. "Of course, in your position of unofficial adviser and helper to everybody who is absolutely puzzled, throughout three continents, you are brought in contact with all that is strange and bizarre. But here"—I picked up the morning paper from the ground—"let us put it to a practical test. Here is the first heading upon which I come. 'A husband's cruelty to his wife.' There is half a column of print, but I know without reading it that it is all perfectly familiar to me. There is, of course, the other woman, the drink, the push, the blow, the bruise, the sympathetic sister or landlady. The crudest of writers could invent nothing more crude."

"Indeed, your example is an unfortunate one for your argument," said Holmes, taking the paper, and glancing his eye down it. "This is the Dundas separation case, and, as it happens, I was engaged in clearing up some small points in connection with it. The husband was a teetotaler, there was no other woman, and the conduct complained of was that he had drifted into the habit of winding up every meal by taking out his false teeth and hurling them at his wife, which you will allow is not an action likely to occur to the imagination of the average story-teller. Take a pinch of snuff, doctor, and acknowledge that I have scored over you in your example."

He held out his snuffbox of old gold, with a great amethyst in the centre of the lid. Its splendour was in such contrast to his homely ways and simple life that I could not help commenting upon it.

"Ah," said he, "I forgot that I had not seen you for some weeks. It is a little souvenir from the King of Bohemia in return for my assistance in the case of the Irene Adler papers."

"And the ring?" I asked, glancing at a remarkable brilliant which sparked upon his finger.

"It was from the reigning family of Holland, though the matter in which I served them was of such delicacy that I cannot confide it even to you, who have been good enough to chronicle one or two of my little problems."

"And have you any on hand just now?" I asked with interest.

"Some ten or twelve, but none which present any feature of interest. They are important, you understand, without being interesting. Indeed, I have found that it is usually in unimportant matters that there is a field for the observation, and for the quick analysis of cause and effect which gives the charm to an investigation. The larger crimes are apt to be the simpler, for the bigger the crime, the more obvious, as a rule, is the motive. In these cases, save for one rather intricate matter which has been referred to me from Marseilles, there is nothing which presents any features of interest. It is possible, however, that I may have something better before very many minutes are over, for this is one of my clients, or I am much mistaken."

He had risen from his chair, and was standing between the parted blinds, gazing down into the dull, neutral-tinted London street. Looking over his shoulder I saw that on the pavement opposite there stood a large woman with a heavy fur boa round her neck, and a large curling red feather in a broad-brimmed hat which was tilted in a coquettish Duchess-of-Devonshire fashion over her ear. From under this great panoply she peeped up in a nervous, hesitating fashion at our windows, while her body oscillated backwards and forwards, and her fingers fidgetted with her glove buttons. Suddenly, with a plunge, as of the swimmer who leaves the bank, she hurried across the road, and we heard the sharp clang of the bell.

"I have seen those symptoms before," said Holmes, throwing his cigarette into the fire. "Oscillation upon the pavement always means an *affaire de cœur*. She would like advice, but is not sure that the matter is not too delicate for communication. And yet even here we may discriminate. When a woman has been seriously wronged by a man she no longer oscillates, and the usual symptom is a broken bell wire. Here we may take it that there is a love matter, but that the maiden is not so much angry as perplexed, or grieved. But here she comes in person to resolve our doubts."

As he spoke there was a tap at the door, and the boy in buttons entered to announce Miss Mary Sutherland, while the lady herself loomed behind his small black figure like a full-sailed merchant-

man behind a tiny pilot boat. Sherlock Holmes welcomed her with the easy courtesy for which he was remarkable, and having closed the door, and bowed her into an armchair, he looked her over in the minute, and yet abstracted fashion which was peculiar to him.

"Do you not find," he said, "that with your short sight it is a little trying to do so much typewriting?"

"I did at first," she answered, "but now I know where the letters are without looking." Then, suddenly realising the full purport of his words, she gave a violent start, and looked up with fear and astonishment upon her broad, good-humoured face. "You've heard about me, Mr. Holmes," she cried, "else how could you know all that?"

"Never mind," said Holmes, laughing, "It is my business to know things. Perhaps I have trained myself to see what others overlook. If not, why should you come to consult me?"

"SHERLOCK HOLMES WELCOMED HER."

"I came to you, sir, because I heard of you from Mrs. Etherege, whose husband you found so easy when the police and everyone had given him up for dead. Oh, Mr. Holmes, I wish you would do as much for me. I'm not rich, but still I have a hundred a year in my own right, besides the little that I make by the machine, and I would give it all to know what has become of Mr. Hosmer Angel."

"Why did you come away to consult me in such a hurry?" asked Sherlock Holmes, with his finger tips together, and his eyes to the ceiling.

Again a startled look came over the somewhat vacuous face of Miss Mary Sutherland. "Yes, I did bang out of the house," she said, "for it made me angry to see the easy way in which Mr. Windibank —that is, my father—took it all. He would not go to the police, and he would not go to you, and so at last, as he would do nothing, and kept on saying that there was no harm done, it made me mad, and I just on with my things and came right away to you."

"Your father," said Holmes, "your stepfather, surely, since the name is different."

"Yes, my stepfather. I call him father, though it sounds funny, too, for he is only five years and two months older than myself."

"And your mother is alive?"

"Oh yes, mother is alive and well. I wasn't best pleased, Mr. Holmes, when she married again so soon after father's death, and a man who was nearly fifteen years younger than herself. Father was a plumber in the Tottenham Court-road, and he left a tidy business behind him, which mother carried on with Mr. Hardy, the foreman, but when Mr. Windibank came he made her sell the business, for he was very superior, being a traveller in wines. They got four thousand seven hundred for the goodwill and interest, which wasn't near as much as father could have got if he had been alive."

I had expected to see Sherlock Holmes impatient under this rambling and inconsequential narrative, but, on the contrary, he had listened with the greatest concentration of attention.

"Your own little income," he asked, "does it come out of the business?"

"Oh no, sir. It is quite separate, and was left me by my Uncle Ned in Auckland. It is in New Zealand Stock, paying 4½ per cent. Two thousand five hundred pounds was the amount, but I can only touch the interest."

"You interest me extremely," said Holmes. "And since you draw so large a sum as a hundred a year, with what you earn into the bargain, you no doubt travel a little, and indulge yourself in every way. I believe that a single lady can get on very nicely upon an income of about sixty pounds."

"I could do with much less than that, Mr. Holmes, but you understand that as long as I live at home I don't wish to be a burden to them, and so they have the use of the money just while I am staying with them. Of course that is only just for the time. Mr. Windibank draws my interest every quarter, and pays it over to mother, and I find that I can do pretty well with what I earn at typewriting. It brings me twopence a sheet, and I can often do from fifteen to twenty sheets in a day."

"You have made your position very clear to me," said Holmes. "This is my friend, Dr. Watson, before whom you can speak as freely as before myself. Kindly tell us now all about your connection with Mr. Hosmer Angel."

A flush stole over Miss Sutherland's face, and she picked nervously at the fringe of her jacket. "I met him first at the gasfitters' ball," she said. "They used to send father tickets when he was alive, and then afterwards they remembered us, and sent them to mother. Mr. Windibank did not wish us to go. He never did wish us to go anywhere. He would get quite mad if I wanted so much as to join a Sunday-school treat. But this time I was set on going, and I would go, for what right had he to prevent? He said the folk were not fit for us to know, when all father's friends were to be there. And he said that I had nothing fit to wear, when I had my purple plush that I had never so much as taken out of the drawer. At last when nothing else would do he went off to France upon the business of the firm, but we went, mother and I, with Mr. Hardy, who used to be our foreman, and it was there I met Mr. Hosmer Angel."

"I suppose," said Holmes, "that when Mr. Windibank came back from France, he was very annoyed at your having gone to the ball."

"Oh, well, he was very good about it. He laughed, I remember, and shrugged his shoulders, and said there was no use denying anything to a woman, for she would have her way."

"I see. Then at the gasfitters' ball you met, as I understand, a gentleman called Mr. Hosmer Angel."

"Yes, sir. I met him that night, and he

"AT THE GASFITTERS' BALL."

called next day to ask if we had got home all safe, and after that we met him—that is to say, Mr. Holmes, I met him twice for walks, but after that father came back again, and Mr. Hosmer Angel could not come to the house any more."

"No?"

"Well, you know, father didn't like anything of the sort He wouldn't have any visitors if he could help it, and he used to say that a woman should be happy in her own family circle. But then, as I used to say to mother, a woman wants her own circle to begin with, and I had not got mine yet."

"But how about Mr. Hosmer Angel? Did he make no attempt to see you?"

"Well, father was going off to France again in a week, and Hosmer wrote and

said that it would be safer and better not to see each other until he had gone. We could write in the meantime, and he used to write every day. I took the letters in in the morning, so there was no need for father to know."

"Were you engaged to the gentleman at this time?"

"Oh yes, Mr. Holmes. We were engaged after the first walk that we took. Hosmer —Mr. Angel—was a cashier in an office in Leadenhall-street—and—"

"What office?"

"That's the worst of it, Mr. Holmes, I don't know."

"Where did he live, then?"

"He slept on the premises."

"And you don't know his address?"

"No—except that it was Leadenhall-street."

"Where did you address your letters, then?"

"To the Leadenhall-street Post Office, to be left till called for. He said that if they were sent to the office he would be chaffed by all the other clerks about having letters from a lady, so I offered to typewrite them, like he did his, but he wouldn't have that, for he said that when I wrote them they seemed to come from me, but when they were typewritten he always felt that the machine had come between us. That will just show you how fond he was of me, Mr. Holmes, and the little things that he would think of."

"It was most suggestive," said Holmes, "It has long been an axiom of mine that the little things are infinitely the most important. Can you remember any other little things about Mr. Hosmer Angel?"

"He was a very shy man, Mr. Holmes. He would rather walk with me in the evening than in the daylight, for he said that he hated to be conspicuous. Very retiring and gentlemanly he was. Even his voice was gentle. He'd had the quinsy and swollen glands when he was young, he told me, and it had left him with a weak throat, and a hesitating, whispering fashion or speech. He was always well-dressed, very neat and plain, but his eyes were weak, just as mine are, and he wore tinted glasses against the glare."

"Well, and what happened when Mr. Windibank, your stepfather, returned to France?"

"Mr. Hosmer Angel came to the house again, and proposed that we should marry before father came back. He was in dreadful earnest, and made me swear, with my hands on the Testament, that whatever happened I would always be true to him. Mother said he was quite right to make me swear, and that it was a sign of his passion. Mother was all in his favour from the first, and was even fonder of him than I was. Then, when they talked of marrying within the week, I began to ask about father; but they both said never to mind about father, but just to tell him afterwards, and mother said she would make it all right with him. I didn't quite like that, Mr. Holmes. It seemed funny that I should ask his leave, as he was only a few years older than me; but I didn't want to do anything on the sly, so I wrote to father at Bordeaux, where the Company has its French offices, but the letter came back to me on the very morning of the wedding."

" It missed him, then ? "

" Yes, sir, for he had started to England just before it arrived."

put us both into it, and stepped himself into a four-wheeler, which happened to be the only other cab in the street. We got to the church first, and when the four-wheeler drove up we waited for him to step out, but he never did, and when the cabman got down from the box and looked, there was no one there ! The cabman said that he could not imagine what had become of him, for he had seen him get in with his own eyes. That was last Friday, Mr. Holmes, and I have never seen or heard anything since then to throw any light upon what became of him."

" It seems to me that you have been very shamefully treated," said Holmes.

" Oh no, sir ! He was too good and kind to leave me so. Why, all the morning he was saying to me that, whatever happened, I was to be true ; and that even if something quite unforeseen occurred to separate us, I was always to remember that I was pledged to him, and that he would claim his pledge

" THERE WAS NO ONE THERE."

" Ha ! that was unfortunate. Your wedding was arranged, then, for the Friday. Was it to be in church ? "

" Yes, sir, but very quietly. It was to be at St. Saviour's, near King's-cross, and we were to have breakfast afterwards at the St. Pancras Hotel. Hosmer came for us in a hansom, but as there were two of us, he

sooner or later. It seemed strange talk for a wedding morning, but what has happened since gives a meaning to it."

" Most certainly it does. Your own opinion is, then, that some unforeseen catastrophe has occurred to him ? "

" Yes, sir. I believe that he foresaw some danger, or else he would not have talked so. And then I think that what he foresaw happened."

"But you have no notion as to what it could have been?"

"None."

"One more question. How did your mother take the matter?"

"She was angry, and said that I was never to speak of the matter again."

"And your father? Did you tell him?"

"Yes, and he seemed to think, with me, that something had happened, and that I should hear of Hosmer again. As he said, what interest could anyone have in bringing me to the doors of the church, and then leaving me? Now, if he had borrowed my money, or if he had married me and got my money settled on him, there might be some reason; but Hosmer was very independent about money, and never would look at a shilling of mine. And yet what could have happened? And why could he not write? Oh, it drives me half mad to think of! and I can't sleep a wink at night." She pulled a little handkerchief out of her muff, and began to sob heavily into it.

"I shall glance into the case for you," said Holmes, rising, "and I have no doubt that we shall reach some definite result. Let the weight of the matter rest upon me now, and do not let your mind dwell upon it further. Above all, try to let Mr. Hosmer Angel vanish from your memory, as he has done from your life."

"Then you don't think I'll see him again?"

"I fear not."

"Then what has happened to him?"

"You will leave that question in my hands. I should like an accurate description of him, and any letters of his which you can spare."

"I advertised for him in last Saturday's *Chronicle*," said she. "Here is the slip, and here are four letters from him."

"Thank you. And your address?"

"31, Lyon-place, Camberwell."

"Mr. Angel's address you never had, I understand. Where is your father's place of business?"

"He travels for Westhouse & Marbank, the great claret importers of Fenchurch-street."

"Thank you. You have made your statement very clearly. You will leave the papers here, and remember the advice which I have given you. Let the whole incident be a sealed book, and do not allow it to affect your life."

"You are very kind, Mr. Holmes, but I cannot do that. I shall be true to Hosmer. He shall find me ready when he comes back."

For all the preposterous hat and the vacuous face, there was something noble in the simple faith of our visitor which compelled our respect. She laid her little bundle of papers upon the

"SHE LAID A LITTLE BUNDLE UPON THE TABLE."

table, and went her way, with a promise to come again whenever she might be summoned.

Sherlock Holmes sat silent for a few minutes with his finger tips still pressed together, his legs stretched out in front of him, and his gaze directed upwards to the ceiling. Then he took down from the rack the old and oily clay pipe, which was to him as a counsellor, and, having lit it, he leaned back in his chair, with the thick blue cloudwreaths spinning up from him, and a look of infinite languor in his face.

"Quite an interesting study, that maiden,"

he observed. "I found her more interesting than her little problem, which, by the
way, is rather a trite one. You will find
parallel cases, if you consult my index, in
Andover in '77, and there was something
of the sort at the Hague last year. Old as
is the idea, however, there were one or two
details which were new to me. But the
maiden herself was most instructive."

"You appeared to read a good deal upon
her which was quite invisible to me," I
remarked.

"Not invisible, but unnoticed, Watson.
You did not know where to look, and so
you missed all that was important. I can
never bring you to realise the importance
of sleeves, the suggestiveness of thumb-
nails, or the great issues that may hang
from a bootlace. Now what did you
gather from that woman's appearance ?
Describe it."

"Well, she had a slate-coloured, broad-
brimmed straw hat, with a feather of a
brickish red. Her jacket was black, with
black beads sewn upon it, and a fringe of
little black jet ornaments. Her dress was
brown, rather darker than coffee colour,
with a little purple plush at the neck and
sleeves. Her gloves were greyish, and
were worn through at the right forefinger.
Her boots I didn't observe. She had small
round, hanging gold earrings, and a general
air of being fairly well to do, in a vulgar,
comfortable, easy-going way."

Sherlock Holmes clapped his hands
softly together and chuckled.

"'Pon my word, Watson, you are coming
along wonderfully. You have really done
very well indeed. It is true that you have
missed everything of importance, but you
have hit upon the method, and you have a
quick eye for colour. Never trust to
general impressions, my boy, but concentrate yourself upon details. My first glance
is always at a woman's sleeve. In a man it
is perhaps better first to take the knee of
the trouser. As you observe, this woman
had plush upon her sleeves, which is a most
useful material for showing traces. The
double line a little above the wrist, where
the typewritist presses against the table,
was beautifully defined. The sewing-
machine, of the hand type, leaves a similar
mark, but only on the left arm, and on the
side of it farthest from the thumb, instead
of being right across the broadest part, as
this was. I then glanced at her face, and
observing the dint of a pince-nez at either
side of her nose, I ventured a remark upon
short sight and typewriting, which seemed
to surprise her.

"It surprised me."

"But, surely, it was very obvious. I
was then much surprised and interested on
glancing down to observe that, though the
boots which she was wearing were not unlike each other, they were really odd ones,
the one having a slightly decorated toe-cap,
and the other a plain one. One was buttoned only in the two lower buttons out of
five, and the other at the first, third, and
fifth. Now, when you see that a young
lady, otherwise neatly dressed, has come
away from home with odd boots, half-but-
toned, it is no great deduction to say that
she came away in a hurry."

"And what else ? " I asked, keenly interested, as I always was, by my friend's
incisive reasoning.

"I noted, in passing, that she had written
a note before leaving home, but after being
fully dressed. You observed that her right
glove was torn at the forefinger, but you
did not apparently see that both glove and
finger were stained with violet ink. She
had written in a hurry, and dipped her pen
too deep. It must have been this morning,
or the mark would not remain clear upon
the finger. All this is amusing, though
rather elementary, but I must go back to
business, Watson. Would you mind reading me the advertised description of Mr.
Hosmer Angel ? "

I held the little printed slip to the light.
"Missing," it said, " on the morning of the
14th, a gentleman named Hosmer Angel.
About 5 ft. 7 in. in height ; strongly built,
sallow complexion, black hair, a little bald in
the centre, bushy, black side whiskers and
moustache ; tinted glasses, slight infirmity
of speech. Was dressed, when last seen,
in black frock coat faced with silk, black
waistcoat, gold Albert chain, and grey
Harris tweed trousers, with brown gaiters
over elastic-sided boots. Known to have
been employed in an office in Leadenhall-
street. Anybody bringing," &c., &c.

"That will do," said Holmes. "As to
the letters," he continued, glancing over
them, " they are very commonplace. Absolutely no clue in them to Mr. Angel, save
that he quotes Balzac once. There is one
remarkable point, however, which will no
doubt strike you."

"They are typewritten," I remarked.

"Not only that, but the signature is type-
written. Look at the neat little 'Hosmer
Angel' at the bottom. There is a date, you

see, but no superscription except Leaden-hall-street, which is rather vague. The point about the signature is very suggestive —in fact, we may call it conclusive."

" Of what ? "

" My dear fellow, is it possible you do not see how strongly it bears upon the case."

" I cannot say that I do, unless it were that he wished to be able to deny his signature if an action for breach of promise were in-stituted."

" No, that was not the point. However, I shall write two letters which should settle the matter. One is to a firm in the City, the other is to the young lady's stepfather, Mr. Windibank, asking him whether he could meet us here at six o'clock to-morrow evening. It is just as well that we should do business with the male relatives. And now, doctor, we can do nothing until the answers to those letters come, so we may put our little problem upon the shelf for the in-terim."

I had had so many reasons to believe in my friend's subtle powers of reasoning, and extraordinary energy in action, that I felt that he must have some solid grounds for the assured and easy demeanour with which he treated the singular mystery which he had been called upon to fathom. Once only had I known him to fail, in the case of the King of Bohemia and of the Irene Adler photograph, but when I looked back to the weird business of the Sign of Four, and the extraordinary circumstances con-nected with the Study in Scarlet, I felt that it would be a strange tangle indeed which he could not unravel.

I left him then, still puffing at his black clay pipe, with the conviction that when I came again on the next evening I would find that he held in his hands all the clues which would lead up to the identity of the disappearing bridegroom of Miss Mary Sutherland.

A professional case of great gravity was engaging my own attention at the time, and the whole of next day I was busy at the bedside of the sufferer. It was not until close upon six o'clock that I found my-self free, and was able to spring into a hansom

"I FOUND SHERLOCK HOLMES HALF ASLEEP.

and drive to Baker-street, half afraid that I might be too late to assist at the *dénouement* of the little mystery. I found Sherlock Holmes alone, however, half asleep, with his long, thin form curled up in the recesses of his armchair. A formidable array of bottles and test-tubes, with the pungent cleanly smell of hydro-chloric acid, told me that he had spent his day in the chemical work which was so dear to him.

" Well, have you solved it ? " I asked as I entered.

" Yes. It was the bisulphate of baryta."

" No, no, the mystery ! " I cried.

" Oh, that ! I thought of the salt that I have been working upon. There was never any mystery in the matter, though, as I said yesterday, some of the details are or interest. The only drawback is that there is no law, I fear, that can touch the scoundrel."

"Who was he, then, and what was his object in deserting Miss Sutherland?"

The question was hardly out of my mouth, and Holmes had not yet opened his lips to reply, when we heard a heavy footfall in the passage, and a tap at the door.

"This is the girl's stepfather, Mr. James Windibank," said Holmes. "He has written to me to say that he would be here at six. Come in!"

The man who entered was a sturdy middle-sized fellow, some thirty years of age, clean shaven, and sallow skinned, with a bland, insinuating manner, and a pair of wonderfully sharp and penetrating grey eyes. He shot a questioning glance at each of us, placed his shiny top hat upon the sideboard, and, with a slight bow, sidled down into the nearest chair.

"Good evening, Mr. James Windibank," said Holmes. "I think that this type-written letter is from you, in which you made an appointment with me for six o'clock?"

"Yes, sir. I am afraid that I am a little late, but I am not quite my own master, you know. I am sorry that Miss Sutherland has troubled you about this little matter, for I think it is far better not to wash linen of the sort in public. It was quite against my wishes that she came, but she is a very excitable, impulsive girl, as you may have noticed, and she is not easily controlled when she has made up her mind on a point. Of course, I did not mind you so much, as you are not connected with the official police, but it is not pleasant to have a family misfortune like this noised abroad. Besides it is a useless expense, for how could you possibly find this Hosmer Angel?"

"On the contrary," said Holmes, quietly; "I have every reason to believe that I will succeed in discovering Mr. Hosmer Angel."

Mr. Windibank gave a violent start, and dropped his gloves. "I am delighted to hear it," he said.

"It is a curious thing," remarked Holmes, "that a typewriter has really quite as much individuality as a man's hand-writing. Unless they are quite new, no two of them write exactly alike. Some letters get more worn than others, and some wear only on one side. Now, you remark in this note of yours, Mr. Windi-bank, that in every case there is some little slurring over of the 'e,' and a slight defect in the tail of the 'r.' There are fourteen other characteristics, but those are the more obvious."

"We do all our correspondence with this machine at the office, and no doubt it is a little worn," our visitor answered, glancing keenly at Holmes with his bright little eyes.

"And now I will show you what is really a very interesting study, Mr. Windibank," Holmes continued. "I think of writing another little monograph some of these days on the typewriter and its relation to crime. It is a subject to which I have devoted some little attention. I have here four letters which purport to come from the missing man. They are all type-written. In each case, not only are the 'e's' slurred and the 'r's' tailless, but you will observe, if you care to use my magni-fying lens, that the fourteen other charac-teristics to which I have alluded are there as well."

Mr. Windibank sprang out of his chair, and picked up his hat. "I cannot waste time over this sort of fantastic talk, Mr. Holmes," he said. "If you can catch the man, catch him, and let me know when you have done it."

"Certainly," said Holmes, stepping over and turning the key in the door. "I let you know, then, that I have caught him!"

"What! where?" shouted Mr. Windi-bank, turning white to his lips, and glancing about him like a rat in a trap.

"Oh, it won't do—really it won't," said Holmes, suavely. "There is no possible getting out of it, Mr. Windibank. It is quite too transparent, and it was a very bad compliment when you said that it was impossible for me to solve so simple a question. That's right! Sit down, and let us talk it over."

Our visitor collapsed into a chair, with a ghastly face, and a glitter of moisture on his brow. "It—it's not actionable," he stammered.

"I am very much afraid that it is not. But between ourselves, Windibank, it was as cruel, and selfish, and heartless a trick in a petty way as ever came before me. Now, let me just run over the course of events, and you will contradict me, if I go wrong."

The man sat huddled up in his chair, with his head sunk upon his breast, like one who is utterly crushed. Holmes stuck his feet up on the corner of the mantel-piece, and, leaning back with his hands in

"GLANCING ABOUT HIM LIKE A RAT IN A TRAP."

his pockets, began talking, rather to himself, as it seemed, than to us.

"The man married a woman very much older than himself for her money," said he, "and he enjoyed the use of the money of the daughter as long as she lived with them. It was a considerable sum, for people in their position, and the loss of it would have made a serious difference. It was worth an effort to preserve it. The daughter was of a good, amiable disposition, but affectionate and warm-hearted in her ways, so that it was evident that with her fair personal advantages, and her little income, she would not be allowed to remain single long. Now her marriage would mean, of course, the loss of a hundred a year, so what does her stepfather do to prevent it? He takes the obvious course of keeping her at home, and forbidding her to seek the company of people of her own age. But soon he found that that would not answer for ever. She became restive, insisted upon her rights, and finally announced her positive intention of going to a certain ball. What does her

clever stepfather do then? He conceives an idea more creditable to his head than to his heart. With the connivance and assistance of his wife he disguised himself, covered those keen eyes with tinted glasses, masked the face with a moustache and a pair of bushy whiskers, sunk that clear voice into an insinuating whisper, and, doubly secure on account of the girl's short sight, he appears as Mr. Hosmer Angel, and keeps off other lovers by making love himself."

"It was only a joke at first," groaned our visitor. "We never thought that she would have been so carried away."

"Very likely not. However that may be, the young lady was very decidedly carried away, and having quite made up her mind that her stepfather was in France, the suspicion of treachery never for an instant entered her mind. She was flattered by the gentleman's attentions, and the effect was increased by the loudly expressed admiration of her mother. Then Mr. Angel began to call, for it was obvious that the matter should be pushed as far as it would go, if a real effect were to be produced. There were meetings, and an engagement, which would finally secure the girl's affections from turning towards anyone else. But the deception could not be kept up for ever. These pretended journeys to France were rather cumbrous. The thing to do was clearly to bring the business to an end in such a dramatic manner that it would leave a permanent impression upon the young lady's mind, and prevent her from looking upon any other suitor for some time to come. Hence those vows of fidelity exacted upon a Testament, and hence also the allusions to a possibility of something happening on the very morning of the wedding. James Windibank wished Miss Sutherland to be so bound to Hosmer Angel, and so uncertain as to his fate, that for ten years to come, at any rate, she would not listen to another man. As far as the church door he brought her, and then, as he could go no further, he conveniently vanished away by the old trick of stepping in at one door of a four-wheeler, and out at the other. I think that that was the chain of events, Mr. Windibank!"

Our visitor had recovered something of his assurance while Holmes had been talking, and he rose from his chair now with a cold sneer upon his pale face.

"It may be so, or it may not, Mr. Holmes," said he, "but if you are so very sharp you ought to be sharp enough to know that it is you who are breaking the law now, and not me. I have done nothing actionable from the first, but as long as you keep that door locked you lay yourself open to an action for assault and illegal constraint."

"The law cannot, as you say, touch you," said Holmes, unlocking and throwing open the door, "yet there never was a man who deserved punishment more. If the young lady has a brother or a friend, he ought to lay a whip across your shoulders. By Jove!" he continued, flushing up at the sight of the bitter sneer upon the man's face, "it is not part of my duties to my client, but here's a hunting crop handy, and I think I shall just treat myself to——" He took two swift steps to the whip, but before he could grasp it there was a wild clatter of steps upon the stairs, the heavy hall door banged, and from the window we could see Mr. James Windibank running at the top of his speed down the road.

"There's a cold-blooded scoundrel!" said Holmes, laughing, as he threw himself down into his chair once more. "That fellow will rise from crime to crime until he does something very bad, and ends on a

"HE TOOK TWO SWIFT STEPS TO THE WHIP.'

gallows. The case has, in some respects, been not entirely devoid of interest."

"I cannot now entirely see all the steps of your reasoning," I remarked.

"Well, of course it was obvious from the first that this Mr. Hosmer Angel must have some strong object for his curious conduct, and it was equally clear that the only man who really profited by the incident, as far as we could see, was the stepfather. Then the fact that the two men were never together, but that the one always appeared when the other was away, was suggestive. So were the tinted spectacles and the curious voice, which both hinted at a disguise, as did the bushy whiskers. My suspicions were all confirmed by his peculiar action in typewriting his signature, which of course inferred that his handwriting was so familiar to her that she would recognise even the smallest sample of it. You see all these isolated facts, together with many minor ones, all pointed in the same direction."

"And how did you verify them?"

"Having once spotted my man, it was easy to get corroboration. I knew the firm for which this man worked. Having taken the printed description, I eliminated every-thing from it which could be the result of a disguise—the whiskers, the glasses, the voice, and I sent it to the firm, with a request that they would inform me whether it answered to the description of any of their travellers. I had already noticed the peculiarities of the typewriter, and I wrote to the man himself at his business address, asking him if he would come here. As I expected, his reply was typewritten, and revealed the same trivial but characteristic defects. The same post brought me a letter from Westhouse & Marbank, of Fenchurch-street, to say that the description tallied in every respect with that of their employé, James Windibank. *Voila tout!*"

"And Miss Sutherland?"

"If I tell her she will not believe me. You may remember the old Persian saying, 'There is danger for him who taketh the tiger cub, and danger also for whoso snatches a delusion from a woman.' There is as much sense in Hafiz as in Horace, and as much knowledge of the world."

Adventures of Sherlock Holmes.

ADVENTURE IV.—THE BOSCOMBE VALLEY MYSTERY.

By A. Conan Doyle.

E were seated at breakfast one morning, my wife and I, when the maid brought in a telegram. It was from Sherlock Holmes, and ran in this way : "Have you a couple of days to spare ? Have just been wired for from the West of England in connection with Boscombe Valley tragedy. Shall be glad if you will come with me. Air and scenery perfect. Leave Paddington by the 11.15."

"What do you say, dear ? " said my wife, looking across at me. "Will you go ? "

"I really don't know what to say. I have a fairly long list at present."

"Oh, Anstruther would do your work for you. You have been looking a little pale lately. I think that the change would do you good, and you are always so interested in Mr. Sherlock Holmes' cases."

"I should be ungrateful if I were not, seeing what I gained through one of them," I answered. "But if I am to go I must pack at once, for I have only half an hour."

My experience of camp life in Afghanistan had at least had the effect of making me a prompt and ready traveller. My wants were few and simple, so that in less than the time stated I was in a cab with my valise, rattling away to Paddington Station. Sherlock Holmes was pacing up and down the platform, his tall, gaunt figure made even gaunter and taller by his long grey travelling cloak, and close-fitting cloth cap.

"It is really very good of you to come, Watson," said he. "It makes a considerable difference to me, having someone with me on whom I can thoroughly rely. Local aid is always either worthless or else biassed. If you will keep the two corner seats I shall get the tickets."

We had the carriage to ourselves save for an immense litter of papers which Holmes had brought with him. Among these he rummaged and read, with intervals of note-taking and of meditation, until we were past Reading. Then he suddenly rolled them all into a gigantic ball, and tossed them up on to the rack.

"Have you heard anything of the case ? " he asked.

"Not a word. I have not seen a paper for some days."

"The London press has not had very full accounts. I have just been looking through all the recent papers in order to master the particulars. It seems, from what I gather, to be one of those simple cases which are so extremely difficult."

"WE HAD THE CARRIAGE TO OURSELVES."

159

"That sounds a little paradoxical."

"But it is profoundly true. Singularity is almost invariably a clue. The more featureless and commonplace a crime is, the more difficult is it to bring it home. In this case, however, they have established a very serious case against the son of the murdered man."

"It is a murder, then ?"

"Well, it is conjectured to be so. I shall take nothing for granted until I have the opportunity of looking personally into it. I will explain the state of things to you, as far as I have been able to understand it, in a very few words.

"Boscombe Valley is a country district not very far from Ross, in Herefordshire. The largest landed proprietor in that part is a Mr. John Turner, who made his money in Australia, and returned some years ago to the old country. One of the farms which he held, that of Hatherley, was let to Mr. Charles McCarthy, who was also an ex-Australian. The men had known each other in the Colonies, so that it was not unnatural that when they came to settle down they should do so as near each other as possible. Turner was apparently the richer man, so McCarthy became his tenant, but still remained, it seems, upon terms of perfect equality, as they were frequently together. McCarthy had one son, a lad of eighteen, and Turner had an only daughter of the same age, but neither of them had wives living. They appear to have avoided the society of the neighbouring English families, and to have led retired lives, though both the McCarthys were fond of sport, and were frequently seen at the race meetings of the neighbourhood. McCarthy kept two servants—a man and a girl. Turner had a considerable household, some half-dozen at the least. That is as much as I have been able to gather about the families. Now for the facts.

"On June 3, that is, on Monday last, McCarthy left his house at Hatherley about three in the afternoon, and walked down to the Boscombe Pool, which is a small lake formed by the spreading out of the stream which runs down the Boscombe Valley. He had been out with his serving-man in the morning at Ross, and he had told the man that he must hurry, as he had an appointment of importance to keep at three. From that appointment he never came back alive.

"From Hatherley Farmhouse to the Boscombe Pool is a quarter of a mile, and two people saw him as he passed over this ground. One was an old woman, whose name is not mentioned, and the other was William Crowder, a gamekeeper in the employ of Mr. Turner. Both these witnesses depose that Mr. McCarthy was walking alone. The gamekeeper adds that within a few minutes of his seeing Mr. McCarthy pass he had seen his son, Mr. James McCarthy, going the same way with a gun under his arm. To the best of his belief, the father was actually in sight at the time, and the son was following him. He thought no more of the matter until he heard in the evening of the tragedy that had occurred.

"The two McCarthys were seen after the time when William Crowder, the gamekeeper, lost sight of them. The Boscombe Pool is thickly wooded round, with just a fringe of grass and of reeds round the edge. A girl of fourteen, Patience Moran, who is the daughter of the lodge-keeper of the Boscombe Valley Estate, was in one of the woods picking flowers. She states that while she was there she saw, at the border of the wood and close by the lake, Mr. McCarthy and his son, and that they appeared to be having a violent quarrel. She heard Mr. McCarthy the elder using very strong language to his son, and she saw the latter raise up his hand as if to strike his father. She was so frightened by their violence that she ran away, and told her mother when she reached home that she had left the two McCarthys quarrelling near Boscombe Pool, and that she was afraid that they were going to fight. She had hardly said the words when young Mr. McCarthy came running up to the lodge to say that he had found his father dead in the wood, and to ask for the help of the lodge-keeper. He was much excited, without either his gun or his hat, and his right hand and sleeve were observed to be stained with fresh blood. On following him they found the dead body stretched out upon the grass beside the Pool. The head had been beaten in by repeated blows of some heavy and blunt weapon. The injuries were such as might very well have been inflicted by the butt-end of his son's gun, which was found lying on the grass within a few paces of the body. Under these circumstances the young man was instantly arrested, and a verdict of 'Wilful Murder' having been returned at the inquest on Tuesday, he was on Wednesday brought before the magistrates at Ross, who have referred the case to the next assizes. Those are the main facts of the case as they came out before the coroner and at the police-court."

"I could hardly imagine a more damning case," I remarked. "If ever circumstantial evidence pointed to a criminal it does so here."

"Circumstantial evidence is a very tricky thing," answered Holmes, thoughtfully. "It may seem to point very straight to one thing, but if you shift your own point of view a little, you may find it pointing in an equally uncompromising manner to something entirely different. It must be confessed, however, that the case looks exceedingly grave against the young man, and it is very possible that he is indeed the culprit. There are several people in the neighbourhood, however, and among them Miss Turner, the daughter of the neighbouring landowner, who believe in his innocence, and who have retained Lestrade, whom you may recollect in connection with the Study in Scarlet, to work out the case in his interest. Lestrade, being rather puzzled, has referred the case to me, and hence it is that two middle-aged gentlemen are flying westward at fifty miles an hour, instead of quietly digesting their breakfasts at home."

"I am afraid," said I, "that the facts are so obvious that you will find little credit to be gained out of this case."

"There is nothing more deceptive than an obvious fact," he answered, laughing.

"THEY FOUND THE BODY."

"Besides, we may chance to hit upon some other obvious facts which may have been by no means obvious to Mr. Lestrade. You know me too well to think that I am boasting when I say that I shall either confirm or destroy his theory by means which he is quite incapable of employing, or even of understanding. To take the first example to hand, I very clearly perceive that in your bedroom the window is upon the right-hand side, and yet I question whether Mr. Lestrade would have noted even so self-evident a thing as that."

"How on earth——!"

"My dear fellow, I know you well. I know the military neatness which characterises you. You shave every morning, and in this season you shave by the sunlight, but since your shaving is less and less complete as we get further back on the left side, until it becomes positively slovenly as we get round the angle of the jaw, it is surely very clear that that side is less well illuminated than the other. I could not imagine a man of your habits looking at himself in an equal light, and being satisfied with such a result. I only quote this as a trivial example of observation and inference. Therein lies my *métier*, and it is just possible that it may be of some service in the investigation which lies before us. There are one or two minor points which were brought out in the inquest, and which are worth considering."

"What are they?"

"It appears that his arrest did not take place at once, but after the return to Hatherley Farm. On the inspector of constabulary informing him that he was a prisoner, he remarked that he was not surprised to hear it, and that it was no more than his deserts. This observation of his had the natural effect of removing any traces of doubt which might have remained in the minds of the coroner's jury."

"It was a confession," I ejaculated.

"No, for it was followed by a protestation of innocence."

"Coming on the top of such a damning series of events, it was at least a most suspicious remark."

"On the contrary," said Holmes, "it is the brightest rift which I can at present see in the clouds. However innocent he might be, he could not be such an absolute imbecile as not to see that the circumstances were very black against him. Had he appeared surprised at his own arrest, or feigned indignation at it, I should have looked upon it as highly suspicious, because such surprise or anger would not be natural under the circumstances, and yet might appear to be the best policy to a scheming man. His frank acceptance of the situation marks him as either an innocent man, or else as a man of considerable self-restraint and firmness. As to his remark about his deserts, it was also not unnatural if you consider that he stood beside the dead body of his father, and that there is no doubt that he had that very day so far forgotten his filial duty as to bandy words with him, and even, according to the little girl whose evidence is so important, to raise his hand as if to strike him. The self-reproach and contrition which are displayed in his remark appear to me to be the signs of a healthy mind, rather than of a guilty one."

I shook my head. "Many men have been hanged on far slighter evidence," I remarked.

"So they have. And many men have been wrongfully hanged."

"What is the young man's own account of the matter?"

"It is, I am afraid, not very encouraging to his supporters, though there are one or two points in it which are suggestive. You will find it here, and may read it for yourself."

He picked out from his bundle a copy of the local Herefordshire paper, and having turned down the sheet, he pointed out the paragraph in which the unfortunate young man had given his own statement of what had occurred. I settled myself down in the corner of the carriage, and read it very carefully. It ran in this way:—

"Mr. James McCarthy, the only son of the deceased, was then called, and gave evidence as follows:—'I had been away from home for three days at Bristol, and had only just returned upon the morning of last Monday, the 3rd. My father was absent from home at the time of my arrival, and I was informed by the maid that he had driven over to Ross with John Cobb, the groom. Shortly after my return I heard the wheels of his trap in the yard, and, looking out of my window, I saw him get out and walk rapidly out of the yard, though I was not aware in which direction he was going. I then took my gun, and strolled out in the direction of the Boscombe Pool, with the intention of visiting the rabbit warren which is upon the other side. On my way I saw William Crowder, the gamekeeper, as he has stated in his evidence; but he is mistaken in thinking that I was following my father. I had no idea that he was in front of me. When about a hundred yards from the Pool I heard a cry of "Cooee!" which was a usual signal between my father and myself. I then hurried forward, and found him standing by the Pool. He appeared to be much surprised at seeing me, and asked me rather roughly what I was doing there. A conversation ensued, which led to high words, and almost to blows, for my father was a man of a very violent temper. Seeing that his passion was becoming ungovernable, I left him, and returned towards Hatherley Farm. I had not gone more than one hundred and fifty yards, however, when I heard a hideous outcry behind me, which caused me to run back again. I found my father expiring upon the ground, with his head terribly injured. I dropped my gun, and held him in my arms, but he almost instantly expired. I knelt besides him for some minutes, and then made my way to Mr. Turner's lodge-keeper, his house being the nearest, to ask for assistance. I saw no one near my father when I returned, and I have no idea how he came by his injuries. He was not a popular man, being somewhat cold and forbidding in his manners; but he had, as far as I know, no active enemies. I know nothing further of the matter.'"

"The Coroner: Did your father make any statement to you before he died?

"I HELD HIM IN MY ARMS."

"Witness: He mumbled a few words, but I could only catch some allusion to a rat.

"The Coroner: What did you understand by that?

"Witness: It conveyed no meaning to me. I thought that he was delirious.

"The Coroner: What was the point upon which you and your father had this final quarrel?

"Witness: I should prefer not to answer.

"The Coroner: I am afraid that I must press it.

"Witness: It is really impossible for me to tell you. I can assure you that it has nothing to do with the sad tragedy which followed.

"The Coroner: That is for the Court to decide. I need not point out to you that your refusal to answer will prejudice your case considerably in any future proceedings which may arise.

"Witness: I must still refuse.

"The Coroner: I understand that the cry of 'Cooee' was a common signal between you and your father?

"Witness: It was.

"The Coroner: How was it, then, that he uttered it before he saw you, and before he even knew that you had returned from Bristol?

"Witness (with considerable confusion): I do not know.

"A Juryman: Did you see nothing which aroused your suspicions when you returned on hearing the cry, and found your father fatally injured?

"Witness: Nothing definite.

"The Coroner: What do you mean?

"Witness: I was so disturbed and excited as I rushed out into the open, that I could think of nothing except of my father. Yet I have a vague impression that as I ran forward something lay upon the ground to the left of me. It seemed to me to be something grey in colour, a coat of some sort, or a plaid perhaps. When I rose from my father I looked round for it, but it was gone.

"'Do you mean that it disappeared before you went for help?'

"'Yes, it was gone.'

"'You cannot say what it was?'

"'No, I had a feeling something was there.'

"'How far from the body?'

"'A dozen yards or so.'

"'And how far from the edge of the wood?'

"'About the same.'

"'Then if it was removed it was while you were within a dozen yards of it?'

"'Yes, but with my back towards it.'

"This concluded the examination of the witness."

"I see," said I, as I glanced down the column, "that the coroner in his concluding remarks was rather severe upon young McCarthy. He calls attention, and with reason, to the discrepancy about his father having signalled to him before seeing him, also to his refusal to give details of his conversation with his father, and his singular account of his father's dying words. They are all, as he remarks, very much against the son."

Holmes laughed softly to himself, and stretched himself out upon the cushioned seat. "Both you and the coroner have been at some pains," said he, "to single out the very strongest points in the young man's favour. Don't you see that you alternately give him credit for having too much imagination and too little? Too little, if he could not invent a cause of quarrel which would give him the sympathy of the jury; too much, if he evolved from his own inner consciousness anything so *outré* as a dying reference to a rat, and the incident of the vanishing cloth. No, sir, I shall approach this case from the point of view that what this young man says is true, and we shall see whither that hypothesis will lead us. And now here is my pocket Petrarch, and not another word shall I say of this case until we are on the scene of action. We lunch at Swindon, and I see that we shall be there in twenty minutes."

It was nearly four o'clock when we at last, after passing through the beautiful Stroud Valley, and over the broad gleaming Severn, found ourselves at the pretty little country town of Ross. A lean, ferret-like man, furtive and sly-looking, was waiting for us upon the platform. In spite of the light brown dustcoat and leather leggings which he wore in deference to his rustic surroundings, I had no difficulty in recognising Lestrade, of Scotland Yard. With him we drove to the "Hereford Arms," where a room had already been engaged for us.

"I have ordered a carriage," said Lestrade, as we sat over a cup of tea. "I knew your energetic nature, and that you would not be happy until you had been on the scene of the crime."

"It was very nice and complimentary of you," Holmes answered. "It is entirely a question of barometric pressure."

Lestrade looked startled. "I do not quite follow," he said.

"How is the glass? Twenty-nine, I see. No wind, and not a cloud in the sky. I have a caseful of cigarettes here which need smoking, and the sofa is very much superior to the usual country hotel abomination. I do not think that it is probable that I shall use the carriage to-night."

Lestrade laughed indulgently. "You have, no doubt, already formed your conclusions from the newspapers," he said. "The case is as plain as a pikestaff, and the more one

goes into it the plainer it becomes. Still, of course, one can't refuse a lady, and such a very positive one, too. She had heard of you, and would have your opinion, though I repeatedly told her that there was nothing which you could do which I had not already done. Why, bless my soul! here is her carriage at the door."

He had hardly spoken before there rushed into the room one of the most lovely young women that I have ever seen in my life. Her violet eyes shining, her lips parted, a pink flush upon her cheeks, all thought of her natural reserve lost in her overpowering excitement and concern.

"Oh, Mr. Sherlock Holmes!" she cried, glancing from one to the other of us, and finally, with a woman's quick intuition, fastening upon my companion, "I am so glad that you have come. I have driven down to tell you so. I know that James didn't do it. I know it, and I want you to start upon your work knowing it, too. Never let yourself doubt upon that point. We have know each other since we were little children, and I know his faults as no one else does; but he is too tender-hearted to hurt a fly. Such a charge is absurd to anyone who really knows him."

"I hope we may clear him, Miss Turner," said Sherlock Holmes. "You may rely upon my doing all that I can."

"But you have read the evidence. You have formed some conclusion? Do you not see some loophole, some flaw? Do you not yourself think that he is innocent?"

"I think that it is very probable."

"There now!" she cried, throwing back her head, and looking defiantly at Lestrade. "You hear! He gives me hopes."

Lestrade shrugged his shoulders. "I am afraid that my colleague has been a little quick in forming his conclusions," he said.

"But he is right. Oh! I know that he is right. James never did it. And about his quarrel with his father, I am sure that the reason why he would not speak about it to the coroner was because I was concerned in it."

"In what way?" asked Holmes.

"It is no time for me to hide anything. James and his father had many disagreements about me. Mr. McCarthy was very anxious that there should be a marriage between us. James and I have always loved each other as brother and sister, but of course he is young, and has seen very little

"LESTRADE SHRUGGED HIS SHOULDERS."

of life yet, and—and—well, he naturally did not wish to do anything like that yet. So there were quarrels, and this, I am sure, was one of them."

"And your father?" asked Holmes. "Was he in favour of such a union?"

"No, he was averse to it also. No one but Mr. McCarthy was in favour of it." A quick blush passed over her fresh young face as Holmes shot one of his keen, questioning glances at her.

"Thank you for this information," said he. "May I see your father if I call to-morrow?"

"I am afraid the doctor won't allow it."

"The doctor?"

"Yes, have you not heard? Poor father has never been strong for years back, but this has broken him down completely. He has taken to his bed, and Dr. Willows says that he is a wreck, and that his nervous system is shattered. Mr. McCarthy was the only man alive who had known dad in the old days in Victoria."

"Ha! In Victoria! That is important."

"Yes, at the mines."

"Quite so; at the gold mines, where, as I understand, Mr. Turner made his money."

"Yes, certainly."

"Thank you, Miss Turner. You have been of material assistance to me."

"You will tell me if you have any news to-morrow. No doubt you will go to the prison to see James. Oh, if you do, Mr. Holmes, do tell him that I know him to be innocent."

"I will, Miss Turner."

"I must go home now, for dad is very ill, and he misses me so if I leave him. Good-bye, and God help you in your undertaking." She hurried from the room as impulsively as she had entered, and we heard the wheels of her carriage rattle off down the street.

"I am ashamed of you, Holmes," said Lestrade with dignity, after a few minutes' silence. "Why should you raise up hopes which you are bound to disappoint? I am not over tender of heart, but I call it cruel."

"I think that I see my way to clearing James McCarthy," said Holmes. "Have you an order to see him in prison."

"Yes, but only for you and me."

"Then I shall reconsider my resolution about going out. We have still time to take a train to Hereford and see him to-night?"

"Ample."

"Then let us do so. Watson, I fear that you will find it very slow, but I shall only be away a couple of hours."

I walked down to the station with them, and then wandered through the streets of the little town, finally returning to the hotel, where I lay upon the sofa and tried to interest myself in a yellow-backed novel. The puny plot of the story was so thin, however, when compared to the deep mystery through which we were groping, and I found my attention wander so continually from the fiction to the fact, that I at last flung it across the room, and gave myself up entirely to a consideration of the events of the day. Supposing that this unhappy young man's story was absolutely true, then what hellish thing, what absolutely unforeseen and extraordinary calamity could have occurred between the time when he parted from his father, and the moment when, drawn back by his screams, he rushed into the glade? It was something terrible and deadly. What could it be? Might not the nature of the injuries reveal something to my medical instincts? I rang the bell, and called for the weekly county paper, which contained a verbatim account of the inquest. In the surgeon's deposition it was stated that the posterior third of the left parietal bone and the left half of the occi-

"I TRIED TO INTEREST MYSELF IN A YELLOW-BACKED NOVEL."

pital bone had been shattered by a heavy blow from a blunt weapon. I marked the spot upon my own head. Clearly such a blow must have been struck from behind. That was to some extent in favour of the accused, as when seen quarrelling he was face to face with his father. Still, it did not go for very much, for the older man might have turned his back before the blow fell. Still, it might be worth while to call Holmes' attention to it. Then there was the peculiar dying reference to a rat. What could that mean? It could not be delirium. A man dying from a sudden blow does not commonly become delirious. No, it was more likely to be an attempt to explain how he met his fate. But what could it indicate? I cudgelled my brains to find some possible

explanation. And then the incident of the grey cloth, seen by young McCarthy. If that were true, the murderer must have dropped some part of his dress, presumably his overcoat, in his flight, and must have had the hardihood to return and to carry it away at the instant when the son was kneeling with his back turned not a dozen paces off. What a tissue of mysteries and improbabilities the whole thing was! I did not wonder at Lestrade's opinion, and yet I had so much faith in Sherlock Holmes' insight that I could not lose hope as long as every fresh fact seemed to strengthen his conviction of young McCarthy's innocence.

It was late before Sherlock Holmes returned. He came back alone, for Lestrade was staying in lodgings in the town.

"The glass still keeps very high," he remarked, as he sat down. "It is of importance that it should not rain before we are able to go over the ground. On the other hand, a man should be at his very best and keenest for such nice work as that, and I did not wish to do it when fagged by a long journey. I have seen young McCarthy."

"And what did you learn from him?"

"Nothing."

"Could he throw no light?"

"None at all. I was inclined to think at one time that he knew who had done it, and was screening him or her, but I am convinced now that he is as puzzled as everyone else. He is not a very quick-witted youth, though comely to look at, and, I should think, sound at heart."

"I cannot admire his taste," I remarked, "if it is indeed a fact that he was averse to a marriage with so charming a young lady as this Miss Turner."

"Ah, thereby hangs a rather painful tale. This fellow is madly, insanely in love with her, but some two years ago, when he was only a lad, and before he really knew her, for she had been away five years at a boarding-school, what does the idiot do but get into the clutches of a barmaid in Bristol, and marry her at a registry office? No one knows a word of the matter, but you can imagine how maddening it must be to him to be upbraided for not doing what he would give his very eyes to do, but what he knows to be absolutely impossible. It was sheer frenzy of this sort which made him throw his hands up into the air when his father, at their last interview, was goading him on to propose to Miss Turner. On the other hand, he had no means of supporting himself, and his father, who was by all accounts a very hard man, would have thrown him over utterly had he known the truth. It was with his barmaid wife that he had spent the last three days in Bristol, and his father did not know where he was. Mark that point. It is of importance. Good has come out of evil, however, for the barmaid, finding from the papers that he is in serious trouble, and likely to be hanged, has thrown him over utterly, and has written to him to say that she has a husband already in the Bermuda Dockyard, so that there is really no tie between them. I think that that bit of news has consoled young McCarthy for all that he has suffered."

"But if he is innocent, who has done it?"

"Ah! who? I would call your attention very particularly to two points. One is that the murdered man had an appointment with someone at the Pool, and that the someone could not have been his son, for his son was away, and he did not know when he would return. The second is that the murdered man was heard to cry, 'Cooee!' before he knew that his son had returned. Those are the crucial points upon which the case depends. And now let us talk about George Meredith, if you please, and we shall leave all minor matters until to-morrow."

There was no rain, as Holmes had fore-told, and the morning broke bright and cloudless. At nine o'clock Lestrade called for us with the carriage, and we set off for Hatherley Farm and the Boscombe Pool.

"There is serious news this morning," Lestrade observed. "It is said that Mr. Turner, of the Hall, is so ill that his life is despaired of."

"An elderly man, I presume?" said Holmes.

"About sixty; but his constitution has been shattered by his life abroad, and he has been in failing health for some time. This business has had a very bad effect upon him. He was an old friend of McCarthy's, and, I may add, a great benefactor to him, for I have learned that he gave him Hatherley Farm rent free."

"Indeed! That is interesting," said Holmes.

"Oh, yes! In a hundred other ways he has helped him. Everybody about here speaks of his kindness to him."

"Really! Does it not strike you as a little singular that this McCarthy, who appears to have had little of his own, and to have been under such obligations to Turner, should still talk of marrying his son to Turner's daughter, who is, presumably, heiress to the estate, and that in such a very cocksure manner, as if it were merely a case of a proposal and all else would follow? It is the more strange, since we know that Turner himself was averse to the idea. The daughter told us as much. Do you not deduce something from that?"

"We have got to the deductions and the inferences," said Lestrade, winking at me. "I find it hard enough to tackle facts, Holmes, without flying away after theories and fancies."

"You are right," said Holmes, demurely; "you do find it very hard to tackle the facts."

"Anyhow, I have grasped one fact which you seem to find it difficult to get hold of," replied Lestrade, with some warmth.

"And that is?"

"That McCarthy, senior, met his death from McCarthy, junior, and that all theories to the contrary are the merest moonshine."

"Well, moonshine is a brighter thing than fog," said Holmes, laughing. "But I am very much mistaken if this is not Hatherley Farm upon the left."

"Yes, that is it." It was a widespread, comfortable-looking building, two-storied slate roofed, with great yellow blotches of lichen upon the grey walls. The drawn blinds and the smokeless chimneys, how-ever, gave it a stricken look, as though the weight of this horror still lay heavy upon it. We called at the door, when the maid at Holmes' request, showed us the boots which her master wore at the time of his death, and also a pair of the son's, though not the pair which he had then had. Hav-

"THE MAID SHOWED US THE BOOTS."

dead, and once he made quite a little *détour* into the meadow. Lestrade and I walked behind him, the detective indifferent and contemptuous, while I watched my friend with the interest which sprang from the conviction that every one of his actions was directed towards a definite end.

The Boscombe Pool, which is a little reed-girt sheet of water some fifty yards across, is situated at the boundary between the Hatherley Farm and the private park of the wealthy Mr. Turner. Above the woods which lined it upon the further side we could see the red jutting pinnacles which marked the site of the rich landowner's dwelling. On the Hatherley side of the Pool the woods grew very thick, and there was a narrow belt of sodden grass twenty paces across between the edge of the trees and the reeds which lined the lake. Lestrade showed us the exact spot at which the body had been found, and, indeed, so moist was the ground, that I could plainly see the traces which had been left by the fall of the stricken man. To Holmes, as I could see by his eager face and peering eyes, very many other things were to be read upon the trampled grass. He ran round, like a dog who is picking up a scent, and then turned upon my companion.

"What did you go into the Pool for?" he asked.

"I fished about with a rake. I thought there might be some weapon or other trace. But how on earth——?"

"Oh, tut, tut! I have no time! That left foot of yours with its inward twist is all over the place. A mole could trace it, and there it vanishes among the reeds. Oh, how simple it would all have been had I been here before they came like a herd of

ing measured these very carefully from seven or eight different points, Holmes desired to be led to the courtyard, from which we all followed the winding track which led to Boscombe Pool.

Sherlock Holmes was transformed when he was hot upon such a scent as this. Men who had only known the quiet thinker and logician of Baker-street would have failed to recognise him. His face flushed and darkened. His brows were drawn into two hard, black lines, while his eyes shone out from beneath them with a steely glitter. His face was bent downwards, his shoulders bowed, his lips compressed, and the veins stood out like whipcord in his long, sinewy neck. His nostrils seemed to dilate with a purely animal lust for the chase, and his mind was so absolutely concentrated upon the matter before him, that a question or remark fell unheeded upon his ears, or at the most, only provoked a quick, impatient snarl in reply. Swiftly and silently he made his way along the track which ran through the meadows, and so by way of the woods to the Boscombe Pool. It was damp, marshy ground, as is all that district, and there were marks of many feet, both upon the path, and amid the short grass which bounded it on either side. Sometimes Holmes would hurry on, sometimes stop buffalo, and wallowed all over it. Here is where the party with the lodge-keeper came, and they have covered all tracks for six or eight feet round the body. But here are and this also he carefully examined and retained. Then he followed a pathway through the wood until he came to the high road, where all traces were lost.

"FOR A LONG TIME HE REMAINED THERE."

three separate tracks of the same feet." He drew out a lens, and lay down upon his waterproof to have a better view, talking all the time rather to himself than to us. "These are young McCarthy's feet. Twice he was walking, and once he ran swiftly so that the soles are deeply marked, and the heels hardly visible. That bears out his story. He ran when he saw his father on the ground. Then here are the father's feet as he paced up and down. What is this, then? It is the butt-end of the gun as the son stood listening. And this? Ha, ha! What have we here? Tip-toes! tip-toes! Square, too, quite unusual boots! They come, they go, they come again—of course that was for the cloak. Now where did they come from?" He ran up and down, sometimes losing, sometimes finding the track until we were well within the edge of the wood, and under the shadow of a great beech, the largest tree in the neighbourhood. Holmes traced his way to the further side of this, and lay down once more upon his face with a little cry of satisfaction. For a long time he remained there, turning over the leaves and dried sticks, gathering up what seemed to me to be dust into an envelope, and examining with his lens not only the ground, but even the bark of the tree as far as he could reach. A jagged stone was lying among the moss,

"It has been a case of considerable interest," he remarked, returning to his natural manner. "I fancy that this grey house on the right must be the lodge. I think that I will go in and have a word with Moran, and perhaps write a little note. Having done that, we may drive back to our luncheon. You may walk to the cab, and I shall be with you presently."

It was about ten minutes before we regained our cab, and drove back into Ross, Holmes still carrying with him the stone which he had picked up in the wood.

"This may interest you, Lestrade," he remarked, holding it out. "The murder was done with it."

"I see no marks."

"There are none."

"How do you know, then?"

"The grass was growing under it. It had only lain there a few days. There was no sign of a place whence it had been taken. It corresponds with the injuries. There is no sign of any other weapon."

"And the murderer?"

"Is a tall man, left-handed, limps with the right leg, wears thick-soled shooting boots and a grey cloak, smokes Indian cigars, uses a cigar-holder, and carries a blunt penknife in his pocket. There are several other indications, but these may be enough to aid us in our search."

Lestrade laughed. "I am afraid that I am still a sceptic," he said. "Theories are all very well, but we have to deal with a hard-headed British jury."

"*Nous verrons*," answered Holmes, calmly. "You work your own method, and I shall work mine. I shall be busy this afternoon, and shall probably return to London by the evening train."

"And leave your case unfinished?"

"No, finished."

"But the mystery?"

"It is solved."

"Who was the criminal, then?"

"The gentleman I describe."

"But who is he?"

"Surely it would not be difficult to find out. This is not such a populous neighbourhood."

Lestrade shrugged his shoulders. "I am a practical man," he said, "and I really cannot undertake to go about the country looking for a left-handed gentleman with a game leg. I should become the laughing-stock of Scotland Yard."

"All right," said Holmes, quietly. "I have given you the chance. Here are your lodgings. Good-bye. I shall drop you a line before I leave."

Having left Lestrade at his rooms we drove to our hotel, where we found lunch upon the table. Holmes was silent and buried in thought with a pained expression upon his face, as one who finds himself in a perplexing position.

"Look here, Watson," he said, when the cloth was cleared; "just sit down in this chair and let me preach to you

"HE HAD STOOD BEHIND THAT TREE."

for a little. I don't quite know what to do, and I should value your advice. Light a cigar, and let me expound."

"Pray do so."

"Well, now, in considering this case there are two points about young McCarthy's narrative which struck us both instantly, although they impressed me in his favour and you against him. One was the fact that his father should, according to his account, cry 'Cooee!' before seeing him. The other was his singular dying reference to a rat. He mumbled several words, you understand, but that was all that caught the son's ear. Now from this double point our research must commence, and we will begin it by presuming that what the lad says is absolutely true."

"What of this 'Cooee!' then?"

"Well, obviously it could not have been meant for the son. The son, as far as he knew, was in Bristol. It was mere chance that he was within earshot. The 'Cooee!' was meant to attract the attention of whoever it was that he had the appointment with. But 'Cooee' is a distinctly Australian cry, and one which is used between Australians. There is a strong presumption that the person whom McCarthy expected to meet him at Boscombe Pool was someone who had been in Australia."

"What of the rat, then?"

Sherlock Holmes took a folded paper from his pocket and flattened it out on the table. "This is a map of the Colony of Victoria," he said. "I wired to Bristol for it last night." He put his hand over part of the map. "What do you read?" he asked.

"ARAT," I read.

"And now?" He raised his hand.

"BALLARAT."

"Quite so. That was the word the man uttered, and of which his son only caught the last two syllables. He was trying to utter the name of his murderer. So-and-so, of Ballarat."

"It is wonderful!" I exclaimed.

"It is obvious. And now, you see, I had narrowed the field down considerably. The possession of a grey garment was a third point which, granting the son's statement to be correct, was a certainty. We have come now out of mere vagueness to the definite conception of an Australian from Ballarat with a grey cloak."

"Certainly."

"And one who was at home in the district, for the Pool can only be approached by the farm or by the estate, where strangers could hardly wander."

"Quite so."

"Then comes our expedition of to-day. By an examination of the ground I gained the trifling details which I gave to that imbecile Lestrade, as to the personality of the criminal."

"But how did you gain them?"

"You know my method. It is founded upon the observance of trifles."

"His height I know that you might roughly judge from the length of his stride. His boots, too, might be told from their traces."

"Yes, they were peculiar boots."

"But his lameness?"

"The impression of his right foot was always less distinct than his left. He put less weight upon it. Why? Because he limped—he was lame."

"But his left-handedness."

"You were yourself struck by the nature of the injury as recorded by the surgeon at the inquest. The blow was struck from immediately behind, and yet was upon the left side. Now, how can that be unless it were by a left-handed man? He had stood behind that tree during the interview between the father and son. He had even smoked there. I found the ash of a cigar, which my special knowledge of tobacco ashes enabled me to pronounce as an Indian cigar. I have, as you know, devoted some attention to this, and written a little monograph on the ashes of 140 different varieties of pipe, cigar, and cigarette tobacco. Having found the ash, I then looked round and discovered the stump among the moss where he had tossed it. It was an Indian cigar, of the variety which are rolled in Rotterdam."

"And the cigar-holder?"

"I could see that the end had not been in his mouth. Therefore he used a holder. The tip had been cut off, not bitten off, but the cut was not a clean one, so I deduced a blunt penknife."

"Holmes," I said, "you have drawn a net round this man from which he cannot escape, and you have saved an innocent human life as truly as if you had cut the cord which was hanging him. I see the direction in which all this points. The culprit is——"

"Mr. John Turner," cried the hotel waiter, opening the door of our sitting-room, and ushering in a visitor.

The man who entered was a strange and impressive figure. His slow, limping step and bowed shoulders gave the appearance of decrepitude, and yet his hard, deep-lined, craggy features, and his enormous limbs showed that he was possessed of unusual

"MR. JOHN TURNER," SAID THE WAITER.

strength of body and of character. His tangled beard, grizzled hair, and outstanding, drooping eyebrows combined to give an air of dignity and power to his appearance, but his face was of an ashen white, while his lips and the corners of his nostrils were tinged with a shade of blue. It was clear to me at a glance that he was in the grip of some deadly and chronic disease.

"Pray sit down on the sofa," said Holmes, gently. "You had my note?"

"Yes, the lodge-keeper brought it up. You said that you wished to see me here to avoid scandal."

"I thought people would talk if I went to the Hall."

"And why did you wish to see me?" He looked across at my companion with despair in his weary eyes, as though his question were already answered.

"Yes," said Holmes, answering the look rather than the words. "It is so. I know all about McCarthy."

The old man sank his face in his hands. "God help me!" he cried. "But I would not have let the young man come to harm. I give you my word that I would have spoken out if it went against him at the Assizes."

"I am glad to hear you say so," said Holmes, gravely.

"I would have spoken now had it not been for my dear girl. It would break her heart—it will break her heart when she hears that I am arrested."

"It may not come to that," said Holmes. "What!"

"I am no official agent. I understand that it was your daughter who required my presence here, and I am acting in her interests. Young McCarthy must be got off, however."

"I am a dying man," said old Turner. "I have had diabetes for years. My doctor says it is a question whether I shall live a month. Yet I would rather die under my own roof than in a gaol."

Holmes rose and sat down at the table with his pen in his hand and a bundle of paper before him. "Just tell us the truth," he said. "I shall jot down the facts. You will sign it, and Watson here can witness it. Then I could produce your confession at the last extremity to save young McCarthy. I promise you that I shall not use it unless it is absolutely needed."

"It's as well," said the old man; "it's a question whether I shall live to the Assizes, so it matters little to me, but I should wish to spare Alice the shock. And now I will make the thing clear to you; it has been a long time in the acting, but will not take me long to tell.

"You didn't know this dead man, McCarthy. He was a devil incarnate. I tell you that. God keep you out of the clutches of such a man as he. His grip has been upon me these twenty years, and he has blasted my life. I'll tell you first how I came to be in his power.

"It was in the early sixties at the diggings. I was a young chap then, hot-blooded and reckless, ready to turn my hand to anything; I got among bad companions, took to drink, had no luck with my claim, took to the bush, and in a word became what you would call over here a highway robber. There were six of us, and we had a wild, free life of it, sticking up a station from time to time, or stopping the waggons on the road to the diggings. Black Jack of Ballarat was the name I went under, and our party is still remembered in the colony as the Ballarat Gang.

"One day a gold convoy came down from Ballarat to Melbourne, and we lay in wait for it and attacked it. There were six troopers and six of us, so it was a close thing, but we emptied four of their saddles at the first volley. Three of our boys were killed, however, before we got the swag. I put my pistol to the head of the waggon-driver, who was this very man McCarthy. I wish to the Lord that I had shot him then, but I spared him, though I saw his wicked little eyes fixed on my face, as though to remember every feature. We got away with the gold, became wealthy men, and made our way over to England without being suspected. There I parted from my old pals, and determined to settle down to a quiet and respectable life. I bought this estate which chanced to be in the market, and I set myself to do a little good with my money, to make up for the way in which I had earned it. I married, too, and though my wife died young, she left me my dear little Alice. Even when she was just a baby her wee hand seemed to lead me down the right path as nothing else had ever done. In a word, I turned over a new leaf, and did my best to make up for the past. All was going well when McCarthy laid his grip upon me.

"I had gone up to town about an investment, and I met him in Regent-street with hardly a coat to his back or a boot to his foot.

"'Here we are, Jack,' says he, touching me on the arm; 'we'll be as good as a family to you. There's two of us, me and my son, and you can have the keeping of us. If ycu don't—it's a fine, law-abiding country is England, and there's always a policeman within hail.'

"Well, down they came to the West country, there was no shaking them off, and there they have lived rent free on my best land ever since. There was no rest for me, no peace, no forgetfulness; turn where I would, there was his cunning, grinning face at my elbow. It grew worse as Alice grew up, for he soon saw I was more afraid of her knowing my past than of the police. Whatever he wanted he must have, and whatever it was I gave him without question, land, money, houses, until at last he asked a thing which I could not give. He asked for Alice.

"His son, you see, had grown up, and so had my girl, and as I was known to be in weak health, it seemed a fine stroke to him that his lad should step into the whole property. But there I was firm. I would not have his cursed stock mixed with mine; not that I had any dislike to the lad, but his blood was in him, and that, was enough. I stood firm. McCarthy threatened. I braved him to do his worst. We were to meet at the Pool midway between our houses to talk it over.

"When I went down there I found him talking with his son, so I smoked a cigar, and waited behind a tree until he should be alone. But as I listened to his talk all that was black and bitter in me seemed to come uppermost. He was urging his son to marry my daughter with as little regard for what she

might think as if she were a slut from off the streets. It drove me mad to think that I and all that I held most dear should be in the power of such a man as this. Could I not snap the bond? I was already a dying and a desperate man. Though clear of mind and fairly strong of limb, I knew that my own fate was sealed. But my memory and my girl! Both could be saved, if I could but silence that foul tongue. I did it, Mr. Holmes. I would do it again. Deeply as I have sinned, I have led a life of martyrdom to atone for it. But that my girl should be entangled in the same meshes which held me was more than I could suffer. I struck him down with no more compunction than if he had been some foul and venomous beast. His cry brought back his son; but I had gained the cover of the wood, though I was forced to go back to fetch the cloak which I had dropped in my flight. That is the true story, gentlemen, of all that occurred."

"Well, it is not for me to judge you," said Holmes, as the old man signed the statement which had been drawn out. "I pray that we may never be exposed to such a temptation."

"I pray not, sir. And what do you intend to do?"

"In view of your health, nothing. You are yourself aware that you will soon have to answer for your deed at a higher Court than the assizes. I will keep your confession, and, if McCarthy is condemned, I shall be forced to use it. If not, it shall never be seen by mortal eye; and your secret, whether you be alive or dead, shall be safe with us."

"Farewell! then," said the old man, solemnly. "Your own death-beds, when they come, will be the easier for the thought of the peace which

"'FAREWELL, THEN,' SAID THE OLD MAN."

you have given to mine." Tottering and shaking in all his giant frame, he stumbled slowly from the room.

"God help us !" said Holmes. after a long silence. "Why does fate play such tricks with poor helpless worms ? I never hear of such a case as this that I do not think of Baxter's words, and say, 'There, but for the grace of God, goes Sherlock Holmes.'"

James McCarthy was acquitted at the assizes, on the strength of a number of objections which had been drawn out by Holmes, and submitted to the defending counsel. Old Turner lived for seven months after our interview, but he is now dead ; and there is every prospect that the son and daughter may come to live happily together, in ignorance of the black cloud which rests upon their past.

Adventures of Sherlock Holmes.

ADVENTURE V.—THE FIVE ORANGE PIPS.

By A. Conan Doyle.

HEN I glance over my notes and records of the Sherlock Holmes cases between the years '82 and '90, I am faced by so many which present strange and interesting features, that it is no easy matter to know which to choose and which to leave. Some, however, have already gained publicity through the papers, and others have not offered a field for those peculiar qualities which my friend possessed in so high a degree, and which it is the object of these papers to illustrate. Some, too, have baffled his analytical skill, and would be, as narratives, beginnings without an ending, while others have been but partially cleared up, and have their explanations founded rather upon conjecture and surmise than on that absolute logical proof which was so dear to him. There is, however, one of these last which was so remarkable in its details and so startling in its results, that I am tempted to give some account of it, in spite of the fact that there are points in connection with it which never have been, and probably never will be, entirely cleared up.

The year '87 furnished us with a long series of cases of greater or less interest, of which I retain the records. Among my headings under this one twelve months, I find an account of the adventure of the Paradol Chamber, of the Amateur Mendicant Society, who held a luxurious club in the lower vault of a furniture warehouse, of the facts connected with the loss of the British barque *Sophy Anderson*, of the singular adventures of the Grice Patersons in the island of Uffa, and finally of the Camberwell poisoning case. In the latter, as may be remembered, Sherlock Holmes was able, by winding up the dead man's watch, to prove that it had been wound up two hours ago, and that therefore the deceased had gone to bed within that time—a deduction which was of the greatest importance in clearing up the case. All these I may sketch out at some future date, but none of them present such singular features as the strange train of circumstances which I have now taken up my pen to describe.

It was in the latter days of September, and the equinoctial gales had set in with exceptional violence. All day the wind had screamed and the rain had beaten against the windows, so that even here in the heart of great, hand-made London we were forced to raise our minds for the instant from the routine of life, and to recognise the presence of those great elemental forces which shriek at mankind through the bars of his civilisation, like untamed beasts in a cage. As evening drew in the storm grew higher and louder, and the wind cried and sobbed like a child in the chimney. Sherlock Holmes sat moodily at one side of the fireplace cross-indexing his records of crime, whilst I at the other was deep in one of Clark Russell's fine sea-stories, until the howl of the gale from without seemed to blend with the text, and the splash of the rain to lengthen out into the long swash of the sea waves. My wife was on a visit to her mother's, and for a few days I was a dweller once more in my old quarters at Baker-street.

"Why," said I, glancing up at my companion, "that was surely the bell. Who could come to-night? Some friend of yours, perhaps?"

"Except yourself I have none," he answered. "I do not encourage visitors."

"A client, then?"

"If so, it is a serious case. Nothing less would bring a man out on such a day, and at such an hour. But I take it that it is more likely to be some crony of the landlady's."

Sherlock Holmes was wrong in his conjecture, however, for there came a step in the passage, and a tapping at the door. He stretched out his long arm to turn the lamp away from himself and towards the vacant chair upon which a new-comer must sit. "Come in!" said he.

The man who entered was young, some two-and-twenty at the outside, well groomed and trimly clad, with something of refinement and delicacy in his bearing. The streaming umbrella which he held in his hand, and his long shining waterproof told of the fierce weather through which he had come. He looked about him anxiously in the glare of the lamp, and I could see that his face was pale and his eyes heavy, like those of a man who is weighed down with some great anxiety.

"I owe you an apology," he said, raising his golden *pince-nez* to his eyes. "I trust that I am not intruding. I fear that I have brought some traces of the storm and the rain into your snug chamber."

"Give me your coat and umbrella," said Holmes. "They may rest here on the hook, and will be dry presently. You have come up from the south-west, I see."

"Yes, from Horsham."

"That clay and chalk mixture which I see upon your toe-caps is quite distinctive."

"I have come for advice."

"That is easily got."

"And help."

"That is not always so easy."

"I have heard of you, Mr. Holmes. I heard from Major Prendergast how you saved him in the Tankerville Club Scandal."

"Ah, of course. He was wrongfully accused of cheating at cards."

"He said that you could solve anything."

"He said too much."

"That you are never beaten."

"I have been beaten four times—three times by men, and once by a woman."

"But what is that compared with the number of your successes?"

"It is true that I have been generally successful."

"Then you may be so with me."

"I beg that you will draw your chair up to the fire, and favour me with some details as to your case."

"It is no ordinary one."

"None of those which come to me are I am the last court of appeal."

"HE LOOKED ABOUT HIM ANXIOUSLY."

"And yet I question, sir, whether, in all your experience, you have ever listened to a more mysterious and inexplicable chain of events than those which have happened in my own family."

"You fill me with interest," said Holmes. "Pray give us the essential facts from the commencement, and I can afterwards question you as to those details which seem to me to be most important."

The young man pulled his chair up, and pushed his wet feet out towards the blaze.

"My name," said he, "is John Openshaw, but my own affairs have, as far as I can understand it, little to do with this awful business. It is a hereditary matter, so in order to give you an idea of the facts, I must go back to the commencement of the affair.

"You must know that my grandfather had two sons—my uncle Elias and my father Joseph. My father had a small factory at Coventry, which he enlarged at the time of the invention of bicycling. He was the patentee of the Openshaw unbreakable tire, and his business met with such success that he was able to sell it, and to retire upon a handsome competence.

"My uncle Elias emigrated to America when he was a young man, and became a planter in Florida, where he was reported to have done very well. At the time of the war he fought in Jackson's army, and afterwards under Hood, where he rose to be a colonel. When Lee laid down his arms my uncle returned to his plantation, where he remained for three or four years. About 1869 or 1870 he came back to Europe, and took a small estate in Sussex, near Horsham. He had made a very considerable fortune in the States, and his reason for leaving them was his aversion to the negroes, and his dislike of the Republican policy in extending the franchise to them. He was a singular man, fierce and quick-tempered, very foul-mouthed when he was angry, and of a most retiring disposition. During all the years that he lived at Horsham I doubt if ever he set foot in the town. He had a garden and two or three fields round his house, and there he would take his exercise, though very often for weeks on end he would never leave his room. He drank a great deal of brandy, and smoked very heavily, but he would see no society, and did not want any friends, not even his own brother.

"He didn't mind me, in fact he took a fancy to me, for at the time when he saw me first I was a youngster of twelve or so. That would be in the year 1878, after he had been eight or nine years in England. He begged my father to let me live with him, and he was very kind to me in his way. When he was sober he used to be fond of playing backgammon and draughts with me, and he would make me his representative both with the servants and with the tradespeople, so that by the time that I was sixteen I was quite master of the house. I kept all the keys, and could go where I liked and do what I liked, so long as I did not disturb him in his privacy. There was one singular exception, however, for he had a single room, a lumber room up among the attics, which was invariably locked, and which he would never permit either me or anyone else to enter. With a boy's curiosity I have peeped through the keyhole, but I was never able to see more than such a collection of old trunks and bundles as would be expected in such a room.

"One day—it was in March, 1883—a letter with a foreign stamp lay upon the table in front of the Colonel's plate. It was not a common thing for him to receive letters, for his bills were all paid in ready money, and he had no friends of any sort. 'From India!' said he, as he took it up, ' Pondicherry postmark! What can this be?' Opening it hurriedly, out there jumped five little dried orange pips, which pattered down upon his plate. I began to laugh at this, but the laugh was struck from my lips at the sight of his face. His lip had fallen, his eyes were protruding, his skin the colour of putty, and he glared at the envelope which he still held in his trembling hand. 'K. K. K.' he shrieked, and then, ' My God, my God, my sins have overtaken me.'

"'What is it, uncle?' I cried.

"' Death,' said he, and rising from the table he retired to his room, leaving me palpitating with horror. I took up the envelope, and saw scrawled in red ink upon the inner flap, just above the gum, the letter K three times repeated. There was nothing else save the five dried pips. What could be the reason of his overpowering terror? I left the breakfast table, and as I ascended the stair I met him coming down with an old rusty key, which must have belonged to the attic, in one hand, and a small brass box, like a cash box, in the other.

"' They may do what they like, but I'll checkmate them still,' said he, with an oath. ' Tell Mary that I shall want a fire in my room to-day, and send down to Fordham, the Horsham lawyer.'

"I did as he ordered, and when the lawyer arrived I was asked to step up to the room. The fire was burning brightly, and in the grate there was a mass of black, fluffy ashes, as of burned paper, while the brass box stood open and empty beside it. As I glanced at the box I noticed, with a start, that upon the lid were printed the treble K which I had read in the morning upon the envelope.

"' I wish you, John,' said my uncle, ' to witness my will. I leave my estate, with all its advantages and all its disadvantages to my brother, your father, whence it will, no doubt, descend to you. If you can enjoy it in peace, well and good! If you find you cannot, take my advice, my boy, and leave it to your deadliest enemy. I am sorry to give you such a two-edged thing, but I can't say what turn things are going to take. Kindly sign the paper where Mr. Fordham shows you.'

"I signed the paper as directed, and the lawyer took it away with him. The singular incident made, as you may think, the deepest impression upon me, and I pondered over it, and turned it every way in my mind without being able to make anything of it. Yet I could not shake off the vague feeling of dread which it left behind it, though the sensation grew less keen as the weeks passed, and nothing happened to disturb the usual routine of our lives. I could see a change in my uncle, however. He drank more than ever, and he was less inclined for any sort of society. Most of his time he would spend in his room, with the door locked upon the inside, but sometimes he would emerge in a sort of drunken frenzy, and would burst out of the house and tear about the garden with a revolver in his hand, screaming out that he was afraid of no man, and that he was not to be cooped up, like a sheep in a pen, by man or devil. When these hot fits were over, however, he would rush tumultuously in at the door, and lock and bar it behind him, like a man who can brazen it out no longer against the terror which lies at the roots of his soul. At such times I have seen his face, even on a cold day, glisten with moisture as though it were new raised from a basin.

" Well, to come to an end of the matter, Mr. Holmes, and not to abuse your patience, there came a night when he made one of those drunken sallies from which he never came back. We found him, when we went to search for him, face downwards in a little green-scummed pool, which lay at the foot of the garden. There was no sign of any violence, and the water was but two feet deep, so that the jury, having regard to his known eccentricity, brought in a verdict of suicide. But I, who knew how he winced from the very thought of death, had much ado to persuade myself that he had gone out of his way to meet it. The matter passed, however, and my father entered into possession of the estate, and of some fourteen thousand

property, he, at my request, made a careful examination of the attic, which had been always locked up. We found the brass box there, although its contents had been destroyed. On the inside of the cover was a paper label, with the initials K. K. K. repeated upon it, and ' Letters, memoranda, receipts, and a register ' written beneath. These, we presume, indicated the nature of the papers which had been destroyed by Colonel Openshaw. For the rest, there was nothing of much importance in the attic, save a great many scattered papers and notebooks bearing upon my uncle's life in America. Some of them were of the war

د۲

"WE FOUND HIM FACE DOWNWARDS IN A LITTLE GREEN SCUMMED POOL."

pounds, which lay to his credit at the bank."

" One moment," Holmes interposed. " Your statement is, I foresee, one of the most remarkable to which I have ever listened. Let me have the date of the reception by your uncle of the letter, and the date of his supposed suicide."

" The latter arrived on March the tenth, 1883. His death was seven weeks later, upon the night of the second of May."

" Thank you. Pray proceed."

" When my father took over the Horsham

time, and showed that he had done his duty well, and had borne the repute of being a brave soldier. Others were of a date during the reconstruction of the Southern States, and were mostly concerned with politics, for he had evidently taken a strong part in opposing the carpet bag politicians who had been sent down from the North.

" Well, it was the beginning of '84 when my father came to live at Horsham, and all went as well as possible with us until the January of '85. On the fourth day after the New Year I heard my father give a sharp cry of surprise as we sat together at the breakfast table. There he was, sitting with a newly-opened envelope in one hand and five dried orange-pips in the out-stretched palm of the other one. He had always laughed at what he called my cock-and-a-bull story about the Colonel, but he looked very scared and puzzled now that the same thing had come upon himself.

"'Why, what on earth does this mean, John?' he stammered.

"My heart had turned to lead. 'It is K. K. K.' said I.

"He looked inside the envelope. 'So it is,' he cried. 'Here are the very letters. But what is this written above them?'

"'Put the papers on the sun-dial,' I read, peeping over his shoulder.

"'What papers? What sun-dial?' he asked.

"'The sun-dial in the garden. There is no other,' said I; 'but the papers must be those that are de-stroyed.'

"'Pooh!' said he, gripping hard at his courage. 'We are in a civilised land here, and we can't have tomfoolery of this kind. Where does the thing come from?'

"'From Dundee,' I an-swered, glancing at the postmark.

"'Some preposterous prac-tical joke,' said he. 'What have I to do with sun-dials and papers? I shall take no notice of such nonsense.'

"'I should certainly speak to the police,' I said.

"'And be laughed at for my pains. Nothing of the sort.'

"'Then let me do so?'

"'No, I forbid you. I won't have a fuss made about such nonsense.'

"It was in vain to argue with him, for he was a very obstinate man. I went about, however, with a heart which was full of forebodings.

"On the third day after the coming of the letter my father went from home to visit an old friend of his, Major Freebody, who is in command of one of the forts upon Portsdown Hill. I was glad that he should go, for it seemed to me that he was further from danger when he was away from home. In that, however, I was in error. Upon the

second day of his absence I received a tele-gram from the Major, imploring me to come at once. My father had fallen over one of the deep chalk-pits which abound in the neighbourhood, and was lying senseless, with a shattered skull. I hurried to him, but he passed away without having ever recovered his consciousness. He had, as it appears, been returning from Fareham in the twilight, and as the country was un-known to him, and the chalk-pit unfenced, the jury had no hesitation in bringing in a verdict of 'Death from accidental causes.' Carefully as I examined every fact con-nected with his death, I was unable to find

'WHAT ON EARTH DOES THIS MEAN?"

anything which could suggest the idea of murder. There were no signs of violence, no footmarks, no robbery, no record or strangers having been seen upon the roads. And yet I need not tell you that my mind was far from at ease, and that I was well-nigh certain that some foul plot had been woven round him.

"In this sinister way I came into my inheritance. You will ask me why I did not dispose of it? I answer because I was well convinced that our troubles were in some way dependent upon an incident in my uncle's life, and that the danger would be as pressing in one house as in another.

"It was in January, '85, that my poor father met his end, and two years and eight months have elapsed since then. During that time I have lived happily at Horsham, and I had begun to hope that this curse had passed away from the family, and that it had ended with the last generation. I had begun to take comfort too soon, however ; yesterday morning the blow fell in the very shape in which it had come upon my father."

The young man took from his waistcoat a crumpled envelope, and, turning to the table, he shook out upon it five little dried orange pips.

"This is the envelope," he continued. "The postmark is London—eastern division. Within are the very words which were upon my father's last message. 'K. K. K.'; and then 'Put the papers on the sun-dial.'"

"What have you done?" asked Holmes.

"Nothing."

"Nothing?"

"To tell the truth"—he sank his face into his thin, white hands— "I have felt helpless. I have felt like one of those poor rabbits when the snake is writhing towards it. I seem to be in the grasp of some resistless, inexorable evil, which no foresight and no precautions can guard against."

"Tut! Tut!" cried Sherlock Holmes. "You must act, man, or you are lost. Nothing but energy can save you. This is no time for despair."

"I have seen the police."

"Ah?"

"But they listened to my story with a smile. I am convinced that the inspector has formed the opinion that the letters are all practical jokes, and that the deaths of my relations were really accidents, as the jury stated, and were not to be connected with the warnings."

Holmes shook his clenched hands in the air. "Incredible imbecility!" he cried.

"They have, however, allowed me a policeman, who may remain in the house with me."

"Has he come with you to-night?"

"No. His orders were to stay in the house.

Again Holmes raved in the air.

"Why did you come to me?" he said ; "and, above all, why did you not come at once?"

"I did not know. It was only to-day

that I spoke to Major Prendergast about my troubles, and was advised by him to come to you."

"It is really two days since you had the letter. We should have acted before this. You have no further evidence, I suppose, than that which you have placed before us—no suggestive detail which might help us?"

"There is one thing," said John Openshaw. He rummaged in his coat pocket, and, drawing out a piece of discoloured, blue-tinted paper, he laid it out upon the table. "I have some remembrance," said

"SHOOK OUT FIVE LITTLE DRIED ORANGE PIPS."

he, "that on the day when my uncle burned the papers I observed that the small, unburned margins which lay amid the ashes were of this particular colour. I found this single sheet upon the floor of his room, and I am inclined to think that it may be one of the papers which has, perhaps, fluttered out from among the others, and in that way have escaped destruction. Beyond the mention of pips, I do not see that it helps us much. I think myself that it is a page from some private diary. The writing is undoubtedly my uncle's."

Holmes moved the lamp, and we both bent over the sheet of paper, which showed by its ragged edge that it had indeed been torn from a book. It was headed, "March,

1869," and beneath were the following enigmatical notices :—

" 4th. Hudson came. Same old platform.

" 7th. Set the pips on McCauley, Paramore, and John Swain of St. Augustine.

" 9th. McCauley cleared.

" 10th. John Swain cleared.

" 12th. Visited Paramore. All well."

" Thank you ! " said Holmes, folding up the paper, and returning it to our visitor. " And now you must on no account lose another instant. We cannot spare time even to discuss what you have told me. You must get home instantly, and act."

" What shall I do ? "

" There is but one thing to do. It must be done at once. You must put this piece of paper which you have shown us into the brass box which you have described. You must also put in a note to say that all the other papers were burned by your uncle, and that this is the only one which remains. You must assert that in such words as will carry conviction with them. Having done this, you must at once put the box out upon the sun-dial, as directed. Do you understand ? "

" Entirely."

" Do not think of revenge, or anything of the sort, at present. I think that we may gain that by means of the law ; but we have our web to weave, while theirs is already woven. The first consideration is to remove the pressing danger which threatens you. The second is to clear up the mystery, and to punish the guilty parties."

" I thank you," said the young man, rising, and pulling on his overcoat. " You have given me fresh life and hope. I shall certainly do as you advise."

" Do not lose an instant. And, above all, take care of yourself in the meanwhile, for I do not think that there can be a doubt that you are threatened by a very real and imminent danger. How do you go back ? "

" By train from Waterloo."

" It is not yet nine. The streets will be crowded, so I trust that you may be in safety. And yet you cannot guard yourself too closely."

" I am armed."

" That is well. To-morrow I shall set to work upon your case."

" I shall see you at Horsham, then ? "

" No, your secret lies in London. It is there that I shall seek it."

" Then I shall call upon you in a day, or in two days, with news as to the box and the papers. I shall take your advice in every particular." He shook hands with us, and took his leave. Outside the wind still screamed, and the rain splashed and pattered against the windows. This strange, wild story seemed to have come to us from amid the mad elements—blown in upon us like a sheet of sea-weed in a gale—and now to have been reabsorbed by them once more.

Sherlock Holmes sat for some time in silence with his head sunk forward, and his eyes bent upon the red glow of the fire. Then he lit his pipe, and leaning back in his chair he watched the blue smoke rings as they chased each other up to the ceiling.

" I think, Watson," he remarked at last, " that of all our cases we have had none more fantastic than this."

" Save, perhaps, the Sign of Four."

" Well, yes. Save, perhaps, that. And yet this John Openshaw seems to me to be walking amid even greater perils than did the Sholtos."

" But have you," I asked, " formed any definite conception as to what these perils are ? "

" There can be no question as to their nature," he answered.

" Then what are they ? Who is this K. K. K., and why does he pursue this unhappy family ? "

Sherlock Holmes closed his eyes, and placed his elbows upon the arms of his chair, with his finger-tips together. " The ideal reasoner," he remarked, " would, when he has once been shown a single fact in all its bearings, deduce from it not only all the chain of events which led up to it, but also all the results which would follow from it. As Cuvier could correctly describe a whole animal by the contemplation of a single bone, so the observer who has thoroughly understood one link in a series of incidents, should be able to accurately state all the other ones, both before and after. We have not yet grasped the results which the reason alone can attain to. Problems may be solved in the study which have baffled all those who have sought a solution by the aid of their senses. To carry the art, however, to its highest pitch, it is necessary that the reasoner should be able to utilise all the facts which have come to his knowledge, and this in itself implies, as you will readily see, a possession of all knowledge, which, even in these days of

"HIS EYES BENT UPON THE GLOW OF THE FIRE."

free education and encyclopædias, is a somewhat rare accomplishment. It is not so impossible, however, that a man should possess all knowledge which is likely to be useful to him in his work, and this I have endeavoured in my case to do. If I remember rightly, you on one occasion, in the early days of our friendship, defined my limits in a very precise fashion."

"Yes," I answered, laughing. "It was a singular document. Philosophy, Astronomy, and Politics were marked at zero, I remember. Botany variable, Geology profound as regards the mud-stains from any region within fifty miles of town, chemistry eccentric, anatomy unsystematic, sensational literature and crime records unique, violin player, boxer, swordsman, lawyer, and self-poisoner by cucaine and tobacco. Those, I think, were the main points of my analysis."

Holmes grinned at the last item. "Well," he said, "I say now, as I said then, that a man should keep his little brain attic stocked with all the furniture that he is likely to use, and the rest he can put away in the lumber room of his library, where he can get it if he wants it. Now, for such a case as the one which has been submitted to us to-night, we need certainly to muster all our resources. Kindly hand me down the letter K of the American Encyclopædia which stands upon the shelf beside you. Thank you. Now let us consider the situation, and see what may be deduced from it. In the first place, we may start with a strong presumption that Colonel Openshaw had some very strong reason for leaving America. Men at his time of life do not change all their habits, and exchange willingly the charming climate of Florida for the lonely life of an English provincial town. His extreme love of solitude in England suggests the idea that he was in fear of someone or something, so we may assume as a working hypothesis that it was fear of someone or something which drove him from America. As to what it was he feared, we can only deduce that by considering the formidable letters which were received by himself and his successors. Did you remark the postmarks of those letters?"

"The first was from Pondicherry, the second from Dundee, and the third from London."

"From East London. What do you deduce from that?"

"They are all sea ports. That the writer was on board of a ship."

"Excellent. We have already a clue. There can be no doubt that the probability —the strong probability—is that the writer was on board of a ship. And now let us consider another point. In the case of Pondicherry seven weeks elapsed between the threat and its fulfilment, in Dundee it was only some three or four days. Does that suggest anything?"

"A greater distance to travel."

"But the letter had also a greater distance to come."

"Then I do not see the point."

"There is at least a presumption that the vessel in which the man or men are is a sailing ship. It looks as if they always sent their singular warning or token before them when starting upon their mission. You see how quickly the deed followed the sign when it came from Dundee. If they had come from Pondicherry in a steamer they would have arrived almost as soon as their letter. But as a matter of fact seven weeks elapsed. I think that those seven weeks represented the difference between the mail boat which brought the letter, and the sailing vessel which brought the writer."

"It is possible."

"More than that. It is probable. And now you see the deadly urgency of this new case, and why I urged young Openshaw to caution. The blow has always fallen at the end of the time which it would take the senders to travel the distance. But this one comes from London, and therefore we cannot count upon delay."

"Good God!" I cried. "What can it mean, this relentless persecution?"

"The papers which Openshaw carried are obviously of vital importance to the person or persons in the sailing ship. I think that it is quite clear that there must be more than one of them. A single man could not have carried out two deaths in such a way as to deceive a coroner's jury. There must have been several in it, and they must have been men of resource and determination. Their papers they mean to have, be the holder of them who it may. In this way you see K. K. K. ceases to be the initials of an individual, and becomes the badge of a society."

"But of what society?"

"Have you never—" said Sherlock Holmes, bending forward and sinking his voice—"have you never heard of the Ku Klux Klan?"

"I never have."

Holmes turned over the leaves of the book upon his knee. "Here it is," said he, presently, "Ku Klux Klan. A name derived from a fanciful resemblance to the sound produced by cocking a rifle. This terrible secret society was formed by some ex-Confederate soldiers in the Southern States after the Civil War, and it rapidly formed local branches in different parts of the country, notably in Tennessee, Louisiana, the Carolinas, Georgia, and Florida. Its power was used for political purposes, principally for the terrorising of the negro voters, and the murdering or driving from the country of those who were opposed to its views. Its outrages were usually preceded by a warning sent to the marked man in some fantastic but generally recognised shape—a sprig of oak-leaves in some parts, melon seeds or orange pips in others. On receiving this the victim might either openly abjure his former ways, or might fly from the country. If he braved the matter out, death would unfailingly come upon him, and usually in some strange and unforeseen manner. So perfect was the organisation of the society, and so systematic its methods, that there is hardly a case upon record where any man succeeded in braving it with impunity, or in which any of its outrages were traced home to the perpetrators. For some years the organisation flourished, in spite of the efforts of the United States Government, and of the better classes of the community in the South. Eventually, in the year 1869, the movement rather suddenly collapsed, although there have been sporadic outbreaks of the same sort since that date."

"You will observe," said Holmes, laying down the volume, "that the sudden breaking up of the society was coincident with the disappearance of Openshaw from America with their papers. It may well have been cause and effect. It is no wonder that he and his family have some of the more implacable spirits upon their track. You can understand that this register and diary may implicate some of the first men in the South, and that there may be many who will not sleep easy at night until it is recovered."

"Then the page which we have seen—"

"Is such as we might expect. It ran, if I remember right, 'sent the pips to A, B, and C,'—that is, sent the society's warning to them. Then there are successive entries that A and B cleared, or left the country, and finally that C was visited, with, I fear, a sinister result for C. Well, I think, Doctor, that we may let some light into this dark place, and I believe that the only chance young Openshaw has in the meantime is to do what I have told him. There is nothing more to be said or to be done to-night, so hand me over my violin and let us try to forget for half an hour the miserable weather, and the still more miserable ways of our fellow men."

It had cleared in the morning, and the sun was shining with a subdued brightness through the dim veil which hangs over the great city. Sherlock Holmes was already at breakfast when I came down.

"You will excuse me for not waiting for you," said he; "I have, I foresee, a very busy day before me in looking into this case of young Openshaw's."

"What steps will you take?" I asked.

"It will very much depend upon the results of my first inquiries. I may have to go down to Horsham after all."

"You will not go there first?"

"No, I shall commence with the City.

"HOLMES," I CRIED. "YOU ARE TOO LATE."

Just ring the bell and the maid will bring up your coffee."

As I waited, I lifted the unopened newspaper from the table and glanced my eye over it. It rested upon a heading which sent a chill to my heart.

"Holmes," I cried, "you are too late."

"Ah!" said he, laying down his cup, "I feared as much. How was it done?" He spoke calmly, but I could see that he was deeply moved.

"My eye caught the name of Openshaw, and the heading 'Tragedy near Waterloo Bridge.' Here is the account : 'Between nine and ten last night Police-constable Cooke, of the H Division, on duty near Waterloo Bridge, heard a cry for help and a splash in the water. The night, however, was extremely dark and stormy, so that, in spite of the help of several passers-by, it was quite impossible to effect a rescue. The alarm, however, was given, and, by the aid of the water police, the body was eventually recovered. It proved to be that of a young gentleman whose name, as it appears from an envelope which was found in his pocket, was John Openshaw, and whose residence is near Horsham. It is conjectured that he may have been hurrying down to catch the last train from Waterloo Station, and that in his haste and the extreme darkness, he missed his path, and walked over the edge of one of the small landing-places for river steamboats. The body exhibited no traces of violence, and there can be no doubt that the deceased had been the victim of an unfortunate accident, which should have the effect of calling the attention of the authorities to the condition of the riverside landing stages."

We sat in silence for some minutes, Holmes more depressed and shaken than I had ever seen him.

"That hurts my pride, Watson," he said at last. "It is a petty feeling, no doubt, but it hurts my pride. It becomes a personal matter with me now, and, if God sends me health, I shall set my hand upon this gang. That he should come to me for help, and that I should send him away to his death——!" He sprang from his chair, and paced about the room in uncontrollable agitation, with a flush upon his sallow cheeks, and a nervous clasping and unclasping of his long, thin hands.

"They must be cunning devils," he exclaimed, at last. "How could they have decoyed him down there? The Embankment is not on the direct line to the station.

The bridge, no doubt, was too crowded, even on such a night, for their purpose. Well, Watson, we shall see who will win in the long run. I am going out now ! "

" To the police ? "

" No ; I shall be my own police. When I have spun the web they may take the flies, but not before."

All day I was engaged in my professional work, and it was late in the evening before I returned to Baker-street. Sherlock Holmes had not come back yet. It was nearly ten o'clock before he entered, looking pale and worn. He walked up to the sideboard, and, tearing a piece from the loaf, he devoured it voraciously, washing it down with a long draught of water.

" You are hungry," I remarked.

" Starving. It had escaped my memory. I have had nothing since breakfast."

" Nothing ? "

" Not a bite. I had no time to think of it."

" And how have you succeeded ? "

" Well."

" You have a clue ? "

" I have them in the hollow of my hand. Young Openshaw shall not long remain unavenged. Why, Watson, let us put their own devilish trade-mark upon them. It is well thought of ! "

" What do you mean ? "

He took an orange from the cupboard, and, tearing it to pieces, he squeezed out the pips upon the table. Of these he took five, and thrust them into an envelope. On the inside of the flap he wrote " S. H. for J. O." Then he sealed it and addressed it to " Captain James Calhoun, Barque *Lone Star*, Savannah, Georgia."

" That will await him when he enters port," said he, chuckling. " It may give him a sleepless night. He will find it as sure a precursor of his fate as Openshaw did before him."

" And who is this Captain Calhoun ? "

" The leader of the gang. I shall have the others, but he first."

" How did you trace it, then ? "

He took a large sheet of paper from his pocket, all covered with dates and names.

" I have spent the whole day," said he, " over Lloyd's registers and the files of the old papers, following the future career of every vessel which touched at Pondicherry in January and February in '83. There were thirty-six ships of fair tonnage which

were reported there during those months. Of these, one, the *Lone Star*, instantly attracted my attention, since, although it was reported as having cleared from London, the name is that which is given to one of the States of the Union."

" Texas, I think."

" I was not and am not sure which ; but I knew that the ship must have an American origin."

" What then ? "

" I searched the Dundee records, and when I found that the barque *Lone Star* was there in January, '85, my suspicion became a certainty. I then inquired as to the vessels which lay at present in the port of London."

" Yes ? "

" The *Lone Star* had arrived here last week. I went down to the Albert Dock, and found that she had been taken down the river by the early tide this morning, homeward bound to Savannah. I wired to Gravesend, and learned that she had passed some time ago, and as the wind is easterly, I have no doubt that she is now past the Goodwins, and not very far from the Isle of Wight."

" What will you do, then ? "

" Oh, I have my hand upon him. He and the two mates are, as I learn, the only native born Americans in the ship. The others are Finns and Germans. I know also that they were all three away from the ship last night. I had it from the stevedore who has been loading their cargo. By the time that their sailing ship reaches Savannah the mail-boat will have carried this letter, and the cable will have informed the police of Savannah that these three gentlemen are badly wanted here upon a charge of murder."

There is ever a flaw, however, in the best laid of human plans, and the murderers of John Openshaw were never to receive the orange pips which would show them that another, as cunning and as resolute as themselves, was upon their track. Very long and very severe were the equinoctial gales that year. We waited long for news of the *Lone Star* of Savannah, but none ever reached us. We did at last hear that somewhere far out in the Atlantic, a shattered sternpost of a boat was seen swinging in the trough of a wave, with the letters " L. S." carved upon it, and that is all which we shall ever know of the fate of the *Lone Star*.

Adventures of Sherlock Holmes.

ADVENTURE VI.—THE MAN WITH THE TWISTED LIP.

By A. Conan Doyle.

ISA WHITNEY, brother of the late Elias Whitney, D.D., Principal of the Theological College of St. George's, was much addicted to opium. The habit grew upon him, as I understand, from some foolish freak when he was at college, for having read De Quincey's description of his dreams and sensations, he had drenched his tobacco with laudanum in an attempt to produce the same effects. He found, as so many more have done, that the practice is easier to attain than to get rid of, and for many years he continued to be a slave to the drug, an object of mingled horror and pity to his friends and relatives. I can see him now, with yellow, pasty face, drooping lids and pin-point pupils, all huddled in a chair, the wreck and ruin of a noble man.

One night—it was in June, '89—there came a ring to my bell, about the hour when a man gives his first yawn, and glances at the clock. I sat up in my chair, and my wife laid her needlework down in her lap and made a little face of disappointment.

"A patient!" said she. "You'll have to go out."

I groaned, for I was newly come back from a weary day.

We heard the door open, a few hurried words, and then quick steps upon the linoleum. Our own door flew open, and a lady, clad in some dark-coloured stuff, with a black veil, entered the room.

"You will excuse my calling so late," she began, and then, suddenly losing her self-control, she ran forward, threw her arms about my wife's neck, and sobbed upon her shoulder. "Oh, I'm in such trouble!" she cried; "I do so want a little help.

"Why," said my wife, pulling up her veil, "it is Kate Whitney. How you startled me, Kate! I had not an idea who you were when you came in."

"I didn't know what to do, so I came straight to you." That was always the way. Folk who were in grief came to my wife like birds to a lighthouse.

"It was very sweet of you to come. Now, you must have some wine and water, and sit here comfortably and tell us all about it. Or should you rather that I sent James off to bed?"

"Oh, no, no. I want the Doctor's advice and help too. It's about Isa. He has not been home for two days. I am so frightened about him!"

It was not the first time that she had spoken to us of her husband's trouble, to me as a doctor, to my wife as an old friend and school companion. We soothed and comforted her by such words as we could find. Did she know where her husband was? Was it possible that we could bring him back to her?

It seemed that it was. She had the surest information that of late he had, when the fit was on him, made use of an opium den in the furthest east of the City. Hitherto his orgies had always been confined to one day, and he had come back, twitching and shattered, in the evening. But now the spell had been upon him eight and forty hours, and he lay there, doubtless among the dregs of the docks, breathing in the poison or sleeping off the effects. There he was to be found, she was sure of it, at the "Bar of Gold," in Upper Swandam-lane. But what was she to do? How could she, a young and timid woman, make her way into such a place, and pluck her husband out from among the ruffians who surrounded him?

There was the case, and of course there was but one way out of it. Might I not escort her to this place? And, then, as a second thought, why should she come at all? I was Isa Whitney's medical adviser, and as such I had influence over him. I could manage it better if I were alone. I promised her on my word that I would send him home in a cab within two hours if he were indeed at the address which she had given me. And so in ten minutes I had left my arm-chair and cheery sitting-room behind me, and was speeding eastward in a hansom on a strange errand, as it seemed to me at the time, though the future only could show how strange it was to be.

But there was no great difficulty in the first stage of my adventure. Upper Swandam-lane is a vile alley lurking behind the high wharves which line the north side of the river to the east of London Bridge. Between a slop shop and a gin shop, approached by a steep flight of steps leading down to a black gap like the mouth of a cave, I found the den of which I was in search. Ordering my cab to wait, I passed down the steps, worn hollow in the centre by the ceaseless tread of drunken feet, and by the light of a flickering oil lamp above the door I found the latch and made my way into a long, low room, thick and heavy with the brown opium smoke, and terraced with wooden berths, like the forecastle of an emigrant ship.

"STARING INTO THE FIRE."

Through the gloom one could dimly catch a glimpse of bodies lying in strange fantastic poses, bowed shoulders, bent knees, heads thrown back and chins pointing upwards, with here and there a dark, lacklustre eye turned upon the new comer. Out of the black shadows there glimmered little red circles of light, now bright, now faint, as the burning poison waxed or waned in the bowls of the metal pipes. The most lay silent but some muttered to themselves, and others talked together in a strange, low, monotonous voice, their conversation coming in gushes, and then suddenly tailing off into silence, each mumbling out his own thoughts, and paying little heed to the words of his neighbour. At the further end was a small brazier of burning charcoal, besides which on a three-legged wooden stool there sat a tall, thin old man with his jaw resting upon his two fists, and his elbows upon his knees, staring into the fire.

As I entered, a sallow Malay attendant had hurried up with a pipe for me and a supply of the drug, beckoning me to an empty berth.

"Thank you, I have not come to stay," said I. "There is a friend of mine here, Mr. Isa Whitney, and I wish to speak with him."

There was a movement and an exclamation from my right, and, peering through the gloom, I saw Whitney, pale, haggard, and unkempt, staring out at me.

"My God! It's Watson," said he. He was in a pitiable state of reaction, with every nerve in a twitter. "I say, Watson, what o'clock is it?"

"Nearly eleven."

"Of what day?"

"Of Friday, June 19."

"Good heavens! I thought it was Wednesday. It *is* Wednesday. What d'you want to frighten a chap for?" He sank his face on to his arms, and began to sob in a high treble key.

"I tell you that it is Friday, man. Your wife has been waiting this two days for you. You should be ashamed of yourself!"

"So I am. But you've got mixed, Watson, for I have only been here a few hours, three pipes, four pipes—I forget how many. But I'll go home with you. I wouldn't frighten Kate—poor little Kate. Give me your hand ! Have you a cab ? "

" Yes, I have one waiting."

" Then I shall go in it. But I must owe something. Find what I owe, Watson. I am all off colour. I can do nothing for myself."

I walked down the narrow passage between the double row of sleepers, holding my breath to keep out the vile, stupefying fumes of the drug, and looking about for the manager. As I passed the tall man who sat by the brazier I felt a sudden pluck at my skirt and a low voice whispered, " Walk past me, and then look back at me." The words fell quite distinctly upon my ear. I glanced down. They could only have come from the old man at my side, and yet he sat now as absorbed as ever, very thin, very wrinkled, bent with age, an opium

" ' HOLMES ! ' I WHISPERED."

pipe dangling down from between his knees, as though it had dropped in sheer lassitude from his fingers. I took two steps forward and looked back. It took all my self-control to prevent me from breaking out into a

cry of astonishment. He had turned his back so that none could see him but I. His form had filled out, his wrinkles were gone, the dull eyes had regained their fire, and there, sitting by the fire, and grinning at my surprise, was none other than Sherlock Holmes. He made a slight motion to me to approach him, and instantly, as he turned his face half round to the company once more, subsided into a doddering, loose-lipped senility.

" Holmes ! " I whispered, " what on earth are you doing in this den ? "

" As low as you can," he answered, " I have excellent ears. If you would have the great kindness to get rid of that sottish friend of yours I should be exceedingly glad to have a little talk with you."

" I have a cab outside."

" Then pray send him home in it. You may safely trust him, for he appears to be too limp to get into any mischief. I should recommend you also to send a note by the cabman to your wife to say that you have thrown in your lot with me. If you will wait outside, I shall be with you in five minutes."

It was difficult to refuse any of Sherlock Holmes' requests, for they were always so exceedingly definite, and put forward with such a quiet air of mastery. I felt, however, that when Whitney was once confined in the cab, my mission was practically accomplished ; and for the rest, I could not wish anything better than to be associated with my friend in one of those singular adventures which were the normal condition of his existence. In a few minutes I had written my note, paid Whitney's bill, led him out to the cab, and seen him driven through the darkness. In a very short time a decrepit figure had emerged from the opium den, and I was walking down the street with Sherlock Holmes. For two streets he shuffled along with a bent back and an uncertain foot,

Then glancing quickly round, he straightened himself out and burst into a hearty fit of laughter.

"I suppose, Watson," said he, "that you imagine that I have added opium-smoking to cucaine injections and all the other little weaknesses on which you have favoured me with your medical views."

"I was certainly surprised to find you there."

"But not more so than I to find you."

"I came to find a friend."

"And I to find an enemy."

"An enemy?"

"Yes, one of my natural enemies, or shall I say, my natural prey. Briefly, Watson, I am in the midst of a very remarkable inquiry, and I have hoped to find a clue in the incoherent ramblings of these sots, as I have done before now. Had I been recognised in that den my life would not have been worth an hour's purchase, for I have used it before now for my own purposes, and the rascally Lascar who runs it has sworn to have vengeance upon me. There is a trap-door at the back of that building, near the corner of Paul's Wharf, which could tell some strange tales of what has passed through it upon the moonless nights."

"What! You do not mean bodies?"

"Aye, bodies, Watson. We should be rich men if we had a thousand pounds for every poor devil who has been done to death in that den. It is the vilest murder-trap on the whole river-side, and I fear that Neville St. Clair has entered it never to leave it more. But our trap should be here!" He put his two fore-fingers between his teeth and whistled shrilly, a signal which was answered by a similar whistle from the distance, followed shortly by the rattle of wheels and the clink of horses' hoofs.

"Now, Watson," said Holmes, as a tall dog-cart dashed up through the gloom, throwing out two golden tunnels of yellow light from its side lanterns. "You'll come with me, won't you?"

"If I can be of use."

"Oh, a trusty comrade is always of use. And a chronicler

still more so. My room at The Cedars is a double-bedded one."

"The Cedars?"

"Yes; that is Mr. St. Clair's house. I am staying there while I conduct the inquiry."

"Where is it, then?"

"Near Lee, in Kent. We have a seven-mile drive before us."

"But I am all in the dark."

"Of course you are. You'll know all about it presently. Jump up here! All right, John, we shall not need you. Here's half-a-crown. Look out for me to-morrow, about eleven. Give her her head! So long, then!"

He flicked the horse with his whip, and we dashed away through the endless succession of sombre and deserted streets, which widened gradually, until we were flying across a broad balustraded bridge, with the murky river flowing sluggishly beneath us. Beyond lay another dull wilderness of bricks and mortar, its silence broken only by the heavy, regular footfall of the policeman, or the songs and shouts of some belated party of revellers. A dull wrack was drifting slowly across the sky,

"HE FLICKED THE HORSE WITH HIS WHIP.'

and a star or two twinkled dimly here and there through the rifts of the clouds. Holmes drove in silence, with his head sunk upon his breast, and the air of a man who is lost in thought, whilst I sat beside him, curious to learn what this new quest might be which seemed to tax his powers so sorely, and yet afraid to break in upon the current of his thoughts. We had driven several miles, and were beginning to get to the fringe of the belt of suburban villas, when he shook himself, shrugged his shoulders, and lit up his pipe with the air of a man who has satisfied himself that he is acting for the best.

"You have a grand gift of silence, Watson," said he. "It makes you quite invaluable as a companion. 'Pon my word, it is a great thing for me to have someone to talk to, for my own thoughts are not over pleasant. I was wondering what I should say to this dear little woman to-night when she meets me at the door."

"You forget that I know nothing about it."

"I shall just have time to tell you the facts of the case before we get to Lee. It seems absurdly simple, and yet, somehow, I can get nothing to go upon. There's plenty of thread, no doubt, but I can't get the end of it into my hand. Now, I'll state the case clearly and concisely to you, Watson, and maybe you may see a spark where all is dark to me."

"Proceed then."

"Some years ago—to be definite, in May, 1884—there came to Lee a gentleman, Neville St. Clair by name, who appeared to have plenty of money. He took a large villa, laid out the grounds very nicely, and lived generally in good style. By degrees he made friends in the neighbourhood, and in 1887 he married the daughter of a local brewer, by whom he has now had two children. He had no occupation, but was interested in several companies, and went into town as a rule in the morning, returning by the 5.14 from Cannon-street every night. Mr. St. Clair is now 37 years of age, is a man of temperate habits, a good husband, a very affectionate father, and a man who is popular with all who know him. I may add that his whole debts at the present moment, as far as we have been able to ascertain, amount to £88 10s., while he has £220 standing to his credit in the Capital and Counties Bank. There is no reason, therefore, to think that money troubles have been weighing upon his mind.

"Last Monday Mr. Neville St. Clair went into town rather earlier than usual, remarking before he started that he had two important commissions to perform, and that he would bring his little boy home a box of bricks. Now, by the merest chance his wife received a telegram upon this same Monday, very shortly after his departure, to the effect that a small parcel of considerable value which she had been expecting was waiting for her at the offices of the Aberdeen Shipping Company. Now, if you are well up in your London, you will know that the office of the company is in Fresno-street, which branches out of Upper Swandam-lane, where you found me to-night. Mrs. St. Clair had her lunch, started for the City, did some shopping, proceeded to the company's office, got her packet, and found herself exactly at 4.35 walking through Swandam-lane on her way back to the station. Have you followed me so far?"

"It is very clear.

"If you remember, Monday was an exceedingly hot day, and Mrs. St. Clair walked slowly, glancing about in the hope of seeing a cab, as she did not like the neighbourhood in which she found herself. While she walked in this way down Swandam-lane she suddenly heard an ejaculation or cry, and was struck cold to see her husband looking down at her, and, as it seemed to her, beckoning to her from a second-floor window. The window was open, and she distinctly saw his face, which she describes as being terribly agitated. He waved his hands frantically to her, and then vanished from the window so suddenly that it seemed to her that he had been plucked back by some irresistible force from behind. One singular point which struck her quick feminine eye was that, although he wore some dark coat, such as he had started to town in, he had on neither collar nor necktie.

"Convinced that something was amiss with him, she rushed down the steps—for the house was none other than the opium den in which you found me to-night—and, running through the front room, she attempted to ascend the stairs which led to the first floor. At the foot of the stairs, however, she met this Lascar scoundrel of whom I have spoken, who thrust her back, and, aided by a Dane, who acts as assistant there, pushed her out into the street. Filled with the most maddening doubts and fears, she rushed down the lane, and, by rare good fortune, met, in Fresno-street, a num-

SP

"AT THE FOOT OF THE STAIRS SHE MET THIS LASCAR SCOUNDREL."

which lay upon the table, and tore the lid from it. Out there fell a cascade of children's bricks. It was the toy which he had promised to bring home.

"This discovery, and the evident confusion which the cripple showed, made the inspector realise that the matter was serious. The rooms were carefully examined, and results all pointed to an abominable crime. The front room was plainly furnished as a sitting-room, and led into a small bedroom, which looked out upon the back of one of the wharves. Between the wharf and the bedroom window is a narrow strip, which is dry at low tide, but is covered at high tide with at least four and a half feet of water. The bed-room window was a broad one, and opened from below. On examination traces of blood were to be seen upon the window sill, and several scattered drops were visible upon the wooden floor of the bedroom. Thrust away behind a curtain in the front room were all the clothes of Mr. Neville St. Clair, with the exception of his coat. His boots, his socks, his hat, and his watch—all were there. There were no signs of violence upon any of these garments, and there were no other traces of Mr. Neville St. Clair. Out of the window he must apparently have gone, for no other exit could be discovered, and the ominous bloodstains upon the sill gave little promise that he could save himself by swimming, for the tide was at its very highest at the moment of the tragedy.

"And now as to the villains who seemed to be immediately implicated in the matter. The Lascar was known to be a man of the vilest antecedents, but as by Mrs. St. Clair's story he was known to have been at the foot of the stair within a very few seconds of her husband's appearance at the window, he could hardly have been more than an accessory to the crime. His defence was one of absolute ignorance, and he protested that he had no knowledge as to the doings of Hugh Boone, his lodger, and that he could not account in any way for the presence of the missing gentleman's clothes.

"So much for the Lascar manager. Now

ber of constables with an inspector, all on their way to their beat. The inspector and two men accompanied her back, and, in spite of the continued resistance of the proprietor, they made their way to the room in which Mr. St. Clair had last been seen. There was no sign of him there. In fact, in the whole of that floor there was no one to be found, save a crippled wretch of hideous aspect, who, it seems, made his home there. Both he and the Lascar stoutly swore that no one else had been in the front room during the afternoon. So determined was their denial that the inspector was staggered, and had almost come to believe that Mrs. St. Clair had been deluded when, with a cry, she sprang at a small deal box for the sinister cripple who lives upon the second floor of the opium den, and who was certainly the last human being whose eyes rested upon Neville St. Clair. His name is Hugh Boone, and his hideous face is one which is familiar to every man who goes much to the City. He is a professional beggar, though in order to avoid the police regulations he pretends to a small trade in wax vestas. Some little distance down Threadneedle-street upon the left hand side there is, as you may have remarked, a small angle in the wall. Here it is that the creature takes his daily seat, cross-legged, with his tiny stock of matches on his lap, and as he is a piteous spectacle a small rain of charity descends into the greasy leather cap which lies upon the pavement beside him. I have watched the fellow more than once, before ever I thought of making his professional acquaintance, and I have been surprised at the harvest which he has reaped in a short time. His appearance, you see, is so remarkable, that no one can pass

"HE IS A PROFESSIONAL BEGGAR."

him without observing him. A shock of orange hair, a pale face disfigured by a horrible scar, which, by its contraction, has turned up the outer edge of his upper lip, a bull-dog chin, and a pair of very penetrating dark eyes, which present a singular contrast to the colour of his hair, all mark him out from amid the common crowd of mendicants, and so, too, does his wit, for he is ever ready with a reply to any piece of chaff which may be thrown at him by the passers-by. This is the man whom we now learn to have been the lodger at the opium den,

and to have been the last man to see the gentleman of whom we are in quest."

"But a cripple!" said I. "What could he have done singlehanded against a man in the prime of life?"

"He is a cripple in the sense that he walks with a limp; but, in other respects, he appears to be a powerful and well-nurtured man. Surely your medical experience would tell you, Watson, that weakness in one limb is often compensated for by exceptional strength in the others."

"Pray continue your narrative."

"Mrs. St. Clair had fainted at the sight of the blood upon the window, and she was escorted home in a cab by the police, as her presence could be of no help to them in their investigations. Inspector Barton, who had charge of the case, made a very careful examination of the premises, but without finding anything which threw any light upon the matter. One mistake had been made in not arresting Boone instantly, as he was allowed some few minutes during which he might have communicated with his friend the Lascar, but this fault was soon remedied, and he was seized and searched, without anything being found which could incriminate him. There were, it is true, some bloodstains upon his right shirt-sleeve, but he pointed to his ring finger, which had been cut near the nail, and explained that the bleeding came from there, adding that he had been to the window not long before, and that the stains which had been observed there came doubtless from the same source. He denied strenuously having ever seen Mr. Neville St. Clair, and swore that the presence of the clothes in his room was as much a mystery to him as to the police. As to Mrs. St. Clair's assertion that she had actually seen her husband at the window, he declared that she must have been either mad or dreaming. He was removed, loudly protesting, to the police station, while the inspector remained upon the premises in the hope that the ebbing tide might afford some fresh clue.

" And it did, though they hardly found upon the mudbank what they had feared to find. It was Neville St. Clair's coat, and not Neville St. Clair, which lay uncovered as the tide receded. And what do you think they found in the pockets? "

" I cannot imagine."

" No, I don't think you would guess. Every pocket stuffed with pennies and half-pennies—four hundred and twenty-one pennies, and two hundred and seventy halfpennies. It was no wonder that it had not been swept away by the tide. But a human body is a different matter. There is a fierce eddy between the wharf and the house. It seemed likely enough that the weighted coat had remained when the stripped body had been sucked away into the river."

" But I understand that all the other clothes were found in the room. Would the body be dressed in a coat alone ? "

" No, sir, but the facts might be met speciously enough. Suppose that this man Boone had thrust Neville St. Clair through the window, there is no human eye which could have seen the deed. What would he do then ? It would of course instantly strike him that he must get rid of the tell-tale garments. He would seize the coat then, and be in the act of throwing it out when it would occur to him that it would swim and not sink. He has little time, for he has heard the scuffle downstairs when the wife tried to force her way up, and perhaps he has already heard from his Lascar confederate that the police are hurrying up the street. There is not an instant to be lost. He rushes to some secret horde, where he has accumulated the fruits of his beggary, and he stuffs all the coins upon which he can lay his hands into the pockets to make sure of the coat's sinking. He throws it out, and would have done the same with the other garments had not he heard the rush of steps below, and only just had time to close the window when the police appeared."

" It certainly sounds feasible "

" Well, we will take it as a working hypothesis for want of a better. Boone, as I have told you, was arrested and taken to the station, but it could not be shown that there had ever before been anything against him. He had for years been known as a professional beggar, but his life appeared to have been a very quiet and innocent one. There the matter stands at present, and the questions which have to be solved, what Neville St. Clair was doing in the opium den, what happened to him when there, where is he now, and what Hugh Boone had to do with his disappearance, are all as far from a solution as ever. I confess

"STUFFS ALL THE COINS INTO THE POCKETS."

that I cannot recall any case within my experience which looked at the first glance so simple, and yet which presented such difficulties."

Whilst Sherlock Holmes had been detailing this singular series of events we had been whirling through the outskirts of the great town until the last straggling houses had been left behind, and we rattled along with a country hedge upon either side of us. Just as he finished, however, we drove through two scattered villages, where a few lights still glimmered in the windows.

"We are on the outskirts of Lee," said my companion. "We have touched on three English counties in our short drive, starting in Middlesex, passing over an angle of Surrey, and ending in Kent. See that light among the trees? That is The Cedars, and beside that lamp sits a woman whose anxious ears have already, I have little doubt, caught the clink of our horse's feet."

"But why are you not conducting the case from Baker-street?" I asked.

"Because there are many inquiries which must be made out here. Mrs. St. Clair has most kindly put two rooms at my disposal, and you may rest assured that she will have nothing but a welcome for my friend and colleague. I hate to meet her, Watson, when I have no news of her husband. Here we are. Whoa, there, whoa!"

We had pulled up in front of a large villa which stood within its own grounds. A stable-boy had run out to the horse's head, and, springing down, I followed Holmes up the small, winding gravel drive which led to the house. As we approached, the door flew open, and a little blonde woman stood in the opening, clad in some sort of light mousseline de soie, with a touch of fluffy pink chiffon at her neck and wrists. She stood with her figure outlined against the flood of light, one hand upon the door, one half raised in her eagerness, her body slightly bent, her head and face protruded, with eager eyes and parted lips, a standing question.

"Well?" she cried, "well?" And then, seeing that there were two of us, she gave a cry of hope which sank into a groan as she saw that my companion shook his head and shrugged his shoulders.

"No good news?"

"None."

"No bad?"

"No."

"Thank God for that. But come in.

You must be weary, for you have had a long day."

"This is my friend, Dr. Watson. He has been of most vital use to me in several of my cases, and a lucky chance has made it possible for me to bring him out and associate him with this investigation."

"I am delighted to see you," said she, pressing my hand warmly. "You will, I am sure, forgive anything which may be wanting in our arrangements, when you consider the blow which has come so suddenly upon us."

"My dear madam," said I, "I am an old campaigner, and if I were not, I can very well see that no apology is needed. If I can be of any assistance, either to you or to my friend here, I shall be indeed happy."

"Now, Mr. Sherlock Holmes," said the lady, as we entered a well-lit dining-room, upon the table of which a cold supper had been laid out. "I should very much like to ask you one or two plain questions, to which I beg that you will give a plain answer."

"Certainly, madam."

"Do not trouble about my feelings. I am not hysterical, nor given to fainting. I simply wish to hear your real, real opinion."

"Upon what point?"

"In your heart of hearts do you think that Neville is alive?"

Sherlock Holmes seemed to be embarrassed by the question. "Frankly now!" she repeated, standing upon the rug, and looking keenly down at him, as he leaned back in a basket chair.

"Frankly then, madam, I do not."

"You think that he is dead?"

"I do."

"Murdered?"

"I don't say that. Perhaps."

"And on what day did he meet his death?"

"On Monday."

"Then perhaps, Mr. Holmes, you will be good enough to explain how it is that I have received a letter from him to-day."

Sherlock Holmes sprang out of his chair as if he had been galvanised.

"What!" he roared.

"Yes, to-day." She stood smiling, holding up a little slip of paper in the air.

"May I see it?"

"Certainly."

He snatched it from her in his eagerness, and smoothing it out upon the table, he drew over the lamp, and examined it

"'FRANKLY, NOW,' SHE REPEATED."

intently. I had left my chair, and was gazing at it over his shoulder. The envelope was a very coarse one, and was stamped with the Gravesend post-mark, and with the date of that very day, or rather of the day before, for it was considerably after midnight.

"Coarse writing!" murmured Holmes. "Surely this is not your husband's writing, madam."

"No, but the enclosure is."

"I perceive also that whoever addressed the envelope had to go and inquire as. to the address."

"How can you tell that?"

"The name, you see, is in perfectly black ink, which has dried itself. The rest is of the greyish colour which shows that blotting-paper has been used. If it had been written straight off, and then blotted, none would be of a deep black shade. This man has written the name, and there has then been a pause before he wrote the address, which can only mean that he was not familiar with it. It is, of course, a trifle, but there is nothing so important as trifles. Let us now see the letter! Ha! there has been an enclosure here!"

"Yes, there was a ring. His signet ring."

"And you are sure that this is your husband's hand?"

"One of his hands."

"One?"

"His hand when he wrote hurriedly. It is very unlike his usual writing, and yet I know it well."

"'Dearest, do not be frightened. All will come well. There is a huge error which it may take some little time to rectify. Wait in patience. — Neville.' Written in pencil upon the fly-leaf of a book, octavo size, no watermark. Hum! Posted to-day in Gravesend by a man with a dirty thumb. Ha! And the flap has been gummed, if I am not very much in error, by a person who had been chewing tobacco. And you have no doubt that it is your husband's hand, madam?"

"None. Neville wrote those words."

"And they were posted to-day at Gravesend. Well, Mrs. St. Clair, the clouds lighten, though I should not venture to say that the danger is over."

"But he must be alive, Mr. Holmes."

"Unless this is a clever forgery to put us on the wrong scent. The ring, after all, proves nothing. It may have been taken from him."

"No, no; it is, it is, it is his very own writing!"

"Very well. It may, however, have been written on Monday, and only posted to-day."

"That is possible."

"If so, much may have happened between."

"Oh, you must not discourage me, Mr. Holmes. I know that all is well with him. There is so keen a sympathy between us that I should know if evil came upon him. On the very day that I saw him last he cut himself in the bedroom, and yet I in the dining-room rushed upstairs instantly with the utmost certainty that something had happened. Do you think that I would respond to such a trifle, and yet be ignorant of his death?"

"I have seen too much not to know that the impression of a woman may be more valuable than the conclusion of an analytical reasoner. And in this letter you certainly have a very strong piece of evidence to corroborate your view. But if your husband is alive, and able to write letters, why should he remain away from you?"

"I cannot imagine. It is unthinkable."

"And on Monday he made no remarks before leaving you?"

"No."

"And you were surprised to see him in Swandam-lane?"

"Very much so."

"Was the window open?"

"Yes."

"Then he might have called to you?"

"He might."

"He only, as I understand, gave an inarticulate cry?"

"Yes."

"A call for help, you thought?"

"Yes. He waved his hands."

"But it might have been a cry of surprise. Astonishment at the unexpected sight of you might cause him to throw up his hands?"

"It is possible."

"And you thought he was pulled back?"

"He disappeared so suddenly."

"He might have leaped back. You did not see anyone else in the room?"

"No, but this horrible man confessed to having been there, and the Lascar was at the foot of the stairs."

"Quite so. Your husband, as far as you could see, had his ordinary clothes on?"

"But without his collar or tie. I distinctly saw his bare throat."

"Had he ever spoken of Swandam-lane?"

"Never."

"Had he ever shown any signs of having taken opium?"

"Never."

"Thank you, Mrs. St. Clair. Those are the principal points about which I wished to be absolutely clear. We shall now have a little supper and then retire, for we may have a very busy day to-morrow."

A large and comfortable double-bedded room had been placed at our disposal, and I was quickly between the sheets, for I was weary after my night of adventure. Sherlock Holmes was a man, however, who when he had an unsolved problem upon his mind would go for days, and even for a week, without rest, turning it over, rearranging his facts, looking at it from every point of view, until he had either fathomed it, or convinced himself that his data were insufficient. It was soon evident to me that he was now preparing for an all night sitting. He took off his coat and waistcoat, put on a large blue dressing gown, and then wandered about the room collecting pillows from his bed, and cushions from the sofa and arm-chairs. With these he constructed a sort of Eastern divan, upon which he perched himself cross-legged, with an ounce of shag tobacco and a box of matches laid out in front of him. In the dim light of the lamp I saw him sitting there, an old brier pipe between his lips, his eyes fixed vacantly upon the corner of the ceiling, the blue smoke curling up from him, silent, motionless, with the light shining upon his strong set aquiline features. So he sat as I dropped off to sleep, and so he sat when a sudden ejaculation caused me to wake up, and I found the summer sun shining into the apartment. The pipe was still between his lips, the smoke still curled upwards, and the room was full of a dense tobacco haze, but nothing remained of the heap of shag which I had seen upon the previous night.

"Awake, Watson?" he asked.

"Yes."

"Game for a morning drive?"

"Certainly."

"Then dress. No one is stirring yet, but I know where the stable boy sleeps, and we shall soon have the trap out." He chuckled to himself as he spoke, his eyes twinkled, and he seemed a different man to the sombre thinker of the previous night.

As I dressed I glanced at my watch. It was no wonder that no one was stirring. It was twenty-five minutes past four. I had hardly finished when Holmes returned with the news that the boy was putting in the horse.

"I want to test a little theory of mine," said he, pulling on his boots. "I think, Watson, that you are now standing in the presence of one of the most absolute fools in Europe. I deserve to be kicked from here to Charing-cross. But I think I have the key of the affair now."

"And where is it?" I asked, smiling.

"In the bath-room," he answered. "Oh, yes, I am not joking," he continued, seeing my look of incredulity. "I have just been there, and I have taken it out, and I have got it in this Gladstone bag. Come on, my boy, and we shall see whether it will not fit the lock."

We made our way downstairs as quietly

" THE PIPE WAS STILL BETWEEN HIS LIPS."

as possible, and out into the bright morning sunshine. In the road stood our horse and trap, with the half-clad stable boy waiting at the head. We both sprang in, and away we dashed down the London-road. A few country carts were stirring, bearing in vegetables to the metropolis, but the lines of villas on either side were as silent and lifeless as some city in a dream.

"It has been in some points a singular case," said Holmes, flicking the horse on into a gallop. "I confess that I have been as blind as a mole, but it is better to learn wisdom late, than never to learn it at all."

In town, the earliest risers were just beginning to look sleepily from their windows as we drove through the streets of the Surrey side. Passing down the Waterloo Bridge-road we crossed over the river, and dashing up Wellington-street wheeled sharply to the right, and found ourselves in Bow-street. Sherlock Holmes was well known to the Force, and the two constables at the door saluted him. One of them held the horse's head while the other led us in.

"Who is on duty?" asked Holmes.

"Inspector Bradstreet, sir."

"Ah, Bradstreet, how are you?" A tall, stout official had come down the stone-flagged passage, in a peaked cap and frogged

jacket. "I wish to have a quiet word with you, Bradstreet."

"Certainly, Mr. Holmes. Step into my room here."

It was a small office-like room, with a huge ledger upon the table, and a telephone projecting from the wall. The inspector sat down at his desk.

"What can I do for you, Mr. Holmes?"

"I called about that beggarman, Boone—the one who was charged with being concerned in the disappearance of Mr. Neville St. Clair, of Lee."

"Yes. He was brought up and remanded for further inquiries."

"So I heard. You have him here?"

"In the cells."

"Is he quiet?"

"Oh, he gives no trouble. But he is a dirty scoundrel."

"Dirty?"

"Yes, it is all we can do to make him wash his hands, and his face is as black as a tinker's. Well, when once his case has been settled he will have a regular prison bath; and I think, if you saw him, you would agree with me that he needed it."

"I should like to see him very much."

"Would you? That is easily done. Come this way. You can leave your bag."

"No, I think that I'll take it."

"Very good. Come this way, if you please." He led us down a passage, opened a barred door, passed down a winding stair, and brought us to a white-washed corridor with a line of doors on each side.

"The third on the right is his," said the inspector. "Here it is!" He quietly shot back a panel in the upper part of the door, and glanced through.

"He is asleep," said he. "You can see him very well."

We both put our eyes to the grating. The prisoner lay with his face towards us, in a very deep sleep, breathing slowly and heavily. He was a middle-sized man, coarsely clad as became his calling, with a coloured shirt protruding through the rents in his tattered coat. He was, as the inspector had said, extremely dirty, but the grime which covered his face could not conceal its repulsive ugliness. A broad wheal from an old scar ran right across it from eye to chin, and by its contraction had turned up one side of the upper lip, so that three teeth were exposed in a perpetual snarl. A shock of very bright red hair grew low over his eyes and forehead.

"He's a beauty, isn't he?" said the inspector.

"He certainly needs a wash," remarked Holmes. "I had an idea that he might, and I took the liberty of bringing the tools with me." He opened his Gladstone bag as he spoke, and took out, to my astonishment, a very large bath sponge.

"He! he! You are a funny one," chuckled the inspector.

"Now, if you will have the great goodness to open that door very quietly, we will soon make him cut a much more respectable figure."

"Well, I don't know why not," said the inspector. "He doesn't look a credit to the Bow-street cells, does he?" He slipped his key into the lock, and we all very quietly entered the cell. The sleeper half turned, and then settled down once more into a deep slumber. Holmes stooped to the water jug, moistened his sponge, and then rubbed it twice vigorously across and down the prisoner's face.

"Let me introduce you," he shouted, "to Mr. Neville St. Clair, of Lee, in the county of Kent."

Never in my life have I seen such a sight. The man's face peeled off under the sponge like the bark from a tree. Gone was the

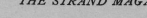

"HE TOOK OUT A VERY LARGE BATH SPONGE."

coarse brown tint! Gone, too, the horrid scar which had seamed it across, and the twisted lip which had given the repulsive sneer to the face! A twitch brought away the tangled red hair, and there, sitting up in his bed, was a pale, sad-faced, refined-looking man, black-haired and smooth-skinned, rubbing his eyes, and staring about him with sleepy bewilderment. Then suddenly realising the exposure, he broke into a scream, and threw himself down with his face to the pillow.

"Great heaven!" cried the inspector, "it is, indeed, the missing man. I know him from the photograph."

The prisoner turned with the reckless air of a man who abandons himself to his destiny. "Be it so," said he. "And pray, what am I charged with?"

"With making away with Mr. Neville St.—— Oh, come, you can't be charged with that, unless they make a case of attempted suicide of it," said the inspector, with a grin. "Well, I have been twenty-seven years in the force, but this really takes the cake."

"If I am Mr. Neville St. Clair, then it is obvious that no crime has been committed, and that, therefore, I am illegally detained."

"No crime, but a very great error has been committed," said Holmes. "You would have done better to have trusted your wife."

"It was not the wife, it was the children," groaned the prisoner. "God help me, I would not have them ashamed of their

"HE BROKE INTO A SCREAM."

father. My God! What an exposure! What can I do?"

Sherlock Holmes sat down beside him on the couch, and patted him kindly on the shoulder.

"If you leave it to a court of law to clear the matter up," said he, "of course you can hardly avoid publicity. On the other hand, if you convince the police authorities that there is no possible case against you, I do not know that there is any reason that the details should find their way into the papers. Inspector Bradstreet would, I am sure, make notes upon anything which you might tell us, and submit it to the proper authorities. The case would then never go into court at all."

"God bless you!" cried the prisoner, passionately. "I would have endured imprisonment, aye, even execution, rather than have left my miserable secret as a family blot to my children.

"You are the first who have ever heard my story. My father was a schoolmaster in Chesterfield, where I received an excellent education. I travelled in my youth, took to the stage, and finally became a reporter on an evening paper in London. One day my editor wished to have a series of articles upon begging in the metropolis, and I volunteered to supply them. There was the point from which all my adventures started. "It was only by trying begging as an amateur that I could get the facts upon which to base my articles. When an actor I had, of course, learned all the secrets of making up, and had been famous in the green-room for my skill. I took advantage now of my attainments. I painted my face, and, to make myself as pitiable as possible I made a good scar and fixed one side of my lip in a twist by the aid of a small slip of flesh-coloured plaster. Then with a red head of hair, and an appropriate dress, I took my station in the busiest part of the City, ostensibly as a match-seller, but really as a beggar. For seven hours I plied my trade, and when I returned home in the evening I found, to my surprise, that I had received no less than twenty-six shillings and fourpence.

"I wrote my articles, and thought little more of the matter until, some time later, I backed a bill for a friend, and had a writ served upon me for £25. I was at my wits' end where to get the money, but a sudden idea came to me. I begged a fortnight's grace from the creditor, asked for a holiday from my employers, and spent the time in begging in the City under my disguise. In ten days I had the money, and had paid the debt.

"Well, you can imagine how hard it was to settle down to arduous work at two pounds a week, when I knew that I could earn as much in a day by smearing my face with a little paint, laying my cap on the ground, and sitting still. It was a long fight between my pride and the money, but the dollars won at last, and I threw up reporting, and sat day after day in the corner which I had first chosen, inspiring pity by my ghastly face, and filling my pockets with coppers. Only one man knew my secret. He was the keeper of a low den in which I used to lodge in Swandamlane, where I could every morning emerge as a squalid beggar, and in the evenings transform myself into a well-dressed man about town. This fellow, a Lascar, was well paid by me for his rooms, so that I knew that my secret was safe in his possession.

"Well, very soon I found that I was saving considerable sums of money. I do not mean that any beggar in the streets of London could earn seven hundred pounds a year—which is less than my average takings—but I had exceptional advantages in my power of making up, and also in a facility in repartee, which improved by practice, and made me quite a recognised character in the City. All day a stream of pennies, varied by silver, poured in upon me, and it was a very bad day upon which I failed to take two pounds.

"As I grew richer I grew more ambitious, took a house in the country, and eventually married, without anyone having a suspicion as to my real occupation. My dear wife knew that I had business in the City. She little knew what.

"Last Monday I had finished for the day, and was dressing in my room above the opium den, when I looked out of the window, and saw, to my horror and astonishment, that my wife was standing in the street, with her eyes fixed full upon me. I gave a cry of surprise, threw up my arms to cover my face, and, rushing to my confidant, the Lascar, entreated him to prevent anyone from coming up to me. I heard her voice downstairs, but I knew that she could not ascend. Swiftly I threw off my clothes, pulled on those of a beggar, and put on my pigments and wig. Even a wife's eyes could not pierce so complete a disguise. But then it occurred to me that there might be a search in the room, and that the clothes might betray me. I threw open the window, re-opening by my violence a small cut which I had inflicted upon myself in the bedroom that morning. Then I seized my coat, which was weighted by the coppers which I had just transferred to it from the leather bag in which I carried my takings. I hurled it out of the window, and it disappeared into the Thames. The other clothes would have followed, but at that moment there was a rush of constables up the stair, and a few minutes after I found, rather, I confess, to my relief, that instead of being identified as Mr. Neville St. Clair, I was arrested as his murderer.

"I do not know that there is anything else for me to explain. I was determined to preserve my disguise as long as possible, and hence my preference for a dirty face. Knowing that my wife would be terribly anxious, I slipped off my ring, and confided it to the Lascar at a moment when no constable was watching me, together with a hurried scrawl, telling her that she had no cause to fear."

"That note only reached her yesterday," said Holmes.

"Good God! What a week she must have spent."

"The police have watched this Lascar," said Inspector Bradstreet, "and I can quite understand that he might find it difficult to post a letter unobserved. Probably he handed it to some sailor customer of his, who forgot all about it for some days."

"That was it," said Holmes, nodding approvingly, "I have no doubt of it. But have you never been prosecuted for begging?"

"Many times; but what was a fine to me?"

"It must stop here, however," said Bradstreet. "If the police are to hush this thing up, there must be no more of Hugh Boone."

"I have sworn it by the most solemn oaths which a man can take."

"In that case I think that it is probable that no further steps may be taken. But if you are found again, then all must come out. I am sure, Mr. Holmes, that we are very much indebted to you for having cleared the matter up. I wish I knew how you reach your results."

"I reached this one," said my friend, "by sitting upon five pillows and consuming an ounce of shag. I think, Watson, that if we drive to Baker-street we shall just be in time for breakfast."

Adventures of Sherlock Holmes.

VII.—THE ADVENTURE OF THE BLUE CARBUNCLE.

By A. Conan Doyle.

I HAD called upon my friend Sherlock Holmes upon the second morning after Christmas, with the intention of wishing him the compliments of the season. He was lounging upon the sofa in a purple dressing-gown, a pipe-rack within his reach upon the right, and a pile of crumpled morning papers, evidently newly studied, near at hand. Beside the couch was a wooden chair, and on the angle of the back hung a very seedy and disreputable hard felt hat, much the worse for wear, and cracked in several places. A lens and a forceps lying upon the seat of the chair suggested that the hat had been suspended in this manner for the purpose of examination.

"You are engaged," said I; "perhaps I interrupt you."

"Not at all. I am glad to have a friend with whom I can discuss my results. The matter is a perfectly trivial one" (he jerked his thumb in the direction of the old hat), "but there are points in connection with it which are not entirely devoid of interest, and even of instruction."

I seated myself in his armchair, and warmed my hands before his crackling fire, for a sharp frost had set in, and the windows were thick with the ice crystals. "I suppose," I remarked, "that, homely as it looks, this thing has some deadly story linked on to it—that it is the clue which will guide you in the solution of some mystery, and the punishment of some crime."

"No, no. No crime," said Sherlock Holmes, laughing. "Only one of those whimsical little incidents which will happen when you have four million human beings all jostling each other within the space of a few square miles. Amid the action and reaction of so dense a swarm of humanity, every possible combination of events may be expected to take place, and many a little problem will be presented which may be striking and bizarre without being criminal. We have already had experience of such."

"A VERY SEEDY HARD FELT HAT."

"So much so," I remarked, "that, of the last six cases which I have added to my notes, three have been entirely free of any legal crime."

"Precisely. You allude to my attempt to recover the Irene Adler papers, to the singular case of Miss Mary Sutherland, and to the adventure of the man with the twisted lip. Well, I have no doubt that this small matter will fall into the same innocent category. You know Peterson, the commissionaire?"

"Yes."

"It is to him that this trophy belongs."

"It is his hat."

"No, no; he found it. Its owner is unknown. I beg that you will look upon it, not as a battered billycock, but as an intellectual problem. And, first, as to how it came here. It arrived upon Christmas morning, in company with a good fat goose, which is, I have no doubt, roasting at this moment in front of Peterson's fire. The facts are these. About four o'clock on Christmas morning, Peterson, who, as you know, is a very honest fellow, was returning from some small jollification, and was making his way homewards down Tottenham Court-road. In front of him he saw, in the gaslight, a tallish man, walking with a slight stagger, and carrying a white goose slung over his shoulder. As he reached the corner of Goodge-street, a row broke out between this stranger and a little knot of roughs. One of the latter knocked off the man's hat, on which he raised his stick to defend himself, and, swinging it over his head, smashed the shop window behind him. Peterson had rushed forward to protect the stranger from his assailants, but the man, shocked at having broken the

"THE ROUGHS HAD FLED AT THE APPEARANCE OF PETERSON."

window, and seeing an official-looking person in uniform rushing towards him, dropped his goose, took to his heels, and vanished amid the labyrinth of small streets which lie at the back of Tottenham Court-road. The roughs had also fled at the appearance of Peterson, so that he was left in possession of the field of battle, and also of the spoils of victory in the shape of this battered hat and a most unimpeachable Christmas goose."

"Which surely he restored to their owner?"

"My dear fellow, there lies the problem. It is true that 'For Mrs. Henry Baker' was printed upon a small card which was tied to the bird's left leg, and it is also true that the initials 'H. B.' are legible upon the lining of this hat; but, as there are some thousands of Bakers, and some hundreds of Henry Bakers in this city of ours, it is not easy to restore lost property to any one of them."

"What, then, did Peterson do?"

"He brought round both hat and goose to me on Christmas morning, knowing that even the smallest problems are of interest to me. The goose we retained until this morning, when there were signs that, in spite of the slight frost, it would be well that it should be eaten without unnecessary delay. Its finder has carried it off, therefore, to fulfil the ultimate destiny of a goose, while I continue to retain the hat of the unknown gentleman who lost his Christmas dinner."

" Did he not advertise ? "

" No."

" Then, what clue could you have as to his identity ? "

" Only as much as we can deduce."

" From his hat ? "

" Precisely."

"But you are joking. What ca.. you gather from this old battered felt ? "

" Here is my lens. You know my methods. What can you gather yourself as to the individuality of the man who has worn this article ? "

I took the tattered object in my hands, and turned it over rather ruefully. It was a very ordinary black hat of the usual round shape, hard, and much the worse for wear. The lining had been of red silk, but was a good deal discoloured. There was no maker's name ; but, as Holmes had remarked, the initials " H. B." were scrawled upon one side. It was pierced in the brim for a hat-securer, but the elastic was missing. For the rest, it was cracked, exceedingly dusty, and spotted in several places, although there seemed to have been some attempt to hide the discoloured patches by smearing them with ink.

" I can see nothing," said I, handing it back to my friend.

" On the contrary, Watson, you can see everything. You fail, however, to reason from what you see. You are too timid in drawing your inferences."

" Then, pray tell me what it is that you can infer from this hat ? "

He picked it up, and gazed at it in the peculiar introspective fashion which was characteristic of him. "It is perhaps less suggestive than it might have been," he remarked, " and yet there are a few inferences which are very distinct, and a few others which represent at least a strong balance of probability. That the man was highly intellectual is of course obvious upon the face of it, and also that he was fairly well-to-do within the last three years, although he has now fallen upon evil days. He had foresight, but has less now than formerly, pointing to a moral retrogression, which, when taken with the decline of his fortunes, seems to indicate some evil influence, probably drink, at work upon him. This may account also for the obvious fact that his wife has ceased to love. him."

" My dear Holmes ! "

" He has, however, retained some degree of self-respect," he continued, disregarding my remonstrance. " He is a man who leads a sedentary life, goes out little, is out of training entirely, is middle-aged, has grizzled hair which he has had cut within the last few days, and which he anoints with lime-cream. These are the more patent facts which are to be deduced from his hat. Also, by the way, that it is extremely improbable that he has gas laid on in his house."

" You are certainly joking, Holmes."

." Not in the least. Is it possible that even now when I give you these results you are unable to see how they are attained ? "

" I have no doubt that I am very stupid ; but I must. confess that I am unable to follow you. For example, how did you deduce that this man was intellectual ? "

For answer Holmes clapped the hat upon his head. It came right over the forehead and settled upon the bridge of his nose. "It is a question of cubic capacity," said he ; " a man with so large a brain must have something in it."

" The decline of his fortunes, then ? "

" This hat is three years old. These flat brims curled at the edge came in then. It is a hat of the very best quality. Look at the band of ribbed silk, and the excellent lining. If this man could afford to buy so expensive a hat three years ago, and has had no hat since, then he has assuredly gone down in the world."

" Well, that is clear enough, certainly. But how about the foresight, and the moral retrogression ? "

Sherlock Holmes laughed. " Here is the foresight," said he, putting his finger upon the little disc and loop of the hat-securer. "They are never sold upon hats. If this man ordered one, it is a sign of a certain amount of foresight, since he went out of his way to take this precaution against the wind. But since we see that he has broken the elastic, and has not troubled to replace it, it is obvious that he has less foresight now than formerly, which is a distinct proof of a weakening nature. On the other hand, he has endeavoured to conceal some of these stains upon the felt by daubing them with ink, which is a sign that he has not entirely lost his self-respect."

"Your reasoning is certainly plausible."

"The further points, that he is middle-aged, that his hair is grizzled, that it has been recently cut, and that he uses lime-cream, are all to be gathered from a close examination of the lower part of the lining. The lens discloses a large number of hair ends, clean cut by the scissors of the barber. They all appear to be adhesive, and there is a distinct odour of lime-cream. This dust, you will observe, is not the gritty, grey dust of the street, but the fluffy brown dust of the house, showing that it has been hung up indoors most of the time ; while the marks of moisture upon the inside are proof positive that the wearer perspired very freely, and could, therefore, hardly be in the best of training."

"But his wife—you said that she had ceased to love him."

"This hat has not been brushed for weeks. When I see you, my dear Watson, with a week's accumulation of dust upon your hat, and when your wife allows you to go out in such a state, I shall fear that you also have been unfortunate enough to lose your wife's affection."

"But he might be a bachelor."

"Nay, he was bringing home the goose as a peace-offering to his wife. Remember the card upon the bird's leg."

"You have an answer to everything. But how on earth do you deduce that the gas is not laid on in his house ? "

"One tallow stain, or even two, might come by chance ; but, when I see no less than five, I think that there can be little doubt that the individual must be brought into frequent contact with burning tallow —walks upstairs at night probably with his hat in one hand and a guttering candle in the other. Anyhow, he never got tallow stains from a gas jet. Are you satisfied ? "

"Well, it is very ingenious," said I,

laughing ; "but, since, as you said just now, there has been no crime committed, and no harm done save the loss of a goose, all this seems to be rather a waste of energy."

Sherlock Holmes had opened his mouth to reply, when the door flew open, and Peterson the commissionaire rushed into the apartment with flushed cheeks and the face of a man who is dazed with astonishment.

"The goose, Mr. Holmes ! The goose, sir !" he gasped.

"Eh ? What of it, then ? Has it returned to life, and flapped off through the kitchen window ? " Holmes twisted himself round upon the sofa to get a fairer view of the man's excited face.

"SEE WHAT MY WIFE FOUND IN ITS CROP ! "

"See here, sir ! See what my wife found in its crop ! " He held out his hand, and displayed upon the centre of the palm a brilliantly scintillating blue stone, rather smaller than a bean in size, but of such purity and radiance that it twinkled like an electric point in the dark hollow of his hand.

Sherlock Holmes sat up with a whistle. "By Jove, Peterson ! " said he, "this is treasure trove indeed. I suppose you know what you have got ? "

"A diamond, sir ! A precious stone ! It cuts into glass as though it were putty."

"It's more than a precious stone. It's *the* precious stone."

"Not the Countess of Morcar's blue carbuncle ! " I ejaculated.

"Precisely so. I ought to know its size and shape, seeing that I have read the advertisement about it in *The Times* every day lately. It is absolutely unique, and its value can only be conjectured, but the reward offered of a thousand pounds is certainly not within a twentieth part of the market price."

"A thousand pounds ! Great Lord of mercy ! " The commissionaire plumped down into a chair, and stared from one to the other of us.

"That is the reward, and I have reason to know that there are sentimental considerations in the background which would induce the Countess to part with half her fortune, if she could but recover the gem."

"It was lost, if I remember aright, at the Hotel Cosmopolitan," I remarked.

"Precisely so, on the twenty-second of December, just five days ago. John Horner, a plumber, was accused of having abstracted it from the lady's jewel case. The evidence against him was so strong that the case has been referred to the Assizes. I have some account of the matter here, I believe." He rummaged amid his newspapers, glancing over the dates, until at last he smoothed one out, doubled it over, and read the following paragraph :—

"Hotel Cosmopolitan Jewel Robbery. John Horner, 26, plumber, was brought up upon the charge of having upon the 22nd inst. abstracted from the jewel case of the Countess of Morcar the valuable gem known as the blue carbuncle. James Ryder, upperattendant at the hotel, gave his evidence to the effect that he had shown Horner up to the dressing-room of the Countess of Morcar upon the day of the robbery, in order that he might solder the second bar of the grate, which was loose. He had remained with Horner some little time, but had finally been called away. On returning, he found that Horner had disappeared, that the bureau had been forced open, and that the small morocco casket in which, as it afterwards transpired, the Countess was accustomed to keep her jewel was lying empty upon the dressing-table. Ryder instantly gave the alarm, and Horner was arrested the same evening ; but the stone could not be found either upon his person or in his rooms. Catherine Cusack, maid to the Countess, deposed to having heard Ryder's cry of dismay on discovering the robbery,

and to having rushed into the room, where she found matters as described by the last witness. Inspector Bradstreet, B division, gave evidence as to the arrest of Horner, who struggled frantically, and protested his innocence in the strongest terms. Evidence of a previous conviction for robbery having been given against the prisoner, the magistrate refused to deal summarily with the offence, but referred it to the Assizes. Horner, who had shown signs of intense emotion during the proceedings, fainted away at the conclusion, and was carried out of court."

"Hum ! So much for the police-court," said Holmes, thoughtfully, tossing aside the paper. "The question for us now to solve is the sequence of events leading from a rifled jewel case at one end to the crop of a goose in Tottenham Court-road at the other. You see, Watson, our little deductions have suddenly assumed a much more important and less innocent aspect. Here is the stone ; the stone came from the goose, and the goose came from Mr. Henry Baker, the gentleman with the bad hat and all the other characteristics with which I have bored you. So now we must set ourselves very seriously to finding this gentleman, and ascertaining what part he has played in this little mystery. To do this, we must try the simplest means first, and these lie undoubtedly in an advertisement in all the evening papers. If this fail, I shall have recourse to other methods."

"What will you say ? "

"Give me a pencil, and that slip of paper. Now, then: 'Found at the corner of Goodge-street, a goose and a black felt hat. Mr. Henry Baker can have the same by applying at 6.30 this evening at 221B, Baker-street.' That is clear and concise."

"Very. But will he see it ? "

"Well, he is sure to keep an eye on the papers, since, to a poor man, the loss was a heavy one. He was clearly so scared by his mischance in breaking the window, and by the approach of Peterson, that he thought of nothing but flight ; but since then he must have bitterly regretted the impulse which caused him to drop his bird. Then, again, the introduction of his name will cause him to see it, for everyone who knows him will direct his attention to it. Here you are, Peterson, run down to the advertising agency, and have this put in the evening papers."

"In which, sir."

"Oh, in the *Globe, Star, Pall Mall, St.*

James's, Evening News, Standard, Echo, and any others that occur to you."

"Very well, sir. And this stone?"

"Ah, yes, I shall keep the stone. Thank you. And, I say, Peterson, just buy a goose on your way back, and leave it here with me, for we must have one to give to this gentleman in place of the one which your family is now devouring."

When the commissionaire had gone, Holmes took up the stone and held it against the light. "It's a bonny thing," said he. "Just see how it glints and sparkles. Of course it is a nucleus and focus of crime. Every good stone is. They are the devil's pet baits. In the larger and older jewels every facet may stand for a bloody deed. This stone is not yet twenty years old. It was found in the banks of the Amoy River in Southern China, and is remarkable in having every characteristic of the carbuncle, save that it is blue in shade, instead of ruby red. In spite of its youth, it has already a sinister history. There have been two murders, a vitriol-throwing, a suicide, and several robberies brought about for the sake of this forty-grain weight of crystallised charcoal. Who would think that so-pretty a toy would be a purveyor to the gallows and the prison? I'll lock it up in my strong box now, and drop a line to the Countess to say that we have it."

"Do you think that this man Horner is innocent?"

"I cannot tell."

"Well, then, do you imagine that this other one, Henry Baker, had anything to do with the matter?"

"It is, I think, much more likely that Henry Baker is an absolutely innocent man, who had no idea that the bird which he was carrying was of considerably more value than if it were made of solid gold. That, however, I shall determine by a very simple test, if we have an answer to our advertisement."

"And you can do nothing until then?"

"Nothing."

"In that case I shall continue my professional round. But I shall come back in the evening at the hour you have mentioned, for I should like to see the solution of so tangled a business."

"Very glad to see you. I dine at seven. There is a woodcock, I believe. By the way, in view of recent occurrences, perhaps I ought to ask Mrs. Hudson to examine its crop."

I had been delayed at a case, and it was a little after half-past six when I found myself in Baker-street once more. As I approached the house I saw a tall man in a Scotch bonnet, with a coat which was buttoned up to his chin, waiting outside in the bright semicircle which was thrown from the fanlight. Just as I arrived, the door was opened, and we were shown up together to Holmes' room.

"Mr. Henry Baker, I believe," said he, rising from his armchair, and greeting his visitor with the easy air of geniality which he could so readily assume. "Pray take this chair by the fire, Mr. Baker. It is a cold night, and I observe that your circulation is more adapted for summer than for winter. Ah, Watson, you have just come at the right time. Is that your hat, Mr. Baker?"

"Yes, sir, that is undoubtedly my hat."

He was a large man, with rounded shoulders, a massive head, and a broad, intelligent face, sloping down to a pointed beard of grizzled brown. A touch of red in nose and cheeks, with a slight tremor of his extended hand, recalled Holmes' surmise as to his habits. His rusty black frock coat was buttoned right up in front, with the collar turned up, and his lank wrists protruded from his sleeves without a sign of cuff or shirt. He spoke in a slow staccato fashion, choosing his words with care, and gave the impression generally of a man of learning and letters who had had ill-usage at the hands of fortune.

"We have retained these things for some days," said Holmes, "because we expected to see an advertisement from you giving your address. I am at a loss to know now why you did not advertise."

Our visitor gave a rather shame-faced laugh. "Shillings have not been so plentiful with me as they once were," he remarked. "I had no doubt that the gang of roughs who assaulted me had carried off both my hat and the bird. I did not care to spend more money in a hopeless attempt at recovering them."

"Very naturally. By the way, about the bird, we were compelled to eat it."

"To eat it!" Our visitor half rose from his chair in his excitement.

"Yes, it would have been no use to anyone had we not done so. But I presume that this other goose upon the sideboard, which is about the same weight and perfectly fresh, will answer your purpose equally well?"

"Oh, certainly, certainly!" answered Mr. Baker, with a sigh of relief.

"Of course, we still have the feathers, legs, crop, and so on of your own bird, so if you wish——"

The man burst into a hearty laugh. "They might be useful to me as relics of my adventure," said he, "but beyond that I can hardly see what use the *disjecta membra* of my late acquaintance are going to be to me. No, sir, I think that, with your permission, I will confine my attentions to the excellent bird which I perceive upon the sideboard."

Sherlock Holmes glanced sharply across at me with a slight shrug of his shoulders.

"There is your hat, then, and there your bird," said he. "By the way, would it bore you to tell me where you got the other one from? I am somewhat of a fowl fancier, and I have seldom seen a better-grown goose."

"Certainly, sir," said Baker, who had risen and tucked his newly-gained property under his arm. "There are a few of us who frequent the 'Alpha' Inn, near the Museum—we are to be found in the Museum itself during the day, you understand. This year our good host, Windigate by name, instituted a goose club, by which, on consideration of some few pence every week, we were each to receive a bird at Christmas. My pence were duly paid, and the rest is familiar to you. I am much

"HE BOWED SOLEMNLY TO BOTH OF US."

indebted to you, sir, for a Scotch bonnet is fitted neither to my years nor my gravity." With a comical pomposity of manner he bowed solemnly to both of us, and strode off upon his way.

"So much for Mr. Henry Baker," said Holmes, when he had closed the door behind him. "It is quite certain that he knows nothing whatever about the matter. Are you hungry, Watson?"

"Not particularly."

"Then I suggest that we turn our dinner into a supper, and follow up this clue while it is still hot."

"By all means."

It was a bitter night, so we drew on our ulsters and wrapped cravats about our throats. Outside, the stars were shining coldly in a cloudless sky, and the breath of the passers-by blew out into smoke like so many pistol shots. Our footfalls rang out crisply and loudly as we swung through the Doctors' quarter, Wimpole-street, Harley-street, and so through Wigmore-street into Oxford-street. In a quarter of an hour we were in Bloomsbury at the "Alpha" Inn, which is a small public-house at the corner of one of the streets which runs down into Holborn. Holmes pushed open the door of the private bar, and ordered two glasses of beer from the ruddy-faced, white-aproned landlord.

"Your beer should be excellent if it is as good as your geese," said he.

"My geese!" The man seemed surprised.

"Yes. I was speaking only half an hour ago to Mr. Henry Baker, who was a member of your goose-club."

"Ah! yes, I see. But you see, sir, them's not *our* geese."

"Indeed! Whose, then?"

"Well, I got the two dozen from a salesman in Covent Garden."

"Indeed! I know some of them. Which was it?"

"Breckinridge is his name."

"Ah! I don't know him. Well, here's your good health, landlord, and prosperity to your house. Good-night!"

"Now for Mr. Breckinridge," he continued, buttoning up his coat, as we came out into the frosty air. "Remember, Watson, that though we have so homely a thing as a goose at one end of this chain, we have at the other a man who will certainly get seven years' penal servitude, unless we can establish his innocence. It is possible that our inquiry may but confirm his guilt ; but, in any case, we have a line of investigation which has been missed by the police, and which a singular chance has placed in our hands. Let us follow it out to the bitter end. Faces to the south, then, and quick march !"

We passed across Holborn, down Endell-street, and so through a zigzag of slums to Covent Garden Market. One of the largest stalls bore the name of Breckinridge upon it, and the proprietor, a horsey-looking man, with a sharp face and trim side-whiskers, was helping a boy to put up the shutters.

"Good evening. It's a cold night," said Holmes.

The salesman nodded, and shot a questioning glance at my companion.

"Sold out of geese, I see," continued Holmes, pointing at the bare slabs of marble.

"Let you have five hundred to-morrow morning."

"That's no good."

"Well, there are some on the stall with the gas flare."

"Ah, but I was recommended to you."

"Who by ? "

"The landlord of the ' Alpha.' "

"Oh, yes ; I sent him a couple of dozen."

"Fine birds they were, too. Now where did you get them from ? "

To my surprise the question provoked a burst of anger from the salesman.

"Now, then, mister," said he, with his head cocked and his arms akimbo, "what are you driving at ? Let's have it straight, now."

"It is straight enough. I should like to know who sold you the geese which you supplied to the ' Alpha.' "

"Well, then, I sha'n't tell you. So now !"

"Oh, it is a matter of no importance ; but I don't know why you should be so warm over such a trifle."

"Warm ! You'd be as warm, maybe, if you were as pestered as I am. When I pay good money for a good article there should be an end of the business ; but it's ' Where are the geese ? ' and ' Who did you sell the geese to ? ' and ' What will you take for the geese ? ' One would think they were the only geese in the world, to hear the fuss that is made over them."

"Well, I have no connection with any other people who have been making inquiries," said Holmes, carelessly. " If you won't tell us the bet is off, that is all. But I'm always ready to back my opinion on a matter of fowls, and I have a fiver on it that the bird I ate is country bred."

"Well, then, you've lost your fiver, for it's town bred," snapped the salesman.

"It's nothing of the kind."

"I say it is."

"I don't believe it."

"D'you think you know more about fowls than I, who have handled them ever since I was a nipper ? I tell you, all those birds that went to the ' Alpha ' were town bred."

"You'll never persuade me to believe that."

"Will you bet, then ? "

"It's merely taking your money, for I know that I am right. But I'll have a sovereign on with you, just to teach you not to be obstinate."

The salesman chuckled grimly. " Bring me the books, Bill," said he.

The small boy brought round a small thin volume and a great greasy-backed one, laying them out together beneath the hanging lamp.

"Now then, Mr. Cocksure," said the salesman, " I thought that I was out of geese, but before I finish you'll find that there is still one left in my shop. You see this little book ? "

"Well ? "

"That's the list of the folk from whom I buy. D'you see ? Well, then, here on this page are the country folk, and the numbers after their names are where their accounts are in the big ledger. Now, then ! You see this other page in red ink ? Well, that is a list of my town suppliers. Now, look at that third name. Just read it out to me."

"Mrs. Oakshott, 117, Brixton-road—249," read Holmes.

"Quite so. Now turn that up in the ledger."

Holmes turned to the page indicated. "Here you are,'Mrs. Oakshott, 117, Brixton-road, egg and poultry supplier.' "

"Now, then, what's the last entry ? "

" ' December 22. Twenty-four geese at 7s. 6d.' "

"Quite so. There you are. And underneath ? "

" ' Sold to Mr. Windigate of the "Alpha" at 12s.' "

"What have you to say now ? "

"JUST READ IT OUT TO ME."

Sherlock Holmes looked deeply chagrined. He drew a sovereign from his pocket and threw it down upon the slab, turning away with the air of a man whose disgust is too deep for words. A few yards off he stopped under a lamp-post, and laughed in the hearty, noiseless fashion which was peculiar to him.

" When you see a man with whiskers of that cut and the ' pink 'un ' protruding out of his pocket, you can always draw him by a bet," said he. " I daresay that if I had put a hundred pounds down in front of him that man would not have given me such complete information as was drawn from him by the idea that he was doing me on a wager. Well, Watson, we are, I fancy, nearing the end of our quest, and the only point which remains to be determined is whether we should go on to this Mrs. Oakshott to-night, or whether we should reserve it for to-morrow. It is clear from what that surly fellow said that there are others besides ourselves who are anxious about the matter, and I should——"

His remarks were suddenly cut short by a loud hubbub which broke out from the stall which we had just left. Turning round we saw a little rat-faced fellow standing in the centre of the circle of yellow light which was thrown by the swinging lamp, while Breckinridge the salesman, framed in the door of his stall, was shaking his fists fiercely at the cringing figure.

" I've had enough of you and your geese," he shouted. " I wish you were all at the devil together. If you come pestering me any more with your silly talk I'll set the dog at you. You bring Mrs. Oakshott here and I'll answer her, but what have you to do with it ? Did I buy the geese off you ? "

" No ; but one of them was mine all the same," whined the little man.

" Well, then, ask Mrs. Oakshott for it."

" She told me to ask you."

" Well, you can ask the King of Proosia for all I care. I've had enough of it. Get out of this ! " He rushed fiercely forward, and the inquirer flitted away into the darkness.

" Ha, this may save us a visit to Brixtonroad," whispered Holmes. " Come with me, and we will see what is to be made of this fellow." Striding through the scattered knots of people who lounged round the flaring stalls, my companion speedily overtook the little man and touched him upon the shoulder. He sprang round, and I could see in the gaslight that every vestige of colour had been driven from his face.

" Who are you, then ? What do you want ? " he asked in a quavering voice.

" You will excuse me," said Holmes

blandly, " but I could not help overhearing the questions which you put to the salesman just now. I think that I could be of assistance to you."

"You? Who are you? How could you know anything of the matter?"

"My name is Sherlock Holmes. It is my business to know what other people don't know."

"But you can know nothing of this?"

"Excuse me, I know everything of it. You are endeavouring to trace some geese which were sold by Mrs. Oakshott, of

"YOU ARE THE VERY MAN."

Brixton-road, to a salesman named Breck-inridge, by him in turn to Mr. Windigate, of the ' Alpha;' and by him to his club, of which Mr. Henry Baker is a member."

"Oh, sir, you are the very man whom I have longed to meet," cried the little fellow, with outstretched hands and quivering fingers. " I can hardly explain to you how interested I am in this matter."

Sherlock Holmes hailed a four-wheeler

which was passing. " In that case we had better discuss it in a cosy room rather than in this windswept market-place," said he. " But pray tell me, before we go further, who it is that I have the pleasure of assisting."

The man hesitated for an instant. " My name is John Robinson," he answered, with a sidelong glance.

"No, no ; the real name," said Holmes, sweetly. " It is always awkward doing business with an *alias*."

A flush sprang to the white cheeks of the stranger. " Well, then," said he, " my real name is James Ryder."

"Precisely so. Head attendant at the Hotel Cosmopolitan. Pray step into the cab, and I shall soon be able to tell you everything which you would wish to know."

The little man stood glancing from one to the other of us with half-frightened, half-hopeful eyes, as one who is not sure whether he is on the verge of a windfall or of a catastrophe. Then he stepped into the cab, and in half an hour we were back in the sitting-room at Baker-street. Nothing had been said during our drive, but the high thin breathing of our new companion, and the claspings and unclaspings of his hands spoke of the nervous tension within him.

"Here we are!" said Holmes, cheerily, as we filed into the room. " The fire looks very seasonable in this weather. You look cold, Mr. Ryder. Pray take the basket chair. I will just put on my slippers before we settle this little matter of yours. Now, then ! You want to know what became of those geese?"

"Yes, sir."

"Or rather, I fancy, of that goose. It was one bird, I imagine, in which you were interested—white, with a black bar across the tail."

Ryder quivered with emotion. "Oh,

sir, he cried, "can you tell me where it went to?"

"It came here."

"Here?"

"Yes, and a most remarkable bird it proved. I don't wonder that you should take an interest in it. It laid an egg after it was dead—the bonniest, brightest little blue egg that ever was seen. I have it here in my museum."

Our visitor staggered to his feet, and clutched the mantelpiece with his right hand. Holmes unlocked his strong box, and held up the blue carbuncle, which shone out like a star, with a cold, brilliant, many-pointed radiance. Ryder stood glaring with a drawn face, uncertain whether to claim or to disown it.

"The game's up, Ryder," said Holmes, quietly. "Hold up, man, or you'll be into the fire. Give him an arm back into his chair, Watson. He's not got blood enough to go in for felony with impunity. Give him a dash of brandy. So! Now he looks a little more human. What a shrimp it is, to be sure!"

For a moment he had staggered and nearly fallen, but the brandy brought a tinge of colour into his cheeks, and he sat staring with frightened eyes at his accuser.

"I have almost every link in my hands, and all the proofs which I could possibly need, so there is little which you need tell me. Still that little may as well be cleared up to make the case complete. You had heard, Ryder, of this blue stone of the Countess of Morcar's?"

"It was Catherine Cusack who told me of it," said he, in a crackling voice.

"I see. Her ladyship's waiting maid. Well, the temptation of sudden wealth so easily acquired was too much for you, as it has been for better men before you; but you were not very scrupulous in the means you used. It seems to me, Ryder, that there is the making of a very pretty villain in you. You knew that this man Horner, the plumber, had been concerned in some such matter before, and that suspicion would rest the more readily upon him. What did you do, then? You made some small job in my lady's room—you and your confederate Cusack—and you managed that he should be the man sent for. Then, when he had left, you rifled the jewel case, raised the alarm, and had this unfortunate man arrested. You then——"

Ryder threw himself down suddenly upon the rug, and clutched at my companion's knees. "For God's sake, have mercy!" he shrieked. "Think of my father! Of my mother! It would break their hearts. I never went wrong before! I never will

"'HAVE MERCY!' HE SHRIEKED."

again. I swear it. I'll swear it on a Bible. Oh, don't bring it into court! For Christ's sake, don't!"

"Get back into your chair!" said Holmes, sternly. "It is very well to cringe and crawl now, but you thought little enough of this poor Horner in the dock for a crime of which he knew nothing."

"I will fly, Mr. Holmes. I will leave the country, sir. Then the charge against him will break down."

"Hum! We will talk about that. And now let us hear a true account of the next act. How came the stone into the goose, and how came the goose into the open market? Tell us the truth, for there lies your only hope of safety."

Ryder passed his tongue over his parched lips. "I will tell you it just as it happened, sir," said he. "When Horner had been arrested, it seemed to me that it would be best for me to get away with the stone at once, for I did not know at what moment the police might not take it into their heads to search me and my room. There was no place about the hotel where it would be safe. I went out, as if on some commission, and I made for my sister's house. She had married a man named Oakshott, and lived in Brixton-road, where she fattened fowls for the market. All the way there every man I met seemed to me to be a policeman or a detective, and for all that it was a cold night, the sweat was pouring down my face before I came to the Brixton-road. My sister asked me what was the matter, and why I was so pale; but I told her that I had been upset by the jewel robbery at the hotel. Then I went into the back yard, and smoked a pipe, and wondered what it would be best to do.

"I had a friend once called Maudsley, who went to the bad, and has just been serving his time in Pentonville. One day he had met me, and fell into talk about the ways of thieves and how they could get rid of what they stole. I knew that he would be true to me, for I knew one or two things about him, so I made up my mind to go right on to Kilburn, where he lived, and take him into my confidence. He would show me how to turn the stone into money. But how to get to him in safety. I thought of the agonies I had gone through in coming from the hotel. I might at any moment be seized and searched, and there would be the stone in my waistcoat pocket. I was leaning against the wall at the time, and looking at the geese which were waddling

about round my feet, and suddenly an idea came into my head which showed me how I could beat the best detective that ever lived.

"My sister had told me some weeks before that I might have the pick of her geese for a Christmas present, and I knew that she was always as good as her word. I would take my goose now, and in it I would carry my stone to Kilburn. There was a little shed in the yard, and behind this I drove one of the birds, a fine big one, white with a barred tail. I caught it, and, prizing its bill open, I thrust the stone down its throat as far as my finger could reach. The bird gave a gulp, and I felt the stone pass along its gullet and down into its crop. But the creature flapped and struggled, and out came my sister to know what was the matter. As I turned to speak to her the brute broke loose, and fluttered off among the others.

"'Whatever were you doing with that bird, Jem?' says she.

"'Well,' said I, 'you said you'd give me one for Christmas, and I was feeling which was the fattest.'

"'Oh,' says she, 'we've set yours aside for you. Jem's bird, we call it. It's the big, white one over yonder. There's twenty-six of them, which makes one for you, and one for us, and two dozen for the market.'

"'Thank you, Maggie,' says I; 'but if it is all the same to you I'd rather have that one I was handling just now.'

"'The other is a good three pound heavier,' said she, 'and we fattened it expressly for you.'

"'Never mind. I'll have the other, and I'll take it now,' said I.

"'Oh, just as you like,' said she, a little huffed. 'Which is it you want, then?'

"'That white one, with the barred tail, right in the middle of the flock.'

"'Oh, very well. Kill it and take it with you.'

"Well, I did what she said, Mr. Holmes, and I carried the bird all the way to Kilburn. I told my pal what I had done, for he was a man that it was easy to tell a thing like that to. He laughed until he choked, and we got a knife and opened the goose. My heart turned to water, for there was no sign of the stone, and I knew that some terrible mistake had occurred. I left the bird, rushed back to my sister's, and hurried into the back yard. There was not a bird to be seen there.

"'Where are they all, Maggie?' I cried.

"'Gone to the dealer's, Jim.'

"'Which dealer's?'

"'Breckinridge, of Covent Garden.

"'But was there another with a barred tail?' I asked, 'the same as the one I chose?'

"'Yes, Jem, there were two barred-tailed ones, and I could never tell them apart.'

"Well, then, of course, I saw it all, and I ran off as hard as my feet would carry me

"What, sir! Oh, heaven bless you!"

"No more words. Get out!"

And no more words were needed. There was a rush, a clatter upon the stairs, the bang of a door, and the crisp rattle of running footfalls from the street.

"HE BURST INTO CONVULSIVE SOBBING."

to this man Breckinridge; but he had sold the lot at once, and not one word would he tell me as to where they had gone. You heard him yourselves to-night. Well, he has always answered me like that. My sister thinks that I am going mad. Sometimes I think that I am myself. And now—and now I am myself a branded thief, without ever having touched the wealth for which I sold my character. God help me! God help me!" He burst into convulsive sobbing, with his face buried in his hands.

There was a long silence, broken only by his heavy breathing, and by the measured tapping of Sherlock Holmes' finger-tips upon the edge of the table. Then my friend rose, and threw open the door.

"Get out!" said he.

"After all, Watson," said Holmes, reaching up his hand for his clay pipe, "I am not retained by the police to supply their deficiencies. If Horner were in danger it would be another thing, but this fellow will not appear against him, and the case must collapse. I suppose that I am commuting a felony, but it is just possible that I am saving a soul. This fellow will not go wrong again. He is too terribly frightened. Send him to gaol now, and you make him a gaol-bird for life. Besides, it is the season of forgiveness. Chance has put in our way a most singular and whimsical problem, and its solution is its own reward. If you will have the goodness to touch the bell, Doctor, we will begin another investigation, in which also a bird will be the chief feature."

Adventures of Sherlock Holmes.

VIII.—THE ADVENTURE OF THE SPECKLED BAND.

By A. Conan Doyle.

N glancing over my notes of the seventy odd cases in which I have during the last eight years studied the methods of my friend Sherlock Holmes, I find many tragic, some comic, a large number merely strange, but none commonplace ; for, working as he did rather for the love of his art than for the acquirement of wealth, he refused to associate himself with any investigation which did not tend towards the unusual, and even the fantastic. Of all these varied cases, however, I cannot recall any which presented more singular features than that which was associated with the well-known Surrey family of the Roylotts of Stoke Moran. The events in question occurred in the early days of my association with Holmes, when we were sharing rooms as bachelors, in Baker-street. It is possible that I might have placed them upon record before, but a promise of secrecy was made at the time; from which I have only been freed during the last month by the untimely death of the lady to whom the pledge was given. It is perhaps as well that the facts should now come to light, for I have reasons to know that there are widespread rumours as to the death of Dr. Grimesby Roylott which tend to make the matter even more terrible than the truth.

It was early in April in the year '83 that I woke one morning to find Sherlock Holmes standing, fully dressed, by the side of my bed. He was a late riser as a rule, and, as the clock on the mantelpiece showed me that it was only a quarter past seven, I blinked up at him in some surprise, and perhaps just a little resentment, for I was myself regular in my habits.

"Very sorry to knock you up, Watson," said he, "but it's the common lot this morning. Mrs. Hudson has been knocked up, she retorted upon me, and I on you."

"What is it, then ? A fire ?"

"No, a client. It seems that a young lady has arrived in a considerable state of excitement, who insists upon seeing me. She is waiting now in the sitting-room. Now, when young ladies wander about the Metropolis at this hour of the morning, and knock sleepy people up out of their beds, I presume that it is something very pressing which they have to communicate. Should it prove to be an interesting case, you would, I am sure, wish to follow it from the outset. I thought at any rate that I should call you, and give you the chance."

"My dear fellow, I would not miss it for anything."

I had no keener pleasure than in following Holmes in his professional investigations, and in admiring the rapid deductions, as swift as intuitions, and yet always founded on a logical basis, with which he unravelled the problems which were submitted to him. I rapidly threw on my clothes, and was ready in a few minutes to accompany my friend down to the sitting-room. A lady dressed in black and heavily veiled, who had been sitting in the window, rose as we entered.

"Good morning, madam," said Holmes, cheerily. "My name is Sherlock Holmes. This is my intimate friend and associate, Dr. Watson, before whom you can speak as freely as before myself. Ha, I am glad to see that Mrs. Hudson has had the good sense to light the fire. Pray draw up to it, and I shall order you a cup of hot coffee, for I observe that you are shivering."

"It is not cold which makes me shiver," said the woman in a low voice, changing her seat as requested.

"What then ?"

"It is fear, Mr. Holmes. It is terror." She raised her veil as she spoke, and we could see that she was indeed in a pitiable state of agitation, her face all drawn and grey, with restless, frightened eyes, like those of some hunted animal. Her features and figure were those of a woman of thirty,

"SHE RAISED HER VEIL."

but her hair was shot with premature grey, and her expression was weary and haggard. Sherlock Holmes ran her over with one of his quick, all-comprehensive glances.

"You must not fear," said he, soothingly, bending forward and patting her forearm. "We shall soon set matters right, I have no doubt. You have come in by train this morning, I see."

"You know me, then?"

"No, but I observe the second half of a return ticket in the palm of your left glove. You must have started early, and yet you had a good drive in a dog-cart, along heavy roads, before you reached the station."

The lady gave a violent start, and stared in bewilderment at my companion.

"There is no mystery, my dear madam," said he, smiling. "The left arm of your jacket is spattered with mud in no less than seven places. The marks are perfectly fresh. There is no vehicle save a dog-cart which throws up mud in that way, and then only when you sit on the left hand side of the driver."

"Whatever your reasons may be, you are perfectly correct," said she. "I started from home before six, reached Leatherhead at twenty past, and came in by the first train to Waterloo. Sir, I can stand this strain no longer, I shall go mad if it continues. I have no one to turn to—none, save only one, who cares for me, and he,

poor fellow, can be of little aid. I have heard of you, Mr. Holmes; I have heard of you from Mrs. Farintosh, whom you helped in the hour of her sore need. It was from her that I had your address. Oh, sir, do you not think that you could help me too, and at least throw a little light through the dense darkness which surrounds me? At present it is out of my power to reward you for your services, but in a month or six weeks I shall be married, with the control of my own income, and then at least you shall not find me ungrateful."

Holmes turned to his desk, and unlocking it, drew out a small case-book which he consulted.

"Farintosh," said he. "Ah, yes, I recall the case; it was concerned with an opal tiara. I think it was before your time, Watson. I can only say, madam, that I shall be happy to devote the same care to your case as I did to that of your friend. As to reward, my profession is its own reward; but you are at liberty to defray whatever expenses I may be put to, at the time which suits you best. And now I beg that you will lay before us everything that may help us in forming an opinion upon the matter."

"Alas!" replied our visitor. "The very horror of my situation lies in the fact that my fears are so vague, and n.y suspicions depend so entirely upon small points, which might seem trivial to another, that even he to whom of all others I have a right to look for help and advice looks upon all that I tell him about it as the fancies of a nervous woman. He does not say so, but I can read it from his soothing answers and averted eyes. But I have heard, Mr. Holmes, that you can see deeply into the manifold wickedness of the human heart.

You may advise me how to walk amid the dangers which encompass me."

"I am all attention, madam."

"My name is Helen Stoner, and I am living with my stepfather, who is the last survivor of one of the oldest Saxon families in England, the Roylotts of Stoke Moran, on the western border of Surrey."

Holmes nodded his head. "The name is familiar to me," said he.

"The family was at one time among the richest in England, and the estates extended over the borders into Berkshire in the north, and Hampshire in the west. In the last century, however, four successive heirs were of a dissolute and wasteful disposition, and the family ruin was eventually completed by a gambler, in the days of the Regency. Nothing was left save a few acres of ground, and the two-hundred-year-old house, which is itself crushed under a heavy mortgage. The last squire dragged out his existence there, living the horrible life of an aristocratic pauper ; but his only son, my stepfather, seeing that he must adapt himself to the new conditions, obtained an advance from a relative, which enabled him to take a medical degree, and went out to Calcutta, where, by his professional skill and his force of character, he established a large practice. In a fit of anger, however, caused by some robberies which had been perpetrated in the house, he beat his native butler to death, and narrowly escaped a capital sentence. As it was, he suffered a long term of imprisonment, and afterwards returned to England a morose and disappointed man.

"When Dr. Roylott was in India he married my mother, Mrs. Stoner, the young widow of Major-General Stoner, of the Bengal Artillery. My sister Julia and I were twins, and we were only two years old at the time of my mother's remarriage. She had a considerable sum of money, not less than a thousand a year, and this she bequeathed to Dr. Roylott entirely whilst we resided with him, with a provision that a certain annual sum should be allowed to each of us in the event of our marriage. Shortly after our return to England my mother died—she was killed eight years ago in a railway accident near Crewe. Dr. Roylott then abandoned his attempts to establish himself in practice in London, and took us to live with him in the old ancestral house at Stoke Moran. The money which my mother had left

was enough for all our wants, and there seemed to be no obstacle to our happiness.

"But a terrible change came over our stepfather about this time. Instead of making friends and exchanging visits with our neighbours, who had at first been overjoyed to see a Roylott of Stoke Moran back in the old family seat, he shut himself up in his house, and seldom came out save to indulge in ferocious quarrels with whoever might cross his path. Violence of temper approaching to mania has been hereditary in the men of the family, and in my stepfather's case it had, I believe, been intensified by his long residence in the tropics. A series of disgraceful brawls took place, two of which ended in the police-court, until at last he became the terror of the village, and the folks would fly at his approach, for he is a man of immense strength, and absolutely uncontrollable in his anger.

"Last week he hurled the local blacksmith over a parapet into a stream, and it was only by paying over all the money which I could gather together that I was able to avert another public exposure. He had no friends at all save the wandering gipsies, and he would give these vagabonds leave to encamp upon the few acres of

"HE HURLED THE BLACKSMITH OVER A PARAPET."

bramble-covered land which represent the family estate, and would accept in return the hospitality of their tents, wandering away with them sometimes for weeks on end. He has a passion also for Indian animals, which are sent over to him by a correspondent, and he has at this moment a cheetah and a baboon, which wander freely over his grounds, and are feared by the villagers almost as much as their master.

"You can imagine from what I say that my poor sister Julia and I had no great pleasure in our lives. No servant would stay with us, and for a long time we did all the work of the house. She was but thirty at the time of her death, and yet her hair had already begun to whiten, even as mine has."

"Your sister is dead, then?"

"She died just two years ago, and it is of her death that I wish to speak to you. You can understand that, living the life which I have described, we were little likely to see anyone of our own age and position. We had, however, an aunt, my mother's maiden sister, Miss Honoria Westphail, who lives near Harrow, and we were occasionally allowed to pay short visits at this lady's house. Julia went there at Christmas two years ago, and met there a half-pay Major of Marines, to whom she became engaged. My stepfather learned of the engagement when my sister returned, and offered no objection to the marriage; but within a fortnight of the day which had been fixed for the wedding, the terrible event occurred which has deprived me of my only companion."

Sherlock Holmes had been leaning back in his chair with his eyes closed, and his head sunk in a cushion, but he half opened his lids now, and glanced across at his visitor.

"Pray be precise as to details," said he.

"It is easy for me to be so, for every event of that dreadful time is seared into my memory. The manor house is, as I have already said, very old, and only one wing is now inhabited. The bedrooms in this wing are on the ground floor, the sitting-rooms being in the central block of the buildings. Of these bedrooms the first is Dr. Roylott's, the second my sister's, and the third my own. There is no communication between them, but they all open out into the same corridor. Do I make myself plain?"

"Perfectly so."

"The windows of the three rooms open out upon the lawn. That fatal night Dr. Roylott had gone to his room early, though we knew that he had not retired to rest, for my sister was troubled by the smell of the strong Indian cigars which it was his custom to smoke. She left her room, therefore, and came into mine, where she sat for some time, chatting about her approaching wedding. At eleven o'clock she rose to leave me, but she paused at the door and looked back.

"'Tell me, Helen,' said she, 'have you ever heard anyone whistle in the dead of the night?'

"'Never,' said I.

"'I suppose that you could not possibly whistle yourself in your sleep?'

"'Certainly not. But why?'

"'Because during the last few nights I have always, about three in the morning, heard a low clear whistle. I am a light sleeper, and it has awakened me. I cannot tell where it came from—perhaps from the next room, perhaps from the lawn. I thought that I would just ask you whether you had heard it.'

"'No, I have not. It must be those wretched gipsies in the plantation.'

"'Very likely. And yet if it were on the lawn I wonder that you did not hear it also.'

"'Ah, but I sleep more heavily than you.'

"'Well, it is of no great consequence at any rate,' she smiled back at me, closed my door, and a few moments later I heard her key turn in the lock."

"Indeed," said Holmes. "Was it your custom always to lock yourselves in at night?"

"Always."

"And why?"

"I think that I mentioned to you that the Doctor kept a cheetah and a baboon. We had no feeling of security unless our doors were locked."

"Quite so. Pray proceed with your statement."

"I could not sleep that night. A vague feeling of impending misfortune impressed me. My sister and I, you will recollect, were twins, and you know how subtle are the links which bind two souls which are so closely allied. It was a wild night. The wind was howling outside, and the rain was beating and splashing against the windows. Suddenly, amidst all the hubbub of the gale, there burst forth the wild scream of a terrified woman. I knew that it was my sister's voice. I sprang from my bed, wrapped a shawl round me, and rushed into the corridor. As I opened my door I seemed to hear a low whistle, such as my sister described, and a few moments later a clanging sound, as if a mass of metal had fallen. As I ran down the passage my sister's door was unlocked, and revolved slowly upon its hinges. I stared at it horror-stricken, not knowing what was about to issue from it. By the light of the corridor lamp I saw my sister appear at the opening, her face blanched with terror, her hands groping for help, her whole figure swaying to and fro like that of a drunkard. I ran to her and threw my arms round her, but at that moment her knees seemed to give way and she fell to the ground. She writhed as one who is in terrible pain, and her limbs were dreadfully convulsed. At first I thought that she had not recognised me, but as I bent over her she suddenly

she was unconscious, and though he poured brandy down her throat, and sent for medical aid from the village, all efforts were in vain, for she slowly sank and died without having recovered her consciousness. Such was the dreadful end of my beloved sister."

" One moment," said Holmes ; " are you sure about this whistle and metallic sound ? Could you swear to it ? "

"That was what the county coroner asked me at the inquiry. It is my strong impression that I heard it, and yet among the crash of the gale, and the creaking of an old house, I may possibly have been deceived."

" Was your sister dressed ? "

" No, she was in her nightdress. In her right hand was found the charred stump of a match, and in her left a matchbox."

" HER FACE BLANCHED WITH TERROR."

shrieked out in a voice which I shall never forget, ' Oh, my God ! Helen ! It was the band ! The speckled band !' There was something else which she would fain have said, and she stabbed with her finger into the air in the direction of the Doctor's room, but a fresh convulsion seized her and choked her words. I rushed out, calling loudly for my stepfather, and I met him hastening from his room in his dressing-gown. When he reached my sister's side

"Showing that she had struck a light and looked about her when the alarm took place. That is important. And what conclusions did the coroner come to ? "

" He investigated the case with great care, for Dr. Roylott's conduct had long been notorious in the county, but he was unable to find any satisfactory cause of death. My evidence showed that the door had been fastened upon the inner side, and the windows were blocked by old-fashioned shutters with broad iron bars, which were secured every night. The walls were carefully sounded, and were shown to be quite solid all round, and the flooring was also thoroughly examined, with the same result. The chimney is wide, but is barred up by four large staples. It is certain, therefore, that my sister was quite alone when she met her end. Besides, there were no marks of any violence upon her."

" How about poison ? "

" The doctors examined her for it, but without success."

" What do you think that this unfortunate lady died of, then ? "

" It is my belief that she died of pure fear and nervous shock, though what it was which frightened her I cannot imagine."

" Were there gipsies in the plantation at the time ? "

" Yes, there are nearly always some there."

" Ah, and what did you gather from this allusion to a band—a speckled band ? "

" Sometimes I have thought that it was merely the wild talk of delirium, sometimes that it may have referred to some band of people, perhaps to these very gipsies in the plantation. I do not know whether the spotted handkerchiefs which so many of them wear over their heads might have suggested the strange adjective which she used."

Holmes shook his head like a man who is far from being satisfied.

" These are very deep waters," said he ; " pray go on with your narrative."

" Two years have passed since then, and my life has been until lately lonelier than ever. A month ago, however, a dear friend, whom I have known for many years, has done me the honour to ask my hand in marriage. His name is Armitage—Percy Armitage—the second son of Mr. Armitage, of Crane Water, near Reading. My stepfather has offered no opposition to the match, and we are to be married in the course of the spring. Two days ago some repairs were started in the west wing of the building, and my bedroom wall has been pierced, so that I have had to move into the chamber in which my sister died, and to sleep in the very bed in which she slept. Imagine, then, my thrill of terror when last night, as I lay awake, thinking over her terrible fate, I suddenly heard in the silence of the night the low whistle which had been the herald of her own death. I sprang up and lit the lamp, but nothing was to be seen in the room. I was too shaken to go to bed again, however, so I dressed, and as soon as it was daylight I slipped down, got a dogcart at the ' Crown ' inn, which is opposite, and drove to Leatherhead, from whence I have come on this morning with the one object of seeing you and asking your advice."

" You have done wisely," said my friend. " But have you told me all ? "

" Yes, all."

" Miss Roylott, you have not. You are screening your stepfather."

" Why, what do you mean ? "

For answer Holmes pushed back the frill of black lace which fringed the hand that lay upon our visitor's knee. Five little livid spots, the marks of four fingers and a thumb, were printed upon the white wrist.

" You have been cruelly used," said Holmes.

The lady coloured deeply, and covered over her injured wrist. " He is a hard man," she said, " and perhaps he hardly knows his own strength."

There was a long silence, during which Holmes leaned his chin upon his hands and stared into the crackling fire.

" This is a very deep business," he said at last. " There are a thousand details which I should desire to know before I decide upon our course of action. Yet we have not a moment to lose. If we were to come to Stoke Moran to-day, would it be possible for us to see over these rooms without the knowledge of your stepfather ? "

" As it happens, he spoke of coming into town to-day upon some most important business. It is probable that he will be away all day, and that there would be nothing to disturb you. We have a housekeeper now, but she is old and foolish, and I could easily get her out of the way."

" Excellent. You are not averse to this trip, Watson ? "

" By no means."

" Then we shall both come. What are you going to do yourself ? "

" I have one or two things which I would wish to do now that I am in town. But I shall return by the twelve o'clock train, so as to be there in time for your coming."

" And you may expect us early in the afternoon. I have myself some small business matters to attend to. Will you not wait and breakfast ? "

" No, I must go. My heart is lightened already since I have confided my trouble to you. I shall look forward to seeing you again this afternoon." She dropped her thick black veil over her face, and glided from the room.

"And what do you think of it all, Watson?" asked Sherlock Holmes, leaning back in his chair.

"It seems to me to be a most dark and sinister business."

"Dark enough, and sinister enough."

"Yet if the lady is correct in saying that the flooring and walls are sound, and that the door, window, and chimney are impassable, then her sister must have been undoubtedly alone when she met her mysterious end."

"What becomes, then, of these nocturnal whistles, and what of the very peculiar words of the dying woman?"

"I cannot think."

"When you combine the ideas of whistles at night, the presence of a band of gipsies who are on intimate terms with this old Doctor, the fact that we have every reason to believe that the Doctor has an interest in preventing his stepdaughter's marriage, the dying allusion to a band, and finally, the fact that Miss Helen Stoner heard a metallic clang, which might have been caused by one of those metal bars which secured the shutters falling back into their place, I think that there is good ground to think that the mystery may be cleared along those lines."

"But what, then, did the gipsies do?"

"I cannot imagine."

"I see many objections to any such theory."

"And so do I. It is precisely for that reason that we are going to Stoke Moran this day. I want to see whether the objec-

"WHICH OF YOU IS HOLMES?"

tions are fatal, or if they may be explained away. But what, in the name of the devil!"

The ejaculation had been drawn from my companion by the fact that our door had been suddenly dashed open, and that a huge man had framed himself in the aperture. His costume was a peculiar mixture of the professional and of the agricultural, having a black top hat, a long frock coat, and a pair of high gaiters, with a hunting crop swinging in his hand. So tall was he that his hat actually brushed the cross bar of the doorway, and his breadth seemed to span it across from side to side. A large face, seared with a thousand wrinkles, burned yellow with the sun, and marked with every evil passion, was turned from one to the other of us, while his deep-set, bile-shot eyes, and his high thin fleshless nose, gave him somewhat the resemblance to a fierce old bird of prey.

"Which of you is Holmes?" asked this apparition.

"My name, sir, but you have the advantage of me," said my companion, quietly.

"I am Dr. Grimesby Roylott, of Stoke Moran."

"Indeed, Doctor," said Holmes, blandly. "Pray take a seat."

"I will do nothing of the kind. My stepdaughter has been here. I have traced her. What has she been saying to you?"

"It is a little cold for the time of the year," said Holmes.

"What has she been saying to you?" screamed the old man furiously.

"But I have heard that the crocuses promise well," continued my companion imperturbably.

"Ha! You put me off, do you?" said our new visitor, taking a step forward, and shaking his hunting crop. "I know you, you scoundrel! I have heard of you before. You are Holmes the meddler."

My friend smiled.

"Holmes the busybody!"

His smile broadened.

"Holmes the Scotland-yard Jack-in-office!"

Holmes chuckled heartily. "Your conversation is most entertaining," said he. "When you go out close the door, for there is a decided draught."

"I will go when I have said my say. Don't you dare to meddle with my affairs. I know that Miss Stoner has been here—I traced her! I am a dangerous man to fall foul of! See here." He stepped swiftly forward, seized the poker, and bent it into a curve with his huge brown hands.

"See that you keep yourself out of my grip," he snarled, and hurling the twisted poker into the fireplace, he strode out of the room.

"He seems a very amiable person," said Holmes, laughing. "I am not quite so bulky, but if he had remained I might have shown him that my grip was not much more feeble than his own." As he spoke he picked up the steel poker, and with a sudden effort straightened it out again.

"Fancy his having the insolence to confound me with the official detective force! This incident gives zest to our investigation, however, and I only trust that our little friend will not suffer from her imprudence in allowing this brute to trace her. And now, Watson, we shall order breakfast, and afterwards I shall walk down to Doctors' Commons, where I hope to get some data which may help us in this matter."

It was nearly one o'clock when Sherlock Holmes returned from his excursion. He held in his hand a sheet of blue paper, scrawled over with notes and figures.

"I have seen the will of the deceased wife," said he. "To determine its exact meaning I have been obliged to work out the present prices of the investments with which it is concerned. The total income, which at the time of the wife's death was little short of £1,100, is now through the fall in agricultural prices not more than £750. Each daughter can claim an income of £250, in case of marriage. It is evident, therefore, that if both girls had married

this beauty would have had a mere pittance, while even one of them would cripple him to a very serious extent. My morning's work has not been wasted, since it has proved that he has the very strongest motives for standing in the way of anything of the sort. And now, Watson, this is too serious for dawdling, especially as the old man is aware that we are interesting ourselves in his affairs, so if you are ready we shall call a cab and drive to Waterloo. I should be very much obliged if you would slip your revolver into your pocket. An Eley's No. 2 is an excellent argument with gentlemen who can twist steel pokers into knots. That and a tooth-brush are, I think, all that we need."

At Waterloo we were fortunate in catching a train for Leatherhead, where we hired a trap at the station inn, and drove for four or five miles through the lovely Surrey lanes. It was a perfect day, with a bright sun and a few fleecy clouds in the heavens. The trees and wayside hedges were just throwing out their first green shoots, and the air was full of the pleasant smell of the moist earth. To me at least there was a strange contrast between the sweet promise of the spring and this sinister quest upon which we were engaged. My companion sat in the front of the trap, his arms folded, his hat pulled down over his eyes, and his chin sunk upon his breast, buried in the deepest thought. Suddenly, however, he started, tapped me on the shoulder, and pointed over the meadows.

"Look there!" said he.

A heavily-timbered park stretched up in a gentle slope, thickening into a grove at the highest point. From amidst the branches there jutted out the grey gables and high roof-tree of a very old mansion.

"Stoke Moran?" said he.

"Yes, sir, that be the house of Dr. Grimesby Roylott," remarked the driver.

"There is some building going on there," said Holmes; "that is where we are going."

"There's the village," said the driver, pointing to a cluster of roofs some distance to the left; "but if you want to get to the house, you'll find it shorter to get over this stile, and so by the footpath over the fields. There it is, where the lady is walking."

"And the lady, I fancy, is Miss Stoner," observed Holmes, shading his eyes. "Yes, I think we had better do as you suggest."

We got off, paid our fare, and the trap rattled back on its way to Leatherhead.

"WE GOT OFF, PAID OUR FARE."

"I thought it as well," said Holmes, as we climbed the stile, "that this fellow should think we had come here as architects, or on some definite business. It may stop his gossip. Good afternoon, Miss Stoner. You see that we have been as good as our word."

Our client of the morning had hurried forward to meet us with a face which spoke her joy. "I have been waiting so eagerly for you," she cried, shaking hands with us warmly. "All has turned out splendidly. Dr. Roylott has gone to town, and it is unlikely that he will be back before evening."

"We have had the pleasure of making the Doctor's acquaintance," said Holmes, and in a few words he sketched out what had occurred. Miss Stoner turned white to the lips as she listened.

"Good heavens!" she cried, "he has followed me, then."

"So it appears."

"He is so cunning that I never know when I am safe from him. What will he say when he returns?"

"He must guard himself, for he may find that there is someone more cunning than himself upon his track. You must lock yourself up from him to-night. If he is violent, we shall take you away to your aunt's at Harrow. Now, we must make the best use of our time, so kindly take us at once to the rooms which we are to examine."

The building was of grey, lichen-blotched stone, with a high central portion, and two curving wings, like the claws of a crab, thrown out on each side. In one of these wings the windows were broken, and blocked with wooden boards, while the roof was partly caved in, a picture of ruin. The central portion was in little better repair, but the right-hand block was comparatively modern, and the blinds in the windows, with the blue smoke curling up from the chimneys, showed that this was where the family resided. Some scaffolding had been erected against the end wall, and the stonework had been broken into, but there were no signs of any workmen at the moment of our visit. Holmes walked slowly up and down the ill-trimmed lawn, and examined with deep attention the outsides of the windows.

"This, I take it, belongs to the room in which you used to sleep, the centre one to your sister's, and the one next to the main building to Dr. Roylott's chamber?"

"Exactly so. But I am now sleeping in the middle one."

"Pending the alterations, as I understand. By the way, there does not seem to be any very pressing need for repairs at that end wall."

"There were none. I believe that it was an excuse to move me from my room."

"Ah! that is suggestive. Now, on the other side of this narrow wing runs the corridor from which these three rooms open. There are windows in it, of course?"

"Yes, but very small ones. Too narrow for anyone to pass through."

"As you both locked your doors at night your rooms were unapproachable from that side. Now, would you have the kindness to go into your room, and to bar your shutters."

Miss Stoner did so, and Holmes, after a careful examination through the open window, endeavoured in every way to force the shutter open, but without success. There was no slit through which a knife could be passed to raise the bar. Then with his lens he tested the hinges, but they were of solid iron, built firmly into the massive masonry. "Hum!" said he, scratching his chin in some perplexity, "my theory certainly presents some difficulties. No one could pass these shutters if they were bolted. Well, we shall see if the inside throws any light upon the matter."

A small side door led into the white-washed corridor from which the three bed-rooms opened. Holmes refused to examine the third chamber, so we passed at once to the second, that in which Miss Stoner was now sleeping, and in which her sister had met with her fate. It was a homely little room, with a low ceiling and a gaping fire-place, after the fashion of old country houses. A brown chest of drawers stood in one corner, a narrow white-counterpaned bed in another, and a dressing-table on the left-hand side of the window. These articles, with two small wickerwork chairs, made up all the furniture in the room, save for a square of Wilton carpet in the centre. The boards round and the panelling of the walls were of brown, worm-eaten oak, so old and discoloured that it may have dated from the original building of the house. Holmes drew one of the chairs into a corner and sat silent, while his eyes travelled round and round and up and down, taking in every detail of the apartment.

"Where does that bell communicate with?" he asked at last, pointing to a thick bell-rope which hung down beside the bed, the tassel actually lying upon the pillow.

"It goes to the housekeeper's room."

"It looks newer than the other things?"

"Yes, it was only put there a couple of years ago."

"Your sister asked for it, I suppose?"

"No, I never heard of her using it. We used always to get what we wanted for ourselves."

"Indeed, it seemed unnecessary to put so nice a bell-pull there. You will excuse me for a few minutes while I satisfy myself as to this floor." He threw himself down upon his face with his lens in his hand, and crawled swiftly backwards and forwards, examining minutely the cracks between the boards. Then he did the same with the woodwork with which the chamber was

panelled. Finally he walked over to the bed and spent some time in staring at it, and in running his eye up and down the wall. Finally he took the bell-rope in his hand and gave it a brisk tug.

"Why, it's a dummy," said he.

"Won't it ring?"

".No, it is not even attached to a wire. This is very interesting. You can see now that it is fastened to a hook just above where the little opening for the ventilator is."

"How very absurd! I never noticed that before."

"Very strange!" muttered Holmes, pulling at the rope. "There are one or two very singular points about this room. For example, what a fool a builder must be to open a ventilator into another room, when, with the same trouble, he might have communicated with the outside air!"

"That is also quite modern," said the lady.

"Done about the same time as the bell-rope?" remarked Holmes.

"Yes, there were several little changes carried out about that time."

"They seem to have been of a most interesting character—dummy bell-ropes, and ventilators which do not ventilate. With your permission, Miss Stoner, we shall now carry our researches into the inner apartment."

Dr. Grimesby Roylott's chamber was larger than that of his step-daughter, but was as plainly furnished. A camp bed, a small wooden shelf full of books, mostly of a technical character, an armchair beside the bed, a plain wooden chair against the wall, a round table, and a large iron safe were the principal things which met the eye. Holmes walked slowly round and examined each and all of them with the keenest interest.

"What's in here?" he asked, tapping the safe.

"My stepfather's business papers."

"Oh! you have seen inside, then?"

"Only once, some years ago. I remember that it was full of papers."

"There isn't a cat in it, for example?"

"No. What a strange idea!"

"Well, look at this!" He took up a small saucer of milk which stood on the top of it.

"No; we don't keep a cat. But there is a cheetah and a baboon."

"Ah, yes, of course! Well, a cheetah is just a big cat, and yet a saucer of milk does not go very far in satisfying its wants, I daresay. There is one point which I should wish to determine." He squatted down in front of the wooden chair, and examined the seat of it with the greatest attention.

"Thank you. That is quite settled," said he, rising and putting his lens in his pocket. "Hullo! here is something interesting!"

"WELL, LOOK AT THIS."

The object which had caught his eye was a small dog lash hung on one corner of the bed. The lash, however, was curled upon itself, and tied so as to make a loop of whipcord.

"What do you make of that, Watson?"

"It's a common enough lash. But I don't know why it should be tied."

"That is not quite so common, is it? Ah, me! it's a wicked world, and when a clever man turns his brains to crime it is the worst of all. I think that I have seen enough now, Miss Stoner, and, with your permission, we shall walk out upon the lawn."

I had never seen my friend's face so grim, or his brow so dark, as it was when we turned from the scene of this investigation. We had walked several times up and down the lawn, neither Miss Stoner nor myself liking to break in upon his thoughts, before he roused himself from his reverie.

"It is very essential, Miss Stoner," said he, "that you should absolutely follow my advice in every respect."

"I shall most certainly do so."

"The matter is too serious for any hesitation. Your life may depend upon your compliance."

"I assure that I am in your hands."

"In the first place, both my friend and I must spend the night in your room."

Both Miss Stoner and I gazed at him in astonishment.

"Yes, it must be so. Let me explain. I believe that that is the village inn over there?"

"Yes, that is the 'Crown.'"

"Very good. Your windows would be visible from there?"

"Certainly."

"You must confine yourself to your room, on pretence of a headache, when your stepfather comes back. Then when you hear him retire for the night, you must open the shutters of your window, undo the hasp, put your lamp there as a signal to us, and then withdraw quietly with everything which you are likely to want into the room which you used to occupy. I have no doubt that, in spite of the repairs, you could manage there for one night."

"Oh, yes, easily."

"The rest you will leave in our hands."

"But what will you do?"

"We shall spend the night in your room, and we shall investigate the cause of this noise which has disturbed you."

"I believe, Mr. Holmes, that you have already made up your mind," said Miss Stoner, laying her hand upon my companion's sleeve.

"Perhaps I have."

"Then for pity's sake tell me what was the cause of my sister's death."

"I should prefer to have clearer proofs before I speak."

"You can at least tell me whether my own thought is correct, and if she died from some sudden fright."

"No, I do not think so. I think that there was probably some more tangible cause. And now, Miss Stoner, we must leave you, for if Dr. Roylott returned and

The trap drove on, and a few minutes later we saw a sudden light spring up among the trees as the lamp was lit in one of the sitting-rooms.

"Do you know, Watson," said Holmes, as we sat together in the gathering darkness, "I have really some scruples as to taking you to-night. There is a distinct element of danger."

"Can I be of assistance?"

"Your presence might be invaluable."

"Then I shall certainly come."

"It is very kind of you."

"You speak of danger. You have evidently seen more in these rooms than was visible to me."

"No, but I fancy that I may have deduced a little more. I imagine that you saw all that I did."

"I saw nothing remarkable save the bell rope, and what purpose that could answer I confess is more than I can imagine."

"You saw the ventilator, too?"

"Yes, but I do not think that it is such a very unusual thing to have a small opening between two rooms. It was so small that a rat could hardly pass through."

"I knew that we should find a ventilator before ever we came to Stoke Moran."

"My dear Holmes!"

"Oh, yes, I did. You remember in her statement she said that her sister could smell Dr. Roylott's cigar. Now, of course that suggested at once that there must be a communication between the two rooms. It could only be a small one, or it would have been remarked upon at the Coroner's inquiry. I deduced a ventilator."

"But what harm can there be in that?"

"Well, there is at least a curious coincidence of dates. A ventilator is made, a cord is hung, and a lady who sleeps in the bed dies. Does not that strike you?"

"I cannot as yet see any connection."

"Did you observe anything very peculiar about that bed?"

"No."

"It was clamped to the floor. Did you ever see a bed fastened like that before?"

"I cannot say that I have."

"GOOD-BYE, AND BE BRAVE."

saw us, our journey would be in vain. Good-bye, and be brave, for if you will do what I have told you, you may rest assured that we shall soon drive away the dangers that threaten you."

Sherlock Holmes and I had no difficulty in engaging a bedroom and sitting-room at the "Crown" Inn. They were on the upper floor, and from our window we could command a view of the avenue gate, and of the inhabited wing of Stoke Moran Manor House. At dusk we saw Dr. Grimesby Roylott drive past, his huge form looming up beside the little figure of the lad who drove him. The boy had some slight difficulty in undoing the heavy iron gates, and we heard the hoarse roar of the doctor's voice, and saw the fury with which he shook his clenched fists at him.

"The lady could not move her bed. It must always be in the same relative position to the ventilator and to the rope—for so we may call it, since it was clearly never meant for a bell-pull."

"Holmes," I cried, "I seem to see dimly what you are hinting at. We are only just in time to prevent some subtle and horrible crime."

"Subtle enough, and horrible enough. When a doctor does go wrong, he is the first of criminals. He has nerve and he has knowledge. Palmer and Pritchard were among the heads of their profession. This man strikes even deeper, but I think, Watson, that we shall be able to strike deeper still. But we shall have horrors enough before the night is over ; for goodness' sake let us have a quiet pipe, and turn our minds for a few hours to something more cheerful."

About nine o'clock the light among the trees was extinguished, and all was dark in the direction of the Manor House. Two hours passed slowly away, and then, suddenly, just at the stroke of eleven, a single bright light shone out right in front of us.

"That is our signal," said Holmes, springing to his feet ; "it comes from the middle window."

As we passed out he exchanged a few words with the landlord, explaining that we were going on a late visit to an acquaintance, and that it was possible that we might spend the night there. A moment later we were out on the dark road, a chill wind blowing in our faces, and one yellow light twinkling in front of us through the gloom to guide us on our sombre errand.

There was little difficulty in entering the grounds, for unrepaired breaches gaped in the old park wall. Making our way among the trees, we reached the lawn, crossed it, and were about to enter through the window, when out from a clump of laurel bushes there darted what seemed to be a hideous and distorted child, who threw itself upon the grass with writhing limbs, and then ran swiftly across the lawn into the darkness.

"My God !" I whispered ; "did you see it ?"

Holmes was for the moment as startled as I. His hand closed like a vice upon my wrist in his agitation. Then he broke into a low laugh, and put his lips to my ear.

"It is a nice household," he murmured. "That is the baboon,"

I had forgotten the strange pets which the Doctor affected. There was a cheetah, too ; perhaps we might find it upon our shoulders at any moment. I confess that I felt easier in my mind when, after following Holmes' example and slipping off my shoes, I found myself inside the bedroom. My companion noiselessly closed the shutters, moved the lamp on to the table, and cast his eyes round the room. All was as we had seen it in the day-time. Then creeping up to me and making a trumpet of his hand, he whispered into my ear again so gently that it was all that I could do to distinguish the words.

"The least sound would be fatal to our plans."

I nodded to show that I had heard.

"We must sit without light. He would see it through the ventilator."

I nodded again.

"Do not go asleep ; your very life may depend upon it. Have your pistol ready in case we should need it. I will sit on the side of the bed, and you in that chair."

I took out my revolver and laid it on the corner of the table.

Holmes had brought up a long thin cane, and this he placed upon the bed beside him. By it he laid the box of matches and the stump of a candle. Then he turned down the lamp, and we were left in darkness.

How shall I ever forget that dreadful vigil ? I could not hear a sound, not even the drawing of a breath, and yet I knew that my companion sat open-eyed, within a few feet of me, in the same state of nervous tension in which I was myself. The shutters cut off the least ray of light, and we waited in absolute darkness. From outside came the occasional cry of a night bird, and once at our very window a long drawn, cat-like whine, which told us that the cheetah was indeed at liberty. Far away we could hear the deep tones of the parish clock, which boomed out every quarter of an hour. How long they seemed, those quarters ! Twelve struck, and one, and two, and three, and still we sat waiting silently for whatever might befall.

Suddenly there was the momentary gleam of a light up in the direction of the ventilator, which vanished immediately, but was succeeded by a strong smell of burning oil and heated metal. Someone in the next room had lit a dark lantern. I heard a gentle sound of movement, and then all was silent once more, though the

"HOLMES LASHED FURIOUSLY."

smell grew stronger. For half an hour I sat with straining ears. Then suddenly another sound became audible—a very gentle, soothing sound, like that of a small jet of steam escaping continually from a kettle. The instant that we heard it, Holmes sprang from the bed, struck a match, and lashed furiously with his cane at the bell-pull.

"You see it, Watson?" he yelled. "You see it?"

But I saw nothing. At the moment when Holmes struck the light I heard a low, clear whistle, but the sudden glare flashing into my weary eyes made it impossible for me to tell what it was at which my friend lashed so savagely. I could, however, see that his face was deadly pale, and filled with horror and loathing.

He had ceased to strike, and was gazing up at the ventilator, when suddenly there broke from the silence of the night the most horrible cry to which I have ever listened. It swelled up louder and louder, a hoarse yell of pain and fear and anger all mingled in the one dreadful shriek. They say that away down in the village, and even in the distant parsonage, that cry raised the sleepers from their beds. It struck cold to our hearts, and I stood gazing at Holmes, and

he at me, until the last echoes of it had died away into the silence from which it rose.

"What can it mean?" I gasped.

"It means that it is all over," Holmes answered. "And perhaps, after all, it is for the best. Take your pistol, and we shall enter Dr. Roylott's room."

With a grave face he lit the lamp, and led the way down the corridor. Twice he struck at the chamber door without any reply from within. Then he turned the handle and entered, I at his heels, with the cocked pistol in my hand.

It was a singular sight which met our eyes. On the table stood a dark lantern with the shutter half open, throwing a brilliant beam of light upon the iron safe, the door of which was ajar. Beside this table, on the wooden chair, sat Dr. Grimesby Roylott, clad in a long grey dressing-gown, his bare ankles protruding beneath, and his feet thrust into red heelless Turkish slippers. Across his lap lay the short stock with the long lash which we had noticed during the day. His chin was cocked upwards, and his eyes were fixed in a dreadful rigid stare at the corner of the ceiling. Round his brow he had a peculiar yellow band, with brownish speckles, which seemed to be bound tightly round his head. As we entered he made neither sound nor motion.

"The band! the speckled band!" whispered Holmes.

I took a step forward. In an instant his strange headgear began to move, and there reared itself from among his hair the squat diamond-shaped head and puffed neck of a loathsome serpent.

Dr. Grimesby Roylott, of Stoke Moran. It is not necessary that I should prolong a narrative which has already run to too great a length, by telling how we broke the sad news to the terrified girl, how we conveyed her by the morning train to the care of her good aunt at Harrow, of how the slow process of official inquiry came to the conclusion that the Doctor met his fate while indiscreetly playing with a dangerous

"HE MADE NEITHER SOUND NOR MOTION."

"It is a swamp adder!" cried Holmes— "the deadliest snake in India. He has died within ten seconds of being bitten. Violence does, in truth, recoil upon the violent, and the schemer falls into the pit which he digs for another. Let us thrust this creature back into its den, and we can then remove Miss Stoner to some place of shelter, and let the county police know what has happened."

As he spoke he drew the dog whip swiftly from the dead man's lap, and throwing the noose round the reptile's neck, he drew it from its horrid perch, and, carrying it at arm's length threw it into the iron safe, which he closed upon it.

Such are the true facts of the death of

pet. The little which I had yet to learn of the case was told me by Sherlock Holmes as we travelled back next day.

"I had," said he, "come to an entirely erroneous conclusion, which shows, my dear Watson, how dangerous it always is to reason from insufficient data. The presence of the gipsies, and the use of the word 'band,' which was used by the poor girl, no doubt, to explain the appearance which she had caught a hurried glimpse of by the light of her match, were sufficient to put me upon an entirely wrong scent. I can only claim the merit that I instantly reconsidered my position when, however, it became clear to me that whatever danger threatened an occupant of the room could not come either from the window or the door. My attention was speedily drawn, as I have already remarked to you, to this ventilator, and to the bell rope which hung down to the bed. The discovery that this was a dummy, and that the bed was clamped to the floor, instantly gave rise to the suspicion that the rope was there as a bridge for something passing through the hole, and coming to the bed. The idea of a snake instantly occurred to me, and when I coupled it with my knowledge that the Doctor was furnished with a supply of creatures from India, I felt that I was probably on the right track. The idea of using a form of poison which could not possibly be discovered by any chemical test was just such a one as would occur to a clever and ruthless man who had had an Eastern training. The rapidity with which such a poison would take effect would also, from his point of view, be an advantage. It would be a sharp-eyed coroner indeed who could distinguish the two little dark punctures which would show where the poison fangs had done their work. Then I thought of the whistle. Of course, he must recall the snake before the morning light revealed it to the victim. He had trained it, probably by the use of the milk which we saw, to return to him when summoned. He would put it through this ventilator at the hour that he thought best, with the certainty that it would crawl down the rope, and land on the bed. It might or might not bite the occupant, perhaps she might escape every night for a week, but sooner or later she must fall a victim.

"I had come to these conclusions before ever I had entered his room. An inspection of his chair showed me that he had been in the habit of standing on it, which, of course, would be necessary in order that he should reach the ventilator. The sight of the safe, the saucer of milk, and the loop of whipcord were enough to finally dispel any doubts which may have remained. The metallic clang heard by Miss Stoner was obviously caused by her father hastily closing the door of his safe upon its terrible occupant. Having once made up my mind, you know the steps which I took in order to put the matter to the proof. I heard the creature hiss, as I have no doubt that you did also, and I instantly lit the light and attacked it."

"With the result of driving it through the ventilator."

"And also with the result of causing it to turn upon its master at the other side. Some of the blows of my cane came home, and roused its snakish temper, so that it flew upon the first person it saw. In this way I am no doubt indirectly responsible for Dr. Grimesby Roylott's death, and I cannot say that it is likely to weigh very heavily upon my conscience."

IX.—THE ADVENTURE OF THE ENGINEER'S THUMB.

BY A. CONAN DOYLE.

OF all the problems which have been submitted to my friend Mr. Sherlock Holmes for solution during the years of our intimacy, there were only two which I was the means of introducing to his notice, that of Mr. Hatherley's thumb and that of Colonel Warburton's madness. Of these the latter may have afforded a finer field for an acute and original observer, but the other was so strange in its inception and so dramatic in its details, that it may be the more worthy of being placed upon record, even if it gave my friend fewer openings for those deductive methods of reasoning by which he achieved such remarkable results. The story has, I believe, been told more than once in the newspapers, but, like all such narratives, its effect is much less striking when set forth *en bloc* in a single half-column of print than when the facts slowly evolve before your own eyes and the mystery clears gradually away as each new discovery furnishes a step which leads on to the complete truth. At the time the circumstances made a deep impression upon me, and the lapse of two years has hardly served to weaken the effect.

It was in the summer of '89, not long after my marriage, that the events occurred which I am now about to summarise. I had returned to civil practice, and had finally abandoned Holmes in his Baker-street rooms, although I continually visited him, and occasionally even persuaded him to forego his Bohemian habits so far as to come and visit us. My practice had steadily increased, and as I happened to live at no very great distance from Paddington Station, I got a few patients from among the officials. One of these whom I had cured of a painful and lingering disease, was never weary of advertising my virtues, and of endeavouring to send me on every sufferer over whom he might have any influence.

One morning, at a little before seven o'clock, I was awakened by the maid tapping at the door, to announce that two men had come from Paddington, and were waiting in the consulting room. I dressed hurriedly, for I knew by experience that railway cases were seldom trivial, and hastened downstairs. As I descended, my old ally, the guard, came out of the room, and closed the door tightly behind him.

"I've got him here," he whispered, jerking his thumb over his shoulder ; "he's all right."

"What is it, then ? " I asked, for his manner suggested that it was some strange creature which he had caged up in my room.

"It's a new patient," he whispered. " I thought I'd bring him round myself ; then he couldn't slip away. There he is, all safe and sound. I must go now, doctor, I have my dooties, just the same as you." And off he went, this trusty tout, without even giving me time to thank him.

I entered my consulting room, and found a gentleman seated by the table. He was quietly dressed in a suit of heather tweed, with a soft cloth cap, which he had laid down upon my books. Round one of his hands he had a handkerchief wrapped, which was mottled all over with bloodstains. He was young, not more than five-and-twenty, I should say, with a strong masculine face ; but he was exceedingly pale, and gave me the impression of a man who was suffering from some strong agitation, which it took all his strength of mind to control.

"I am sorry to knock you up so early, doctor," said he. " But I have had a very serious accident during the night. I came in by train this morning, and on inquiring at Paddington as to where I might find a doctor a worthy fellow very kindly escorted me here. I gave the maid a card, but I see that she has left it upon the side table."

I took it up and glanced at it. " Mr.

Victor Hatherley, hydraulic engineer, 16A, Victoria-street (3rd floor)." That was the name, style, and abode of my morning visitor. "I regret that I have kept you waiting," said I, sitting down in my library chair. "You are fresh from a night journey, I understand, which is in itself a monotonous occupation."

"Oh, my night could not be called monotonous," said he, and laughed. He laughed very heartily, with a high ringing note, leaning back in his chair, and shaking his sides. All my medical instincts rose up against that laugh.

"Stop it!" I cried. "Pull yourself together!" and I poured out some water from a caraffe.

It was useless, however. He was off in one of those hysterical outbursts which come upon a strong nature when some great crisis is over and gone. Presently he came to himself once more, very weary and blushing hotly.

"I have been making a fool of myself," he gasped.

"Not at all. Drink this!" I dashed some brandy into the water, and the colour began to come back to his bloodless cheeks.

"That's better!" said he. "And now, doctor, perhaps you would kindly attend to my thumb, or rather to the place where my thumb used to be."

He unwound the handkerchief and held out his hand. It gave even my hardened nerves a shudder to look at it. There were four protruding fingers and a horrid red spongy surface where the thumb should have been. It had been hacked or torn right out from the roots.

"Good heavens!" I cried, "this is a terrible injury. It must have bled considerably."

"Yes, it did. I fainted when it was done; and I think that I must have been senseless for a long time. When I came to, I found that it was still bleeding, so I tied one end of my handkerchief very tightly round the wrist, and braced it up with a twig."

"Excellent! You should have been a surgeon."

"It is a question of hydraulics, you see, and came within my own province."

"This has been done," said I, examining the wound, "by a very heavy and sharp instrument."

"A thing like a cleaver," said he.

"An accident, I presume?"

"By no means."

"What, a murderous attack!"

"Very murderous indeed."

"You horrify me."

I sponged the wound, cleaned it, dressed it; and, finally, covered it over with cotton wadding and carbolised bandages. He lay back without wincing, though he bit his lip from time to time.

"How is that?" I asked, when I had finished.

"Capital! Between your brandy and your bandage, I feel a new man. I was very weak, but I have had a good deal to go through."

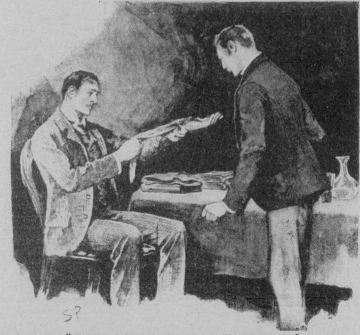

"HE UNWOUND THE HANDKERCHIEF, AND HELD OUT HIS HAND."

"Perhaps you had better not speak of the matter. It is evidently trying to your nerves."

"Oh, no ; not now. I shall have to tell my tale to the police ; but, between ourselves, if it were not for the convincing evidence of this wound of mine, I should be surprised if they believed my statement, for it is a very extraordinary one, and I

"HE SETTLED OUR NEW ACQUAINTANCE ON THE SOFA.

have not much in the way of proof with which to back it up. And, even if they believe me, the clues which I can give them are so vague that it is a question whether justice will be done."

"Ha ! " cried I, "if it is anything in the nature of a problem which you desire to see solved, I should strongly recommend you to come to my friend Mr. Sherlock Holmes before you go to the official police."

"Oh, I have heard of that fellow," answered my visitor, "and I should be very glad if he would take the matter up, though of course I must use the official police as well. Would you give me an introduction to him ? "

"I'll do better. I'll take you round to him myself."

"I should be immensely obliged to you."

"We'll call a cab, and go together. We shall just be in time to have a little breakfast with him. Do you feel equal to it ? "

"Yes, I shall not feel easy until I have told my story."

"Then my servant will call a cab, and I shall be with you in an instant." I rushed upstairs, explained the matter shortly to my wife, and in five minutes was inside a hansom, driving with my new acquaintance to Baker-street.

Sherlock Holmes was, as I expected, lounging about his sitting-room in his dressing-gown, reading the agony column of The Times, and smoking his before-breakfast pipe, which was composed of all the plugs and dottels left from his smokes of the day before, all carefully dried and collected on the corner of the mantel-piece. He received us in his quietly genial fashion, ordered fresh rashers and eggs, and joined us in a hearty meal. When it was concluded he settled our new acquaintance upon the sofa, placed a pillow beneath his head, and laid a glass of brandy and water within his reach.

"It is easy to see that your experience has been no common one, Mr. Hatherley," said he. "Pray lie down there and make yourself absolutely at home. Tell us what you can, but stop when you are tired, and keep up your strength with a little stimulant."

"Thank you," said my patient, "but I have felt another man since the doctor bandaged me, and I think that your breakfast has completed the cure. I shall take up as little of your valuable time as possible, so I shall start at once upon my peculiar experiences."

Holmes sat in his big armchair with the weary, heavy-lidded expression which veiled his keen and eager nature, while I sat opposite to him, and we listened in silence to the strange story which our visitor detailed to us.

"You must know," said he, "that I am an orphan and a bachelor, residing alone in lodgings in London. By profession I am a hydraulic engineer, and I have had considerable experience of my work during the seven years that I was apprenticed to Venner and Matheson, the well-known firm, of Greenwich. Two years ago, having served my time, and having also come into a fair sum of money through my poor father's death, I determined to start in business for myself, and took professional chambers in Victoria-street.

"I suppose that everyone finds his first independent start in business a dreary experience. To me it has been exceptionally so. During two years I have had three consultations and one small job, and that is absolutely all that my profession has brought me. My gross takings amount to twenty-seven pounds ten. Every day, from nine in the morning until four in the afternoon, I waited in my little den, until at last my heart began to sink, and I came to believe that I should never have any practice at all.

"Yesterday, however, just as I was thinking of leaving the office, my clerk entered

"COLONEL LYSANDER STARK."

to say there was a gentleman waiting who wished to see me upon business. He brought up a card, too, with the name of "Colonel Lysander Stark" engraved upon it. Close at his heels came the Colonel himself, a man rather over the middle size but of an exceeding thinness. I do not think that I have ever seen so thin a man. His whole face sharpened away into nose and chin, and the skin of his cheeks was drawn quite tense over his outstanding bones. Yet this emaciation seemed to be his natural habit, and due to no disease, for his eye was bright, his step brisk, and his bearing assured. He was plainly but neatly dressed, and his age, I should judge, would be nearer forty than thirty.

"'Mr. Hatherley?' said he, with something of a German accent. 'You have been recommended to me, Mr. Hatherley, as being a man who is not only proficient in his profession, but is also discreet and capable of preserving a secret.'

"I bowed, feeling as flattered as any young man would at such an address. 'May I ask who it was who gave me so good a character?' I asked.

"'Well, perhaps it is better that I should not tell you that just at this moment. I have it from the same source that you are both an orphan and a bachelor, and are residing alone in London.'

"'That is quite correct,' I answered, 'but you will excuse me if I say that I cannot see how all this bears upon my professional qualifications. I understood that it was on a professional matter that you wished to speak to me?'

"'Undoubtedly so. But you will find that all I say is really to the point. I have a professional commission for you, but absolute secrecy is quite essential—*absolute* secrecy, you understand, and of course we may expect that more from a man who is alone than from one who lives in the bosom of his family.'

"'If I promise to keep a secret,' said I, 'you may absolutely depend upon my doing so.'

"He looked very hard at me as I spoke, and it seemed to me that I had never seen so suspicious and questioning an eye.

"'You do promise, then?' said he at last.

"'Yes, I promise.'

"'Absolute and complete silence, before, during, and after? No reference to the matter at all, either in word or writing?'

"'I have already given you my word.'

"'Very good.' He suddenly sprang up,

and darting like lightning across the room he flung open the door. The passage outside was empty.

" ' That's all right,' said he, coming back. ' I know that clerks are sometimes curious as to their master's affairs. Now we can talk in safety.' He drew up his chair very close to mine, and began to stare at me again with the same questioning and thoughtful look.

" A feeling of repulsion, and of something akin to fear had begun to rise within me at the strange antics of this fleshless man. Even my dread of losing a client could not restrain me from showing my impatience.

" ' I beg that you will state your business, sir,' said I ; ' my time is of value.' Heaven forgive me for that last sentence, but the words came to my lips.

" ' How would fifty guineas for a night's work suit you ? ' he asked.

" ' Most admirably.'

" ' I say a night's work, but an hour's would be nearer the mark. I simply want your opinion about a hydraulic stamping machine which has got out of gear. If you show us what is wrong we shall soon set it right ourselves. What do you think of such a commission as that ? '

" ' The work appears to be light, and the pay munificent.'

" ' Precisely so. We shall want you to come to-night by the last train.'

" ' Where to ? '

" ' To Eyford, in Berkshire. It is a little place near the borders of Oxfordshire, and within seven miles of Reading. There is a train from Paddington which would bring you in there at about eleven fifteen.'

" ' Very good.'

" ' I shall come down in a carriage to meet you.'

" ' There is a drive, then ? '

" ' Yes, our little place is quite out in the country. It is a good seven miles from Eyford Station.'

" ' Then we can hardly get there before midnight. I suppose there would be no chance of a train back. I should be compelled to stop the night.'

" ' Yes, we could easily give you a shake-down.'

" ' That is very awkward. Could I not come at some more convenient hour ? '

" ' We have judged it best that you should come late. It is to recompense you for any inconvenience that we are paying to you, a young and unknown man, a fee which would buy an opinion from the very heads of your profession. Still, of course, if you would like to draw out of the business, there is plenty of time to do so.'

" I thought of the fifty guineas, and of how very useful they would be to me. ' Not at all,' said I, ' I shall be very happy to accommodate myself to your wishes. I should like, however, to understand a little more clearly what it is that you wish me to do.'

" ' Quite so. It is very natural that the pledge of secrecy which we have exacted from you should have aroused your curiosity. I have no wish to commit you to anything without your having it all laid before you. I suppose that we are absolutely safe from eavesdroppers ? '

" ' Entirely.'

" ' Then the matter stands thus. You are probably aware that fuller's earth is a valuable product, and that it is only found in one or two places in England ? '

" ' I have heard so.'

" Some little time ago I bought a small place—a very small place—within ten miles of Reading. I was fortunate enough to discover that there was a deposit of fuller's earth in one of my fields. On examining it, however, I found that this deposit was a comparatively small one, and that it formed a link between two very much larger ones upon the right and the left—both of them, however, in the grounds of my neighbours. These good people were absolutely ignorant that their land contained that which was quite as valuable as a gold mine. Naturally, it was to my interest to buy their land before they discovered its true value ; but, unfortunately, I had no capital by which I could do this. I took a few of my friends into the secret, however, and they suggested that we should quietly and secretly work our own little deposit, and that in this way we should earn the money which would enable us to buy the neighbouring fields. This we have now been doing for some time, and in order to help us in our operations we erected a hydraulic press. This press, as I have already explained, has got out of order, and we wish your advice upon the subject. We guard our secret very jealously, however, and if it once became known that we had hydraulic engineers coming to our little house, it would soon rouse inquiry, and then, if the facts came out, it would be good-bye to any chance of getting these fields and carrying out our plans. That is why I have made you promise me that you will not tell a human being that you are going to Eyford to-night. I hope that I make it all plain?'

"'I quite follow you,' said I. 'The only point which I could not quite understand, was what use you could make of a hydraulic press in excavating fuller's earth, which, as I understand, is dug out like gravel from a pit.'

"'Ah!' said he, carelessly, 'we have our own process. We compress the earth into bricks, so as to remove them without revealing what they are. But that is a mere detail. I have taken you fully into my confidence now, Mr. Hatherley, and I have shown you how I trust you.' He rose as he spoke. 'I shall expect you, then, at Eyford at 11.15.'

"'I shall certainly be there.'

"'NOT A WORD TO A SOUL!'"

"'And not a word to a soul.' He looked at me with a last long, questioning gaze, and then, pressing my hand in a cold, dank grasp, he hurried from the room.

"Well, when I came to think it all over in cool blood I was very much astonished, as you may both think, at this sudden commission which had been entrusted to me. On the one hand, of course, I was glad, for the fee was at least tenfold what I should have asked had I set a price upon my own services, and it was possible that this order might lead to other ones. On the other hand, the face and manner of my patron had made an unpleasant impression upon me, and I could not think that his explanation of the fuller's earth was sufficient to explain the necessity for my coming at midnight, and his extreme anxiety lest I should tell anyone of my errand. However, I threw all fears to the winds, ate a hearty supper, drove to Paddington, and started off, having obeyed to the letter the injunction as to holding my tongue.

"At Reading I had to change not only my carriage but my station. However, I was in time for the last train to Eyford, and I reached the little dim lit station after eleven o'clock. I was the only passenger who got out there, and there was no one upon the platform save a single sleepy porter with a lantern. As I passed out through the wicket gate, however, I found my acquaintance of the morning waiting in the shadow upon the other side. Without a word he grasped my arm and hurried me into a carriage, the door of which was standing open. He drew up the windows on either side, tapped on the woodwork, and away we went as hard as the horse could go."

"One horse?" interjected Holmes.

"Yes, only one."

"Did you observe the colour?"

U

" Yes, I saw it by the sidelights when I was stepping into the carriage. It was a chestnut."

" Tired-looking or fresh ? "

" Oh, fresh and glossy."

" Thank you. I am sorry to have interrupted you. Pray continue your most interesting statement."

" Away we went then, and we drove for at least an hour. Colonel Lysander Stark had said that it was only seven miles, but I should think, from the rate that we seemed to go, and from the time that we took, that it must have been nearer twelve. He sat at my side in silence all the time, and I was aware, more than once when I glanced in his direction, that he was looking at me with great intensity. The country roads seem to be not very good in that part of the world, for we lurched and jolted terribly. I tried to look out of the windows to see something of where we were, but they were made of frosted glass, and I could make out nothing save the occasional bright blurr of a passing light. Now and then I hazarded some remark to break the monotony of the journey, but the Colonel answered only in monosyllables, and the conversation soon flagged. At last, however, the bumping of the road was exchanged for the crisp smoothness of a gravel drive, and the carriage came to a stand. Colonel Lysander Stark sprang out, and, as I followed after him, pulled me swiftly into a porch which gaped in front of us. We stepped, as it were, right out of the carriage and into the hall, so that I failed to catch the most fleeting glance of the front of the house. The instant that I had crossed the threshold the door slammed heavily behind us, and I heard faintly the rattle of the wheels as the carriage drove away.

" It was pitch dark inside the house, and the Colonel fumbled about looking for matches, and muttering under his breath. Suddenly a door opened at the other end of the passage, and a long, golden bar of light shot out in our direction. It grew broader, and a woman appeared with a lamp in her hand, which she held above her head, pushing her face forward and peering at us. I could see that she was pretty, and from the gloss with which the light shone upon her dark dress I knew that it was a rich material. She spoke a few words in a foreign tongue in a tone as though asking a question, and when my companion answered in a gruff monosyllable she gave such a start that the lamp nearly fell from her

hand. Colonel Stark went up to her, whispered something in her ear, and then, pushing her back into the room from whence she had come, he walked towards me again with the lamp in his hand.

" ' Perhaps you will have the kindness to wait in this room for a few minutes,' said he, throwing open another door. It was a quiet little, plainly furnished room, with a round table in the centre, on which several German books were scattered. Colonel Stark laid down the lamp on the top of a harmonium beside the door. ' I shall not keep you waiting an instant,' said he, and vanished into the darkness.

" I glanced at the books upon the table, and in spite of my ignorance of German I could see that two of them were treatises on science, the others being volumes of poetry. Then I walked across to the window, hoping that I might catch some glimpse of the country side, but an oak shutter, heavily barred, was folded across it. It was a wonderfully silent house. There was an old clock ticking loudly somewhere in the passage, but otherwise everything was deadly still. A vague feeling of uneasiness began to steal over me. Who were these German people, and what were they doing, living in this strange, out-of-the-way place ? And where was the place ? I was ten miles or so from Eyford, that was all I knew, but whether north, south, east, or west I had no idea. For that matter, Reading, and possibly other large towns, were within that radius, so the place might not be so secluded after all. Yet it was quite certain from the absolute stillness that we were in the country. I paced up and down the room, humming a tune under my breath to keep up my spirits, and feeling that I was thoroughly earning my fifty-guinea fee.

" Suddenly, without any preliminary sound in the midst of the utter stillness, the door of my room swung slowly open. The woman was standing in the aperture, the darkness of the hall behind her, the yellow light from my lamp beating upon her eager and beautiful face. I could see at a glance that she was sick with fear, and the sight sent a chill to my own heart. She held up one shaking finger to warn me to be silent, and she shot a few whispered words of broken English at me, her eyes glancing back, like those of a frightened horse, into the gloom behind her.

" ' I would go,' said she, trying hard, as it seemed to me, to speak calmly ; ' I would go. I should not stay here. There is no good for you to do.'

"'But, madam,' said I, 'I have not yet done what I came for. I cannot possibly leave until I have seen the machine.'

"'It is not worth your while to wait,' she went on. 'You can pass through the door; no one hinders.' And then, seeing that I smiled and shook my head, she suddenly threw aside her constraint, and made a step forward, with her hands wrung together. 'For the love of Heaven!' she

"' GET AWAY FROM HERE BEFORE IT IS TOO LATE.'"

whispered, ' get away from here before it is too late!'

"But I am somewhat headstrong by nature, and the more ready to engage in an affair when there is some obstacle in the way. I thought of my fifty-guinea fee, of my wearisome journey, and of the unpleasant night which seemed to be before me. Was it all to go for nothing ? Why should I slink away without having carried out my commission, and without the payment which was my due ? This woman

might, for all I knew, be a monomaniac. With a stout bearing, therefore, though her manner had shaken me more than I cared to confess, I still shook my head, and declared my intention of remaining where I was. She was about to renew her entreaties when a door slammed overhead, and the sound of several footsteps were heard upon the stairs. She listened for an instant, threw up her hands with a despairing gesture, and vanished as suddenly and as noiselessly as she had come.

"The newcomers were Colonel Lysander Stark, and a short thick man with a chinchilla beard growing out of the creases of his double chin, who was introduced to me as Mr. Ferguson.

"'This is my secretary and manager,' said the Colonel. 'By the way, I was under the impression that I left this door shut just now. I fear that you have felt the draught.'

"'On the contrary,' said I, 'I opened the door myself, because I felt the room to be a little close.'

"He shot one of his suspicious glances at me. 'Perhaps we had better proceed to business, then,' said he. 'Mr. Ferguson and I will take you up to see the machine.'

"'I had better put my hat on, I suppose.'

"'Oh no, it is in the house.'

"'What, you dig fuller's earth in the house?'

"'No, no. This is only where we compress it. But never mind that! All we wish you to do is to examine the machine, and to let us know what is wrong with it.'

"We went upstairs together, the Colonel first with the lamp, the fat manager, and I behind him. It was a labyrinth of an old house, with corridors, passages, narrow winding staircases, and little low doors, the thresholds of which were hollowed out by the generations who had crossed them. There were no carpets, and no signs of any furniture above the ground floor, while the plaster was peeling off the walls, and the damp was breaking through in green, unhealthy blotches. I tried to put on as unconcerned an air as possible, but I had not forgotten the warnings of the lady, even though I disregarded them, and I kept a keen eye upon my two companions. Ferguson appeared to be a morose and silent man, but I could see from the little that he said that he was at least a fellow-countryman.

"Colonel Lysander Stark stopped at last before a low door, which he unlocked. Within was a small square room, in which the three of us could hardly get at one time. Ferguson remained outside, and the Colonel ushered me in.

"'We are now,' said he, 'actually within the hydraulic press, and it would be a particularly unpleasant thing for us if any-one were to turn it on. The ceiling of this small chamber is really the end of the descending piston, and it comes down with the force of many tons upon this metal floor. There are small lateral columns of water outside which receive the force, and which transmit and multiply it in the manner which is familiar to you. The machine goes readily enough, but there is some stiffness in the working of it, and it has lost a little of its force. Perhaps you will have the goodness to look it over, and to show us how we can set it right.'

"I took the lamp from him, and I examined the machine very tho-roughly. It was indeed a gigantic one, and capable of exercising enormous pressure. When I passed outside, however, and pressed down the levers which controlled it, I knew at once by the whishing sound that there was a slight leakage, which al-lowed a regurgitation of water through one of the side cylinders. An examination showed that one of the indiarubber bands which was round the head of a driving rod had shrunk so as not quite to fill the socket along which it worked. This was clearly the cause of the loss of power, and I pointed it out to my companions, who followed my remarks very carefully, and asked several prac-tical questions as to how they should proceed to set it right. When I had made it clear to them, I returned to the main chamber of the machine, and took a good look at it to satisfy my own curiosity. It was obvious at a glance that the story of the fuller's earth was the merest fabrication, for it would be absurd to suppose

that so powerful an engine could be de-signed for so inadequate a purpose. The walls were of wood, but the floor consisted of a large iron trough, and when I came to examine it I could see a crust of metallic deposit all over it. I had stooped and was scraping at this to see exactly what it was, when I heard a muttered exclamation in German, and saw the cadaverous face of the Colonel looking down at me.

"'What are you doing there?' he asked.

"I felt angry at having been tricked by so elaborate a story as that which he had told me. 'I was admiring your fuller's earth,' said I; 'I think that I should be better able to advise you as to your machine if I knew what the exact purpose was for which it was used.'

"The instant that I uttered the words I regretted the rashness of my speech. His face set hard, and a baleful light sprang up in his grey eyes.

"'Very well,' said he, 'you shall know all about the machine.' He took a step

"I RUSHED TO THE DOOR."

backward, slammed the little door, and turned the key in the lock. I rushed towards it and pulled at the handle, but it was quite secure, and did not give in the least to my kicks and shoves. 'Hullo!' I yelled. 'Hullo! Colonel! Let me out!'

"And then suddenly in the silence I heard a sound which sent my heart into my mouth. It was the clank of the levers, and the swish of the leaking cylinder. He had set the engine at work. The lamp still stood upon the floor where I had placed it when examining the trough. By its light I saw that the black ceiling was coming down upon me, slowly, jerkily, but, as none knew better than myself, with a force which must within a minute grind me to a shapeless pulp. I threw myself, screaming, against the door, and dragged with my nails at the lock. I implored the Colonel to let me out, but the remorseless clanking of the levers drowned my cries. The ceiling was only a foot or two above my head, and with my hand upraised I could feel its hard, rough surface. Then it flashed through my mind that the pain of my death would depend very much upon the position in which I met it. If I lay on my face the weight would come upon my spine, and I shuddered to think of that dreadful snap. Easier the other way, perhaps, and yet had I the nerve to lie and look up at that deadly black shadow wavering down upon me? Already I was unable to stand erect, when my eye caught something which brought a gush of hope back to my heart.

"I have said that though floor and ceiling were of iron, the walls were of wood. As I gave a last hurried glance around, I saw a thin line of yellow light between two of the boards, which broadened and broadened as a small panel was pushed backwards. For an instant I could hardly believe that here was indeed a door which led away from death. The next I threw myself through, and lay half-fainting upon the other side. The panel had closed again behind me, but the crash of the lamp, and a few moments afterwards the clang of the two slabs of metal, told me how narrow had been my escape.

"I was recalled to myself by a frantic plucking at my wrist, and I found myself lying upon the stone floor of a narrow corridor, while a woman bent over me and tugged at me with her left hand, while she held a candle in her right. It was the same good friend whose warning I had so foolishly rejected.

"'Come! come!' she cried, breathlessly. 'They will be here in a moment. They will see that you are not there. Oh, do not waste the so precious time, but come!'

"This time, at least, I did not scorn her advice. I staggered to my feet, and ran with her along the corridor and down a winding stair. The latter led to another broad passage, and, just as we reached it, we heard the sound of running feet, and the shouting of two voices—one answering the other—from the floor on which we were, and from the one beneath. My guide stopped, and looked about her like one who is at her wits' end. Then she threw open a door which led into a bedroom, through the window of which the moon was shining brightly.

"'It is your only chance,' said she. 'It is high, but it may be that you can jump it.'

"As she spoke a light sprang into view at the further end of the passage, and I saw the lean figure of Colonel Lysander Stark rushing forward with a lantern in one hand, and a weapon like a butcher's cleaver in the other. I rushed across the bedroom, flung open the window, and looked out. How quiet and sweet and wholesome the garden looked in the moonlight, and it could not be more than thirty feet down. I clambered out upon the sill, but I hesitated to jump, until I should have heard what passed between my saviour and the ruffian who pursued me. If she were ill-used, then at any risks I was determined to go back to her assistance. The thought had hardly flashed through my mind before he was at the door, pushing his way past her; but she threw her arms round him, and tried to hold him back.

"'Fritz! Fritz!' she cried in English, 'remember your promise after the last time. You said it should not be again. He will be silent! Oh, he will be silent!'

"'You are mad, Elise!' he shouted, struggling to break away from her. 'You will be the ruin of us. He has seen too much. Let me pass, I say!' He dashed her to one side, and, rushing to the window, cut at me with his heavy weapon. I had let myself go, and was hanging by the hands to the sill, when his blow fell. I was conscious of a dull pain, my grip loosened, and I fell into the garden below.

"I was shaken, but not hurt by the fall; so I picked myself up, and rushed off among the bushes as hard as I could run, for I

" ' HE CUT AT ME.' "

sprang to my feet with the feeling that I might hardly yet be safe from my pursuers. But, to my astonishment, when I came to look round me, neither house nor garden were to be seen. I had been lying in an angle of the hedge close by the high road, and just a little lower down was a long building, which proved, upon my approaching it, to be the very station at which I had arrived upon the previous night. Were it not for the ugly wound upon my hand, all that had passed during those dreadful hours might have been an evil dream.

"Half dazed, I went into the station, and asked about the morning train. There would be one to Reading in less than an hour. The same porter was on duty, I found, as had been there when I arrived. I inquired from him whether he had ever heard of Colonel Lysander Stark. The name was strange to him. Had he observed a carriage the night before waiting for me? No, he had not. Was there a police station anywhere near? There was one about three miles off.

"It was too far for me to go, weak and ill as I was. I determined to wait until I got back to town before telling my story to the police. It was a little past six when I arrived, so I went first to have my wound dressed, and then the doctor was kind enough to bring me along here. I put the case into your hands, and shall do exactly what you advise."

We both sat in silence for some little time after, listening to this extraordinary narrative. Then Sherlock Holmes pulled down from the shelf one of the ponderous commonplace books in which he placed his cuttings.

"Here is an advertisement which will interest you," said he. "It appeared in all the papers about a year ago. Listen to this :—'Lost, on the 9th inst., Mr. Jeremiah Hayling, aged 26, a hydraulic engineer. Left his lodgings at ten o'clock at night, and has not been heard of since. Was dressed in,' &c., &c. Ha! That represents the last time that the Colonel needed to have his machine overhauled, I fancy."

"Good heavens!" cried my patient. "Then that explains what the girl said."

understood that I was far from being out of danger yet. Suddenly, however, as I ran, a deadly dizziness and sickness came over me. I glanced down at my hand, which was throbbing painfully, and then, for the first time, saw that my thumb had been cut off, and that the blood was pouring from my wound. I endeavoured to tie my handkerchief round it, but there came a sudden buzzing in my ears, and next moment I fell in a dead faint among the rose-bushes.

"How long I remained unconscious I cannot tell. It must have been a very long time, for the moon had sunk, and a bright morning was breaking when I came to myself. My clothes were all sodden with dew, and my coat-sleeve was drenched with blood from my wounded thumb. The smarting of it recalled in an instant all the particulars of my night's adventure, and I

" Undoubtedly. It is quite clear that the Colonel was a cool and desperate man, who was absolutely determined that nothing should stand in the way of his little game, like those out-and-out pirates who will leave no survivor from a captured ship. Well, every moment now is precious, so, if you feel equal to it, we shall go down to Scotland Yard at once as a preliminary to starting for Eyford."

Some three hours or so afterwards we were all in the train together, bound from Reading to the little Berkshire village. There were Sherlock Holmes, the hydraulic engineer, Inspector Bradstreet of Scotland-yard, a plain-clothes man, and myself. Bradstreet had spread. an ordnance map of the county out upon the seat, and was busy with his compasses drawing a circle with Eyford for its centre.

" There you are," said he. " That circle is drawn at a radius of ten miles from the village. The place we want must be somewhere near that line. You said ten miles, I think, sir ? "

" It was an hour's good drive."

" And you think that they brought you back all that way when you were unconscious ? "

" They must have done so. I have a confused memory, too, of having been lifted and conveyed somewhere."

" What I cannot understand," said I, " is why they should have spared you when they found you lying fainting in the garden. Perhaps the villain was softened by the woman's entreaties."

" I hardly think that likely. I never saw a more inexorable face in my life."

" Oh, we shall soon clear up all that," said Bradstreet. " Well, I have drawn my circle, and I only wish I knew at what point upon it the folk that we are in search of are to be found."

" I think I could lay my finger on it," said Holmes, quietly.

" Really, now ! " cried the Inspector, " you have formed your opinion ! Come now, we shall see who agrees with you. I say it is south, for the country is more deserted there."

" And I say east," said my patient.

" I am for west," remarked the plain-clothes man. " There are several quiet little villages up there."

" And I am for north," said I ; " because there are no hills there, and our friend says that he did not notice the carriage go up any."

" Come," cried the Inspector, laughing ; " it's a very pretty diversity of opinion. We have boxed the compass among us. Who do you give your casting vote to ? "

" You are all wrong."

" But we can't *all* be."

" Oh yes, you can. This is my point," he placed his finger in the centre of the circle. " This is where we shall find them."

" But the twelve-mile drive?" gasped Hatherley.

" Six out and six back. Nothing simpler. You say yourself that the horse was fresh and glossy when you got in. How could it be that, if it had gone twelve miles over heavy roads ? "

" Indeed it is a likely ruse enough," observed Bradstreet, thoughtfully. " Of course there can be no doubt as to the nature of this gang."

" None at all," said Holmes. " They are coiners on a large scale, and have used the machine to form the amalgam which has taken the place of silver."

" We have known for some time that a clever gang was at work," said the Inspector. " They have been turning out half-crowns by the thousand. We even traced them as far as Reading, but could get no further ; for they had covered their traces in a way that showed that they were very old hands. But now, thanks to this lucky chance, I think that we have got them right enough."

But the Inspector was mistaken, for those criminals were not destined to fall into the hands of justice. As we rolled into Eyford Station we saw a gigantic column of smoke which streamed up from behind a small clump of trees in the neighbourhood, and hung like an immense ostrich feather over the landscape.

" A house on fire ? " asked Bradstreet, as the train steamed off again on its way.

" Yes, sir ! " said the station-master.

" When did it break out ? "

" I hear that it was during the night, sir, but it has got worse, and the whole place is in a blaze."

" Whose house is it ? "

" Dr. Becher's."

" Tell me," broke in the engineer, " is Dr. Becher a German, very thin, with a long sharp nose ? "

The station-master laughed heartily. " No, sir, Dr. Becher is an Englishman, and there isn't a man in the parish who has a better-lined waistcoat. But he has a gentleman staying with him, a patient, as I understand, who is a foreigner, and he looks as if a little good Berkshire beef would do him no harm."

The station-master had not finished his speech before we were all hastening in the direction of the fire. The road topped a low hill, and there was a great widespread white-washed building in front of us, spouting fire at every chink and window, while in the garden in

"A HOUSE ON FIRE?"

front three fire-engines were vainly striving to keep the flames under.

"That's it!" cried Hatherley, in intense excitement. "There is the gravel drive, and there are the rose-bushes where I lay. That second window is the one that I jumped from."

"Well, at least," said Holmes, "you have had your revenge upon them. There can be no question that it was your oil lamp which, when it was crushed in the press, set fire to the wooden walls, though no doubt they were too excited in the chase after you to observe it at the time. Now keep your eyes open in this crowd for your friends of last night, though I very much fear that they are a good hundred miles off by now."

And Holmes' fears came to be realised, for from that day to this no word has ever been heard either of the beautiful woman, the sinister German, or the morose Englishman. Early that morning a peasant had

met a cart containing several people and some very bulky boxes driving rapidly in the direction of Reading, but there all traces of the fugitives disappeared, and even Holmes' ingenuity failed ever to discover the least clue as to their whereabouts.

The firemen had been much perturbed at the strange arrangements which they had found within, and still more so by discovering a newly severed human thumb upon a window-sill of the second floor. About sunset, however, their efforts were at last successful, and they subdued the flames, but not before the roof had fallen in, and the whole place been reduced to such absolute ruin that, save some twisted cylinders and iron piping, not a trace remained of the machinery which had cost our unfortunate acquaintance so dearly. Large masses of nickel and of tin were discovered stored in an outhouse, but no coins were to be found, which may have explained the presence of those bulky boxes which have been already referred to.

How our hydraulic engineer had been conveyed from the garden to the spot where he recovered his senses might have remained for ever a mystery were it not for the soft mould, which told us a very plain tale. He had evidently been carried down by two persons, one of whom had remarkably small feet and the other unusually large ones. On the whole, it was most probable that the silent Englishman, being less bold or less murderous than his companion, had assisted the woman to bear the unconscious man out of the way of danger.

"Well," said our engineer ruefully, as we took our seats to return once more to London, "it has been a pretty business for me! I have lost my thumb, and I have lost a fifty-guinea fee, and what have I gained?"

"Experience," said Holmes laughing. "Indirectly it may be of value, you know; you have only to put it into words to gain the reputation of being excellent company for the remainder of your existence."

Adventures of Sherlock Holmes.

X.—THE ADVENTURE OF THE NOBLE BACHELOR.

By A. Conan Doyle.

THE Lord St. Simon marriage, and its curious termination, have long ceased to be a subject of interest in those exalted circles in which the unfortunate bridegroom moves. Fresh scandals have eclipsed it, and their more piquant details have drawn the gossips away from this four-year-old drama. As I have reason to believe, however, that the full facts have never been revealed to the general public, and as my friend Sherlock Holmes had a considerable share in clearing the matter up, I feel that no memoir of him would be complete without some little sketch of this remarkable episode.

It was a few weeks before my own marriage, during the days when I was still sharing rooms with Holmes in Baker-street, that he came home from an afternoon stroll to find a letter on the table waiting for him. I had remained indoors all day, for the weather had taken a sudden turn to rain, with high autumnal winds, and the jezail bullet which I had brought back in one of my limbs as a relic of my Afghan campaign, throbbed with dull persistency. With my body in one easy chair and my legs upon another, I had surrounded myself with a cloud of newspapers, until at last, saturated with the news of the day, I tossed them all aside and lay listless, watching the huge crest and monogram upon the envelope upon the table, and wondering lazily who my friend's noble correspondent could be.

"Here is a very fashionable epistle," I remarked as he entered. "Your morning letters, if I remember right, were from a fishmonger and a tide waiter."

"Yes, my correspondence has certainly the charm of variety," he answered, smiling, "and the humbler are usually the more interesting. This looks like one of those

"HE BROKE THE SEAL AND GLANCED OVER THE CONTENTS."

unwelcome social summonses which call upon a man either to be bored or to lie."

He broke the seal, and glanced over the contents.

"Oh, come, it may prove to be something of interest after all."

"Not social, then?"

"No, distinctly professional."

"And from a noble client?"

"One of the highest in England."

"My dear fellow, I congratulate you."

"I assure you, Watson, without affectation, that the status of my client is a matter of less moment to me than the interest of his case. It is just possible, however, that that also may not be wanting in this new investigation. You have been reading the papers diligently of late, have you not?"

"It looks like it," said I, ruefully, pointing to a huge bundle in the corner. "I have had nothing else to do."

"It is fortunate, for you will perhaps be able to post me up. I read nothing except the criminal news and the agony column. The latter is always instructive. But if you have followed recent events so closely you must have read about Lord St. Simon and his wedding?"

"Oh, yes, with the deepest interest."

"That is well. The letter which I hold in my hand is from Lord St. Simon. I will read it to you, and in return you must turn over these papers and let me have whatever bears upon the matter. This is what he says:—

"'My dear Mr. Sherlock Holmes,—Lord Backwater tells me that I may place implicit reliance upon your judgment and discretion. I have determined, therefore, to call upon you, and to consult you in reference to the very painful event which has occurred in connection with my wedding. Mr. Lestrade, of Scotland Yard, is acting already in the matter, but he assures me that he sees no objection to your co-operation, and that he even thinks that it might be of some assistance. I will call at four o'clock in the afternoon, and, should you have any other engagement at that time, I hope that you will postpone it, as this matter is of paramount importance.— Yours faithfully,			ST. SIMON.'

"It is dated from Grosvenor Mansions, written with a quill pen, and the noble lord has had the misfortune to get a smear of ink upon the outer side of his right little finger," remarked Holmes, as he folded up the epistle.

"He says four o'clock. It is three now. He will be here in an hour."

"Then I have just time, with your assistance, to get clear upon the subject. Turn over those papers, and arrange the extracts in their order of time, while I take a glance as to who our client is." He picked a red-covered volume from a line of books of reference beside the mantelpiece. "Here he is," said he, sitting down and flattening it out upon his knee. "Lord Robert Walsingham de Vere St. Simon, second son of the Duke of Balmoral—Hum! Arms: Azure, three caltrops in chief over a fess sable. Born in 1846. He's forty-one years of age, which is mature for marriage. Was Under-Secretary for the Colonies in a late Administration. The Duke, his father, was at one time Secretary for Foreign Affairs. They inherit Plantagenet blood by direct descent, and Tudor on the distaff side. Ha! Well, there is nothing very instructive in all this. I think that I must turn to you, Watson, for something more solid."

"I have very little difficulty in finding what I want," said I, "for the facts are quite recent, and the matter struck me as remarkable. I feared to refer them to you, however, as I knew that you had an inquiry on hand, and that you disliked the intrusion of other matters."

"Oh, you mean the little problem of the Grosvenor-square furniture van. That is quite cleared up now—though, indeed, it was obvious from the first. Pray give me the results of your newspaper selections."

"Here is the first notice which I can find. It is in the personal column of *The Morning Post*, and dates, as you see, some weeks back. 'A marriage has been arranged,' it says, 'and will, if rumour is correct, very shortly take place, between Lord Robert St. Simon, second son of the Duke of Balmoral, and Miss Hatty Doran, the only daughter of Aloysius Doran, Esq., of San Francisco, Cal., U.S.A.' That is all."

"Terse and to the point," remarked Holmes, stretching his long, thin legs towards the fire.

"There was a paragraph amplifying this in one of the society papers of the same week. Ah, here it is. 'There will soon be a call for protection in the marriage market, for the present free-trade principle appears to tell heavily against our home product. One by one the management of the noble houses of Great Britain is passing into the hands of our fair cousins from across the Atlantic. An important addition has been made during the last week to the list of the prizes which have been borne away by these charming invaders. Lord St. Simon, who has shown himself for over twenty years proof against the little god's arrows, has now definitely announced his approaching marriage with Miss Hatty Doran, the fascinating daughter of a Californian millionaire. Miss Doran, whose graceful figure and striking face attracted much attention at the Westbury House festivities, is an only child, and it is currently reported that her dowry will run to considerably over the six figures, with expectancies for the future. As it is an open secret that the Duke of Balmoral has been compelled to sell his pictures within the last few years, and as Lord St. Simon has no property of his own, save the small estate of Birchmoor, it is obvious that the Californian heiress is not the only gainer by an alliance which will enable her to make the easy and common transition from a Republican lady to a British peeress.' "

"Anything else?" asked Holmes, yawning.

"Oh yes; plenty. Then there is another note in *The Morning Post* to say that the marriage would be an absolutely quiet one, that it would be at St. George's, Hanover-square, that only half a dozen intimate friends would be invited, and that the party would return to the furnished house at Lancaster-gate which has been taken by Mr. Aloysius Doran. Two days later— that is, on Wednesday last—there is a curt announcement that the wedding had taken place, and that the honeymoon would be passed at Lord Backwater's place, near Petersfield. Those are all the notices which appeared before the disappearance of the bride."

"Before the what?" asked Holmes, with a start.

"The vanishing of the lady."

"When did she vanish, then?"

"At the wedding breakfast."

"Indeed. This is more interesting than it promised to be; quite dramatic, in fact."

"Yes; it struck me as being a little out of the common."

"They often vanish before the ceremony, and occasionally during the honeymoon; but I cannot call to mind anything quite so prompt as this. Pray let me have the details."

"I warn you that they are very incomplete."

"Perhaps we may make them less so."

"Such as they are, they are set forth in a single article of a morning paper of yesterday, which I will read to you. It is headed, 'Singular Occurrence at a Fashionable Wedding':—

"'The family of Lord Robert St. Simon has been thrown into the greatest consternation by the strange and painful episodes which have taken place in connection with his wedding. The ceremony, as shortly announced in the papers of yesterday, occurred on the previous morning; but it is only now that it has been possible to confirm the strange rumours which have been so persistently floating about. In spite of the attempts of the friends to hush the matter up, so much public attention has now been drawn to it that no good purpose can be served by affecting to disregard what is a common subject for conversation.

"'The ceremony, which was performed at St. George's, Hanover-square, was a very quiet one, no one being present save the father of the bride, Mr. Aloysius Doran, the Duchess of Balmoral, Lord Backwater, Lord Eustace and Lady Clara St. Simon (the younger brother and sister of the bridegroom), and Lady Alicia Whittington. The whole party proceeded afterwards to the house of Mr. Aloysius Doran, at Lancaster Gate, where breakfast had been prepared. It appears that some little trouble was caused by a woman, whose name has not been ascertained, who endeavoured to force her way into the house after the bridal party, alleging that she had some claim upon Lord St. Simon. It was only after a painful and prolonged scene that she was ejected by the butler and the footman. The bride, who had fortunately entered the house before this unpleasant interruption, had sat down to breakfast with the rest, when she complained of a sudden indisposition, and retired to her room. Her prolonged absence having caused some comment, her father followed her; but learned from her maid that she had only come up to her chamber for an instant, caught up an ulster and bonnet, and hurried down to the passage. One of the footmen declared that he had seen a lady leave the house thus apparelled; but had refused to credit that it was his mistress, believing her to be with the company. On ascertaining that his daughter had disappeared, Mr. Aloysius Doran, in conjunction with the bridegroom, instantly put themselves into communication with the police, and very energetic inquiries are being made, which will pro-she has known the bride-groom for some years. There are no further particulars, and the whole case is in your hands now—so far as it has been set forth in the public press."

"And an exceedingly interesting case it appears to be. I would not have missed it for worlds. But there is a ring at the bell, Watson, and as the clock makes it a few minutes after four, I have no doubt that this will prove to be our noble client. Do not dream of going, Watson, for I very much prefer having a witness, if only as a check to my own memory."

"Lord Robert St. Simon," announced our page boy, throwing open the door. A gentleman entered, with a pleasant, cultured face, high-nosed and pale, with something perhaps of petulance about the mouth, and with the steady, well-opened eye of a man whose pleasant lot it had ever been to command and to be obeyed. His manner was brisk, and yet his general appearance gave an undue impression of age, for he had a slight forward stoop, and a little

"SHE WAS EJECTED BY THE BUTLER AND THE FOOTMAN."

bably result in a speedy clearing up of this very singular business. Up to a late hour last night, however, nothing had transpired as to the whereabouts of the missing lady. There are rumours of foul play in the matter, and it is said that the police have caused the arrest of the woman who had caused the original disturbance, in the belief that, from jealousy or some other motive, she may have been concerned in the strange disappearance of the bride.' "

"And is that all?"

"Only one little item in another of the morning papers, but it is a suggestive one."

"And it is?"

"That Miss Flora Millar, the lady who had caused the disturbance, has actually been arrested. It appears that she was formerly a *danseuse* at the Allegro, and that

bend ot the knees as he walked. His hair, too, as he swept off his very curly-brimmed hat, was grizzled round the edges, and thin upon the top. As to his dress, it was careful to the verge of foppishness, with high collar, black frock coat, white waistcoat, yellow gloves, patent-leather shoes, and light-coloured gaiters. He advanced slowly into the room, turning his head from left to right, and swinging in his right hand the cord which held his golden eye-glasses.

"Good day, Lord St. Simon," said Holmes, rising and bowing. "Pray take the basket chair. This is my friend and colleague, Dr. Watson. Draw up a little to the fire, and we shall talk this matter over."

"A most painful matter to me, as you can most readily imagine, Mr. Holmes. I have been cut to the quick. I understand that you have already managed several delicate cases of this sort, sir, though I presume that they were hardly from the same class of society."

"No, I am descending."

"I beg pardon ? "

"My last client of the sort was a king."

"Oh, really! I had no idea. And which king ? "

"The King of Scandinavia."

"What! Had he lost his wife ? "

"You can understand," said Holmes, suavely, " that I extend to the affairs of my other clients the same secrecy which I promise to you in yours."

"Of course! Very right! very right! I'm sure I beg pardon. As to my own case, I am ready to give you any information which may assist you in forming an opinion."

"Thank you. I have already learned all that is in the public prints, nothing more. I presume that I may take it as correct—this article, for example, as to the disappearance of the bride."

Lord St. Simon glanced over it. " Yes, it is correct, as far as it goes."

"But it needs a great deal of supplementing before anyone could offer an opinion. I think that I may arrive at my facts most directly by questioning you."

"Pray do so."

"When did you first meet Miss Hatty Doran ? "

"In San Francisco, a year ago."

"You were travelling in the States ? "

"Yes."

"Did you become engaged then ? "

"No."

"But you were on a friendly footing ? "

"I was amused by her society, and she could see that I was amused."

"Her father is very rich ? "

"He is said to be the richest man on the Pacific slope."

"And how did he make his money ? "

"In mining. He had nothing a few years ago. Then he struck gold, invested it, and came up by leaps and bounds."

"Now, what is your own impression as to the young lady's —your wife's character ? "

The nobleman swung his glasses a little faster and stared down into the fire. "You see, Mr. Holmes," said he, " my wife was twenty before her father became a rich man. During that time she ran free in a mining camp, and wandered through woods or mountains, so that her education has come from Nature rather than from the schoolmaster. She is what we call in England a tomboy, with a strong nature, wild and free, unfettered by any sort of traditions. She is impetuous—volcanic, I was about to say. She is swift in making up her mind, and fearless in carrying out her resolutions. On the other hand, I would not have given her the name which I have the honour to bear" (he gave a little stately cough) " had I not thought her to be at bottom a noble woman. I believe that she is capable of heroic self-sacrifice, and that anything dishonourable would be repugnant to her."

"Have you her photograph ? "

"I brought this with me." He opened a locket, and showed us the full face of a very lovely woman. It was not a photograph, but an ivory miniature, and the artist had brought out the full effect of the lustrous black hair, the large dark eyes, and the exquisite mouth. Holmes gazed long and earnestly at it. Then he closed the

" LORD ROBERT ST. SIMON."

locket and handed it back to Lord St. Simon.

"The young lady came to London, then, and you renewed your acquaintance?"

"Yes, her father brought her over for this last London season. I met her several times, became engaged to her, and have now married her."

"She brought, I understand, a considerable dowry?"

"A fair dowry. Not more than is usual in my family."

"And this, of course, remains to you, since the marriage is a *fait accompli*?"

"I really have made no inquiries on the subject."

"Very naturally not. Did you see Miss Doran on the day before the wedding?"

"Yes."

"Was she in good spirits?"

"Never better. She kept talking of what we should do in our future lives."

"Indeed. That is very interesting. And on the morning of the wedding?"

"She was as bright as possible—at least, until after the ceremony."

"And did you observe any change in her then?"

"Well, to tell the truth, I saw then the first signs that I had ever seen that her temper was just a little sharp. The incident, however, was too trivial to relate, and can have no possible bearing upon the case."

"Pray let us have it, for all that."

"Oh, it is childish. She dropped her bouquet as we went towards the vestry. She was passing the front pew at the time, and it fell over into the pew. There was a moment's delay, but the gentleman in the pew handed it up to her again, and it did not appear to be the worse for the fall. Yet, when I spoke to her of the matter, she answered me abruptly; and in the carriage, on our way home, she seemed absurdly agitated over this trifling cause."

"Indeed. You say that there was a gentleman in the pew. Some of the general public were present, then?"

"Oh yes. It is impossible to exclude them when the church is open."

"This gentleman was not one of your wife's friends?"

"No, no; I call him a gentleman by courtesy, but he was quite a common-looking person. I hardly noticed his appearance. But really I think that we are wandering rather far from the point."

'THE GENTLEMAN IN THE PEW HANDED IT UP TO HER."

"Lady St. Simon, then, returned from the wedding in a less cheerful frame of mind than she had gone to it. What did she do on re-entering her father's house?"

"I saw her in conversation with her maid."

"And who is her maid?"

"Alice is her name. She is an American, and came from California with her."

"A confidential servant?"

"A little too much so. It seemed to me that her mistress allowed her to take great liberties. Still, of course, in America they look upon these things in a different way."

"How long did she speak to this Alice?"

"Oh, a few minutes. I had something else to think of."

"You did not overhear what they said?"

"Lady St. Simon said something about 'jumping a claim.' She was accustomed to use slang of the kind. I have no idea what she meant."

"American slang is very expressive sometimes. And what did your wife do when she had finished speaking to her maid?"

"She walked into the breakfast room."

"On your arm?"

"No, alone. She was very independent in little matters like that. Then, after we had sat down for ten minutes or so, she rose hurriedly, muttered some words of apology, and left the room. She never came back."

"But this maid Alice, as I understand, deposes that she went to her room, covered her bride's dress with a long ulster, put on a bonnet, and went out."

"Quite so. And she was afterwards seen walking into Hyde-park in company with Flora Millar, a woman who is now in custody, and who had already made a disturbance at Mr. Doran's house that morning."

"Ah, yes. I should like a few particulars as to this young lady, and your relations to her."

Lord St. Simon shrugged his shoulders, and raised his eyebrows. "We have been on a friendly footing for some years—I may say on a *very* friendly footing. She used to be at the Allegro. I have not treated her ungenerously, and she has no just cause of complaint against me, but you know what women are, Mr. Holmes. Flora was a dear little thing, but exceedingly hot-headed, and devotedly attached to me. She wrote me dreadful letters when she heard that I was about to be married, and to tell the truth the reason why I had the marriage celebrated so quietly was that I feared lest there might be a scandal in the church. She came to Mr. Doran's door just after we returned, and she endeavoured to push her way in, uttering very abusive expressions towards my wife, and even threatening her, but I had foreseen the possibility of something of the sort, and I had two police fellows there in private clothes, who soon pushed her out again. She was quiet when she saw that there was no good in making a row."

"Did your wife hear all this?"

"No, thank goodness, she did not."

"And she was seen walking with this very woman afterwards?"

"Yes. That is what Mr. Lestrade, of Scotland Yard, looks upon as so serious. It is thought that Flora decoyed my wife out, and laid some terrible trap for her."

"Well, it is a possible supposition."

"You think so, too?"

"I did not say a probable one. But you do not yourself look upon this as likely?"

"I do not think Flora would hurt a fly."

"Still, jealousy is a strange transformer of characters. Pray what is your own theory as to what took place?"

"Well, really, I came to seek a theory, not to propound one. I have given you all the facts. Since you ask me, however, I may say that it has occurred to me as possible that the excitement of this affair, the consciousness that she had made so immense a social stride, had the effect of causing some little nervous disturbance in my wife."

"In short, that she had become suddenly deranged?"

"Well, really, when I consider that she has turned her back—I will not say upon me, but upon so much that many have aspired to without success—I can hardly explain it in any other fashion."

"Well, certainly that is also a conceivable hypothesis," said Holmes, smiling. "And now, Lord St. Simon, I think that I have nearly all my data. May I ask whether you were seated at the breakfast-table so that you could see out of the window?"

"We could see the other side of the road, and the Park."

"Quite so. Then I do not think that I need detain you longer. I shall communicate with you."

"Should you be fortunate enough to solve this problem," said our client, rising.

"I have solved it."

"Eh? What was that?"

"I say that I have solved it."

"Where, then, is my wife?"

"That is a detail which I shall speedily supply."

Lord St. Simon shook his head. "I am afraid that it will take wiser heads than yours or mine," he remarked, and bowing in a stately, old-fashioned manner, he departed.

"It is very good of Lord St. Simon to honour my head by putting it on a level with his own," said Sherlock Holmes, laughing. "I think that I shall have a whisky and soda and a cigar after all this cross-questioning. I had formed my conclusions as to the case before our client came into the room."

"My dear Holmes!"

"I have notes of several similar cases, though none, as I remarked before, which were quite as prompt. My whole examination served to turn my conjecture into a certainty. Circumstantial evidence is occasionally very convincing, as when you find a trout in the milk, to quote Thoreau's example."

"But I have heard all that you have heard."

"Without, however, the knowledge of pre-existing cases which serves me so well. There was a parallel instance in Aberdeen some years back, and something on very much the same lines at Munich the year after the Franco-Prussian war. It is one of these cases—but hullo, here is Lestrade! Good afternoon, Lestrade! You will find an extra tumbler upon the sideboard, and there are cigars in the box."

The official detective was attired in a pea-jacket and cravat, which gave him a decidedly nautical appearance, and he carried a black canvas bag in his hand. With a short greeting he seated himself, and lit the cigar which had been offered to him.

"What's up, then?" asked Holmes, with a twinkle in his eye. "You look dissatisfied."

"And I feel dissatisfied. It is this infernal St. Simon marriage case. I can make neither head nor tail of the business."

"Really! You surprise me."

"Who ever heard of such a mixed affair? Every clue seems to slip through my fingers. I have been at work upon it all day."

"And very wet it seems to have made you," said Holmes, laying his hand upon the arm of the pea-jacket.

"Yes, I have been dragging the Serpentine."

"In heaven's name, what for?"

"In search of the body of Lady St. Simon."

Sherlock Holmes leaned back in his chair and laughed heartily.

"Have you dragged the basin of the Trafalgar-square fountain?" he asked.

"Why? What do you mean?"

"Because you have just as good a chance of finding this lady in the one as in the other."

Lestrade shot an angry glance at my companion. "I suppose you know all about it," he snarled.

"Well, I have only just heard the facts, but my mind is made up."

"Oh, indeed! Then you think that the Serpentine plays no part in the matter?"

"'THERE,' SAID HE."

"I think it very unlikely."

"Then perhaps you will kindly explain how it is that we found this in it?" He opened his bag as he spoke, and tumbled on to the floor a wedding dress of watered silk, a pair of white satin shoes, and a bride's wreath and veil, all discoloured and soaked in water. "There," said he, putting a new wedding-ring upon the top of the pile. "There is a little nut for you to crack, Master Holmes."

"Oh, indeed," said my friend, blowing blue rings into the air. "You dragged them from the Serpentine?"

"No. They were found floating near the margin by a park-keeper. They have been identified as her clothes, and it seemed to me that if the clothes were there the body would not be far off."

"By the same brilliant reasoning, every man's body is to be found in the neighbourhood of his wardrobe. And pray what did you hope to arrive at through this?"

"At some evidence implicating Flora Millar in the disappearance."

"I am afraid that you will find it difficult."

"Are you indeed, now?" cried Lestrade, with some bitterness. "I am afraid, Holmes, that you are not very practical with your deductions and your inferences. You have made two blunders in as many minutes. This dress does implicate Miss Flora Millar."

"And how?"

"In the dress is a pocket. In the pocket is a card-case. In the card-case is a note. And here is the very note." He slapped it down upon the table in front of him. "Listen to this. 'You will see me when all is ready. Come at once. F. H. M.' Now my theory all along has been that Lady St. Simon was decoyed away by Flora Millar, and that she, with confederates no doubt, was responsible for her disappearance. Here, signed with her initials, is the very note which was no doubt quietly slipped into her hand at the door, and which lured her within their reach."

"Very good, Lestrade," said Holmes, laughing. "You really are very fine indeed. Let me see it." He took up the paper in a listless way, but his attention instantly became riveted, and he gave a little cry of satisfaction. "This is indeed important," said he.

"Ha, you find it so?"

"Extremely so. I congratulate you warmly."

Lestrade rose in his triumph and bent his head to look. "Why," he shrieked, "you're looking at the wrong side."

"On the contrary, this is the right side."

"The right side? You're mad! Here is the note written in pencil over here."

"And over here is what appears to be the fragment of a hotel bill, which interests me deeply."

"There's nothing in it. I looked at it before," said Lestrade, "'Oct. 4th, rooms 8s., breakfast 2s. 6d , cocktail 1s., lunch 2s. 6d., glass sherry, 8d.' I see nothing in that."

"Very likely not. It is most important all the same. As to the note, it is important also, or at least the initials are, so I congratulate you again."

"I've wasted time enough," said Lestrade, rising, "I believe in hard work, and not in sitting by the fire spinning fine theories. Good-day, Mr. Holmes, and we shall see which gets to the bottom of the matter first." He gathered up the garments, thrust them into the bag, and made for the door.

"Just one hint to you, Lestrade," drawled Holmes, before his rival vanished; "I will tell you the true solution of the matter. Lady St. Simon is a myth. There is not, and there never has been, any such person."

Lestrade looked sadly at my companion. Then he turned to me, tapped his forehead three times, shook his head solemnly, and hurried away.

He had hardly shut the door behind him when Holmes rose and put on his overcoat. "There is something in what the fellow says about outdoor work," he remarked, "so I think, Watson, that I must leave you to your papers for a little."

It was after five o'clock when Sherlock Holmes left me, but I had no time to be lonely, for within an hour there arrived a confectioner's man with a very large flat box. This he unpacked with the help of a youth whom he had brought with him, and presently, to my very great astonishment, a quite epicurean little cold supper began to be laid out upon our humble lodging-house mahogany. There were a couple of brace of cold woodcock, a pheasant, a *pâté de foie gras* pie, with a group of ancient and cobwebby bottles. Having laid out all these luxuries, my two visitors vanished away, like the genii of the Arabian Nights, with no explanation save that the things had been paid for, and were ordered to this address.

Just before nine o'clock Sherlock Holmes

stepped briskly into the room. His features were gravely set, but there was a light in his eye which made me think that he had not been disappointed in his conclusions.

"They have laid the supper, then," he said, rubbing his hands.

"You seem to expect company. They have laid for five."

"Yes, I fancy we may have some company dropping in," said he. "I am surprised that Lord St. Simon has not already arrived. Ha! I fancy that I hear his step now upon the stairs."

It was indeed our visitor of the morning who came bustling in, dangling his glasses more vigorously than ever, and with a very perturbed expression upon his aristocratic features.

"My messenger reached you, then?" asked Holmes.

"Yes, and I confess that the contents startled me beyond measure. Have you good authority for what you say?"

"The best possible."

Lord St. Simon sank into a chair, and passed his hand over his forehead.

"What will the duke say," he murmured, "when he hears that one of the family has been subjected to such a humiliation?"

"It is the purest accident. I cannot allow that there is any humiliation."

"Ah, you look on these things from another standpoint."

"I fail to see that anyone is to blame. I can hardly see how the lady could have acted otherwise, though her abrupt method of doing it was undoubtedly to be regretted. Having no mother she had no one to advise her at such a crisis."

"It was a slight, sir, a public slight," said Lord St. Simon, tapping his fingers upon the table.

"You must make allowance for this poor girl, placed in so unprecedented a position."

"I will make no allowance. I am very angry indeed, and I have been shamefully used."

"I think that I heard a ring," said Holmes. "Yes, there are steps on the landing. If I cannot persuade you to take a lenient view of the matter, Lord St. Simon, I have brought an advocate here who may be more successful." He opened the door and ushered in a lady and gentleman. "Lord St. Simon," said he, "allow me to introduce you to Mr. and Mrs. Francis Hay Moulton. The lady, I think, you have already met."

At the sight of these new-comers our client had sprung from his seat, and stood very erect, with his eyes cast down and his hand thrust into the breast of his frock coat, a picture of offended dignity. The lady had taken a quick step forward and had held out her hand to him, but he still refused

"A PICTURE OF OFFENDED DIGNITY."

to raise his eyes. It was as well for his resolution, perhaps, for her pleading face was one which it was hard to resist.

"You're angry, Robert," said she. "Well, I guess you have every cause to be."

"Pray make no apology to me," said Lord St. Simon, bitterly.

"Oh yes, I know that I treated you real bad, and that I should have spoken to you before I went; but I was kind of rattled, and from the time when I saw Frank here again, I just didn't know what I was doing or saying. I only wonder I didn't fall down and do a faint right there before the altar."

"Perhaps, Mrs. Moulton, you would like my friend and me to leave the room while you explain this matter?"

"If I may give an opinion," remarked the strange gentleman, "we've had just a little too much secrecy over this business already. For my part, I should like all Europe and America to hear the rights of it." He was a small, wiry, sunburned man, clean shaven, with a sharp face and alert manner.

"Then I'll tell our story right away," said the lady. "Frank here and I met in '84, in McQuire's camp, near the Rockies, where Pa was working a claim. We were engaged to each other, Frank and I; but then one day father struck a rich pocket, and made a pile, while poor Frank here had a claim that petered out and came to nothing. The richer Pa grew, the poorer was Frank; so at last Pa wouldn't hear of our engagement lasting any longer, and he took me away to 'Frisco. Frank wouldn't throw up his hand, though; so he followed me there, and he saw me without Pa knowing anything about it. It would only have made him mad to know, so we just fixed it all up for ourselves. Frank said that he would go and make his pile, too, and never come back to claim me until he had as much as Pa. So then I promised to wait for him to the end of time, and pledged myself not to marry any-one else while he lived. 'Why shouldn't we be married right away, then,' said he, 'and then I will feel sure of you; and I won't claim to be your husband until I come back.' Well, we talked it over, and he had fixed it all up so nicely, with a clergyman all ready in waiting, that we just did it right there; and then Frank went off to seek his fortune, and I went back to Pa.

"The next that I heard of Frank was that he was in Montana, and then he went prospecting into Arizona, and then I heard of him from New Mexico. After that came a long newspaper story about how a miners' camp had been attacked by Apache Indians, and there was my Frank's name among the killed. I fainted dead away, and I was very sick for months after. Pa thought I had a decline, and took me to half the doctors in 'Frisco. Not a word of news came for a year and more, so that I never doubted that Frank was really dead. Then Lord St. Simon came to 'Frisco, and we came to London, and a marriage was arranged, and Pa was very pleased, but I felt all the time that no man on this earth would ever take the place in my heart that had been given to my poor Frank.

"Still, if I had married Lord St. Simon, of course I'd have done my duty by him. We can't command our love, but we can our actions. I went to the altar with him with the intention that I would make him just as good a wife as it was in me to be. But you may imagine what I felt when, just as I came to the altar rails, I glanced back and saw Frank standing looking at me out of the first pew. I thought it was his ghost at first; but, when I looked again, there he was still, with a kind of question in his eyes as if to ask me whether I were glad or sorry to see him. I wonder I didn't drop. I know that everything was turning round, and the words of the clergy-man were just like the buzz of a bee in my ear. I didn't know what to do. Should I stop the service and make a scene in the church? I glanced at him again, and he seemed to know what I was thinking, for he raised his finger to his lips to tell me to to be still. Then I saw him scribble on a piece of paper, and I knew that he was writing me a note. As I passed his pew on the way out I dropped my bouquet over to him, and he slipped the note into my hand when he returned me the flowers. It was only a line asking me to join him when he made the sign to me to do so. Of course, I never doubted for a moment that my first duty now was to him, and I determined to do just whatever he might direct.

"When I got back I told my maid, who had known him in California, and had always been his friend. I ordered her to say nothing, but to get a few things packed and my ulster ready. I know I ought to have spoken to Lord St. Simon, but it was dreadful hard before his mother and all those great people. I just made up my mind to run away, and explain afterwards. I hadn't been at the table ten minutes before I saw Frank out of the window at the other side of the road. He beckoned to me, and then began walking into the Park. I slipped out, put on my things, and followed him. Some woman came talking

"SOME WOMAN CAME TALKING ABOUT LORD ST. SIMON."

something or other about Lord St. Simon to me—seemed to me from the little I heard as if he had a little secret of his own before marriage also—but I managed to get away from her, and soon over took Frank. We got into a cab together, and away we drove to some lodgings he had taken in Gordon-square, and that was my true wedding after all those years of waiting. Frank had been a prisoner among the Apaches, had escaped, came on to 'Frisco, found that I had given him up for dead and had gone to England, followed me there, and had come upon me at last on the very morning of my second wedding."

"I saw it in a paper," explained the

American. "It gave the name and the church, but not where the lady lived."

"Then we had a talk as to what we should do, and Frank was all for openness, but I was so ashamed of it all that I felt as if I would like to vanish away and never see any of them again, just sending a line to Pa, perhaps, to show him that I was alive. It was awful to me to think of all those lords and ladies sitting round that breakfast table, and waiting for me to come back. So Frank took my wedding clothes and things, and made a bundle of them so that I should not be traced, and dropped them away somewhere where no one should find them. It is likely that we should have gone on to Paris to-morrow, only that this good gentleman, Mr. Holmes, came round to us this evening, though how he found us is more than I can think, and he showed us very clearly and kindly that I was wrong and that Frank was right, and that we should put ourselves in the wrong if we were so secret. Then he offered to give us a chance of talking to Lord St. Simon alone, and so we came right away round to his rooms at once. Now, Robert, you have heard it all, and I am very sorry if I have given you pain, and I hope that you do not think very meanly of me."

Lord St. Simon had by no means relaxed his rigid attitude, but had listened with a frowning brow and a compressed lip to this long narrative.

"Excuse me," he said, "but it is not my custom to discuss my most intimate personal affairs in this public manner."

"Then you won't forgive me? You won't shake hands before I go?"

"Oh, certainly, if it would give you any pleasure." He put out his hand and coldly grasped that which she extended to him.

"I had hoped," suggested Holmes, "that you would have joined us in a friendly supper."

"I think that there you ask a little too much," responded his lordship. "I may be forced to acquiesce in these recent developments, but I can hardly be expected to make merry over them. I think that, with

obvious to me, the one that the lady had been quite willing to undergo the wedding ceremony, the other that she had repented of it within a few minutes of returning home. Obviously something had occurred

"I WILL WISH YOU ALL A VERY GOOD NIGHT."

your permission, I will now wish you all a very good night." He included us all in a sweeping bow, and stalked out of the room.

"Then I trust that you at least will honour me with your company," said Sherlock Holmes. "It is always a joy to me to meet an American, Mr. Moulton, for I am one of those who believe that the folly of a monarch and the blundering of a Minister in far gone years will not prevent our children from being some day citizens of the same world-wide country under a flag which shall be a quartering of the Union Jack with the Stars and Stripes."

"The case has been an interesting one," remarked Holmes, when our visitors had left us, "because it serves to show very clearly how simple the explanation may be of an affair which at first sight seems to be almost inexplicable. Nothing could be more natural than the sequence of events as narrated by this lady, and nothing stranger than the result when viewed, for instance, by Mr. Lestrade of Scotland Yard.

"You were not yourself at fault at all, then?"

"From the first, two facts were very

during the morning, then, to cause her to change her mind. What could that something be? She could not have spoken to anyone when she was out, for she had been in the company of the bridegroom. Had she seen someone, then? If she had, it must be someone from America, because she had spent so short a time in this country that she could hardly have allowed anyone to acquire so deep an influence over her that the mere sight of him would induce her to change her plans so completely. You see we have already arrived, by a process of exclusion, at the idea that she might have seen an American. Then who could this American be, and why should he possess so much influence over her? It might be a lover; it might be a husband. Her young womanhood had, I knew, been spent in rough scenes, and under strange conditions. So far I had got before ever I heard Lord St. Simon's narrative. When he told us of a man in a pew, of the change in the bride's manner, of so transparent a device for obtaining a note as the dropping of a bouquet, of her resort to her confidential maid, and of her very significant allusion to claim-jumping, which in miners' parlance means taking possession of that which another person has a prior claim to, the whole situation became absolutely clear. She had gone off with a man, and the man was either a lover or was a previous husband, the chances being in favour of the latter."

"And how in the world did you find them ? "

" It might have been difficult, but friend Lestrade held information in his hands the value of which he did not himself know. The initials were of course of the highest importance, but more valuable still was it to know that within a week he had settled his bill at one of the most select London hotels."

" How did you deduce the select ? "

"By the select prices. Eight shillings for a bed and eightpence for a glass of sherry, pointed to one of the most expensive hotels. There are not many in London which charge at that rate. In the second one which I visited in Northumberland-avenue, I learned by an inspection of the book that Francis H. Moulton, an American gentleman, had left only the day before,

and on looking over the entries against him, I came upon the very items which I had seen in the duplicate bill. His letters were to be forwarded to 226, Gordon-square, so thither I travelled, and being fortunate enough to find the loving couple at home, I ventured to give them some paternal advice, and to point out to them that it would be better in every way that they should make their position a little clearer, both to the general publ'c and to Lord St. Simon in particular. I invited them to meet him here, and as you see, I made him keep the appointment."

"But with no very good result," I remarked. "His conduct was certainly not very gracious."

" Ah ! Watson," said Holmes, smiling, " perhaps you would not be very gracious either, if, after all the trouble of wooing and wedding, you found yourself deprived in an instant of wife and of fortune. I think that we may judge Lord St. Simon very mercifully, and thank our stars that we are never likely to find ourselves in the same position. Draw your chair up, and hand me my violin, for the only problem which we have still to solve is how to while away these bleak autumnal evenings."

XI.—THE ADVENTURE OF THE BERYL CORONET.

"HOLMES," said I, as I stood one morning in our bow window looking down the street, "here is a madman coming along. It seems rather sad that his relatives should allow him to come out alone."

My friend rose lazily from his arm-chair, and stood with his hands in the pockets of his dressing gown, looking over my shoulder. It was a bright, crisp February morning, and the snow of the day before still lay deep upon the ground, shimmering brightly in the wintry sun. Down the centre of Baker-street it had been ploughed into a brown crumbly band by the traffic, but at either side and on the heaped-up edges of the footpaths it still lay as white as when it fell. The grey pavement had been cleaned and scraped, but was still dangerously slippery, so that there were fewer passengers than usual. Indeed, from the direction of the Metropolitan Station no one was coming save the single gentleman whose eccentric conduct had drawn my attention.

He was a man of about fifty, tall, portly, and imposing, with a massive, strongly marked face and a commanding figure. He was dressed in a sombre yet rich style, in black frock-coat, shining hat, neat brown gaiters, and well cut pearl grey trousers. Yet his actions were in absurd contrast to the dignity of his dress and features, for he was running hard, with occasional little springs, such as a weary man gives who is little accustomed to set any tax upon his legs. As he ran he jerked his hands up and down, waggled his head, and writhed his face into the most extraordinary contortions.

"What on earth can be the matter with him?" I asked. "He is looking up at the numbers of the houses."

"I believe that he is coming here," said Holmes, rubbing his hands.

"Here?"

"Yes; I rather think he is coming to consult me professionally. I think that I recognise the symptoms. Ha! did I not tell you?" As he spoke, the man, puffing and blowing, rushed at our door, and pulled at our bell until the whole house resounded with the clanging.

A few moments later he was in our room, still puffing, still gesticulating, but with so fixed a look of grief and despair in his eyes that our smiles were turned in an instant to horror and pity. For a while he could not get his words out, but swayed his body and plucked at his hair like one who has been driven to the extreme limits of his reason. Then, suddenly springing

"WITH A LOOK OF GRIEF AND DESPAIR."

to his feet, he beat his head against the wall with such force that we both rushed upon him, and tore him away to the centre of the room. Sherlock Holmes pushed him down into the easy-chair, and, sitting beside him, patted his hand, and chatted with him in the easy, soothing tones which he knew so well how to employ.

"You have come to me to tell your story, have you not?" said he. "You are fatigued with your haste. Pray wait until you have recovered yourself, and then I shall be most happy to look into any little problem which you may submit to me."

The man sat for a minute or more with a heaving chest, fighting against his emotion. Then he passed his handkerchief over his brow, set his lips tight, and turned his face towards us.

"No doubt you think me mad?" said he.

"I see that you have had some great trouble," responded Holmes.

"God knows I have!—a trouble which is enough to unseat my reason, so sudden and so terrible is it. Public disgrace I might have faced, although I am a man whose character has never yet borne a stain. Private affliction also is the lot of every man; but the two coming together, and in so frightful a form, have been enough to shake my very soul. Besides, it is not I alone. The very noblest in the land may suffer, unless some way be found out of this horrible affair."

"Pray compose yourself, sir," said Holmes, "and let me have a clear account of who you are, and what it is that has befallen you."

"My name," answered our visitor, "is probably familiar to your ears. I am Alexander Holder, of the banking firm of Holder & Stevenson, of Threadneedle-street."

The name was indeed well known to us, as belonging to the senior partner in the second largest private banking concern in the City of London. What could have happened, then, to bring one of the foremost citizens of London to this most pitiable pass? We waited, all curiosity, until with another effort he braced himself to tell his story.

"I feel that time is of value," said he, "that is why I hastened here when the police inspector suggested that I should secure your co-operation. I came to Baker-street by the Undergound, and hurried from there on foot, for the cabs go slowly through this snow. That is why I was so out of breath, for I am a man who take very little exercise. I feel better now, and I will put the facts before you as shortly and yet as clearly as I can.

"It is, of course, well known to you that in a successful banking business as much depends upon our being able to find remunerative investments for our funds, as upon our increasing our connection and the number of our depositors. One of our most lucrative means of laying out money is in the shape of loans, where the security is unimpeachable. We have done a good deal in this direction during the last few years, and there are many noble families to whom we have advanced large sums upon the security of their pictures, libraries, or plate.

"Yesterday morning I was seated in my office at the Bank, when a card was brought in to me by one of the clerks. I started when I saw the name, for it was that of none other than—— well, perhaps even to you I had better say no more than that it was a name which is a household word all over the earth—one of the highest, noblest, most exalted names in England. I was overwhelmed by the honour, and attempted, when he entered, to say so, but he plunged at once into business with the air of a man who wishes to hurry quickly through a disagreeable task.

"'Mr. Holder,' said he, 'I have been informed that you are in the habit of advancing money.'

"'The firm do so when the security is good,' I answered.

"'It is absolutely essential to me,' said he, 'that I should have fifty thousand pounds at once. I could of course borrow so trifling a sum ten times over from my friends, but I much prefer to make it a matter of business, and to carry out that business myself. In my position you can readily understand that it is unwise to place oneself under obligations.'

"'For how long, may I ask, do you want this sum?' I asked.

"'Next Monday I have a large sum due to me, and I shall then most certainly repay what you advance, with whatever interest you think it right to charge. But it is very essential to me that the money should be paid at once.'

"'I should be happy to advance it without further parley from my own private purse,' said I, 'were it not that the strain would be rather more than it could bear. If, on the other hand, I am to do it in the name of the firm, then in justice to my partner I must insist that, even in your case, every businesslike precaution should be taken.'

"'I should much prefer to have it so,' said he, raising up a square, black morocco case which he had laid beside his chair. 'You have doubtless heard of the Beryl coronet?'

"'One of the most precious public possessions of the Empire,' said I.

"'Precisely.' He opened the case, and there, embedded in soft, flesh-coloured velvet, lay the magnificent piece of jewellery which he had named. 'There are thirty-

"I TOOK THE PRECIOUS CASE."

nine enormous beryls,' said he, 'and the price of the gold chasing is incalculable. The lowest estimate would put the worth of the coronet at double the sum which I have asked. I am prepared to leave it with you as my security.'

"I took the precious case into my hands and looked in some perplexity from it to my illustrious client.

"'You doubt its value?' he asked.

"'Not at all. I only doubt——'

"'The propriety of my leaving it. You may set your mind at rest about that. I should not dream of doing so were it not

absolutely certain that I should be able in four days to reclaim it. It is a pure matter of form. Is the security sufficient?'

"'Ample.'

"'You understand, Mr. Holder, that I am giving you a strong proof of the confidence which I have in you, founded upon all that I have heard of you. I rely upon you not only to be discreet and to refrain from all gossip upon the matter, but, above all, to preserve this coronet with every possible precaution, because I need not say that a great public scandal would be caused if any harm were to befall it. Any injury to it would be almost as serious as its complete loss, for there are no beryls in the world to match these, and it would be impossible to replace them. I leave it with you, however, with every confidence, and I shall call for it in person on Monday morning.'

"Seeing that my client was anxious to leave, I said no more; but, calling for my cashier, I ordered him to pay over fifty thousand-pound notes. When I was alone once more, however, with the precious case lying upon the table in front of me, I could not but think with some misgivings of the immense responsibility which it entailed upon me. There could be no doubt that, as it was a national possession, a horrible scandal would ensue if any misfortune should occur to it. I already regretted having ever consented to take charge of it. However, it was too late to alter the matter now, so I locked it up in my private safe, and turned once more to my work.

"When evening came, I felt that it would be an imprudence to leave so precious a thing in the office behind me. Bankers' safes had been forced before now, and why should not mine be? If so, how terrible would be the position in which I should find myself! I determined, therefore, that for the next few days I would always carry the case backwards and forwards with me, so that it might never be really out of my reach. With this intention, I called a cab, and drove out to my house at Streatham, carrying the jewel with me. I did not breathe freely until I had taken it upstairs, and locked it in the bureau of my dressing-room.

"And now a word as to my household, Mr. Holmes, for I wish you to thoroughly understand the situation. My groom and my page sleep out of the house, and may be set aside altogether. I have three maid-servants who have been with me a number of years, and whose absolute reliability is quite above suspicion. Another, Lucy Parr, the second waiting-maid, has only been in my service a few months. She came with an excellent character, however, and has always given me satisfaction. She is a very pretty girl, and has attracted admirers who have occasionally hung about the place. That is the only drawback which we have found to her, but we believe her to be a thoroughly good girl in every way.

"So much for the servants. My family itself is so small that it will not take me long to describe it. I am a widower, and have an only son, Arthur. He has been a disappointment to me, Mr. Holmes—a grievous disappointment. I have no doubt that I am myself to blame. People tell me that I have spoiled him. Very likely I have. When my dear wife died I felt that he was all I had to love. I could not bear to see the smile fade even for a moment from his face. I have never denied him a wish. Perhaps it would have been better for both of us had I been sterner, but I meant it for the best.

"It was naturally my intention that he should succeed me in my business, but he was not of a business turn. He was wild, wayward, and, to speak the truth, I could not trust him in the handling of large sums of money. When he was young he became a member of an aristocratic club, and there, having charming manners, he was soon the intimate of a number of men with long purses and expensive habits. He learned to play heavily at cards and to squander money on the turf, until he had again and again to come to me and implore me to give him an advance upon his allowance, that he might settle his debts of honour. He tried more than once to break away from the dangerous company which he was keeping, but each time the influence of his friend Sir George Burnwell was enough to draw him back again.

"And, indeed, I could not wonder that such a man as Sir George Burnwell should gain an influence over him, for he has frequently brought him to my house, and I have found myself that I could hardly resist the fascination of his manner. He is older than Arthur, a man of the world to his finger-tips, one who had been everywhere, seen everything, a brilliant talker, and a man of great personal beauty. Yet when I think of him in cold blood, far away from the glamour of his presence, I am convinced from his cynical speech, and the look which I have caught in his eyes, that he is one who should be deeply distrusted. So I think, and so, too, thinks my little Mary, who has a woman's quick insight into character.

"And now there is only she to be described. She is my niece; but when my brother died five years ago and left her alone in the world I adopted her, and have looked upon her ever since as my daughter. She is a sunbeam in my house—sweet, loving, beautiful, a wonderful manager and housekeeper, yet as tender and quiet and gentle as a woman could be. She is my right hand. I do not know what I could do without her. In only one matter has she ever gone against my wishes. Twice my boy has asked her to marry him, for he loves her devotedly, but each time she has refused him. I think that if anyone could have drawn him into the right path it would have been she, and that his marriage might have changed his whole life; but now, alas! it is too late—for ever too late!

"Now, Mr. Holmes, you know the people who live under my roof, and I shall continue with my miserable story.

"When we were taking coffee in the drawing-room that night, after dinner, I told Arthur and Mary my experience, and of the precious treasure which we had under our roof, suppressing only the name of my client. Lucy Parr, who had brought in the coffee, had, I am sure, left the room; but I cannot swear that the door was closed. Mary and Arthur were much interested, and wished to see the famous coronet, but I thought it better not to disturb it.

"'Where have you put it?' asked Arthur.

"'In my own bureau.'

"'Well, I hope to goodness the house won't be burgled during the night,' said he.

"'It is locked up,' I answered.

"'Oh, any old key will fit that bureau. When I was a youngster I have opened it myself with the key of the box-room cupboard.'

"He often had a wild way of talking, so that I thought little of what he said. He

"OH, ANY OLD KEY WILL FIT THAT BUREAU."

followed me to my room, however, that night with a very grave face.

"'Look here, dad,' said he, with his eyes cast down. 'Can you let me have two hundred pounds ?'

"'No, I cannot !' I answered, sharply. 'I have been far too generous with you in money matters.'

"'You h ve been very kind,' said he ; 'but I must have this money, or else I can never show my face inside the club again.'

"'And a very good thing, too !' I cried.

"'Yes, but you would not have me leave it a dishonoured man,' said he. 'I could not bear the disgrace. I must raise the money in some way, and if you will not let me have it, then I must try other means.'

"I was very angry, for this was the third demand during the month. 'You shall not have a farthing from me,' I cried, on which he bowed and left the room without another word.

"When he was gone I unlocked my bureau, made sure that my treasure was safe, and locked it again. Then I started to go round the house to see that all was secure—a duty which I usually leave to Mary, but which I thought it well to perform myself that night. As I came down the stairs I saw Mary herself at the side window of the hall, which she closed and fastened as I approached.

"'Tell me, dad,' said she, looking, I thought, a little disturbed, 'did you give Lucy, the maid, leave to go out to-night ?'

"'Certainly not.'

"'She came in just now by the back door. I have no doubt that she has only been to the side gate to see someone, but I think that it is hardly safe, and should be stopped.'

"'You must speak to her in the morning, or I will, if you prefer it. Are you sure that everything is fastened ?'

"'Quite sure, dad.'

"'Then, good-night.' I kissed her, and went up to my bedroom again, where I was soon asleep.

"I am endeavouring to tell you everything, Mr. Holmes, which may have any bearing upon the case, but I beg that you will question me upon any point which I do not make clear."

"On the contrary, your statement is singularly lucid."

"I come to a part of my story now in which I should wish to be particularly so. I am not a very heavy sleeper, and the anxiety in my mind tended, no doubt, to make me even less so than usual. About two in the morning, then, I was awakened by some sound in the house. It had ceased ere I was wide awake, but it had left an impression behind it as though a window had gently closed somewhere. I lay listening with all my ears. Suddenly, to my horror, there was a distinct sound of footsteps moving softly in the next room. I slipped out of bed, all palpitating with fear, and peeped round the corner of my dressing-room door.

"'Arthur!' I screamed, 'you villain! you thief! How dare you touch that coronet?'

"AT MY CRY HE DROPPED IT."

"The gas was half up, as I had left it, and my unhappy boy, dressed only in his shirt and trousers, was standing beside the light, holding the coronet in his hands. He appeared to be wrenching at it, or bending it with all his strength. At my cry he dropped it from his grasp, and turned as pale as death. I snatched it up and examined it. One of the gold corners, with three of the beryls in it, was missing.

"'You blackguard!' I shouted, beside myself with rage. 'You have destroyed it! You have dishonoured me for ever! Where are the jewels which you have stolen?'

"'Stolen!' he cried.

"'Yes, you thief!' I roared, shaking him by the shoulder.

"'There are none missing. There cannot be any missing,' said he.

"'There are three missing. And you know where they are. Must I call you a liar as well as a thief? Did I not see you trying to tear off another piece?'

"'You have called me names enough,' said he, 'I will not stand it any longer. I shall not say another word about this business since you have chosen to insult me. I will leave your house in the morning, and make my own way in the world.'

"'You shall leave it in the hands of the police!' I cried, half mad with grief and rage. 'I shall have this matter probed to the bottom.'

"'You shall learn nothing from me,' said he, with a passion such as I should not have thought was in his nature. 'If you choose to call the police, let the police find what they can.'

"By this time the whole house was astir, for I had raised my voice in my anger. Mary was the first to rush into my room, and, at the sight of the coronet and of Arthur's face, she read the whole story, and, with a scream, fell down senseless on the ground. I sent the housemaid for the police, and put the investigation into their hands at once. When the inspector and a constable entered the house, Arthur, who had stood sullenly with his arms folded, asked me whether it was my intention to charge him with theft. I answered that it had ceased to be a private matter, but had become a public one, since the ruined coronet was national property. I was determined that the law should have its way in everything.

"'At least,' said he, 'you will not have me arrested at once. It would be to your advantage as well as mine if I might leave the house for five minutes.'

"'That you may get away, or perhaps that you may conceal what you have stolen,' said I. And then realising the dreadful position in which I was placed, I implored him to remember that not only my honour, but that of one who was far greater than I was at stake; and that he threatened to raise a scandal which would convulse the nation. He might avert it all if he would but tell me what he had done with the three missing stones.

"'You may as well face the matter,' said I; 'you have been caught in the act, and no confession could make your guilt more heinous. If you but make such reparation as is in your power, by telling us where the beryls are, all shall be forgiven and forgotten.'

"'Keep your forgiveness for those who ask for it,' he answered, turning away from me with a sneer. I saw that he was too hardened for any words of mine to influence him. There was but one way for it. I called in the inspector, and gave him into custody. A search was made at once, not only of his person, but of his room, and of every portion of the house where he could possibly have concealed the gems ; but no trace of them could be found, nor would the wretched boy open his mouth for all our persuasions and our threats. This morning he was removed to a cell, and I, after going through all the police formalities, have hurried round to you, to implore you to use your skill in unravelling the matter. The police have openly confessed that they can at present make nothing of it. You may go to any expense which you think necessary. I have already offered a reward of a thousand pounds. My God, what shall I do ! I have lost my honour, my gems, and my son in one night. Oh, what shall I do !"

He put a hand on either side of his head, and rocked himself to and fro, droning to himself like a child whose grief has got beyond words.

Sherlock Holmes sat silent for some few minutes, with his brows knitted and his eyes fixed upon the fire.

"Do you receive much company ? " he asked.

"None, save my partner with his family, and an occasional friend of Arthur's. Sir George Burnwell has been several times lately. No one else, I think."

"Do you go out much in society ? "

"Arthur does. Mary and I stay at home. We neither of us care for it."

"That is unusual in a young girl."

"She is of a quiet nature. Besides, she is not so very young. She is four and twenty."

"This matter, from what you say, seems to have been a shock to her also."

"Terrible ! She is even more affected than I."

"You have neither of you any doubt as to your son's guilt ?"

"How can we have, when I saw him with my own eyes with the coronet in his hands."

"I hardly consider that a conclusive proof. Was the remainder of the coronet at all injured ? "

"Yes, it was twisted."

"Do you not think, then, that he might have been trying to straighten it ? "

"God bless you ! You are doing what you can for him and for me. But it is too heavy a task. What was he doing there at all ? If his purpose were innocent, why did he not say so ? "

"Precisely. And if it were guilty, why did he not invent a lie ? His silence appears to me to cut both ways. There are several singular points about the case. What did the police think of the noise which awoke you from your sleep ? "

"They considered that it might be caused by Arthur's closing his bedroom door."

"A likely story ! As if a man bent on felony would slam his door so as to wake a household. What did they say, then, of the disappearance of these gems ? "

"They are still sounding the planking, and probing the furniture in the hope of finding them."

"Have they thought of looking outside the house ? "

"Yes, they have shown extraordinary energy. The whole garden has already been minutely examined."

"Now, my dear sir," said Holmes, " is it not obvious to you now that this matter really strikes very much deeper than either you or the police were at first inclined to think ? It appeared to you to be a simple case ; to me it seems exceedingly complex. Consider what is involved by your theory. You suppose that your son came down from his bed, went, at great risk, to your dressing-room, opened your bureau, took out your coronet, broke off by main force a small portion of it, went off to some other place, concealed three gems out of the thirty-nine, with such skill that nobody can find them, and then returned with the other thirty-six into the room in which he exposed himself to the greatest danger of being discovered. I ask you now, is such a theory tenable ? "

"But what other is there ? " cried the banker with a gesture of despair. " If his motives were innocent, why does he not explain them ? "

"It is our task to find that out," replied Holmes, " so now, if you please, Mr. Holder, we wi'l set off for Streatham together, and devote an hour to glancing a little more closely into details."

My friend insisted upon my accompanying them in their expedition, which I was eager enough to do, for my curiosity and sympathy were deeply stirred by the story to which we had listened. I confess that the guilt of the banker's son appeared to me to be as obvious as it did to his unhappy father, but still I had such faith in Holmes' judgment that I felt that there must be some grounds for hope as long as he was dissatisfied with the accepted explanation. He hardly spoke a word the whole way out to the southern suburb, but sat with his chin upon his breast, and his hat drawn over his eyes, sunk in the deepest thought. Our client appeared to have taken fresh heart at the little glimpse of hope which had been presented to him, and he even broke into a desultory chat with me over his business affairs. A short railway journey, and a shorter walk, brought us to Fairbank, the modest residence of the great financier.

Fairbank was a good - sized square house of white stone, standing back a little from the road. A double carriage sweep, with a snowclad lawn, stretched down in front to the two large iron gates which closed the entrance. On the right side was a small wooden thicket which led into a narrow path between two neat hedges stretching from the road to the kitchen door, and forming the tradesmen's entrance. On the left ran a lane which led to the stables, and was not itself within the grounds at all, being a public, though little used, thoroughfare. Holmes left us standing at the door, and walked slowly all round the house, across the front, down the tradesmen's path, and so round by the garden behind into the stable lane. So long was he that Mr. Holder and I went into the dining-room, and waited

by the fire until he should return. We were sitting there in silence when the door opened, and a young lady came in. She was rather above the middle height, slim, with dark hair and eyes, which seemed the darker against the absolute pallor of her skin. I do not think that I have ever seen such deadly paleness in a woman's face. Her lips, too, were bloodless, but her eyes were flushed with crying. As she swept silently into the room she impressed me with a greater sense of grief than the banker had done in the morning, and it was the more striking in her as she was evidently a woman of strong character, with immense capacity for self-restraint. Disregarding my presence, she went straight to her uncle, and passed her hand over his head with a sweet womanly caress.

"You have given orders that Arthur should be liberated, have you not, dad?" she asked.

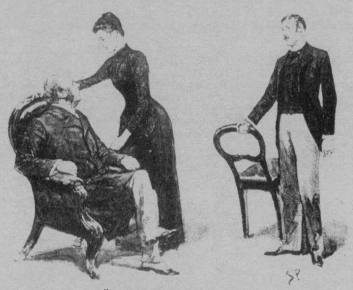

"SHE WENT STRAIGHT TO HER UNCLE."

"No, no, my girl, the matter must be probed to the bottom."

"But I am so sure that he is innocent. You know what women's instincts are. I know that he has done no harm, and that you will be sorry for having acted so harshly."

"Why is he silent, then, if he is innocent?"

"Who knows? Perhaps because he was so angry that you should suspect him."

"How could I help suspecting him, when I actually saw him with the coronet in his hand?"

"Oh, but he had only picked it up to look at it. Oh, do, do take my word for it that he is innocent. Let the matter drop, and say no more. It is so dreadful to think of our dear Arthur in prison!"

"I shall never let it drop until the gems are found—never, Mary! Your affection for Arthur blinds you as to the awful consequences to me. Far from hushing the thing up, I have brought a gentleman down from London to inquire more deeply into it."

"This gentleman?" she asked, facing round to me.

"No, his friend. He wished us to leave him alone. He is round in the stable lane now."

"The stable lane?" She raised her dark eyebrows. "What can he hope to find there! Ah! this, I suppose, is he. I trust, sir, that you will succeed in proving, what I feel sure is the truth, that my cousin Arthur is innocent of this crime."

"I fully share your opinion, and, I trust with you, that we may prove it," returned Holmes, going back to the mat to knock the snow from his shoes. "I believe I have the honour of addressing Miss Mary Holder. Might I ask you a question or two?"

"Pray do, sir, if it may help to clear this horrible affair up."

"You heard nothing yourself last night?"

"Nothing, until my uncle here began to

"SOMETHING LIKE FEAR SPRANG UP IN THE YOUNG LADY'S EYES."

speak loudly. I heard that, and I came down."

"You shut up the windows and doors the night before. Did you fasten all the windows?"

"Yes."

"Were they all fastened this morning?"

"Yes."

"You have a maid who has a sweetheart? I think that you remarked to your uncle last night that she had been out to see him?"

"Yes, and she was the girl who waited in the drawing-room, and who may have heard uncle's remarks about the coronet."

"I see. You infer that she may have gone out to tell her sweetheart, and that the two may have planned the robbery."

"But what is the good of all these vague theories," cried the banker, impatiently, "when I have told you that I saw Arthur with the coronet in his hands?"

"Wait a little, Mr. Holder. We must come back to that. About this girl, Miss Holder. You saw her return by the kitchen door, I presume?"

"Yes; when I went to see if the door was fastened for the night I met her slipping in. I saw the man, too, in the gloom."

"Do you know him?"

"Oh, yes; he is the greengrocer who brings our vegetables round. His name is Francis Prosper."

"He stood," said Holmes, "to the left of the door—that is to say, further up the path than is necessary to reach the door?"

"Yes, he did."

"And he is a man with a wooden leg?"

Something like fear sprang up in the young lady's expressive black eyes. "Why, you are like a magician," said she. " How do you know that ? " She smiled, but there was no answering smile in Holmes' thin, eager face.

" I should be very glad now to go upstairs," said he. " I shall probably wish to go over the outside of the house again. Perhaps I had better take a look at the lower windows before I go up."

He walked swiftly round from one to the other, pausing only at the large one which looked from the hall on to the stable lane. This he opened, and made a very careful examination of the sill with his powerful magnifying lens. " Now we shall go upstairs," said he, at last.

The banker's dressing-room was a plainly furnished little chamber with a grey carpet, a large bureau, and a long mirror. Holmes went to the bureau first, and looked hard at the lock.

" Which key was used to open it ? " he asked.

" That which my son himself indicated— that of the cupboard of the lumber-room."

" Have you it here ? "

" That is it on the dressing-table."

Sherlock Holmes took it up and opened the bureau.

" It is a noiseless lock," said he. " It is no wonder that it did not wake you. This case, I presume, contains the coronet. We must have a look at it." He opened the case, and, taking out the diadem, he laid it upon the table. It was a magnificent specimen of the jeweller's art, and the thirty-six stones were the finest that I have ever seen. At one side of the coronet was a crooked cracked edge, where a corner holding three gems had been torn away.

" Now, Mr. Holder," said Holmes ; " here is the corner which corresponds to that which has been so unfortunately lost. Might I beg that you will break it off."

The banker recoiled in horror. "I should not dream of trying," said he.

" Then I will." Holmes suddenly bent his strength upon it, but without result. " I feel it give a little," said he ; " but, though I am exceptionally strong in the fingers, it would take me all my time to break it. An ordinary man could not do it. Now, what do you think would happen if I did break it, Mr. Holder ? There would be a noise like a pistol shot. Do you tell me that all this happened within a few yards of your bed, and that you heard nothing of it ? "

" I do not know what to think. It is all dark to me."

" But perhaps it may grow lighter as we go. What do you think, Miss Holder ? "

" I confess that I still share my uncle's perplexity."

" Your son had no shoes or slippers on when you saw him ? "

" He had nothing on save only his trousers and shirt."

" Thank you. We have certainly been favoured with extraordinary luck during this inquiry, and it will be entirely our own fault if we do not succeed in clearing the matter up. With your permission, Mr. Holder, I shall now continue my investigations outside."

He went alone, at his own request, for he explained that any unnecessary footmarks might make his task more difficult. For an hour or more he was at work, returning at last with his feet heavy with snow and his features as inscrutable as ever.

" I think that I have seen now all that there is to see, Mr. Holder," said he; " I can serve you best by returning to my rooms."

" But the gems, Mr. Holmes. Where are they ? "

" I cannot tell."

The banker wrung his hands. " I shall never see them again ! " he cried. " And my son ? You give me hopes ? "

" My opinion is in no way altered."

" Then for God's sake what was this dark business which was acted in my house last night ? "

" If you can call upon me at my Baker-street rooms to-morrow morning between nine and ten I shall be happy to do what I can to make it clearer. I understand that you give me *carte blanche* to act for you, provided only that I get back the gems, and that you place no limit on the sum I may draw."

" I would give my fortune to have them back."

" Very good. I shall look into the matter between this and then. Good-bye, it is just possible that I may have to come over here again before evening."

It was obvious to me that my companion's mind was now made up about the case, although what his conclusions were was more than I could even dimly imagine. Several times during our homeward journey I endeavoured to sound him upon the point, but he always glided away to some other topic, until at last I gave it over in despair. It was not yet three when we found our-

"DRESSED AS A COMMON LOAFER."

selves in our room once more. He hurried to his chamber and was down again in a few minutes dressed as a common loafer. With his collar turned up, his shiny seedy coat, his red cravat, and his worn boots, he was a perfect sample of the class.

"I think that this should do," said he, glancing into the glass above the fireplace. "I only wish that you could come with me, Watson, but I fear that it won't do. I may be on the trail in this matter, or I may be following a will o' the wisp, but I shall soon know which it is. I hope that I may be back in a few hours." He cut a slice of beef from the joint upon the sideboard, sandwiched it between two rounds of bread, and, thrusting this rude meal into his pocket, he started off upon his expedition.

I had just finished my tea when he returned, evidently in excellent spirits, swinging an old elastic-sided boot in his hand. He chucked it down into a corner and helped himself to a cup of tea.

"I only looked in as I passed," said he. "I am going right on."

"Where to ?"

"Oh, to the other side of the West-end. It may be some time before I get back. Don't wait up for me in case I should be late."

"How are you getting on ?"

"Oh, so so. Nothing to complain of. I have been out to Streatham since I saw you last, but I did not call at the house. It is a very sweet little problem, and I would not have missed it for a good deal. However, I must not sit gossiping here, but must get these disreputable clothes off and return to my highly respectable self."

I could see by his manner that he had stronger reasons for satisfaction than his words alone would imply. His eyes twinkled, and there was even a touch of colour upon his sallow cheeks. He hastened upstairs, and a few minutes later I heard the slam of the hall door, which told me that he was off once more upon his congenial hunt.

I waited until midnight, but there was no sign of his return, so I retired to my room. It was no uncommon thing for him to be away for days and nights on end when he was hot upon a scent, so that his lateness caused me no surprise. I do not know at what hour he came in, but when I came down to breakfast in the morning, there he was with a cup of coffee in one hand and the paper in the other, as fresh and trim as possible.

"You will excuse my beginning without you, Watson," said he; "but you remember that our client has rather an early appointment this morning."

"Why, it is after nine now," I answered. "I should not be surprised if that were he. I thought I heard a ring."

It was, indeed, our friend the financier. I was shocked by the change which had come over him, for his face, which was naturally of a broad and massive mould, was now pinched and fallen in, while his hair seemed to me at least a shade whiter. He entered with a weariness and lethargy which was even more painful than his violence of the morning before, and he dropped heavily into the arm-chair which I pushed forward for him.

"I do not know what I have done to be so severely tried," said he. "Only two days ago I was a happy and prosperous man, without a care in the world. Now I am left to a lonely and dishonoured age. One sorrow comes close upon the heels of another. My niece, Mary, has deserted me."

"Deserted you?"

"Yes. Her bed this morning had not been slept in, her room was empty, and a note lay for me upon the hall table. I had said to her last night, in sorrow and not in anger, that if she had married my boy all might have been well with him. Perhaps it was thoughtless of me to say so. It is to that remark that she refers in this note : 'My dearest Uncle,—I feel that I have brought trouble upon you, and that if I had acted differently this terrible misfortune might never have occurred. I cannot, with this thought in my mind, ever again be happy under your roof, and I feel that I must leave you for ever. Do not worry about my future, for that is provided for ; and, above all, do not search for me, for it will be fruitless labour, and an ill service to me. In life or in death, I am ever your loving,—MARY.' What could she mean by that note, Mr. Holmes? Do you think it points to suicide?"

"No, no, nothing of the kind. It is perhaps the best possible solution. I trust, Mr. Holder, that you are nearing the end of your troubles."

"Ha! You say so! You have heard something, Mr. Holmes ; you have learned something! Where are the gems?"

"You would not think a thousand pounds apiece an excessive sum for them?"

"I would pay ten."

"That would be unnecessary. Three thousand will cover the matter. And there is a little reward, I fancy. Have you your cheque-book? Here is a pen. Better make it out for four thousand pounds."

With a dazed face the banker made out the required cheque. Holmes walked over to his desk, took out a little triangular piece of gold with three gems in it, and threw it down upon the table.

With a shriek of joy our client clutched it up.

"You have it!" he gasped. "I am saved! I am saved!"

The reaction of joy was as passionate as his grief had been, and he hugged his recovered gems to his bosom.

"There is one other thing you owe," Mr. Holder," said Sherlock Holmes, rather sternly

"Owe!" He caught up a pen. "Name the sum, and I will pay it."

"No, the debt is not to me. You owe a very humble apology to that noble lad, your son, who has carried himself in this matter as I should be proud to see my own son do, should I ever chance to have one."

"Then it was not Arthur who took them?"

"I told you yesterday, and I repeat to-day, that it was not."

"You are sure of it! Then let us hurry to him at once, to let him know that the truth is known."

"He knows it already. When I had cleared it all up I had an interview with him, and, finding that he would not tell me the story, I told it to him, on which he had to confess that I was right, and to add the very few details which were not yet quite clear to me. Your news of this morning, however, may open his lips."

"For Heaven's sake, tell me, then, what is this extraordinary mystery!"

"I will do so, and I will show you the steps by which I reached it. And let me say to you, first, that which it is hardest for me to say and for you to hear. There has been an understanding between Sir George Burnwell, and your niece Mary. They have now fled together."

"My Mary? Impossible!"

"It is, unfortunately, more than possible ; it is certain. Neither you nor your son knew the true character of this man when you admitted him into your family circle. He is one of the most dangerous men in England—a ruined gambler, an absolutely desperate villain ; a man without heart or conscience. Your niece knew nothing of such men. When he breathed his vows to her, as he had done to a hundred before her, she flattered herself that she alone had touched his heart. The devil knows best what he said, but at least she became his tool, and was in the habit of seeing him nearly every evening."

"I cannot, and I will not, believe it!" cried the banker, with an ashen face.

"I will tell you, then, what occurred in your house last night. Your niece, when you had, as she thought, gone to your room, slipped down and talked to her lover through the window which leads into the stable lane. His footmarks had pressed right through the snow, so long had he stood there. She told him of the coronet. His wicked lust for gold kindled at the news, and he bent her to his will. I have no doubt that she loved you, but there are women in whom the love of a lover extinguishes all other loves, and I think that she must have been one. She had hardly listened to his instructions when she saw you coming down stairs, on which she closed the window rapidly, and told you about one of the servants' escapade with her wooden-legged lover, which was all perfectly true.

"Your boy, Arthur, went to bed after his interview with you, but he slept badly on account of his uneasiness about his club debts. In the middle of the night he heard a soft tread pass his door, so he rose, and looking out was surprised to see his cousin walking very stealthily along the passage, until she disappeared into your dressing-room. Petrified with astonishment the lad slipped on some clothes, and waited there in the dark to see what would come of this strange affair. Presently she emerged from the room again, and in the light of the passage lamp your son saw that she carried the precious coronet in her hands. She passed down the stairs, and he, thrilling with horror, ran along and slipped behind the curtain near your door, whence he could see what passed in the hall beneath. He saw her stealthily open the window, hand out the coronet to someone in the gloom, and then closing it once more hurry back to her room, passing quite close to where he stood hid behind the curtain.

"As long as she was on the scene he could not take any action without a horrible exposure of the woman whom he loved. But the instant that she was gone he realised how crushing a misfortune this would be for you, and how all-important it was to set it right. He rushed down, just as he was, in his bare feet, opened the window, sprang out into the snow, and ran down the lane, where he could see a dark

"ARTHUR CAUGHT HIM."

figure in the moonlight. Sir George Burnwell tried to get away, but Arthur caught him, and there was a struggle between them, your lad tugging at one side of the coronet, and his opponent at the other. In the scuffle, your son struck Sir George, and cut him over the eye. Then something suddenly snapped, and your son, finding that he had the coronet in his hands, rushed back, closed the window, ascended to your room, and had just observed that the coronet had been twisted in the struggle, and was endeavouring to straighten it, when you appeared upon the scene."

"Is it possible?" gasped the banker.

"You then roused his anger by calling him names at a moment when he felt that he had deserved your warmest thanks. He could not explain the true state of affairs without betraying one who certainly deserved little enough consideration at his hands. He took the more chivalrous view, however, and preserved her secret."

"And that was why she shrieked and fainted when she saw the coronet," cried Mr. Holder. "Oh, my God! what a blind fool I have been. And his asking to be allowed to go out for five minutes! The dear fellow wanted to see if the missing piece were at the scene of the struggle. How cruelly I have misjudged him!"

"When I arrived at the house," continued Holmes, "I at once went very carefully round it to observe if there were any traces in the snow which might help me. I knew that none had fallen since the evening before, and also that there had been a strong frost to preserve impressions. I passed along the tradesmen's path, but found it all trampled down and indistinguishable. Just beyond it, however, at the far side of the kitchen door, a woman had stood and talked with a man, whose round impressions on one side showed that he had a wooden leg. I could even tell that they had been disturbed, for the woman had run back swiftly to the door, as was shown by the deep toe and light heelmarks, while Wooden-leg had waited a little, and then had gone away. I thought at the time that this might be the maid and her sweetheart, of whom you had already spoken to me, and inquiry showed it was so. I passed round the garden without seeing anything more than random tracks, which I took to be the police; but when I got into the stable lane a very long and complex story was written in the snow in front of me.

"There was a double line of tracks of a booted man, and a second double line which I saw with delight belonged to a man with naked feet. I was at once convinced from what you had told me that the latter was your son. The first had walked both ways, but the other had run swiftly, and, as his tread was marked in places over the depression of the boot, it was obvious that he had passed after the other. I followed them up, and found that they led to the hall window, where Boots had worn all the snow away while waiting. Then I walked to the other end, which was a hundred yards or more down the lane. I saw where Boots had faced round, where the snow was cut up as though there had been a struggle, and, finally, where a few drops of blood had fallen, to show me that I was not mistaken. Boots had then run down

the lane, and another little smudge of blood showed that it was he who had been hurt. When he came to the high road at the other end, I found that the pavement had been cleared, so there was an end to that clue.

"On entering the house, however, I examined, as you remember, the sill and framework of the hall window with my lens, and I could at once see that someone had passed out. I could distinguish the outline of an instep where the wet foot had been placed in coming in. I was then beginning to be able to form an opinion as to what had occurred. A man had waited outside the window, someone had brought him the gems; the deed had been overseen by your son, he had pursued the thief, had struggled with him, they had each tugged at the coronet, their united strength causing injuries which neither alone could have effected. He had returned with the prize, but had left a fragment in the grasp of his opponent. So far I was clear. The question now was, who was the man, and who was it brought him the coronet?

"It is an old maxim of mine that when you have excluded the impossible, whatever remains, however improbable, must be the truth. Now, I knew that it was not you who had brought it down, so there only remained your niece and the maids. But if it were the maids, why should your son allow himself to be accused in their place? There could be no possible reason. As he loved his cousin, however, there was an excellent explanation why he should retain her secret—the more so as the secret was a disgraceful one. When I remembered that you had seen her at that window, and how she had fainted on seeing the coronet again, my conjecture became a certainty.

"And who could it be who was her confederate? A lover evidently, for who else could outweigh the love and gratitude which she must feel to you? I knew that you went out little, and that your circle of friends was a very limited one. But among them was Sir George Burnwell. I had heard of him before as being a man of evil reputation among women. It must have been he who wore those boots, and retained the missing gems. Even though he knew that Arthur had discovered him, he might still flatter himself that he was safe, for the lad could not say a word without compromising his own family.

"Well, your own good sense will suggest what measures I took next. I went in the shape of a loafer to Sir George's house, managed to pick up an acquaintance with his valet, learned that his master had cut his head the night before, and finally, at the expense of six shillings, made all sure by buying a pair of his cast-off shoes. With these I journeyed down to Streatham, and saw that they exactly fitted the tracks."

"I saw an ill-dressed vaga-bond in the lane yesterday evening," said Mr. Holder.

"Precisely. It was I. I found that I had my man, so I came home and changed my clothes. It was a delicate part which I had to play then, for I saw that a prosecution must be avoided to avert scandal, and I knew that so astute a villain would see that our hands were tied in the matter. I went and saw him. At first, of course, he denied everything. But when I gave him every particular that had occurred, he tried to bluster, and took down a life-preserver from the wall. I knew my man, however, and I clapped a pistol to his head before he could strike. Then he became a little more reasonable. I told him that we would give him a price for the stones he held—a thousand pounds apiece. That brought out the first signs of grief that he had shown.

"I CLAPPED A PISTOL TO HIS HEAD."

'Why, dash it all!' said he, 'I've let them go at six hundred for the three!' I soon managed to get the address of the receiver who had them, on promising him that there would be no prosecution. Off I set to him, and after much chaffering I got our stones at a thousand apiece. Then I looked in upon your son, told him that all was right, and eventually got to my bed about two o'clock, after what I may call a really hard day's work."

"A day which has saved England from a great public scandal," said the banker, rising. "Sir, I cannot find words to thank you, but you shall not find me ungrateful for what you have done. Your skill has indeed exceeded all that I have ever heard of it. And now I must fly to my dear boy to apologise to him for the wrong which I have done him. As to what you tell me of poor Mary, it goes to my very heart. Not even your skill can inform me where she is now."

"I think that we may safely say," returned Holmes, "that she is wherever Sir George Burnwell is. It is equally certain, too, that whatever her sins are, they will soon receive a more than sufficient punishment."

Adventures of Sherlock Holmes.

XII.—THE ADVENTURE OF THE COPPER BEECHES.

By A. Conan Doyle.

"TO the man who loves art for its own sake," remarked Sherlock Holmes, tossing aside the advertisement sheet of *The Daily Telegraph*, "it is frequently in its least important and lowliest manifestations that the keenest pleasure is to be derived. It is pleasant to me to observe, Watson, that you have so far grasped this truth that in these little records of our cases which you have been good enough to draw up, and, I am bound to say, occasionally to embellish, you have given prominence not so much to the many *causes célèbres* and sensational trials in which I have figured, but rather to those incidents which may have been trivial in themselves, but which have given room for those faculties of deduction and of logical synthesis which I have made my special province."

"And yet," said I, smiling, "I cannot quite hold myself absolved from the charge of sensationalism which has been urged against my records."

"You have erred, perhaps," he observed, taking up a glowing cinder with the tongs, and lighting with it the long cherrywood pipe which was wont to replace his clay when he was in a disputatious, rather than a meditative mood—"you have erred perhaps in attempting to put colour and life into each of your statements, instead of confining yourself to the task of placing upon record that severe reasoning from cause to effect which is really the only notable feature about the thing."

"It seems to me that I have done you full justice in the matter," I remarked, with some coldness, for I was repelled by the egotism which I had more than once observed to be a strong factor in my friend's singular character.

"No, it is not selfishness or conceit," said he, answering, as was his wont, my thoughts rather than my words. "If I claim full justice for my art, it is because it is an impersonal thing—a thing beyond myself. Crime is common. Logic is rare. Therefore it is upon the logic rather than upon the crime that you should dwell. You have degraded what should have been a course of lectures into a series of tales."

It was a cold morning of the early spring, and we sat after breakfast on either side of a cheery fire in the old room at Baker-street. A thick fog rolled down between the lines of dun-coloured houses, and the opposing windows loomed like dark, shapeless blurs through the heavy yellow wreaths. Our gas was lit, and shone on the white cloth, and glimmer of china and metal, for the table had not been cleared yet. Sherlock Holmes had been

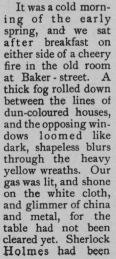

"TAKING UP A GLOWING CINDER WITH THE TONGS."

silent all the morning, dipping continuously into the advertisement columns of a succession of papers, until at last, having apparently given up his search, he had emerged in no very sweet temper to lecture me upon my literary shortcomings.

"At the same time," he remarked, after a pause, during which he had sat puffing at his long pipe and gazing down into the fire, "you can hardly be open to a charge of sensationalism, for out of these cases which you have been so kind as to interest yourself in, a fair proportion do not treat of crime, in its legal sense, at all. The small matter in which I endeavoured to help the King of Bohemia, the singular experience of Miss Mary Sutherland, the problem connected with the man with the twisted lip, and the incident of the noble bachelor, were all matters which are outside the pale of the law. But in avoiding the sensational, I fear that you may have bordered on the trivial."

"The end may have been so," I answered, "but the methods I hold to have been novel and of interest."

"Pshaw, my dear fellow, what do the public, the great unobservant public, who could hardly tell a weaver by his tooth or a compositor by his left thumb, care about the finer shades of analysis and deduction ! But, indeed, if you are trivial, I cannot blame you, for the days of the great cases are past. Man, or at least criminal man, has lost all enterprise and originality. As to my own little practice, it seems to be degenerating into an agency for recovering lost lead pencils, and giving advice to young ladies from boarding-schools. I think that I have touched bottom at last, however. This note I had this morning marks my zero point, I fancy. Read it ! " He tossed a crumpled letter across to me.

It was dated from Montague-place upon the preceding evening, and ran thus :—

"DEAR MR. HOLMES,—I am very anxious to consult you as to whether I should or should not accept a situation which has been offered to me as governess. I shall call at half-past ten to-morrow, if I do not inconvenience you.—Yours faithfully,

VIOLET HUNTER."

"Do you know the young lady ? " I asked.

"Not I."

"It is half-past ten now."

"Yes, and I have no doubt that is her ring."

"It may turn out to be of more interest than you think. You remember that the affair of the blue carbuncle, which appeared to be a mere whim at first, developed into a serious investigation. It may be so in this case, also."

"Well, let us hope so ! But our doubts will very soon be solved, for here, unless I am much mistaken, is the person in question."

As he spoke the door opened, and a young lady entered the room. She was plainly but neatly dressed, with a bright, quick face, freckled like a plover's egg, and with the brisk manner of a woman who has had her own way to make in the world.

"You will excuse my troubling you, I am sure," said she, as my companion rose to greet her ; "but I have had a very strange experience, and as I have no parents or relations of any sort from whom I could ask advice, I thought that perhaps you would be kind enough to tell me what I should do."

"Pray take a seat, Miss Hunter. I shall be happy to do anything that I can to serve you."

I could see that Holmes was favourably impressed by the manner and speech of his new client. He looked her over in his searching fashion, and then composed himself with his lids drooping and his finger tips together to listen to her story.

"I have been a governess for five years," said she, "in the family of Colonel Spence Munro, but two months ago the Colonel received an appointment at Halifax, in Nova Scotia, and took his children over to America with him, so that I found myself without a situation. I advertised, and I answered advertisements, but without success. At last the little money which I had saved began to run short, and I was at my wit's end as to what I should do.

"There is a well-known agency for governesses in the West-end called Westaway's, and there I used to call about once a week in order to see whether anything had turned up which might suit me. Westaway was the name of the founder of the business, but it is really managed by Miss Stoper. She sits in her own little office, and the ladies who are seeking employment wait in an ante-room, and are then shown in one by one, when she consults her ledgers, and sees whether she has anything which would suit them.

"Well, when I called last week I was

shown into the little office as usual, but I found that Miss Stoper was not alone. A prodigiously stout man with a very smiling face, and a great heavy chin which rolled down in fold upon fold over his throat, sat at her elbow with a pair of glasses on his nose, looking very earnestly at the ladies who entered. As I came in he gave quite a jump in his chair, and turned quickly to Miss Stoper:

"'That will do,' said he; 'I could not ask for anything better. Capital! capital!

French, a little German, music and drawing——'

"'Tut, tut!' he cried. 'This is all quite beside the question. The point is, have you or have you not the bearing and deportment of a lady? There it is in a nutshell. If you have not, you are not fitted for the rearing of a child who may some day play a considerable part in the history of the country. But if you have, why, then, how could any gentleman ask you to condescend to accept anything

"CAPITAL."

He seemed quite enthusiastic, and rubbed his hands together in the most genial fashion. He was such a comfortable-looking man that it was quite a pleasure to look at him.

"'You are looking for a situation, miss?' he asked.

"'Yes, sir.'

"'As governess?'

"'Yes, sir.'

"'And what salary do you ask?'

"'I had four pounds a month in my last place with Colonel Spence Munro.'

"'Oh, tut, tut! sweating—rank sweating!' he cried, throwing his fat hands out into the air like a man who is in a boiling passion. 'How could anyone offer so pitiful a sum to a lady with such attractions and accomplishments?'

"'My accomplishments, sir, may be less than you imagine,' said I. 'A little

under the three figures? Your salary with me, madam, would commence at a hundred pounds a year.'

"You may imagine, Mr. Holmes, that to me, destitute as I was, such an offer seemed almost too good to be true. The gentleman, however, seeing perhaps the look of incredulity upon my face, opened a pocket-book and took out a note.

"'It is also my custom,' said he, smiling in the most pleasant fashion until his eyes were just two little shining slits, amid the white creases of his face, 'to advance to my young ladies half their salary beforehand, so that they may meet any little expenses of their journey and their wardrobe.'

"It seemed to me that I had never met so fascinating and so thoughtful a man. As I was already in debt to my tradesmen the advance was a great convenience, and yet there was something unnatural about the whole transaction which made me wish to know a little more before I quite committed myself.

"'May I ask where you live, sir?' said I.

"'Hampshire. Charming rural place. The Copper Beeches, five miles on the far side of Winchester. It is the most lovely country, my dear young lady, and the dearest old country house.'

"'And my duties, sir? I should be glad to know what they would be.'

"'One child—one dear little romper just six years old. Oh, if you could see him killing cockroaches with a slipper! Smack! smack! smack! Three gone before you could wink!' He leaned back in his chair and laughed his eyes into his head again.

"I was a little startled at the nature of the child's amusement, but the father's laughter made me think that perhaps he was joking.

"'My sole duties, then,' I asked, 'are to take charge of a single child?'

"'No, no, not the sole, not the sole, my dear young lady,' he cried. 'Your duty would be, as I am sure your good sense would suggest, to obey any little commands which my wife might give, provided always that they were such commands as a lady might with propriety obey. You see no difficulty, heh?'

"'I should be happy to make myself useful.'

"'Quite so. In dress now, for example! We are faddy people, you know—faddy but kind-hearted. If you were asked to wear any dress which we might give you, you would not object to our little whim. Heh?'

"'No,' said I, considerably astonished at his words.

"'Or to sit here, or sit there, that would not be offensive to you?'

"'Oh, no.'

"'Or to cut your hair quite short before you come to us.'

"I could hardly believe my ears. As you may observe, Mr. Holmes, my hair is somewhat luxuriant, and of a rather peculiar tint of chestnut. It has been considered artistic. I could not dream of sacrificing it in this offhand fashion.

"'I am afraid that that is quite impossible,' said I. He had been watching me eagerly out of his small eyes, and I could see a shadow pass over his face as I spoke.

"'I am afraid that it is quite essential,' said he. 'It is a little fancy of my wife's, and ladies' fancies, you know, madam, ladies'

fancies must be consulted. And so you won't cut your hair?'

"'No, sir, I really could not,' I answered firmly.

"'Ah, very well; then that quite settles the matter. It is a pity, because in other respects you would really have done very nicely. In that case, Miss Stoper, I had best inspect a few more of your young ladies.'

"The manageress had sat all this while busy with her papers without a word to either of us, but she glanced at me now with so much annoyance upon her face that I could not help suspecting that she had lost a handsome commission through my refusal.

"'Do you desire your name to be kept upon the books?' she asked.

"'If you please, Miss Stoper.'

"'Well, really, it seems rather useless, since you refuse the most excellent offers in this fashion,' said she sharply. 'You can hardly expect us to exert ourselves to find another such opening for you. Good day to you, Miss Hunter.' She struck a gong upon the table, and I was shown out by the page.

"Well, Mr. Holmes, when I got back to my lodgings and found little enough in the cupboard, and two or three bills upon the table, I began to ask myself whether I had not done a very foolish thing. After all, if these people had strange fads, and expected obedience on the most extraordinary matters, they were at least ready to pay for their eccentricity. Very few governesses in England are getting a hundred a year. Besides, what use was my hair to me? Many people are improved by wearing it short, and perhaps I should be among the number. Next day I was inclined to think that I had made a mistake, and by the day after I was sure of it. I had almost overcome my pride, so far as to go back to the agency and inquire whether the place was still open, when I received this letter from the gentleman himself. I have it here, and I will read it to you :—

"'The Copper Beeches, near Winchester.

"'Dear Miss Hunter,—Miss Stoper has very kindly given me your address, and I write from here to ask you whether you have reconsidered your decision. My wife is very anxious that you should come, for she has been much attracted by my description of you. We are willing to give thirty pounds a quarter, or £120 a year, so as to recompense you for any little inconvenience which our fads may cause you. They are not very exacting after all. My wife is fond of a particular shade of electric blue, and would like you to wear such a dress indoors in the morning. You need not, however, go to the expense of purchasing one, as we have one belonging to my dear daughter Alice (now in Philadelphia) which would, I should think, fit you very well. Then, as to sitting here or there, or amusing yourself in any manner indicated, that need cause you no inconvenience. As regards your hair, it is no doubt a pity, especially as I could not help remarking its beauty during our short interview, but I am afraid that I must remain firm upon this point, and I only hope that the increased salary may recompense you for the loss. Your duties, as far as the child is concerned, are very light. Now do try to come, and I shall meet you with the dogcart at Winchester. Let me know your train.—Yours faithfully,

JEPHRO RUCASTLE.'

"That is the letter which I have just received, Mr. Holmes, and my mind is made up that I will accept it. I thought, however, that before taking the final step, I should like to submit the whole matter to your consideration."

"Well, Miss Hunter, if your mind is made up, that settles the question," said Holmes, smiling.

"But you would not advise me to refuse?"

"I confess that it is not the situation which I should like to see a sister of mine apply for."

"What is the meaning of it all, Mr. Holmes?"

"Ah, I have no data. I cannot tell. Perhaps you have yourself formed some opinion?"

"Well, there seems to me to be only one possible solution. Mr. Rucastle seemed to be a very kind, good-natured man. Is it not possible that his wife is a lunatic, that he desires to keep the matter quiet for fear she should be taken to an asylum, and that he humours her fancies in every way in order to prevent an outbreak."

"That is a possible solution—in fact, as matters stand, it is the most probable one. But in any case it does not seem to be a nice household for a young lady."

"But the money, Mr. Holmes, the money!"

"Well, yes, of course the pay is good—too good. That is what makes me uneasy. Why should they give you £120 a year, when they could have their pick for £40? There must be some strong reason behind."

"I thought that if I told you the circumstances you would understand afterwards if I wanted your help. I should feel so much stronger if I felt that you were at the back of me."

"Oh, you may carry that feeling away with you. I assure you that your little problem promises to be the most interesting which has come my way for some months. There is something distinctly novel about some of the features. If you should find yourself in doubt or in danger——"

"Danger! What danger do you foresee?"

Holmes shook his head gravely. "It would cease to be a danger if we could define it," said he. "But at any time, day or night, a telegram would bring me down to your help."

"HOLMES SHOOK HIS HEAD GRAVELY."

S S

"That is enough." She rose briskly from her chair with the anxiety all swept from her face. "I shall go down to Hampshire quite easy in my mind now. I shall write to Mr. Rucastle at once, sacrifice my poor hair to-night, and start for Winchester to-morrow." With a few grateful words to Holmes she bade us both good-night and bustled off upon her way.

"At least," said I, as we heard her quick, firm step descending the stairs, "she seems to be a young lady who is very well able to take care of herself."

"And she would need to be," said Holmes, gravely; "I am much mistaken if we do not hear from her before many days are past."

It was not very long before my friend's prediction was fulfilled. A fortnight went by, during which I frequently found my thoughts turning in her direction, and wondering what strange side-alley of human experience this lonely woman had strayed into. The unusual salary, the curious conditions, the light duties, all pointed to something abnormal, though whether a fad or a plot, or whether the man were a philanthropist or a villain, it was quite beyond my powers to determine. As to Holmes, I observed that he sat frequently for half an hour on end, with knitted brows and an abstracted air, but he swept the matter away with a wave of his hand when I mentioned it. "Data! data! data!" he cried impatiently. "I can't make bricks without clay." And yet he would always wind up by muttering that no sister of his should ever have accepted such a situation.

The telegram which we eventually received came late one night, just as I was thinking of turning in, and Holmes was settling down to one of those all-night chemical researches which he frequently indulged in, when I would leave him stooping over a retort and a test-tube at night, and find him in the same position when I came down to breakfast in the morning. He opened the yellow envelope, and then, glancing at the message, threw it across to me.

"Just look up the trains in Bradshaw," said he, and turned back to his chemical studies.

The summons was a brief and urgent one.

"Please be at the 'Black Swan' Hotel at Winchester at midday to-morrow," it said. "Do come! I am at my wit's end.

"HUNTER."

"Will you come with me?" asked Holmes, glancing up.

"I should wish to."

"Just look it up, then."

"There is a train at half-past nine," said I, glancing over my Bradshaw. "It is due at Winchester at 11.30."

"That will do very nicely. Then perhaps I had better postpone my analysis of the acetones, as we may need to be at our best in the morning."

By eleven o'clock the next day we were well upon our way to the old English capital. Holmes had been buried in the morning papers all the way down, but after we had passed the Hampshire border he threw them down, and began to admire the scenery. It was an ideal spring day, a light blue sky, flecked with little fleecy white clouds drifting across from west to east. The sun was shining very brightly, and yet there was an exhilarating nip in the air, which set an edge to a man's energy. All over the countryside, away to the rolling hills around Aldershot, the little red and grey roofs of the farm-steadings peeped out from amidst the light green of the new foliage.

"Are they not fresh and beautiful?" I cried, with all the enthusiasm of a man fresh from the fogs of Baker-street.

But Holmes shook his head gravely.

"Do you know, Watson," said he, "that it is one of the curses of a mind with a turn like mine that I must look at everything with reference to my own special subject. You look at these scattered houses, and you are impressed by their beauty. I look at them, and the only thought which comes to me is a feeling of their isolation, and of the impunity with which crime may be committed there."

"Good heavens!" I cried. "Who would associate crime with these dear old homesteads?"

"They always fill me with a certain horror. It is my belief, Watson, founded upon my experience, that the lowest and vilest alleys in London do not present a more dreadful record of sin than does the smiling and beautiful countryside."

"You horrify me!"

"But the reason is very obvious. The pressure of public opinion can do in the town what the law cannot accomplish. There is no lane so vile that the scream of a tortured child, or the thud of a drunkard's blow, does not beget sympathy and indignation among the neighbours, and then the whole machinery of justice is ever so close that a word of complaint can set it going, and there is but a step between the crime and the dock. But look at these lonely houses, each in its own fields, filled for the most part with poor ignorant folk who know little of the law. Think of the deeds of hellish cruelty, the hidden wickedness which may go on, year in, year out, in such places, and none the wiser. Had this lady who appeals to us for help gone to live in Winchester, I should never have had a fear for her. It is the five miles of country which makes the danger. Still, it is clear that she is not personally threatened."

"No. If she can come to Winchester to meet us she can get away."

"Quite so. She has her freedom."

"What *can* be the matter, then? Can you suggest no explanation?"

"I have devised seven separate explanations, each of which would cover the facts as far as we know them. But which of these is correct can only be determined by the fresh information which we shall no doubt find waiting for us. Well, there is the tower of the Cathedral, and we shall soon learn all that Miss Hunter has to tell."

The "Black Swan" is an inn of repute in the High-street, at no distance from the station, and there we found the young lady waiting for us. She had engaged a sitting-room, and our lunch awaited us upon the table.

"I am so delighted that you have come," she said, earnestly. "It is so very kind of you both; but indeed I do not know what I should do. Your advice will be altogether invaluable to me."

"Pray tell us what has happened to you."

"I will do so, and I must be quick, for I have promised Mr. Rucastle to be back

before three. I got his leave to come into town this morning, though he little knew for what purpose."

"Let us have everything in its due

"I AM SO DELIGHTED THAT YOU HAVE COME."

order." Holmes thrust his long thin legs out towards the fire, and composed himself to listen.

"In the first place, I may say that I have met, on the whole, with no actual ill-treatment from Mr. and Mrs. Rucastle. It is only fair to them to say that. But I cannot understand them, and I am not easy in my mind about them."

"What can you not understand?"

"Their reasons for their conduct. But you shall have it all just as it occurred. When I came down Mr. Rucastle met me here, and drove me in his dogcart to the Copper Beeches. It is, as he said, beautifully situated, but it is not beautiful in itself, for it is a large square block of a house, whitewashed, but all stained and streaked with damp and bad weather. There are grounds round it, woods on three sides, and on the fourth a field which slopes down to the Southampton high road, which curves past about a hundred yards from the front door. This ground in front belongs to the house, but the woods all round are part of Lord Southerton's preserves. A clump of copper beeches immediately in front of the hall door has given its name to the place.

"I was driven over by my employer, who was as amiable as ever, and was introduced by him that evening to his wife and the child. There was no truth, Mr. Holmes, in the conjecture which seemed to us to be probable in your rooms at Baker-street. Mrs. Rucastle is not mad. I found her to be a silent, pale-faced woman, much younger than her husband, not more than thirty, I should think, while he can hardly be less than forty-five. From their conversation I have gathered that they have been married about seven years, that he was a widower, and that his only child by the first wife was the daughter who has gone to Philadelphia. Mr. Rucastle told me in private that the reason why she had left them was that she had an unreasoning aversion to her step-mother. As the daughter could not have been less than twenty I can quite imagine that her position must have been uncomfortable with her father's young wife.

"Mrs. Rucastle seemed to me to be colourless in mind as well as in feature. She impressed me neither favourably nor the reverse. She was a nonentity. It was easy to see that she was passionately devoted both to her husband and to her little son. Her light grey eyes wandered continually from one to the other, noting every little want and forestalling it if possible. He was kind to her also in his bluff boisterous fashion, and on the whole they seemed to be a happy couple. And yet she had some secret sorrow, this woman. She would often be lost in deep thought, with the saddest look upon her face. More than once I have surprised her in tears. I have thought sometimes that it was the disposition of her child which weighed upon her mind, for I have never met so utterly spoilt and so ill-natured a little creature. He is small for his age, with a head which is quite disproportionately large. His whole life appears to be spent in an alternation between savage fits of passion, and gloomy intervals of sulking. Giving pain to any creature weaker than himself seems to be his one idea of amusement, and he shows quite remarkable talent in planning the capture of mice, little birds, and insects. But I

would rather not talk about the creature, Mr. Holmes, and, indeed, he has little to do with my story."

"I am glad of all details," remarked my friend, "whether they seem to you to be relevant or not."

"I shall try not to miss anything of importance. The one unpleasant thing about the house, which struck me at once, was the appearance and conduct of the servants. There are only two, a man and his wife. Toller, for that is his name, is a rough, uncouth man, with grizzled hair and whiskers, and a perpetual smell of drink. Twice since I have been with them he has been quite drunk, and yet Mr. Rucastle seemed to take no notice of it. His wife is a very tall and strong woman with a sour face, as silent as Mrs. Rucastle, and much less amiable. They are a most unpleasant couple, but fortunately I spend most of my time in the nursery and my own room, which are next to each other in one corner of the building.

"For two days after my arrival at the Copper Beeches my life was very quiet; on the third, Mrs. Rucastle came down just after breakfast and whispered something to her husband.

"'Oh yes,' said he, turning to me; 'we are very much obliged to you, Miss Hunter, for falling in with our whims so far as to cut your hair. I assure you that it has not detracted in the tiniest iota from your appearance. We shall now see how the electric blue dress will become you. You will find it laid out upon the bed in your room, and if you would be so good as to put it on we should both be extremely obliged.'

"The dress which I found waiting for me was of a peculiar shade of blue. It was of excellent material, a sort of beige, but it bore unmistakable signs of having been worn before. It could not have been a better fit if I had been measured for it. Both Mr. and Mrs. Rucastle expressed a delight at the look of it which seemed quite exaggerated in its vehemence. They were waiting for me in the drawing-room, which is a very large room, stretching along the entire front of the house, with three long windows reaching down to the floor. A chair had been placed close to the central window, with its back turned towards it. In this I was asked to sit, and then Mr. Rucastle, walking up and down on the other side of the room, began to tell me a series of the funniest stories that I have ever listened to. You cannot imagine how comical he was, and I laughed until I was quite weary. Mrs. Rucastle, however, who has evidently no sense of humour, never so much as smiled, but sat with her hands in her lap, and a sad, anxious look upon her face. After an hour or so, Mr. Rucastle suddenly remarked that it was time to commence the duties of the day, and that I might change my dress, and go to little Edward in the nursery.

"Two days later this same performance was gone through under exactly similar circumstances. Again I changed my dress, again I sat in the window, and again I laughed very heartily at the funny stories of which my employer had an immense *répertoire*, and which he told inimitably. Then he handed me a yellow-backed novel, and, moving my chair a little sideways, that my own shadow might not fall upon

"I READ FOR ABOUT TEN MINUTES."

the page, he begged me to read aloud to him. I read for about ten minutes, beginning in the heart of a chapter, and then suddenly, in the middle of a sentence, he

ordered me to cease and to change my dress.

"You can easily imagine, Mr. Holmes, how curious I became as to what the meaning of this extraordinary performance could possibly be. They were always very careful, I observed, to turn my face away from the window, so that I became consumed with the desire to see what was going on behind my back. At first it seemed to be impossible, but I soon devised a means. My hand mirror had been broken, so a happy thought seized me, and I concealed a piece of the glass in my handkerchief. On the next occasion, in the midst of my laughter, I put my handkerchief up to my eyes, and was able with a little management to see all that there was behind me. I confess that I was disappointed. There was nothing.

"At least, that was my first impression. At the second glance, however, I perceived that there was a man standing in the Southampton Road, a small bearded man in a grey suit, who seemed to be looking in my direction. The road is an important highway, and there are usually people there. This man, however, was leaning against the railings which bordered our field, and was looking earnestly up. I lowered my handkerchief, and glanced at Mrs. Rucastle to find her eyes fixed upon me with a most searching gaze. She said nothing, but I am convinced that she had divined that I had a mirror in my hand, and had seen what was behind me. She rose at once.

"'Jephro,' said she, 'there is an impertinent fellow upon the road there who stares up at Miss Hunter.'

"'No friend of yours, Miss Hunter?' he asked.

"'No; I know no one in these parts.'

"'Dear me! How very impertinent! Kindly turn round, and motion to him to go away!'

"'Surely it would be better to take no notice.'

"'No, no, we should have him loitering here always. Kindly turn round, and wave him away like that.'

"I did as I was told, and at the same instant Mrs. Rucastle drew down the blind. That was a week ago, and from that time I have not sat again in the window, nor have

I worn the blue dress, nor seen the man in the road."

"Pray continue," said Holmes. "Your narrative promises to be a most interesting one."

"You will find it rather disconnected, I fear, and there may prove to be little relation between the different incidents of which I speak. On the very first day that I was at the Copper Beeches, Mr. Rucastle took me to a small outhouse which stands near the kitchen door. As we approached it I heard the sharp rattling of a chain, and the sound as of a large animal moving about.

"'Look in here!' said Mr. Rucastle, showing me a slit between two planks. 'Is he not a beauty?'

"I looked through, and was conscious of two glowing eyes, and of a vague figure huddled up in the darkness.

"'Don't be frightened,' said my employer, laughing at the start which I had given. 'It's only Carlo, my mastiff. I call him mine, but really old Toller, my groom, is the only man who can do anything with him. We feed him once a day, and not too much then, so that he is always as keen as mustard. Toller lets him loose every night, and God help the trespasser whom he lays his fangs upon. For goodness' sake don't you ever on any pretext set your foot over the threshold at night, for it is as much as your life is worth.'

"The warning was no idle one, for two nights later I happened to look out of my bedroom window about two o'clock in the morning. It was a beautiful moonlight night, and the lawn in front of the house was silvered over and almost as bright as day. I was standing, wrapt in the peaceful beauty of the scene, when I was aware that something was moving under the shadow of the copper beeches. As it emerged into the moonshine I saw what it was. It was a giant dog, as large as a calf, tawny tinted, with hanging jowl, black muzzle, and huge projecting bones. It walked slowly across the lawn and vanished into the shadow upon the other side. That dreadful silent sentinel sent a chill to my heart which I do not think that any burglar could have done.

"And now I have a very strange experience to tell you. I had, as you know, cut off my hair in London, and I had placed it in a great coil at the bottom of my trunk. One evening, after the child was in bed, I began to amuse myself by examining the furniture of my room, and by rearranging my own little things. There was an old chest of drawers in the room, the two upper ones empty and open, the lower one locked. I had filled the two first with my linen, and, as I had still much to pack away, I was naturally annoyed at not having the use of the third drawer. It struck me that it might have been fastened by a mere oversight, so I took out my bunch of keys and tried to open it. The very first key fitted to perfection, and I drew the drawer open. There was only one thing in it, but I am sure that you would never guess what it was. It was my coil of hair.

"I took it up and examined it. It was of the same peculiar tint, and the same thickness. But then the impossibility of the thing obtruded itself upon me. How *could* my hair have been locked in the drawer?

"I TOOK IT UP AND EXAMINED IT."

With trembling hands I undid my trunk turned out the contents, and drew from the bottom my own hair. I laid the two tresses together, and I assure you that they were identical. Was it not extraordinary? Puzzle as I would, I could make nothing at all of what it meant. I returned the strange hair to the drawer, and I said nothing of the matter to the Rucastles, as I felt that I had put myself in the wrong by opening a drawer which they had locked.

"I am naturally observant, as you may have remarked, Mr. Holmes, and I soon had a pretty good plan of the whole house in my head. There was one wing, however, which appeared not to be inhabited at all. A door which faced that which led into the quarters of the Tollers opened into this suite, but it was invariably locked. One day, however, as I ascended the stair, I met Mr. Rucastle coming out through this door, his keys in his hand, and a look on his face which made him a very different person to the round, jovial man to whom I was accustomed. His cheeks were red, his brow was all crinkled with anger, and the veins stood out at his temples with passion. He locked the door, and hurried past me without a word or a look.

"This aroused my curiosity; so when I went out for a walk in the grounds with my charge, I strolled round to the side from which I could see the windows of this part of the house. There were four of them in a row, three of which were simply dirty, while the fourth was shuttered up. They were evidently all deserted. As I strolled up and down, glancing at 'them occasionally, Mr. Rucastle came out to me, looking as merry and jovial as ever.

"'Ah!' said he, 'you must not think me rude if I passed you without a word, my dear young lady. I was pre-occupied with business matters.'

"I assured him that I was not offended. 'By the way,' said I, 'you seem to have quite a suite of spare rooms up there, and one of them has the shutters up.'

"He looked surprised, and, as it seemed to me, a little startled at my remark.

"'Photography is one of my hobbies,' said he. 'I have made my dark room up there. But, dear me! what an observant young lady we have come upon. Who would have believed it? Who would have ever believed it?' He spoke in a jesting tone, but there was no jest in his eyes as he looked at me. I read suspicion there, and annoyance, but no jest.

"Well, Mr. Holmes, from the moment that I understood that there was something about that suite of rooms which I was not to know, I was all on fire to go over them. It was not mere curiosity, though I have my share of that. It was more a feeling of duty—a feeling that some good might come from my penetrating to this place. They talk of woman's instinct; perhaps it was woman's instinct which gave me that feeling. At any rate, it was there; and I was keenly on the look-out for any chance to pass the forbidden door.

"It was only yesterday that the chance came. I may tell you that, besides Mr. Rucastle, both Toller and his wife find something to do in these deserted rooms, and I once saw him carrying a large black linen bag with him through the door. Recently he has been drinking hard, and yesterday evening he was very drunk; and, when I came upstairs, there was the key in the door. I have no doubt at all that he had left it there. Mr. and Mrs. Rucastle were both downstairs, and the child was with them, so that I had an admirable opportunity. I turned the key gently in the lock, opened the door, and slipped through.

"There was a little passage in front of me, unpapered and uncarpeted, which turned at a right angle at the further end. Round this corner were three doors in a line, the first and third of which were open. They each led into an empty room, dusty and cheerless, with two windows in the one, and one in the other, so thick with dirt that the evening light glimmered dimly through them. The centre door was closed, and across the outside of it had been fastened one of the broad bars of an iron bed, padlocked at one end to a ring in the wall, and fastened at the other with stout cord. The door itself was locked as well, and the key was not there. This barricaded door corresponded clearly with the shuttered window outside, and yet I could see by the glimmer from beneath it that the room was not in darkness. Evidently there was a skylight which let in light from above. As I stood in the passage gazing at this sinister door, and wondering what secret it might veil, I suddenly heard the sound of steps within the room, and saw a shadow pass backwards and forwards against the little slit of dim light which shone out from under the door. A mad, unreasoning terror rose up in me at the sight, Mr. Holmes. My overstrung nerves failed me suddenly, and I turned and ran—ran as though some dreadful hand were behind me, clutching at the skirt of my dress. I rushed down the passage, through the door, and straight into the arms of Mr. Rucastle, who was waiting outside.

"'So,' said he, smiling, 'it was you, then. I thought that it must be when I saw the door open.'

"'Oh, I am so frightened!' I panted.

"'My dear young lady! my dear young lady!'—you cannot think how caressing and soothing his manner was—'and what has frightened you, my dear young lady?'

"But his voice was just a little too coaxing. He overdid it. I was keenly on my guard against him.

"'I was foolish enough to go into the empty wing,' I answered. 'But it is so lonely and eerie in this dim light that I was frightened and ran out again. Oh, it is so dreadfully still in there!'

"'Only that?' said he, looking at me keenly.

"'OH! I AM SO FRIGHTENED!' I PANTED."

"'Why, what did you think?' I asked.

"'Why do you think that I lock this door?'

"'I am sure that I do not know.'

"'It is to keep people out who have no business there. Do you see?' He was still smiling in the most amiable manner.

"'I am sure if I had known——'

"'Well, then, you know now. And if you ever put your foot over that threshold again—' here in an instant the smile hardened into a grin of rage, and he glared down at me with the face of a demon, 'I'll throw you to the mastiff.'

"I was so terrified that I do not know what I did. I suppose that I must have rushed past him into my room. I remember nothing until I found myself lying on my bed trembling all over. Then I thought of you, Mr. Holmes. I could not live there longer without some advice. I was frightened of the house, of the man, of the woman, of the servants, even of the child. They were all horrible to me. If I could only bring you down all would be well. Of course I might have fled from the house, but my curiosity was almost as strong as my fears. My mind was soon made up. I would send you a wire. I put on my hat and cloak, went down to the office, which is about half a mile from the house, and then returned, feeling very much easier. A horrible doubt came into my mind as I approached the door lest the dog might be loose, but I remembered that Toller had drunk himself into a state of insensibility that evening, and I knew that he was the only one in the household who had any influence with the savage creature, or who would venture to set him free. I slipped in in safety, and lay awake half the night in my joy at the thought of seeing you. I had no difficulty in getting leave to come into Winchester this morning, but I must be back before three o'clock, for Mr. and Mrs. Rucastle are going on a visit, and will be away all the evening, so that I must look after the child. Now I have told you all my adventures, Mr. Holmes, and I should be very glad if you could tell me what it all means, and, above all, what I should do."

Holmes and I had listened spell-bound to this extraordinary story.

My friend rose now, and paced up and down the room, his hands in his pockets, and an expression of the most profound gravity upon his face.

" Is Toller still drunk ? " he asked.

" Yes. I heard his wife tell Mrs. Rucastle that she could do nothing with him."

" That is well. And the Rucastles go out to-night ? "

" Yes."

" Is there a cellar with a good strong lock ? "

" Yes, the wine cellar."

" You seem to me to have acted all through this matter like a very brave and sensible girl, Miss Hunter. Do you think that you could perform one more feat ? I should not ask it of you if I did not think you a quite exceptional woman."

" I will try. What is it ? "

" We shall be at the Copper Beeches by seven o'clock, my friend and I. The Rucastles will be gone by that time, and Toller will, we hope, be incapable. There only remains Mrs. Toller, who might give the alarm. If you could send her into the cellar on some errand, and then turn the key upon her, you would facilitate matters immensely."

" I will do it."

" Excellent ! We shall then look thoroughly into the affair. Of course there is only one feasible explanation. You have been brought there to personate someone, and the real person is imprisoned in this chamber. That is obvious. As to who this prisoner is, I have no doubt that it is the daughter, Miss Alice Rucastle, if I remember right, who was said to have gone to America. You were chosen, doubtless, as resembling her in height, figure, and the colour of your hair. Hers had been cut off, very possibly in some illness through which she has passed, and so, of course, yours had to be sacrificed also. By a curious chance you came upon her tresses. The man in the road was, undoubtedly, some friend of hers—possibly her *fiancé*—and no doubt as you wore the girl's dress, and were so like her, he was convinced from your laughter, whenever he saw you, and afterwards from your gesture, that Miss Rucastle was perfectly happy, and that she no longer desired his attentions. The dog is let loose at night to prevent him from endeavouring to communicate with her. So much is fairly clear. The most serious point in the case is the disposition of the child."

" What on earth has that to do with it ? " I ejaculated.

" My dear Watson, you as a medical man are continually gaining light as to the tendencies of a child by the study of the parents. Don't you see that the converse is equally valid. I have frequently gained my first real insight into the character of parents by studying their children. This child's disposition is abnormally cruel, merely for cruelty's sake, and whether he derives this from his smiling father, as I should suspect, or from his mother, it bodes evil for the poor girl who is in their power."

" I am sure that you are right, Mr. Holmes," cried our client. " A thousand things come back to me which make me certain that you have hit it. Oh, let us lose not an instant in bringing help to this poor creature."

" We must be circumspect, for we are dealing with a very cunning man. We can do nothing until seven o'clock. At that hour we shall be with you, and it will not be long before we solve the mystery."

We were as good as our word, for it was just seven when we reached the Copper Beeches, having put up our trap at a wayside publichouse. The group of trees, with their dark leaves shining like burnished metal in the light of the setting sun, were sufficient to mark the house even had Miss Hunter not been standing smiling on the doorstep.

" Have you managed it ? " asked Holmes.

A loud thudding noise came from somewhere downstairs. " That is Mrs. Toller in the cellar," said she. " Her husband lies snoring on the kitchen rug. Here are his keys, which are the duplicates of Mr. Rucastle's."

" You have done well indeed ! " cried Holmes, with enthusiasm. " Now lead the way, and we shall soon see the end of this black business."

We passed up the stair, unlocked the door, followed on down a passage, and found ourselves in front of the barricade which Miss Hunter had described. Holmes cut the cord and removed the transverse bar. Then he tried the various keys in the lock, but without success. No sound came from within, and at the silence Holmes' face clouded over.

" I trust that we are not too late," said he. " I think, Miss Hunter, that we had better go in without you. Now, Watson, put your shoulder to it, and we shall see whether we cannot make our way in."

"It was an old rickety door, and gave at once before our united strength. Together we rushed into the room. It was empty. There was no furniture save a little pallet bed, a small table, and a basketful of linen. The skylight above was open, and the prisoner gone.

"There has been some villainy here," said Holmes, "this beauty has guessed Miss Hunter's intentions, and has carried his victim off."

"But how?"

"Through the skylight. We shall soon see how he managed it." He swung himself up on to the roof. "Ah, yes," he cried, "here's the end of a long light ladder against the eaves. That is how he did it."

"But it is impossible," said Miss Hunter, "the ladder was not there when the Rucastles went away."

"He has come back and done it. I tell you that he is a clever and dangerous man. I should not be very much surprised if this were he whose step I hear now upon the stair. I think, Watson, that it would be as well for you to have your pistol ready."

The words were hardly out of his mouth before a man appeared at the door of the room, a very fat and burly man, with a heavy stick in his hand. Miss Hunter screamed and shrunk against the wall at the sight of him, but Sherlock Holmes sprang forward and confronted him.

"You villain!" said he, "where's your daughter?"

The fat man cast his eyes round, and then up at the open skylight.

"It is for me to ask you that," he shrieked, "you thieves! Spies and thieves! I have caught you, have I? You are in my power. I'll serve you!" He turned and clattered down the stairs as hard as he could go.

"'YOU VILLAIN!' SAID HE. 'WHERE'S YOUR DAUGHTER?'"

"He's gone for the dog!" cried Miss Hunter.

"I have my revolver," said I.

"Better close the front door," cried Holmes, and we all rushed down the stairs together. We had hardly reached the hall when we heard the baying of a hound, and then a scream of agony, with a horrible worrying sound which it was dreadful to listen to. An elderly man with a red face and shaking limbs came staggering out at a side door.

"My God!" he cried. "Some one has loosed the dog. It's not been fed for two days. Quick, quick, or it'll be too late!"

Holmes and I rushed out, and round the angle of the house, with Toller hurrying behind us. There was the huge famished brute, its black muzzle buried in Rucastle's throat, while he writhed and screamed upon the ground. Running up, I blew its brains out, and it fell over with its keen white teeth still meeting in the great creases of his neck. With much labour we separated them, and carried him, living but horribly mangled, into the house. We laid him upon the drawing-room sofa, and, having despatched the sobered Toller to bear the news to his wife, I did what I could to relieve his pain. We were all assembled

there's police-court business over this, you'll remember that I was the one that stood your friend, and that I was Miss Alice's friend too.

"She was never happy at home, Miss Alice wasn't, from the time that her father married again. She was slighted like, and had no say in anything; but it never really became bad for her until after she met Mr. Fowler at a friend's house. As well as I could learn, Miss Alice had rights of her own by will, but she was so quiet and patient, she was, that she never said a word about them, but just left everything in Mr. Rucastle's hands. He knew he was safe

RUNNING UP, I BLEW ITS BRAINS OUT.'

round him when the door opened, and a tall, gaunt woman entered the room.

"Mrs. Toller!" cried Miss Hunter.

"Yes, miss. Mr. Rucastle let me out when he came back before he went up to you. Ah, miss, it is a pity you didn't let me know what you were planning, for I would have told you that your pains were wasted."

"Ha!" said Holmes, looking keenly at her. "It is clear that Mrs. Toller knows more about this matter than anyone else."

"Yes, sir, I do, and I am ready enough to tell what I know."

"Then, pray, sit down, and let us hear it, for there are several points on which I must confess that I am still in the dark."

"I will soon make it clear to you," said she; "and I'd have done so before now if I could ha' got out from the cellar. If

with her; but when there was a chance of a husband coming forward, who would ask for all that the law would give him, then her father thought it time to put a stop on it. He wanted her to sign a paper so that whether she married or not, he could use her money. When she wouldn't do it, he kept on worrying her until she got brain fever, and for six weeks was at death's door. Then she got better at last, all worn to a shadow, and with her beautiful hair cut off; but that didn't make no change in her young man, and he stuck to her as true as man could be.

"Ah," said Holmes, "I think that what you have been good enough to tell us makes the matter fairly clear, and that I can deduce all that remains. Mr. Rucastle then, I presume, took to this system of imprisonment?"

" Yes, sir."

" And brought Miss Hunter down from London in order to get rid of .the disagreeable persistence of Mr. Fowler."

" That was it, sir."

" But Mr. Fowler being a persevering man, as a good seaman should be, blockaded the house, and, having met you, succeeded by certain arguments, metallic or otherwise, in convincing you that your interests were the same as his."

" Mr. Fowler was a very kind-spoken, free-handed gentleman," said Mrs. Toller serenely.

" And in this way he managed that your good man should have no want of drink, and that a ladder should be ready at the moment when your master had gone out."

" You have it, sir, just as it happened."

" I am sure we owe you an apology, Mrs. Toller," said Holmes, " for you have certainly cleared up everything which puzzled us. And here comes the country surgeon and Mrs. Rucastle, so I think, Watson, that we had best escort Miss Hunter back to Winchester, as it seems to me that our *locus standi* now is rather a questionable one."

And thus was solved the mystery of the sinister house with the copper beeches in front of the door. Mr. Rucastle survived, but was always a broken man, kept alive solely through the care of his devoted wife. They still live with their old servants, who probably know so much of Rucastle's past life that he finds it difficult to part from them. Mr. Fowler and Miss Rucastle were married, by special licence, in Southampton the day after their flight, and he is now the holder of a Government appointment in the Island of Mauritius. As to Miss Violet Hunter, my friend Holmes, rather to my disappointment, manifested no further interest in her when once she had ceased to be the centre of one of his problems, and she is now the head of a private school at Walsall, where I believe that she has met with considerable success.

THE ADVENTURES
OF SHERLOCK HOLMES

*Facsimile from the Strand Magazine, Volumes IV, V and VI,
December 1892 – December 1893.*

Adventures of Sherlock Holmes.*

XIII.—THE ADVENTURE OF SILVER BLAZE.

By A. Conan Doyle.

"I AM afraid, Watson, that I shall have to go," said Holmes, as we sat down together to our breakfast one morning.

"Go! Where to?"

"To Dartmoor—to King's Pyland."

I was not surprised. Indeed, my only wonder was that he had not already been mixed up in this extraordinary case, which was the one topic of conversation through the length and breadth of England. For a whole day my companion had rambled about the room with his chin upon his chest and his brows knitted, charging and re-charging his pipe with the strongest black tobacco, and absolutely deaf to any of my questions or remarks. Fresh editions of every paper had been sent up by our newsagent only to be glanced over and tossed down into a corner. Yet, silent as he was, I knew perfectly well what it was, over which he was brooding. There was but one problem before the public which could challenge his powers of analysis, and that was the singular disappearance of the favourite for the Wessex Cup and the tragic murder of its trainer. When, therefore, he suddenly announced his intention of setting out for the scene of the drama, it was only what I had both expected and hoped for.

"I should be most happy to go down with you if I should not be in the way," said I.

"My dear Watson, you would confer a great favour upon me by coming. And I think that your time will not be mis-spent, for there are points about this case which promise to make it an absolutely unique one. We have, I think, just time to catch our train at Paddington, and I will go further into the matter upon our journey. You would oblige me by bringing with you your very excellent field-glass."

And so it happened that an hour or so later I found myself in the corner of a first-class carriage, flying along, en route for Exeter, while Sherlock Holmes, with his sharp, eager face framed in his earflapped travelling cap, dipped rapidly into the bundle of fresh papers which he had procured at Paddington. We had left Reading far behind us before he thrust the last of them under the seat, and offered me his cigar case.

"We are going well," said he, looking out of the window, and glancing at his watch. "Our rate at present is fifty-three and a half miles an hour."

"I have not observed the quarter-mile posts," said I.

"Nor have I. But the telegraph posts upon this line are sixty yards apart, and the calculation is a simple one. I presume that you have already looked into this matter of the murder of John Straker and the disappearance of Silver Blaze?"

"I have seen what the *Telegraph* and the *Chronicle* have to say."

"It is one of those cases where the art of the reasoner should be used rather for the sifting of details than for the acquiring of fresh evidence. The tragedy has been so uncommon, so complete, and of such personal importance to so many people that we are suffering from a plethora of surmise, conjecture, and hypothesis. The difficulty is to detach the framework of fact—of absolute, undeniable fact — from the embellishments of theorists and reporters. Then, having established ourselves upon this sound basis, it is our duty to see what inferences may be drawn, and which are the special points upon which the whole mystery turns. On Tuesday evening I received telegrams, both from Colonel Ross, the owner of the horse, and from Inspector Gregory, who is looking after the case, inviting my co-operation."

"Tuesday evening!" I exclaimed. "And this is Thursday morning. Why did you not go down yesterday?"

"Because I made a blunder, my dear Watson—which is, I am afraid, a more common occurrence than anyone would think who only knew me through your memoirs.

The fact is that I could not believe it possible that the most remarkable horse in England could long remain concealed, especially in so sparsely inhabited a place as the north of Dartmoor. From hour to hour yesterday I expected to hear that he had been found, and that his abductor was the murderer of John Straker. When, however, another morning had come and I found that, beyond the arrest of young Fitzroy Simpson, nothing had been done, I felt that it was time for me to take action. Yet in some ways I feel that yesterday has not been wasted."

"You have formed a theory then?"

"At least I have got a grip of the essential facts of the case. I shall enumerate them to you, for nothing clears up a case so much as stating it to another person, and I can hardly expect your co-operation if I do not show you the position from which we start."

"HOLMES GAVE ME A SKETCH OF THE EVENTS."

I lay back against the cushions, puffing at my cigar, while Holmes, leaning forward, with his long thin forefinger checking off the points upon the palm of his left hand, gave me a sketch of the events which had led to our journey.

"Silver Blaze," said he, "is from the

Isonomy stock, and holds as brilliant a record as his famous ancestor. He is now in his fifth year, and has brought in turn each of the prizes of the turf to Colonel Ross, his fortunate owner. Up to the time of the catastrophe he was first favourite for the Wessex Cup, the betting being three to one on. He has always, however, been a prime favourite with the racing public, and has never yet disappointed them, so that even at those odds enormous sums of money have been laid upon him. It is obvious, therefore, that there were many people who had the strongest interest in preventing Silver Blaze from being there at the fall of the flag, next Tuesday.

"This fact was, of course, appreciated at King's Pyland, where the Colonel's training stable is situated. Every precaution was taken to guard the favourite. The trainer, John Straker, is a retired jockey, who rode in Colonel Ross's colours before he became too heavy for the weighing chair. He has served the Colonel for five years as jockey, and for seven as trainer, and has always shown himself to be a zealous and honest servant. Under him were three lads, for the establishment was a small one, containing only four horses in all. One of these lads sat up each night in the stable, while the others slept in the loft. All three bore excellent characters. John Straker, who is a married man, lived in a small villa about two hundred yards from the stables. He has no children, keeps one maid-servant, and is comfortably off. The country round is very lonely, but about half a mile to the north there is a small cluster of villas which have been built by a Tavistock contractor for the use of invalids and others who may wish to enjoy the pure Dartmoor air. Tavistock itself lies two miles to the west, while across the moor, also about two miles distant, is the larger training establishment of Mapleton, which belongs to Lord Backwater, and is managed by Silas Brown. In every other direction the moor is a complete wilderness, inhabited only by a few roaming gipsies. Such was the general situation last Monday night when the catastrophe occurred.

"On that evening the horses had been exercised and watered as usual, and the stables were locked up at nine o'clock. Two of the lads walked up to the trainer's house, where they had supper in the kitchen, while the third, Ned Hunter, remained on guard. At a few minutes after nine the maid, Edith Baxter, carried down to the stables his supper, which consisted of a dish of curried mutton. She took no liquid, as there was a water-tap in the stables, and it was the rule that the lad on duty should drink nothing else. The maid carried a lantern with her, as it was very dark, and the path ran across the open moor.

"A MAN APPEARED OUT OF THE DARKNESS."

"Edith Baxter was within thirty yards of the stables when a man appeared out of the darkness and called to her to stop. As he stepped into the circle of yellow light thrown by the lantern she saw that he was a person of gentlemanly bearing, dressed in a grey suit of tweed with a cloth cap. He wore gaiters, and carried a heavy stick with a knob to it. She was most impressed, however, by the extreme pallor of his face and by the nervousness of his manner. His age, she thought, would be rather over thirty than under it.

"'Can you tell me where I am?' he asked. 'I had almost made up my mind to sleep on the moor when I saw the light of your lantern.'

"'You are close to the King's Pyland training stables,' she said.

"'Oh, indeed! What a stroke of luck!' he cried. 'I understand that a stable boy sleeps there alone every night. Perhaps that is his supper which you are carrying to him. Now I am sure that you would not be too proud to earn the price of a new dress, would you?' He took a piece of white paper folded up out of his waistcoat pocket. 'See that the boy has this to-night, and you shall have the prettiest frock that money can buy.'

"She was frightened by the earnestness of his manner, and ran past him to the window through which she was accustomed to hand the meals. It was already open, and Hunter was seated at the small table inside. She had begun to tell him of what had happened, when the stranger came up again.

"'Good evening,' said he, looking through the window, 'I wanted to have a word with you.' The girl has sworn that as he spoke she noticed the corner of the little paper packet protruding from his closed hand.

"'What business have you here?' asked the lad.

" ' It's business that may put something into your pocket,' said the other. ' You've two horses in for the Wessex Cup—Silver Blaze and Bayard. Let me have the straight tip, and you won't be a loser. Is it a fact that at the weights Bayard could give the other a hundred yards in five furlongs, and that the stable have put their money on him ?'

" ' So you're one of those damned touts,' cried the lad. ' I'll show you how we serve them in King's Pyland.' He sprang up and rushed across the stable to unloose the dog. The girl fled away to the house, but as she ran she looked back, and saw that the stranger was leaning through the window. A minute later, however, when Hunter rushed out with the hound he was gone, and though the lad ran all round the buildings he failed to find any trace of him."

" One moment!" I asked. " Did the stable-boy, when he ran out with the dog, leave the door unlocked behind him ? "

" Excellent, Watson; excellent!" murmured my companion. " The importance of the point struck me so forcibly, that I sent a special wire to Dartmoor yesterday to clear the matter up. The boy locked the door before he left it. The window, I may add, was not large enough for a man to get through.

" Hunter waited until his fellow grooms had returned, when he sent a message up to the trainer and told him what had occurred. Straker was excited at hearing the account, although he does not seem to have quite realized its true significance. It left him, however, vaguely uneasy, and Mrs. Straker, waking at one in the morning, found that he was dressing. In reply to her inquiries, he said that he could not sleep on account of his anxiety about the horses, and that he intended to walk down to the stables to see that all was well. She begged him to remain at home, as she could hear the rain pattering against the windows, but in spite of her entreaties he pulled on his large mackintosh and left the house.

" Mrs. Straker awoke at seven in the morning, to find that her husband had not yet returned. She dressed herself hastily, called the maid, and set off for the stables. The door was open; inside, huddled together upon a chair, Hunter was sunk in a state of absolute stupor, the favourite's stall was empty, and there were no signs of his trainer.

" The two lads who slept in the chaff-cutting loft above the harness-room were quickly aroused. They had heard nothing during the night, for they are both sound sleepers. Hunter was obviously under the influence of some powerful drug; and, as no sense could be got out of him, he was left to sleep it off while the two lads and the two women ran out in search of the absentees. They still had hopes that the trainer had for some reason taken out the horse for early exercise, but on ascending the knoll near the house, from which all the neighbouring moors were visible, they not only could see no signs of the favourite, but they perceived something which warned them that they were in the presence of a tragedy.

" About a quarter of a mile from the stables, John Straker's overcoat was flapping from a

"THEY FOUND THE DEAD BODY OF THE UNFORTUNATE TRAINER.

furze bush. Immediately beyond there was a bowl-shaped depression in the moor, and at the bottom of this was found the dead body of the unfortunate trainer. His head had been shattered by a savage blow from some heavy weapon, and he was wounded in the thigh, where there was a long, clean cut, inflicted evidently by some very sharp instrument. It was clear, however, that Straker had defended himself vigorously against his assailants, for in his right hand he held a small knife, which was clotted with blood up to the handle, while in his left he grasped a red and black silk cravat, which was recognised by the maid as having been worn on the preceding evening by the stranger who had visited the stables.

"Hunter, on recovering from his stupor, was also quite positive as to the ownership of the cravat. He was equally certain that the same stranger had, while standing at the window, drugged his curried mutton, and so deprived the stables of their watchman.

"As to the missing horse, there were abundant proofs in the mud which lay at the bottom of the fatal hollow, that he had been there at the time of the struggle. But from that morning he has disappeared ; and although a large reward has been offered, and all the gipsies of Dartmoor are on the alert, no news has come of him. Finally an analysis has shown that the remains of his supper, left by the stable lad, contain an appreciable quantity of powdered opium, while the people at the house partook of the same dish on the same night without any ill effect.

"Those are the main facts of the case, stripped of all surmise and stated as baldly as possible. I shall now recapitulate what the police have done in the matter.

"Inspector Gregory, to whom the case has been committed, is an extremely competent officer. Were he but gifted with imagination he might rise to great heights in his profession. On his arrival he promptly found and arrested the man upon whom suspicion naturally rested. There was little difficulty in finding him, for he inhabited one of those villas which I have mentioned. His name, it appears, was Fitzroy Simpson. He was a man of excellent birth and education, who had squandered a fortune upon the turf, and who lived now by doing a little quiet and genteel bookmaking in the sporting clubs of London. An examination of his betting-book shows that bets to the amount of five thousand pounds had been registered by him against the favourite.

"On being arrested he volunteered the statement that he had come down to Dartmoor in the hope of getting some information about the King's Pyland horses, and also about Desborough, the second favourite, which was in charge of Silas Brown, at the Mapleton stables. He did not attempt to deny that he had acted as described upon the evening before, but declared that he had no sinister designs, and had simply wished to obtain first-hand information. When confronted with his cravat he turned very pale, and was utterly unable to account for its presence in the hand of the murdered man. His wet clothing showed that he had been out in the storm of the night before, and his stick, which was a Penang lawyer, weighted with lead, was just such a weapon as might, by repeated blows, have inflicted the terrible injuries to which the trainer had succumbed.

"On the other hand, there was no wound upon his person, while the state of Straker's knife would show that one, at least, of his assailants must bear his mark upon him. There you have it all in a nutshell, Watson, and if you can give me any light I shall be infinitely obliged to you."

I had listened with the greatest interest to the statement which Holmes, with characteristic clearness, had laid before me. Though most of the facts were familiar to me, I had not sufficiently appreciated their relative importance, nor their connection to each other.

"Is it not possible," I suggested, "that the incised wound upon Straker may have been caused by his own knife in the convulsive struggles which follow any brain injury?"

"It is more than possible ; it is probable," said Holmes. "In that case, one of the main points in favour of the accused disappears."

"And yet," said I, "even now I fail to understand what the theory of the police can be."

"I am afraid that whatever theory we state has very grave objections to it," returned my companion. "The police imagine, I take it, that this Fitzroy Simpson, having drugged the lad, and having in some way obtained a duplicate key, opened the stable door, and took out the horse, with the intention, apparently, of kidnapping him altogether. His bridle is missing, so that Simpson must have put this on. Then, having left the door open behind him, he was leading the horse away over the moor, when he was either met or overtaken by the trainer. A row naturally ensued, Simpson beat out the trainer's brains with his heavy stick without receiving any injury from the small knife which Straker used in self-defence, and then the thief either led the horse on to some secret hiding-place, or else it may have bolted during the struggle, and be now wandering out on the moors. That is the case as it appears to the police, and improbable as it is, all other explanations are more improbable still. However, I shall very quickly test the matter when I am once upon the spot, and until then I really cannot see how we can get much further than our present position."

It was evening before we reached the little town of Tavistock, which lies, like the boss of a shield, in the middle of the huge circle of Dartmoor. Two gentlemen were awaiting us at the station; the one a tall fair man with lion-like hair and beard, and curiously penetrating light blue eyes, the other a small alert person, very neat and dapper, in a frockcoat and gaiters, with trim little side-whiskers and an eye-glass. The latter was Colonel Ross, the well-known sportsman, the other Inspector Gregory, a man who was rapidly making his name in the English detective service.

"I am delighted that you have come down, Mr. Holmes," said the Colonel. "The Inspector here has done all that could possibly be suggested; but I wish to leave no stone unturned in trying to avenge poor Straker, and in recovering my horse."

"Have there been any fresh developments?" asked Holmes.

"I am sorry to say that we have made very little progress," said the Inspector. "We have an open carriage outside, and as you would no doubt like to see the place before the light fails, we might talk it over as we drive."

A minute later we were all seated in a comfortable landau and were rattling through the quaint old Devonshire town. Inspector Gregory was full of his case, and poured out a stream of remarks, while Holmes threw in an occasional question or interjection. Colonel Ross leaned back with his arms folded and his hat tilted over his eyes, while I listened with interest to the dialogue of the two detectives. Gregory was formulating his theory, which was almost exactly what Holmes had foretold in the train.

"The net is drawn pretty close round Fitzroy Simpson," he remarked, "and I believe myself that he is our man. At the same time, I recognise that the evidence is purely circumstantial, and that some new development may upset it."

"How about Straker's knife?"

"We have quite come to the conclusion that he wounded himself in his fall."

"My friend Dr. Watson made that suggestion to me as we came down. If so, it would tell against this man Simpson."

"Undoubtedly. He has neither a knife nor any sign of a wound. The evidence against him is certainly very strong. He had a great interest in the

"I AM DELIGHTED THAT YOU HAVE COME DOWN, MR. HOLMES.'

disappearance of the favourite, he lies under the suspicion of having poisoned the stable boy, he was undoubtedly out in the storm, he was armed with a heavy stick, and his cravat was found in the dead man's hand. I really think we have enough to go before a jury."

Holmes shook his head. "A clever counsel would tear it all to rags," said he. "Why should he take the horse out of the stable? If he wished to injure it, why could he not do it there? Has a duplicate key been found in his possession? What chemist sold him the powdered opium? Above all, where could he, a stranger to the district, hide a horse, and such a horse as this? What is his own explanation as to the paper which he wished the maid to give to the stable-boy?"

"He says that it was a ten-pound note. One was found in his purse. But your other difficulties are not so formidable as they seem. He is not a stranger to the district. He has twice lodged at Tavistock in the summer. The opium was probably brought from London. The key, having served its purpose, would be hurled away. The horse may lie at the bottom of one of the pits or old mines upon the moor."

"What does he say about the cravat?"

"He acknowledges that it is his, and declares that he had lost it. But a new element has been introduced into the case which may account for his leading the horse from the stable."

Holmes pricked up his ears.

"We have found traces which show that a party of gipsies encamped on Monday night within a mile of the spot where the murder took place. On Tuesday they were gone. Now, presuming that there was some understanding between Simpson and these gipsies, might he not have been leading the horse to them when he was overtaken, and may they not have him now?"

"It is certainly possible."

"The moor is being scoured for these gipsies. I have also examined every stable and outhouse in Tavistock, and for a radius of ten miles."

"There is another training stable quite close, I understand?"

"Yes, and that is a factor which we must certainly not neglect. As Desborough, their horse, was second in the betting, they had an interest in the disappearance of the favourite. Silas Brown, the trainer, is known to have had large bets upon the event, and he was no friend to poor Straker. We have, however, examined the stables, and there is nothing to connect him with the affair."

"And nothing to connect this man Simpson with the interests of the Mapleton stables?"

"Nothing at all."

Holmes leaned back in the carriage and the conversation ceased. A few minutes later our driver pulled up at a neat little red-brick villa with overhanging eaves, which stood by the road. Some distance off, across a paddock, lay a long grey-tiled out-building. In every other direction the low curves of the moor, bronze-coloured from the fading ferns, stretched away to the sky-line, broken only by the steeples of Tavistock, and by a cluster of houses away to the westward, which marked the Mapleton stables. We all sprang out with the exception of Holmes, who continued to lean back with his eyes fixed upon the sky in front of him, entirely absorbed in his own thoughts. It was only when I touched his arm that he roused himself with a violent start and stepped out of the carriage.

"Excuse me," said he, turning to Colonel Ross, who had looked at him in some surprise. "I was day-dreaming." There was a gleam in his eyes and a suppressed excitement in his manner which convinced me, used as I was to his ways, that his hand was upon a clue, though I could not imagine where he had found it.

"Perhaps you would prefer at once to go on to the scene of the crime, Mr. Holmes?" said Gregory.

"I think that I should prefer to stay here a little and go into one or two questions of detail. Straker was brought back here, I presume?"

"Yes, he lies upstairs. The inquest is to-morrow."

"He has been in your service some years, Colonel Ross?"

"I have always found him an excellent servant."

"I presume that you made an inventory of what he had in his pockets at the time of his death, Inspector?"

"I have the things themselves in the sitting-room if you would care to see them."

"I should be very glad."

We all filed into the front room and sat round the central table, while the Inspector unlocked a square tin box and laid a small heap of things before us. There was a box of vestas, two inches of tallow candle, an A.D.P. briar-root pipe, a pouch of sealskin with half an ounce of long-cut Cavendish, a silver watch with a gold chain, five sovereigns in gold, an aluminium pencil-case, a few papers, and an ivory-handled knife with a very delicate inflexible blade marked Weiss and Co., London.

"This is a very singular knife," said Holmes, lifting it up and examining it minutely. "I presume, as I see bloodstains upon it, that it is the one which was found in the dead man's grasp. Watson, this knife is surely in your line."

"It is what we call a cataract knife," said I.

"I thought so. A very delicate blade devised for very delicate work. A strange thing for a man to carry with him upon a rough expedition, especially as it would not shut in his pocket."

"The tip was guarded by a disc of cork which we found beside his body," said the Inspector. "His wife tells us that the knife had lain for some days upon the dressing-table, and that he had picked it up as he left the room. It was a poor weapon, but perhaps the best that he could lay his hand on at the moment."

"Very possibly. How about these papers?"

"Three of them are receipted hay - dealers' accounts. One of them is a letter of instructions from Colonel Ross. This other is a milliner's account for thirty-seven pounds fifteen, made out by Madame Lesurier, of Bond Street, to William Darbyshire. Mrs. Straker tells us that Darbyshire was a friend of her husband's, and that occasionally his letters were addressed here."

"Madame Darbyshire had somewhat expensive tastes," remarked Holmes, glancing down the account. "Twenty-two guineas is rather heavy for a single costume. However, there appears to be nothing more to learn, and we may now go down to the scene of the crime."

As we emerged from the sitting-room a woman who had been waiting in the passage took a step forward and laid her hand upon the Inspector's sleeve. Her face was haggard, and thin, and eager ; stamped with the print of a recent horror.

"Have you got them? Have you found them ? " she panted.

"No, Mrs. Straker ; but Mr. Holmes, here, has come from London to help us, and we shall do all that is possible."

"Surely I met you in Plymouth, at a garden party, some little time ago, Mrs. Straker," said Holmes.

"No, sir ; you are mistaken."

"HAVE YOU FOUND THEM?" SHE PANTED.

"Dear me ; why, I could have sworn to it. You wore a costume of dove-coloured silk, with ostrich feather trimming."

"I never had such a dress, sir," answered the lady.

"Ah ; that quite settles it," said Holmes ; and, with an apology, he followed the Inspector outside. A short walk across the moor took us to the hollow in which the body had been found. At the brink of it was the furze bush upon which the coat had been hung.

"There was no wind that night, I understand," said Holmes.

"None : but very heavy rain."

"In that case the overcoat was not blown against the furze bushes, but placed there."

"Yes, it was laid across the bush."

"You fill me with interest. I perceive that the ground has been trampled up a good deal. No doubt many feet have been there since Monday night."

"A piece of matting has been laid here at the side, and we have all stood upon that."

"Excellent."

"In this bag I have one of the boots which Straker wore, one of Fitzroy Simpson's shoes, and a cast horseshoe of Silver Blaze."

"My dear Inspector, you surpass yourself!" Holmes took the bag, and descending into the hollow he pushed the matting into a more central position. Then stretching himself upon his face and leaning his chin upon his hands he made a careful study of the trampled mud in front of him.

"Halloa!" said he, suddenly, "what's this?"

It was a wax vesta, half burned, which was so coated with mud that it looked at first like a little chip of wood.

"I cannot think how I came to overlook it," said the Inspector, with an expression of annoyance.

"It was invisible, buried in the mud. I only saw it because I was looking for it."

"What! You expected to find it?"

"I thought it not unlikely." He took the boots from the bag and compared the impressions of each of them with marks upon the ground. Then he clambered up to the rim of the hollow and crawled about among the ferns and bushes.

"I am afraid that there are no more tracks," said the Inspector. "I have examined the ground very carefully for a hundred yards in each direction."

"Indeed!" said Holmes, rising, "I should not have the impertinence to do it again after what you say. But I should like to take a little walk over the moor before it grows dark, that I may know my ground to-morrow, and I think that I shall put this horseshoe into my pocket for luck."

Colonel Ross, who had shown some signs of impatience at my companion's quiet and systematic method of work, glanced at his watch.

"I wish you would come back with me, Inspector," said he. "There are several points on which I should like your advice, and especially as to whether we do not owe it to the public to remove our horse's name from the entries for the Cup."

"Certainly not," cried Holmes, with decision : "I should let the name stand."

The Colonel bowed. "I am very glad to have had your opinion, sir," said he. "You will find us at poor Straker's house when you have finished your walk, and we can drive together into Tavistock."

He turned back with the Inspector, while Holmes and I walked slowly across the moor. The sun was beginning to sink behind the stables of Mapleton, and the long sloping plain in front of us was tinged with gold, deepening into rich, ruddy brown where the faded ferns and brambles caught the evening light. But the glories of the landscape were all wasted upon my companion, who was sunk in the deepest thought.

"It's this way, Watson," he said at last. "We may leave the question of who killed John Straker for the instant, and confine ourselves to finding out what has become of the horse. Now, supposing that he broke away during or after the tragedy, where could he have gone to? The horse is a very gregarious creature. If left to himself his instincts would have been either to return to King's Pyland, or go over to Mapleton. Why should he run wild upon the moor? He would surely have been seen by now. And why should gipsies kidnap him? These people always clear out when they hear of trouble, for they do not wish to be pestered by the police. They could not hope to sell such a horse. They would run a great risk and gain nothing by taking him. Surely that is clear."

"Where is he, then?"

"I have already said that he must have gone to King's Pyland or to Mapleton. He is not at King's Pyland, therefore he is at Mapleton. Let us take that as a working hypothesis and see what it leads us to. This part of the moor, as the Inspector remarked, is very hard and dry. But it falls away towards Mapleton, and you can see from here that there is a long hollow over yonder, which must have been very wet on Monday night. If our supposition is correct, then the horse must have crossed that, and there is the point where we should look for his tracks."

We had been walking briskly during this conversation, and a few more minutes brought us to the hollow in question. At Holmes' request I walked down the bank to the right and he to the left, but I had not taken fifty paces before I heard him give a shout, and saw him waving his hand to me. The track of a horse was plainly outlined in the soft earth in front of him, and the shoe which he took from his pocket exactly fitted the impression.

"See the value of imagination," said Holmes. "It is the one . quality which Gregory lacks. We imagined what might have happened, acted upon the supposition, and find ourselves justified. Let us proceed."

We crossed the marshy bottom and passed over a quarter of a mile of dry, hard turf. Again the ground sloped and again we came on the tracks. Then we lost them for half a mile, but only to pick them up once more quite close to Mapleton. It was Holmes who saw them first, and he stood pointing with a look of triumph upon his face. A man's track was visible beside the horse's.

"The horse was alone before," I cried.

"Quite so. It was alone before. Halloa, what is this?"

The double track turned sharp off and took the direction of King's Pyland. Holmes whistled, and we both followed along after it. His eyes were on the trail, but I happened to look a little to one side, and saw to my surprise the same tracks coming back again in the opposite direction.

"One for you, Watson," said Holmes, when I pointed it out; "you have saved us a long walk which would have brought us back on our own traces. Let us follow the return track."

"BE OFF!"

We had not to go far. It ended at the paving of asphalt which led up to the gates of the Mapleton stables. As we approached a groom ran out from them.

"We don't want any loiterers about here," said he.

"I only wished to ask a question," said Holmes, with his finger and thumb in his waistcoat pocket. "Should I be too early to see your master, Mr. Silas Brown, if I were to call at five o'clock to-morrow morning?"

"Bless you, sir, if anyone is about he will be, for he is always the first stirring. But here he is, sir, to answer your questions for himself. No, sir, no; it's as much as my place is worth to let him see me touch your money. Afterwards, if you like."

As Sherlock Holmes replaced the half-crown which he had drawn from his pocket, a fierce-looking, elderly man strode out from the gate with a hunting-crop swinging in his hand.

"What's this, Dawson?" he cried. "No gossiping! Go about your business! And you—what the devil do you want here?"

"Ten minutes' talk with you, my good sir," said Holmes, in the sweetest of voices.

"I've no time to talk to every gadabout. We want no strangers here. Be off, or you may find a dog at your heels."

Holmes leaned forward and whispered

something in the trainer's ear. He started violently and flushed to the temples.

"It's a lie!" he shouted. "An infernal lie!"

"Very good! Shall we argue about it here in public, or talk it over in your parlour?"

"Oh, come in if you wish to."

Holmes smiled. "I shall not keep you more than a few minutes, Watson," he said. "Now, Mr. Brown, I am quite at your disposal."

It was quite twenty minutes, and the reds had all faded into greys before Holmes and the trainer reappeared. Never have I seen such a change as had been brought about in Silas Brown in that short time. His face was ashy pale, beads of perspiration shone upon his brow, and his hands shook until the hunting-crop wagged like a branch in the wind. His bullying, overbearing manner was all gone too, and he cringed along at my companion's side like a dog with its master.

"Your instructions will be done. It shall be done," said he.

"There must be no mistake," said Holmes, looking round at him. The other winced as he read the menace in his eyes.

"Oh, no, there shall be no mistake. It shall be there. Should I change it first or not?"

Holmes thought a little and then burst out laughing. "No, don't," said he. "I shall write to you about it. No tricks now or——"

"Oh, you can trust me, you can trust me!"

"Yes, I think I can. Well, you shall hear from me to-morrow." He turned upon his heel, disregarding the trembling hand which the other held out to him, and we set off for King's Pyland.

"A more perfect compound of the bully, coward and sneak than Master Silas Brown I have seldom met with," remarked Holmes, as we trudged along together.

"He has the horse, then?"

"He tried to bluster out of it, but I described to him so exactly what his actions had been upon that morning, that he is convinced that I was watching him. Of course, you observed the peculiarly square toes in the impressions, and that his own boots exactly corresponded to them. Again, of course, no subordinate would have dared to have done such a thing. I described to him how when, according to his custom, he was the first down, he perceived a strange horse wandering over the moor; how he went out to it, and his astonishment at recognising from the white forehead which has given the

favourite its name that chance had put in his power the only horse which could beat the one upon which he had put his money. Then I described how his first impulse had been to lead him back to King's Pyland, and how the devil had shown him how he could hide the horse until the race was over, and how he had led it back and concealed it at Mapleton. When I told him every detail he gave it up, and thought only of saving his own skin."

"But his stables had been searched."

"Oh, an old horse-faker like him has many a dodge."

"But are you not afraid to leave the horse in his power now, since he has every interest in injuring it?"

"My dear fellow, he will guard it as the apple of his eye. He knows that his only hope of mercy is to produce it safe."

"Colonel Ross did not impress me as a man who would be likely to show much mercy in any case."

"The matter does not rest with Colonel Ross. I follow my own methods, and tell as much or as little as I choose. That is the advantage of being unofficial. I don't know whether you observed it, Watson, but the Colonel's manner has been just a trifle cavalier to me. I am inclined now to have a little amusement at his expense. Say nothing to him about the horse."

"Certainly not, without your permission."

"And, of course, this is all quite a minor point compared to the question of who killed John Straker."

"And you will devote yourself to that?"

"On the contrary, we both go back to London by the night train."

I was thunderstruck by my friend's words. We had only been a few hours in Devonshire, and that he should give up an investigation which he had begun so brilliantly was quite incomprehensible to me. Not a word more could I draw from him until we were back at the trainer's house. The Colonel and the Inspector were awaiting us in the parlour.

"My friend and I return to town by the midnight express," said Holmes. "We have had a charming little breath of your beautiful Dartmoor air."

The Inspector opened his eyes, and the Colonel's lip curled in a sneer.

"So you despair of arresting the murderer of poor Straker," said he.

Holmes shrugged his shoulders. "There are certainly grave difficulties in the way," said he. "I have every hope, however, that your horse will start upon Tuesday, and I beg that you will have your jockey in readiness. Might I ask for a photograph of Mr. John Straker?"

The Inspector took one from an envelope in his pocket and handed it to him.

"My dear Gregory, you anticipate all my wants. If I might ask you to wait here for an instant, I have a question which I should like to put to the maid."

"I must say that I am rather disappointed in our London consultant," said Colonel Ross, bluntly, as my friend left the room. "I do not see that we are any further than when he came."

"At least, you have his assurance that your horse will run," said I.

"Yes, I have his assurance," said the Colonel, with a shrug of his shoulders. "I should prefer to have the horse."

I was about to make some reply in defence of my friend, when he entered the room again.

"Now, gentlemen," said he, "I am quite ready for Tavistock."

As we stepped into the carriage one of the stable-lads held the door open for us. A sudden idea seemed to occur to Holmes, for he leaned forward and touched the lad upon the sleeve.

"You have a few sheep in the paddock," he said. "Who attends to them?"

"I do, sir."

"Have you noticed anything amiss with them of late?"

"Well, sir, not of much account; but three of them have gone lame, sir."

I could see that Holmes was extremely pleased, for he chuckled and rubbed his hands together.

"A long shot, Watson; a very long shot!" said he, pinching my arm. "Gregory, let me recommend to your attention this singular epidemic among the sheep. Drive on, coachman!"

Colonel Ross still wore an expression which showed the poor opinion which he had formed of my companion's ability, but I saw by the Inspector's face that his attention had been keenly aroused.

"You consider that to be important?" he asked.

"Exceedingly so."

"Is there any other point to which you would wish to draw my attention?"

"HOLMES WAS EXTREMELY PLEASED."

"To the curious incident of the dog in the night-time."

"The dog did nothing in the night-time."

"That was the curious incident," remarked Sherlock Holmes.

Four days later Holmes and I were again in the train bound for Winchester, to see the race for the Wessex Cup. Colonel Ross met us, by appointment, outside the station, and we drove in his drag to the course beyond the town. His face was grave and his manner was cold in the extreme.

"I have seen nothing of my horse," said he.

"I suppose that you would know him when you saw him?" asked Holmes.

The Colonel was very angry. "I have been on the turf for twenty years, and never was asked such a question as that before," said he. "A child would know Silver Blaze with his white forehead and his mottled off fore leg."

"How is the betting?"

"Well, that is the curious part of it. You could have got fifteen to one yesterday, but the price has become shorter and shorter, until you can hardly get three to one now."

"Hum!" said Holmes. "Somebody knows something, that is clear!"

As the drag drew up in the inclosure near the grand stand, I glanced at the card to see the entries. It ran :—

Wessex Plate. 50 sovs. each, h ft, with 1,000 sovs. added, for four and five-year olds. Second £300. Third £200. New course (one mile and five furlongs).

1. Mr. Heath Newton's The Negro (red cap, cinnamon jacket).
2. Colonel Wardlaw's Pugilist (pink cap, blue and black jacket).
3. Lord Backwater's Desborough (yellow cap and sleeves).
4. Colonel Ross's Silver Blaze (black cap, red jacket).
5. Duke of Balmoral's Iris (yellow and black stripes).
6. Lord Singleford's Rasper (purple cap, black sleeves).

"We scratched our other one and put all hopes on your word," said the Colonel. "Why, what is that? Silver Blaze favourite?"

"Five to four against Silver Blaze!" roared the ring. "Five to four against Silver Blaze! Fifteen to five against Desborough! Five to four on the field!"

"There are the numbers up," I cried. "They are all six there."

"All six there! Then my horse is running," cried the Colonel, in great agitation. "But I don't see him. My colours have not passed."

"Only five have passed. This must be he."

As I spoke a powerful bay horse swept out from the weighing inclosure and cantered past us, bearing on its back the well-known black and red of the Colonel.

"That's not my horse," cried the owner. "That beast has not a white hair upon its body. What is this that you have done, Mr. Holmes?"

"Well, well, let us see how he gets on," said my friend, imperturbably. For a few minutes he gazed through my field-glass. "Capital! An excellent start!" he cried suddenly. "There they are, coming round the curve!"

From our drag we had a superb view as they came up the straight. The six horses were so close together that a carpet could have covered them, but half way up the yellow of the Mapleton stable showed to the front. Before they reached us, however, Desborough's bolt was shot, and the Colonel's horse, coming away with a rush, passed the post a good six lengths before its rival, the Duke of Balmoral's Iris making a bad third.

"It's my race anyhow," gasped the Colonel, passing his hand over his eyes. "I confess that I can make neither head nor tail of it. Don't you think that you have kept up your mystery long enough, Mr. Holmes?"

"Certainly, Colonel. You shall know everything. Let us all go round and have a look at the horse together. Here he is," he continued, as we made our way into the weighing inclosure where only owners and their friends find admittance. "You have only to wash his face and his leg in spirits of wine and you will find that he is the same old Silver Blaze as ever."

"You take my breath away!"

"I found him in the hands of a faker, and took the liberty of running him just as he was sent over."

"My dear sir, you have done wonders. The horse looks very fit and well. It never went better in its life. I owe you a thousand apologies for having doubted your ability. You have done me a great service by recovering my horse. You would do me a greater still if you could lay your hands on the murderer of John Straker."

"I have done so," said Holmes, quietly.

The Colonel and I stared at him in amazement. "You have got him! Where is he, then?"

"He is here."

"Here! Where?"

"In my company at the present moment."

The Colonel flushed angrily. "I quite recognise that I am under obligations to you, Mr. Holmes," said he, "but I must regard what you have just said as either a very bad joke or an insult."

Sherlock Holmes laughed. "I assure you that I have not associated you with the entirely unworthy of your confidence. But there goes the bell ; and as I stand to win a little on this next race, I shall defer a more lengthy explanation until a more fitting time."

We had the corner of a Pullman car to

HE LAID HIS HAND UPON THE GLOSSY NECK.

crime, Colonel," said he ; "the real murderer is standing immediately behind you ! "

He stepped past and laid his hand upon the glossy neck of the thoroughbred.

" The horse ! " cried both the Colonel and myself.

" Yes, the horse. And it may lessen his guilt if I say that it was done in self-defence, and that John Straker was a man who was ourselves that evening as we whirled back to London, and I fancy that the journey was a short one to Colonel Ross as well as to myself, as we listened to our companion's narrative of the events which had occurred at the Dartmoor training stables upon that Monday night, and the means by which he had unravelled them.

" I confess," said he, " that any theories

which I had formed from the newspaper reports were entirely erroneous. And yet there were indications there, had they not been overlaid by other details which concealed their true import. I went to Devonshire with the conviction that Fitzroy Simpson was the true culprit, although, of course, I saw that the evidence against him was by no means complete.

"It was while I was in the carriage, just as we reached the trainer's house, that the immense significance of the curried mutton occurred to me. You may remember that I was distrait, and remained sitting after you had all alighted. I was marvelling in my own mind how I could possibly have overlooked so obvious a clue."

" I confess," said the Colonel, "that even now I cannot see how it helps us."

"It was the first link in my chain of reasoning. Powdered opium is by no means tasteless. The flavour is not disagreeable, but it is perceptible. Were it mixed with any ordinary dish, the eater would undoubtedly detect it, and would probably eat no more. A curry was exactly the medium which would disguise this taste. By no possible supposition could this stranger, Fitzroy Simpson, have caused curry to be served in the trainer's family that night, and it is surely too monstrous a coincidence to suppose that he happened to come along with powdered opium upon the very night when a dish happened to be served which would disguise the flavour. That is unthinkable. Therefore Simpson becomes eliminated from the case and our attention centres upon Straker and his wife, the only two people who could have chosen curried mutton for supper that night. The opium was added after the dish was set aside for the stable-boy, for the others had the same for supper with no ill effects. Which of them, then, had access to that dish without the maid seeing them ?

" Before deciding that question I had grasped the significance of the silence of the dog, for one true inference invariably suggests others. The Simpson incident had shown me that a dog was kept in the stables, and yet, though someone had been in and had fetched out a horse, he had not barked enough to arouse the two lads in the loft. Obviously the midnight visitor was someone whom the dog knew well.

"I was already convinced, or almost convinced, that John Straker went down to the stables in the dead of the night and took out Silver Blaze. For what purpose? For a dishonest one, obviously, or why should he drug his own stable-boy ? And yet I was at a loss to know why. There have been cases before now where trainers have made sure of great sums of money by laying against their own horses, through agents, and then preventing them from winning by fraud. Sometimes it is a pulling jockey. Sometimes it is some surer and subtler means. What was it here ? I hoped that the contents of his pockets might help me to form a conclusion.

"And they did so. You cannot have forgotten the singular knife which was found in the dead man's hand, a knife which certainly no sane man would choose for a weapon. It was, as Dr. Watson told us, a form of knife which is used for the most delicate operations known in surgery. And it was to be used for a delicate operation that night. You must know, with your wide experience of turf matters, Colonel Ross, that it is possible to make a slight nick upon the tendons of a horse's ham, and to do it subcutaneously so as to leave absolutely no trace. A horse so treated would develop a slight lameness which would be put down to a strain in exercise or a touch of rheumatism, but never to foul play."

" Villain ! Scoundrel ! " cried the Colonel.

"We have here the explanation of why John Straker wished to take the horse out on to the moor. So spirited a creature would have certainly roused the soundest of sleepers when it felt the prick of the knife. It was absolutely necessary to do it in the open air."

" I have been blind !" cried the Colonel. " Of course, that was why he needed the candle, and struck the match."

" Undoubtedly. But in examining his belongings, I was fortunate enough to discover, not only the method of the crime, but even its motives. As a man of the world, Colonel, you know that men do not carry other people's bills about in their pockets. We have most of us quite enough to do to settle our own. I at once concluded that Straker was leading a double life, and keeping a second establishment. The nature of the bill showed that there was a lady in the case, and one who had expensive tastes. Liberal as you are with your servants, one hardly expects that they can buy twenty - guinea walking dresses for their women. I questioned Mrs. Straker as to the dress without her knowing it, and having satisfied myself that it had never reached her, I made a note of the milliner's address, and felt that by calling there with Straker's photograph, I could easily dispose of the mythical Darbyshire.

" From that time on all was plain. Straker

had led out the horse to a hollow where his light would be invisible. Simpson, in his flight, had dropped his cravat, and Straker had picked it up with some idea, perhaps, that he might use it in securing the horse's leg. Once in the hollow he had got behind the horse, and had struck a light, but the creature, frightened at the sudden glare, and with the strange instinct of animals feeling that some mischief was intended, had lashed out, and the steel shoe had struck Straker full on the forehead. He had already, in spite of the rain, taken off his overcoat in order to do his delicate task, and so, as he fell, his knife gashed his thigh. Do I make it clear?"

"Wonderful!" cried the Colonel. "Wonderful! You might have been there."

"My final shot was, I confess, a very long one. It struck me that so astute a man as Straker would not undertake this delicate tendon - nicking without a little practice. What could he practise on? My eyes fell upon the sheep, and I asked a question which, rather to my surprise, showed that my surmise was correct."

"You have made it perfectly clear, Mr. Holmes."

"When I returned to London I called upon the milliner, who at once recognised Straker as an excellent customer, of the name of Darbyshire, who had a very dashing wife with a strong partiality for expensive dresses. I have no doubt that this woman had plunged him over head and ears in debt, and so led him into this miserable plot."

"You have explained all but one thing," cried the Colonel. "Where was the horse?"

"Ah, it bolted and was cared for by one of your neighbours. We must have an amnesty in that direction, I think. This is Clapham Junction, if I am not mistaken, and we shall be in Victoria in less than ten minutes. If you care to smoke a cigar in our rooms, Colonel, I shall be happy to give you any other details which might interest you."

SILVER BLAZE

The Adventures of Sherlock Holmes.

XIV.—THE ADVENTURE OF THE CARDBOARD BOX.

By Conan Doyle.

IN choosing a few typical cases which illustrate the remarkable mental qualities of my friend, Sherlock Holmes, I have endeavoured, as far as possible, to select those which presented the minimum of sensationalism, while offering a fair field for his talents. It is, however, unfortunately, impossible to entirely separate the sensational from the criminal, and a chronicler is left in the dilemma that he must either sacrifice details which are essential to his statement, and so give a false impression of the problem, or he must use matter which chance, and not choice, has provided him with. With this short preface I shall turn to my notes of what proved to be a strange, though a peculiarly terrible, chain of events.

It was a blazing hot day in August. Baker Street was like an oven, and the glare of the sunlight upon the yellow brickwork of the houses across the road was painful to the eye. It was hard to believe that these were the same walls which loomed so gloomily through the fogs of winter. Our blinds were half-drawn, and Holmes lay curled upon the sofa, reading and re-reading a letter which he had received by the morning post. For myself, my term of service in India had trained me to stand heat better than cold, and a thermometer at 90 was no hardship. But the morning paper was uninteresting.

Parliament had risen. Everybody was out of town, and I yearned for the glades of the New Forest or the shingle of Southsea. A depleted bank account had caused me to postpone my holiday, and as to my companion, neither the country nor the sea presented the slightest attraction to him. He loved to lie in the very centre of five millions of people, with his filaments stretching out and running through them, responsive to every little rumour or suspicion of unsolved crime. Appreciation of Nature found no place among his many gifts, and his only change was when he turned his mind from the evil-doer of the town to track down his brother of the country.

Finding that Holmes was too absorbed for conversation I had tossed aside the barren paper and, leaning back in my chair, I fell into a brown study. Suddenly my companion's voice broke in upon my thoughts.

"You are right, Watson," said he. "It does seem a most preposterous way of settling a dispute."

"I FELL INTO A BROWN STUDY."

307

"Most preposterous!" I exclaimed, and then suddenly realizing how he had echoed the inmost thought of my soul, I sat up in my chair and stared at him in blank amazement.

"What is this, Holmes?" I cried. "This is beyond anything which I could have imagined."

He laughed heartily at my perplexity.

"You remember," said he, "that some little time ago when I read you the passage in one of Poe's sketches in which a close reasoner follows the unspoken thoughts of his companion, you were inclined to treat the matter as a mere *tour-de-force* of the author. On my remarking that I was constantly in the habit of doing the same thing you expressed incredulity."

"Oh, no!"

"Perhaps not with your tongue, my dear Watson, but certainly with your eyebrows. So when I saw you throw down your paper and enter upon a train of thought, I was very happy to have the opportunity of reading it off, and eventually of breaking into it, as a proof that I had been in rapport with you."

But I was still far from satisfied. "In the example which you read to me," said I, "the reasoner drew his conclusions from the actions of the man whom he observed. If I remember right, he stumbled over a heap of stones, looked up at the stars, and so on. But I have been seated quietly in my chair, and what clues can I have given you?"

"You do yourself an injustice. The features are given to man as the means by which he shall express his emotions, and yours are faithful servants."

"Do you mean to say that you read my train of thoughts from my features?"

"Your features, and especially your eyes. Perhaps you cannot yourself recall how your reverie commenced?"

"No, I cannot."

"Then I will tell you. After throwing down your paper, which was the action which drew my attention to you, you sat for half a minute with a vacant expression. Then your eyes fixed themselves upon your newly-framed picture of General Gordon, and I saw by the alteration in your face that a train of thought had been started. But it did not lead very far. Your eyes flashed across to the unframed portrait of Henry Ward Beecher which stands upon the top of your books. You then glanced up at the wall, and of course your meaning was obvious. You were thinking that if the portrait were framed, it would just cover that bare space and correspond with Gordon's picture over there."

"You have followed me wonderfully!" I exclaimed.

"So far I could hardly have gone astray. But now your thoughts went back to Beecher, and you looked hard across as if you were studying the character in his features. Then your eyes ceased to pucker, but you continued to look across, and your face was thoughtful. You were recalling the incidents of Beecher's career. I was well aware that you could not do this without thinking of the mission which he undertook on behalf of the North at the time of the Civil War, for I remember your expressing your passionate indignation at the way in which he was received by the more turbulent of our people. You felt so strongly about it, that I knew you could not think of Beecher without thinking of that also. When a moment later I saw your eyes wander away from the picture, I suspected that your mind had now turned to the Civil War, and when I observed that your lips set, your eyes sparkled, and your hands clenched, I was positive that you were indeed thinking of the gallantry which was shown by both sides in that desperate struggle. But then, again, your face grew sadder; you shook your head. You were dwelling upon the sadness and horror and useless waste of life. Your hand stole towards your own old wound and a smile quivered on your lips, which showed me that the ridiculous side of this method of settling international questions had forced itself upon your mind. At this point I agreed with you that it was preposterous, and was glad to find that all my deductions had been correct."

"Absolutely!" said I. "And now that you have explained it, I confess that I am as amazed as before."

"It was very superficial, my dear Watson, I assure you. I should not have intruded it upon your attention had you not shown some incredulity the other day. But I have in my hands here a little problem which may prove to be more difficult of solution than my small essay in thought reading. Have you observed in the paper a short paragraph referring to the remarkable contents of a packet sent through the post to Miss Susan Cushing, of Cross Street, Croydon?"

"No, I saw nothing."

"Ah! then you must have overlooked it. Just toss it over to me. Here it is, under the financial column. Perhaps you would be good enough to read it aloud."

I picked up the paper which he had

thrown back to me, and read the paragraph indicated. It was headed, "A Gruesome Packet."

"Miss Susan Cushing, living at Cross Street, Croydon, has been made the victim of what must be regarded as a peculiarly revolting practical joke, unless some more sinister meaning should prove to be attached to the incident. At two o'clock yesterday afternoon a small packet, wrapped in brown paper, was handed in by the postman. A cardboard box was inside, which was filled with coarse salt. On emptying this, Miss Cushing was horrified to find two human ears, apparently quite freshly severed. The box had been sent by parcel post from Belfast upon the morning before. There is no indication as to the sender, and the matter is the more mysterious as Miss Cushing, who is a maiden lady of fifty, has led a most retired life, and has so few acquaintances or correspondents that it is a rare event for her to receive anything through the post. Some years ago, however, when she resided at Penge, she let apartments in her house to three young medical students, whom she was obliged to get rid of on account of their noisy and irregular habits. The police are of opinion that this outrage may have been perpetrated upon Miss Cushing by these youths, who owed her a grudge, and who hoped to frighten her by sending her these relics of the dissecting-rooms. Some probability is lent to the theory by the fact that one of these students came from the north of Ireland, and, to the best of Miss Cushing's belief, from Belfast. In the meantime, the matter is being actively investigated, Mr. Lestrade, one of the very smartest of our detective officers, being in charge of the case."

"So much for the *Daily Chronicle*," said Holmes, as I finished reading. "Now for our friend Lestrade. I had a note from him this morning, in which

he says : ' I think that this case is very much in your line. We have every hope of clearing the matter up, but we find a little difficulty in getting anything to work upon. We have, of course, wired to the Belfast post-office, but a large number of parcels were handed in upon that day, and they have no means of identifying this particular one, or of remembering the sender. The box is a half-pound box of honeydew tobacco, and does not help us in any way. The medical student theory still appears to me to be the most feasible, but if you should have a few hours to spare, I should be very happy to see you out here. I shall be either at the house or in the police-station all day.' What say you, Watson? Can you rise superior to the heat, and run down to Croydon with me on the off chance of a case for your annals ?"

"I was longing for something to do."

"You shall have it, then. Ring for our boots, and tell them to order a cab. I'll be back in a moment, when I have changed my dressing-gown and filled my cigar-case."

A shower of rain fell while we were in the train, and the heat was far less oppressive in Croydon than in town. Holmes had sent on a wire, so that Lestrade, as wiry, as dapper, and as ferret-like as ever, was waiting for us at the station. A walk of five minutes took us to Cross Street, where Miss Cushing resided.

"MISS CUSHING."

It was a very long street of two-story brick houses, neat and prim, with whitened stone steps and little groups of aproned women gossiping at the doors. Half-way down, Lestrade stopped and tapped at a door, which was opened by a small servant girl. Miss Cushing was sitting in the front room, into which we were ushered. She was a placid-faced woman with large, gentle eyes, and grizzled hair curving down over her temples on each side. A worked antimacassar lay upon her lap and a basket of coloured silks stood upon a stool beside her.

" They are in the outhouse, those dreadful things," said she, as Lestrade entered. " I wish that you would take them away altogether."

" So I shall, Miss Cushing. I only kept them here until my friend, Mr. Holmes, should have seen them in your presence."

" Why in my presence, sir ? "

" In case he wished to ask any questions."

" What is the use of asking me questions, when I tell you that I know nothing whatever about it ? "

" Quite so, madam," said Holmes, in his soothing way. " I have no doubt that you have been annoyed more than enough already over this business."

" Indeed, I have, sir. I am a quiet woman and live a retired life. It is something new for me to see my name in the papers and to find the police in my house. I won't have those things in here, Mr. Lestrade. If you wish to see them you must go to the outhouse."

It was a small shed in the narrow garden which ran down behind the house. Lestrade went in and brought out a yellow cardboard box, with a piece of brown paper and some string. There was a bench at the edge of the path, and we all sat down while Holmes examined, one by one, the articles which Lestrade had handed to him.

" The string is exceedingly interesting," he remarked, holding it up to the light and sniffing at it. " What do you make of this string, Lestrade ? "

" It has been tarred."

" Precisely. It is a piece of tarred twine. You have also, no doubt, re

marked that Miss Cushing has cut the cord with a scissors, as can be seen by the double fray on each side. This is of importance."

" I cannot see the importance," said Lestrade.

" The importance lies in the fact that the knot is left intact, and that this knot is of a peculiar character."

" It is very neatly tied. I had already made a note to that effect," said Lestrade, complacently.

" So much for the string then," said Holmes, smiling; " now for the box wrapper. Brown paper, with a distinct smell of coffee. What, you did not observe it ? I think there can be no doubt of it. Address printed in rather straggling characters : ' Miss S. Cushing, Cross Street, Croydon.' Done with a broad pointed pen, probably a J, and with very inferior ink. The word Croydon has been spelt originally with an i, which has been changed to y. The parcel was directed, then, by a man—the printing is distinctly masculine—of limited education and unacquainted with the town of Croydon. So far, so good ! The box is a yellow, half-pound honeydew box, with nothing distinctive save two thumb marks at the left bottom corner. It is filled with rough salt of the quality used for preserving hides and other of the coarser commercial purposes. And embedded in it are these very singular inclosures."

He took out the two ears as he spoke, and laying a board across his knees, he examined them minutely, while Lestrade and I, bending forward on each side of him, glanced

" HE EXAMINED THEM MINUTELY.'

alternately at these dreadful relics and at the thoughtful, eager face of our companion. Finally he returned them to the box once more, and sat for a while in deep thought.

"You have observed, of course," said he at last, "that the ears are not a pair."

"Yes, I have noticed that. But if this were the practical joke of some students from the dissecting-rooms, it would be as easy for them to send two odd ears as a pair."

"Precisely. But this is not a practical joke."

"You are sure of it?"

"The presumption is strongly against it. Bodies in the dissecting-rooms are injected with preservative fluid. These ears bear no signs of this. They are fresh, too. They have been cut off with a blunt instrument, which would hardly happen if a student had done it. Again, carbolic or rectified spirits would be the preservatives which would suggest themselves to the medical mind, certainly not rough salt. I repeat that there is no practical joke here, but that we are investigating a serious crime."

A vague thrill ran through me as I listened to my companion's words and saw the stern gravity which had hardened his features. This brutal preliminary seemed to shadow forth some strange and inexplicable horror in the background. Lestrade, however, shook his head like a man who is only half convinced.

"There are objections to the joke theory, no doubt," said he; "but there are much stronger reasons against the other. We know that this woman has led a most quiet and respectable life at Penge and here for the last twenty years. She has hardly been away from her home for a day during that time. Why on earth, then, should any criminal send her the proofs of his guilt, especially as, unless she is a most consummate actress, she understands quite as little of the matter as we do?"

"That is the problem which we have to solve," Holmes answered, "and for my part I shall set about it by presuming that my reasoning is correct, and that a double murder has been committed. One of these ears is a woman's, small, finely formed, and pierced for an earring. The other is a man's, sunburned, discoloured, and also pierced for an earring. These two people are presumably dead, or we should have heard their story before now. To-day is Friday. The packet was posted on Thursday morning. The tragedy, then, occurred on Wednesday or Tuesday, or earlier. If the two people were murdered, who but their murderer would have sent this sign of his work to Miss Cushing? We may take it that the sender of the packet is the man whom we want. But he must have some strong reason for sending Miss Cushing this packet. What reason, then? It must have been to tell her that the deed was done; or to pain her, perhaps. But in that case she knows who it is. Does she know? I doubt it. If she knew, why should she call the police in? She might have buried the ears, and no one would have been the wiser. That is what she would have done if she had wished to shield the criminal. But if she does not wish to shield him she would give his name. There is a tangle here which needs straightening out." He had been talking in a high, quick voice, staring blankly up over the garden fence, but now he sprang briskly to his feet and walked towards the house.

"I have a few questions to ask Miss Cushing," said he.

"In that case I may leave you here," said Lestrade, "for I have another small business on hand. I think that I have nothing further to learn from Miss Cushing. You will find me at the police-station."

"We shall look in on our way to the train," answered Holmes. A moment later he and I were back in the front room, where the impassive lady was still quietly working away at her antimacassar. She put it down on her lap as we entered, and looked at us with her frank, searching blue eyes.

"I am convinced, sir," she said, "that this matter is a mistake, and that the parcel was never meant for me at all. I have said this several times to the gentleman from Scotland Yard, but he simply laughs at me. I have not an enemy in the world, as far as I know, so why should anyone play me such a trick?"

"I am coming to be of the same opinion, Miss Cushing," said Holmes, taking a seat beside her. "I think that it is more than probable——" he paused, and I was surprised on glancing round to see that he was staring with singular intentness at the lady's profile. Surprise and satisfaction were both for an instant to be read upon his eager face, though when she glanced round to find out the cause of his silence he had become as demure as ever. I stared hard myself at her flat, grizzled hair, her trim cap, her little gilt earrings, her placid features; but I could see nothing which could account for my companion's evident excitement.

"There were one or two questions——"

"Oh, I am weary of questions!" cried Miss Cushing, impatiently.

"You have two sisters, I believe."

"How could you know that?"

"I observed the very instant that I entered the room that you have a portrait group of three ladies upon the mantelpiece, one of whom is undoubtedly yourself, while the others are so exceedingly like you that there could be no doubt of the relationship."

"Yes, you are quite right. Those are my sisters, Sarah and Mary."

"And here at my elbow is another portrait, taken at Liverpool, of your younger sister, in the company of a man who appears to be a steward by his uniform. I observe that she was unmarried at the time."

"You are very quick at observing."

"That is my trade."

"Well, you are quite right. But she was married to Mr. Browner a few days afterwards. He was on the South American line when that was taken, but he was so fond of her that he couldn't abide to leave her for so long, and he got into the Liverpool and London boats."

"Ah, the *Conqueror*, perhaps?"

"No, the *May Day*, when last I heard. Jim came down here to see me once. That was before he broke the pledge; but afterwards he would always take drink when he was ashore, and a little drink would send him stark, staring mad. Ah! it was a bad day that ever he took a glass in his hand again. First he dropped me, and then he quarrelled with Sarah, and now that Mary has stopped writing we don't know how things are going with them."

It was evident that Miss Cushing had come upon a subject on which she felt very deeply. Like most people who lead a lonely life, she was shy at first, but ended by becoming extremely communicative. She told us many details about her brother-in-law the steward, and then wandering off on to the subject of her former lodgers, the medical students, she gave us a long account of their delinquencies, with their names and those of their hospitals

Holmes listened attentively to everything, throwing in a question from time to time.

"About your second sister, Sarah," said he. "I wonder, since you are both maiden ladies, that you do not keep house together."

"Ah! you don't know Sarah's temper, or you would wonder no more. I tried it when I came to Croydon, and we kept on until about two months ago, when we had to part. I don't want to say a word against my own sister, but she was always meddlesome and hard to please, was Sarah."

"You say that she quarrelled with your Liverpool relations."

"Yes, and they were the best of friends at one time. Why, she went up there to live just in order to be near them. And now she has no word hard enough for Jim Browner. The last six months that she was here she would speak of nothing but his drinking and his ways. He had caught her meddling, I suspect, and given her a bit of his mind, and that was the start of it."

"Thank you, Miss Cushing," said Holmes, rising and bowing. "Your sister Sarah lives, I think you said, at New Street, Wallington? Good-bye, and I am very sorry that you should have been troubled over a case with which, as you say, you have nothing whatever to do."

There was a cab passing as we came out, and Holmes hailed it.

"How far to Wallington?" he asked.

"Only about a mile, sir."

"HOW FAR TO WALLINGTON?"

"Very good. Jump in, Watson. We must strike while the iron is hot. Simple as the case is, there have been one or two very instructive details in connection with it. Just pull up at a telegraph office as you pass, cabby."

Holmes sent off a short wire, and for the rest of the drive lay back in the cab with his hat tilted over his nose to keep the sun from his face. Our driver pulled up at a house which was not unlike the one which we had just quitted. My companion ordered him to wait, and had his hand upon the knocker, when the door opened and a grave young gentleman in black, with a very shiny hat, appeared on the step.

"Is Miss Sarah Cushing at home?" asked Holmes.

"Miss Sarah Cushing is extremely ill," said he. "She has been suffering since yesterday from brain symptoms of great severity. As her medical adviser, I cannot possibly take the responsibility of allowing anyone to see her. I should recommend you to call again in ten days." He drew on his gloves, closed the door, and marched off down the street.

"Well, if we can't, we can't," said Holmes, cheerfully.

"Perhaps she could not, or would not have told you much."

"I did not wish her to tell me anything. I only wanted to look at her. However, I think that I have got all that I want. Drive us to some decent hotel, cabby, where we may have some lunch, and afterwards we shall drop down upon friend Lestrade at the police-station."

We had a pleasant little meal together, during which Holmes would talk about nothing but violins, narrating with great exultation how he had purchased his own Stradivarius, which was worth at least five hundred guineas, at a Jew broker's in Tottenham Court Road for fifty-five shillings. This led him to Paganini, and we sat for an hour over a bottle of claret while he told me anecdote after anecdote of that extraordinary man. The afternoon was far advanced and the hot glare had softened into a mellow glow before we found ourselves at the police-station. Lestrade was waiting for us at the door.

"A telegram for you, Mr Holmes," said he.

"Ha! It is the answer!" He tore it open, glanced his eyes over it, and crumpled it into his pocket. "That's all right," said he.

"Have you found out anything?"

"I have found out everything!"

"What!" Lestrade stared at him in amazement. "You are joking."

"I was never more serious in my life. A shocking crime has been committed, and I think that I have now laid bare every detail of it."

"And the criminal?"

Holmes scribbled a few words upon the back of one of his visiting cards and threw it over to Lestrade.

"That is it," he said; "you cannot effect an arrest until to-morrow night at the earliest. I should prefer that you would not mention my name at all in connection with the case, as I choose to be associated only with those crimes which present some difficulty in their solution. Come on, Watson." We strode off together to the station, leaving Lestrade still staring with a delighted face at the card which Holmes had thrown him.

"The case," said Sherlock Holmes, as we chatted over our cigars that night in our rooms at Baker Street, "is one where, as in the investigations which you have chronicled under the names of the 'Study in Scarlet' and of the 'Sign of Four,' we have been compelled to reason backward from effects to causes. I have written to Lestrade asking him to supply us with the details which are now wanting, and which he will only get after he has secured his man. That he may be safely trusted to do, for although he is absolutely devoid of reason, he is as tenacious as a bulldog when he once understands what he has to do, and indeed it is just this tenacity which has brought him to the top at Scotland Yard."

"Your case is not complete, then?" I asked.

"It is fairly complete in essentials. We know who the author of the revolting business is, although one of the victims still escapes us. Of course, you have formed your own conclusions."

"I presume that this Jim Browner, the steward of a Liverpool boat, is the man whom you suspect?"

"Oh! it is more than a suspicion."

"And yet I cannot see anything save very vague indications."

"On the contrary, to my mind nothing could be more clear. Let me run over the principal steps. We approached the case, you remember, with an absolutely blank mind, which is always an advantage. We had formed no theories. We were simply there to observe and to draw inferences from our observations. What did we see first?

A very placid and respectable lady, who seemed quite innocent of any secret, and a portrait which showed me that she had two younger sisters. It instantly flashed across my mind that the box might have been meant for one of these. I set the idea aside as one which could be disproved or confirmed at our leisure. Then we went to the garden, as you remember, and we saw the very singular contents of the little yellow box.

"The string was of the quality which is used by sail-makers aboard ship, and at once a whiff of the sea was perceptible in our investigation. When I observed that the knot was one which is popular with sailors, that the parcel had been posted at a port, and that the male ear was pierced for an earring which is so much more common among sailors than landsmen, I was quite certain that all the actors in the tragedy were to be found among our seafaring classes.

"When I came to examine the address of the packet I observed that it was to Miss S. Cushing. Now, the oldest sister would, of course, be Miss Cushing, and although her initial was 'S.,' it might belong to one of the others as well. In that case we should have to commence our investigation from a fresh basis altogether. I therefore went into the house with the intention of clearing up this point. I was about to assure Miss Cushing that I was convinced that a mistake had been made, when you may remember that I came suddenly to a stop. The fact was that I had just seen something which filled me with surprise, and at the same time narrowed the field of our inquiry immensely.

"As a medical man, you are aware, Watson, that there is no part of the body which varies so much as the human ear. Each ear is as a rule quite distinctive, and differs from all other ones. In last year's *Anthropological Journal* you will find two short monographs from my

"JIM BROWNER."

pen upon the subject. I had therefore examined the ears in the box with the eyes of an expert, and had carefully noted their anatomical peculiarities. Imagine my surprise then, when, on looking at Miss Cushing, I perceived that her ear corresponded exactly with the female ear which I had just inspected. The matter was entirely beyond coincidence. There was the same shortening of the pinna, the same broad curve of the upper lobe, the same convolution of the inner cartilage. In all essentials it was the same ear.

"Of course, I at once saw the enormous importance of the observation. It was evident that the victim was a blood relation, and probably a very close one. I began to talk to her about her family, and you remember that she at once gave us some exceedingly valuable details.

"In the first place, her sister's name was Sarah, and her address had, until recently, been the same, so that it was quite obvious how the mistake had occurred, and whom the packet was meant for. Then we heard of this steward, married to the third sister, and learned that he had at one time been so intimate with Miss Sarah that she had actually gone up to Liverpool to be near the Browners, but a quarrel had afterwards divided them. This quarrel had put a stop to all communications for some months, so that if Browner had occasion to address a packet to Miss Sarah, he would undoubtedly have done so to her old address.

"And now the matter had begun to straighten itself out wonderfully. We had learned of the existence of this steward, an impulsive man, of strong passions — you remember that he threw up what must have been a very superior berth, in order to be nearer to his wife—subject, too, to occasional fits of hard drinking. We had reason to believe that his wife had been murdered, and that a man—presumably a seafaring man

—had been murdered at the same time. Jealousy, of course, at once suggests itself as the motive for the crime. And why should these proofs of the deed be sent to Miss Sarah Cushing? Probably because during her residence in Liverpool she had some hand in bringing about the events which led to the tragedy. You will observe that this line of boats calls at Belfast, Dublin, and Waterford; so that, presuming that Browner had committed the deed, and had embarked at once upon his steamer, the *May Day*, Belfast would be the first place at which he could post his terrible packet.

"A second solution was at this stage obviously possible, and although I thought it exceedingly unlikely, I was determined to elucidate it before going further. An unsuccessful lover might have killed Mr. and Mrs. Browner, and the male ear might have belonged to the husband. There were many grave objections to this theory, but it was conceivable. I therefore sent off a telegram to my friend Algar, of the Liverpool force, and asked him to find out if Mrs. Browner were at home, and if Browner had departed in the *May Day*. Then we went on to Wallington to visit Miss Sarah.

"I was curious, in the first place, to see how far the family ear had been reproduced in her. Then, of course, she might give us very important information, but I was not sanguine that she would. She must have heard of the business the day before, since all Croydon was ringing with it, and she alone could have understood whom the packet was meant for. If she had been willing to help justice she would probably have communicated with the police already. However, it was clearly our duty to see her, so we went. We found that the news of the arrival of the packet—for her illness dated from that time—had such an effect upon her as to bring on brain fever. It was clearer than ever that she understood its full significance, but equally clear that we should have to wait some time for any assistance from her.

"However, we were really independent of her help. Our answers were waiting for us at the police-station, where I had directed Algar to send them. Nothing could be more conclusive. Mrs. Browner's house had been closed for more than three days, and the neighbours were of opinion that she had gone south to see her relatives. It had been ascertained at the shipping offices that Browner had left aboard of the *May Day*, and I calculate that she is due in the Thames tomorrow night. When he arrives he will be met by the obtuse but resolute Lestrade, and I have no doubt that we shall have all our details filled in."

Sherlock Holmes was not disappointed in his expectations. Two days later he received a bulky envelope, which contained a short note from the detective, and a type-written document, which covered several pages of foolscap.

"Lestrade has got him all right," said Holmes, glancing up at me. "Perhaps it would interest you to hear what he says."

"My dear Mr. Holmes,—In accordance with the scheme which we had formed in order to test our theories"—"the 'we' is rather fine, Watson, is it not?"—"I went down to the Albert Dock yesterday at 6 p.m., and boarded the ss. *May Day*, belonging to the Liverpool, Dublin, and London Steam Packet Company. On inquiry, I found that there was a steward on board of the name of James Browner, and that he had acted during the voyage in such an extraordinary manner that the captain had been compelled to relieve him of his duties. On descending to his berth, I found him seated upon a chest with his head sunk upon his hands, rocking himself to and fro. He is a big, powerful chap, clean-shaven, and very swarthy—something like Aldridge, who helped us in the bogus laundry affair. He jumped up when he heard my business, and I had my whistle to my lips to call a couple of river police, who were round the corner, but he seemed to have no heart in him, and he held out his hands quietly enough for the darbies. We brought him along to the cells, and his box as well, for we thought there might be something incriminating; but, bar a big sharp knife, such as most sailors have, we got nothing for our trouble. However, we find that we shall want no more evidence, for, on being brought before the inspector at the station, he asked leave to make a statement, which was, of course, taken down, just as he made it, by our shorthand man. We had three copies type-written, one of which I inclose. The affair proves, as I always thought it would, to be an extremely simple one, but I am obliged to you for assisting me in my investigation. With kind regards, yours very truly,—G. LESTRADE."

"Hum! The investigation really was a very simple one," remarked Holmes; "but I don't think it struck him in that light when he first called us in. However, let us see what Jim Browner has to say for himself. This is his statement, as made before Inspector Mont-

"HE HELD OUT HIS HANDS QUIETLY."

gomery at the Shadwell Police Station, and it has the advantage of being verbatim."

"Have I anything to say? Yes, I have a deal to say. I have to make a clean breast of it all. You can hang me, or you can leave me alone. I don't care a plug which you do. I tell you I've not shut an eye in sleep since I did it, and I don't believe I ever will again until I get past all waking. Sometimes it's his face, but most generally it's hers. I'm never without one or the other before me. He looks frowning and black-like, but she has a kind o' surprise upon her face. Aye, the white lamb, she might well be surprised when she read death on a face that had seldom looked anything but love upon her before.

"But it was Sarah's fault, and may the curse of a broken man put a blight on her and set the blood rotting in her veins! It's not that I want to clear myself. I know that I went back to drink, like the beast that I was. But she would have forgiven me; she would have stuck as close to me as a rope to a block if that woman had never darkened our door. For Sarah Cushing loved me—that's the root of the business—she loved me, until all her love turned to poisonous hate when she knew that I thought more of my wife's foot-

mark in the mud than I did of her whole body and soul.

"There were three sisters altogether. The old one was just a good woman, the second was a devil, and the third was an angel. Sarah was thirty-three, and Mary was twenty-nine when I married. We were just as happy as the day was long when we set up house together, and in all Liverpool there was no better woman than my Mary. And then we asked Sarah up for a week, and the week grew into a month, and one thing led to another, until she was just one of ourselves.

"I was blue ribbon at that time, and we were putting a little money by, and all was as bright as a new dollar. My God, whoever would have thought that it could have come to this? Whoever would have dreamed it?

"I used to be home for the week-ends very often, and sometimes if the ship were held back for cargo I would have a whole week at a time, and in this way I saw a deal of my sister-in-law, Sarah. She was a fine tall woman, black and quick and fierce, with a proud way of carrying her head, and a glint from her eye like the spark from a flint. But when little Mary was there I had never a thought for her, and that I swear as I hope for God's mercy.

"It had seemed to me sometimes that she liked to be alone with me, or to coax me out for a walk with her, but I had never thought anything of that. But one evening my eyes were opened. I had come up from the ship and found my wife out, but Sarah at home. 'Where's Mary?' I asked. 'Oh, she has gone to pay some accounts.' I was impatient and paced up and down the room. 'Can't you be happy for five minutes without Mary, Jim?' says she. 'It's a bad compliment to me that you can't be contented with my society for so short a time.' 'That's all right, my lass," said I, putting out my hand towards her in a kindly way, but she had it in both hers in an instant, and they burned as if they were in a fever. I looked into her eyes and I read it all there. There was no need for her to speak, nor for me either. I frowned and drew my hand away. Then she stood by my side in silence for a bit, and then put up her hand and patted me on the shoulder.

" ' THAT'S ALL RIGHT, MY LASS,' SAID I."

'Steady old Jim!' said she; and, with a kind o' mocking laugh, she ran out of the room.

"Well, from that time Sarah hated me with her whole heart and soul, and she is a woman who can hate, too. I was a fool to let her go on biding with us—a besotted fool—but I never said a word to Mary, for I knew it would grieve her. Things went on much as before, but after a time I began to find that there was a bit of a change in Mary herself. She had always been so trusting and so innocent, but now she became queer and suspicious, wanting to know where I had been and what I had been doing, and whom my letters were from, and what I had in my pockets, and a thousand such follies. Day by day she grew queerer and more irritable, and we had causeless rows about nothing. I was fairly puzzled by it all. Sarah avoided me now, but she and Mary were just inseparable. I can see now how she was plotting and scheming and poisoning my wife's mind against me, but I was such a blind beetle that I could not understand it at the time. Then I broke my blue ribbon and began to drink again, but I think I should not have done it if Mary had been the same as ever. She had some reason to be disgusted with me now, and the gap between us began to be wider and wider. And then this Alec Fairbairn chipped in, and things became a thousand times blacker.

"It was to see Sarah that he came to my house first, but soon it was to see us, for he was a man with winning ways, and he made friends wherever he went. He was a dashing, swaggering chap, smart and curled, who had seen half the world, and could talk of what he had seen. He was good company, I won't deny it, and he had wonderful polite ways with him for a sailor man, so that I think there must have been a time when he knew more of the poop than the forecastle. For a month he was in and out of my house, and never once did it cross my mind that harm might come of his soft, tricky ways. And then at last something made me suspect, and from that day my peace was gone for ever.

"It was only a little thing, too. I had come into the parlour unexpected, and as I walked in at the door I saw a light of welcome on my wife's face. But as she saw who it was it faded again, and she turned away with a look of disappointment. That was enough for me. There was no one but Alec Fairbairn whose step she could have mistaken for mine. If I could have seen him then I should have killed him, for I have always been like a madman when my temper gets loose. Mary saw the devil's light in my eyes, and she ran forward with her hands on my sleeve. 'Don't, Jim, don't!' says she. 'Where's Sarah?' I asked. 'In the kitchen,' says she. 'Sarah,' says I, as I went in, 'this man Fairbairn is never to darken my door again.' 'Why not?' says she. 'Because I order it.' 'Oh!' says she, 'if my friends are not good enough for this house, then I am not good enough for it either.' 'You can do what you like,' says I, 'but if Fairbairn shows his face here again, I'll send you one of his ears for a keepsake.' She was frightened by my face, I think, for she never answered a word, and the same evening she left my house.

"Well, I don't know now whether it was pure devilry on the part of this woman, or whether she thought that she could turn me against my wife by encouraging her to misbehave. Anyway, she took a house just two streets off, and let lodgings to sailors. Fairbairn used to stay there, and Mary would go round to have tea with her sister and him. How often she went I don't know, but I followed her one day, and as I broke in at the door Fairbairn got away over the back garden wall, like the cowardly skunk that he was. I swore to my wife that I would kill her if I found her in his company again, and I led her back with me, sobbing and trembling, and as white as a piece of paper. There was no trace of love between us any longer. I could see that she hated me and feared me, and when the thought of it drove me to drink, then she despised me as well.

"Well, Sarah found that she could not make a living in Liverpool, so she went back, as I understand, to live with her sister in Croydon, and things jogged on much the same as ever at home. And then came this last week and all the misery and ruin.

"It was in this way. We had gone on the *May Day* for a round voyage of seven days, but a hogshead got loose and started one of our plates, so that we had to put back into port for twelve hours. I left the ship and came home, thinking what a surprise it would be for my wife, and hoping that maybe she would be glad to see me so soon. The thought was in my head as I turned into my own street, and at that moment a cab passed me, and there she was, sitting by the side of Fairbairn, the two chatting and laughing, with never a thought for me as I stood watching them from the footpath.

"I tell you, and I give you my word on it, that from that moment I was not my own master, and it is all like a dim dream when I look back on it. I had been drinking hard of late, and the two things together fairly turned my brain. There's something throbbing in my head now, like a docker's hammer, but that morning I seemed to have all Niagara whizzing and buzzing in my ears.

"Well, I took to my heels, and I ran after the cab. I had a heavy oak stick in my hand, and I tell you that I saw red from the first; but as I ran I got cunning, too, and hung back a little to see them without being seen. They pulled up soon at the railway station. There was a good crowd round the booking-office, so I got quite close to them without being seen. They took tickets for New Brighton. So did I, but I got in three carriages behind them. When we reached it they walked along the Parade, and I was never more than a hundred yards from them. At last I saw them hire a boat and start for a row, for it was a very hot day, and they thought no doubt that it would be cooler on the water.

"It was just as if they had been given into my hands. There was a bit of a haze, and you could not see more than a few hundred yards. I hired a boat for myself, and I pulled after them. I could see the blurr of their craft, but they were going nearly as fast as I, and they must have been a long mile from the shore before I caught them up. The haze was like a curtain all round us, and there were we three in the middle of it. My God, shall I ever forget their faces when they saw who was in the boat that was closing in upon them? She screamed out. He swore like a madman, and jabbed at me with an oar, for he must have seen death in my eyes. I got past it and got one in with my stick, that crushed his head like an egg. I would have spared her, perhaps, for all my madness, but she threw her arms round him, crying out to him, and calling him 'Alec.' I struck again, and she lay stretched beside him. I was like a wild beast then that had tasted blood. If Sarah had been there, by the Lord, she should have joined them. I pulled out my knife, and— well, there! I've said enough. It gave me a kind of savage joy when I thought how Sarah would feel when she had such signs as these of what her meddling had brought about. Then

I tied the bodies into the boat, stove a plank, and stood by until they had sunk. I knew very well that the owner would think that they had lost their bearings in the haze, and had drifted off out to sea. I cleaned myself up, got back to land, and joined my ship without a soul having a suspicion of what had passed. That night I made up the packet for Sarah Cushing, and next day I sent it from Belfast.

"There you have the whole truth of it. You can hang me, or do what you like with me, but you cannot punish me as I have been punished already. I cannot shut my eyes but I see those two faces staring at me —staring at me as they stared when my boat broke through the haze. I killed them quick, but they are killing me slow; and if I have another night of it I shall be either mad or dead before morning. You won't put me alone into a cell, sir? For pity's sake don't, and may you be treated in your day of agony as you treat me now."

"What is the meaning of it, Watson?" said Holmes, solemnly, as he laid down the paper. "What object is served by this circle of misery and violence and fear? It must tend to some end, or else our universe is ruled by chance, which is unthinkable. But what end? There is the great standing perennial problem to which human reason is as far from an answer as ever."

The Adventures of Sherlock Holmes.

XV.—THE ADVENTURE OF THE YELLOW FACE.

By A. Conan Doyle.

N publishing these short sketches, based upon the numerous cases which my companion's singular gifts have made me the listener to, and eventually the actor in some strange drama, it is only natural that I should dwell rather upon his successes than upon his failures. And this not so much for the sake of his reputation, for indeed it was when he was at his wits' end that his energy and his versatility were most admirable, but because where he failed it happened too often that no one else succeeded, and that the tale was left for ever without a conclusion. Now and again, however, it chanced that even when he erred the truth was still discovered. I have notes of some half-dozen cases of the kind of which "The Adventure of the Musgrave Ritual" and that which I am now about to recount are the two which present the strongest features of interest.

Sherlock Holmes was a man who seldom took exercise for exercise's sake. Few men were capable of greater muscular effort, and he was undoubtedly one of the finest boxers of his weight that I have ever seen, but he looked upon aimless bodily exertion as a waste of energy, and he seldom bestirred himself save where there was some professional object to be served. Then he was absolutely untiring and indefatigable. That he should have kept himself in training under such circumstances is remarkable, but his diet was usually of the sparest, and his habits were simple to the verge of austerity. Save for the occasional use of cocaine he had no vices, and he only turned to the drug as a protest against the monotony of existence when cases were scanty and the papers uninteresting.

One day in early spring he had so far relaxed as to go for a walk with me in the Park, where the first faint shoots of green were breaking out upon the elms, and the sticky spearheads of the chestnuts were just beginning to burst into their five-fold leaves. For two hours we rambled about together, in silence for the most part, as befits two men who know each other intimately. It was nearly five before we were back in Baker Street once more.

"Beg pardon, sir," said our page-boy, as he opened the door; "there's been a gentleman here asking for you, sir."

Holmes glanced reproachfully at me. "So much for afternoon walks!" said he. "Has this gentleman gone, then?"

"Yes, sir."

"Didn't you ask him in?"

"Yes, sir; he came in."

"How long did he wait?"

"Half an hour, sir. He was a very restless gentleman, sir, a-walkin' and a-stampin' all the time he was here. I was waitin' outside the door, sir, and I could hear him. At last he goes out into the passage and he cries: 'Is that man never goin' to come?' Those were his very words, sir. 'You'll only need to wait a little longer,' says I. 'Then I'll wait in the open air, for I feel half choked,' says he. 'I'll be back before long,' and with that he ups and he outs, and all I could say wouldn't hold him back."

"Well, well, you did your best," said Holmes, as we walked into our room. "It's very annoying though, Watson. I was badly in need of a case, and this looks, from the man's impatience, as if it were of importance. Halloa! that's not your pipe on the table! He must have left his behind him. A nice old briar, with a good long stem of what the tobacconists call amber. I wonder how many real amber mouthpieces there are in London. Some people think a fly in it is a sign. Why, it is quite a branch of trade the putting of sham flies into the sham amber. Well, he must have been disturbed in his mind to leave a pipe behind him which he evidently values highly."

"How do you know that he values it highly?" I asked.

"Well, I should put the original cost of the pipe at seven-and-sixpence. Now it has, you see, been twice mended: once in the wooden stem and once in the amber. Each of these mends, done, as you observe, with silver bands, must have cost more than the pipe did originally. The man must value the pipe highly when he prefers to patch it up rather than buy a new one with the same money."

"Anything else?" I asked, for Holmes

"HE HELD IT UP.

was turning the pipe about in his hand and staring at it in his peculiar, pensive way.

He held it up and tapped on it with his long, thin forefinger as a professor might who was lecturing on a bone.

"Pipes are occasionally of extraordinary interest," said he. "Nothing has more individuality save, perhaps, watches and boot-laces. The indications here, however, are neither very marked nor very important. The owner is obviously a muscular man, left-handed, with an excellent set of teeth, careless in his habits, and with no need to practise economy."

My friend threw out the information in a very off-hand way, but I saw that he cocked his eye at me to see if I had followed his reasoning.

"You think a man must be well-to-do if he smokes a seven-shilling pipe?" said I.

"This is Grosvenor mixture at eightpence an ounce," Holmes answered, knocking a little out on his palm. "As he might get an excellent smoke for half the price, he has no need to practise economy."

"And the other points?"

"He has been in the habit of lighting his pipe at lamps and gas-jets. You can see

that it is quite charred all down one side. Of course, a match could not have done that. Why should a man hold a match to the side of his pipe? But you cannot light it at a lamp without getting the bowl charred. And it is all on the right side of the pipe. From that I gather that he is a left-handed man. You hold your own pipe to the lamp, and see how naturally you, being right-handed, hold the left side to the flame. You might do it once the other way, but not as a constancy. This has always been held so. Then he has bitten through his amber. It takes a muscular, energetic fellow, and one with a good set of teeth to do that. But if I am not mistaken I hear him upon the stair, so we shall have something more interesting than his pipe to study."

An instant later our door opened, and a tall young man entered the room. He was well but quietly dressed in a dark-grey suit, and carried a brown wideawake in his hand. I should have put him at about thirty, though he was really some years older.

"I beg your pardon," said he, with some embarrassment; "I suppose I should have knocked. Yes, of course I should have knocked. The fact is that I am a little upset, and you must put it all down to that." He passed his hand over his forehead like a man who is half dazed, and then fell, rather than sat, down upon a chair.

"I can see that you have not slept for a night or two," said Holmes, in his easy, genial way. "That tries a man's nerves more than work, and more even than pleasure. May I ask how I can help you?"

"I wanted your advice, sir. I don't know what to do, and my whole life seems to have gone to pieces."

"You wish to employ me as a consulting detective?"

"Not that only. I want your opinion as a judicious man—as a man of the world. I want to know what I ought to do next. I hope to God you'll be able to tell me,"

He spoke in little, sharp, jerky outbursts, and it seemed to me that to speak at all was very painful to him, and that his will all through was overriding his inclinations.

"It's a very delicate thing," said he. "One does not like to speak of one's domestic affairs to strangers. It seems dreadful to discuss the conduct of one's wife with two men whom I have never seen before. It's horrible to have to do it. But I've got to the end of my tether, and I must have advice."

"My dear Mr. Grant Munro———" began Holmes.

Our visitor sprang from his chair. "What!" he cried. "You know my name?"

"If you wish to preserve your *incognito*," said Holmes, smiling, "I should suggest that you cease to write your name upon the lining of your hat, or else that you turn the

"OUR VISITOR SPRANG FROM HIS CHAIR."

crown towards the person whom you are addressing. I was about to say that my friend and I have listened to many strange secrets in this room, and that we have had the good fortune to bring peace to many troubled souls. I trust that we may do as much for you. Might I beg you, as time may prove to be of importance, to furnish me with the facts of your case without further delay?"

Our visitor again passed his hand over his forehead as if he found it bitterly hard. From every gesture and expression I could see that he was a reserved, self-contained man, with a dash of pride in his nature, more likely to hide his wounds than to expose them. Then suddenly with a fierce gesture of his closed hand, like one who throws reserve to the winds, he began.

"The facts are these, Mr. Holmes," said he. "I am a married man, and have been so

for three years. During that time my wife and I have loved each other as fondly, and lived as happily, as any two that ever were joined. We have not had a difference, not one, in thought, or word, or deed. And now, since last Monday, there has suddenly sprung up a barrier between us, and I find that there is something in her life and in her thoughts of which I know as little as if she were the woman who brushes by me in the street. We are estranged, and I want to know why.

"Now there is one thing that I want to impress upon you before I go any further, Mr. Holmes. Effie loves me. Don't let there be any mistake about that. She loves me with her whole heart and soul, and never more than now. I know it—I feel it. I don't want to argue about that. A man can tell easily enough when a woman loves him. But there's this secret between us, and we can never be the same until it is cleared."

"Kindly let me have the facts, Mr. Munro," said Holmes, with some impatience.

"I'll tell you what I know about Effie's history. She was a widow when I met her first, though quite young—only twenty-five. Her name then was Mrs. Hebron. She went out to America when she was young and lived in the town of Atlanta, where she married this Hebron, who was a lawyer with a good practice. They had one child, but the yellow fever broke out badly in the place, and both husband and child died of it. I have seen his death certificate. This sickened her of America, and she came back to live with a maiden aunt at Pinner, in Middlesex. I may mention that her husband had left her comfortably off, and that she had a capital of about four thousand five hundred pounds, which had been so well invested by him that it returned an average of 7 per cent. She had only been six months at Pinner when I met her; we fell in love with each other, and we married a few weeks afterwards.

"I am a hop merchant myself, and as I have an income of seven or eight hundred, we found ourselves comfortably off, and took a nice eighty-pound-a-year villa at Norbury. Our little place was very countrified, considering that it is so close to town. We had an inn and two houses a little above us, and a single cottage at the other side of the field which faces us, and except those there were no houses until you got half-way to the station. My business took me into town at certain seasons, but in summer I had less to do, and then in our country home my wife and I were just as happy as could be wished. I tell you that there never was a shadow between us until this accursed affair began.

"There's one thing I ought to tell you before I go further. When we married, my wife made over all her property to me— rather against my will, for I saw how awkward it would be if my business affairs went wrong. However, she would have it so, and it was done. Well, about six weeks ago she came to me.

"'Jack,' said she, 'when you took my money you said that if ever I wanted any I was to ask you for it.'

"'Certainly,' said I, 'it's all your own.'

"'Well,' said she, 'I want a hundred pounds.'

"I was a bit staggered at this, for I had imagined it was simply a new dress or something of the kind that she was after.

"'What on earth for?' I asked.

"'Oh,' said she, in her playful way, 'you said that you were only my banker, and bankers never ask questions, you know.'

"'If you really mean it, of course you shall have the money,' said I.

"'Oh, yes, I really mean it.'

"'And you won't tell me what you want it for?'

"'Some day, perhaps, but not just at present, Jack.'

"So I had to be content with that, though it was the first time that there had ever been any secret between us. I gave her a cheque, and I never thought any more of the matter. It may have nothing to do with what came afterwards, but I thought it only right to mention it.

"Well, I told you just now that there is a cottage not far from our house. There is just a field between us, but to reach it you have to go along the road and then turn down a lane. Just beyond it is a nice little grove of Scotch firs, and I used to be very fond of strolling down there, for trees are always neighbourly kinds of things. The cottage had been standing empty this eight months, and it was a pity, for it was a pretty two-storied place, with an old-fashioned porch and honeysuckle about it. I have stood many a time and thought what a neat little homestead it would make.

"Well, last Monday evening I was taking a stroll down that way when I met an empty van coming up the lane, and saw a pile of carpets and things lying about on the grass-plot beside the porch. It was clear that the cottage had at last been let. I walked past it, and then stopping, as an idle man might, I ran my eye over it, and wondered what sort of folk they were who had come to live so near us. And as I looked I suddenly became aware that a face was watching me out of one of the upper windows.

"I don't know what there was about that face, Mr. Holmes, but it seemed to send a chill right down my back. I was some little way off, so that I could not make out the features, but there was something unnatural and inhuman about the face. That was the impression I had, and I moved quickly forwards to get a nearer view of the person who was watching me. But as I did so the face suddenly disappeared, so suddenly that it seemed to have been plucked away into the darkness of the room. I stood for five minutes thinking the business over, and trying to analyze my impressions. I could not tell if the face was that of a man or a woman. It had been too far from me for that. But its colour was what had impressed me most. It was of a livid, dead yellow, and with something set and rigid about it, which was shockingly unnatural. So disturbed was I, that I determined to see a little more of the new inmates of the cottage. I approached and knocked at the door, which was instantly opened by a tall, gaunt woman, with a harsh, forbidding face.

"'What may you be wantin'?' she asked, in a northern accent.

"'I am your neighbour over yonder,' said I, nodding towards my house. 'I see that you have only just moved in, so I thought that if I could be of any help to you in any——'

"'Aye, we'll just ask ye when we want ye,' said she, and shut the door in my face. Annoyed at the churlish rebuff, I turned my back and walked home. All the evening,

"WHAT MAY YOU BE WANTIN'?"

though I tried to think of other things, my mind would still turn to the apparition at the window and the rudeness of the woman. I determined to say nothing about the former to my wife, for she is a nervous, highly-strung woman, and I had no wish that she should share the unpleasant impression which had been produced upon myself. I remarked to her, however, before I fell asleep that the cottage was now occupied, to which she returned no reply.

" I am usually an extremely sound sleeper. It has been a standing jest in the family that nothing could ever wake me during the night ; and yet somehow on that particular night, whether it may have been the slight excitement produced by my little adventure or not, I know not, but I slept much more lightly than usual. Half in my dreams I was dimly conscious that something was going on in the room, and gradually became aware that my wife had dressed herself and was slipping on her mantle and her bonnet. My lips were parted to murmur out some sleepy words of surprise or re-monstrance at this untimely preparation,

when suddenly my half-opened eyes fell upon her face, illuminated by the candle light, and astonishment held me dumb. She wore an expression such as I had never seen before—such as I should have thought her incapable of assuming. She was deadly pale, and breathing fast, glancing furtively towards the bed, as she fastened her mantle, to see if she had disturbed me. Then, thinking that I was still asleep, she slipped noiselessly from the room, and an instant later I heard a sharp creaking, which could only come from the hinges of the front door. I sat up in bed and rapped my knuckles against the rail to make certain that I was truly awake. Then I took my watch from under the pillow. It was three in the morning. What on this earth could my wife be doing out on the country road at three in the morning ?

" I had sat for about twenty minutes turning the thing over in my mind and trying to find some possible explanation. The more I thought the more extraor-dinary and inexplicable did it appear. I was still puzzling over it when I heard the door gently close again and her footsteps coming up the stairs.

" 'Where in the world have you been, Effie ? ' I asked, as she entered.

" She gave a violent start and a kind of gasping cry when I spoke, and that cry and start troubled me more than all the rest, for there was something indescribably guilty about them. My wife had always been a woman of a frank, open nature, and it gave me a chill to see her slinking into her own room, and crying out and wincing when her own husband spoke to her.

" ' You awake, Jack ? ' she cried, with a nervous laugh. ' Why, I thought that nothing could awaken you.'

" ' Where have you been ? ' I asked, more sternly.

" ' I don't wonder that you are surprised,' said she, and I could see that her fingers were trembling as she undid the fastenings of her mantle. ' Why, I never remember having done such a thing in my life before. The fact is, that I felt as though I were choking, and had a perfect longing for a breath of fresh air. I really think that I should have fainted if I had not gone out. I stood at the door for a few minutes, and now I am quite myself again.'

" All the time that she was telling me this story she never once looked in my direction, and her voice was quite unlike her usual tones. It was evident to me that she was saying what was false. I said nothing in reply, but turned my face to the wall, sick at heart, with my mind filled with a thousand venomous doubts and suspicions. What was it that my wife was concealing from me? Where had she been during that strange expedition? I felt that I should have no peace until I knew, and yet I shrank from asking her again after once she had told me what was false. All the rest of the night I tossed and tumbled, framing theory after theory, each more unlikely than the last.

"I should have gone to the City that day, but I was too perturbed in my mind to be able to pay attention to business matters. My wife seemed to be as upset as myself, and I could see from the little questioning glances which she kept shooting at me, that she understood that I disbelieved her statement and that she was at her wits' ends what to do. We hardly exchanged a word during breakfast, and immediately afterwards I went out for a walk that I might think the matter out in the fresh morning air.

" ' TRUST ME, JACK !' SHE CRIED."

"I went as far as the Crystal Palace, spent an hour in the grounds, and was back in Norbury by one o'clock. It happened that my way took me past the cottage, and I stopped for an instant to look at the windows and to see if I could catch a glimpse of the strange face which had looked out at me on the day before. As I stood there, imagine my surprise, Mr. Holmes, when the door suddenly opened and my wife walked out!

"I was struck dumb with astonishment at the sight of her, but my emotions were nothing to those which showed themselves upon her face when our eyes met. She seemed for an instant to wish to shrink back inside the house again, and then, seeing how useless all concealment must be, she came forward with a very white face and frightened eyes which belied the smile upon her lips.

" 'Oh, Jack!' she said, 'I have just been in to see if I can be of any assistance to our new neighbours. Why do you look at me like that, Jack? You are not angry with me?'

" 'So,' said I, 'this is where you went during the night?'

" 'What do you mean?' she cried.

" 'You came here. I am sure of it. Who are these people that you should visit them at such an hour?'

" 'I have not been here before.'

" 'How can you tell me what you know is false?' I cried. 'Your very voice changes as you speak. When have I ever had a secret from you? I shall enter that cottage and I shall probe the matter to the bottom.'

" 'No, no, Jack, for God's sake!' she gasped, in incontrollable emotion. Then as I approached the door she seized my sleeve and pulled me back with convulsive strength.

" 'I implore you not to do this, Jack,' she cried. 'I swear that I will tell you everything some day, but nothing but misery can come of it if you enter that cottage.' Then, as I tried to shake her off, she clung to me in a frenzy of entreaty.

" 'Trust me, Jack!' she cried. 'Trust me only this once. You will never have cause to regret it. You know that I would not have a secret from you if it were not for your own sake. Our whole lives are at stake on this. If you come home with me all will be well. If you force your way into that cottage, all is over between us.'

"There was such earnestness, such despair in her manner that her words arrested me, and I stood irresolute before the door.

"'I will trust you on one condition, and on one condition only,' said I at last. 'It is that this mystery comes to an end from now. You are at liberty to preserve your secret, but you must promise me that there shall be no more nightly visits, no more doings which are kept from my knowledge. I am willing to forget those which are passed if you will promise that there shall be no more in the future.'

"'I was sure that you would trust me,' she cried, with a great sigh of relief. 'It shall be just as you wish. Come away, oh, come away up to the house!' Still pulling at my sleeve she led me away from the cottage. As we went I glanced back, and there was that yellow livid face watching us out of the upper window. What link could there be between that creature and my wife? Or how could the coarse, rough woman whom I had seen the day before be connected with her? It was a strange puzzle, and yet I knew that my mind could never know ease again until I had solved it.

"For two days after this I stayed at home, and my wife appeared to abide loyally by our engagement, for, as far as I know, she never stirred out of the house. On the third day, however, I had ample evidence that her solemn promise was not enough to hold her back from this secret influence which drew her away from her husband and her duty.

"I had gone into town on that day, but I returned by the 2.40 instead of the 3.36, which is my usual train. As I entered the house the maid ran into the hall with a startled face.

"'Where is your mistress?' I asked.

"'I think that she has gone out for a walk,' she answered.

"My mind was instantly filled with suspicion. I rushed upstairs to make sure that she was not in the house. As I did so I happened to glance out of one of the upper windows, and saw the maid with whom I had just been speaking running across the field in the direction of the cottage. Then, of course, I saw exactly what it all meant. My wife had gone over there and had asked the servant to call her if I should return. Tingling with anger, I rushed down and hurried across, determined to end the matter once and for ever. I saw my wife and the maid hurrying back together along the lane, but I did not stop to speak with them. In the cottage lay the secret which was casting a shadow over my life. I vowed that, come what might, it should be a secret no longer. I did not even knock when I reached it, but turned the handle and rushed into the passage.

"It was all still and quiet upon the ground-floor. In the kitchen a kettle was singing on the fire, and a large black cat lay coiled up in a basket, but there was no sign of the woman whom I had seen before. I ran into the other room, but it was equally deserted. Then I rushed up the stairs, but only to find two other rooms empty and deserted at the top. There was no one at all in the whole house. The furniture and pictures were of the most common and vulgar description save in the one chamber at the window of which I had seen the strange face. That was comfortable and elegant, and all my suspicions rose into a fierce, bitter blaze when I saw that on the mantelpiece stood a full-length photograph of my wife, which had been taken at my request only three months ago.

"I stayed long enough to make certain that the house was absolutely empty. Then I left it, feeling a weight at my heart such as I had never had before. My wife came out into the hall as I entered my house, but I was too hurt and angry to speak with her, and pushing past her I made my way into my study. She followed me, however, before I could close the door.

"'I am sorry that I broke my promise, Jack,' said she, 'but if you knew all the circumstances I am sure that you would forgive me.'

"'Tell me everything, then,' said I.

"'I cannot, Jack, I cannot!' she cried.

"'Until you tell me who it is that has been living in that cottage, and who it is to whom you have given that photograph, there can never be any confidence between us,' said I, and breaking away from her I left the house. That was yesterday, Mr. Holmes, and I have not seen her since, nor do I know anything more about this strange business. It is the first shadow that has come between us, and it has so shaken me that I do not know what I should do for the best. Suddenly this morning it occurred to me that you were the man to advise me, so I have hurried to you now, and I place myself unreservedly in your hands. If there is any point which I have not made clear, pray question me about it. But above all tell me

"'TELL ME EVERYTHING,' SAID I."

quickly what I have to do, for this misery is more than I can bear."

Holmes and I had listened with the utmost interest to this extraordinary statement, which had been delivered in the jerky, broken fashion of a man who is under the influence of extreme emotion. My companion sat silent how for some time, with his chin upon his hand, lost in thought.

"Tell me," said he at last, "could you swear that this was a man's face which you saw at the window?"

"Each time that I saw it I was some distance away from it, so that it is impossible for me to say."

"You appear, however, to have been disagreeably impressed by it."

"It seemed to be of an unnatural colour and to have a strange rigidity about the features. When I approached, it vanished with a jerk."

"How long is it since your wife asked you for a hundred pounds?"

"Nearly two months."

"Have you ever seen a photograph of her first husband?"

"No, there was a great fire at Atlanta very shortly after his death, and all her papers were destroyed."

"And yet she had a certificate of death. You say that you saw it?"

"Yes, she got a duplicate after the fire."

"Did you ever meet anyone who knew her in America?"

"No."

"Did she ever talk of revisiting the place?"

"No."

"Or get letters from it?"

"Not to my knowledge."

"Thank you. I should like to think over the matter a little now. If the cottage is permanently deserted we may have some difficulty; if on the other hand, as I fancy is more likely, the inmates were warned of your coming, and left before you entered yesterday, then they may be back now, and we should clear it all up easily. Let me advise you, then, to return to Norbury and to examine the windows of the cottage again. If you have reason to believe that it is inhabited do not force your way in, but send a wire to my friend and me. We shall be with you within an hour of receiving it, and we shall then very soon get to the bottom of the business."

"And if it is still empty?"

"In that case I shall come out to-morrow and talk it over with you. Good-bye, and above all do not fret until you know that you really have a cause for it."

"I am afraid that this is a bad business, Watson," said my companion, as he returned after accompanying Mr. Grant Munro to the door. "What did you make of it?"

"It had an ugly sound," I answered.

"Yes. There's blackmail in it, or I am much mistaken."

"And who is the blackmailer?"

"Well, it must be this creature who lives in the only comfortable room in the place, and has her photograph above his fireplace. Upon my word, Watson, there is something very attractive about that livid face at the window, and I would not have missed the case for worlds."

"You have a theory?"

"Yes, a provisional one. But I shall be surprised if it does not turn out to be correct. This woman's first husband is in that cottage."

"Why do you think so?"

"How else can we explain her frenzied anxiety that her second one should not enter it? The facts, as I read them, are something like this: This woman was married in America. Her husband developed some hateful qualities, or, shall we say, that he contracted some loathsome disease, and became a leper or an imbecile. She fled from him at last, returned to England, changed her name, and started her life, as she thought, afresh. She had been married three years, and believed that her position was quite secure —having shown her husband the death certificate of some man, whose name she had assumed—when suddenly her whereabouts was discovered by her first husband, or, we may suppose, by some unscrupulous woman, who had attached herself to the invalid. They write to the wife and threaten to come and expose her. She asks for a hundred pounds and endeavours to buy them off. They come in spite of it, and when the husband mentions casually to the wife that there are new-comers in the cottage, she knows in some way that they are her pursuers. She waits until her husband is asleep, and then she rushes down to endeavour to persuade them to leave her in peace. Having no success, she goes again next morning, and her husband meets her, as he has told us, as she came out. She promises him then not to go there again, but two days afterwards, the hope of getting rid of those dreadful neighbours is too strong for her, and she makes another attempt, taking down with her the photograph which had probably been demanded from her. In the midst of this interview the maid rushes in to say that the master has come home, on which the wife, knowing that he would come straight down to the cottage, hurries the inmates out at the back door, into that grove of fir trees probably which was mentioned as standing near. In this way he finds the place deserted. I shall be very much surprised, however, if it is still so when he reconnoitres it this evening. What do you think of my theory?"

"It is all surmise."

"But at least it covers all the facts. When new facts come to our knowledge, which cannot be covered by it, it will be time enough to reconsider it. At present we can do nothing until we have a fresh message from our friend at Norbury."

But we had not very long to wait. It came just as we had finished our tea. "The cottage is still tenanted," it said. "Have seen the face again at the window. I'll meet the seven o'clock train, and take no steps until you arrive."

He was waiting on the platform when we stepped out, and we could see in the light of the station lamps that he was very pale, and quivering with agitation.

"They are still there, Mr. Holmes," said he, laying his hand upon my friend's sleeve. "I saw lights in the cottage as I came down. We shall settle it now, once and for all."

"What is your plan, then?" asked Holmes, as we walked down the dark, tree-lined road.

"I am going to force my way in, and see for myself who is in the house. I wish you both to be there as witnesses."

"You are quite determined to do this, in spite of your wife's warning that it was better that you should not solve the mystery?"

"Yes, I am determined."

"Well, I think that you are in the right. Any truth is better than indefinite doubt. We had better go up at once. Of course, legally we are putting ourselves hopelessly in the wrong, but I think that it is worth it."

It was a very dark night and a thin rain began to fall as we turned from the high road into a narrow lane, deeply rutted, with hedges on either side. Mr. Grant Munro pushed impatiently forward, however, and we stumbled after him as best we could.

"There are the lights of my house," he murmured, pointing to a glimmer among the trees, "and here is the cottage which I am going to enter."

We turned a corner in the lane as he spoke, and there was the building close beside us. A yellow bar falling across the black foreground showed that the door was not quite closed, and one window in the upper story was brightly illuminated. As we looked we saw a dark blurr moving across the blind.

"There is that creature," cried Grant Munro; "you can see for yourselves that someone is there. Now follow me, and we shall soon know all."

We approached the door, but suddenly a woman appeared out of the shadow and stood in the golden track of the lamp light. I could not see her face in the darkness, but her arms were thrown out in an attitude of entreaty.

"For God's sake, don't, Jack!" she cried. "I had a presentiment that you would come this evening. Think better of it, dear! Trust me again, and you will never have cause to regret it."

"I have trusted you too long, Effie!" he cried, sternly. "Leave go of me! I must pass you. My friends and I are going to settle this matter once and for ever." He pushed her to one side and we followed closely after him. As he threw the door open, an elderly woman ran out in front of him and tried to bar his passage, but he thrust her back, and an instant afterwards we were all upon the stairs. Grant Munro rushed into the lighted room at the top, and we entered it at his heels.

It was a cosy, well-furnished apartment, with two candles burning upon the table and two upon the mantelpiece. In the corner, stooping over a desk, there sat what appeared to be a little girl. Her face was turned away as we entered, but we could see that she was dressed in a red frock, and that she had long white gloves on. As she whisked round to us I gave a cry of surprise and horror. The face which she turned towards us was of the strangest livid tint, and the features were absolutely levoid of any expression. An instant later the mystery was explained. Holmes, with a laugh, passed his hand behind the child's ear, a mask peeled off from her countenance, and there was a little coal-black negress with all her white teeth flashing in amusement at our amazed faces. I burst out laughing out

"THERE WAS A LITTLE COAL-BLACK NEGRESS."

of sympathy with her merriment, but Grant Munro stood staring, with his hand clutching at his throat.

"My God!" he cried, "what can be the meaning of this?"

"I will tell you the meaning of it," cried the lady, sweeping into the room with a proud, set face. "You have forced me against my own judgment to tell you, and now we must both make the best of it. My husband died at Atlanta. My child survived."

"Your child!"

She drew a large silver locket from her bosom. "You have never seen this open."

"I understood that it did not open."

She touched a spring, and the front hinged back. There was a portrait within of a man, strikingly handsome and intelligent, but bearing unmistakable signs upon his features of his African descent.

"That is John Hebron, of Atlanta," said the lady, "and a nobler man never walked the earth. I cut myself off from my race in order to wed him; but never once while he lived did I for one instant regret it. It was our misfortune that our only child took after his people rather than mine. It is often so in such matches, and little Lucy is darker far than ever her father was. But, dark or fair, she is my own dear little girlie, and her mother's pet." The little creature ran across at the words and nestled up against the lady's dress.

"When I left her in America," she continued, "it was only because her health was weak, and the change might have done her harm. She was given to the care of a faithful Scotch-woman who had once been our servant. Never for an instant did I dream of disowning her as my child. But when chance threw you in my way, Jack, and I learned to love you, I feared to tell you about my child. God forgive me, I feared that I should lose you, and I had not the courage to tell you. I had to choose between you, and in my weakness I turned away from my own little girl. For three years I have kept her existence a secret from you, but I heard from the nurse, and I knew that all was well with her. At last, however, there came an overwhelming desire to see the child once more. I struggled against it, but in vain. Though I knew the danger I determined to have the child over, if it were but for a few weeks. I sent a hundred pounds to the nurse, and I gave her instructions about this cottage, so that she might come as a neighbour without my appearing to be in any way

child only just escaped from the back door as you rushed in at the front one. And now to-night you at last know all, and I ask you what is to become of us, my child and me?" She clasped her hands and waited for an answer.

It was a long two minutes before Grant Munro broke the silence, and when his answer came it was one of which I love to think. He lifted the little child, kissed her, and

"HE LIFTED THE LITTLE CHILD."

connected with her. I pushed my precautions so far as to order her to keep the child in the house during the daytime, and to cover up her little face and hands, so that even those who might see her at the window should not gossip about there being a black child in the neighbourhood. If I had been less cautious I might have been more wise, but I was half crazy with fear lest you should learn the truth.

"It was you who told me first that the cottage was occupied. I should have waited for the morning, but I could not sleep for excitement, and so at last I slipped out, knowing how difficult it is to awaken you. But you saw me go, and that was the beginning of my troubles. Next day you had my secret at your mercy, but you nobly refrained from pursuing your advantage. Three days later, however, the nurse and

then, still carrying her, he held his other hand out to his wife and turned towards the door.

"We can talk it over more comfortably at home," said he. "I am not a very good man, Effie, but I think that I am a better one than you have given me credit for being."

Holmes and I followed them down to the lane, and my friend plucked at my sleeve as we came out. "I think," said he, "that we shall be of more use in London than in Norbury."

Not another word did he say of the case until late that night when he was turning away, with his lighted candle, for his bedroom.

"Watson," said he, "if it should ever strike you that I am getting a little over-confident in my powers, or giving less pains to a case than it deserves, kindly whisper 'Norbury' in my ear, and I shall be infinitely obliged to you."

The Adventures of Sherlock Holmes.

XVI.—THE ADVENTURE OF THE STOCKBROKER'S CLERK.

By A. Conan Doyle.

SHORTLY after my marriage I had bought a connection in the Paddington district. Old Mr. Farquhar, from whom I purchased it, had at one time an excellent general practice, but his age, and an affliction of the nature of St. Vitus' dance, from which he suffered, had very much thinned it. The public, not unnaturally, goes upon the principle that he who would heal others must himself be whole, and looks askance at the curative powers of the man whose own case is beyond the reach of his drugs. Thus, as my predecessor weakened, his practice declined, until when I purchased it from him it had sunk from twelve hundred to little more than three hundred a year. I had confidence, however, in my own youth and energy, and was convinced that in a very few years the concern would be as flourishing as ever.

For three months after taking over the practice I was kept very closely at work, and saw little of my friend Sherlock Holmes, for I was too busy to visit Baker Street, and he seldom went anywhere himself save upon professional business. I was surprised, therefore, when one morning in June, as I sat reading the *British Medical Journal* after breakfast, I heard a ring at the bell followed by the high, somewhat strident, tones of my old companion's voice.

"Ah, my dear Watson," said he, striding into the room. "I am very delighted to see you. I trust that Mrs. Watson has entirely recovered from all the little excitements connected with our adventure of the 'Sign of Four.'"

"Thank you, we are both very well," said I, shaking him warmly by the hand.

"And I hope also," he continued, sitting down in the rocking-chair, "that the cares of medical practice have not entirely obliterated the interest which you used to take in our little deductive problems."

"On the contrary," I answered; "it was only last night that I was looking over my old notes and classifying some of our past results."

"I trust that you don't consider your collection closed?"

"Not at all. I should wish nothing better than to have some more of such experiences."

"To-day, for example?"

"Yes; to-day, if you like."

"And as far off as Birmingham?"

"Certainly, if you wish it."

"And the practice?"

"I do my neighbour's when he goes. He is always ready to work off the debt."

"Ha! Nothing could be better!" said Holmes, leaning back in his chair and looking keenly at me from under his half-closed lids. "I perceive that you have been

" ' NOTHING COULD BE BETTER, SAID HOLMES·

unwell lately Summer colds are always a little trying"

"I was confined to the house by a severe chill for three days last week. I thought, however, that I had cast off every trace of it."

"So you have. You look remarkably robust."

"How, then, did you know of it?"

"My dear fellow, you know my methods."

"You deduced it, then?"

"Certainly."

"And from what?"

"From your slippers."

I glanced down at the new patent leathers which I was wearing. "How on earth——?" I began, but Holmes answered my question before it was asked.

"Your slippers are new," he said. "You could not have had them more than a few weeks. The soles which you are at this moment presenting to me are slightly scorched. For a moment I thought they might have got wet and been burned in the drying. But near the instep there is a small circular wafer of paper with the shopman's hieroglyphics upon it. Damp would of course have removed this. You had then been sitting with your feet outstretched to the fire, which a man would hardly do even in so wet a June as this if he were in his full health."

Like all Holmes's reasoning the thing seemed simplicity itself when it was once explained. He read the thought upon my features, and his smile had a tinge of bitterness.

"I am afraid that I rather give myself away when I explain," said he. "Results without causes are much more impressive. You are ready to come to Birmingham, then?"

"Certainly. What is the case?"

"You shall hear it all in the train. My client is outside in a four-wheeler. Can you come at once?"

"In an instant." I scribbled a note to my neighbour, rushed upstairs to explain the matter to my wife, and joined Holmes upon the doorstep.

"Your neighbour is a doctor?" said he, nodding at the brass plate.

"Yes. He bought a practice as I did."

"An old-established one?"

"Just the same as mine. Both have been ever since the houses were built."

"Ah, then you got hold of the best of the two."

"I think I did. But how do you know?"

"By the steps, my boy. Yours are worn three inches deeper than his. But this gentleman in the cab is my client, Mr. Hall Pycroft. Allow me to introduce you to him. Whip your horse up, cabby, for we have only just time to catch our train."

The man whom I found myself facing was a well-built, fresh-complexioned young fellow with a frank, honest face and a slight, crisp, yellow moustache. He wore a very shiny top-hat and a neat suit of sober black, which made him look what he was—a smart young City man, of the class who have been labelled Cockneys, but who give us our crack Volunteer regiments, and who turn out more fine athletes and sportsmen than any body of men in these islands. His round, ruddy face was naturally full of cheeriness, but the corners of his mouth seemed to me to be pulled down in a half-comical distress. It was not, however, until we were all in a first-class carriage and well started upon our journey to Birmingham, that I was able to learn what the trouble was which had driven him to Sherlock Holmes.

"We have a clear run here of seventy minutes," Holmes remarked. "I want you, Mr. Hall Pycroft, to tell my friend your very interesting experience exactly as you have told it to me, or with more detail if possible. It will be of use to me to hear the succession of events again. It is a case, Watson, which may prove to have something in it, or may prove to have nothing, but which at least presents those unusual and *outré* features which are as dear to you as they are to me. Now, Mr. Pycroft, I shall not interrupt you again."

Our young companion looked at me with a twinkle in his eye.

"The worst of the story is," said he, "that I show myself up as such a confounded fool. Of course, it may work out all right, and I don't see that I could have done otherwise; but if I have lost my crib and get nothing in exchange, I shall feel what a soft Johnny I have been. I'm not very good at telling a story, Dr. Watson, but it is like this with me.

"I used to have a billet at Coxon and Woodhouse, of Drapers' Gardens, but they were let in early in the spring through the Venezuelan loan, as no doubt you remember, and came a nasty cropper. I had been with them five years, and old Coxon gave me a ripping good testimonial when the smash came; but, of course, we clerks were all turned adrift, the twenty-seven of us. I tried here and tried there, but there were lots of other chaps on the same lay as myself, and it was a perfect frost for a long time. I had been taking three pounds a week at Coxon's, and I had saved about seventy of them, but I soon worked my way through that and out at the other end. I was fairly at the end of my tether at last, and could hardly find the stamps to answer the advertisements or the envelopes to stick them to. I had worn out my boots padding up office stairs, and I seemed just as far from getting a billet as ever.

"At last I saw a vacancy at Mawson and Williams', the great stockbroking firm in Lombard Street. I daresay E.C. is not much in your line, but I can tell you that this is about the richest house in London. The advertisement was to be answered by letter only. I sent in my testimonial and application, but without the least hope of getting it. Back came an answer by return saying that if I would appear next Monday I might take over my new duties at once, provided that my appearance was satisfactory. No one knows how these things are worked. Some people say the manager just

"'MR. HALL PYCROFT, I BELIEVE?' SAID HE."

plunges his hand into the heap and takes the first that comes. Anyhow, it was my innings that time, and I don't ever wish to feel better pleased. The screw was a pound a week rise, and the duties just about the same as at Coxon's.

"And now I come to the queer part of the business. I was in diggings out Hampstead way—17, Potter's Terrace, was the address. Well, I was sitting doing a smoke that very evening after I had been promised the appointment, when up came my landlady with a card which had 'Arthur Pinner, financial agent,' printed upon it. I had never heard

the name before, and could not imagine what he wanted with me, but of course I asked her to show him up. In he walked—a middle-sized, dark-haired, dark-eyed, black-bearded man, with a touch of the sheeny about his nose. He had a brisk kind of way with him and spoke sharply, like a man that knew the value of time.

"'Mr. Hall Pycroft, I believe?' said he.

"'Yes, sir,' I answered, and pushed a chair towards him.

"'Lately engaged at Coxon and Woodhouse's?'

"'Yes, sir.'

"'And now on the staff of Mawson's?'

"'Quite so.'

"'Well,' said he. 'The fact is that I have heard some really extraordinary stories about your financial ability. You remember Parker who used to be Coxon's manager? He can never say enough about it.'

"'Of course I was pleased to hear this. I had always been pretty smart in the office, but I had never dreamed that I was talked about in the City in this fashion.

"'You have a good memory?' said he.

"'Pretty fair,' I answered, modestly.

"'Have you kept in touch with the market while you have been out of work?' he asked.

"'Yes; I read the Stock Exchange List every morning.'

"'Now, that shows real application!' he cried. 'That is the way to prosper! You won't mind my testing you, will you? Let me see! How are Ayrshires?'

"'One hundred and six and a quarter to one hundred and five and seven-eighths,' I answered.

"'And New Zealand Consolidated?'

" ' A hundred and four.'

' ' And British Broken Hills?

" Seven to seven and six.'

" 'Wonderful!' he cried, with his hands up. 'This quite fits in with all that I had heard. My boy, my boy, you are very much too good to be a clerk at Mawson's!'

" This outburst rather astonished me, as you can think. 'Well,' said I, 'other people don't think quite so much of me as you seem to do, Mr. Pinner. I had a hard enough fight to get this berth, and I am very glad to have it.'

" ' Pooh, man, you should soar above it. You are not in your true sphere. Now I'll tell you how it stands with me. What I have to offer is little enough when measured by your ability, but when compared with Mawson's it is light to dark. Let me see! When do you go to Mawson's?'

" ' On Monday.'

" ' Ha! ha! I think I would risk a little sporting flutter that you don't go there at all.'

" ' Not go to Mawson's?'

" ' No, sir. By that day you will be the business manager of the Franco-Midland Hardware Company, Limited, with one hundred and thirty-four branches in the towns and villages of France, not counting one in Brussels and one in San Remo.'

" This took my breath away. 'I never heard of it,' said I.

" ' Very likely not. It has been kept very quiet, for the capital was all privately subscribed, and it is too good a thing to let the public into. My brother, Harry Pinner, is promoter, and joins the board after allotment as managing director. He knew that I was in the swim down here, and he asked me to pick up a good man cheap—a young, pushing man with plenty of snap about him. Parker spoke of you, and that brought me here to-night. We can only offer you a beggarly five hundred to start with——'

" ' Five hundred a year!' I shouted.

" ' Only that at the beginning, but you are to have an over-riding commission of 1 per cent. on all business done by your agents, and you may take my word for it that this will come to more than your salary.'

" ' But I know nothing about hardware.'

" ' Tut, my boy, you know about figures.'

" My head buzzed, and I could hardly sit still in the chair. But suddenly a little chill of doubt came over me.

" ' I must be frank with you,' said I. 'Mawson only gives me two hundred, but Mawson is safe. Now, really, I know so little about your company that —— '

" ' Ah, smart, smart!' he cried, in a kind of ecstasy of delight. 'You are the very man for us! You are not to be talked over, and quite right too. Now, here's a note for a hundred pounds; and if you think that we can do business you may just slip it into your pocket as an advance upon your salary.'

" ' That is very handsome,' said I. 'When should I take over my new duties?'

" ' Be in Birmingham to-morrow at one,' said he. 'I have a note in my pocket here which you will take to my brother. You will find him at 126B, Corporation Street, where the temporary offices of the company are situated. Of course he must confirm your engagement, but between ourselves it will be all right.'

" ' Really, I hardly know how to express my gratitude, Mr. Pinner,' said I.

" ' Not at all, my boy. You have only got your deserts. There are one or two small things—mere formalities—which I must arrange with you. You have a bit of paper beside you there. Kindly write upon it, " I am perfectly willing to act as business manager to the Franco-Midland Hardware Company, Limited, at a minimum salary of £500." '

" I did as he asked, and he put the paper in his pocket.

" ' There is one other detail,' said he. 'What do you intend to do about Mawson's?'

" I had forgotten all about Mawson's in my joy.

" ' I'll write and resign,' said I.

" ' Precisely what I don't want you to do. I had a row over you with Mawson's manager. I had gone up to ask him about you, and he was very offensive—accused me of coaxing you away from the service of the firm, and that sort of thing. At last I fairly lost my temper. " If you want good men you should pay them a good price," said I. " He would rather have our small price than your big one," said he. " I'll lay you a fiver," said I, " that when he has my offer you will never so much as hear from him again." " Done!" said he. " We picked him out of the gutter, and he won't leave us so easily." Those were his very words.'

" 'The impudent scoundrel!' I cried. 'I've never so much as seen him in my life. Why should I consider him in any way? I shall certainly not write if you would rather that I didn't.'

" ' Good! That's a promise!' said he, rising from his chair. 'Well, I am delighted to have got so good a man for my brother.

Here is your advance of a hundred pounds, and here is the letter. Make a note of the address, 126B, Corporation Street, and remember that one o'clock to-morrow is your appointment. Good-night, and may you have all the fortune that you deserve.'

"That's just about all that passed between us as near as I can remember it. You can imagine, Dr. Watson, how pleased I was at such an extraordinary bit of good fortune. I sat up half the night hugging myself over it, and next day I was off to Birmingham in a train that would take me in plenty of time for my appointment. I took my things to an hotel in New Street, and then I made my way to the address which had been given me.

"It was a quarter of an hour before my time, but I thought that would make no difference. 126B was a passage between two large shops which led to a winding stone stair, from which there were many flats, let as offices to companies or professional men. The names of the occupants were painted up at the bottom on the wall, but there was no such name as the Franco-Midland Hardware Company, Limited. I stood for a few minutes with my heart in my boots, wondering whether the whole thing was an elaborate hoax or not, when up came a man and addressed me. He was very like the chap that I had seen the night before, the same figure and voice, but he was clean shaven and his hair was lighter.

"'Are you Mr. Hall Pycroft?' he asked.

"'Yes,' said I.

"'Ah! I was expecting you, but you are a trifle before your time. I had a note from my brother this morning, in which he sang your praises very loudly.'

" UP CAME A MAN AND ADDRESSED ME."

"'I was just looking for the offices when you came.'

"'We have not got our name up yet, for we only secured these temporary premises last week. Come up with me and we will talk the matter over.'

"I followed him to the top of a very lofty stair, and there right under the slates were a couple of empty and dusty little rooms, uncarpeted and uncurtained, into which he led me. I had thought of a great office with shining tables and rows of clerks such as I was used to, and I daresay I stared rather straight at the two deal chairs and one little table, which, with a ledger and a waste-paper basket, made up the whole furniture.

"'Don't be disheartened, Mr. Pycroft,' said my new acquaintance, seeing the length of my face. 'Rome was not built in a day, and we have lots of money at our backs, though we don't cut much dash yet in offices. Pray sit down and let me have your letter.'

"I gave it to him, and he read it over very carefully.

"'You seem to have made a vast impression upon my brother, Arthur,' said he, 'and I know that he is a pretty shrewd judge. He swears by London, you know, and I by Birmingham, but this time I shall follow his advice. Pray consider yourself definitely engaged.'

"'What are my duties?' I asked.

"'You will eventually manage the great depôt in Paris, which will pour a flood of English crockery into the shops of one hundred and thirty-four agents in France. The purchase will be completed in a week, and meanwhile you will remain in Birmingham and make yourself useful.'

"'How?'

"For answer he took a big red book out of a drawer. 'This is a directory of Paris,' said he, 'with the trades after the names of the people. I want you to take it home with you, and to mark off all the hardware sellers with their addresses. It would be of the greatest use to me to have them.'

"'Surely, there are classified lists?' I suggested.

"'Not reliable ones. Their system is different to ours. Stick at it and let me have the lists by Monday, at twelve. Good-day, Mr. Pycroft; if you continue to show zeal and intelligence, you will find the company a good master.'

"I went back to the hotel with the big book under my arm, and with very conflicting feelings in my breast. On the one hand I was definitely engaged, and had a hundred pounds in my pocket. On the other, the look of the offices, the absence of name on the wall, and other of the points which would strike a business man had left a bad impression as to the position of my employers. However, come what might, I had my money, so I settled down to my task. All Sunday I was kept hard at work, and yet by Monday I had only got as far as H. I went round to my employer, found him in the same dismantled kind of room, and was told to keep at it until Wednesday, and then come again. On Wednesday it was still unfinished, so I hammered away until Friday—that is, yesterday. Then I brought it round to Mr. Harry Pinner.

"'Thank you very much,' said he. 'I fear that I underrated the difficulty of the task. This list will be of very material assistance to me.'

"'It took some time,' said I.

"'And now,' said he, 'I want you to make a list of the furniture shops, for they all sell crockery.'

"'Very good.'

"'And you can come up to-morrow evening at seven, and let me know how you are getting on. Don't overwork yourself. A couple of hours at Day's Music-Hall in the evening would do you no harm after your labours.' He laughed as he spoke, and I saw with a thrill that his second tooth upon the left-hand side had been very badly stuffed with gold."

Sherlock Holmes rubbed his hands with delight, and I stared in astonishment at our client.

"You may well look surprised, Dr. Watson, but it is this way," said he. "When I was speaking to the other chap in London at the time that he laughed at my not going to Mawson's, I happened to notice that his tooth was stuffed in this very identical fashion. The glint of the gold in each case caught my eye, you see. When I put that with the voice and figure being the same, and only those things altered which might be changed by a razor or a wig, I could not doubt that it was the same man. Of course, you expect two brothers to be alike, but not that they should have the same tooth stuffed in the same way. He bowed me out and I found myself in the street, hardly knowing whether I was on my head or my heels. Back I went to my hotel, put my head in a basin of cold water, and tried to think it out. Why had he sent me from London to Birmingham; why had he got there before me; and why had he written a letter from himself to himself? It was altogether too much for me, and I could make no sense of it. And then suddenly it struck me that what was dark to me might be very light to Mr. Sherlock Holmes. I had just time to get up to town by the night train, to see him this morning, and to bring you both back with me to Birmingham."

There was a pause after the stockbroker's clerk had concluded his surprising experience. Then Sherlock Holmes cocked his eye at me, leaning back on the cushions with a pleased and yet critical face, like a connoisseur who had just taken his first sip of a comet vintage.

"Rather fine, Watson, is it not?" said he. "There are points in it which please me. I think you will agree with me that an interview with Mr. Arthur Harry Pinner in the temporary offices of the Franco-Midland Hardware Company, Limited, would be a rather interesting experience for both of us."

"But how can we do it?" I asked.

"Oh, easily enough," said Hall Pycroft, cheerily. "You are two friends of mine who are in want of a billet, and what could be more natural than that I should bring you both round to the managing director?"

"Quite so! Of course!" said Holmes. "I should like to have a look at the gentleman and see if I can make anything of his little game. What qualities have you, my friend, which would make your services so valuable? or is it possible that——" he began biting his nails and staring blankly out of the window, and we hardly drew another word from him until we were in New Street.

At seven o'clock that evening we were walking, the three of us, down Corporation Street to the company's offices.

" It is of no use our being at all before our time," said our client. " He only comes there to see me apparently, for the place is deserted up to the very hour he names."

" That is suggestive," remarked Holmes.

" By Jove, I told you so!" cried the clerk. " That's he walking ahead of us there."

He pointed to a smallish, blonde, well-dressed man, who was bustling along the other side of the road. As we watched him he looked across at a boy who was bawling out the latest edition of the evening paper, and, running over among the cabs and 'buses, he bought one from him. Then clutching it in his hand he vanished through a doorway.

" There he goes!" cried Hall Pycroft. " Those are the company's offices into which he has gone. Come with me and I'll fix it up as easily as possible."

Following his lead we ascended five stories, until we found ourselves outside a half-opened door, at which our client tapped. A voice within bade us " Come in," and we entered a bare, unfurnished room, such as Hall Pycroft had described. At the single table sat the man whom we had seen in the street, with his evening paper spread out in front of him, and as he looked up at us it seemed to me

" HE LOOKED UP AT US."

that I had never looked upon a face which bore such marks of grief, and of something beyond grief—of a horror such as comes to few men in a lifetime. His brow glistened with perspiration, his cheeks were of the dull dead white of a fish's belly, and his eyes were wild and staring. He looked at his clerk as though he failed to recognise him, and I could see, by the astonishment depicted upon our conductor's face, that this was by no means the usual appearance of his employer.

" You look ill, Mr. Pinner," he exclaimed.

" Yes, I am not very well," answered the other, making obvious efforts to pull himself together, and licking his dry lips before he spoke. " Who are these gentlemen whom you have brought with you ? "

" One is Mr. Harris, of Bermondsey, and the other is Mr. Price, of this town," said our clerk, glibly. " They are friends of mine, and gentlemen of experience, but they have been out of a place for some little time, and they hoped that perhaps you might find an opening for them in the company's employment."

" Very possibly! Very possibly!" cried Mr. Pinner, with a ghastly smile. " Yes, I have no doubt that we shall be able to do something for you. What is your particular line, Mr. Harris ? "

" I am an accountant," said Holmes.

" Ah, yes, we shall want something of the sort. And you, Mr. Price ? "

" A clerk," said I.

" I have every hope that the company may accommodate you. I will let you know about it as soon as we come to any conclusion. And now I beg that you will go. For God's sake, leave me to myself ! "

These last words were shot out of him, as though the constraint which he was evidently setting upon himself had suddenly and utterly burst asunder. Holmes and I glanced at each other, and Hall Pycroft took a step towards the table.

" You forget, Mr. Pinner, that I am here

by appointment to receive some directions from you," said he.

"Certainly, Mr. Pycroft, certainly," the other answered in a calmer tone. "You may wait here a moment, and there is no reason why your friends should not wait with you. I will be entirely at your service in three minutes, if I might trespass upon your patience so far." He rose with a very courteous air, and bowing to us he passed out through a door at the further end of the room, which he closed behind him.

"What now?" whispered Holmes. "Is he giving us the slip?"

"Impossible," answered Pycroft.

"Why so?"

"That door leads into an inner room."

"There is no exit?"

"None."

"Is it furnished?"

"It was empty yesterday."

"Then what on earth can he be doing? There is something which I don't understand in this matter. If ever a man was three parts mad with terror, that man's name is Pinner. What can have put the shivers on him?"

"He suspects that we are detectives," I suggested.

"That's it," said Pycroft.

Holmes shook his head. "He did not turn pale. He *was* pale when we entered the room," said he. "It is just possible that—"

His words were interrupted by a sharp rat-tat from the direction of the inner door.

"What the deuce is he knocking at his own door for?" cried the clerk.

Again and much louder came the rat-tat-tat. We all gazed expectantly at the closed door. Glancing at

"WE FOUND OURSELVES IN THE INNER ROOM,"

Holmes I saw his face turn rigid, and he leaned forward in intense excitement. Then suddenly came a low gurgling, gargling sound and a brisk drumming upon woodwork. Holmes sprang frantically across the room and pushed at the door. It was fastened on the inner side. Following his example, we threw ourselves upon it with all our weight. One hinge snapped, then the other, and down came the door with a crash. Rushing over it we found ourselves in the inner room.

It was empty.

But it was only for a moment that we were at fault. At one corner, the corner nearest the room which we had left, there was a second door. Holmes sprang to it and pulled it open. A coat and waistcoat were lying on the floor, and from a hook behind the door, with his own braces round his neck, was hanging the managing director of the Franco-Midland Hardware Company. His knees were drawn up, his head hung at a dreadful angle to his body, and the clatter of his heels against the door made the noise which had broken in upon our conversation. In an instant I had caught him round the waist and held him up, while Holmes and Pycroft untied the elastic bands which had disappeared between the livid creases of skin. Then we carried him into the other room, where he lay with a clay-coloured face, puffing his purple lips in and out with every breath—a dreadful wreck of all that he had been but five minutes before.

"What do you think of him, Watson?" asked Holmes.

I stooped over him and examined him.

His pulse was feeble and intermittent, but his breathing grew longer, and there was a little shivering of his eyelids which showed a thin white slit of ball beneath.

"It has been touch and go with him," said I, "but he'll live now. Just open that window and hand me the water carafe." I undid his collar, poured the cold water over his face, and raised and sank his arms until he drew a long natural breath.

"It's only a question of time now," said I, as I turned away from him.

Holmes stood by the table with his hands deep in his trousers pockets and his chin upon his breast.

"I suppose we ought to call the police in now," said he; "and yet I confess that I like to give them a complete case when they come."

"It's a blessed mystery to me," cried Pycroft, scratching his head. "Whatever they wanted to bring me all the way up here for, and then——"

"Pooh! All that is clear enough," said Holmes, impatiently. "It is this last sudden move."

"You understand the rest, then?"

"I think that it is fairly obvious. What do you say, Watson?"

I shrugged my shoulders.

"I must confess that I am out of my depths," said I.

"Oh, surely, if you consider the events at first they can only point to one conclusion."

"What do you make of them?"

"Well, the whole thing hinges upon two points. The first is the making of Pycroft write a declaration by which he entered the service of this preposterous company. Do you not see how very suggestive that is?"

"I am afraid I miss the point."

"Well, why did they want him to do it? Not as a business matter, for these arrangements are usually verbal, and there was no earthly business reason why this should be an exception. Don't you see, my young friend, that they were very anxious to obtain a specimen of your handwriting, and had no other way of doing it?"

"And why?"

"Quite so. Why? When we answer that, we have made some progress with our little problem. Why? There can be only one adequate reason. Someone wanted to learn to imitate your writing, and had to procure a specimen of it first. And now if we pass on to the second point, we find that each throws light upon the other. That point is the request made by Pinner that you should not resign your place, but should leave the manager of this important business in the full expectation that a Mr. Hall Pycroft, whom he had never seen, was about to enter the office upon the Monday morning."

"My God!" cried our client, "what a blind beetle I have been!"

"Now you see the point about the handwriting. Suppose that someone turned up in your place who wrote a completely different hand from that in which you had applied for the vacancy, of course the game would have been up. But in the interval the rogue learnt to imitate you, and his position was therefore secure, as I presume that nobody in the office had ever set eyes upon you?"

"Not a soul," groaned Hall Pycroft.

"Very good. Of course, it was of the utmost importance to prevent you from thinking better of it, and also to keep you from coming into contact with anyone who might tell you that your double was at work in Mawson's office. Therefore they gave you a handsome advance on your salary, and ran you off to the Midlands, where they gave you enough work to do to prevent your going to London, where you might have burst their little game up. That is all plain enough."

"But why should this man pretend to be his own brother?"

"Well, that is pretty clear also. There are evidently only two of them in it. The other is personating you at the office. This one acted as your engager, and then found that he could not find you an employer without admitting a third person into his plot. That he was most unwilling to do. He changed his appearance as far as he could, and trusted that the likeness, which you could not fail to observe, would be put down to a family resemblance. But for the happy chance of the gold stuffing your suspicions would probably have never been aroused."

Hall Pycroft shook his clenched hands in the air. "Good Lord!" he cried. "While I have been fooled in this way, what has this other Hall Pycroft been doing at Mawson's? What should we do, Mr. Holmes? Tell me what to do!"

"We must wire to Mawson's."

"They shut at twelve on Saturdays."

"Never mind; there may be some door-keeper or attendant——"

"Ah, yes; they keep a permanent guard there on account of the value of the securities that they hold. I remember hearing it talked of in the City."

"PYCROFT SHOOK HIS CLENCHED HANDS IN THE AIR."

"Very good, we shall wire to him, and see if all is well, and if a clerk of your name is working there. That is clear enough, but what is not so clear is why at sight of us one of the rogues should instantly walk out of the room and hang himself."

"The paper!" croaked a voice behind us. The man was sitting up, blanched and ghastly, with returning reason in his eyes, and hands which rubbed nervously at the broad red band which still encircled his throat.

"The paper! Of course!" yelled Holmes, in a paroxysm of excitement. "Idiot that I was! I thought so much of our visit that the paper never entered my head for an instant. To be sure the secret must lie there." He flattened it out upon the table, and a cry of triumph burst from his lips.

"Look at this, Watson!" he cried. "It is a London paper, an early edition of the *Evening Standard.* Here is what we want. Look at the headlines—'Crime in the City. Murder at Mawson and Williams'. Gigantic Attempted Robbery; Capture of the Criminal.'

Here, Watson, we are all equally anxious to hear it, so kindly read it aloud to us."

It appeared from its position in the paper to have been the one event of importance in town, and the account of it ran in this way:—

"A desperate attempt at robbery, culminating in the death of one man and the capture of the criminal, occurred this afternoon in the City. For some time back Mawson and Williams, the famous financial house, have been the guardians of securities which amount in the aggregate to a sum of considerably over a million sterling. So conscious was the manager of the responsibility which devolved upon him in consequence of the great interests at stake, that safes of the very latest construction have been employed, and an armed watchman has been left day and night in the building. It appears that last week a new clerk, named Hall Pycroft, was engaged by the firm. This person appears to have been none other than Beddington, the famous forger and cracksman, who, with his brother, has only recently emerged from a five years' spell of penal servitude. By some means, which are not yet clear, he succeeded in winning, under a false name, this official position in the office, which he utilized in order to obtain mouldings of various locks, and a thorough knowledge of the position of the strong room and the safes.

"It is customary at Mawson's for the clerks to leave at midday on Saturday. Sergeant Tuson, of the City Police, was somewhat surprised therefore to see a gentleman with a carpet bag come down the steps at twenty minutes past one. His suspicions being aroused, the sergeant followed the man, and with the aid of Constable Pollock succeeded, after a most desperate resistance, in arresting him. It was at once clear that a daring and gigantic robbery had been committed. Nearly a hundred thousand pounds worth of American railway bonds, with a large amount of scrip in other mines and companies, were discovered in the bag. On examining the premises the body of the unfortunate watchman was found doubled up and thrust into the largest of the safes, where it would not have been discovered until Monday morning had it not been for the prompt action of Sergeant Tuson. The man's skull had been shattered by a blow from a poker, delivered from behind. There at present be ascertained, although the police are making energetic inquiries as to his whereabouts."

"Well, we may save the police some little trouble in that direction," said Holmes, glancing at the haggard figure huddled up by the window. "Human nature is a strange mixture, Watson. You see that even a villain and a murderer can inspire

"GLANCING AT THE HAGGARD FIGURE.

could be no doubt that Beddington had obtained entrance by pretending that he had left something behind him, and having murdered the watchman, rapidly rifled the large safe, and then made off with his booty. His brother, who usually works with him, has not appeared in this job, so far as can such affection that his brother turns to suicide when he learns that his neck is forfeited. However, we have no choice as to our action. The doctor and I will remain on guard, Mr. Pycroft, if you will have the kindness to step out for the police."

The Adventures of Sherlock Holmes.

XVII.—THE ADVENTURE OF THE "GLORIA SCOTT."

By A. Conan Doyle.

"I HAVE some papers here," said my friend, Sherlock Holmes, as we sat one winter's night on either side of the fire, "which I really think, Watson, it would be worth your while to glance over. These are the documents in the extraordinary case of the *Gloria Scott*, and this is the message which struck Justice of the Peace Trevor dead with horror when he read it."

He had picked from a drawer a little tarnished cylinder, and, undoing the tape, he handed me a short note scrawled upon a half sheet of slate-grey paper.

"The supply of game for London is going steadily up," it ran. "Head-keeper Hudson, we believe, has been now told to receive all orders for fly-paper, and for preservation of your hen pheasant's life."

As I glanced up from reading this enigmatical message I saw Holmes chuckling at the expression upon my face.

"You look a little bewildered," said he.

"I cannot see how such a message as this could inspire horror. It seems to me to be rather grotesque than otherwise."

"Very likely. Yet the fact remains that the reader, who was a fine, robust old man, was knocked clean down by it, as if it had been the butt-end of a pistol."

"You arouse my curiosity," said I. "But why did you say just now that there were very particular reasons why I should study this case ?"

"Because it was the first in which I was ever engaged."

I had often endeavoured to elicit from my companion what had first turned his mind in the direction of criminal research, but I had never caught him before in a communicative humour. Now he sat forward in his arm-chair, and spread out the documents upon his knees. Then he lit his pipe and sat for some time smoking and turning them over.

"You never heard me talk of Victor Trevor ?" he asked. "He was the only friend I made during the two years that I was at college. I was never a very sociable fellow, Watson, always rather fond of moping in my rooms and working out my own little methods of thought, so that I never mixed much with the men of my year. Bar fencing and boxing I had few athletic tastes, and then my line of study was quite distinct from that of the other fellows, so that we had no points of contact at all. Trevor was the only man I knew, and that only through the accident of his bull-terrier freezing on to my ankle one morning as I went down to chapel.

"It was a prosaic way of forming a friendship, but it was effective. I was laid by the heels for ten days, and Trevor used to come in to inquire after me. At first it was only a minute's chat, but soon his visits lengthened, and before the end of the term we were close friends. He was a hearty, full-blooded fellow, full of spirits and energy, the very opposite to me in most respects ; but we found we had some subjects in common, and it was a bond of union when I found that he was as friendless as I. Finally, he invited me down to his father's place at Donnithorpe, in Norfolk, and I accepted his hospitality for a month of the long vacation.

"Old Trevor was evidently a man of some wealth and consideration, a J.P. and a landed proprietor. Donnithorpe is a little hamlet just to the north of Langmere, in the country of the Broads. The house was an old-fashioned, wide-spread, oak-beamed, brick building, with a fine lime-lined avenue leading up to it. There was excellent wild duck shooting in the fens, remarkably good fishing, a small but select library, taken over, as I understood, from a former occupant, and a tolerable cook, so that it would be a fastidious man who could not put in a pleasant month there.

"Trevor senior was a widower, and my friend was his only son. There had been a daughter, I heard, but she had died of diphtheria while on a visit to Birmingham. The father interested me extremely. He was a man of little culture, but with a considerable amount of rude strength both physically and mentally. He knew hardly any books, but he had travelled far, had seen much of the world, and had remembered all that he had learned. In person he was a thick-set, burly man, with a shock of grizzled

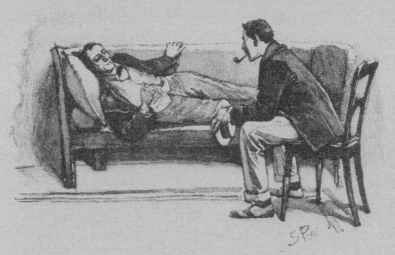

"TREVOR USED TO COME IN TO INQUIRE AFTER ME."

hair, a brown, weather-beaten face, and blue eyes which were keen to the verge of fierceness. Yet he had a reputation for kindness and charity on the country side, and was noted for the leniency of his sentences from the bench.

"One evening, shortly after my arrival, we were sitting over a glass of port after dinner, when young Trevor began to talk about those habits of observation and inference which I had already formed into a system, although I had not yet appreciated the part which they were to play in my life. The old man evidently thought that his son was exaggerating in his description of one or two trivial feats which I had performed.

"'Come now, Mr. Holmes,' said he, laughing good-humouredly, 'I'm an excellent subject, if you can deduce anything from me.'

"'I fear there is not very much,' I answered. 'I might suggest that you have gone about in fear of some personal attack within the last twelve months.'

"The laugh faded from his lips and he stared at me in great surprise.

"'Well, that's true enough,' said he. 'You know, Victor,' turning to his son, 'when we broke up that poaching gang, they swore to knife us; and Sir Edward Hoby has actually been attacked. I've always been on my guard since then, though I have no idea how you know it.'

"'You have a very handsome stick,' I answered. 'By the inscription, I observed

that you had not had it more than a year. But you have taken some pains to bore the head of it and pour melted lead into the hole, so as to make it a formidable weapon. I argued that you would not take such precautions unless you had some danger to fear.'

"'Anything else?' he asked, smiling.

"'You have boxed a good deal in your youth.'

"'Right again. How did you know it? Is my nose knocked a little out of the straight?'

"'No,' said I. 'It is your ears. They have the peculiar flattening and thickening which marks the boxing man.'

"'Anything else?'

"'You have done a great deal of digging, by your callosities.'

"'Made all my money at the gold-fields.'

"'You have been in New Zealand.'

"'Right again.'

"'You have visited Japan.'

"'Quite true.'

"'And you have been most intimately associated with someone whose initials were J. A., and whom you afterwards were eager to entirely forget.'

"Mr. Trevor stood slowly up, fixed his large blue eyes upon me with a strange, wild stare, and then pitched forward with his face among the nutshells which strewed the cloth, in a dead faint.

"You can imagine, Watson, how shocked both his son and I were. His attack did not last long, however, for when we undid his collar and sprinkled the water from one of the finger-glasses over his face, he gave a gasp or two and sat up.

"'Ah, boys!' said he, forcing a smile. 'I hope I haven't frightened you. Strong as I look, there is a weak place in my heart, and it does not take much to knock me over. I don't know how you manage this, Mr. Holmes, but it seems to me that all the detectives of fact and of fancy would be children in your hands. That's your line of life, sir, and you may take the word of a man who has seen something of the world.'

"And that recommendation, with the exaggerated estimate of my ability with which he prefaced it, was, if you will believe me, Watson, the very first thing which ever made me feel that a profession might be made out of what had up to that time been the merest hobby. At the moment, however, I was too much concerned at the sudden illness of my host to think of anything else.

"'I hope that I have said nothing to pain you,' said I.

"'Well, you certainly touched upon rather a tender point. Might I ask how you know and how much you know?' He spoke now in a half jesting fashion, but a look of terror still lurked at the back of his eyes.

"'It is simplicity itself,' said I. 'When you bared your arm to draw that fish into the boat I saw that "J. A." had been tattooed in the bend of the elbow. The letters were still legible, but it was perfectly clear from their blurred appearance, and from the staining of the skin round them, that efforts had been made to obliterate them. It was obvious, then, that those initials had once been very familiar to you, and that you had afterwards wished to forget them.'

"'What an eye you have!' he cried, with a sigh of relief. 'It is just as you say. But we won't talk of it. Of all ghosts, the ghosts of our old loves are the worst. Come into the billiard-room and have a quiet cigar.'

"From that day, amid all his cordiality, there was always a touch of suspicion in Mr. Trevor's manner towards me. Even his son remarked it. 'You've given the governor such a turn,' said he, 'that he'll never be sure again of what you know and what you don't know.' He did not mean to show it, I am sure, but it was so strongly in his mind that it peeped out at every action. At last I became so convinced that I was causing him uneasiness, that I drew my visit to a close. On the very day, however, before I left an incident occurred which proved in the sequel to be of importance.

"We were sitting out upon the lawn on garden chairs, the three of us, basking in the sun and admiring the view across the Broads, when the maid came out to say that there was a man at the door who wanted to see Mr. Trevor.

"'What is his name?' asked my host.

"'He would not give any.'

"'What does he want, then?'

"'He says that you know him, and that he only wants a moment's conversation.'

"'Show him round here.' An instant afterwards there appeared a little wizened fellow, with a cringing manner and a shambling style of walking. He wore an open jacket, with a splotch of tar on the sleeve, a red and black check shirt, dungaree trousers, and heavy boots badly worn. His face was thin and brown and crafty, with a perpetual smile upon it, which showed an irregular line of yellow teeth, and his crinkled hands were half-closed in a way that is distinctive of sailors. As he came slouching across the lawn I heard Mr. Trevor make a sort of hiccoughing noise in his throat, and, jumping out of his chair, he ran into the house. He was back in a moment, and I smelt a strong reek of brandy as he passed me.

"'Well, my man,' said he, 'what can I do for you?'

"The sailor stood looking at him with puckered eyes, and with the same loose-lipped smile upon his face.

"'You don't know me?' he asked.

"'Why, dear me, it is surely Hudson!' said Mr. Trevor, in a tone of surprise.

"'Hudson it is, sir,' said the seaman. 'Why, it's thirty year and more since I saw you last. Here you are in your house, and me still picking my salt meat out of the harness cask.'

"'Tut, you will find that I have not forgotten old times,' cried Mr. Trevor, and, walking towards the sailor, he said something in a low voice. 'Go into the kitchen,' he continued out loud, 'and you will get food and drink. I have no doubt that I shall find you a situation.'

"'Thank you, sir,' said the seaman, touching his forelock. 'I'm just off a two-yearer in an eight-knot tramp, short-handed at that, and I wants a rest. I thought I'd get it either with Mr. Beddoes or with you.'

"'Ah!' cried Mr. Trevor, 'you know where Mr. Beddoes is?'

"'Bless you, sir, I know where all my old friends are,' said the fellow, with a sinister smile, and slouched off after the maid to the

"'HUDSON IT IS, SIR,' SAID THE SEAMAN."

kitchen. Mr. Trevor mumbled something to us about having been shipmates with the man when he was going back to the diggings, and then, leaving us on the lawn, he went indoors. An hour later, when we entered the house we found him stretched dead drunk upon the dining-room sofa. The whole incident left a most ugly impression upon my mind, and I was not sorry next day to leave Donnithorpe behind me, for I felt that my presence must be a source of embarrassment to my friend.

"All this occurred during the first month of the long vacation. I went up to my London rooms, where I spent seven weeks working out a few experiments in organic chemistry. One day, however, when the autumn was far advanced and the vacation drawing to a close, I received a telegram from my friend imploring me to return to Donnithorpe, and saying that he was in great need of my advice and assistance. Of course I dropped everything, and set out for the north once more.

"He met me with the dog-cart at the station, and I saw at a glance that the last two months had been very trying ones for him. He had grown thin and careworn, and had lost the loud, cheery manner for which he had been remarkable.

"'The governor is dying,' were the first words he said.

"'Impossible!' I cried. 'What is the matter?'

"'Apoplexy. Nervous shock. He's been on the verge all day. I doubt if we shall find him alive.'

"I was, as you may think, Watson, horrified at this unexpected news.

"'What has caused it?' I asked.

"'Ah, that is the point. Jump in, and we can talk it over while we drive. You remember that fellow who came upon the evening before you left us?'

"'Perfectly.'

"'Do you know who it was that we let into the house that day?'

"'I have no idea.'

"'It was the Devil, Holmes!' he cried.

"I stared at him in astonishment.

"'Yes; it was the Devil himself. We have not had a peaceful hour since—not one. The governor has never held up his head from that evening, and now the life has been crushed out of him, and his heart broken all through this accursed Hudson.'

"'What power had he, then?'

"'Ah! that is what I would give so much to know. The kindly, charitable, good old governor ! How could he have fallen into the clutches of such a ruffian ? But I am so glad that you have come, Holmes. I trust very much to your judgment and discretion, and I know that you will advise me for the best.'

"We were dashing along the smooth, white country road, with the long stretch of the Broads in front of us glimmering in the red light of the setting sun. From a grove upon our left I could already see the high chimneys and the flag-staff which marked the squire's dwelling.

"'My father made the fellow gardener,' said my companion, 'and then, as that did not satisfy him, he was promoted to be butler. The house seemed to be at his mercy, and he wandered about and did what he chose in it. The maids complained of his drunken habits and his vile language. The dad raised their wages all round to recompense them for the annoyance. The fellow would take the boat and my father's best gun and treat himself to little shooting parties. And all this with such a sneering, leering, insolent face, that I would have knocked him down twenty times over if he had been a man of my own age. I tell you, Holmes, I have had to keep a tight hold upon myself all this time, and now I am asking myself whether, if I had let myself go a little more, I might not have been a wiser man.

"'Well, matters went from bad to worse with us, and this animal, Hudson, became more and more intrusive, until at last, on his making some insolent reply to my father in my presence one day, I took him by the shoulder and turned him out of the room. He slunk away with a livid face, and two venomous eyes which uttered more threats than his tongue could do. I don't know what passed between the poor dad and him after that, but the dad came to me next day and asked me whether I would mind apologizing to Hudson. I refused, as you can imagine, and asked my father how he could allow such a wretch to take such liberties with himself and his household.

"'Ah, my boy,' said he, 'it is all very well to talk, but you don't know how I am placed. But you shall know, Victor. I'll see that you shall know, come what may ! You wouldn't believe harm of your poor old father, would you, lad ?' He was very much moved, and shut himself up in the study all day, where I could see through the window that he was writing busily.

"'That evening there came what seemed to me to be a grand release, for Hudson told us that he was going to leave us. He walked into the dining-room as we sat after dinner, and announced his intention in the thick voice of a half-drunken man.

"'I've had enough of Norfolk,' said he. 'I'll run down to Mr. Beddoes, in Hampshire. He'll be as glad to see me as you were, I daresay.'

"'You're not going away in an unkind spirit, Hudson, I hope,' said my father, with a tameness which made my blood boil.

"'I've not had my 'pology,'" said he, sulkily, glancing in my direction.

"'Victor, you will acknowledge

"'I'VE NOT HAD MY 'POLOGY,' SAID HE, SULKILY."

that you have used this worthy fellow rather roughly?' said the dad, turning to me.

"'On the contrary, I think that we have

both shown extraordinary patience towards him,' I answered.

"'Oh, you do, do you?' he snarled. 'Very good, mate. We'll see about that!' He slouched out of the room, and half an hour afterwards left the house, leaving my father in a state of pitiable nervousness. Night after night I heard him pacing his room, and it was just as he was recovering his confidence that the blow did at last fall.

"'And how?' I asked, eagerly.

"'In a most extraordinary fashion. A letter arrived for my father yesterday evening, bearing the Fordingbridge postmark. My father read it, clapped both his hands to his head and began running round the room in little circles like a man who has been driven out of his senses. When I at last drew him down on to the sofa, his mouth and eyelids were all puckered on one side, and I saw that he had a stroke. Dr. Fordham came over at once, and we put him to bed; but the paralysis has spread, he has shown no sign of returning consciousness, and I think that we shall hardly find him alive.'

"'You horrify me, Trevor!' I cried. 'What, then, could have been in this letter to cause so dreadful a result?'

"'Nothing. There lies the inexplicable part of it. The message was absurd and trivial. Ah, my God, it is as I feared!'

"As he spoke we came round the curve of the avenue, and saw in the fading light that every blind in the house had been drawn down. As we dashed up to the door, my friend's face convulsed with grief, a gentleman in black emerged from it.

"'When did it happen, doctor?' asked Trevor.

"'Almost immediately after you left.'

"'Did he recover consciousness?'

"'For an instant before the end.'

"'Any message for me?'

"'Only that the papers were in the back drawer of the Japanese cabinet.'

"My friend ascended with the doctor to the chamber of death, while I remained in the study, turning the whole matter over and over in my head, and feeling as sombre as ever I had done in my life. What was the past of this Trevor: pugilist, traveller, and gold-digger; and how had he placed himself in the power of this acid-faced seaman? Why, too, should he faint at an allusion to the half-effaced initials upon his arm, and die of fright when he had a letter from Fordingbridge? Then I remembered that Fording-bridge was in Hampshire, and that this Mr. Beddoes, whom the seaman had gone to visit, and presumably to blackmail, had also been mentioned as living in Hampshire. The letter, then, might either come from Hudson, the seaman, saying that he had betrayed the guilty secret which appeared to exist, or it might come from Beddoes, warning an old confederate that such a betrayal was imminent. So far it seemed clear enough. But, then, how could the letter be trivial and grotesque, as described by the son? He must have misread it. If so, it must have been one of those ingenious secret codes which mean one thing while they seem to mean another. I must see this letter. If there were a hidden meaning in it, I was confident that I could pluck it forth. For an hour I sat pondering over it in the gloom, until at last a weeping maid brought in a lamp, and close at her heels came my friend Trevor, pale but composed, with these very papers which lie upon my knee held in his grasp. He sat down opposite to me, drew the lamp to the edge of the table, and handed me a short note scribbled, as you see, upon a single sheet of grey paper. 'The supply of game for London is going steadily up,' it ran. 'Head-keeper Hudson, we believe, has been now told to receive all orders for fly-paper and for preservation of your hen pheasant's life.'

"I daresay my face looked as bewildered as yours did just now when first I read this message. Then I re-read it very carefully. It was evidently as I had thought, and some second meaning must lie buried in this strange combination of words. Or could it be that there was a prearranged significance to such phrases as 'fly-paper' and 'hen pheasant'? Such a meaning would be arbitrary, and could not be deduced in any way. And yet I was loth to believe that this was the case, and the presence of the word 'Hudson' seemed to show that the subject of the message was as I had guessed, and that it was from Beddoes rather than the sailor. I tried it backwards, but the combination, 'Life pheasant's hen,' was not encouraging. Then I tried alternate words, but neither 'The of for' nor 'supply game London' promised to throw any light upon it. And then in an instant the key of the riddle was in my hands, and I saw that every third word beginning with the first would give a message which might well drive old Trevor to despair.

"It was short and terse, the warning, as I now read it to my companion:—

"THE KEY OF THE RIDDLE WAS IN MY HANDS."

" 'The game is up. Hudson has told all. Fly for your life.'

"Victor Trevor sank his face into his shaking hands. 'It must be that, I suppose,' said he. 'This is worse than death, for it means disgrace as well. But what is the meaning of these " head-keepers " and " hen pheasants " ?

" ' It means nothing to the message, but it might mean a good deal to us if we had no other means of discovering the sender. You see that he has begun by writing, " The . . . . . game . . . . . is," and so on. Afterwards he had, to fulfil the prearranged cipher, to fill in any two words in each space. He would naturally use the first words which came to his mind, and if there were so many which referred to sport among them, you may be tolerably sure that he is either an ardent shot cr interested in breeding. Do you know anything of this Beddoes ?'

" 'Why, now that you mention it,' said he, 'I remember that my poor father used to have an invitation from him to shoot over his preserves every autumn.'

" ' Then it is undoubtedly from him that the note comes,' said I. 'It only remains for us to find out what this secret was which the sailor Hudson seems to have held over the heads of these two wealthy and respected men.'

" ' Alas, Holmes, I fear that it is one of sin and shame ! ' cried my friend. ' But from you I shall have no secrets. Here is the statement which was drawn up by my father when he knew that the danger from Hudson had become imminent. I found it in the Japanese cabinet, as he told the doctor. Take it and read it to me, for I have neither the strength nor the courage to do it myself.'

" These are the very papers, Watson, which he handed to me, and I will read them to you as I read them in the old study that night to him. They are indorsed outside, as you see : 'Some particulars of the voyage of the barque *Gloria Scott*, from her leaving Falmouth on the 8th October, 1855, to her destruction in N. lat. 15° 20', W. long. 25° 14', on November 6th.' It is in the form of a letter, and runs in this way :—

" My dear, dear son,—Now that approaching disgrace begins to darken the closing years of my life, I can write with all truth and honesty that it is not the terror of the law, it is not the loss of my position in the county, nor is it my fall in the eyes of all who have known me, which cuts me to the heart ; but it is the thought that you should come to blush for me—you who love me, and who have seldom, I hope, had reason to do other than respect me. But if the blow falls which is for ever hanging over me, then I should wish you to read this that you may know straight from me how far I have been to blame. On the other hand, if all should go well (which may kind God Almighty giant !), then if by any chance this paper should be still undestroyed, and should fall into your hands, I conjure you by all you hold sacred, by the memory of your dear mother, and by the love which has been between us, to hurl it into the fire, and to never give one thought to it again.

" If, then, your eye goes on to read this line, I know that I shall already have been exposed and dragged from my home, or, as is more likely—for you know that my heart is weak—be lying with my tongue sealed for ever in death. In either case the time for suppression is past, and every word which I tell you is the naked truth ; and this I swear as I hope for mercy.

" My name, dear lad, is not Trevor. I was James Armitage in my younger days, and you can understand now the shock that it was to me a few weeks ago when your college friend addressed me in words which seemed to imply that he had surmised my secret. As Armitage it was that I entered a London banking house, and as Armitage I was convicted of breaking my country's laws, and was sentenced to transportation. Do not think very harshly of me, laddie. It was a debt of honour, so-called, which I had to pay, and I used money which was not my own to do it, in the certainty that I could replace it before there could be any possibility of its being missed. But the most dreadful ill-luck pursued me. The money which I had reckoned upon never came to hand, and a premature examination of accounts exposed my deficit. The case might have been dealt leniently with, but the laws were more harshly administered thirty years ago than now, and on my twenty-third birthday I found myself chained as a felon with thirty-seven other convicts in the 'tween decks of the barque *Gloria Scott*, bound for Australia.

" It was the year '55, when the Crimean War was at its height, and the old convict ships had been largely used as transports in the Black Sea. The Government was compelled therefore to use smaller and less suitable vessels for sending out their prisoners. The *Gloria Scott* had been in the Chinese tea trade, but she was an old-fashioned, heavy-bowed, broad-beamed craft, and the new clippers had cut her out. She was a 500-ton boat, and besides her thirty-eight gaol-birds, she carried twenty-six of a crew, eighteen soldiers, a captain, three mates, a doctor, a chaplain, and four warders. Nearly a hundred souls were in her, all told, when we set sail from Falmouth.

" The partitions between the cells of the convicts, instead of being of thick oak, as is usual in convict ships, were quite thin and frail. The man next to me upon the aft side was one whom I had particularly noticed when we were led down the quay. He was a young man with a clear, hairless face, a long thin nose, and rather nutcracker jaws. He carried his head very jauntily in the air, had a swaggering style of walking, and was above all else remarkable for his extraordinary height. I don't think any of our heads would come up to his shoulder, and I am sure that he could not have measured less than six and a half feet. It was strange among so many sad and weary faces to see one which was full of energy and resolution. The sight of it was to me like a fire in a snowstorm. I was glad then to find that he was my neighbour, and gladder still when, in the dead of the night, I heard a whisper close to my ear, and found that he had managed to cut an opening in the board which separated us.

" ' Halloa, chummy ! ' said he, ' what's your name, and what are you here for ? '

" I answered him, and asked in turn who I was talking with.

" ' I'm Jack Prendergast,' said he, ' and, by God, you'll learn to bless my name before you've done with me ! '

" I remembered hearing of his case, for it was one which had made an immense sensation throughout the country, some time before my own arrest. He was a man of good family and of great ability, but of incurably vicious habits, who had, by an ingenious system of fraud, obtained huge sums of money from the leading London merchants.

" ' Ah, ha ! You remember my case ? ' said he, proudly.

" ' Very well indeed.'

" ' Then maybe you remember something queer about it ? '

" ' What was that, then ? '

" ' I'd had nearly a quarter of a million, hadn't I ? '

" ' So it was said.'

" ' But none was recovered, eh ? '

" ' No.'

" ' Well, where d'ye suppose the balance is ? ' he asked.

" ' I have no idea,' said I.

" ' Right between my finger and thumb,' he cried. ' By God, I've got more pounds to my name than you have hairs on your head. And if you've money, my son, and know how to handle it and spread it, you can do *anything !* Now, you don't think it likely that a man who could do anything is going to wear his breeches out sitting in the stinking hold of a rat-gutted, beetle-ridden, mouldy old coffin of a China coaster ? No, sir, such a man will look after himself, and will look after his chums. You may lay to that ! You hold on to him, and you may kiss the Book that he'll haul you through.'

"That was his style of talk, and at first I thought it meant nothing, but after a while, when he had tested me and sworn me in with all possible solemnity, he let me understand that there really was a plot to gain command of the vessel. A dozen of the prisoners had hatched it before they came aboard; Prendergast was the leader, and his money was the motive power.

" 'I'd a partner,' said he, 'a rare good man, as true as a stock to a barrel. He's got the dibbs, he has, and where do you think he is at this moment ? Why, he's the chaplain of this ship — the chaplain, no less ! He came aboard with a black coat and his papers right, and money enough in his box to buy the thing right up from keel to main-truck. The crew are his, body and soul. He could buy 'em at so much a gross with a cash discount, and he did it before ever they signed on. He's got two of the warders and Mercer

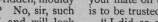

JACK PRENDERGAST.

the second mate, and he'd get the captain himself if he thought him worth it.'

" 'What are we to do, then ? ' I asked.

" 'What do you think ? ' said he. 'We'll make the coats of some of these soldiers redder than ever the tailor did.'

" 'But they are armed,' said I.

" 'And so shall we be, my boy. There's a brace of pistols for every mother's son of us, and if we can't carry this ship, with the crew at our back, it's time we were all sent to a young Miss's boarding school. You speak to your mate on the left to-night, and see if he is to be trusted.'

" I did so, and found my other neighbour to be a young fellow in much the same position as myself, whose crime had been forgery. His name was Evans, but he afterwards changed it, like myself, and he is now a rich and prosperous man in the South of England. He was ready enough to join the conspiracy, as the only means of saving ourselves, and before we had crossed the Bay there were only two of the prisoners who were not in the secret. One of these was of weak mind, and we did not dare to trust him, and the other was suffering from jaundice, and could not be of any use to us.

" From the beginning there was really nothing to prevent us taking possession of the ship. The crew were a set of ruffians, specially picked for the job. The sham chaplain came into our cells to exhort us, carrying a black bag, supposed to be full of tracts ; and so often did he come that by the third day we had each stowed away at the foot of our bed a file, a brace of pistols, a pound of powder, and twenty slugs. Two of the warders were agents of Prendergast, and the second mate was his right-hand man. The captain, the two mates, two warders, Lieutenant Martin, his eighteen soldiers, and the doctor were all that we had against us. Yet, safe as it was, we determined to neglect no precaution, and to make our attack suddenly at night. It came, however, more quickly than we expected, and in this way :—

" One evening, about the third week after our start, the doctor had come down to see one of the prisoners, who was ill, and, putting his hand down on the bottom of his bunk, he felt the outline of the pistols. If he had been silent he might have blown the whole thing; but he was a nervous little chap, so he gave a cry of surprise and turned so pale, that the man knew what was up in an instant and seized him. He was gagged before he could give the alarm, and tied down upon the bed. He had unlocked the door that led to the deck, and we were through it in a rush. The two sentries were shot down, and so was a corporal who came running to see what was the matter. There were two more soldiers at the door of the state-room, and their muskets seemed not to be loaded, for they never fired upon us, and they were shot while trying to fix their bayonets. Then we rushed on into the captain's cabin, but as we pushed open the door there was an explosion from within, and there he lay with his head on the chart of the Atlantic, which was pinned upon the table, while the chaplain stood, with a smoking pistol in his hand,

more. There were lockers all round, and Wilson, the sham chaplain, knocked one of them in, and pulled out a dozen of brown sherry. We cracked off the necks of the bottles, poured the stuff out into tumblers, and were just tossing them off, when in an instant, without warning, there came the roar of muskets in our ears, and the saloon was so full of smoke that we could not see across the table. When it cleared again the place was a shambles. Wilson and eight others were wriggling on the top of each other on the floor, and the blood and the brown sherry on that table turn me sick now when I think of it. We were so cowed by the sight that I think we should have given the job up if it had not been for Prendergast. He bellowed like a bull, and rushed for the door with all that were left alive at his heels. Out we ran, and there on the poop were the lieutenant and ten of his men. The swing skylights above the saloon table had been a bit open, and they had fired on us through the slit. We got on them before they could load, and they stood to it like men, but we had the upper hand of them, and in five minutes it was all over. My God! was there ever a slaughter-house like that ship? Prendergast was like a raging devil, and he picked the soldiers up as if they had been children and threw them overboard, alive or dead. There was one sergeant that was horribly wounded, and yet kept on swimming for a surprising time, until

"THE CHAPLAIN STOOD WITH A SMOKING PISTOL IN HIS HAND."

at his elbow. The two mates had both been seized by the crew, and the whole business seemed to be settled.

"The state-room was next the cabin, and we flocked in there and flopped down on the settees all speaking together, for we were just mad with the feeling that we were free once

someone in mercy blew out his brains. When the fighting was over there was no one left of our enemies except just the warders, the mates, and the doctor.

"It was over them that the great quarrel arose. There were many of us who were glad enough to win back our freedom, and yet who had no wish to have murder on our souls. It was one thing to knock the soldiers over with their muskets in their hands, and it was another to stand by while men were being killed in cold blood. Eight of us, five convicts and three sailors, said that we would not see it done. But there was no moving Prendergast and those who were with him. Our only chance of safety lay in making a clean job of it, said he, and he would not leave a tongue with power to wag in a witness-box. It nearly came to our sharing the fate of the prisoners, but at last he said that if we wished we might take a boat and go. We jumped at the offer, for we were already sick of these bloodthirsty doings, and we saw that there would be worse before it was done. We were given a suit of sailors' togs each, a barrel of water, two casks, one of junk and one of biscuits, and a compass. Prendergast threw us over a chart, told us that we were shipwrecked mariners whose ship had foundered in lat. 15° N. and long. 25° W., and then cut the painter and let us go.

"And now I come to the most surprising part of my story, my dear son. The seamen had hauled the foreyard aback during the rising, but now as we left them they brought it square again, and, as there was a light wind from the north and east, the barque began to draw slowly away from us. Our boat lay, rising and falling, upon the long, smooth rollers, and Evans and I, who were the most educated of the party, were sitting in the sheets working out our position and planning what coast we should make for. It was a nice question, for the Cape de Verds were about 500 miles to the north of us, and the African coast about 700 miles to the east. On the whole, as the wind was coming round to north, we thought that Sierra Leone might be best, and turned our

head in that direction, the barque being at that time nearly hull down on our starboard quarter. Suddenly as we looked at her we saw a dense black cloud of smoke shoot up from her, which hung like a monstrous tree upon the sky-line. A few seconds later a roar like thunder burst upon our ears, and as the smoke thinned away there was no sign left of the *Gloria Scott*. In an instant we swept the boat's head round again, and pulled with all our strength for the place where the haze, still trailing over the water, marked the scene of this catastrophe.

"It was a long hour before we reached it, and at first we feared that we had come too late to save anyone. A splintered boat and a number of crates and fragments of spars rising and falling on the waves showed us where the vessel had foundered, but there was no sign of life, and we had turned away in despair when we heard a cry for help, and saw at some distance a piece of wreckage with a man lying stretched across it. When we pulled him aboard the boat he proved to be a young seaman of the name of Hudson, who was so burned and exhausted that he could give us no account of what bad happened until the following morning.

"It seemed that after we had left, Prendergast and his gang had proceeded to put to death the five remaining prisoners: the two warders had been shot and thrown overboard,

"WE PULLED HIM ABOARD THE BOAT."

and so also had the third mate. Prendergast then descended into the 'tween decks, and with his own hands cut the throat of the unfortunate surgeon. There only remained the first mate, who was a bold and active man. When he saw the convict approaching him with the bloody knife in his hand, he kicked off his bonds, which he had somehow contrived to loosen, and rushing down the deck he plunged into the after-hold.

"A dozen convicts who descended with their pistols in search of him found him with a match-box in his hand seated beside an open powder barrel, which was one of a hundred carried on board, and swearing that he would blow all hands up if he were in any way molested. An instant later the explosion occurred, though Hudson thought it was caused by the misdirected bullet of one of the convicts rather than the mate's match. Be the cause what it may, it was the end of the *Gloria Scott*, and of the rabble who held command of her.

"Such, in a few words, my dear boy, is the history of this terrible business in which I was involved. Next day we were picked up by the brig *Hotspur*, bound for Australia, whose captain found no difficulty in believing that we were the survivors of a passenger ship which had foundered. The transport ship, *Gloria Scott*, was set down by the Admiralty as being lost at sea, and no word has ever leaked out as to her true fate. After an excellent voyage the *Hotspur* landed us at Sydney, where Evans and I changed our names and made our way to the diggings, where, among the crowds who were gathered from all nations, we had no difficulty in losing our former identities.

"The rest I need not relate. We prospered, we travelled, we came back as rich Colonials to England, and we bought country estates. For more than twenty years we have led peaceful and useful lives, and we hoped that our past was for ever buried. Imagine, then, my feelings when in the seaman who came to us I recognised instantly the man who had been picked off the wreck! He had tracked us down somehow, and had set himself to live upon our fears. You will understand now how it was that I strove to keep peace with him, and you will in some measure sympathize with me in the fears which fill me, now that he has gone from me to his other victim with threats upon his tongue.

"Underneath is written, in a hand so shaky as to be hardly legible, 'Beddoes writes in cipher to say that H. has told all. Sweet Lord, have mercy on our souls!'

"That was the narrative which I read that night to young Trevor, and I think, Watson, that under the circumstances it was a dramatic one. The good fellow was heartbroken at it, and went out to the Terai tea planting, where I hear that he is doing well. As to the sailor and Beddoes, neither of them was ever heard of again after that day on which the letter of warning was written. They both disappeared utterly and completely. No complaint had been lodged with the police, so that Beddoes had mistaken a threat for a deed. Hudson had been seen lurking about, and it was believed by the police that he had done away with Beddoes, and had fled. For myself, I believe that the truth was exactly the opposite. I think that it is most probable that Beddoes, pushed to desperation, and believing himself to have been already betrayed, had revenged himself upon Hudson, and had fled from the country with as much money as he could lay his hands on. Those are the facts of the case, Doctor, and if they are of any use to your collection, I am sure that they are very heartily at your service."

The Adventures of Sherlock Holmes.

XVIII.—THE ADVENTURE OF THE MUSGRAVE RITUAL.

By A. Conan Doyle.

N anomaly which often struck me in the character of my friend Sherlock Holmes was that, although in his methods of thought he was the neatest and most methodical of mankind, and although also he affected a certain quiet primness of dress, he was none the less in his personal habits one of the most untidy men that ever drove a fellow-lodger to distraction. Not that I am in the least conventional in that respect myself. The rough-and-tumble work in Afghanistan, coming on the top of a natural Bohemianism of disposition, has made me rather more lax than befits a medical man. But with me there is a limit, and when I find a man who keeps his cigars in the coal-scuttle, his tobacco in the toe end of a Persian slipper, and his unanswered correspondence transfixed by a jack-knife into the very centre of his wooden mantelpiece, then I begin to give myself virtuous airs. I have always held, too, that pistol practice should distinctly be an open-air pastime ; and when Holmes in one of his queer humours would sit in an arm-chair, with his hair-trigger and a hundred Boxer cartridges, and proceed to adorn the opposite wall with a patriotic V. R. done in bullet-pocks, I felt strongly that neither the atmosphere nor the appearance of our room was improved by it.

Our chambers were always full of chemicals and of criminal relics, which had a way of wandering into unlikely positions, and of turning up in the butter-dish, or in even less desirable places. But his papers were my great crux. He had a horror of destroying documents, especially those which were connected with his past cases, and yet it was only once in every year or two that he would muster energy to docket and arrange them, for as I have mentioned somewhere in these incoherent memoirs, the outbursts of passionate energy when he performed the remarkable feats with which his name is associated were followed by reactions of lethargy, during which he would lie about with his violin and his books, hardly moving, save from the sofa to the table. Thus month after month his papers accumulated, until every corner of the room was stacked with bundles of manuscript which were on no account to be burned, and which could not be put away save by their owner.

One winter's night, as we sat together by the fire, I ventured to suggest to him that as he had finished pasting extracts into his commonplace book he might employ the next two hours in making our room a little more habitable. He could not deny the justice of my request, so with a rather rueful face he went off to his bedroom, from which he returned presently pulling a large tin box behind him. This he placed in the middle of the floor, and squatting down upon a stool in front of it he threw back the lid. I could see that it was already a third full of bundles of paper tied up with red tape into separate packages.

"There are cases enough here, Watson," said he, looking at me with mischievous eyes. "I think that if you knew all that I had in this box you would ask me to pull some out instead of putting others in."

"These are the records of your early work, then ? " I asked. "I have often wished that I had notes of those cases."

"Yes, my boy ; these were all done prematurely, before my biographer had come to glorify me." He lifted bundle after bundle in a tender, caressing sort of way. "They are not all successes, Watson," said he, "but there are some pretty little problems among them. Here's the record of the Tarleton murders, and the case of Vamberry, the wine merchant, and the adventure of the old Russian woman, and the singular affair of the aluminium crutch, as well as a full account of Ricoletti of the club foot and his abominable wife. And here—ah, now ! this really is something a little recherché."

He dived his arm down to the bottom of the chest, and brought up a small wooden box, with a sliding lid, such as children's toys are kept in. From within he produced a crumpled piece of paper, an old-fashioned brass key, a peg of wood with a ball of string be glad that you should add this case to your annals, for there are points in it which make it quite unique in the criminal records of this or, I believe, of any other country. A collection of my trifling achievements would certainly be incomplete which contained no account of this very singular business.

"A CURIOUS COLLECTION."

attached to it, and three rusty old discs of metal.

"Well, my boy, what do you make of this lot?" he asked, smiling at my expression.

"It is a curious collection."

"Very curious, and the story that hangs round it will strike you as being more curious still."

"These relics have a history, then?"

"So much so that they *are* history."

"What do you mean by that?"

Sherlock Holmes picked them up one by one, and laid them along the edge of the table. Then he reseated himself in his chair, and looked them over with a gleam of satisfaction in his eyes.

"These," said he, "are all that I have left to remind me of 'The Adventure of the Musgrave Ritual.'"

I had heard him mention the case more than once, though I had never been able to gather the details.

"I should be so glad," said I, "if you would give me an account of it."

"And leave the litter as it is," he cried, mischievously. "Your tidiness won't bear much strain, after all, Watson. But I should

"You may remember how the affair of the *Gloria Scott*, and my conversation with the unhappy man whose fate I told you of, first turned my attention in the direction of the profession which has become my life's work. You see me now when my name has become known far and wide, and when I am generally recognised both by the public and by the official force as being a final court of appeal in doubtful cases. Even when you knew me first, at the time of the affair which you have commemorated in 'A Study in Scarlet,' I had already established a considerable, though not a very lucrative, connection. You can hardly realize, then, how difficult I found it at first, and how long I had to wait before I succeeded in making any headway.

"When I first came up to London I had rooms in Montague Street, just round the corner from the British Museum, and there I waited, filling in my too abundant leisure time by studying all those branches of science which might make me more efficient. Now and again cases came in my way, principally through the introduction of old fellow students, for during my last years at the university there was a good deal of talk there about myself and my methods. The third of these cases was that of the Musgrave Ritual, and it is to the interest which was aroused by that singular chain of events, and the large issues which proved to be at stake, that I trace my first stride towards the position which I now hold.

"Reginald Musgrave had been in the same college as myself, and I had some slight acquaintance with him. He was not generally popular among the undergraduates, though it always seemed to me that what was set down as pride was really an attempt to cover extreme natural diffidence. In appearance he was a man of an exceedingly aristocratic type, thin, high-nosed, and large-eyed, with languid and yet courtly manners. He was indeed a scion of one of the very oldest families in the kingdom, though his branch was a cadet one which had separated from the Northern Musgraves some time in the sixteenth century, and had established itself in Western Sussex, where the manor house of Hurlstone is perhaps the oldest inhabited building in the county. Something of his birthplace seemed to cling to the man, and I never looked at his pale, keen face, or the poise of his head without associating him with grey archways and mullioned windows and all the venerable wreckage of a feudal keep. Once or twice we drifted into talk, and I can remember that more than once he expressed a keen interest in my methods of observation and inference.

"For four years I had seen nothing of him, until one morning he walked into my room in Montague Street. He had changed little, was dressed like a young man of fashion—he was always a bit of a dandy—and preserved the same quiet, suave manner which had formerly distinguished him.

"'How has all gone with you, Musgrave?' I asked, after we had cordially shaken hands.

"'You probably heard of my poor father's death,' said he. 'He was carried off about two years ago. Since then I have, of course, had the Hurlstone estates to manage, and as

I am member for my district as well, my life has been a busy one; but I understand, Holmes, that you are turning to practical ends those powers with which you used to amaze us?'

"'Yes,' said I, 'I have taken to living by my wits.'

"'I am delighted to hear it, for your advice at present would be exceedingly valuable to me. We have had some very strange doings at Hurlstone, and the police have been able to throw no light upon the matter. It is really the most extraordinary and inexplicable business.'

REGINALD MUSGRAVE

"You can imagine with what eagerness I listened to him, Watson, for the very chance for which I had been panting during all those months of inaction seemed to have come within my reach. In my inmost heart I believed that I could succeed where others failed, and now I had the opportunity to test myself.

"'Pray let me have the details,' I cried.

"Reginald Musgrave sat down opposite to me, and lit the cigarette which I had pushed towards him.

"'You must know,' said he, 'that though I am a bachelor I have to keep up a considerable staff of servants at Hurlstone, for it is a rambling old place, and takes a good deal of looking after. I preserve, too, and in the pheasant months I usually have a house party, so that it would not do to be short-handed. Altogether there are eight maids, the cook, the butler, two footmen, and a boy. The garden and the stables, of course, have a separate staff.

" ' Of these servants the one who had been longest in our service was Brunton, the butler. He was a young schoolmaster out of place when he was first taken up by my father, but he was a man of great energy and character, and he soon became quite invaluable in the household. He was a well-grown, handsome man, with a splendid forehead, and though he has been with us for twenty years he cannot be more than forty now. With his personal advantages and his extraordinary gifts, for he can speak several languages and play nearly every musical instrument, it is wonderful that he should have been satisfied so long in such a position, but I suppose that he was comfortable and lacked energy to make any change. The butler of Hurlstone is always a thing that is remembered by all who visit us.

" ' But this paragon has one fault. He is a bit of a Don Juan, and you can imagine that for a man like him it is not a very difficult part to play in a quiet country district.

" ' When he was married it was all right, but since he has been a widower we have had no end of trouble with him. A few months ago we were in hopes that he was about to settle down again, for he became engaged to Rachel Howells, our second housemaid, but he has thrown her over since then and taken up with Janet Tregellis, the daughter of the head gamekeeper. Rachel, who is a very good girl, but of an excitable Welsh temperament, had a sharp touch of brain fever, and goes about the house now—or did until yesterday —like a black-eyed shadow of her former self. That was our first drama at Hurlstone, but a second one came to drive it from our minds, and it was prefaced by 'the disgrace and dismissal of butler Brunton.

" ' This is how it came about. I have said that the man was intelligent, and this very intelligence has caused his ruin, for it seems to have led to an insatiable curiosity about things which did not in the least concern him. I had no idea of the lengths to which this would carry him until the merest accident opened my eyes to it.

" ' I have said that the house is a rambling one. One night last week—on Thursday night, to be more exact—I found that I could not sleep, having foolishly taken a cup of strong *café noir* after my dinner. After struggling against it until two in the morning I felt that it was quite hopeless, so I rose and lit the candle with the intention of continuing a novel which I was reading. The book, however, had been left in the billiard-room, so I pulled on my dressing-gown and started off to get it.

" ' In order to reach the billiard-room I had to descend a flight of stairs, and then to cross the head of a passage which led to the library and the gun-room. You can imagine my surprise when as I looked down this corridor I saw a glimmer of light coming from the open door of the library. I had myself extinguished the lamp and closed the door before coming to bed. Naturally, my first thought was of burglars. The corridors at Hurlstone have their walls largely decorated with trophies of old weapons. From one of these I picked a battle-axe, and then, leaving my candle behind me, I crept on tip-toe down the passage and peeped in at the open door.

" 'Brunton, the butler, was in the library. He was sitting, fully dressed, in an easy chair, with a slip of paper, which looked like a map, upon his knee, and his forehead sunk forward upon his hand in deep thought. I stood, dumb with astonishment, watching him from the darkness. A small taper on the edge of the table shed a feeble light, which sufficed to show me that he was fully dressed. Suddenly, as I looked, he rose from his chair, and walking over to a bureau at the side he unlocked it and drew out one of the drawers. From this he took a paper, and, returning to his seat, he flattened it out beside the taper on the edge of the table, and began to study it with minute attention. My indignation at this calm examination of our family documents overcame me so far that I took a step forward, and Brunton looking up saw me standing in the doorway. He sprang to his feet, his face turned livid with fear, and he thrust into his breast the chart-like paper which he had been originally studying.

" 'So !' said I, 'this is how you repay the trust which we have reposed in you ! You will leave my service to-morrow.'

" ' He bowed with the look of a man who is utterly crushed, and slunk past me without a word. The taper was still on the table, and by its light I glanced to see what the paper was which Brunton had taken from the bureau. To my surprise it was nothing of

"HE SPRANG TO HIS FEET."

my station in life, and disgrace would kill me. My blood will be on your head, sir—it will, indeed—if you drive me to despair. If you cannot keep me after what has passed, then for God's sake let me give you notice and leave in a month, as if of my own free will. I could stand that, Mr. Musgrave, but not to be cast out before all the folk that I know so well.'

"'You don't deserve much consideration, Brunton,' I answered. 'Your conduct has been most infamous. However, as you have been a long time in the family, I have no wish to bring public disgrace upon you. A month, however, is too long. Take yourself away in a week, and give what reason you like for going.'

"'Only a week, sir?' he cried in a despairing voice. 'A fortnight—say at least a fortnight.'

"'A week,' I repeated, 'and you may consider yourself to have been very leniently dealt with.'

"'He crept away, his face sunk upon his breast, like a broken man, while I put out the light and returned to my room.

"'For two days after this Brunton was most assiduous in his attention to his duties. I made no allusion to what had passed, and waited with some curiosity to see how he would cover his disgrace. On the third morning, however, he did not appear, as was his custom, after breakfast to receive my instructions for the day. As I left the dining-room I happened to meet Rachel Howells, the maid. I have told you that she had only recently recovered from an illness, and was looking so wretchedly pale and wan that I remonstrated with her for being at work.

"'You should be in bed,' I said. 'Come back to your duties when you are stronger.'

"'She looked at me with so strange an expression that I began to suspect that her brain was affected.

"'I am strong enough, Mr. Musgrave,' said she.

"'We will see what the doctor says,' I answered. 'You must stop work now, and when you go downstairs just say that I wish to see Brunton.'

"'The butler is gone,' said she.

"'Gone! Gone where?'

any importance at all, but simply a copy of the questions and answers in the singular old observance called the Musgrave Ritual. It is a sort of ceremony peculiar to our family, which each Musgrave for centuries past has gone through upon his coming of age—a thing of private interest, and perhaps of some little importance to the archæologist, like our own blazonings and charges, but of no practical use whatever.'

"'We had better come back to the paper afterwards,' said I.

"'If you think it really necessary,' he answered, with some hesitation. 'To continue my statement, however, I re-locked the bureau, using the key which Brunton had left, and I had turned to go, when I was surprised to find that the butler had returned and was standing before me.

"'Mr. Musgrave, sir,' he cried, in a voice which was hoarse with emotion, 'I can't bear disgrace, sir. I've always been proud above

"'He is gone. No one has seen him. He is not in his room. Oh, yes, he is gone—he is gone!' She fell back against the wall with shriek after shriek of laughter, while I, horrified at this sudden hysterical attack, rushed to the bell to summon help. The girl was taken to her room, still screaming and sobbing, while I made inquiries about Brunton. There was no doubt about it that he had disappeared. His bed had not been slept in; he had been seen by no one since he had retired to his room the night before; and yet it was difficult to see how he could have left the house, as both windows and doors were found to be fastened in the morning. His clothes, his watch, and even his money were in his room—but the black suit which he usually wore was missing. His slippers, too, were gone, but his boots were left behind. Where, then, could butler Brunton have gone in the night, and what could have become of him now?

"'Of course we searched the house from cellar to garret, but there was no trace of him. It is as I have said a labyrinth of an old house, especially the original wing, which is now practically uninhabited, but we ransacked every room and cellar without discovering the least sign of the missing man. It was incredible to me that he could have gone away leaving all his property behind him, and yet where could he be? I called in the local police, but without success. Rain had fallen on the night before, and we examined the lawn and the paths all round the house, but in vain. Matters were in this state when a new development quite drew our attention away from the original mystery.

"'For two days Rachel Howells had been so ill, sometimes delirious, sometimes hysterical, that a nurse had been employed to sit up with her at night. On the third night after Brunton's disappearance the nurse, finding her patient sleeping nicely, had dropped into a nap in the arm-chair, when she woke in the early morning to find the bed empty, the window open, and no signs of the invalid. I was instantly aroused, and with the two footmen started off at once in search of the missing girl. It was not difficult to tell the direction which she had taken, for, starting from under her window, we could follow her footmarks easily across the lawn to the edge of the mere, where they vanished, close to the gravel path which leads out of the grounds. The lake there is 8ft. deep, and you can imagine our feelings when we saw that the trail of the poor demented girl came to an end at the edge of it.

"'Of course, we had the drags at once, and set to work to recover the remains; but no trace of the body could we find. On the other hand, we brought to the surface an object of a most unexpected kind. It was a linen bag, which contained within it a mass of old rusted and discoloured metal and several dull-coloured pieces of pebble or glass. This strange find was all that we could get from the mere, and although we made every possible search and inquiry yesterday, we know nothing of the fate either of Rachel Howells or Richard Brunton. The county police are at their wits' end, and I have come up to you as a last resource.'

"You can imagine, Watson, with what eagerness I listened to this extraordinary sequence of events, and endeavoured to piece them together, and to devise some common thread upon which they might all hang.

"The butler was gone. The maid was gone. The maid had loved the butler, but had afterwards had cause to hate him. She was of Welsh blood, fiery and passionate. She had been terribly excited immediately after his disappearance. She had flung into the lake a bag containing some curious contents. These were all factors which had to be taken into consideration, and yet none of them got quite to the heart of the matter. What was the starting point of this chain of events? There lay the end of this tangled line.

"'I must see that paper, Musgrave,' said I, 'which this butler of yours thought it worth his while to consult, even at the risk of the loss of his place.'

"'It is rather an absurd business, this Ritual of ours,' he answered, 'but it has at least the saving grace of antiquity to excuse it. I have a copy of the questions and answers here, if you care to run your eye over them.'

"He handed me the very paper which I have here, Watson, and this is the strange catechism to which each Musgrave had to submit when he came to man's estate. I will read you the questions and answers as they stand:—

"'Whose was it?
"'His who is gone.
"'Who shall have it?
"'He who will come.
"'Where was the sun?
"'Over the oak.
"'Where was the shadow?
"'Under the elm.
"'How was it stepped?
"'North by ten and by ten, east by five

and by five, south by two and by two, west by one and by one, and so under.

" ' What shall we give for it ?

" ' All that is ours.

" ' Why should we give it ?

" ' For the sake of the trust.'

" ' The original has no date, but is in the spelling of the middle of the seventeenth century,' remarked Musgrave. ' I am afraid, however, that 'it can be of little help to you in solving this mystery.'

" ' At least,' said I, ' it gives us another mystery, and one which is even more interesting than the first. It may be that the solution of the one may prove to be the solution of the other. You will excuse me, Musgrave, if I say that your butler appears to me to have been a very clever man, and to have had a clearer insight than ten generations of his masters.'

" ' I hardly follow you,' said Musgrave. ' The paper seems to me to be of no practical importance.'

" ' But to me it seems immensely practical, and I fancy that Brunton took the same view. He had probably seen it before that night on which you caught him.'

" ' It is very possible. We took no pains to hide it.'

" ' He simply wished, I should imagine, to refresh his memory upon that last occasion. He had, as I understand, some sort of map or chart which he was comparing with the manuscript, and which he thrust into his pocket when you appeared ? '

" ' That is true. But what could he have to do with this old family custom of ours, and what does this rigmarole mean ? '

" ' I don't think that we should have much difficulty in determining that,' said I. ' With your permission we will take the first train down to Sussex and go a little more deeply into the matter upon the spot.'

" The same afternoon saw us both at Hurlstone. Possibly you have seen pictures and read descriptions of the famous old building, so I will confine my account of it to saying that it is built in the shape of an L, the long arm being the more modern portion, and the shorter the ancient nucleus from which the other has developed. Over the low, heavy-lintelled door, in the centre of this old part, is chiselled the date 1607, but experts are agreed that the beams and stonework are really much older than this. The enormously thick walls and tiny windows of this part had in the last century driven the family into building the new wing, and the old one was used now as a storehouse and a cellar when it was used at all. A splendid park, with fine old timber, surrounded the house, and the lake, to which my client had referred, lay close to the avenue, about two hundred yards from the building.

" I was already firmly convinced, Watson, that there were not three separate mysteries here, but one only, and that if I could read the Musgrave Ritual aright, I should hold in my hand the clue which would lead me to the truth concerning both the butler Brunton and the maid Howells. To that, then, I turned all my energies. Why should this servant be so anxious to master this old

"IT HAS A GIRTH OF TWENTY-THREE FEET.

formula ? Evidently because he saw some-thing in it which had escaped all those generations of country squires, and from which he expected some personal advantage. What was it, then, and how had it affected his fate ?

"It was perfectly obvicus to me on reading the Ritual that the measurements must refer to some spot to which the rest of the document alluded, and that if we could find that spot we should be in a fair way towards knowing what the secret was which the old Musgraves had thought it necessary to embalm in so curious a fashion. There were two guides given us to start with, an oak and an elm. As to the oak, there could be no question at all. Right in front of the house, upon the left-hand side of the drive, there stood a patriarch among oaks, one of the most magnificent trees that I have ever seen.

"'That was there when your Ritual was drawn up?' said I, as we drove past it.

"'It was there at the Norman Conquest, in all probability,' he answered. 'It has a girth of 23ft.'

"Here was one of my fixed points secured.

"'Have you any old elms?' I asked.

"'There used to be a very old one over yonder, but it was struck by lightning ten years ago, and we cut down the stump.'

"'You can see where it used to be?'

"'Oh, yes.'

"'There are no other elms?'

"'No old ones, but plenty of beeches.'

"'I should like to see where it grew.'

"'We had driven up in a dog-cart, and my client led me away at once, without our entering the house, to the scar on the lawn where the elm had stood. It was nearly midway between the oak and the house. My investigation seemed to be progressing.

"'I suppose it is impossible to find out how high the elm was?' I asked.

"'I can give you it at once. It was 64ft.'

"'How do you come to know it?' I asked in surprise.

"'When my old tutor used to give me an exercise in trigonometry it always took the shape of measuring heights. When I was a lad I worked out every tree and building on the estate.'

"This was an unexpected piece of luck. My data were coming more quickly than I could have reasonably hoped.

"'Tell me,' I asked, 'did your butler ever ask you such a question?'

"Reginald Musgrave looked at me in astonishment. 'Now that you call it to my mind,' he answered, 'Brunton *did* ask me about the height of the tree some months ago, in connection with some little argument with the groom.'

"This was excellent news, Watson, for it showed me that I was on the right road. I looked up at the sun. It was low in the heavens, and I calculated that in less than an hour it would lie just above the topmost branches of the old oak. One condition mentioned in the Ritual would then be ful-filled. And the shadow of the elm must mean the further end of the shadow, other-wise the trunk would have been chosen as the guide. I had then to find where the far end of the shadow would fall when the sun was just clear of the oak."

"That must have been difficult, Holmes, when the elm was no longer there."

"Well, at least, I knew that if Brunton could do it I could also. Besides, there was no real difficulty. I went with Musgrave to his study and whittled myself this peg, to which I tied this long string, with a knot at each yard. Then I took two lengths of a fishing-rod, which came to just six feet, and I went back with my client to where the elm had been. The sun was just grazing the top of the oak. I fastened the rod on end, marked out the direction of the shadow, and measured it. It was 9ft. in length.

"Of course, the calculation now was a simple one. If a rod of 6ft. threw a shadow of 9ft., a tree of 64ft. would throw one of 96ft., and the line of the one would of course be the line of the other. I measured out the distance, which brought me almost to the wall of the house, and I thrust a peg into the spot. You can imagine my exultation, Watson, when within 2in. of my peg I saw a conical depression in the ground. I knew that it was the mark made by Brunton in his measurements, and that I was still upon his trail.

"From this starting point I proceeded to step, having first taken the cardinal points by my pocket compass. Ten steps with each foot took me along parallel with the wall of the house, and again I marked my spot with a peg. Then I carefully paced off five to the east and two to the south. It brought me to the very threshold of the old door. Two steps to the west meant now that I was to go two paces down the stone-flagged passage, and this was the place indicated by the Ritual.

"Never have I felt such a cold chill of dis-appointment, Watson. For a moment it seemed to me that there must be some radical mistake in my calculations. The

"THIS WAS THE PLACE INDICATED."

setting sun shone full upon the passage floor, and I could see that the old foot-worn grey stones, with which it was paved, were firmly cemented together, and had certainly not been moved for many a long year. Brunton had not been at work here. I tapped upon the floor, but it sounded the same all over, and there was no sign of any crack or crevice. But fortunately, Musgrave, who had begun to appreciate the meaning of my proceedings, and who was now as excited as myself, took out his manuscript to check my calculations.

"'And under,' he cried : 'you have omitted the "and under."'

"I had thought that it meant that we were to dig, but now of course I saw at once that I was wrong. 'There is a cellar under this, then?' I cried.

"'Yes, and as old as the house. Down here, through this door.'

"We went down a winding stone stair, and my companion, striking a match, lit a large lantern which stood on a barrel in the corner. In an instant it was obvious that we had at last come upon the true place, and that we had not been the only people to visit the spot recently.

"It had been used for the storage of wood, but the billets, which had evidently been littered over the floor, were now piled at the sides so as to leave a clear space in the middle. In this space lay a large and heavy flagstone, with a rusted iron ring in the centre, to which a thick shepherd's check muffler was attached.

"'By Jove!' cried my client, 'that's Brunton's muffler. I have seen it on him, and could swear to it. What has the villain been doing here?'

"At my suggestion a couple of the county police were summoned to be present, and I then endeavoured to raise the stone by pulling on the cravat. I could only move it slightly, and it was with the aid of one of the constables that I succeeded at last in carrying it to one side. A black hole yawned beneath, into which we all peered, while Musgrave, kneeling at the side, pushed down the lantern.

"A small chamber about 7ft. deep and 4ft. square lay open to us. At one side of this was a squat, brass-bound, wooden box, the lid of which was hinged upwards, with this curious, old-fashioned key projecting from the lock. It was furred outside by a thick layer of dust, and damp and worms had eaten through the wood so that a crop of livid fungi was growing on the inside of it. Several discs of metal—old coins apparently—such as I hold here, were scattered over the bottom of the box, but it contained nothing else.

"At the moment, however, we had no thought for the old chest, for our eyes were riveted upon that which crouched beside it. It was the figure of a man, clad in a suit of black, who squatted down upon his hams with his forehead sunk upon the edge of the box and his two arms thrown out on each side of it. The attitude had drawn all the stagnant blood to the face, and no man could have recognised that distorted, liver-coloured countenance ; but his height, his dress, and his hair were all sufficient to show my client, when we had drawn the body up, that it was, indeed, his missing butler. He had been dead some days, but there was no wound or bruise upon his person to show how he had met his dreadful end. When his body had been carried from the cellar we found ourselves still confronted with a problem which was almost as formidable as that with which we had started.

"IT WAS THE FIGURE OF A MAN."

"I confess that so far, Watson, I had been disappointed in my investigation. I had reckoned upon solving the matter when once I had found the place referred to in the Ritual; but now I was there, and was apparently as far as ever from knowing what it was which the family had concealed with such elaborate precautions. It is true that I had thrown a light upon the fate of Brunton, but now I had to ascertain how that fate had come upon him, and what part had been played in the matter by the woman who had disappeared. I sat down upon a keg in the corner and thought the whole matter carefully over.

"You know my methods in such cases, Watson: I put myself in the man's place, and having first gauged his intelligence, I try to imagine how I should myself have proceeded under the same circumstances. In this case the matter was simplified by Brunton's intelligence being quite first rate, so that it was unnecessary to make any allowance for the personal equation, as the astronomers have dubbed it. He knew that something valuable was concealed. He had spotted the place. He found that the stone which covered it was just too heavy for a man to move unaided. What would he do next? He could not get help from outside, even if he had someone whom he could trust, without the unbarring of doors, and considerable risk of detection. It was better, if he could, to have his helpmate inside the house. But whom could he ask? This girl had been devoted to him. A man always finds it hard to realize that he may have finally lost a woman's love, however badly he may have treated her. He would try by a few attentions to make his peace with the girl Howells, and then would engage her as his accomplice. Together they would come at night to the cellar, and their united force would suffice to raise the stone. So far I could follow their actions as if I had actually seen them.

"But for two of them, and one a woman, it must have been heavy work, the raising of that stone. A burly Sussex policeman and I had found it no light job. What would they do to assist them? Probably what I should have done myself. I rose and examined carefully the different billets of wood which were scattered round the floor. Almost at once I came upon what I expected. One piece, about 3ft. in length, had a marked indentation at one end, while several were flattened at the sides as if they had been compressed by some considerable weight. Evidently as they had dragged the stone up they had thrust the chunks of wood into the chink, until at last, when the opening was large enough to crawl through, they would hold it open by a billet placed lengthwise, which might very well become indented at the lower end, since the whole weight of the stone would press it down on to the edge of this other slab. So far I was still on safe ground.

"And now, how was I to proceed to reconstruct this midnight drama? Clearly only one could get into the hole, and that one was Brunton. The girl must have waited above. Brunton then unlocked the box, handed up the contents, presumably—since they were not to be found—and then—and then what happened?

"What smouldering fire of vengeance had suddenly sprung into flame in this passionate Celtic woman's soul when she saw the man who had wronged her—wronged her perhaps far more than we suspected—in her power? Was it a chance that the wood had slipped and that the stone had shut Brunton into what had become his sepulchre? Had she only been guilty of silence as to his fate? Or had some sudden blow from her hand dashed the support away and sent the slab crashing down into its place. Be that as it might, I seemed to see that woman's figure, still clutching at her treasure-trove, and flying wildly up the winding stair with her ears ringing perhaps with the muffled screams from behind her, and with the drumming of frenzied hands against the slab of stone which was choking her faithless lover's life out.

"Here was the secret of her blanched face, her shaken nerves, her peals of hysterical laughter on the next morning. But what had been in the box? What had she done with that? Of course, it must have been the old metal and pebbles which my client had dragged from the mere. She had thrown them in there at the first opportunity, to remove the last trace of her crime.

"For twenty minutes I had sat motionless thinking the matter out. Musgrave still stood with a very pale face swinging his lantern and peering down into the hole.

"'These are coins of Charles I.,' said he, holding out the few which had been left in the box. 'You see we were right in fixing our date for the Ritual.'

"'We may find something else of Charles I.,' I cried, as the probable meaning of the first two questions of the Ritual broke suddenly upon me. 'Let me see the contents of the bag which you fished from the mere.'

"We ascended to his study, and he laid the débris before me. I could understand his regarding it as of small importance when I looked at it, for the metal was almost black, and the stones lustreless and dull. I rubbed one of them on my sleeve, however, and it glowed afterwards like a spark, in the dark hollow of my hand. The metal-work was in the form of a double ring, but it had been bent and twisted out of its original shape.

"'You must bear in mind,' said I, 'that the Royal party made head in England even after the death of the King, and that when they at last fled they probably left many of their most precious possessions buried behind them, with the intention of returning for them in more peaceful times.'

"'My ancestor, Sir Ralph Musgrave, was a prominent Cavalier, and the right-hand man of Charles II. in his wanderings,' said my friend.

"'Ah, indeed!' I answered. 'Well, now, I think that really should give us the last link that we wanted. I must congratulate you on coming into the possession, though in rather a tragic manner, of a relic which is of great intrinsic value, but of even greater importance as an historical curiosity.'

"'What is it, then?' he gasped in astonishment.

"'It is nothing less than·· ancient crown of the Kings of England.'

"'The crown!'

"'Precisely. Consider what the Ritual says. How does it run? "Whose was it?" "His who is gone." That was after the execution of Charles. Then, "Who shall have it?" "He who will come." That was Charles II., whose advent was already foreseen. There can I think be no doubt that this battered and shapeless diadem once encircled the brows of the Royal Stuarts.'

"'And how came it in the pond?'

"'Ah, that is a question which will take some time to answer,' and with that I sketched out to him the whole long chain of surmise and of proof which I had constructed. The twilight had closed in and the moon was shining brightly in the sky before my narrative was finished.

"'And how was it, then, that Charles did not get his crown when he returned?' asked Musgrave, pushing back the relic into its linen bag.

"'Ah, there you lay your finger upon the one point which we shall probably never be able to clear up. It is likely that the Musgrave who held the secret died in the interval, and by some oversight left this guide to his descendant without explaining the meaning of it. From that day to this it has been handed down from father to son, until at last it came within reach of a man who tore its secret out of it and lost his life in the venture.'

"And that's the story of the Musgrave Ritual, Watson. They have the crown down at Hurlstone—though they had some legal bother, and a considerable sum to pay before they were allowed to retain it. I am sure that if you mentioned my name they would be happy to show it to you. Of the woman nothing was ever heard, and the probability is that she got away out of England, and carried herself, and the memory of her crime, to some land beyond the seas."

The Adventures of Sherlock Holmes.

XIX.—THE ADVENTURE OF THE REIGATE SQUIRE.

By A. Conan Doyle.

IT was some time before the health of my friend, Mr. Sherlock Holmes, recovered from the strain caused by his immense exertions in the spring of '87. The whole question of the Netherland-Sumatra Company and of the colossal schemes of Baron Maupertins are too recent in the minds of the public, and are too intimately concerned with politics and finance, to be fitting subjects for this series of sketches. They led, however, in an indirect fashion to a singular and complex problem, which gave my friend an opportunity of demonstrating the value of a fresh weapon among the many with which he waged his life-long battle against crime.

On referring to my notes, I see that it was upon the 14th of April that I received a telegram from Lyons, which informed me that Holmes was lying ill in the Hotel Dulong. Within twenty-four hours I was in his sick room, and was relieved to find that there was nothing formidable in his symptoms. His iron constitution, however, had broken down under the strain of an investigation which had extended over two months, during which period he had never worked less than fifteen hours a day, and had more than once, as he assured me, kept to his task for five days at a stretch. The triumphant issue of his labours could not save him from reaction after so terrible an exertion, and at a time when Europe was ringing with his name, and when his room was literally ankle-deep with congratulatory telegrams, I found him a prey to the blackest depression. Even the knowledge that he had succeeded where the police of three countries had failed, and that he had outmanœuvred at every point the most accomplished swindler in Europe, were insufficient to rouse him from his nervous prostration.

Three days later we were back in Baker Street together, but it was evident that my friend would be much the better for a change, and the thought of a week of spring-time in the country was full of attractions to me also.

My old friend Colonel Hayter, who had come under my professional care in Afghanistan, had now taken a house near Reigate, in Surrey, and had frequently asked me to come down to him upon a visit. On the last occasion he had remarked that if my friend would only come with me, he would be glad to extend his hospitality to him also. A little diplomacy was needed, but when Holmes understood that the establishment was a bachelor one, and that he would be allowed the fullest freedom, he fell in with my plans, and a week after our return from Lyons we were under the Colonel's roof. Hayter was a fine old soldier, who had seen much of the world, and he soon found, as I had expected, that Holmes and he had plenty in common.

On the evening of our arrival we were sitting in the Colonel's gun-room after dinner, Holmes stretched upon the sofa, while Hayter and I looked over his little armoury of fire-arms.

"By the way," said he, suddenly, "I think I'll take one of these pistols upstairs with me in case we have an alarm."

"An alarm!" said I.

"Yes, we've had a scare in this part lately. Old Acton, who is one of our county magnates, had his house broken into last Monday. No great damage done, but the fellows are still at large."

"No clue?" asked Holmes, cocking his eye at the Colonel.

"None as yet. But the affair is a petty one, one of our little country crimes, which must seem too small for your attention, Mr. Holmes, after this great international affair."

Holmes waved away the compliment, though his smile showed that it had pleased him.

"Was there any feature of interest?"

"I fancy not. The thieves ransacked the library and got very little for their pains. The whole place was turned upside down, drawers burst open and presses ransacked, with the result that an odd volume of Pope's 'Homer,' two plated candlesticks, an ivory letter-weight, a small oak barometer, and a ball of twine, are all that have vanished."

"What an extraordinary assortment!" I exclaimed.

"Oh, the fellows evidently grabbed hold of anything they could get."

Holmes grunted from the sofa.

"The county police ought to make something of that," said he. "Why, it is surely obvious that——"

But I held up a warning finger.

"Neither, sir. It was William, the coachman. Shot through the heart, sir, and never spoke again."

"Who shot him, then?"

"The burglar, sir. He was off like a shot and got clean away. He'd just broke in at the pantry window when William came on him and met his end in saving his master's property."

"I HELD UP A WARNING FINGER."

"You are here for a rest, my dear fellow. For Heaven's sake, don't get started on a new problem when your nerves are all in shreds."

Holmes shrugged his shoulders with a glance of comic resignation towards the Colonel, and the talk drifted away into less dangerous channels.

It was destined, however, that all my professional caution should be wasted, for next morning the problem obtruded itself upon us in such a way that it was impossible to ignore it, and our country visit took a turn which neither of us could have anticipated. We were at breakfast when the Colonel's butler rushed in with all his propriety shaken out of him.

"Have you heard the news, sir?" he gasped. "At the Cunningham's, sir!"

"Burglary!" cried the Colonel, with his coffee cup in mid air.

"Murder!"

The Colonel whistled. "By Jove!" said he, "who's killed, then? The J.P. or his son?"

"What time?"

"It was last night, sir, somewhere about twelve."

"Ah, then, we'll step over presently," said the Colonel, coolly settling down to his breakfast again. "It's a baddish business," he added, when the butler had gone. "He's our leading squire about here, is old Cunningham, and a very decent fellow too. He'll be cut up over this, for the man has been in his service for years, and was a good servant. It's evidently the same villains who broke into Acton's."

"And stole that very singular collection?" said Holmes, thoughtfully.

"Precisely."

"Hum! It may prove the simplest matter in the world; but, all the same, at first glance this is just a little curious, is it not? A gang of burglars acting in the country might be expected to vary the scene of their operations, and not to crack two cribs in the same district within a few days. When you spoke last night of taking precautions, I remember that it passed through my mind that this was probably the last parish in England to which the thief or thieves would be likely to turn their attention; which shows that I have still much to learn."

"I fancy it's some local practitioner," said the Colonel. "In that case, of course, Acton's and Cunningham's are just the places he would go for, since they are far the largest about here."

"And richest?"

"Well, they ought to be; but they've had a law-suit for some years which has sucked the blood out of both of them, I fancy. Old Acton has some claim on half Cunningham's estate, and the lawyers have been at it with both hands."

"If it's a local villain, there should not be much difficulty in running him down," said Holmes, with a yawn. "All right, Watson, I don't intend to meddle."

"Inspector Forrester, sir," said the butler, throwing open the door.

The official, a smart, keen-faced young fellow, stepped into the room. "Good morning, Colonel," said he. "I hope I don't intrude, but we hear that Mr. Holmes, of Baker Street, is here."

The Colonel waved his hand towards my friend, and the Inspector bowed.

"We thought that perhaps you would care to step across, Mr. Holmes."

"The Fates are against you, Watson," said he, laughing. "We were chatting about the matter when you came in, Inspector. Perhaps you can let us have a few details." As he leaned back in his chair in the familiar attitude, I knew that the case was hopeless.

"We had no clue in the Acton affair.

"INSPECTOR FORRESTER."

But here we have plenty to go on, and there's no doubt it is the same party in each case. The man was seen."

"Ah!"

"Yes, sir. But he was off like a deer after the shot that killed poor William Kirwan was fired. Mr. Cunningham saw him from the bedroom window, and Mr. Alec Cunningham saw him from the back passage. It was a quarter to twelve when the alarm broke out. Mr. Cunningham had just got into bed, and Mister Alec was smoking a pipe in his dressing-gown. They both heard William, the coachman, calling for help, and Mister Alec he ran down to see what was the matter. The back door was open, and as he came to the foot of the stairs he saw two men wrestling together outside. One of them fired a shot, the other dropped, and the murderer rushed across the garden and over the hedge. Mr. Cunningham, looking out of his bedroom window, saw the fellow as he gained the road, but lost sight of him at once. Mister Alec stopped to see if he could help the dying man, and so the villain got clean away. Beyond the fact that he was a middle-sized man, and dressed in some dark stuff, we have no personal clue, but we are making energetic inquiries, and if he is a stranger we shall soon find him out."

"What was this William doing there? Did he say anything before he died?"

"Not a word. He lives at the lodge with his mother, and as he was a very faithful fellow, we imagine that he walked up to the house with the intention of seeing that all was right there. Of course, this Acton business has put everyone on their guard.

The robber must have just burst open the door — the lock has been forced — when William came upon him."

"Did William say anything to his mother before going out?"

"She is very old and deaf, and we can get no information from her. The shock has made her half-witted, but I understand that she was never very bright. There is one very important circumstance, however. Look at this!"

He took a small piece of torn paper from a note-book and spread it out upon his knee.

"This was found between the finger and thumb of the dead man. It appears to be a fragment torn from a larger sheet. You will observe that the hour mentioned upon it is the very time at which the poor fellow met his fate. You see that his murderer might have torn the rest of the sheet from him or he might have taken this fragment from the murderer. It reads almost as though it was an appointment."

Holmes took up the scrap of paper, a facsimile of which is here reproduced :—

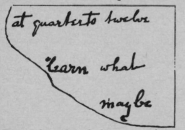

"Presuming that it is an appointment," continued the Inspector, "it is, of course, a conceivable theory that this William Kirwan, although he had the reputation of being an honest man, may have been in league with the thief. He may have met him there, may even have helped him to break in the door, and then they may have fallen out between themselves."

"This writing is of extraordinary interest," said Holmes, who had been examining it with intense concentration. "These are much deeper waters than I had thought." He sank his head upon his hands, while the Inspector smiled at the effect which his case had had upon the famous London specialist.

"Your last remark," said Holmes, presently, "as to the possibility of there being an understanding between the burglar and the servant, and this being a note of appointment from one to the other, is an ingenious and not entirely an impossible supposition. But this writing opens up——" he sank his head into

his hands again and remained for some minutes in the deepest thought. When he raised his face again I was surprised to see that his cheek was tinged with colour and his eyes as bright as before his illness. He sprang to his feet with all his old energy.

"I'll tell you what!" said he. "I should like to have a quiet little glance into the details of this case. There is something in it which fascinates me extremely. If you will permit me, Colonel, I will leave my friend, Watson, and you, and I will step round with the Inspector to test the truth of one or two little fancies of mine. I will be with you again in half an hour."

An hour and a half had elapsed before the Inspector returned alone.

"Mr. Holmes is walking up and down in the field outside," said he. "He wants us all four to go up to the house together."

"To Mr. Cunningham's?"

"Yes, sir."

"What for?"

The Inspector shrugged his shoulders. "I don't quite know, sir. Between ourselves, I think Mr. Holmes has not quite got over his illness yet. He's been behaving very queerly, and he is very much excited."

"I don't think you need alarm yourself," said I. "I have usually found that there was method in his madness."

"Some folk might say there was madness in his method," muttered the Inspector. "But he's all on fire to start, Colonel, so we had best go out, if you are ready."

We found Holmes pacing up and down in the field, his chin sunk upon his breast, and his hands thrust into his trouser pockets.

"The matter grows in interest," said he. "Watson, your country trip has been a distinct success. I have had a charming morning."

"You have been up to the scene of the crime, I understand?" said the Colonel.

"Yes; the Inspector and I have made quite a little reconnaissance together."

"Any success?"

"Well, we have seen some very interesting things. I'll tell you what we did as we walk. First of all we saw the body of this unfortunate man. He certainly died from a revolver wound, as reported."

"Had you doubted it, then?"

"Oh, it is as well to test everything. Our inspection was not wasted. We then had an interview with Mr. Cunningham and his son, who were able to point out the exact spot where the murderer had broken through the garden hedge in his flight. That was of great interest."

"Naturally."

"Then we had a look at this poor fellow's mother. We could get no information from her, however, as she is very old and feeble."

"And what is the result of your investigations?"

"The conviction that the crime is a very peculiar one. Perhaps our visit now may do something to make it less obscure. I think that we are both agreed, Inspector, that the fragment of paper in the dead man's hand, bearing, as it does, the very hour of his death written upon it, is of extreme importance."

"It should give a clue, Mr. Holmes."

"It *does* give a clue. Whoever wrote that note was the man who brought William Kirwan out of his bed at that hour. But where is the rest of that sheet of paper?"

"I examined the ground carefully in the hope of finding it," said the Inspector.

"It was torn out of the dead man's hand. Why was someone so anxious to get possession of it? Because it incriminated him. And what would he do with it? Thrust it into his pocket most likely, never noticing that a corner of it had been left in the grip of the corpse. If we could get the rest of that sheet, it is obvious that we should have gone a long way towards solving the mystery."

"Yes, but how can we get at the criminal's pocket before we catch the criminal?"

"Well, well, it was worth thinking over. Then there is another obvious point. The note was sent to William. The man who wrote it could not have taken it, otherwise of course he might have delivered his own message by word of mouth. Who brought the note, then? Or did it come through the post?"

"I have made inquiries," said the Inspector. "William received a letter by the afternoon post yesterday. The envelope was destroyed by him."

"Excellent!" cried Holmes, clapping the Inspector on the back. "You've seen the postman. It is a pleasure to work with you. Well, here is the lodge, and if you will come up, Colonel, I will show you the scene of the crime."

We passed the pretty cottage where the murdered man had lived, and walked up an oak-lined avenue to the fine old Queen Anne house, which bears the date of Malplaquet upon the lintel of the door. Holmes and the Inspector led us round it until we came to the side gate, which is separated by a stretch of garden from the hedge which lines the road. A constable was standing at the kitchen door.

"Throw the door open, officer," said Holmes. "Now it was on those stairs that young Mr. Cunningham stood and saw the two men struggling just where we are. Old Mr. Cunningham was at that window—the second on the left—and he saw the fellow get away just to the left of that bush. So did the son. They are both sure of it, on account of the bush. Then Mister Alec ran out and knelt beside the wounded man. The ground is very hard, you see, and there are no marks to guide us."

As he spoke two men came down the garden path, from round the angle of the house. The one was an elderly man, with a strong, deep-lined, heavy-eyed face; the other a dashing young fellow, whose bright, smiling expression and showy dress were in strange contrast with the business which had brought us there.

"Still at it, then?" said he to Holmes. "I thought you Londoners were never at fault. You don't seem to be so very quick, after all."

"Ah! you must give us a little time," said Holmes, good-humouredly.

"You'll want it," said young Alec Cunningham. "Why, I don't see that we have any clue at all."

"There's only one," answered the Inspector. "We thought that if we could only find——Good heavens! Mr. Holmes, what is the matter?"

My poor friend's face had suddenly assumed the most dreadful expression. His eyes rolled upwards, his features writhed in agony, and with a suppressed groan he dropped on his face upon the ground. Horrified at the suddenness and severity of the attack, we carried him into the kitchen, where he lay back in a large chair and breathed heavily for some minutes. Finally, with a shame-faced apology for his weakness, he rose once more.

"Watson would tell you that I have only just recovered from a severe illness," he explained. "I am liable to these sudden nervous attacks."

"Shall I send you home in my trap?" asked old Cunningham.

"Well, since I am here, there is one point on which I should like to feel sure. We can very easily verify it."

"What is it?"

"Well, it seems to me that it is just possible that the arrival of this poor fellow William was not before but after the entrance of the burglar into the house. You appear to take it for granted that although the door was forced the robber never got in."

"GOOD HEAVENS! WHAT IS THE MATTER?"

"I fancy that is quite obvious," said Mr. Cunningham, gravely. "Why, my son Alec had not yet gone to bed, and he would certainly have heard anyone moving about."

"Where was he sitting?"

"I was sitting smoking in my dressing-room."

"Which window is that?"

"The last on the left, next my father's."

"Both your lamps were lit, of course?"

"Undoubtedly."

"There are some very singular points here," said Holmes, smiling. "Is it not extraordinary that a burglar—and a burglar who had had some previous experience—should deliberately break into a house at a time when he could see from the lights that two of the family were still afoot?"

"He must have been a cool hand."

"Well, of course, if the case were not an odd one we should not have been driven to ask you for an explanation," said Mister Alec. "But as to your idea that the man had robbed the house before William tackled him, I think it a most absurd notion. Shouldn't we have found the place disarranged and missed the things which he had taken?"

"It depends on what the things were," said Holmes. "You must remember that we are dealing with a burglar who is a very peculiar fellow, and who appears to work on lines of his own. Look, for example, at the queer lot of things which he took from Acton's—what was it?—a ball of string, a letter-weight, and I don't know what other odds and ends!"

"Well, we are quite in your hands, Mr. Holmes," said old Cunningham. "Anything which you or the Inspector may suggest will most certainly be done."

"In the first place," said Holmes, "I should like you to offer a reward—coming from yourself, for the officials may take a little time before they would agree upon the sum, and these things cannot be done too promptly. I have jotted down the form here, if you would not mind signing it. Fifty pounds was quite enough, I thought."

"I would willingly give five hundred," said the J.P., taking the slip of paper and the pencil which Holmes handed to him. "This is not quite correct, however," he added, glancing over the document.

"I wrote it rather hurriedly."

"You see you begin: 'Whereas, at about a quarter to one on Tuesday morning, an attempt was made'—and so on. It was at a quarter to twelve, as a matter of fact."

I was pained at the mistake, for I knew how keenly Holmes would feel any slip of the kind. It was his speciality to be accurate as to fact, but his recent illness had shaken him, and this one little incident was enough to show me that he was still far from being himself. He was obviously embarrassed for an instant, while the Inspector raised his eyebrows and Alec Cunningham burst into a laugh. The old gentleman corrected the mistake, however, and handed the paper back to Holmes.

"Get it printed as soon as possible," he said. "I think your idea is an excellent one."

Holmes put the slip of paper carefully away in his pocket-book.

"And now," said he, "it would really be a good thing that we should all go over the house together and make certain that this rather erratic burglar did not, after all, carry anything away with him."

Before entering, Holmes made an examination of the door which had been forced. It was evident that a chisel or strong knife had been thrust in, and the lock forced back with it. We could see the marks in the wood where it had been pushed in.

"You don't use bars, then?" he asked.

"We have never found it necessary."

"You don't keep a dog?"

"Yes; but he is chained on the other side of the house."

"When do the servants go to bed?"

"About ten."

"I understand that William was usually in bed also at that hour?"

"Yes."

"It is singular that on this particular night he should have been up. Now, I should be very glad if you would have the kindness to show us over the house, Mr. Cunningham."

A stone-flagged passage, with the kitchens branching away from it, led by a wooden staircase directly to the first floor of the house. It came out upon the landing opposite to a second more ornamental stair which led up from the front hall. Out of this landing opened the drawing-room and several bedrooms, including those of Mr. Cunningham and his son. Holmes walked slowly, taking keen note of the architecture of the house. I could tell from his expression that he was on a hot scent, and yet I could not in the least imagine in what direction his inferences were leading him.

"My good sir," said Mr. Cunningham, with some impatience, "this is surely very unnecessary. That is my room at the end of the stairs, and my son's is the one beyond it. I leave it to your judgment whether it was possible for the thief to have come up here without disturbing us."

"You must try round and get on a fresh scent, I fancy," said the son, with a rather malicious smile.

"Still, I must ask you to humour me a little further. I should like, for example, to see how far the windows of the bedrooms command the front. This, I understand, is your son's room "—he pushed open the door—"and that, I presume, is the dressing-room in which he sat smoking when the alarm was given. Where does the window of that look out to?" He stepped across the bedroom, pushed open the door, and glanced round the other chamber.

"I hope you are satisfied now?" said Mr. Cunningham, testily.

"Thank you; I think I have seen all that I wished."

"Then, if it is really necessary, we can go into my room."

"If it is not too much trouble."

The J.P. shrugged his shoulders, and led the way into his own chamber, which was a plainly furnished and commonplace room. As we moved across it in the direction of the window, Holmes fell back until he and I were the last of the group. Near the foot of the bed was a small square table, on which stood a dish of oranges and a carafe of water. As we passed it, Holmes, to my unutterable astonishment, leaned over in front of me and deliberately knocked the whole thing over. The glass smashed into a thousand pieces, and the fruit rolled about into every corner of the room.

"You've done it now, Watson," said he,

HE DELIBERATELY KNOCKED THE WHOLE THING OVER."

coolly. "A pretty mess you've made of the carpet."

I stooped in some confusion and began to pick up the fruit, understanding that for some reason my companion desired me to take the blame upon myself. The others did the same, and set the table on its legs again.

"Halloa!" cried the Inspector, "where's he got to?"

Holmes had disappeared.

"Wait here an instant," said young Alec Cunningham. "The fellow is off his head, in my opinion. Come with me, father, and see where he has got to!"

They rushed out of the room, leaving the Inspector, the Colonel, and me staring at each other.

"'Pon my word, I am inclined to agree with Mister Alec," said the official. "It may be the effect of this illness, but it seems to me that——"

His words were cut short by a sudden scream of "Help! Help! Murder!" With a thrill I recognised the voice as that of my friend. I rushed madly from the room on to the landing. The cries, which had sunk down into a hoarse, inarticulate shouting, came from the room which we had first visited. I dashed in, and on into the dressing-room beyond. The two Cunninghams were bending over the prostrate figure of Sherlock Holmes, the younger clutching his throat with both hands, while the elder seemed to be twisting one of his wrists. In an instant the three of us had torn them away from him, and Holmes staggered to his feet, very pale, and evidently greatly exhausted.

"Arrest these men, Inspector," he gasped.

"On what charge?"

"That of murdering their coachman, William Kirwan!"

The Inspector stared about him in bewilderment. "Oh, come now, Mr. Holmes," said he at last; "I am sure you don't really mean to——"

"Tut, man; look at their faces!" cried Holmes, curtly.

Never, certainly, have I seen a plainer confession of guilt upon human countenances. The older man seemed numbed and dazed, with a heavy, sullen expression upon his strongly-marked face. The son, on the other hand, had dropped all that jaunty, dashing style which had characterized him, and the ferocity of a dangerous wild beast gleamed in his dark eyes and distorted his handsome features. The Inspector said nothing, but, stepping to the door, he blew his whistle. Two of his constables came at the call.

"I have no alternative, Mr. Cunningham," said he. "I trust that this may all prove to be an absurd mistake; but you can see that——Ah, would you? Drop it!" He struck out with his hand, and a revolver, which the younger man was in the act of cocking, clattered down upon the floor.

"BENDING OVER THE PROSTRATE FIGURE OF SHERLOCK HOLMES."

"Keep that," said Holmes, quickly putting his foot upon it. "You will find it useful at the trial. But this is what we really wanted." He held up a little crumpled piece of paper.

"The remainder of the sheet!" cried the Inspector.

"Precisely."

"And where was it?"

"Where I was sure it must be. I'll make the whole matter clear to you presently. I think, Colonel, that you and Watson might return now, and I will be with you again in an hour at the furthest. The Inspector and I must have a word with the prisoners; but you will certainly see me back at luncheon time."

Sherlock Holmes was as good as his word, for about one o'clock he rejoined us in the Colonel's smoking-room. He was accompanied by a little, elderly gentleman, who was introduced to me as the Mr. Acton whose house had been the scene of the original burglary.

"I wished Mr. Acton to be present while I demonstrated this small matter to you," said Holmes, "for it is natural that he should take a keen interest in the details. I am afraid, my dear Colonel, that you must regret the hour that you took in such a stormy petrel as I am."

"On the contrary," answered the Colonel, warmly, "I consider it the greatest privilege to have been permitted to study your methods of working. I confess that they quite surpass my expectations, and that I am utterly unable to account for your result. I have not yet seen the vestige of a clue."

"I am afraid that my explanation may disillusionize you, but it has always been my habit to hide none of my methods, either from my friend Watson or from anyone who might take an intelligent interest in them. But first, as I am rather shaken by the knocking about which I had in the dressing-room, I think that I shall help myself to a dash of your brandy, Colonel. My strength has been rather tried of late."

"I trust you had no more of those nervous attacks."

Sherlock Holmes laughed heartily. "We will come to that in its turn," said he. "I will lay an account of the case before you in its due order, showing you the various points which guided me in my de-

cision. Pray interrupt me if there is any inference which is not perfectly clear to you.

"It is of the highest importance in the art of detection to be able to recognise out of a number of facts which are incidental and which vital. Otherwise your energy and attention must be dissipated instead of being concentrated. Now, in this case there was not the slightest doubt in my mind from the first that the key of the whole matter must be looked for in the scrap of paper in the dead man's hand.

"Before going into this I would draw your attention to the fact that if Alec Cunningham's narrative was correct, and if the assailant after shooting William Kirwan had *instantly* fled, then it obviously could not be he who tore the paper from the dead man's hand. But if it was not he, it must have been Alec Cunningham himself, for by the time that the old man had descended several servants were upon the scene. The point is a simple one, but the Inspector had overlooked it because he had started with the supposition that these county magnates had had nothing to do with the matter. Now, I make a point of never having any prejudices and of following docilely wherever fact may lead me, and so in the very first stage of the investigation I found myself looking a little askance at the part which had been played by Mr. Alec Cunningham.

"THE POINT IS A SIMPLE ONE."

"And now I made a very careful examination of the corner of paper which the Inspector had submitted ↑ us. It was at once clear to me that it formed part of a very remarkable document. Here it is. Do you not now observe something very suggestive about it?"

"It has a very irregular look," said the Colonel.

"My dear sir," cried Holmes, "there cannot be the least doubt in the world that it has been written by two persons doing alternate words. When I draw your attention to the strong t's of 'at' and 'to' and ask you to compare them with the weak ones of 'quarter' and 'twelve,' you will instantly recognise the fact. A very brief analysis of those four words would enable you to say with the utmost confidence that the 'learn' and the 'maybe' are written in the stronger hand, and the 'what' in the weaker."

"By Jove, it's as clear as day!" cried the Colonel. "Why on earth should two men write a letter in such a fashion?"

"Obviously the business was a bad one, and one of the men who distrusted the other was determined that, whatever was done, each should have an equal hand in it. Now, of the two men it is clear that the one who wrote the 'at' and 'to' was the ringleader."

"How do you get at that?"

"We might deduce it from the mere character of the one hand as compared with the other. But we have more assured reasons than that for supposing it. If you examine this scrap with attention you will come to the conclusion that the man with the stronger hand wrote all his words first, leaving blanks for the other to fill up. These blanks were not always sufficient, and you can see that the second man had a squeeze to fit his 'quarter' in between the 'at' and the 'to,' showing that the latter were already written. The man who wrote all his words first is undoubtedly the man who planned this affair."

"Excellent!" cried Mr. Acton.

"But very superficial," said Holmes. "We come now, however, to a point which is of importance. You may not be aware that the deduction of a man's age from his writing is one which has been brought to considerable accuracy by experts. In normal cases one can place a man in his true decade with tolerable confidence. I say normal cases, because ill-health and physical weakness reproduce the signs of old age, even when the invalid is a youth. In this case, looking at the bold, strong hand of the one, and the rather broken-backed appearance of the other, which still retains its legibility, although the t's have begun to lose their crossings, we can say that the one was a young man, and the other was advanced in years without being positively decrepit."

"Excellent!" cried Mr. Acton again.

"There is a further point, however, which is subtler and of greater interest. There is something in common between these hands. They belong to men who are blood-relatives. It may be most obvious to you in the Greek e's, but to me there are many small points which indicate the same thing. I have no doubt at all that a family mannerism can be traced in these two specimens of writing. I am only, of course, giving you the leading results now of my examination of the paper. There were twenty-three other deductions which would be of more interest to experts than to you. They all tended to deepen the impression upon my mind that the Cunninghams, father and son, had written this letter.

"Having got so far, my next step was, of course, to examine into the details of the crime and to see how far they would help us. I went up to the house with the Inspector, and saw all that was to be seen. The wound upon the dead man was, as I was able to determine with absolute confidence, fired from a revolver at the distance of something over four yards. There was no powder-blackening on the clothes. Evidently, therefore, Alec Cunningham had lied when he said that the two men were struggling when the shot was fired. Again, both father and son agreed as to the place where the man escaped into the road. At that point, however, as it happens, there is a broadish ditch, moist at the bottom. As there were no indications of boot-marks about this ditch, I was absolutely sure not only that the Cunninghams had again lied, but that there had never been any unknown man upon the scene at all.

"And now I had to consider the motive of this singular crime. To get at this I endeavoured first of all to solve the reason of the original burglary at Mr. Acton's. I understood from something which the Colonel told us that a law-suit had been going on between you, Mr. Acton, and the Cunninghams. Of course, it instantly occurred to me that they had broken into your library with the intention of getting at some document which might be of importance in the case."

"Precisely so," said Mr. Acton; "there

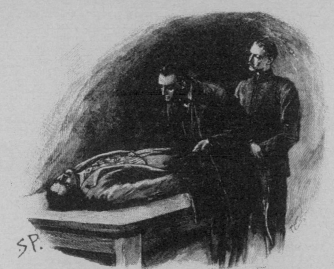

"THERE WAS NO POWDER-BLACKENING ON THE CLOTHES."

can be no possible doubt as to their intentions. I have the clearest claim upon half their present estate, and if they could have found a single paper—which, fortunately, was in the strong box of my solicitors—they would undoubtedly have crippled our case."

"There you are!" said Holmes, smiling. "It was a dangerous, reckless attempt in which I seem to trace the influence of young Alec. Having found nothing, they tried to divert suspicion by making it appear to be an ordinary burglary, to which end they carried off whatever they could lay their hands upon. That is all clear enough, but there was much that was still obscure. What I wanted above all was to get the missing part of that note. I was certain that Alec had torn it out of the dead man's hand, and almost certain that he must have thrust it into the pocket of his dressing-gown. Where else could he have put it? The only question was whether it was still there. It was worth an effort to find out, and for that object we all went up to the house.

"The Cunninghams joined us, as you doubtless remember, outside the kitchen door. It was, of course, of the very first importance that they should not be reminded of the existence of this paper, otherwise they would naturally destroy it without delay. The Inspector was about to tell them the importance which we attached to it when, by the luckiest chance in the world, I tumbled down in a sort of fit and so changed the conversation."

"Good heavens!" cried the Colonel, laughing. "Do you mean to say all our sympathy was wasted and your fit an imposture?"

"Speaking professionally, it was admirably done," cried I, looking in amazement at this man who was for ever confounding me with some new phase of his astuteness.

"It is an art which is often useful," said he. "When I recovered I managed by a device, which had, perhaps, some little merit of ingenuity, to get old Cunningham to write the word 'twelve,' so that I might compare it with the 'twelve' upon the paper."

"Oh, what an ass I have been!" I exclaimed.

"I could see that you were commiserating with me over my weakness," said Holmes, laughing. "I was sorry to cause you the sympathetic pain which I know that you felt. We then went upstairs together, and having entered the room and seen the dressing-gown hanging up behind the door, I contrived by upsetting a table to engage their attention for the moment and slipped back to examine the pockets. I had hardly got the paper, however, which was, as I had expected, in one of them, when the two Cunninghams were on me, and would, I verily believe, have murdered me then and there but for your prompt and friendly aid. As it is, I feel that young man's grip on my throat now, and the father has twisted my wrist round in the effort to get the paper out of my hand. They saw that I must know all about it, you see, and the sudden change from absolute security to complete despair made them perfectly desperate.

"I had a little talk with old Cunningham afterwards as to the motive of the crime. He was tractable enough, though his son was a perfect demon, ready to blow out his own or anybody else's brains if he could have got to his revolver. When Cunningham saw that the case against him was so strong he lost all heart, and made a clean breast of everything. It seems that William had secretly followed his two masters on the night when they made their raid upon Mr. Acton's,

"And the note?" I asked.

Sherlock Holmes placed the subjoined paper before us :—

If you will only come round at quarter to twelve to the east gate you will learn what will very much surprise you and maybe be of the greatest service to you and also to Annie Morrison. But say nothing to anyone upon the matter

and, having thus got them into his power, proceeded under threats of exposure to levy blackmail upon them. Mister Alec, however, was a dangerous man to play games of that sort with. It was a stroke of positive genius on his part to see in the burglary scare, which was convulsing the country side, an opportunity of plausibly getting rid of the man whom he feared. William was decoyed up and shot ; and, had they only got the whole of the note, and paid a little more attention to detail in their accessories, it is very possible that suspicion might never have been aroused."

"It is very much the sort of thing that I expected," said he. "Of course, we do not yet know what the relations may have been between Alec Cunningham, William Kirwan, and Annie Morrison. The result shows that the trap was skilfully baited. I am sure that you cannot fail to be delighted with the traces of heredity shown in the p's and in the tails of the g's. The absence of the i-dots in the old man's writing is also most characteristic. Watson, I think our quiet rest in the country has been a distinct success, and I shall certainly return, much invigorated, to Baker Street to-morrow."

The Adventures of Sherlock Holmes.

XX.—THE ADVENTURE OF THE CROOKED MAN.

By A. Conan Doyle.

ONE summer night, a few months after my marriage, I was seated by my own hearth smoking a last pipe and nodding over a novel, for my day's work had been an exhausting one. My wife had already gone upstairs, and the sound of the locking of the hall door some time before told me that the servants had also retired. I had risen from my seat and was knocking out the ashes of my pipe, when I suddenly heard the clang of the bell.

I looked at the clock. It was a quarter to twelve. This could not be a visitor at so late an hour. A patient, evidently, and possibly an all-night sitting. With a wry face I went out into the hall and opened the door. To my astonishment, it was Sherlock Holmes who stood upon my step.

"Ah, Watson," said he, "I hoped that I might not be too late to catch you."

"My dear fellow, pray come in."

"You look surprised, and no wonder! Relieved, too, I fancy! Hum! you still smoke the Arcadia mixture of your bachelor days, then! There's no mistaking that fluffy ash upon your coat. It's easy to tell that you've been accustomed to wear a uniform, Watson; you'll never pass as a pure-bred civilian as long as you keep that habit of carrying your handkerchief in your sleeve. Could you put me up to-night?"

"With pleasure."

"You told me that you had bachelor quarters for one, and I see that you have no gentleman visitor at present. Your hat-stand proclaims as much."

"I shall be delighted if you will stay."

"Thank you. I'll fill a vacant peg, then. Sorry to see that you've had the British workman in the house. He's a token of evil. Not the drains, I hope?"

"No, the gas."

"Ah! He has left two nail-marks from his boot upon your linoleum just where the light strikes it. No, thank you, I had some supper at Waterloo, but I'll smoke a pipe with you with pleasure."

I handed him my pouch, and he seated himself opposite to me, and smoked for some

377

time in silence. I was well aware that nothing but business of importance could have brought him to me at such an hour, so I waited patiently until he should come round to it.

"I see that you are professionally rather busy just now," said he, glancing very keenly across at me.

"Yes, I've had a busy day," I answered. "It may seem very foolish in your eyes," I added, "but really I don't know how you deduced it."

Holmes chuckled to himself.

"I have the advantage of knowing your habits, my dear Watson," said he. "When your round is a short one you walk, and when it is a long one you use a hansom. As I perceive that your boots, although used, are by no means dirty, I cannot doubt that you are at present busy enough to justify the hansom."

"Excellent!" I cried.

"Elementary," said he. "It is one of those instances where the reasoner can produce an effect which seems remarkable to his neighbour, because the latter has missed the one little point which is the basis of the deduction. The same may be said, my dear fellow, for the effect of some of these little sketches of yours, which is entirely meretricious, depending as it does upon your retaining in your own hands some factors in the problem which are never imparted to the reader. Now, at present I am in the position of these same readers, for I hold in this hand several threads of one of the strangest cases which ever perplexed a man's brain, and yet I lack the one or two which are needful to complete my theory. But I'll have them, Watson, I'll have them!" His eyes kindled and a slight flush sprang into his thin cheeks. For an instant the veil had lifted upon his keen, intense nature, but for an instant only. When I glanced again his face had resumed that Red Indian composure which had made so many regard him as a machine rather than a man.

"The problem presents features of interest," said he; "I may even say very exceptional features of interest. I have already looked into the matter, and have come, as I think, within sight of my solution. If you could accompany me in that last step, you might be of considerable service to me."

"I should be delighted."

"Could you go as far as Aldershot to-morrow?"

"I have no doubt Jackson would take my practice."

"Very good. I want to start by the 11.10 from Waterloo."

"That would give me time."

"Then, if you are not too sleepy, I will give you a sketch of what has happened and of what remains to be done."

"I was sleepy before you came. I am quite wakeful now."

"I will compress the story as far as may be done without omitting anything vital to the case. It is conceivable that you may even have read some account of the matter. It is the supposed murder of Colonel Barclay, of the Royal Mallows, at Aldershot which I am investigating."

"I have heard nothing of it."

"It has not excited much attention yet, except locally. The facts are only two days old. Briefly they are these :—

"The Royal Mallows is, as you know, one of the most famous Irish regiments in the British Army. It did wonders both in the Crimea and the Mutiny, and has since that time distinguished itself upon every possible occasion. It was commanded up to Monday night by James Barclay, a gallant veteran, who started as a full private, was raised to commissioned rank for his bravery at the time of the Mutiny, and so lived to command the regiment in which he had once carried a musket.

"Colonel Barclay had married at the time when he was a sergeant, and his wife, whose maiden name was Miss Nancy Devoy, was the daughter of a former colour-sergeant in the same corps. There was therefore, as can be imagined, some little social friction when the young couple (for they were still young) found themselves in their new surroundings. They appear, however, to have quickly adapted themselves, and Mrs. Barclay has always, I understand, been as popular with the ladies of the regiment as her husband was with his brother officers. I may add that she was a woman of great beauty, and that even now, when she has been married for upwards of thirty years, she is still of a striking appearance.

"Colonel Barclay's family life appears to have been a uniformly happy one. Major Murphy, to whom I owe most of my facts, assures me that he has never heard of any misunderstanding between the pair. On the whole, he thinks that Barclay's devotion to his wife was greater than his wife's to Barclay. He was acutely uneasy if he were absent from her for a day. She, on the other hand, though devoted and faithful, was less obtrusively affectionate. But they were regarded in the regiment as the very model of a middle-aged couple. There was absolutely nothing in their mutual relations to prepare people for the tragedy which was to follow.

"Colonel Barclay himself seems to have had some singular traits in his character. He was a dashing, jovial old soldier in his usual mood, but there were occasions on which he seemed to show himself capable of considerable violence and vindictiveness. This side of his nature, however, appears never to have been turned towards his wife. Another fact which had struck Major Murphy, and three out of five of the other officers with whom I conversed, was the singular sort of depression which came upon him at times. As the Major expressed it, the smile had often been struck from his mouth, as if by some invisible hand, when he has been joining in the gaieties and chaff of the mess table. For days on end when the mood was on him he has been sunk in the deepest gloom. This and a certain tinge of superstition were the only unusual traits in his character which his brother officers had observed. The latter peculiarity took the form of a dislike to being left alone, especially after dark. This puerile feature in a nature which was conspicuously manly had often given rise to comment and conjecture.

"The first battalion of the Royal Mallows (which is the old 117th) has been stationed at Aldershot for some years. The married officers live out of barracks, and the Colonel has during all this time occupied a villa called Lachine, about half a mile from the North Camp. The house stands in its own grounds, but the west side of it is not more than thirty yards from the high road. A coachman and two maids form the staff of servants. These, with their master and mistress, were the sole occupants of Lachine, for the Barclays had no children, nor was it usual for them to have resident visitors.

"Now for the events at Lachine between nine and ten on the evening of last Monday.

"Mrs. Barclay was, it appears, a member of the Roman Catholic Church, and had interested herself very much in the establishment of the Guild of St. George, which was formed in connection with the Watt Street Chapel for the purpose of supplying the poor with cast-off clothing. A meeting of the Guild had been held that evening at eight, and Mrs. Barclay had hurried over her dinner in order to be present at it. When leaving the house, she was heard by the coachman to make some commonplace remark to her husband, and to assure him that she would be back before very long. She then called for Miss Morrison, a young lady who lives in the next villa, and the two went off together to their meeting. It lasted forty minutes, and at a quarter past nine Mrs. Barclay returned home, having left Miss Morrison at her door as she passed.

"There is a room which is used as a morning-room at Lachine. This faces the road and opens by a large glass folding door on to the lawn. The lawn is thirty yards across, and is only divided from the highway by a low wall with an iron rail above it. It was into this room that Mrs. Barclay went upon her return. The blinds were not down, for the room was seldom used in the evening, but Mrs. Barclay herself lit the lamp and then rang the bell, asking Jane Stewart, the housemaid, to bring her a cup of tea, which was quite contrary to her usual habits. The Colonel had been sitting in the dining-room, but hearing that his wife had returned, he joined her in the morning-room. The coachman saw him cross the hall, and enter it. He was never seen again alive.

"The tea which had been ordered was brought up at the end of ten minutes, but the maid, as she approached the door, was surprised to hear the voices of her master and mistress in furious altercation. She knocked without receiving any answer, and even turned the handle, but only to find that the door was locked upon the inside. Naturally enough, she ran down to tell the cook, and the two women with the coachman came up into the hall and listened to the dispute which was still raging. They all agree that only two voices were to be heard, those of Barclay and of his wife. Barclay's remarks were subdued and abrupt, so that none of them were audible to the listeners. The lady's, on the other hand, were most bitter, and, when she raised her voice, could be plainly heard. 'You coward!' she repeated over and over again. 'What can be done now? What can be done now? Give me back my life. I will never so much as breathe the same air as you again! You coward! You coward!' Those were scraps of her conversation, ending in a sudden dreadful cry in the man's voice, with a crash, and a piercing scream from the woman. Convinced that some tragedy had occurred, the coachman rushed to the door and strove to force it, while scream after scream issued from within. He was unable, however, to make his way in, and the maids were too distracted with fear to be of any assistance to him. A

"THE COACHMAN RUSHED TO THE DOOR."

sudden thought struck him, however, and he ran through the hall door and round to the lawn, upon which the long French windows open. One side of the window was open, which I understand was quite usual in the summer-time, and he passed without difficulty into the room. His mistress had ceased to scream, and was stretched insensible upon a couch, while with his feet tilted over the side of an arm-chair, and his head upon the ground near the corner of the fender, was lying the unfortunate soldier, stone dead, in a pool of his own blood.

"Naturally the coachman's first thought, on finding that he could do nothing for his master, was to open the door. But here an unexpected and singular difficulty presented itself. The key was not on the inner side of the door, nor could he find it anywhere in the room. He went out again, therefore, through the window, and having obtained the help of a policeman and of a medical man he returned. The lady, against whom

naturally the strongest suspicion rested, was removed to her room, still in a state of insensibility. The Colonel's body was then placed upon the sofa, and a careful examination made of the scene of the tragedy.

"The injury from which the unfortunate veteran was suffering was found to be a ragged cut, some two inches long, at the back part of his head, which had evidently been caused by a violent blow from a blunt weapon. Nor was it difficult to guess what that weapon may have been. Upon the floor, close to the body, was lying a singular club of hard carved wood with a bone handle. The Colonel possessed a varied collection of weapons brought from the different countries in which he had fought, and it is conjectured by the police that this club was among his trophies. The servants deny having seen it before, but among the numerous curiosities in the house it is possible that it may have been overlooked. Nothing else of importance was discovered in the room by the police, save the inexplicable fact that neither upon Mrs. Barclay's person, nor upon that of the victim, nor in any part of the room was the missing key to be found. The door had eventually to be opened by a locksmith from Aldershot.

"That was the state of things, Watson, when upon the Tuesday morning I, at the request of Major Murphy, went down to Aldershot to supplement the efforts of the police. I think you will acknowledge that the problem was already one of interest, but my observations soon made me realize that it was in truth much more extraordinary than would at first sight appear.

"Before examining the room I cross-questioned the servants, but only succeeded in eliciting the facts which I have already stated. One other detail of interest was remembered by Jane Stewart, the housemaid. You will remember that on hearing the sound of the quarrel she descended and returned with the other servants. On that first occasion, when she was alone, she says that the voices of her master and mistress were sunk so low that she could hear hardly anything, and judged by their tones, rather than their words, that they had fallen out. On my pressing her, however, she remembered that she heard the word 'David' uttered twice by the lady. The point is of the utmost importance as guiding us towards the reason of the sudden quarrel The Colonel's name, you remember, was James.

"There was one thing in the case which had made the deepest impression both upon the servants and the police. This was the contortion of the Colonel's face. It had set, according to their account, into the most dreadful expression of fear and horror which a human countenance is capable of assuming. More than one person fainted at the mere sight of him, so terrible was the effect. It was quite certain that he had foreseen his fate, and that it had caused him the utmost horror. This, of course, fitted in well enough with the police theory, if the Colonel could have seen his wife making a murderous attack upon him. Nor was the fact of the wound being on the back of his head a fatal objection to this, as he might have turned to avoid the blow. No information could be got from the lady herself, who was temporarily insane from an acute attack of brain fever.

"From the police I learned that Miss Morrison, who, you remember, went out that evening with Mrs. Barclay, denied having any knowledge of what it was which had caused the ill-humour in which her companion had returned.

"Having gathered these facts, Watson, I smoked several pipes over them, trying to separate those which were crucial from others which were merely incidental. There could be no question that the most distinctive and suggestive point in the case was the singular disappearance of the door key. A most careful search had failed to discover it in the room. Therefore, it must have been taken from it. But neither the Colonel nor the Colonel's wife could have taken it. That was perfectly clear. Therefore a third person must have entered the room. And that third person could only have come in through the window. It seemed to me that a careful examination of the room and the lawn might possibly reveal some traces of this mysterious individual. You know my methods, Watson. There was not one of them which I did not apply to the inquiry. And it ended by my discovering traces, but very different ones from those which I had expected. There had been a man in the room, and he had crossed the lawn coming from the road. I was able to obtain five very clear impressions of his footmarks—one on the roadway itself, at the point where he had climbed the low wall, two on the lawn, and two very faint ones upon the stained boards near the window where he had entered. He had apparently rushed across the lawn, for his toe marks were much deeper than his heels. But it was not the man who surprised me. It was his companion."

"His companion!"

Holmes pulled a large sheet of tissue paper out of his pocket and carefully unfolded it upon his knee.

"What do you make of that?" he asked.

The paper was covered with tracings of the footmarks of some small animal. It

"WHAT DO YOU MAKE OF THAT?"

had five well-marked footpads, an indication of long nails, and the whole print might be nearly as large as a dessert spoon.

"It's a dog," said I.

"Did ever you hear of a dog running up a curtain? I found distinct traces that this creature had done so."

"A monkey, then?"

"But it is not the print of a monkey."

"What can it be, then?"

"Neither dog, nor cat, nor monkey, nor any creature that we are familiar with. I have tried to reconstruct it from the measurements. Here are four prints where the beast has been standing motionless. You see that it is no less than fifteen inches from fore foot to hind. Add to that the length of neck and head, and you get a creature not much less than two feet long—probably more if there is any tail. But now observe this other measurement. The animal has been moving, and we have the length of its stride. In each case it is only about three inches. You have an indication, you see, of a long body with very short legs attached to it. It has not been considerate enough to leave any of its hair behind it. But its general shape must be what I have indicated, and it can run up a curtain and is carnivorous."

"How do you deduce that?"

"Because it ran up the curtain. A canary's cage was hanging in the window, and its aim seems to have been to get at the bird."

"Then what was the beast?"

"Ah, if I could give it a name it might go a long way towards solving the case. On the whole it was probably some creature of the weasel and stoat tribe—and yet it is larger than any of these that I have seen."

"But what had it to do with the crime?"

"That also is still obscure. But we have learned a good deal, you perceive. We know that a man stood in the road looking at the quarrel between the Barclays—the blinds were up and the room lighted. We know also that he ran across the lawn, entered the room, accompanied by a strange animal, and that he either struck the Colonel, or, as is equally possible, that the Colonel fell down from sheer fright at the sight of him, and cut his head on the corner of the fender. Finally, we have the curious fact that the intruder carried away the key with him when he left."

"Your discoveries seem to have left the business more obscure than it was before," said I.

"Quite so. They undoubtedly showed that the affair was much deeper than was at first conjectured. I thought the matter over, and I came to the conclusion that I must approach the case from another aspect. But really, Watson, I am keeping you up, and I might just as well tell you all this on our way to Aldershot to-morrow."

"Thank you, you've gone rather too far to stop."

"It was quite certain that when Mrs. Barclay left the house at half-past seven she was on good terms with her husband. She was never, as I think I have said, ostentatiously affectionate, but she was heard by the coachman chatting with the Colonel in a friendly fashion. Now, it was equally certain that immediately on her return she had gone to the room in which she was least likely to see her husband, had flown to tea, as an agitated woman will, and, finally, on his coming in to her, had broken into violent recriminations. Therefore, something had occurred between seventhirty and nine o'clock which had completely altered her feelings towards him. But Miss Morrison had been with her during the whole of that hour and a half. It was absolutely certain, therefore, in spite of her denial, that she must know something of the matter.

"My first conjecture was that possibly there had been some passages between this young lady and the old soldier, which the former had now confessed to the wife. That would account for the angry return and also for the girl's denial that anything had occurred. Nor would it be entirely incompatible with most of the words overheard. But there was the reference to David, and there was the known affection of the Colonel for his wife to weigh against it, to say nothing of the tragic intrusion of this other man, which might of course be entirely disconnected with what had gone before. It was not easy to pick one's steps, but on the whole I was inclined to dismiss the idea that there had been anything between the Colonel and Miss Morrison, but more than ever convinced that the young lady held the clue as to what it was which had turned Mrs. Barclay to hatred of her husband. I took the obvious course therefore of calling upon Miss Morrison, of explaining to her that I was perfectly certain that she held the facts in her possession, and of assuring her that her friend, Mrs. Barclay, might find herself in the dock upon a capital charge unless the matter were cleared up.

"Miss Morrison is a little, ethereal slip of a girl, with timid eyes and blonde hair, but I found her by no means wanting in shrewdness and common sense. She sat thinking for some time after I had spoken, and then turning to me with a brisk air of resolution, she broke into a remarkable statement, which I will condense for your benefit.

"'I promised my friend that I would say nothing of the matter, and a promise is a promise,' said she. 'But if I can really help her when so serious a charge is made against her, and when her own mouth, poor darling, is closed by illness, then I think I am absolved from my promise. I will tell you exactly what happened upon Monday evening.

"'We were returning from the Watt Street Mission, about a quarter to nine o'clock. On our way we had to pass through Hudson Street, which is a very quiet thoroughfare. There is only one lamp in it upon the left-hand side, and as we approached this lamp I saw a man coming towards us with his back very bent, and something like a box slung over one of his shoulders. He appeared to be deformed, for he carried his head low, and walked with his knees bent. We were passing him when he raised his face to look at us in the circle of light thrown by the

lamp, and as he did so he stopped and screamed out in a dreadful voice, " My God, it's Nancy ! " Mrs. Barclay turned as white as death, and would have fallen down had the dreadful-looking creature not caught hold of her. I was going to call for the police, but she, to my surprise, spoke quite civilly to the fellow.

"'I thought you had been dead this thirty years, Henry,' said she, in a shaking voice.

"'So I have,' said he, and it was awful to hear the tones that he said it in. He had a very dark, fearsome face, and a gleam in his eyes that comes back to me in my dreams. His hair and whiskers were shot with grey, and his face was all crinkled and puckered like a withered apple.

"'Just walk on a little way, dear,' said Mrs. Barclay. 'I want to have a word with this man. There is nothing to be afraid of.' She tried to speak boldly, but she was still deadly pale, and could hardly get her words out for the trembling of her lips.

"'I did as she asked me, and they talked together for a few minutes. Then she came down the street with her eyes blazing, and I saw the crippled wretch standing by the lamp-post and shaking his clenched fists in the air, as if he were mad with rage. She never said a word until we were at the door here, when she took me by the hand and begged me to tell no one what had happened. 'It is an old acquaintance of mine who has come down in the world,' said she. When I promised her that I would say nothing she kissed me, and I have never seen her since. I have told you now the whole truth, and if I withheld it from the police it is because I did not realize then the danger in which my dear friend stood. I know that it can only be to her advantage that everything should be known.'

"There was her statement, Watson, and to me, as you can imagine, it was like a light on a dark night. Everything which had been disconnected before began at once to as-

" IT'S NANCY ! "

sume its true place, and I had a shadowy presentment of the whole sequence of events. My next step obviously was to find the man who had produced such a remarkable impression upon Mrs. Barclay. If he were still in Aldershot it should not be a very difficult matter. There are not such a very great number of civilians, and a deformed man was sure to have attracted attention. I spent a day in the search, and by evening—this very evening, Watson—I had run him down. The man's name is Henry Wood, and he lives in lodgings in this same street in which the ladies met him. He has only been five days in the place. In the character of a registration agent I had a most interesting gossip with his landlady. The man is by trade a conjurer and performer, going round the canteens after nightfall, and giving a little entertainment at each. He carries some creature about with him in that box, about which the landlady seemed to be in considerable trepidation, for she had never seen an animal like it. He uses it in some of his tricks, according to her account. So much the woman was able to tell me, and also that it was a wonder the man lived, seeing how twisted he was, and that he spoke in a strange tongue sometimes, and that for the last two nights she had heard him groaning and weeping in his bedroom. He was all right as far as money went, but in his deposit he had given her what looked like a bad florin. She showed it to me, Watson, and it was an Indian rupee.

"So now, my dear fellow, you see exactly how we stand and why it is I want you. It is perfectly plain that after the ladies parted from this man he followed them at a distance, that he saw the quarrel between husband and wife through the window, that he rushed in, and that the creature which he carried in his box got loose. That is all very certain. But he is the only person in this world who can tell us exactly what happened in that room."

"And you intend to ask him?"

"Most certainly—but in the presence of a witness."

"And I am the witness?"

"If you will be so good. If he can clear the matter up, well and good. If he refuses, we have no alternative but to apply for a warrant."

"But how do you know he will be there when we return?"

"You may be sure that I took some precautions. I have one of my Baker Street boys mounting guard over him who would

stick to him like a burr, go where he might. We shall find him in Hudson Street to-morrow, Watson ; and meanwhile I should be the criminal myself if I kept you out of bed any longer."

It was midday when we found ourselves at the scene of the tragedy, and, under my companion's guidance, we made our way at once to Hudson Street. In spite of his capacity for concealing his emotions I could easily see that Holmes was in a state of suppressed excitement, while I was myself tingling with that half-sporting, half-intellectual pleasure which I invariably experienced when I associated myself with him in his investigations.

"This is the street," said he, as he turned into a short thoroughfare lined with plain two-storied brick houses—"Ah ! here is Simpson to report."

"He's in all right, Mr. Holmes," cried a small street Arab, running up to us.

"Good, Simpson !" said Holmes, patting him on the head. "Come along, Watson. This is the house." He sent in his card with a message that he had come on important business, and a moment later we were face to face with the man whom we had come to see. In spite of the warm weather he was crouching over a fire, and the little room was like an oven. The man sat all twisted and huddled in his chair in a way which gave an indescribable impression of deformity, but the face which he turned towards us, though worn and swarthy, must at some time have been remarkable for its beauty. He looked suspiciously at us now out of yellow-shot bilious eyes, and, without speaking or rising, he waved towards two chairs.

"Mr. Henry Wood, late of India, I believe?" said Holmes, affably. "I've come over this little matter of Colonel Barclay's death."

"What should I know about that?"

"That's what I wanted to ascertain. You know, I suppose, that unless the matter is cleared up, Mrs. Barclay, who is an old friend of yours, will in all probability be tried for murder?"

The man gave a violent start.

"I don't know who you are," he cried, "nor how you come to know what you do know ; but will you swear that this is true that you tell me?"

"Why, they are only waiting for her to come to her senses to arrest her."

"My God ! Are you in the police yourself?"

"MR. HENRY WOOD, I BELIEVE?"

"No."

"What business is it of yours, then?"

"It's every man's business to see justice done."

"You can take my word that she is innocent."

"Then you are guilty?"

"No, I am not."

"Who killed Colonel James Barclay, then?"

"It was a just Providence that killed him. But, mind you this, that if I had knocked his brains out, as it was in my heart to do, he would have had no more than his due from my hands. If his own guilty conscience had not struck him down, it is likely enough that I might have had his blood upon my soul. You want me to tell the story. Well, I don't know why I shouldn't, for there's no cause for me to be ashamed of it.

"It was in this way, sir. You see me now with my back like a camel and my ribs all awry, but there was a time when Corporal Henry Wood was the smartest man in the 117th Foot. We were in India then, in cantonments, at a place we'll call Bhurtee. Barclay, who died the other day, was sergeant in the same company as myself, and the belle of the regiment—aye, and the finest girl that ever had the breath of life between her lips— was Nancy Devoy, the daughter of the colour-sergeant. There were two men who

loved her, and one whom she loved; and you'll smile when you look at this poor thing huddled before the fire, and hear me say that it was for my good looks that she loved me.

"Well, though I had her heart, her father was set upon her marrying Barclay. I was a harum-scarum, reckless lad, and he had had an education, and was already marked for the sword belt. But the girl held true to me, and it seemed that I would have had her, when the Mutiny broke out, and all Hell was loose in the country.

"We were shut up in Bhurtee, the regiment of us with half a battery of artillery, a company of Sikhs, and a lot of civilians and women-folk. There were ten thousand rebels round us, and they were as keen as a set of terriers round a rat-cage. About the second week of it our water gave out, and it was a question whether we could communicate with General Neill's column, which was moving up country. It was our only chance, for we could not hope to fight our way out with all the women and children, so I volunteered to go out and warn General Neill of our danger. My offer was accepted, and I talked it over with Sergeant Barclay, who was supposed to know the ground better than any other man, and who drew up a route by which I might get through the rebel lines. At ten o'clock the same night I started off upon my journey. There were a thousand lives to save, but it was of only one that I was thinking when I dropped over the wall that night.

"My way ran down a dried-up watercourse which we hoped would screen me from the enemy's sentries, but as I crept round the corner of it I walked right into six of them, who were crouching down in the dark waiting for me. In an instant I was stunned with a blow, and bound hand and foot. But the real blow was to my heart and not to my

"I WALKED RIGHT INTO SIX OF THEM."

head, for as I came to and listened to as much as I could understand of their talk, I heard enough to tell me that my comrade, the very man who had arranged the way that I was to take, had betrayed me by means of a native servant into the hands of the enemy.

"Well, there's no need for me to dwell on that part of it. You know now what James Barclay was capable of. Bhurtee was relieved by Neill next day, but the rebels took me away with them in their retreat, and it was many a long year before ever I saw a white face again. I was tortured, and tried to get away, and was captured and tortured again. You can see for yourselves the state in which I was left. Some of them that fled into Nepaul took me with them, and then afterwards I was up past Darjeeling. The hillfolk up there murdered the rebels who had me, and I became their slave for a time until I escaped, but instead of going south I had to go north, until I found myself among the Afghans. There I wandered about for many a year, and at last came back to the Punjab, where I lived mostly among the natives, and picked up a living by the conjuring tricks that I had learned. What use was it for me, a wretched cripple, to go back to England, or to make myself known to my old comrades? Even my wish for revenge would not make me do that. I had

rather that Nancy and my old pals should think of Harry Wood as having died with a straight back, than see him living and crawling with a stick like a chimpanzee. They never doubted that I was dead, and I meant that they never should. I heard that Barclay had married Nancy, and that he was rising rapidly in the regiment, but even that did not make me speak.

"But when one gets old, one has a longing for home. For years I've been dreaming of the bright green fields and the hedges of England. At last I determined to see them before I died. I saved enough to bring me across, and then I came here where the soldiers are, for I know their ways, and how to amuse them, and so earn enough to keep me."

"Your narrative is most interesting," said Sherlock Holmes. "I have already heard of your meeting with Mrs. Barclay and your mutual recognition. You then, as I understand, followed her home and saw through the window an altercation between her husband and her, in which she doubtless cast his conduct to you in his teeth. Your own feelings overcame you and you ran across the lawn and broke in upon them."

"I did, sir, and at the sight of me he looked as I have never seen a man look before, and over he went with his head on the fender. But he was dead before he fell. I read death on his face as plain as I can read that text over the fire. The bare sight of me was like a bullet through his guilty heart."

" And then ? "

" Then Nancy fainted, and I caught up the key of the door from her hand, intending to unlock it and get help. But as I was doing it it seemed to me better to leave it alone and get away, for the thing might look black against me, and any way my secret would be out if I were taken. In my haste I thrust the key into my pocket, and dropped my stick while I was chasing Teddy, who had run up the curtain. When I got him into his box, from which he had slipped, I was off as fast as I could run."

"Who's Teddy?" asked Holmes.

The man leaned over and pulled up the front of a kind of hutch in the corner. In an instant out there slipped a beautiful reddish-brown creature, thin and lithe, with the legs of a stoat, a long thin nose, and a pair of the finest red eyes that ever I saw in an animal's head.

"IT WAS QUITE A SIMPLE CASE AFTER ALL."

" It's a mongoose ! " I cried.

"Well, some call them that, and some call them ichneumon," said the man. "Snake catcher is what I call them, and Teddy is amazing quick on cobras. I have one here without the fangs, and Teddy catches it every night to please the folk in the canteen. Any other point, sir ? "

" Well, we may have to apply to you again if Mrs. Barclay should prove to be in serious trouble."

" In that case, of course, I'd come forward."

" But if not, there is no object in raking up this scandal against a dead man, foully as he has acted. You have, at least, the satisfaction of knowing that for thirty years of his life his conscience bitterly reproached him for this wicked deed. Ah, there goes Major Murphy on the other side of the street. Good-bye, Wood ; I want to learn if anything has happened since yesterday."

We were in time to overtake the Major before he reached the corner.

" Ah, Holmes," he said, "I suppose you have heard that all this fuss has come to nothing ? "

" What, then ? "

" The inquest is just over. The medical evidence showed conclusively that death was due to apoplexy. You see, it was quite a simple case after all."

" Oh, remarkably superficial," said Holmes, smiling. " Come, Watson, I don't think we shall be wanted in Aldershot any more."

" There's one thing," said I, as we walked down to the station, " if the husband's name was James, and the other was Henry, what was this talk about David ? "

" That one word, my dear Watson, should have told me the whole story had I been the ideal reasoner which you are so fond of depicting. It was evidently a term of reproach."

" Of reproach ? "

" Yes, David strayed a little occasionally, you know, and on one occasion in the same direction as Sergeant James Barclay. You remember the small affair of Uriah and Bathsheba. My Biblical knowledge is a trifle rusty, I fear, but you will find the story in the first or second of Samuel."

The Adventures of Sherlock Holmes.

By A. Conan Doyle.

XXI.—THE ADVENTURE OF THE RESIDENT PATIENT.

I N glancing over the somewhat incoherent series of memoirs with which I have endeavoured to illustrate a few of the mental peculiarities of my friend, Mr. Sherlock Holmes, I have been struck by the difficulty which I have experienced in picking out examples which shall in every way answer my purpose. For in those cases in which Holmes has performed some *tour-de-force* of analytical reasoning, and has demonstrated the value of his peculiar methods of investigation, the facts themselves have often been so slight or so commonplace that I could not feel justified in laying them before the public. On the other hand, it has frequently happened that he has been concerned in some research where the facts have been of the most remarkable and dramatic character, but where the share which he has himself taken in determining their causes has been less pronounced than I, as his biographer, could wish. The small matter which I have chronicled under the heading of "A Study in Scarlet," and that other later one connected with the loss of the *Gloria Scott*, may serve as examples of this Scylla and Charybdis which are for ever threatening his historian. It may be that, in the business of which I am now about to write, the part which my friend played is not sufficiently accentuated; and yet the whole train of circumstances is so remarkable that I cannot bring myself to omit it entirely from this series.

I cannot be sure of the exact date, for some of my memoranda upon the matter have been mislaid, but it must have been towards the end of the first year during which Holmes and I shared chambers in Baker Street. It was boisterous October weather, and we had both remained indoors all day, I because I feared with my shaken health to face the keen autumn wind, while he was deep in some of those abstruse chemical investigations which absorbed him utterly as long as he was engaged upon them. Towards evening, however, the breaking of a test-tube brought his research to a premature ending, and he sprang up from his chair with an exclamation of impatience and a clouded brow.

"A day's work ruined, Watson," said he, striding across to the window. "Ha! the stars are out and the wind has fallen. What do you say to a ramble through London?"

I was weary of our little sitting-room, and gladly acquiesced, muffling myself nose-high against the keen night air. For three hours we strolled about together, watching the ever-changing kaleidoscope of life as it ebbs and flows through Fleet Street and the Strand. Holmes had shaken off his temporary ill-humour, and his characteristic talk, with its keen observance of detail and subtle power of inference, held me amused and enthralled. It was ten o'clock before we reached Baker Street again. A brougham was waiting at our door.

"Hum! A doctor's—general practitioner, I perceive," said Holmes. "Not been long in practice, or had much to do. Come to consult us, I fancy! Lucky we came back!"

I was sufficiently conversant with Holmes's methods to be able to follow his reasoning, and to see that the nature and state of the various medical instruments in the wicker basket which hung in the lamp-light inside the brougham had given him the data for his swift deduction. The light in our window above showed that this late visit was indeed intended for us. With some curiosity as to what could have sent a brother medico to us at such an hour, I followed Holmes into our sanctum.

A pale, taper-faced man with sandy whiskers rose up from a chair by the fire as we entered. His age may not have been more than three or four and thirty, but his haggard expression and unhealthy hue told of a life which had sapped his strength and robbed him of his youth. His manner was nervous and shy, like that of a sensitive gentleman,

" WE STROLLED ABOUT TOGETHER."

and the thin white hand which he laid on the mantelpiece as he rose was that of an artist rather than of a surgeon. His dress was quiet and sombre, a black frock-coat, dark trousers, and a touch of colour about his necktie.

"Good evening, Doctor," said Holmes, cheerily; " I am glad to see that you have only been waiting a very few minutes."

"You spoke to my coachman, then ? "

"No, it was the candle on the side-table that told me. Pray resume your seat and let me know how I can serve you."

"My name is Doctor Percy Trevelyan," said our visitor, "and I live at 403, Brook Street."

"Are you not the author of a monograph upon obscure nervous lesions ? " I asked.

His pale cheeks flushed with pleasure at hearing that his work was known to me.

"I so seldom hear of the work that I thought it was quite dead," said he. " My publishers give me a most discouraging

account of its sale. You are yourself, I presume, a medical man ? "

"A retired Army surgeon."

" My own hobby has always been nervous disease. I should wish to make it an absolute specialty, but, of course, a man must take what he can get at first. This, however, is beside the question, Mr. Sherlock Holmes, and I quite appreciate how valuable your time is. The fact is that a very singular train of events has occurred recently at my house in Brook Street, and to-night they came to such a head that I felt it was quite impossible for me to wait another hour before asking for your advice and assistance."

Sherlock Holmes sat down and lit his pipe. "You are very welcome to both," said he. " Pray let me have a detailed account of what the circumstances are which have disturbed you."

"One or two of them are so trivial," said Dr. Trevelyan, "that really I am almost ashamed to mention them. But the matter is so inexplicable, and the recent turn which it has taken is so elaborate, that I shall lay it all before you, and you shall judge what is essential and what is not.

" I am compelled, to begin with, to say something of my own college career. I am a London University man, you know, and I am sure you will not think that I am unduly singing my own praises if I say that my student career was considered by my professors to be a very promising one. After I had graduated I continued to devote myself to research, occupying a minor position in King's College Hospital, and I was fortunate enough to excite considerable interest by my research into the pathology of catalepsy, and finally to win the Bruce Pinkerton prize and medal by the monograph on nervous lesions to which your friend has just alluded. I should not go too far if I were to say that there was a general impression at that time that a distinguished career lay before me.

"But the one great stumbling-block lay in

my want of capital. As you will readily understand, a specialist who aims high is compelled to start in one of a dozen streets in the Cavendish Square quarter, all of which entail enormous rents and furnishing expenses. Besides this preliminary outlay, he must be prepared to keep himself for some years, and to hire a presentable carriage and horse. To do this was quite beyond my power, and I could only hope that by economy I might in ten years' time save enough to enable me to put up my plate. Suddenly, however, an unexpected incident opened up quite a new prospect to me.

"This was a visit from a gentleman of the name of Blessington, who was a complete stranger to me. He came up into my room one morning, and plunged into business in an instant.

"'You are the same Percy Trevelyan who has had so distinguished a career and won a great prize lately?' said he. I bowed.

"'Answer me frankly,' he continued, 'for you will find it to your interest to do so. You have all the cleverness which makes a successful man. Have you the tact?'

"I could not help smiling at the abruptness of the question.

"'I trust that I have my share,' I said.

"'Any bad habits? Not drawn towards drink, eh?'

"'Really, sir!' I cried.

"'Quite right! That's all right! But I was bound to ask. With all these qualities why are you not in practice?'

"I shrugged my shoulders.

"'Come, come!' said he, in his bustling way. 'It's the old story. More in your brains than in your pocket, eh? What would you say if I were to start you in Brook Street?'

"I stared at him in astonishment.

"'Oh, it's for my sake, not for yours,' he cried. 'I'll be perfectly frank with you, and if it suits you it will suit me very well. I have a few thousands to invest, d'ye see, and I think I'll sink them in you.'

"'But why?' I gasped.

"'Well, it's just like any other speculation, and safer than most.'

"'What am I to do, then?'

"'I'll tell you. I'll take the house, furnish it, pay the maids, and run the whole place. All you have to do is just to wear out your chair in the consulting-room. I'll let you have pocket-money and everything. Then you hand over to me three-quarters of what you earn and you keep the other quarter for yourself.'

"This was the strange proposal, Mr. Holmes, with which the man Blessington approached me. I won't weary you with the account of how we bargained and negotiated. It ended in my moving into the house next Lady Day and starting in practice on very much the same conditions as he had suggested. He came himself to live with me in the character of a resident patient. His heart was weak, it appears, and he needed constant medical supervision. He turned the two best rooms on the first floor into a sitting-room and bedroom for himself. He was a man of singular habits, shunning company and very seldom going out. His life was irregular, but in one respect he was regularity itself. Every evening at the same hour he walked into the consulting-room, examined the books, put down five and threepence for every guinea that I had earned, and carried the rest off to the strong box in his own room.

"I STARED AT HIM IN ASTONISHMENT."

"I may say with confidence that he never had occasion to regret his speculation. From the first it was a success. A few good cases and the reputation which I had won in the hospital brought me rapidly to the front, and during the last few years I have made him a rich man.

"So much, Mr. Holmes, for my past history and for my relations with Mr. Blessington. It only remains for me now to tell you what has occurred to bring me here to-night.

"Some weeks ago Mr. Blessington came down to me in, as it seemed to me, a state of considerable agitation. He spoke of some burglary which, he said, had been committed in the West-end, and he appeared, I remember, to be quite unnecessarily excited about it, declaring that a day should not pass before we should add stronger bolts to our windows and doors. For a week he continued to be in quite a peculiar state of restlessness, peering continually out of the windows, and ceasing to take the short walk which had usually been the prelude to his dinner. From his manner it struck me that he was in mortal dread of something or somebody, but when I questioned him upon the point he became so offensive that I was compelled to drop the subject. Gradually as time passed his fears appeared to die away, and he had renewed his former habits, when a fresh event reduced him to the pitiable state of prostration in which he now lies.

"What happened was this. Two days ago I received the letter which I now read to you. Neither address nor date is attached to it.

"'A Russian nobleman who is now resident in England,' it runs, 'would be glad to avail himself of the professional assistance of Dr. Percy Trevelyan. He has been for some years a victim to cataleptic attacks, on which, as is well known, Dr. Trevelyan is an authority. He proposes to call at about a quarter-past six to-morrow evening, if Dr. Trevelyan will make it convenient to be at home.'

"This letter interested me deeply, because the chief difficulty in the study of catalepsy is the rareness of the disease. You may believe, then, that I was in my consulting-room when, at the appointed hour, the page showed in the patient.

"He was an elderly man, thin, demure, and commonplace—by no means the conception one forms of a Russian nobleman. I was much more struck by the appearance of his companion. This was a tall young man, surprisingly handsome, with a dark, fierce face, and the limbs and chest of a Hercules. He had his hand under the other's arm as they entered, and helped him to a chair with

"HELPED HIM TO A CHAIR."

a tenderness which one would hardly have expected from his appearance.

"'You will excuse my coming in, Doctor,'

said he to me, speaking English with a slight lisp. 'This is my father, and his health is a matter of the most overwhelming importance to me.'

"I was touched by this filial anxiety. 'You would, perhaps, care to remain during the consultation,' said I.

"'Not for the world,' he cried, with a gesture of horror. 'It is more painful to me than I can express. If I were to see my father in one of those dreadful seizures, I am convinced that I should never survive it. My own nervous system is an exceptionally sensitive one. With your permission I will remain in the waiting-room while you go into my father's case.'

"To this, of course, I assented, and the young man withdrew. The patient and I then plunged into a discussion of his case, of which I took exhaustive notes. He was not remarkable for intelligence, and his answers were frequently obscure, which I attributed to his limited acquaintance with our language. Suddenly, however, as I sat writing he ceased to give any answer at all to my inquiries, and on my turning towards him I was shocked to see that he was sitting bolt upright in his chair, staring at me with a perfectly blank and rigid face. He was again in the grip of his mysterious malady.

"My first feeling, as I have just said, was one of pity and horror. My second, I fear, was rather one of professional satisfaction. I made notes of my patient's pulse and temperature, tested the rigidity of his muscles, and examined his reflexes. There was nothing markedly abnormal in any of these conditions, which harmonized with my former experiences. I had obtained good results in such cases by the inhalation of nitrite of amyl, and the present seemed an admirable opportunity of testing its virtues. The bottle was downstairs in my laboratory, so, leaving my patient seated in his chair, I ran down to get it. There was some little delay in finding it—five minutes, let us say—and then I returned. Imagine my amazement to find the room empty and the patient gone!

"Of course, my first act was to run into the waiting-room. The son had gone also. The hall door had been closed, but not shut. My page who admits patients is a new boy, and by no means quick. He waits downstairs, and runs up to show patients out when I ring the consulting-room bell. He had heard nothing, and the affair remained a complete mystery. Mr. Blessington came in from his walk shortly afterwards, but I did not say anything to him upon the subject, for,

to tell the truth, I have got in the way of late of holding as little communication with him as possible.

"Well, I never thought that I should see anything more of the Russian and his son, so you can imagine my amazement when at the very same hour this evening they both came marching into my consulting-room, just as they had done before.

"'I feel that I owe you a great many apologies for my abrupt departure yesterday, Doctor,' said my patient.

"'I confess that I was very much surprised at it,' said I.

"'Well, the fact is,' he remarked, 'that when I recover from these attacks my mind is always very clouded as to all that has gone before. I woke up in a strange room, as it seemed to me, and made my way out into the street in a sort of dazed way when you were absent.'

"'And I,' said the son, 'seeing my father pass the door of the waiting-room, naturally thought that the consultation had come to an end. It was not until we had reached home that I began to realize the true state of affairs.'

"'Well,' said I, laughing, 'there is no harm done, except that you puzzled me terribly; so if you, sir, would kindly step into the waiting-room, I shall be happy to continue our consultation, which was brought to so abrupt an ending.'

"For half an hour or so I discussed the old gentleman's symptoms with him, and then, having prescribed for him, I saw him go off on the arm of his son.

"I have told you that Mr. Blessington generally chose this hour of the day for his exercise. He came in shortly afterwards and passed upstairs. An instant later I heard him running down, and he burst into my consulting-room like a man who is mad with panic.

"'Who has been in my room?' he cried.

"'No one,' said I.

"'It's a lie!' he yelled. 'Come up and look.'

"I passed over the grossness of his language, as he seemed half out of his mind with fear. When I went upstairs with him he pointed to several footprints upon the light carpet.

"'D'you mean to say those are mine?' he cried.

"They were certainly very much larger than any which he could have made, and were evidently quite fresh. It rained hard this afternoon, as you know, and my patients were the only people who called. It must have been the case, then, that the man in the

"HF BURST INTO MY CONSULTING-ROOM."

sombre, flat-faced houses which one associates with a West-end practice. A small page admitted us, and we began at once to ascend the broad, well-carpeted stair.

But a singular interruption brought us to a standstill. The light at the top was suddenly whisked out, and from the darkness came a reedy, quavering voice.

"I have a pistol," it cried; "I give you my word that I'll fire if you come any nearer."

"This really grows outrageous, Mr. Blessington," cried Dr. Trevelyan.

"Oh, then it is you, Doctor?" said the voice, with a great heave of relief. "But those other gentlemen, are they what they pretend to be?"

We were conscious of a long scrutiny out of the darkness.

"Yes, yes, it's all right," said the voice at last. "You can come up, and I am sorry if my precautions have annoyed you."

He re-lit the stair gas as he spoke, and we saw before us a singular-looking man, whose appearance, as well as his voice, testified to his jangled nerves. He was very fat, but had apparently at some time been much fatter, so that the skin hung about his face in loose pouches, like the cheeks of a bloodhound. He was of a sickly colour, and his thin sandy hair seemed to bristle up with the intensity of his emotion. In his hand he held a pistol, but he thrust it into his pocket as we advanced.

"Good evening, Mr. Holmes," said he; "I am sure I am very much obliged to you for coming round. No one ever needed your advice more than I do. I suppose that Dr. Trevelyan has told you of this most unwarrantable intrusion into my rooms."

"Quite so," said Holmes. "Who are these two men, Mr. Blessington, and why do they wish to molest you?"

"Well, well," said the resident patient, in a nervous fashion, "of course, it is hard to say

waiting-room had for some unknown reason, while I was busy with the other, ascended to the room of my resident patient. Nothing had been touched or taken, but there were the footprints to prove that the intrusion was an undoubted fact.

"Mr. Blessington seemed more excited over the matter than I should have thought possible, though, of course, it was enough to disturb anybody's peace of mind. He actually sat crying in an arm-chair, and I could hardly get him to speak coherently. It was his suggestion that I should come round to you, and of course I at once saw the propriety of it, for certainly the incident is a very singular one, though he appears to completely overrate its importance. If you would only come back with me in my brougham, you would at least be able to soothe him, though I can hardly hope that you will be able to explain this remarkable occurrence."

Sherlock Holmes had listened to this long narrative with an intentness which showed me that his interest was keenly aroused. His face was as impassive as ever, but his lids had drooped more heavily over his eyes, and his smoke had curled up more thickly from his pipe to emphasize each curious episode in the doctor's tale. As our visitor concluded Holmes sprang up without a word, handed me my hat, picked up his own from the table, and followed Dr. Trevelyan to the door. Within a quarter of an hour we had been dropped at the door of the physician's residence in Brook Street, one of those

IN HIS HAND HE HELD A PISTOL."

that. You can hardly expect me to answer that, Mr. Holmes."

"Do you mean that you don't know?"

"Come in here, if you please. Just have the kindness to step in here."

He led the way into his bedroom, which was large and comfortably furnished.

"You see that," said he, pointing to a big black box at the end of his bed. "I have never been a very rich man, Mr. Holmes—never made but one investment in my life, as Dr. Trevelyan would tell you. But I don't believe in bankers. I would never trust a banker, Mr. Holmes. Between ourselves, what little I have is in that box, so you can understand what it means to me when unknown people force themselves into my rooms."

Holmes looked at Blessington in his questioning way, and shook his head.

"I cannot possibly advise you if you try to deceive me," said he.

"But I have told you everything."

Holmes turned on his heel with a gesture of disgust. "Good-night, Dr. Trevelyan," said he.

"And no advice for me?" cried Blessington, in a breaking voice.

"My advice to you, sir, is to speak the truth."

A minute later we were in the street and walking for home. We had crossed Oxford Street, and were half-way down Harley

Street before I could get a word from my companion.

"Sorry to bring you out on such a fool's errand, Watson," he said at last. "It is an interesting case, too, at the bottom of it."

"I can make little of it," I confessed.

"Well, it is quite evident that there are two men—more, perhaps, but at least two—who are determined for some reason to get at this fellow Blessington. I have no doubt in my mind that both on the first and on the second occasion that young man penetrated to Blessington's room, while his confederate, by an ingenious device, kept the doctor from interfering."

"And the catalepsy!"

"A fraudulent imitation, Watson, though I should hardly dare to hint as much to our specialist. It is a very easy complaint to imitate. I have done it myself."

"And then?"

"By the purest chance Blessington was out on each occasion. Their reason for choosing so unusual an hour for a consultation was obviously to insure that there should be no other patient in the waiting-room. It just happened, however, that this hour coincided with Blessington's constitutional, which seems to show that they were not very well acquainted with his daily routine. Of course, if they had been merely after plunder they would at least have made some attempt to search for it. Besides, I can read in a man's eye when it is his own skin that he is frightened for. It is inconceivable that this fellow could have made two such vindictive enemies as these appear to be without knowing of it. I hold it, therefore, to be certain that he does know who these men are, and that for reasons of his own he suppresses it. It is just possible that tomorrow may find him in a more communicative mood."

"Is there not one alternative," I suggested, "grotesquely improbable, no doubt, but still just conceivable? Might the whole story of the cataleptic Russian and his son be a concoction of Dr. Trevelyan's, who has, for his own purposes, been in Blessington's rooms?"

I saw in the gaslight that Holmes wore an amused smile at this brilliant departure of mine.

"My dear fellow," said he, "it was one of the first solutions which occurred to me, but I was soon able to corroborate the doctor's tale. This young man has left prints upon the stair carpet which made it quite superfluous for me to ask to see those which he had made in the room. When I tell you that his shoes were square-toed, instead of being pointed like Blessington's, and were quite an inch and a third longer than the doctor's, you will acknowledge that there can be no doubt as to his individuality. But we may sleep on it now, for I shall be surprised if we do not hear something further from Brook Street in the morning."

Sherlock Holmes's prophecy was soon fulfilled, and in a dramatic fashion. At half-past seven next morning, in the first dim glimmer of daylight, I found him standing by my bedside in his dressing-gown.

"There's a brougham waiting for us, Watson," said he.

"What's the matter, then?"

"The Brook Street business."

"Any fresh news?"

"Tragic but ambiguous," said he, pulling up the blind. "Look at this—a sheet from a notebook with 'For God's sake, come at once—P. T.' scrawled upon it in pencil. Our friend the doctor was hard put to it when he wrote this. Come along, my dear fellow, for it's an urgent call."

In a quarter of an hour or so we were back at the physician's house. He came running out to meet us with a face of horror.

"Oh, such a business!" he cried, with his hands to his temples.

"What, then?"

"Blessington has committed suicide!"

Holmes whistled.

"Yes, he hanged himself during the night."

We had entered, and the doctor had preceded us into what was evidently his waiting-room.

"I really hardly know what I am doing," he cried. "The police are already upstairs. It has shaken me most dreadfully."

"When did you find it out?"

"He has a cup of tea taken in to him early every morning. When the maid entered about seven, there the unfortunate fellow was hanging in the middle of the room. He had tied his cord to the hook on which the heavy lamp used to hang, and he had jumped off from the top of the very box that he showed us yesterday."

Holmes stood for a moment in deep thought.

"With your permission," said he at last, "I should like to go upstairs and look into the matter." We both ascended, followed by the doctor.

It was a dreadful sight which met us as we entered the bedroom door. I have spoken of the impression of flabbiness which this man Blessington conveyed. As he dangled from the hook it was exaggerated and intensified until he was scarce human in his appearance. The neck was drawn out like a plucked chicken's, making the rest of him seem the more obese and unnatural by the contrast. He was clad only in his long night-dress, and his swollen ankles and ungainly feet protruded starkly from beneath it. Beside him stood a smart-looking police inspector, who was taking notes in a pocket-book.

"Ah, Mr. Holmes," said he, heartily, as my friend entered. "I am delighted to see you."

"Good morning, Lanner," answered Holmes. "You won't think me an intruder, I am sure. Have you heard of the events which led up to this affair?"

"Yes, I heard something of them."

"Have you formed any opinion?"

"As far as I can see, the man has been driven out of his senses by fright. The bed has been well slept in, you see. There's his impression deep enough. It's about five in the morning, you know, that suicides are most common. That would be about his time for hanging himself. It seems to have been a very deliberate affair."

"I should say that he has been dead about three hours, judging by the rigidity of the muscles," said I.

"Noticed anything peculiar about the room?" asked Holmes.

"Found a screwdriver and some screws on the wash-hand stand. Seems to have smoked heavily during the night, too. Here are four cigar ends that I picked out of the fireplace."

"Hum !" said Holmes. "Have you got his cigar-holder ?"

"No, I have seen none."

"His cigar-case, then ?"

"Yes, it was in his coat pocket."

Holmes opened it and smelled the single cigar which it contained.

"Oh, this is a Havana, and these others are cigars of the peculiar sort which are imported by the Dutch from their East Indian colonies. They are usually wrapped in straw, you know, and are thinner for their length than any other brand." He picked up the four ends and examined them with his pocket lens.

"Two of these have been smoked from a holder and two without," said he. "Two have been cut by a not very sharp knife, and two have had the ends bitten off by a set of excellent teeth. This is no suicide, Mr. Lanner. It is a very deeply-planned and cold-blooded murder."

"Impossible !" cried the inspector.

"And why ?"

"Why should anyone murder a man in so clumsy a fashion as by hanging him ? '

"HOLMES OPENED IT AND SMELLED THE SINGLE CIGAR WHICH IT CONTAINED."

"That is what we have to find out."

"How could they get in ?"

"Through the front door."

"It was barred in the morning."

"Then it was barred after them."

"How do you know ?"

"I saw their traces. Excuse me a moment, and I may be able to give you some further information about it."

He went over to the door, and turning the lock he examined it in his methodical fashion. Then he took out the key, which was on the inside, and inspected that also.

The bed, the carpet, the chairs, the mantel-piece, the dead body, and the rope were each in turn examined, until at last he professed himself satisfied, and with my aid and that of the inspector cut down the wretched object, and laid it reverently under a sheet.

"How about this rope ?" he asked.

"It is cut off this," said Dr. Trevelyan, drawing a large coil from under the bed. "He was morbidly nervous of fire, and always kept this beside him, so that he might escape by the window in case the stairs were burning."

"That must have saved them trouble," said Holmes, thoughtfully. "Yes, the actual facts are very plain, and I shall be surprised if by the afternoon I cannot give you the reasons for them as well. I will take this photograph of Blessington which I see upon the mantelpiece, as it may help me in my inquiries."

"But you have told us nothing," cried the doctor.

"Oh, there can be no doubt as to the sequence of events," said Holmes. "There were three of them in it: the young man, the old man, and a third to whose identity I have no clue. The first two, I need hardly remark, are the same who masqueraded as the Russian Count and his son, so we can give a very full description of them. They were admitted by a confederate inside the house. If I might offer you a word of advice, Inspector, it would be to arrest the page, who, as I understand, has only recently come into your service, Doctor."

"The young imp cannot be found," said Dr. Trevelyan; "the maid and the cook have just been searching for him."

Holmes shrugged his shoulders.

"He has played a not unimportant part in this drama," said he. "The three men having ascended the stair, which they did on tiptoe, the elder man first, the younger man second, and the unknown man in the rear——"

" My dear Holmes ! " I ejaculated.

" Oh, there could be no question as to the superimposing of the footmarks. I had the advantage of learning which was which last night. They ascended then to Mr. Blessington's room, the door of which they found to be locked. With the help of a wire, however, they forced round the key. Even without a lens, you will perceive by the scratches on this ward where the pressure was applied.

"On entering the room, their first proceeding must have been to gag Mr. Blessington. He may have been asleep, or he may have been so paralyzed with terror as to have been unable to cry out. These walls are thick, and it is conceivable that his shriek, if he had time to utter one, was unheard.

" Having secured him, it is evident to me that a consultation of some sort was held. Probably it was something in the nature of a judicial proceeding. It must have lasted for some time, for it was then that these cigars were smoked. The older man sat in that wicker chair : it was he who used the cigar-holder. The younger man sat over yonder : he knocked his ash off against the chest of drawers. The third fellow paced up and down. Blessington, I think, sat upright in the bed, but of that I cannot be absolutely certain.

" Well, it ended by their taking Blessington and hanging him. The matter was so pre-arranged that it is my belief that they brought with them some sort of block or pulley which might serve as a gallows. That screwdriver and those screws were, as I conceive, for fixing it up. Seeing the hook, however, they naturally

saved themselves the trouble. Having finished their work they made off, and the door was barred behind them by their confederate."

We had all listened with the deepest interest to this sketch of the night's doings, which Holmes had deduced from signs so subtle and minute, that even when he had pointed them out to us, we could scarcely follow him in his reasonings. The inspector hurried away on the instant to make inquiries about the page, while Holmes and I returned to Baker Street for breakfast.

" I'll be back by three," said he when we had finished our meal. " Both the inspector and the doctor will meet me here at that hour, and I hope by that time to have cleared up any little obscurity which the case may still present."

Our visitors arrived at the appointed time, but it was a quarter to four before my friend put in an appearance. From his expression as he entered, however, I could see that all had gone well with him.

" Any news, Inspector ? "

" We have got the boy, sir."

" Excellent, and I have got the men."

" You have got them ! " we cried all three.

"' YOU HAVE GOT THEM !' WE CRIED."

"Well, at least I have got their identity. This so-called Blessington is, as I expected, well known at headquarters, and so are his assailants. Their names are Biddle, Hayward, and Moffat."

"The Worthingdon bank gang," cried the inspector.

"Precisely," said Holmes.

"Then Blessington must have been Sutton?"

"Exactly," said Holmes.

"Why, that makes it as clear as crystal," said the inspector.

But Trevelyan and I looked at each other in bewilderment.

"You must surely remember the great Worthingdon bank business," said Holmes; "five men were in it, these four and a fifth called Cartwright. Tobin, the caretaker, was murdered, and the thieves got away with seven thousand pounds. This was in 1875. They were all five arrested, but the evidence against them was by no means conclusive. This Blessington, or Sutton, who was the worst of the gang, turned informer. On his evidence, Cartwright was hanged and the other three got fifteen years apiece. When they got out the other day, which was some years before their full term, they set themselves, as you perceive, to hunt down the traitor and to avenge the death of their comrade upon him. Twice they tried to get at him and failed; a third time, you see, it came off. Is there anything further which I can explain, Dr. Trevelyan?"

"I think you have made it all remarkably clear," said the doctor. "No doubt the day on which he was so perturbed was the day when he had read of their release in the newspapers."

"Quite so. His talk about a burglary was the merest blind."

"But why could he not tell you this?"

"Well, my dear sir, knowing the vindictive character of his old associates, he was trying to hide his own identity from everybody as long as he could. His secret was a shameful one, and he could not bring himself to divulge it. However, wretch as he was, he was still living under the shield of British law, and I have no doubt, Inspector, that you will see that, though that shield may fail to guard, the sword of justice is still there to avenge."

Such were the singular circumstances in connection with the resident patient and the Brook Street doctor. From that night nothing has been seen of the three murderers by the police, and it is surmised at Scotland Yard that they were among the passengers of the ill-fated steamer *Norah Creina*, which was lost some years ago with all hands upon the Portuguese coast, some leagues to the north of Oporto. The proceedings against the page broke down for want of evidence, and the "Brook Street Mystery," as it was called, has never, until now, been fully dealt with in any public print.

The Adventures of Sherlock Holmes.

By A. Conan Doyle.

XXII.—THE ADVENTURE OF THE GREEK INTERPRETER.

URING my long and intimate acquaintance with Mr. Sherlock Holmes I had never heard him refer to his relations, and hardly ever to his own early life. This reticence upon his part had increased the somewhat inhuman effect which he produced upon me, until sometimes I found myself regarding him as an isolated phenomenon, a brain without a heart, as deficient in human sympathy as he was pre-eminent in intelligence. His aversion to women, and his disinclination to form new friendships, were both typical of his unemotional character, but not more so than his complete suppression of every reference to his own people. I had come to believe that he was an orphan with no relatives living, but one day, to my very great surprise, he began to talk to me about his brother.

It was after tea on a summer evening, and the conversation, which had roamed in a desultory, spasmodic fashion from golf clubs to the causes of the change in the obliquity of the ecliptic, came round at last to the question of atavism and hereditary aptitudes. The point under discussion was how far any singular gift in an individual was due to his ancestry, and how far to his own early training.

"In your own case," said I, "from all that you have told me it seems obvious that your faculty of observation and your peculiar facility for deduction are due to your own systematic training."

"To some extent," he answered, thoughtfully. "My ancestors were country squires, who appear to have led much the same life, as is natural to their class. But, none the less, my turn that way is in my veins, and may have come with my grandmother, who was the sister of Vernet, the French artist. Art in the blood is liable to take the strangest forms."

"But how do you know that it is hereditary?"

"Because my brother Mycroft possesses it in a larger degree than I do."

This was news to me, indeed. If there were another man with such singular powers in England, how was it that neither police nor public had heard of him? I put the question, with a hint that it was my companion's modesty which made him acknowledge his brother as his superior. Holmes laughed at my suggestion.

"My dear Watson," said he, "I cannot agree with those who rank modesty among the virtues. To the logician all things should be seen exactly as they are, and to underestimate oneself is as much a departure from truth as to exaggerate one's own powers. When I say, therefore, that Mycroft has better powers of observation than I, you may take it that I am speaking the exact and literal truth."

"Is he your junior?"

"Seven years my senior."

"How comes it that he is unknown?"

"Oh, he is very well known in his own circle."

"Where, then?"

"Well, in the Diogenes Club, for example."

I had never heard of the institution, and my face must have proclaimed as much, for Sherlock Holmes pulled out his watch.

"The Diogenes Club is the queerest club in London, and Mycroft, one of the queerest men. He's always there from a quarter to five till twenty to eight. It's six now, so if you care for a stroll this beautiful evening I shall be very happy to introduce you to two curiosities."

Five minutes later we were in the street, walking towards Regent Circus.

"You wonder," said my companion, "why it is that Mycroft does not use his powers for detective work. He is incapable of it."

"But I thought you said——!"

"I said that he was my superior in observation and deduction. If the art of the detective began and ended in reasoning from an arm-chair, my brother would be the greatest criminal agent that ever lived. But

"HOLMES PULLED OUT HIS WATCH."

"Very likely not. There are many men in London, you know, who, some from shyness, some from misanthropy, have no wish for the company of their fellows. Yet they are not averse to comfortable chairs and the latest periodicals. It is for the convenience of these that the Diogenes Club was started, and it now contains the most unsociable and unclubbable men in town. No member is permitted to take the least notice of any other one. Save in the Strangers' Room, no talking is, under any circumstances, permitted, and three offences, if brought to the notice of the committee, render the talker liable to expulsion. My brother was one of the founders, and I have myself found it a very soothing atmosphere."

We had reached Pall Mall as we talked, and were walking down it from the St. James' end. Sherlock Holmes stopped at a door some little distance from the Carlton, and, cautioning me not to speak, he led the way into the hall. Through the glass panelling I caught a glimpse of a large and luxurious room in which a considerable number of men were sitting about and reading papers, each in his own little nook. Holmes showed me into a small chamber which looked out on to Pall Mall, and then, leaving me for a minute, he came back with a companion who I knew could only be his brother.

Mycroft Holmes was a much larger and stouter man than Sherlock. His body was absolutely corpulent, but his face, though massive, had preserved something of the sharpness of expression which was so remarkable in that of his brother. His eyes, which were of a peculiarly light watery grey, seemed to always retain that far-away, introspective look which I had only observed

he has no ambition and no energy. He will not even go out of his way to verify his own solutions, and would rather be considered wrong than take the trouble to prove himself right. Again and again I have taken a problem to him, and have received an explanation which has afterwards proved to be the correct one. And yet he was absolutely incapable of working out the practical points which must be gone into before a case could be laid before a judge or jury."

"It is not his profession, then?"

"By no means. What is to me a means of livelihood is to him the merest hobby of a dilettante. He has an extraordinary faculty for figures, and audits the books in some of the Government departments. Mycroft lodges in Pall Mall, and he walks round the corner into Whitehall every morning and back every evening. From year's end to year's end he takes no other exercise, and is seen nowhere else, except only in the Diogenes Club, which is just opposite his rooms."

"I cannot recall the name."

in Sherlock's when he was exerting his full powers.

"I am glad to meet you, sir," said he, putting out a broad, fat hand, like the flipper of a seal. "I hear of Sherlock everywhere since you became his chronicler. By the way, Sherlock, I expected to see you round last week to consult me over that Manor House case. I thought you might be a little out of your depth."

"No, I solved it," said my friend, smiling.

"It was Adams, of course?"

"Yes, it was Adams."

"I was sure of it from the first." The two sat down together in the bow-window of the club. "To anyone who wishes to study mankind this is the spot," said Mycroft. "Look at the magnificent types! Look at these two men who are coming towards us, for example."

"The billiard-marker and the other?"

"Precisely. What do you make of the other?"

The two men had stopped opposite the window. Some chalk marks over the waist-coat pocket were the only signs of billiards which I could see in one of them. The other was a very small dark fellow, with his hat pushed back and several packages under his arm.

"An old soldier, I perceive," said Sherlock.

"And very recently discharged," remarked the brother.

"Served in India, I see."

"And a non-commissioned officer."

"Royal Artillery, I fancy," said Sherlock.

"And a widower."

"But with a child."

"Children, my dear boy, children."

"Come," said I, laughing, "this is a little too much."

"Surely," answered Holmes, "it is not hard to say that a man with that bearing, expression of authority, and sun-baked skin is a soldier, is more than a private, and is not long from India."

"That he has not left the service long is shown by his still wearing his 'ammunition boots,' as they are called," observed Mycroft.

"He has not the cavalry stride, yet he wore his hat on one side, as is shown by the lighter skin on that side of his brow. His weight is against his being a sapper. He is in the artillery."

"Then, of course, his complete mourning shows that he has lost someone very dear. The fact that he is doing his own shopping looks as though it were his wife. He has been buying things for children you perceive. There is a rattle, which shows that one of them is very young. The wife probably died in child-bed. The fact that he has a picture-book under his arm shows that there is another child to be thought of."

I began to understand what my friend meant when he said that his brother possessed even keener faculties than he did himself. He glanced across at me, and smiled. Mycroft took snuff from a tortoise-shell box, and brushed away the wandering grains from his coat front with a large, red silk handkerchief.

"By the way, Sherlock," said he, "I have had something quite after your own heart—a most singular problem—submitted to my judgment. I really had not the energy to follow it up, save in a very incomplete fashion, but it gave me a basis for some very pleasing speculations. If you would care to hear the facts——"

"My dear Mycroft, I should be delighted."

The brother scribbled a note upon a leaf of his pocket-book, and ringing the bell, he handed it to the waiter.

"I have asked Mr. Melas to step across," said he. "He lodges on the floor above me, and I have some slight acquaintance with him, which led him to come to me in his perplexity. Mr. Melas is a Greek by extraction, as I understand, and he is a remarkable

MYCROFT HOLMES.

linguist. He earns his living partly as interpreter in the law courts, and partly by acting as guide to any wealthy Orientals who may visit the Northumberland Avenue hotels. I think I will leave him to tell his very remarkable experience in his own fashion."

A few minutes later we were joined by a short, stout man, whose olive face and coal-black hair proclaimed his southern origin, though his speech was that of an educated Englishman. He shook hands eagerly with Sherlock Holmes, and his dark eyes sparkled with pleasure when he understood that the specialist was anxious to hear his story.

"I do not believe that the police credit me—on my word I do not," said he, in a wailing voice. "Just because they have never heard of it before, they think that such a thing cannot be. But I know that I shall never be easy in my mind until I know what has become of my poor man with the sticking-plaster upon his face."

"I am all attention," said Sherlock Holmes.

"This is Wednesday evening," said Mr. Melas ; "well, then, it was on Monday night —only two days ago, you understand—that all this happened. I am an interpreter, as, perhaps, my neighbour there has told you. I interpret all languages—or nearly all—but as I am a Greek by birth, and with a Grecian name, it is with that particular tongue that I am principally associated. For many years I have been the chief Greek interpreter in London, and my name is very well known in the hotels.

"It happens, not unfrequently, that I am sent for at strange hours, by foreigners who get into difficulties, or by travellers who arrive late and wish my services. I was not surprised, therefore, on Monday night when a Mr. Latimer, a very fashionably-dressed young man, came up to my rooms and asked me to accompany him in a cab, which was waiting at the door. A Greek friend had come to see him upon business, he said, and, as he could speak nothing but his own tongue, the services of an

interpreter were indispensable. He gave me to understand that his house was some little distance off, in Kensington, and he seemed to be in a great hurry, bustling me rapidly into the cab when we had descended to the street.

"I say into the cab, but I soon became doubtful as to whether it was not a carriage in which I found myself. It was certainly more roomy than the ordinary four-wheeled disgrace to London, and the fittings, though frayed, were of rich quality. Mr. Latimer seated himself opposite to me, and we started off through Charing Cross and up the Shaftesbury Avenue. We had come out upon Oxford Street, and I had ventured some remark as to this being a roundabout way to Kensington, when my words were arrested by the extraordinary conduct of my companion.

"He began by drawing a most formidable-looking bludgeon loaded with lead from his pocket, and switching it backwards and forwards several times, as if to test its weight and strength. Then he placed it, without a word, upon the seat beside him. Having done this he drew up the windows on each side, and I found to my astonishment that they were covered with paper so as to prevent my seeing through them.

"'I am sorry to cut off your view, Mr. Melas,' said he. 'The fact is that I have

"HE DREW UP THE WINDOWS."

no intention that you should see what the place is to which we are driving. It might possibly be inconvenient to me if you could find your way there again.'

"As you can imagine, I was utterly taken aback by such an address. My companion was a powerful, broad-shouldered young fellow, and, apart from the weapon, I should not have had the slightest chance in a struggle with him.

"'This is very extraordinary conduct, Mr. Latimer,' I stammered. 'You must be aware that what you are doing is quite illegal.'

"'It is somewhat of a liberty, no doubt,' said he, 'but we'll make it up to you. But I must warn you, however, Mr. Melas, that if at any time to-night you attempt to raise an alarm or do anything which is against my interests, you will find it a very serious thing. I beg you to remember that no one knows where you are, and that whether you are in this carriage or in my house, you are equally in my power.'

"His words were quiet, but he had a rasping way of saying them which was very menacing. I sat in silence, wondering what on earth could be his reason for kidnapping me in this extraordinary fashion. Whatever it might be, it was perfectly clear that there was no possible use in my resisting, and that I could only wait to see what might befall.

"For nearly two hours we drove without my having the least clue as to where we were going. Sometimes the rattle of the stones told of a paved causeway, and at others our smooth, silent course suggested asphalte, but save by this variation in sound there was nothing at all which could in the remotest way help me to form a guess as to where we were. The paper over each window was impenetrable to light, and a blue curtain was drawn across the glass-work in front. It was a quarter past seven when we left Pall Mall, and my watch showed me that it was ten minutes to nine when we at last came to a standstill. My companion let down the window and I caught a glimpse of a low, arched doorway with a lamp burning above it. As I was hurried from the carriage it swung open, and I found myself inside the house, with a vague impression of a lawn and trees on each side of me as I entered. Whether these were private grounds, however, or *bonâ-fide* country was more than I could possibly venture to say.

"There was a coloured gas-lamp inside which was turned so low that I could see little save that the hall was of some size and hung with pictures. In the dim light I could make out that the person who had opened the door was a small, mean-looking, middle-aged man with rounded shoulders. As he turned towards us the glint of the light showed me that he was wearing glasses.

"'Is this Mr. Melas, Harold?' said he.

"'Yes.'

"'Well done! Well done! No ill-will, Mr. Melas, I hope, but we could not get on without you. If you deal fair with us you'll not regret it; but if you try any tricks, God help you!'

"He spoke in a jerky, nervous fashion, and with little giggling laughs in between, but somehow he impressed me with fear more than the other.

"'What do you want with me?' I asked.

"'Only to ask a few questions of a Greek gentleman who is visiting us, and to let us have the answers. But say no more than you are told to say, or'—here came the nervous giggle again—'you had better never have been born.'

"As he spoke he opened a door and showed the way into a room which appeared to be very richly furnished—but again the only light was afforded by a single lamp half turned down. The chamber was certainly large, and the way in which my feet sank into the carpet as I stepped across it told me of its richness. I caught glimpses of velvet chairs, a high, white marble mantelpiece and what seemed to be a suit of Japanese armour at one side of it. There was a chair just under the lamp, and the elderly man motioned that I should sit in it. The younger had left us, but he suddenly returned through another door, leading with him a gentleman clad in some sort of loose dressing-gown, who moved slowly towards us. As he came into the circle of dim light which enabled me to see him more clearly, I was thrilled with horror at his appearance. He was deadly pale and terribly emaciated, with the protruding, brilliant eyes of a man whose spirit is greater than his strength. But what shocked me more than any signs of physical weakness was that his face was grotesquely criss-crossed with sticking-plaster, and that one large pad of it was fastened over his mouth.

"'Have you the slate, Harold?' cried the older man, as this strange being fell rather than sat down into a chair. 'Are his hands loose? Now then, give him the pencil. You are to ask the questions, Mr. Melas, and he will write the answers. Ask him first of all whether he is prepared to sign the papers.'

"'I care not. *I am a stranger in London.*'

"'Your fate will be on your own head. *How long have you been here?*'

"'Let it be so. *Three weeks.*'

"'The property can never be yours. *What ails you?*'

"'It shall not go to villains. *They are starving me.*'

"'You shall go free if you sign. *What house is this?*'

"'I will never sign. *I do not know.*'

"'You are not doing her any service. *What is your name?*'

"'Let me hear her say so. *Kratides.*'

"'You shall see her if you sign. *Where are you from?*'

"'Then I shall never see her. *Athens.*'

"Another five minutes, Mr. Holmes, and I should have wormed out the whole

"I WAS THRILLED WITH HORROR."

"The man's eyes flashed fire.

"'Never,' he wrote in Greek upon the slate.

"'On no conditions?' I asked at the bidding of our tyrant.

"'Only if I see her married in my presence by a Greek priest whom I know.'

"The man giggled in his venomous way.

"'You know what awaits you then?'

"'I care nothing for myself.'

"These are samples of the questions and answers which made up our strange half-spoken, half-written conversation. Again and again I had to ask him whether he would give in and sign the document. Again and again I had the same indignant reply. But soon a happy thought came to me. I took to adding on little sentences of my own to each question—innocent ones at first to test whether either of our companions knew anything of the matter, and then, as I found that they showed no sign, I played a more dangerous game. Our conversation ran something like this :—

"'You can do no good by this obstinacy. *Who are you?*'

story under their very noses. My very next question might have cleared the matter up, but at that instant the door opened and a woman stepped into the room. I could not see her clearly enough to know more than that she was tall and graceful, with black hair, and clad in some sort of loose, white gown.

"'Harold!' said she, speaking English with a broken accent, 'I could not stay away longer. It is so lonely up there with only—oh, my God, it is Paul!'

"These last words were in Greek, and at the same instant the man, with a convulsive effort, tore the plaster from his lips, and screaming out 'Sophy! Sophy!' rushed into the woman's arms. Their embrace was but for an instant, however, for the younger man seized the woman and pushed her out of the room, while the elder easily overpowered his emaciated victim, and dragged him away through the other door. For a moment I was left alone in the room, and I sprang to my feet with some vague idea that I might in some way get a clue to what this house was in which I found myself. Fortunately, however, I took no steps, for, looking

"SOPHY ! SOPHY !"

beard was thready and ill nourished. He pushed his face forward as he spoke, and his lips and eyelids were continually twitching like a man with St. Vitus's dance. I could not help thinking that his strange, catchy little laugh was also a symptom of some nervous malady. The terror of his face lay in his eyes, however, steel grey, and glistening coldly, with a malignant, inexorable cruelty in their depths.

"'We shall know if you speak of this,' said he. 'We have our own means of information. Now, you will find the carriage waiting, and my friend will see you on your way.'

"I was hurried through the hall, and into the vehicle, again obtaining that momentary glimpse of trees and a garden. Mr. Latimer followed closely at my heels, and took his place opposite to me without a word. In silence we again drove for an interminable distance, with the windows raised, until at last, just after midnight, the carriage pulled up.

"'You will get down here, Mr. Melas,' said my companion. 'I am sorry to leave you so far from your house, but there is no alternative. Any attempt upon your part to follow the carriage can only end in injury to yourself.'

"He opened the door as he spoke, and I had hardly time to spring out when the coachman lashed the horse, and the carriage rattled away. I looked round me in astonishment. I was on some sort of a heathy common, mottled over with dark clumps of furze bushes. Far away stretched a line of houses with a light here and there in the upper windows. On the other side I saw the red signal lamps of a railway.

"The carriage which had brought me was

up, I saw that the older man was standing in the doorway, with his eyes fixed upon me.

"'That will do, Mr. Melas,' said he. 'You perceive that we have taken you into our confidence over some very private business. We should not have troubled you only that our friend who speaks Greek and who began these negotiations has been forced to return to the East. It was quite necessary for us to find someone to take his place, and we were fortunate in hearing of your powers.'

"I bowed.

"'There are five sovereigns here,' said he, walking up to me, 'which will, I hope, be a sufficient fee. But remember,' he added, tapping me lightly on the chest and giggling, 'if you speak to a human soul about this— one human soul mind, well, may God have mercy upon your soul!'

"I cannot tell you the loathing and horror with which this insignificant-looking man inspired me. I could see him better now as the lamp-light shone upon him. His features were peaty and sallow, and his little, pointed already out of sight. I stood gazing round and wondering where on earth I might be, when I saw someone coming towards me in the darkness. As he came up to me I made out that it was a railway porter.

"'Can you tell me what place this is?' I asked.

"'Wandsworth Common,' said he.

"'Can I get a train into town?'

"'If you walk on a mile or so, to Clapham Junction,' said he, 'you'll just be in time for the last to Victoria.'

"So that was the end of my adventure, Mr. Holmes. I do not know where I was nor whom I spoke with, nor anything, save what I have told you. But I

"I SAW SOMEONE COMING TOWARDS ME."

know that there is foul play going on, and I want to help that unhappy man if I can. I told the whole story to Mr. Mycroft Holmes next morning and, subsequently, to the police."

We all sat in silence for some little time after listening to this extraordinary narrative. Then Sherlock looked across at his brother.

"Any steps?" he asked.

Mycroft picked up the *Daily News*, which was lying on a side table.

"'Anybody supplying any information as to the whereabouts of a Greek gentleman named Paul Kratides, from Athens, who is unable to speak English, will be rewarded. A similar reward paid to anyone giving information about a Greek lady whose first name is Sophy. X 2473.' That was in all the dailies. No answer."

"How about the Greek Legation?"

"I have inquired. They know nothing."

"A wire to the head of the Athens police, then."

"Sherlock has all the energy of the family,"
said Mycroft, turning to me. "Well, you take the case up by all means, and let me know if you do any good."

"Certainly," answered my friend, rising from his chair. "I'll let you know, and Mr. Melas also. In the meantime, Mr. Melas, I should certainly be on my guard, if I were you, for, of course, they must know through these advertisements that you have betrayed them."

As we walked home together Holmes stopped at a telegraph office and sent off several wires.

"You see, Watson," he remarked, "our evening has been by no means wasted. Some of my most interesting cases have come to me in this way through Mycroft. The problem which we have just listened to, although it can admit of but one explanation, has still some distinguishing features."

"You have hopes of solving it?"

"Well, knowing as much as we do, it will be singular indeed if we fail to discover the rest. You must yourself have formed some theory which will explain the facts to which we have listened."

"In a vague way, yes."

"What was your idea then?"

"It seemed to me to be obvious that this Greek girl had been carried off by the young Englishman named Harold Latimer."

"Carried off from where?"

"Athens, perhaps."

Sherlock Holmes shook his head. "This young man could not talk a word of Greek. The lady could talk English fairly well. Inference that she had been in England some little time, but he had not been in Greece."

"Well, then, we will presume that she had

come on a visit to England, and that this Harold had persuaded her to fly with him."

"That is the more probable."

"Then the brother—for that, I fancy, must be the relationship—comes over from Greece to interfere. He imprudently puts himself into the power of the young man and his older associate. They seize him and use violence towards him in order to make him sign some papers to make over the girl's fortune—of which he may be trustee—to them. This he refuses to do. In order to negotiate with him they have to get an interpreter, and they pitch upon this Mr. Melas, having used some other one before. The girl is not told of the arrival of her brother, and finds it out by the merest accident."

"Excellent, Watson," cried Holmes. "I really fancy that you are not far from the truth. You see that we hold all the cards, and we have only to fear some sudden act of violence on their part. If they give us time we must have them."

"But how can we find where this house lies ?"

"Well, if our conjecture is correct, and the girl's name is, or was, Sophy Kratides, we should have no difficulty in tracing her. That must be our main hope, for the brother, of course, is a complete stranger. It is clear that some time has elapsed since this Harold established these relations with the girl—some weeks at any rate — since the brother in Greece has had time to hear of it and come across. If they have been living in the same place during this time, it is probable that we shall have some answer to Mycroft's advertisement."

We had reached our house in Baker Street whilst we had been talking. Holmes ascended the stairs first, and as he opened the door of our room he gave a start of surprise. Looking over his shoulder I was equally astonished. His brother Mycroft was sitting smoking in the arm-chair.

"Come in, Sherlock ! Come in, sir," said he,

blandly, smiling at our surprised faces. "You don't expect such energy from me, do you, Sherlock ? But somehow this case attracts me."

"How did you get here ? "

"I passed you in a hansom."

"There has been some new development ? "

"I had an answer to my advertisement."

"Ah ! "

"Yes ; it came within a few minutes of your leaving."

"And to what effect ? "

Mycroft Holmes took out a sheet of paper.

"Here it is," said he, "written with a J pen on royal cream paper by a middle-aged man with a weak constitution. 'Sir,' he says, 'in answer to your advertisement of to-day's date, I beg to inform you that I know the young lady in question very well. If you should care to call upon me, I could give you some particulars as to her painful history. She is living at present at The Myrtles, Beckenham. Yours faithfully, J. DAVENPORT."

"He writes from Lower Brixton," said Mycroft Holmes. "Do you not think that we might drive to him now, Sherlock, and learn these particulars ? "

" 'COME IN,' SAID HE, BLANDLY. "

"My dear Mycroft, the brother's life is more valuable than the sister's story. I think we should call at Scotland Yard for Inspector Gregson, and go straight out to Beckenham. We know that a man is being done to death, and every hour may be vital."

"Better pick up Mr. Melas upon our way," I suggested ; "we may need an interpreter."

"Excellent !" said Sherlock Holmes. "Send the boy for a four-wheeler, and we shall be off at once." He opened the table-drawer as he spoke, and I noticed that he slipped his revolver into his pocket. "Yes," said he, in answer to my glance, "I should say from what we have heard that we are dealing with a particularly dangerous gang."

It was almost dark before we found ourselves in Pall Mall, at the rooms of Mr. Melas. A gentleman had just called for him, and he was gone.

"Can you tell me where ? " asked Mycroft Holmes.

"I don't know, sir," answered the woman who had opened the door. "I only know that he drove away with the gentleman in a carriage."

"Did the gentleman give a name ? "

"No, sir."

"He wasn't a tall, handsome, dark young man ? "

"Oh, no, sir. He was a little gentleman, with glasses, thin in the face, but very pleasant in his ways, for he was laughing all the time that he was talking."

"Come along !" cried Sherlock Holmes, abruptly. "This grows serious!" he observed, as we drove to Scotland Yard. "These men have got hold of Melas again. He is a man of no physical courage, as they are well aware from their experience the other night. This villain was able to terrorize him the instant that he got into his presence. No doubt they want his professional services ; but, having used him, they may be inclined to punish him for what they will regard as his treachery."

Our hope was that by taking train we might get to Beckenham as soon as, or sooner, than the carriage. On reaching Scotland Yard, however, it was more than an hour before we could get Inspector Gregson and comply with the legal formalities which would enable us to enter the house. It was a quarter to ten before we reached London Bridge, and half-past before the four of us alighted on the Beckenham platform. A drive of half a mile brought us to the Myrtles—a large, dark house standing back from the road in its own grounds. Here we dismissed our cab, and made our way up the drive together.

"The windows are all dark," remarked the Inspector. "The house seems deserted."

"Our birds are flown and the nest empty," said Holmes.

"Why do you say so ? "

"A carriage heavily loaded with luggage has passed out during the last hour."

The Inspector laughed. "I saw the wheel tracks in the light of the gate-lamp, but where does the luggage come in ? "

"You may have observed the same wheel-tracks going the other way. But the outward-bound ones were very much deeper—so much so that we can say for a certainty that there was a very considerable weight on the carriage."

"You get a trifle beyond me there," said the Inspector, shrugging his shoulders. "It will not be an easy door to force. But we will try if we cannot make someone hear us."

He hammered loudly at the knocker and pulled at the bell, but without any success. Holmes had slipped away, but he came back in a few minutes.

"I have a window open," said he.

"It is a mercy that you are on the side of the force, and not against it, Mr. Holmes," remarked the Inspector, as he noted the clever way in which my friend had forced back the catch. "Well, I think that, under the circumstances, we may enter without waiting for an invitation."

One after the other we made our way into a large apartment, which was evidently that in which Mr. Melas had found himself. The Inspector had lit his lantern, and by its light we could see the two doors, the curtain, the lamp and the suit of Japanese mail as he had described them. On the table lay two glasses, an empty brandy bottle, and the remains of a meal.

"What is that ? " asked Holmes, suddenly.

We all stood still and listened. A low, moaning sound was coming from somewhere above our heads. Holmes rushed to the door and out into the hall. The dismal noise came from upstairs. He dashed up, the Inspector and I at his heels, while his brother, Mycroft, followed as quickly as his great bulk would permit.

Three doors faced us upon the second floor, and it was from the central of these that the sinister sounds were issuing, sinking sometimes into a dull mumble and rising again into a shrill whine. It was locked, but the key was on the outside. Holmes flung open the door and rushed in, but he was out again in an instant with his hand to his throat.

" It's charcoal," he cried.
" Give it time. It will clear."

Peering in we could see that the only light in the room came from a dull, blue flame, which flickered from a small brass tripod in the centre. It threw a livid, unnatural circle upon the floor, while in the shadows beyond we saw the vague loom of two figures, which crouched against the wall. From the open door there reeked a horrible, poisonous exhalation, which set us gasping and coughing. Holmes rushed to the top of the stairs to draw in the fresh air, and then, dashing into the room, he threw up the window and hurled the brazen tripod out into the garden.

"We can enter in a minute," he gasped, darting out again. "Where is a candle? I doubt if we could strike a match in that atmosphere. Hold the light at the door and we shall get them out, Mycroft. Now!"

With a rush we got to the poisoned men and dragged

"'IT'S CHARCOAL, HE CRIED."

them out on to the landing. Both of them were blue lipped and insensible, with swollen, congested faces and protruding eyes. Indeed, so distorted were their features that save for his black beard and stout figure we might have failed to recognise in one of them the Greek interpreter who had parted from us only a few hours before at the Diogenes Club. His hands and feet were securely strapped together, and he bore over one eye the mark of a violent blow. The other, who was secured in a similar fashion, was a tall man in the last stage of emaciation, with several strips of sticking-plaster arranged in a grotesque pattern over his face. He had ceased to moan as we laid him down, and a glance showed me that for him, at least, our aid had come too late. Mr. Melas, however, still lived, and in less than an hour, with the aid of ammonia and brandy, I had the satisfaction of seeing him open his eyes, and of knowing that my hand had drawn him back from the dark valley in which all paths meet.

It was a simple story which he had to tell, and one which did but confirm our own deductions. His visitor on entering his rooms had drawn a life preserver from his sleeve, and had so impressed him with the fear of instant and inevitable death, that he had kidnapped him for the second time. Indeed, it was almost mesmeric the effect which this giggling ruffian had produced upon the unfortunate linguist, for he could not speak of him save with trembling hands and a blanched cheek. He had been taken swiftly to Beckenham, and had acted as interpreter in a second interview, even more dramatic than the first, in which the two Englishmen had menaced their prisoner with instant death if he did not comply with their demands. Finally, finding him proof against every threat, they had hurled him back into his prison, and after reproaching Melas with his treachery, which appeared from the newspaper advertisement, they had stunned him with a blow from a stick, and he remembered nothing more until he found us bending over him.

And this was the singular case of the

Grecian Interpreter, the explanation of which is still involved in some mystery. We were able to find out, by communicating with the gentleman who had answered the advertisement, that the unfortunate young lady came of a wealthy Grecian family, and that she had been on a visit to some friends in England. While there she had met a young man named Harold Latimer, who had acquired an ascendancy over her, and had eventually persuaded her to fly with him. Her friends, shocked at the event, had contented themselves with informing her brother at Athens, and had then washed their hands of the matter. The brother, on his arrival in England, had imprudently placed himself in the power of Latimer, and of his associate, whose name was Wilson Kemp—a man of the foulest antecedents. These two, finding that through his ignorance of the language he was helpless in their hands, had kept him a prisoner, and had endeavoured, by cruelty and starvation, to make him sign away his own and his sister's property. They had kept him in the house without the girl's knowledge, and the plaster over the face had been for the purpose of making recognition difficult in case she should ever catch a glimpse of him. Her feminine perceptions, however, had instantly seen through the disguise when, on the occasion of the interpreter's first visit, she had seen him for the first time. The poor girl, however, was herself a prisoner, for there was no one about the house except the man who acted as coachman, and his wife, both of whom were tools of the conspirators. Finding that their secret was out and that their prisoner was not to be coerced, the two villains, with the girl, had fled away at a few hours' notice from the furnished house which they had hired, having first, as they thought, taken vengeance both upon the man who had defied and the one who had betrayed them.

Months afterwards a curious newspaper cutting reached us from Buda-Pesth. It told how two Englishmen who had been travelling with a woman had met with a tragic end. They had each been stabbed, it seems, and the Hungarian police were of opinion that they had quarrelled and had inflicted mortal injuries upon each other. Holmes, however, is, I fancy, of a different way of thinking, and he holds to this day that if one could find the Grecian girl one might learn how the wrongs of herself and her brother came to be avenged.

The Adventures of Sherlock Holmes.

By A. Conan Doyle.

XXIII.—THE ADVENTURE OF THE NAVAL TREATY.

THE July which immediately succeeded my marriage was made memorable by three cases of interest in which I had the privilege of being associated with Sherlock Holmes, and of studying his methods. I find them recorded in my notes under the headings of "The Adventure of the Second Stain," "The Adventure of the Naval Treaty," and "The Adventure of the Tired Captain." The first of these, however, deals with interests of such importance, and implicates so many of the first families in the kingdom, that for many years it will be impossible to make it public. No case, however, in which Holmes was ever engaged has illustrated the value of his analytical methods so clearly or has impressed those who were associated with him so deeply. I still retain an almost verbatim report of the interview in which he demonstrated the true facts of the case to Monsieur Dubuque, of the Paris police, and Fritz von Waldbaum, the well-known specialist of Dantzig, both of whom had wasted their energies upon what proved to be side issues. The new century will have come, however, before the story can be safely told. Meanwhile, I pass on to the second upon my list, which promised also, at one time, to be of national importance, and was marked by several incidents which give it a quite unique character.

During my school days I had been intimately associated with a lad named Percy Phelps, who was of much the same age as myself, though he was two classes ahead of me. He was a very brilliant boy, and carried away every prize which the school had to offer, finishing his exploits by winning a scholarship, which sent him on to continue his triumphant career at Cambridge. He was, I remember, extremely well connected, and even when we were all little boys together, we knew that his mother's brother was Lord Holdhurst, the great Conservative politician. This gaudy relationship did him little good at school ; on the contrary, it seemed rather a piquant thing to us to chevy him about the playground and hit him over the shins with a wicket. But it was another thing when he came out into the world. I heard vaguely that his abilities and the influence which he commanded had won him a good position at the Foreign Office, and then he passed completely out of my mind until the following letter recalled his existence :—

"Briarbrae, Woking.

"My Dear Watson,—I have no doubt that you can remember 'Tadpole' Phelps, who was in the fifth form when you were in the third. It is possible even that you may have heard that, through my uncle's influence, I obtained a good appointment at the Foreign Office, and that I was in a situation of trust and honour until a horrible misfortune came suddenly to blast my career.

"There is no use writing the details of that dreadful event. In the event of your acceding to my request, it is probable that I shall have to narrate them to you. I have only just recovered from nine weeks of brain fever, and am still exceedingly weak. Do you think that you could bring your friend, Mr. Holmes, down to see me? I should like to have his opinion of the case, though the authorities assure me that nothing more can be done. Do try to bring him down, and as soon as possible. Every minute seems an hour while I live in this state of horrible suspense. Assure him that if I have not asked his advice sooner it was not because I did not appreciate his talents, but because I have been off my head ever since the blow fell. Now I am clear again, though I dare not think of it too much for fear of a relapse. I am still so weak that I have to write, as you see, by dictating. Do try and bring him.

"Your old schoolfellow,

"Percy Phelps."

There was something that touched me as I read this letter, something pitiable in the reiterated appeals to bring Holmes. So moved was I that, even if it had been a difficult matter, I should have tried it ; but of course I knew well that Holmes loved his art so, that he was ever as ready to bring his aid as his client could be to receive it. My wife agreed with me that not a moment should be lost in laying the matter before him, and so within an hour of breakfast time I found myself back once more in the old rooms in Baker Street.

" HOLMES WAS WORKING HARD OVER A CHEMICAL INVESTIGATION."

chair opposite, and drew up his knees until his fingers clasped round his long, thin shins.

"A very commonplace little murder," said he. "You've got something better, I fancy. You are the stormy petrel of crime, Watson. What is it?"

I handed him the letter, which he read with the most concentrated attention.

"It does not tell us very much, does it?" he remarked, as he handed it back to me.

"Hardly anything."

"And yet the writing is of interest."

"But the writing is not his own."

"Precisely. It is a woman's."

"A man's, surely!" I cried.

"No, a woman's; and a woman of rare character. You see, at the commencement of an investigation, it is something to know that your client is in close contact with someone who for good or evil has an exceptional nature. My interest is already awakened in the case. If you are ready, we will start at once for Woking and see this diplomatist who is in such evil case, and the lady to whom he dictates his letters."

We were fortunate enough to catch an early train at Waterloo, and in a little under an hour we found ourselves among the fir-woods and the heather of Woking. Briarbrae proved to be a large detached house standing in extensive grounds, within a few minutes' walk of the station. On sending in our cards we were shown into an elegantly-appointed drawing-room, where we were joined in a few minutes by a rather stout man, who received us with much hospitality. His age may have been nearer forty than thirty, but his cheeks were so ruddy and his eyes so merry, that he still conveyed the impression of a plump and mischievous boy.

"I am so glad that you have come," said he, shaking our hands with effusion. "Percy has been inquiring for you all the morning. Ah, poor old chap, he clings to any straw. His father and mother asked me to see you,

Holmes was seated at his side table clad in his dressing gown and working hard over a chemical investigation. A large curved retort was boiling furiously in the bluish flame of a Bunsen burner, and the distilled drops were condensing into a two-litre measure. My friend hardly glanced up as I entered, and I, seeing that his investigation must be of importance, seated myself in an armchair and waited. He dipped into this bottle or that, drawing out a few drops of each with his glass pipette, and finally brought a test-tube containing a solution over to the table. In his right hand he had a slip of litmus-paper.

"You come at a crisis, Watson," said he. "If this paper remains blue, all is well. If it turns red, it means a man's life." He dipped it into the test-tube and it flushed at once into a dull, dirty crimson. "Hum! I thought as much!" he cried. "I will be at your service in one instant, Watson. You will find tobacco in the Persian slipper." He turned to his desk and scribbled off several telegrams, which were handed over to the page-boy. Then he threw himself down in the for tne mere mention of the subject is very painful to them."

"We have had no details yet," observed Holmes. "I perceive that you are not your-self a member of the family."

Our acquaintance looked surprised, and then glancing down he began to laugh.

"Of course you saw the 'J. H.' mono-gram on my locket," said he. "For a mo-ment I thought you had done something clever. Joseph Harrison is my name, and as Percy is to marry my sister Annie, I shall at least be a relation by marriage. You will find my sister in his room, for she has nursed him hand-and-foot this two months back. Perhaps we had better go in at once, for I know how impatient he is."

The chamber into which we were shown

He clutched her hand to detain her. "How are you, Watson?" said he, cordially. "I should never have known you under that moustache, and I daresay you would not be prepared to swear to me. This I presume is your celebrated friend, Mr. Sherlock Holmes?"

I introduced him in a few words, and we both sat down. The stout young man had left us, but his sister still remained, with her hand in that of the invalid. She was a striking-looking woman, a little short and thick for symmetry, but with a beautiful olive complexion, large, dark Italian eyes, and a wealth of deep black hair. Her rich tints made the white face of her companion the more worn and haggard by the contrast.

"I won't waste your time," said he, raising

"'I WON'T WASTE YOUR TIME,' SAID HE."

was on the same floor as the drawing-room. It was furnished partly as a sitting and partly as a bedroom, with flowers arranged daintily in every nook and corner. A young man, very pale and worn, was lying upon a sofa near the open window, through which came the rich scent of the garden and the balmy summer air. A woman was sitting beside him, and rose as we entered.

"Shall I leave, Percy?" she asked.

himself upon the sofa. "I'll plunge into the matter without further preamble. I was a happy and successful man, Mr. Holmes, and on the eve of being married, when a sudden and dreadful misfortune wrecked all my prospects in life.

"I was, as Watson may have told you, in the Foreign Office, and through the influence of my uncle, Lord Holdhurst, I rose rapidly to a responsible position. When my uncle became Foreign Minister in this Administration he gave me several missions of trust, and as I always brought them to a successful conclusion, he came at last to have the utmost confidence in my ability and tact.

"Nearly ten weeks ago—to be more accurate, on the 23rd of May—he called me into his private room and, after complimenting me upon the good work which I had done, he informed me that he had a new commission of trust for me to execute.

"'This,' said he, taking a grey roll of paper from his bureau, 'is the original of that secret treaty between England and Italy of which, I regret to say, some rumours have already got into the public Press. It is of enormous importance that nothing further should leak out. The French or Russian Embassies would pay an immense sum to learn the contents of these papers. They should not leave my bureau were it not that it is absolutely necessary to have them copied. You have a desk in your office?'

"'Yes, sir.'

"'Then take the treaty and lock it up there. I shall give directions that you may remain behind when the others go, so that you may copy it at your leisure, without fear of being overlooked. When you have finished, re-lock both the original and the draft in the desk, and hand them over to me personally to-morrow morning.'

"I took the papers and——"

"Excuse me an instant," said Holmes; "were you alone during this conversation?"

"Absolutely."

"In a large room?"

"Thirty feet each way."

"In the centre?"

"Yes, about it."

"And speaking low?"

"My uncle's voice is always remarkably low. I hardly spoke at all."

"Thank you," said Holmes, shutting his eyes; "pray go on."

"I did exactly what he had indicated, and waited until the other clerks had departed. One of them in my room, Charles Gorot, had some arrears of work to make up, so I left him there and went out to dine. When I returned he was gone. I was anxious to hurry my work, for I knew that Joseph, the Mr. Harrison whom you saw just now, was in town, and that he would travel down to Woking by the eleven o'clock train, and I wanted if possible to catch it.

"When I came to examine the treaty I saw at once that it was of such importance that my uncle had been guilty of no exaggeration in what he had said. Without going into details, I may say that it defined the position of Great Britain towards the Triple Alliance, and foreshadowed the policy which this country would pursue in the event of the French fleet gaining a complete ascendency over that of Italy in the Mediterranean. The questions treated in it were purely naval. At the end were the signatures of the high dignitaries who had signed it. I glanced my eyes over it, and then settled down to my task of copying.

"It was a long document, written in the French language, and containing twenty-six separate articles. I copied as quickly as I could, but at nine o'clock I had only done nine articles, and it seemed hopeless for me to attempt to catch my

"THEN TAKE THE TREATY."

train. I was feeling drowsy and stupid, partly from my dinner and also from the effects of a long day's work. A cup of coffee would clear my brain. A commissionaire remains all night in a little lodge at the foot of the stairs, and is in the habit of making coffee at his spirit-lamp for any of the officials who may be working over-time. I rang the bell, therefore, to summon him.

" To my surprise, it was a woman who answered the summons, a large, coarse-faced, elderly woman, in an apron. She explained that she was the commissionaire's wife, who did the charing, and I gave her the order for the coffee.

" I wrote two more articles, and then, feeling more drowsy than ever, I rose and walked up and down the room to stretch my legs. My coffee had not yet come, and I wondered what the cause of the delay could be. Opening the door, I started down the corridor to find out. There was a straight passage dimly lighted which led from the room in which I had been working, and was the only exit from it. It ended in a curving staircase, with the commissionaire's lodge in the passage at the bottom. Half-way down this staircase is a small landing, with another passage running into it at right angles. This second one leads, by means of a second small stair, to a side door used by servants, and also as a short cut by clerks when coming from Charles Street. Here is a rough chart of the place."

" Thank you. I think that I quite follow you," said Sherlock Holmes.

" FAST ASLEEP IN HIS BOX."

" It is of the utmost importance that you should notice this point. I went down the stairs and into the hall, where I found the commissionaire fast asleep in his box, with the kettle boiling furiously upon the spirit-lamp; for the water was spurting over the floor. Then I put out my hand and was about to shake the man, who was still sleeping soundly, when a bell over his head rang loudly, and he woke with a start.

" 'Mr. Phelps, sir!' said he, looking at me in bewilderment.

" 'I came down to see if my coffee was ready.'

" 'I was boiling the kettle when I fell asleep, sir.' He looked at me and then up at the still quivering bell, with an ever-growing astonishment upon his face.

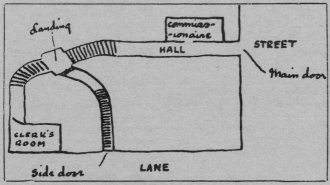

" HERE IS A ROUGH CHART OF THE PLACE."

"'If you was here, sir, then who rang the bell?' he asked.

"'The bell!' I said. 'What bell is it?'

"'It's the bell of the room you were working in.'

"A cold hand seemed to close round my heart. Someone, then, was in that room where my precious treaty lay upon the table. I ran frantically up the stairs and along the passage. There was no one in the corridors, Mr. Holmes. There was no one in the room. All was exactly as I left it, save only that the papers committed to my care had been taken from the desk on which they lay. The copy was there and the original was gone."

Holmes sat up in his chair and rubbed his hands. I could see that the problem was entirely to his heart. "Pray, what did you do then?" he murmured.

"I recognised in an instant that the thief must have come up the stairs from the side door. Of course, I must have met him if he had come the other way."

"You were satisfied that he could not have been concealed in the room all the time, or in the corridor which you have just described as dimly lighted?"

"It is absolutely impossible. A rat could not conceal himself either in the room or the corridor. There is no cover at all."

"Thank you. Pray proceed."

"The commissionaire, seeing by my pale face that something was to be feared, had followed me upstairs. Now we both rushed along the corridor and down the steep steps which led to Charles Street. The door at the bottom was closed but unlocked. We flung it open and rushed out. I can distinctly remember that as we did so there came three chimes from a neighbouring church. It was a quarter to ten."

"That is of enormous importance," said Holmes, making a note upon his shirt cuff.

"The night was very dark, and a thin, warm rain was falling. There was no one in Charles Street, but a great traffic was going on, as usual, in Whitehall at the extremity. We rushed along the pavement, bareheaded as we were, and at the far corner we found a policeman standing.

"'A robbery has been committed,' I gasped. 'A document of immense value has been stolen from the Foreign Office. Has anyone passed this way?'

"'I have been standing here for a quarter of an hour, sir,' said he; 'only one person has passed during that time—a woman, tall and elderly, with a Paisley shawl.'

"'Ah, that is only my wife,' cried the commissionaire. 'Has no one else passed?'

"'No one.'

"'Then it must be the other way that the thief took,' cried the fellow, tugging at my sleeve.

"But I was not satisfied, and the attempts which he made to draw me away increased my suspicions.

"'Which way did the woman go?' I cried.

"'I don't know, sir. I noticed her pass, but I had no special reason for watching her. She seemed to be in a hurry.'

"'How long ago was it?'

"'Oh, not very many minutes.'

"'Within the last five?'

"'Well, it could not be more than five.'

"'You're only wasting your time, sir, and every minute now is of importance,' cried the commissionaire. 'Take my word for it that my old woman has nothing to do with it, and come down to the other end of the street. Well, if you won't I will,' and with that he rushed off in the other direction.

"But I was after him in an instant and caught him by the sleeve.

"'Where do you live?' said I.

"'No. 16, Ivy Lane, Brixton,' he answered; 'but don't let yourself be drawn away upon a false scent, Mr. Phelps. Come to the other end of the street, and let us see if we can hear of anything.'

"Nothing was to be lost by following his advice. With the policeman we both hurried down, but only to find the street full of traffic, many people coming and going, but all only too eager to get to a place of safety upon so wet a night. There was no lounger who could tell us who had passed.

"Then we returned to the office, and searched the stairs and the passage without result. The corridor which led to the room was laid down with a kind of creamy linoleum which shows an impression very easily. We examined it very carefully, but found no outline of any footmark."

"Had it been raining all the evening?"

"Since about seven."

"How is it, then, that the woman who came into the room about nine left no traces with her muddy boots?"

"I am glad you raise the point. It occurred to me at the time. The charwomen are in the habit of taking off their boots at the commissionaire's office, and putting on list slippers."

"That is very clear. There were no marks, then, though the night was a wet one? The chain of events is certainly one of extraordinary interest. What did you do next?"

"We examined the room also. There is no possibility of a secret door, and the windows are quite thirty feet from the ground. Both of them were fastened on the inside. The carpet prevents any possibility of a trap-door, and the ceiling is of the ordinary white-washed kind. I will pledge my life that whoever stole my papers could only have come through the door."

"How about the fireplace?"

"They use none. There is a stove. The bell-rope hangs from the wire just to the right of my desk. Whoever rang it must have come right up to the desk to do it. But why should any criminal wish to ring the bell? It is a most insoluble mystery."

"Certainly the incident was unusual. What were your next steps? You examined the room, I presume, to see if the intruder had left any traces—any cigar end, or dropped glove, or hairpin, or other trifle?"

"There was nothing of the sort."

"No smell?"

"Well, we never thought of that."

"Ah, a scent of tobacco would have been worth a great deal to us in such an investigation."

"I never smoke myself, so I think I should have observed it if there had been any smell of tobacco. There was absolutely no clue of any kind. The only tangible fact was that the commissionaire's wife—Mrs. Tangey was the name—had hurried out of the place. He could give no explanation save that it was about the time when the woman always went home. The policeman and I agreed that our best plan would be to seize the woman before she could get rid of the papers, presuming that she had them.

"The alarm had reached Scotland Yard by this time, and Mr. Forbes, the detective, came round at once and took up the case with a great deal of energy. We hired a hansom, and in half an hour we were at the address which had been given to us. A young woman opened the door, who proved to be Mrs. Tangey's eldest daughter. Her mother had not come back yet, and we were shown into the front room to wait.

"About ten minutes later a knock came at the door, and here we made the one serious mistake for which I blame myself. Instead of opening the door ourselves we allowed the girl to do so. We heard her say, 'Mother, there are two men in the house waiting to see you,' and an instant afterwards we heard the patter of feet rushing down the passage. Forbes flung open the door, and we both ran into the back room or kitchen, but the woman had got there before us. She stared at us with defiant eyes, and then suddenly recognising me, an expres-

"WHY, IF IT ISN'T MR. PHELPS!"

sion of absolute astonishment came over her face.

"'Why, if it isn't Mr. Phelps, of the office!' she cried.

"'Come, come, who did you think we were when you ran away from us?' asked my companion.

"'I thought you were the brokers,' said she. 'We've had some trouble with a trades-man.'

"'That's not quite good enough,' answered Forbes. 'We have reason to believe that you have taken a paper of importance from the Foreign Office, and that you ran in here to dispose of it. You must come back with us to Scotland Yard to be searched.'

"It was in vain that she protested and resisted. A four-wheeler was brought, and we all three drove back in it. We had first made an examination of the kitchen, and especially of the kitchen fire, to see whether she might have made away with the papers during the instant that she was alone. There were no signs, however, of any ashes or scraps. When we reached Scotland Yard she was handed over at once to the female searcher. I waited in an agony of suspense until she came back with her report. There were no signs of the papers.

"Then, for the first time, the horror of my situation came in its full force upon me. Hitherto I had been acting, and action had numbed thought. I had been so confident of regaining the treaty at once that I had not dared to think of what would be the consequence if I failed to do so. But now there was nothing more to be done, and I had leisure to realize my position. It was horrible! Watson there would tell you that I was a nervous, sensitive boy at school. It is my nature. I thought of my uncle and of his colleagues in the Cabinet, of the shame which I had brought upon him, upon myself, upon everyone connected with me. What though I was the victim of an extraordinary accident? No allowance is made for accidents where diplomatic interests are at stake. I was ruined; shamefully, hopelessly ruined. I don't know what I did. I fancy I must have made a scene. I have a dim recollection of a group of officials who crowded round me endeavouring to soothe me. One of them drove down with me to Waterloo and saw me into the Woking train. I believe that he would have come all the way had it not been that Dr. Ferrier, who lives near me, was going down by that very train. The doctor most kindly took charge of me, and it was well he did so, for I had a fit in the station, and before we reached home I was practically a raving maniac.

"You can imagine the state of things here when they were roused from their beds by the doctor's ringing, and found me in this condition. Poor Annie here and my mother were broken-hearted. Dr. Ferrier had just heard enough from the detective at the station to be able to give an idea of what had happened, and his story did not mend matters. It was evident to all that I was in for a long illness, so Joseph was bundled out of this cheery bedroom, and it was turned into a sick room for me. Here I have lain, Mr. Holmes, for over nine weeks, unconscious, and raving with brain fever. If it had not been for Miss Harrison here and for the doctor's care, I should not be speaking to you now. She has nursed me by day, and a hired nurse has looked after me by night, for in my mad fits I was capable of anything. Slowly my reason has cleared, but it is only during the last three days that my memory has quite returned. Sometimes I wish that it never had. The first thing that I did was to wire to Mr. Forbes, who had the case in hand. He came out and assured me that, though everything has been done, no trace of a clue has been discovered. The commissionaire and his wife have been examined in every way without any light being thrown upon the matter. The suspicions of the police then rested upon young Gorot, who, as you may remember, stayed overtime in the office that night. His remaining behind and his French name were really the only two points which could suggest suspicion; but as a matter of fact, I did not begin work until he had gone, and his people are of Huguenot extraction, but as English in sympathy and tradition as you and I are. Nothing was found to implicate him in any way, and there the matter dropped. I turn to you, Mr. Holmes, as absolutely my last hope. If you fail me, then my honour as well as my position are for ever forfeited."

The invalid sank back upon his cushions, tired out by this long recital, while his nurse poured him out a glass of some stimulating medicine. Holmes sat silently with his head thrown back and his eyes closed in an attitude which might seem listless to a stranger, but which I knew betokened the most intense absorption.

"Your statement has been so explicit," said he at last, "that you have really left me very few questions to ask. There is one of the very utmost importance, however. Did you tell anyone that you had this special task to perform?"

"No one."

"Not Miss Harrison here, for example?"

"No. I had not been back to Woking between getting the order and executing the commission."

"And none of your people had by chance been to see you?"

"None."

"Did any of them know their way about in the office?"

"Oh, yes; all of them had been shown over it."

"Still, of course, if you said nothing to any one about the treaty, these inquiries are irrelevant."

"I said nothing."

"Do you know anything of the commissionaire?"

"Nothing, except that he is an old soldier."

"What regiment?"

"Oh, I have heard—Coldstream Guards."

"Thank you. I have no doubt I can get details from Forbes. The authorities are excellent at amassing facts, though they do not always use them to advantage. What a lovely thing a rose is!"

He walked past the couch to the open window, and held up the drooping stalk of a moss rose, looking down at the dainty blend of crimson and green. It

"WHAT A LOVELY THING A ROSE IS."

was a new phase of his character to me, for I had never before seen him show any keen interest in natural objects.

"There is nothing in which deduction is so necessary as in religion," said he, leaning with his back against the shutters. "It can be built up as an exact science by the reasoner. Our highest assurance of the goodness of Providence seems to me to rest in the flowers. All other things, our powers, our desires, our food, are really necessary for our existence in the first instance. But this rose is an extra. Its smell and its colour are an embellishment of life, not a condition of it. It is only goodness which gives extras, and so I say again that we have much to hope from the flowers."

Percy Phelps and his nurse looked at Holmes during this demonstration with surprise and a good deal of disappointment written upon their faces. He had fallen into a reverie, with the moss rose between his fingers. It had lasted some minutes before the young lady broke in upon it.

"Do you see any prospect of solving this mystery, Mr. Holmes?" she asked, with a touch of asperity in her voice.

"Oh, the mystery!" he answered, coming back with a start to the realities of life. "Well, it would be absurd to deny that the case is a very abstruse and complicated one; but I can promise you that I will look into the matter and let you know any points which may strike me."

"Do you see any clue?"

"You have furnished me with seven, but of course I must test them before I can pronounce upon their value."

"You suspect someone?"

"I suspect myself—"

"What?"

"Of coming to conclusions too rapidly."

"Then go to London and test your conclusions."

"Your advice is very excellent, Miss Harrison," said Holmes, rising. "I think, Watson, we cannot do better. Do not allow yourself to indulge in false hopes, Mr. Phelps. The affair is a very tangled one."

"I shall be in a fever until I see you again," cried the diplomatist.

"Well, I'll come out by the same train to-morrow, though it's more than likely that my report will be a negative one."

"God bless you for promising to come," cried our client. "It gives me fresh life to know that something is being done. By the way, I have had a letter from Lord Holdhurst."

"Ha, what did he say?"

"He was cold, but not harsh. I daresay my severe illness prevented him from being that. He repeated that the matter was of the utmost importance, and added that no steps would be taken about my future—by which he means, of course, my dismissal—until my health was restored and I had an opportunity of repairing my misfortune."

"Well, that was reasonable and considerate," said Holmes. "Come, Watson, for we have a good day's work before us in town."

Mr. Joseph Harrison drove us down to the station, and we were soon whirling up in a Portsmouth train. Holmes was sunk in profound thought, and hardly opened his mouth until we had passed Clapham Junction.

"It's a very cheering thing to come into London by any of these lines which run high and allow you to look down upon the houses like this."

I thought he was joking, for the view was sordid enough, but he soon explained himself.

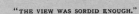

"THE VIEW WAS SORDID ENOUGH."

"Look at those big, isolated clumps of building rising up above the slates, like brick islands in a lead-coloured sea."

"The Board schools."

"Lighthouses, my boy! Beacons of the future! Capsules, with hundreds of bright little seeds in each, out of which will spring the wiser, better England of the future. I suppose that man Phelps does not drink?"

"I should not think so."

"Nor should I. But we are bound to take every possibility into account. The poor devil has certainly got himself into very hot water, and it's a question whether we shall ever be able to get him ashore. What did you think of Miss Harrison?"

"A girl of strong character."

"Yes, but she is a good sort, or I am mistaken. She and her brother are the only children of an ironmaster somewhere up Northumberland way. He got engaged to her when travelling last winter, and she came down to be introduced to his people, with her brother as escort. Then came the smash, and she stayed on to nurse her lover, while brother Joseph, finding himself pretty snug, stayed on too. I've been making a few independent inquiries, you see. But to-day must be a day of inquiries."

"My practice——" I began.

"Oh, if you find your own cases more interesting than mine——" said Holmes, with some asperity.

"I was going to say that my practice could get along very well for a day or two, since it is the slackest time in the year."

"Excellent!" said he, recovering his good humour. "Then we'll look into this matter together. I think that we should begin by seeing Forbes. He can probably tell us all the details we want, until we know from what side the case is to be approached."

"You said you had a clue."

"Well, we have several, but we can only test their value by further inquiry. The most difficult crime to track is the one which is purposeless. Now, this is not purposeless. Who is it that profits by it? There is the

French Ambassador, there is the Russian, there is whoever might sell it to either of these, and there is Lord Holdhurst."

"Lord Holdhurst!"

"Well, it is just conceivable that a statesman might find himself in a position where he was not sorry to have such a document accidentally destroyed."

"Not a statesman with the honourable record of Lord Holdhurst."

"It is a possibility, and we cannot afford to disregard it. We shall see the noble lord to-day, and find out if he can tell us anything. Meanwhile, I have already set inquiries upon foot."

"Already?"

"Yes, I sent wires from Woking Station to every evening paper in London. This advertisement will appear in each of them."

He handed over a sheet torn from a note-book. On it was scribbled in pencil :—

"£10 Reward.—The number of the cab which dropped a fare at or about the door of the Foreign Office in Charles Street, at a quarter to ten in the evening of May 23rd. Apply 221B, Baker Street."

"You are confident that the thief came in a cab?"

"If not, there is no harm done. But if Mr. Phelps is correct in stating that there is no hiding-place either in the room or the corridors, then the person must have come from outside. If he came from outside on so wet a night, and yet left no trace of damp upon the linoleum which was examined within a few minutes of his passing, then it is exceedingly probable that he came in a cab. Yes, I think that we may safely deduce a cab."

"It sounds plausible."

"That is one of the clues of which I spoke. It may lead us to something. And then, of course, there is the bell—which is the most distinctive feature of the case. Why should the bell ring? Was it the thief that did it out of bravado? Or was it someone who was with the thief who did it in order to prevent the crime? Or was it an accident? Or was it —— ?" He sank back into the state of intense and silent thought from which he had emerged, but it seemed to me, accustomed as I was to

his every mood, that some new possibility had dawned suddenly upon him.

It was twenty past three when we reached our terminus, and after a hasty luncheon at the buffet we pushed on at once to Scotland Yard. Holmes had already wired to Forbes, and we found him waiting to receive us: a small, foxy man, with a sharp but by no means amiable expression. He was decidedly frigid in his manner to us, especially when he heard the errand upon which we had come.

"I've heard of your methods before now, Mr. Holmes," said he, tartly. "You are

"I'VE HEARD OF YOUR METHODS BEFORE NOW, MR. HOLMES."

ready enough to use all the information that the police can lay at your disposal, and then you try to finish the case yourself and bring discredit upon them."

"On the contrary," said Holmes; "out of my last fifty-three cases my name has only appeared in four, and the police have had all the credit in forty-nine. I don't blame you for not knowing this, for you are young and inexperienced; but if you wish to get on in your new duties you will work with me, and not against me."

"I'd be very glad of a hint or two," said the detective, changing his manner. "I've certainly had no credit from the case so far."

"What steps have you taken?"

"Tangey, the commissionaire, has been shadowed. He left the Guards with a good character, and we can find nothing against him. His wife is a bad lot, though. I fancy she knows more about this than appears."

"Have you shadowed her?"

"We have set one of our women on to her. Mrs. Tangey drinks, and our woman has been with her twice when she was well on, but she could get nothing out of her."

"I understand that they have had brokers in the house?"

"Yes, but they were paid off."

"Where did the money come from?"

"That was all right. His pension was due. They have not shown any sign of being in funds."

"What explanation did she give of having answered the bell when Mr. Phelps rang for the coffee?"

"She said that her husband was very tired and she wished to relieve him."

"Well, certainly that would agree with his being found, a little later, asleep in his chair. There is nothing against them, then, but the woman's character. Did you ask her why she hurried away that night? Her haste attracted the attention of the police constable."

"She was later than usual, and wanted to get home."

"Did you point out to her that you and Mr. Phelps, who started at least twenty minutes after her, got home before her?"

"She explains that by the difference between a 'bus and a hansom."

"Did she make it clear why, on reaching her house, she ran into the back kitchen?"

"Because she had the money there with which to pay off the brokers."

"She has at least an answer for everything. Did you ask her whether in leaving she met anyone or saw anyone loitering about Charles Street?"

"She saw no one but the constable."

"Well, you seem to have cross-examined her pretty thoroughly. What else have you done?"

"The clerk, Gorot, has been shadowed all these nine weeks, but without result. We can show nothing against him."

"Anything else?"

"Well, we have nothing else to go upon— no evidence of any kind."

"Have you formed any theory about how that bell rang?"

"Well, I must confess that it beats me. It was a cool hand, whoever it was, to go and give the alarm like that."

"Yes, it was a queer thing to do. Many thanks to you for what you have told me. If I can put the man into your hands you shall hear from me. Come along, Watson!"

"Where are we going to now?" I asked, as we left the office.

"We are now going to interview Lord Holdhurst, the Cabinet Minister and future Premier of England."

The Adventures of Sherlock Holmes.

By A. Conan Doyle.

XXIII.—THE ADVENTURE OF THE NAVAL TREATY.

E were fortunate in finding that Lord Holdhurst was still in his chambers at Downing Street, and on Holmes sending in his card we were instantly shown up. The statesman received us with that old-fashioned courtesy for which he is remarkable, and seated us on the two luxurious easy chairs on either side of the fireplace. Standing on the rug between us, with his slight, tall figure, his sharp-featured, thoughtful face, and his curling hair prematurely tinged with grey, he seemed to represent that not too common type, a nobleman who is in truth noble.

"Your name is very familiar to me, Mr. Holmes," said he, smiling. "And, of course, I cannot pretend to be ignorant of the object of your visit. There has only been one occurrence in these offices which could call for your attention. In whose interest are you acting, may I ask?"

"In that of Mr. Percy Phelps," answered Holmes.

"Ah, my unfortunate nephew! You can understand that our kinship makes it the more impossible for me to screen him in any way. I fear that the incident must have a very prejudicial effect upon his career."

"But if the document is found?"

"Ah, that, of course, would be different."

"I had one or two questions which I wished to ask you, Lord Holdhurst."

"A NOBLEMAN."

"I shall be happy to give you any information in my power."

"Was it in this room that you gave your

instructions as to the copying of the document?"

"It was."

"Then you could hardly have been overheard?"

"It is out of the question."

"Did you ever mention to anyone that it was your intention to give out the treaty to be copied?"

"Never."

"You are certain of that?"

"Absolutely."

"Well, since you never said so, and Mr. Phelps never said so, and nobody else knew anything of the matter, then the thief's presence in the room was purely accidental. He saw his chance and he took it."

The statesman smiled. "You take me out of my province there," said he.

Holmes considered for a moment. "There is another very important point which I wish to discuss with you," said he. "You feared, as I understand, that very grave results might follow from the details of this treaty becoming known?"

A shadow passed over the expressive face of the statesman. "Very grave results, indeed."

"And have they occurred?"

"Not yet."

"If the treaty had reached, let us say, the French or Russian Foreign Office, you would expect to hear of it?"

"I should," said Lord Holdhurst, with a wry face.

"Since nearly ten weeks have elapsed then, and nothing has been heard, it is not unfair to suppose that for some reason the treaty has not reached them?"

Lord Holdhurst shrugged his shoulders.

"We can hardly suppose, Mr. Holmes, that the thief took the treaty in order to frame it and hang it up."

"Perhaps he is waiting for a better price."

"If he waits a little longer he will get no price at all. The treaty will cease to be a secret in a few months."

"That is most important," said Holmes. "Of course it is a possible supposition that the thief has had a sudden illness——"

"An attack of brain fever, for example?" asked the statesman, flashing a swift glance at him.

"I did not say so," said Holmes, imperturbably. "And now, Lord Holdhurst, we have already taken up too much of your valuable time, and we shall wish you good-day."

"Every success to your investigation, be the criminal who it may," answered the nobleman, as he bowed us out at the door.

"He's a fine fellow," said Holmes, as we came out into Whitehall. "But he has a struggle to keep up his position. He is far from rich, and has many calls. You noticed, of course, that his boots had been re-soled? Now, Watson, I won't detain you from your legitimate work any longer. I shall do nothing more to-day, unless I have an answer to my cab advertisement. But I should be extremely obliged to you if you would come down with me to Woking to-morrow, by the same train which we took to-day."

I met him accordingly next morning, and we travelled down to Woking together. He had had no answer to his advertisement, he said, and no fresh light had been thrown upon the case. He had, when he so willed it, the utter immobility of countenance of a red Indian, and I could not gather from his appearance whether he was satisfied or not with the position of the case. His conversation, I remember, was about the Bertillon system of measurements, and he expressed his enthusiastic admiration of the French savant.

We found our client still under the charge of his devoted nurse, but looking considerably better than before. He rose from the sofa and greeted us without difficulty when we entered.

"Any news?" he asked, eagerly.

"My report, as I expected, is a negative one," said Holmes. "I have seen Forbes, and I have seen your uncle, and I have set one or two trains of inquiry upon foot which may lead to something."

"You have not lost heart, then?"

"By no means."

"God bless you for saying that!" cried Miss Harrison. "If we keep our courage and our patience, the truth must come out."

"We have more to tell you than you have for us," said Phelps, reseating himself upon the couch.

"I hoped you might have something."

"Yes, we have had an adventure during the night, and one which might have proved to be a serious one," his expression grew very grave as he spoke, and a look of something akin to fear sprang up in his eyes. "Do you know," said he, "that I begin to believe that I am the unconscious centre of some monstrous conspiracy, and that my life is aimed at as well as my honour?"

"Ah!" cried Holmes.

"It sounds incredible, for I have not, as

"' ANY NEWS ?' HE ASKED."

shutters. A man was crouching at the window. I could see little of him, for he was gone like a flash. He was wrapped in some sort of cloak, which came across the lower part of his face. One thing only I am sure of, and that is that he had some weapon in his hand. It looked to me like a long knife. I distinctly saw the gleam of it as he turned to run."

" This is most interesting," said Holmes. " Pray, what did you do then ? "

" I should have followed him through the open window if I had been stronger. As it was, I rang the bell and roused the house. It took me some little time, for the bell rings in the kitchen, and the servants all sleep upstairs. I shouted, however, and that brought Joseph down, and he roused the others. Joseph and the groom found marks on the flower-bed outside the window, but the weather has been so dry lately that they found it hopeless to follow the trail across the grass. There's a place, however, on the wooden fence which skirts the road which shows signs, they tell me, as if someone had got over and had snapped the top of the rail in doing so. I have said nothing to the local police yet, for I thought I had best have your opinion first."

This tale of our client's appeared to have an extraordinary effect upon Sherlock Holmes. He rose from his chair and paced about the room in incontrollable excitement.

" Misfortunes never come singly," said Phelps, smiling, though it was evident that his adventure had somewhat shaken him.

" You have certainly had your share," said Holmes. " Do you think you could walk round the house with me ? "

" Oh, yes, I should like a little sunshine. Joseph will come too."

" And I also," said Miss Harrison.

far as I know, an enemy in the world. Yet from last night's experience I can come to no other conclusion."

" Pray let me hear it."

" You must know that last night was the very first night that I have ever slept without a nurse in the room. I was so much better that I thought I could dispense with one. I had a night-light burning, however. Well, about two in the morning I had sunk into a light sleep, when I was suddenly aroused by a slight noise. It was like the sound which a mouse makes when it is gnawing a plank, and I lay listening to it for some time, under the impression that it must come from that cause. Then it grew louder, and suddenly there came from the window a sharp metallic snick. I sat up in amazement. There could be no doubt what the sounds were now. The faint ones had been caused by someone forcing an instrument through the slit between the sashes, and the second by the catch being pressed back.

" There was a pause then for about ten minutes, as if the person were waiting to see whether the noise had awoken me. Then I heard a gentle creaking as the window was very slowly opened. I could stand it no longer, for my nerves are not what they used to be. I sprang out of bed and flung open the

"I am afraid not," said Holmes, shaking his head. "I think I must ask you to remain sitting exactly where you are."

The young lady resumed her seat with an air of displeasure. Her brother, however, had joined us, and we set off all four together. We passed round the lawn to the outside of the young diplomatist's window. There were, as he had said, marks upon the flower-bed, but they were hopelessly blurred and vague. Holmes stooped over them for an instant, and then rose, shrugging his shoulders.

"I don't think anyone could make much of this," said he. "Let us go round the house and see why this particular room was chosen by the burglar. I should have thought those larger windows of the drawing-room and dining-room would have had more attractions for him."

"They are more visible from the road," suggested Mr. Joseph Harrison.

"Ah, yes, of course. There is a door here which he might have attempted. What is it for?"

"It is the side entrance for tradespeople. Of course, it is locked at night."

"Have you ever had an alarm like this before?"

"Never," said our client.

"Do you keep plate in the house, or anything to attract burglars?"

"Nothing of value."

Holmes strolled round the house with his hands in his pockets, and a negligent air which was unusual with him.

"By the way," said he, to Joseph Harrison, "you found some place, I understand, where

"HOLMES EXAMINED IT CRITICALLY."

the fellow scaled the fence. Let us have a look at that."

The plump young man led us to a spot where the top of one of the wooden rails had been cracked. A small fragment of the wood was hanging down. Holmes pulled it off and examined it critically.

"Do you think that was done last night? It looks rather old, does it not?"

"Well, possibly so."

"There are no marks of anyone jumping down upon the other side. No, I fancy we shall get no help here. Let us go back to the bedroom and talk the matter over."

Percy Phelps was walking very slowly, leaning upon the arm of his future brother-in-law. Holmes walked swiftly across the lawn, and we were at the open window of the bedroom long before the others came up.

"Miss Harrison," said Holmes, speaking with the utmost intensity of manner. "You must stay where you are all day. Let nothing prevent you from staying where you are all day. It is of the utmost importance."

"Certainly, if you wish it, Mr. Holmes," said the girl, in astonishment.

"When you go to bed lock the door of this room on the outside and keep the key. Promise to do this."

"But Percy?"

"He will come to London with us."

"And I am to remain here?"

"It is for his sake. You can serve him! Quick! Promise!"

She gave a quick nod of assent just as the other two came up.

"Why do you sit moping there, Annie?" cried her brother. "Come out into the sunshine!"

"No, thank you, Joseph. I have a slight headache, and this room is deliciously cool and soothing."

"What do you propose now, Mr. Holmes?" asked our client.

"Well, in investigating this minor affair we must not lose sight of our main inquiry. It would be a very great help to me if you would come up to London with us."

"At once?"

"Well, as soon as you conveniently can. Say in an hour."

"I feel quite strong enough, if I can really be of any help."

"The greatest possible."

"Perhaps you would like me to stay there to-night?"

"I was just going to propose it."

"Then if my friend of the night comes to revisit me, he will find the bird flown. We are all in your hands, Mr. Holmes, and you must tell us exactly what you would like done. Perhaps you would prefer that Joseph came with us, so as to look after me?'

"Oh, no; my friend Watson is a medical man, you know, and he'll look after you. We'll have our lunch here, if you will permit us, and then we shall all three set off for town together."

It was arranged as he suggested, though Miss Harrison excused herself from leaving the bedroom, in accordance with Holmes's suggestion. What the object of my friend's manœuvres was I could not conceive, unless it were to keep the lady away from Phelps, who, rejoiced by his returning health and by the prospect of action, lunched with us in the dining-room. Holmes had a still more startling surprise for us, however, for after accompanying us down to the station and seeing us into our carriage, he calmly announced that he had no intention of leaving Woking.

"There are one or two small points which I should

desire to clear up before I go," said he. "Your absence, Mr. Phelps, will in some ways rather assist me. Watson, when you reach London you would oblige me by driving at once to Baker Street with our friend here, and remaining with him until I see you again. It is fortunate that you are old schoolfellows, as you must have much to talk over. Mr. Phelps can have the spare bedroom to-night, and I will be with you in time for breakfast, for there is a train which will take me into Waterloo at eight."

"But how about our investigation in London?" asked Phelps, ruefully.

"We can do that to-morrow. I think that just at present I can be of more immediate use here."

"You might tell them at Briarbrae that I hope to be back to-morrow night," cried Phelps, as we began to move from the platform.

"I hardly expect to go back to Briarbrae,"

I HARDLY EXPECT TO GO BACK TO BRIARBRAE.

answered Holmes, and waved his hand to us cheerily as we shot out from the station.

Phelps and I talked it over on our journey, but neither of us could devise a satisfactory reason for this new development.

"I suppose he wants to find out some clue as to the burglary last night, if a burglar it was. For myself, I don't believe it was an ordinary thief."

"What is your own idea, then?"

"Upon my word, you may put it down to my weak nerves or not, but I believe there is some deep political intrigue going on around me, and that, for some reason that passes my understanding, my life is aimed at by the conspirators. It sounds high-flown and absurd, but consider the facts! Why should a thief try to break in at a bedroom window, where there could be no hope of any plunder, and why should he come with a long knife in his hand?"

"You are sure it was not a housebreaker's jemmy?"

"Oh, no; it was a knife. I saw the flash of the blade quite distinctly."

"But why on earth should you be pursued with such animosity?"

"Ah, that is the question."

"Well, if Holmes takes the same view, that would account for his action, would it not? Presuming that your theory is correct, if he can lay his hands upon the man who threatened you last night, he will have gone a long way towards finding who took the naval treaty. It is absurd to suppose that you have two enemies, one of whom robs you while the other threatens your life."

"But Mr. Holmes said that he was not going to Briarbrae."

"I have known him for some time," said I, "but I never knew him do anything yet without a very good reason," and with that our conversation drifted off into other topics.

But it was a weary day for me. Phelps was still weak after his long illness, and his misfortunes made him querulous and nervous. In vain I endeavoured to interest him in Afghanistan, in India, in social questions, in anything which might take his mind out of the groove. He would always come back to his lost treaty; wondering, guessing, speculating as to what Holmes was doing, what steps Lord Holdhurst was taking, what news we should have in the morning. As the evening wore on, his excitement became quite painful.

"You have implicit faith in Holmes?" he asked.

"I have seen him do some remarkable things."

"But he never brought light into anything quite so dark as this?"

"Oh, yes; I have known him solve questions which presented fewer clues than yours."

"But not where such large interests are at stake?"

"I don't know that. To my certain knowledge he has acted on behalf of three of the reigning Houses of Europe in very vital matters."

"But you know him well, Watson. He is such an inscrutable fellow, that I never quite know what to make of him. Do you think he is hopeful? Do you think he expects to make a success of it?"

"He has said nothing."

"That is a bad sign."

"On the contrary, I have noticed that when he is off the trail he generally says so. It is when he is on a scent, and is not quite absolutely sure yet that it is the right one, that he is most taciturn. Now, my dear fellow, we can't help matters by making ourselves nervous about them, so let me implore you to go to bed, and so be fresh for whatever may await us to-morrow."

I was able at last to persuade my companion to take my advice, though I knew from his excited manner that there was not much hope of sleep for him. Indeed, his mood was infectious, for I lay tossing half the night myself, brooding over this strange problem, and inventing a hundred theories each of which was more impossible than the last. Why had Holmes remained at Woking? Why had he asked Miss Harrison to remain in the sick room all day? Why had he been so careful not to inform the people at Briarbrae that he intended to remain near them? I cudgelled my brains until I fell asleep in the endeavour to find some explanation which would cover all these facts.

It was seven o'clock when I awoke, and I set off at once for Phelps's room, to find him haggard and spent after a sleepless night. His first question was whether Holmes had arrived yet.

"He'll be here when he promised," said I, "and not an instant sooner or later."

And my words were true, for shortly after eight a hansom dashed up to the door and our friend got out of it. Standing in the window, we saw that his left hand was swathed in a bandage and that his face was very grim and pale. He entered the house, but it was some little time before he came upstairs.

"He looks like a beaten man," cried Phelps.

I was forced to confess that he was right. "After all," said I, "the clue of the matter lies probably here in town."

Phelps gave a groan.

"I don't know how it is," said he, "but I had hoped for so much from his return. But surely his hand was not tied up like that yesterday? What can be the matter?"

"You are not wounded, Holmes?" I asked, as my friend entered the room.

"Tut, it is only a scratch through my own clumsiness," he answered, nodding his good morning to us. "This case of yours, Mr. Phelps, is certainly one of the darkest which I have ever investigated."

said Holmes, uncovering a dish of curried chicken. "Her cuisine is a little limited, but she has as good an idea of breakfast as a Scotchwoman. What have you there, Watson?"

"Ham and eggs," I answered.

"Good! What are you going to take, Mr. Phelps: curried fowl, or eggs, or will you help yourself?"

"Thank you, I can eat nothing," said Phelps.

"Oh, come! Try the dish before you."

"Thank you, I would really rather not."

"Well, then," said Holmes, with a mischievous twinkle, "I suppose that you have no objection to helping me?"

Phelps raised the cover and as he did so

'PHELPS RAISED THE COVER.

"I feared that you would find it beyond you."

"It has been a most remarkable experience."

"That bandage tells of adventures," said I. "Won't you tell us what has happened?"

"After breakfast, my dear Watson. Remember that I have breathed thirty miles of Surrey air this morning. I suppose there has been no answer from my cabman advertisement? Well, well, we cannot expect to score every time."

The table was all laid, and, just as I was about to ring, Mrs. Hudson entered with the tea and coffee. A few minutes later she brought in three covers, and we all drew up to the table, Holmes ravenous, I curious, and Phelps in the gloomiest state of depression.

"Mrs. Hudson has risen to the occasion,"

he uttered a scream, and sat there staring with a face as white as the plate upon which he looked. Across the centre of it was lying a little cylinder of blue-grey paper. He caught it up, devoured it with his eyes, and then danced madly about the room, pressing it to his bosom and shrieking out in his delight. Then he fell back into an arm-chair, so limp and exhausted with his own emotions that we had to pour brandy down his throat to keep him from fainting.

"There! there!" said Holmes, soothingly, patting him upon the shoulder. "It was too bad to spring it on you like this; but Watson here will tell you that I never can resist a touch of the dramatic."

Phelps seized his hand and kissed it.

"God bless you!" he cried; "you have saved my honour."

"Well, my own was at stake, you know," said Holmes. "I assure you, it is just as hateful to me to fail in a case as it can be to you to blunder over a commission."

Phelps thrust away the precious document into the innermost pocket of his coat.

"I have not the heart to interrupt your breakfast any further, and yet I am dying to know how you got it and where it was."

Sherlock Holmes swallowed a cup of coffee and turned his attention to the ham and eggs. Then he rose, lit his pipe, and settled himself down into his chair.

"I'll tell you what I did first, and how I came to do it afterwards," said he. "After leaving you at the station I went for a charming walk through some admirable Surrey scenery to a pretty little village called Ripley, where I had my tea at an inn, and took the precaution of filling my flask and of putting a paper of sandwiches in my pocket. There I remained until evening, when I set off for Woking again, and found myself in the high road outside Briarbrae just after sunset.

"Well, I waited until the road was clear—it is never a very frequented one at any time, I fancy—and then I clambered over the fence into the grounds."

"Surely the gate was open?" ejaculated Phelps.

"Yes; but I have a peculiar taste in these matters. I chose the place where the three fir trees stand, and behind their screen I got over without the least chance of anyone in the house being able to see me. I crouched down among the bushes on the other side, and crawled from one to the other—witness the disreputable state of my trouser knees—until I had reached the clump of rhododendrons just opposite to your bedroom window. There I squatted down and awaited developments.

"The blind was not down in your room, and I could see Miss Harrison sitting there reading by the table. It was a quarter past ten when she closed her book, fastened the shutters, and retired. I heard her shut the door, and felt quite sure that she had turned the key in the lock."

"The key?" ejaculated Phelps.

"Yes, I had given Miss Harrison instructions to lock the door on the outside and take the key with her when she went to bed. She carried out every one of my injunctions to the letter, and certainly without her co-operation you would not have that paper in your coat pocket. She departed then and the lights went out, and I was left squatting in the rhododendron bush.

"The night was fine, but still it was a very weary vigil. Of course, it has the sort of excitement about it that the sportsman feels when he lies beside the water-course and waits for the big game. It was very long, though—almost as long, Watson, as when you and I waited in that deadly room when we looked into the little problem of the 'Speckled Band.' There was a church clock down at Woking which struck the quarters, and I thought more than once that it had stopped. At last, however, about two in the morning, I suddenly heard the gentle sound of a bolt being pushed back, and the creaking of a key. A moment later the servants' door was opened, and Mr. Joseph Harrison stepped out into the moonlight."

"JOSEPH HARRISON STEPPED OUT."

"Joseph!" ejaculated Phelps.

"He was bare-headed, but he had a black cloak thrown over his shoulder so that he could conceal his face in an instant, if there were any alarm. He walked on tip-toe under the shadow of the wall, and when he reached the window, he worked a long-bladed knife through the sash and pushed back the catch. Then he flung open the window and, putting his knife through the crack in the shutters, he thrust the bar up and swung them open.

"From where I lay I had a perfect view of the inside of the room and of every one of his movements. He lit the two candles which stand upon the mantelpiece, and then he proceeded to turn back the corner of the carpet in the neigbourhood of the door. Presently he stooped and picked out a square piece of board, such as is usually left to enable plumbers to get at the joints of the gas pipes. This one covered, as a matter of fact, the T-joint which gives off the pipe which supplies the kitchen underneath. Out of this hiding-place he drew that little cylinder of paper, pushed down the board, rearranged the carpet, blew out the candles, and walked straight into my arms as I stood waiting for him outside the window.

"Well, he has rather more viciousness than I gave him credit for, has Master Joseph. He flew at me with his knife, and I had to grass him twice, and got a cut over the knuckles, before I had the upper hand of him. He looked 'murder' out of the only eye he could see with when we had finished, but he listened to reason and gave up the papers. Having got them I let my man go, but I wired full particulars to Forbes this morning. If he is quick enough to catch his bird, well and good! But if, as I shrewdly suspect, he finds the nest empty before he gets there, why, all the better for the Government. I fancy that Lord Holdhurst, for one, and Mr. Percy Phelps for another, would very much rather that the affair never got as far as a police-court."

. "My God!" gasped our client. "Do you tell me that during these long ten weeks of agony, the stolen papers were within the very room with me all the time?"

"So it was."

"And Joseph! Joseph a villain and a thief!"

"Hum! I am afraid Joseph's character is a rather deeper and more dangerous one than one might judge from his appearance. From what I have heard from him this morning, I gather that he has lost heavily in dabbling with stocks, and that he is ready to do anything on earth to better his fortunes. Being an absolutely selfish man, when a chance presented itself he did not allow either his sister's happiness or your reputation to hold his hand."

Percy Phelps sank back in his chair.

"My head whirls," said he; "your words have dazed me."

"The principal difficulty in your case," remarked Holmes, in his didactic fashion, "lay in the fact of there being too much evidence. What was vital was overlaid and hidden by what was irrelevant. Of all the facts which were presented to us, we had to pick just those which we deemed to be essential, and then piece them together in their order, so as to reconstruct this very remarkable chain of events. I had already begun to suspect Joseph, from the fact that you had intended to travel home with him that night, and. that therefore it was a likely enough thing that he should call for you— knowing the Foreign Office well—upon his way. When I heard that someone had been so anxious to get into the bedroom, in which no one but Joseph could have concealed anything—you told us in your narrative how you had turned Joseph out when you arrived with the doctor—my suspicions all changed to certainties, especially as the attempt was made on the first night upon which the nurse was absent, showing that the intruder was well acquainted with the ways of the house."

"How blind I have been!"

"The facts of the case, as far as I have worked them out, are these: This Joseph Harrison entered the office through the Charles Street door, and knowing his way he walked straight into your room the instant after you left it. Finding no one there he promptly rang the bell, and at the instant that he did so his eyes caught the paper upon the table. A glance showed him that chance had put in his way a State document of immense value, and in an instant he had thrust it into his pocket and was gone. A few minutes elapsed, as you remember, before the sleepy commissionaire drew your attention to the bell, and those were just enough to give the thief time to make his escape.

"He made his way to Woking by the first train, and, having examined his booty and assured himself that it really was of immense value, he concealed it in what he thought was a very safe place, with the intention of taking it out again in a day or two, and carrying it to the French Embassy, or wherever he thought that a long price was to be had. Then came your sudden return. He, without a moment's warning, was bundled out of his room, and from that time onwards there were always at least two of you there to prevent him from regaining his treasure. The situation to him must have been a maddening one. But at last he thought he saw his chance. He tried to steal in, but was baffled by your wakefulness. You may remember that you did not take your usual draught that night."

"I remember."

"I fancy that he had taken steps to make that draught efficacious, and that he quite relied upon your being unconscious. Of course, I understood that he would repeat the attempt whenever it could be done with safety. Your leaving the room gave him the

therefore, from the hiding-place, and so saved myself an infinity of trouble. Is there any other point which I can make clear?"

"Why did he try the window on the first occasion," I asked, "when he might have entered by the door?"

"In reaching the door he would have to pass seven bedrooms. On the other hand, he could get out on to the lawn with ease. Anything else?"

"IS THERE ANY OTHER POINT WHICH I CAN MAKE CLEAR?"

chance he wanted. I kept Miss Harrison in it all day, so that he might not anticipate us. Then, having given him the idea that the coast was clear, I kept guard as I have described. I already knew that the papers were probably in the room, but I had no desire to rip up all the planking and skirting in search of them. I let him take them,

"You do not think," asked Phelps, "that he had any murderous intention? The knife was only meant as a tool."

"It may be so," answered Holmes, shrugging his shoulders. "I can only say for certain that Mr. Joseph Harrison is a gentleman to whose mercy I should be extremely unwilling to trust."

THE DEATH OF SHERLOCK HOLMES.

434

The Adventures of Sherlock Holmes.

BY A. CONAN DOYLE.

XXIV.—THE ADVENTURE OF THE FINAL PROBLEM.

IT is with a heavy heart that I take up my pen to write these the last words in which I shall ever record the singular gifts by which my friend Mr. Sherlock Holmes was distinguished. In an incoherent and, as I deeply feel, an entirely inadequate fashion, I have endeavoured to give some account of my strange experiences in his company from the chance which first brought us together at the period of the "Study in Scarlet," up to the time of his interference in the matter of the "Naval Treaty"—an interference which had the unquestionable effect of preventing a serious international complication. It was my intention to have stopped there, and to have said nothing of that event which has created a void in my life which the lapse of two years has done little to fill. My hand has been forced, however, by the recent letters in which Colonel James Moriarty defends the memory of his brother, and I have no choice but to lay the facts before the public exactly as they occurred. I alone know the absolute truth of the matter, and I am satisfied that the time has come when no good purpose is to be served by its suppression. As far as I know, there have been only three accounts in the public Press: that in the *Journal de Genève* upon May 6th, 1891, the Reuter's despatch in the English papers upon May 7th, and finally the recent letters to which I have alluded. Of these the first and second were extremely condensed, while the last is, as I shall now show, an absolute perversion of the facts. It lies with me to tell for the first time what really took place between Professor Moriarty and Mr. Sherlock Holmes.

It may be remembered that after my marriage, and my subsequent start in private practice, the very intimate relations which had existed between Holmes and myself became to some extent modified. He still came to me from time to time when he desired a companion in his investigations, but these occasions grew more and more seldom, until I find that in the year 1890 there were only three cases of which I retain any record. During the winter of that year and the early spring of 1891, I saw in the papers that he had been engaged by the French Government upon a matter of supreme importance, and I received two notes from Holmes, dated from Narbonne and from Nîmes, from which I gathered that his stay in France was likely to be a long one. It was with some surprise, therefore, that I saw him walk into my consulting-room upon the evening of the 24th of April. It struck me that he was looking even paler and thinner than usual.

"Yes, I have been using myself up rather too freely," he remarked, in answer to my look rather than to my words; "I have been a little pressed of late. Have you any objection to my closing your shutters?"

The only light in the room came from the lamp upon the table at which I had been reading. Holmes edged his way round the wall, and flinging the shutters together, he bolted them securely.

"You are afraid of something?" I asked.

"Well, I am."

"Of what?"

"Of air-guns."

"My dear Holmes, what do you mean?"

"I think that you know me well enough, Watson, to understand that I am by no means a nervous man. At the same time, it is stupidity rather than courage to refuse to recognise danger when it is close upon you. Might I trouble you for a match?" He drew in the smoke of his cigarette as if the soothing influence was grateful to him.

"I must apologize for calling so late," said he, "and I must further beg you to be so unconventional as to allow me to leave your house presently by scrambling over your back garden wall."

"But what does it all mean?" I asked.

He held out his hand, and I saw in the light of the lamp that two of his knuckles were burst and bleeding.

"It's not an airy nothing, you see," said he, smiling. "On the contrary, it is solid enough for a man to break his hand over. Is Mrs. Watson in?"

"She is away upon a visit."

"Indeed! You are alone?"

"Quite."

"Then it makes it the easier for me to propose that you should come away with me for a week on to the Continent."

"Where?"

"Oh, anywhere. It's all the same to me."

There was something very strange in all this. It was not Holmes's nature to take an

"TWO OF HIS KNUCKLES WERE BURST AND BLEEDING."

aimless holiday, and something about his pale, worn face told me that his nerves were at their highest tension. He saw the question in my eyes, and, putting his finger-tips together and his elbows upon his knees, he explained the situation.

"You have probably never heard of Professor Moriarty?" said he.

"Never."

"Aye, there's the genius and the wonder of the thing!" he cried. "The man pervades London, and no one has heard of him. That's what puts him on a pinnacle in the records of crime. I tell you, Watson, in all seriousness, that if I could beat that man, if I could free society of him, I should feel that my own career had reached its summit, and I should be prepared to turn to some more placid line in life. Between ourselves, the recent cases in which I have been of assistance to the Royal Family of Scandinavia, and to the French Republic, have left me in such a position that I could continue to live in the quiet fashion which is most congenial to me, and to concentrate my attention upon my chemical researches. But I could not rest, Watson, I could not sit quiet in my chair, if I thought that such a man as Professor Moriarty were walking the streets of London unchallenged."

"What has he done, then?"

"His career has been an extraordinary one. He is a man of good birth and excel-lent education, endowed by Nature with a phenomenal mathematical faculty. At the age of twenty-one he wrote a treatise upon the Binomial Theorem, which has had a European vogue. On the strength of it, he won the Mathematical Chair at one of our smaller Universities and had, to all appearance, a most brilliant career before him. But the man had hereditary tendencies of the most diabolical kind. A criminal strain ran in his blood, which, instead of being modified, was increased and rendered infinitely more dangerous by his extraordinary mental powers. Dark rumours gathered round him in the University town, and eventually he was compelled to resign his Chair and to come down to London, where he set up as an Army coach. So much is known to the world, but what I am telling you now is what I have myself discovered.

"As you are aware, Watson, there is no one who knows the higher criminal world of London so well as I do. For years past I have continually been conscious of some power behind the malefactor, some deep organizing power which for ever stands in the way of the law, and throws its shield over the wrong-doer. Again and again in cases of the most varying sorts—forgery cases, robberies, murders—I have felt the presence of this force, and I have deduced its action in many of those undiscovered crimes in which I have not been personally consulted. For years I have endeavoured to break through the veil which shrouded it, and at last the time came when I seized my thread and followed it, until it led me, after a thousand cunning windings, to ex-Professor Moriarty of mathematical celebrity.

"He is the Napoleon of crime, Watson. He is the organizer of half that is evil and of nearly all that is undetected in this great city. He is a genius, a philosopher, an abstract thinker. He has a brain of the first order. He sits motionless, like a spider in the centre of its web, but that web has a thousand radiations, and he knows well every quiver of each of them. He does little himself. He only plans. But his agents are numerous and splendidly organized. Is there a crime to be done, a paper to be abstracted, we will say, a house to be rifled, a man to be removed — the word is passed to the Professor, the matter is organized and carried out. The agent may be caught. In that case money is found for his bail or his defence. But the central power which uses the agent is never caught—never so much as suspected. This was the organization which I deduced, Watson, and which I devoted my whole energy to exposing and breaking up.

" But the Professor was fenced round with safeguards so cunningly devised that, do what I would, it seemed impossible to get evidence which could convict in a court of law. You know my powers, my dear Watson, and yet at the end of three months I was forced to confess that I had at last met an antagonist who was my

" PROFESSOR MORIARTY STOOD BEFORE ME."

intellectual equal. My horror at his crimes was lost in my admiration at his skill. But at last he made a trip—only a little, little trip—but it was more than he could afford, when I was so close upon him. I had my chance, and, starting from that point, I have woven my net round him until now it is all ready to close. In three days, that is to say on Monday next, matters will be ripe, and the Professor, with all the principal members of his gang, will be in the hands of the police. Then will come the greatest criminal trial of the century, the clearing up of over forty mysteries and the rope for all of them —but if we move at all prematurely, you understand, they may slip out of our hands even at the last moment.

"Now, if I could have done this without the knowledge of Professor Moriarty, all would have been well. But he was too wily for that. He saw every step which I took to draw my toils round him. Again and again he strove to break away, but I as often headed him off. I tell you, my friend, that if a detailed account of that silent contest could be written, it would take its place as the most brilliant bit of thrust-and-parry work in the history of detection. Never have I risen to such a height, and never have I been so hard pressed by an opponent. He cut deep, and yet I just undercut him. This morning the last steps were taken, and three days only were wanted to complete the business. I was sitting in my room thinking the matter over, when the door opened and Professor Moriarty stood before me.

" My nerves are fairly proof, Watson, but I must confess to a start when I saw the very man who had been so much in my thoughts standing there on my threshold. His appearance was quite familiar to me. He is extremely tall and thin, his forehead domes out in a white curve, and his two eyes are deeply sunken in his head. He is clean shaven, pale, and ascetic-looking, retaining something of the professor in his features. His shoulders are rounded from much study, and his face protrudes forward, and is for ever slowly oscillating from side to side in a curiously reptilian fashion. He peered at me with great curiosity in his puckered eyes.

" 'Yo⁻ ᵃave less frontal development than I should have expected,' said he at last. 'It is a dangerous habit to finger loaded firearms in the pocket of one's dressing-gown.'

" The fact is that upon his entrance I had instantly recognised the extreme personal danger in which I lay. The only conceivable escape for him lay in silencing my tongue. In an instant I had slipped the revolver from the drawer into my pocket, and was covering him through the cloth. At his remark I drew the weapon out and laid it cocked upon the table. He still smiled and blinked, but there was something about his eyes which made me feel very glad that I had it there.

" 'You evidently don't know me,' said he.

" 'On the contrary,' I answered, 'I think it is fairly evident that I do. Pray take a chair. I can spare you five minutes if you have anything to say.'

" 'All that I have to say has already crossed your mind,' said he.

" 'Then possibly my answer has crossed yours,' I replied.

" 'You stand fast ? '

" 'Absolutely.'

" He clapped his hand into his pocket, and I raised the pistol from the table. But he merely drew out a memorandum-book in which he had scribbled some dates.

" 'You crossed my path on the 4th of January,' said he. 'On the 23rd you incommoded me ; by the middle of February I was seriously inconvenienced by you ; at the end of March I was absolutely hampered in my plans ; and now, at the close of April, I find myself placed in such a position through your continual persecution that I am in positive danger of losing my liberty. The situation is becoming an impossible one.'

" 'Have you any suggestion to make ? ' I asked.

" 'You must drop it, Mr. Holmes,' said

he, swaying his face about. ' You really must, you know.'

" 'After Monday,' said I.

" 'Tut, tut !' said he. 'I am quite sure that a man of your intelligence will see that there can be but one outcome to this affair. It is necessary that you should withdraw. You have worked things in such a fashion that we have only one resource left. It has been an intellectual treat to me to see the way in which you have grappled with this affair, and I say, unaffectedly, that it would be a grief to me to be forced to take any extreme measure. You smile, sir, but I assure you that it really would.'

" 'Danger is part of my trade,' I remarked.

" 'This is not danger,' said he. 'It is inevitable destruction. You stand in the way not merely of an individual, but of a mighty organization, the full extent of which you, with all your cleverness, have been unable to realize. You must stand clear, Mr. Holmes, or be trodden under foot.'

" 'I am afraid,' said I, rising, 'that in the pleasure of this conversation I am neglecting business of importance which awaits me elsewhere.'

" He rose also and looked at me in silence, shaking his head sadly.

" 'Well, well,' said he at last. ' It seems a pity, but I have done what I could. I know every move of your game. You can do nothing before Monday. It has been a duel between you and me, Mr. Holmes. You hope to place me in the dock. I tell you that I will never stand in the dock. You hope to beat me. I tell you that you will never beat me. If you are clever enough to bring destruction upon me, rest assured that I shall do as much to you.'

" 'You have paid me several compliments, Mr. Moriarty,' said I. ' Let me pay you one in return when I say that if I were assured of the former eventuality I would, in the interests of the public, cheerfully accept the latter.'

" 'I can promise you the one but not the other,' he snarled, and so turned his rounded back upon me and went peering and blinking out of the room.

" That was my singular interview with Professor Moriarty. I confess that it left an unpleasant effect upon my mind. His soft, precise fashion of speech leaves a conviction of sincerity which a mere bully could not produce. Of course, you will say : ' Why not take police precautions against him ? ' The reason is that I am well convinced that it is from his agents the blow would fall. I

S P

"HE TURNED HIS ROUNDED BACK UPON ME."

the day. Now I have come round to you, and on my way I was attacked by a rough with a bludgeon. I knocked him down, and the police have him in custody; but I can tell you with the most absolute confidence that no possible connection will ever be traced between the gentleman upon whose front teeth I have barked my knuckles and the retiring mathematical coach, who is, I daresay, working out problems upon a blackboard ten miles away. You will not wonder, Watson, that my first act on entering your rooms was to close your shutters, and that I have been compelled to ask your permission to leave the house by some less conspicuous exit than the front door."

I had often admired my friend's courage, but never more than now, as he sat quietly checking off a series of incidents which must have combined to make up a day of horror.

"You will spend the night here?" I said.

"No, my friend, you might find me a dangerous guest. I have my plans laid, and all will be well. Matters have gone so far now that they can move without my help as far as the arrest goes, though my presence is necessary for a conviction. It is obvious, therefore, that I cannot do better than get away for the few days which remain before the police are at liberty to act. It would be a great pleasure to me, therefore, if you could come on to the Continent with me."

"The practice is quiet," said I, "and I have an accommodating neighbour. I should be glad to come."

"And to start to-morrow morning?"

"If necessary."

"Oh, yes, it is most necessary. Then these are your instructions, and I beg, my dear Watson, that you will obey them to the letter, for you are now playing a double-handed game with me against the cleverest

have the best of proofs that it would be so."

"You have already been assaulted?"

"My dear Watson, Professor Moriarty is not a man who lets the grass grow under his feet. I went out about midday to transact some business in Oxford Street. As I passed the corner which leads from Bentinck Street on to the Welbeck Street crossing a two-horse van furiously driven whizzed round and was on me like a flash. I sprang for the footpath and saved myself by the fraction of a second. The van dashed round by Marylebone Lane and was gone in an instant. I kept to the pavement after that, Watson, but as I walked down Vere Street a brick came down from the roof of one of the houses, and was shattered to fragments at my feet. I called the police and had the place examined. There were slates and bricks piled upon the roof preparatory to some repairs, and they would have me believe that the wind had toppled over one of these. Of course I knew better, but I could prove nothing. I took a cab after that and reached my brother's rooms in Pall Mall, where I spent rogue and the most powerful syndicate of criminals in Europe. Now listen! You will dispatch whatever luggage you intend to take by a trusty messenger unaddressed to Victoria to-night. In the morning you will send for a hansom, desiring your man to take neither the first nor the second which may present itself. Into this hansom you will jump, and you will drive to the Strand end of the Lowther Arcade, handing the address to the cabman upon a slip of paper, with a request that he will not throw it away. Have your fare ready, and the instant that your cab stops, dash through the Arcade, timing yourself to reach the other side at a quarter-past nine. You will find a small brougham waiting close to the curb, driven by a fellow with a heavy black cloak tipped at the collar with red. Into this you will step, and you will reach Victoria in time for the Continental express."

"Where shall I meet you?"

"At the station. The second first-class carriage from the front will be reserved for us."

"The carriage is our rendezvous, then?"

"Yes."

It was in vain that I asked Holmes to remain for the evening. It was evident to me that he thought he might bring trouble to the roof he was under, and that that was the motive which impelled him to go. With a few hurried words as to our plans for the morrow he rose and came out with me into the garden, clambering over the wall which leads into Mortimer Street, and immediately whistling for a hansom, in which I heard him drive away.

In the morning I obeyed Holmes's injunctions to the letter. A hansom was procured with such precautions as would prevent its being one which was placed ready for us, and I drove immediately after breakfast to the Lowther Arcade, through which I hurried at the top of my speed. A brougham was waiting with a very massive driver wrapped in a dark cloak, who, the instant that I had stepped in, whipped up the horse and rattled off to Victoria Station. On my alighting there he turned the carriage, and dashed away again without so much as a look in my direction.

So far all had gone admirably. My luggage was waiting for me, and I had no difficulty in finding the carriage which Holmes had indicated, the less so as it was the only one in the train which was marked "Engaged." My only source of anxiety now was the non-appearance of Holmes. The station clock marked only seven minutes from the time when we were due to start. In vain I searched among the groups of travellers and leave-takers for the lithe figure of my friend. There was no sign of him. I spent a few minutes in assisting a venerable Italian priest, who was endeavouring to make a porter understand, in his broken English, that his luggage was to be booked through to Paris. Then, having taken another look round, I returned to my carriage, where I found that the porter, in spite of the ticket, had given me my decrepit Italian friend as a travelling companion. It was useless for me to explain to him that his presence was an intrusion, for my Italian was even more limited than his English, so I shrugged my shoulders resignedly, and continued to look out anxiously for my friend. A chill of fear had come over me, as I thought that his absence might mean that some blow had fallen during the night. Already the doors had all been shut and the whistle blown, when—

"My dear Watson," said a voice, "you have not even condescended to say good morning."

I turned in incontrollable astonishment. The aged ecclesiastic had turned his face towards me. For an instant the wrinkles were smoothed away, the nose drew away from the chin, the lower lip ceased to protrude and the mouth to mumble, the dull eyes regained their fire, the drooping figure expanded. The next the whole frame collapsed again, and Holmes had gone as quickly as he had come.

"Good heavens!" I cried. "How you startled me!"

"Every precaution is still necessary," he whispered. "I have reason to think that they are hot upon our trail. Ah, there is Moriarty himself."

The train had already begun to move as Holmes spoke. Glancing back I saw a tall man pushing his way furiously through the crowd and waving his hand as if he desired to have the train stopped. It was too late, however, for we were rapidly gathering momentum, and an instant later had shot clear of the station.

"With all our precautions, you see that we have cut it rather fine," said Holmes, laughing. He rose, and throwing off the black cassock and hat which had formed his disguise, he packed them away in a hand-bag.

"Have you seen the morning paper, Watson?"

"No."

"Yes, it was waiting."

"Did you recognise your coachman?"

"No."

"It was my brother Mycroft. It is an advantage to get about in such a case without taking a mercenary into your confidence. But we must plan what we are to do about Moriarty now."

"As this is an express, and as the boat runs in connection with it, I should think we have shaken him off very effectively."

"My dear Watson, you evidently did not realize my meaning when I said that this man may be taken as being quite on the same intellectual plane as myself. You do not imagine

"MY DECREPIT ITALIAN FRIEND."

"You haven't seen about Baker Street, then?"

"Baker Street?"

"They set fire to our rooms last night. No great harm was done."

"Good heavens, Holmes! This is intolerable."

"They must have lost my track completely after their bludgeon-man was arrested. Otherwise they could not have imagined that I had returned to my rooms. They have evidently taken the precaution of watching you, however, and that is what has brought Moriarty to Victoria. You could not have made any slip in coming?"

"I did exactly what you advised."

"Did you find your brougham?"

that if I were the pursuer I should allow myself to be baffled by so slight an obstacle. Why, then, should you think so meanly of him?"

"What will he do?"

"What I should do."

"What would you do, then?"

"Engage a special."

"But it must be late."

"By no means. This train stops at Canterbury; and there is always at least a quarter of an hour's delay at the boat. He will catch us there."

"One would think that we were the criminals. Let us have him arrested on his arrival."

"It would be to ruin the work of three

months. We should get the big fish, but the smaller would dart right and left out of the net. On Monday we should have them all. No, an arrest is inadmissible."

"What then?"

"We shall get out at Canterbury."

"And then?"

"Well, then we must make a cross-country journey to Newhaven, and so over to Dieppe. Moriarty will again do what I should do. He will get on to Paris, mark down our luggage, and wait for two days at the depôt. In the meantime we shall treat ourselves to a couple of carpet bags, encourage the manufactures of the countries through which we travel, and make our way at our leisure into Switzerland, viâ Luxembourg and Basle."

At Canterbury, therefore, we alighted, only to find that we should' have to wait an hour before we could get a train to Newhaven.

I was still looking rather ruefully after the rapidly disappearing luggage van which contained my wardrobe, when Holmes pulled my sleeve and pointed up the line.

"Already, you see," said he.

Far away, from among the Kentish woods there rose a thin spray of smoke. A minute later a carriage and engine could be seen flying along the open curve which leads to the station. We had hardly time to take our place behind a pile of luggage when it passed with a rattle and a roar, beating a blast of hot air into our faces.

"There he goes," said Holmes, as we watched the carriage swing and rock over the points. "There are limits, you see, to our friend's intelligence. It would have been a *coup-de-maître* had he deduced what I would deduce and acted accordingly."

"And what would he have done had he overtaken us?"

"There cannot be the least doubt that he would have made a murderous attack upon me. It is, however, a game at which two

may play. The question now is whether we should take a premature lunch here, or run our chance of starving before we reach the buffet at Newhaven."

We made our way to Brussels that night and spent two days there, moving on upon the third day as far as Strasburg. On the Monday morning Holmes had telegraphed to the London police, and in the evening we found a reply waiting for us at our hotel. Holmes tore it open, and then with a bitter curse hurled it into the grate.

"IT PASSED WITH A RATTLE AND A ROAR."

"I might have known it!" he groaned. "He has escaped!"

"Moriarty?"

"They have secured the whole gang with the exception of him. He has given them the slip. Of course, when I had left the country there was no one to cope with. him. But I did think that I had put the game in their hands. I think that you had better return to England, Watson."

"Why?"

"Because you will find me a dangerous companion now. This man's occupation is gone. He is lost if he returns to London. If I read his character right he will devote his whole energies to revenging himself upon me. He said as much in our short interview, and I fancy that he meant it. I should certainly recommend you to return to your practice."

It was hardly an appeal to be successful with one who was an old campaigner as well as an old friend. We sat in the Strasburg *salle-à-manger* arguing the question for half an hour, but the same night we had resumed our journey and were well on our way to Geneva.

For a charming week we wandered up the Valley of the Rhone, and then, branching off at Leuk, we made our way over the Gemmi Pass, still deep in snow, and so, by way of Interlaken, to Meiringen. It was a lovely trip, the dainty green of the spring below, the virgin white of the winter above; but it was clear to me that never for one instant did Holmes forget the shadow which lay across him. In the homely Alpine villages or in the lonely mountain passes, I could still tell by his quick glancing eyes and his sharp scrutiny of every face that passed us, that he was well convinced that, walk where we would, we could not walk ourselves clear of the danger which was dogging our footsteps.

Once, I remember, as we passed over the Gemmi, and walked along the border of the melancholy Daubensee, a large rock which had been dislodged from the ridge upon our right clattered down and roared into the lake behind us. In an instant Holmes had raced up on to the ridge, and, standing upon a lofty pinnacle, craned his neck in every direction. It was in vain that our guide assured him that a fall of stones was a common chance in the spring-time at that spot. He said nothing, but he smiled at me with the air of a man who sees the fulfilment of that which he had expected.

And yet for all his watchfulness he was never depressed. On the contrary, I can never recollect having seen him in such exuberant spirits. Again and again he recurred to the fact that if he could be assured that society was freed from

Professor Moriarty he would cheerfully bring his own career to a conclusion.

"I think that I may go so far as to say, Watson, that I have not lived wholly in vain," he remarked. "If my record were closed to-night I could still survey it with equanimity. The air of London is the sweeter for my presence. In over a thousand cases I am not aware that I have ever used my powers upon the wrong side. Of late I have been tempted to look into the problems furnished by Nature rather than those more superficial ones for which our artificial state of society is responsible. Your memoirs will draw to an end, Watson, upon the day that I crown my career by the capture or extinction of the most dangerous and capable criminal in Europe."

I shall be brief, and yet exact, in the little which remains for me to tell. It is not a subject on which I would willingly dwell, and yet I am conscious that a duty devolves upon me to omit no detail.

It was upon the 3rd of May that we reached the little village of Meiringen, where we put up at the Englischer Hof, then kept

"A LARGE ROCK CLATTERED DOWN."

by Peter Steiler the elder. Our landlord was an intelligent man, and spoke excellent English, having served for three years as waiter at the Grosvenor Hotel in London. At his advice, upon the afternoon of the 4th we set off together with the intention of crossing the hills and spending the night at the hamlet of Rosenlaui. We had strict injunctions, however, on no account to pass the falls of Reichenbach, which are about half-way up the hill, without making a small détour to see them.

It is, indeed, a fearful place. The torrent, swollen by the melting snow, plunges into a tremendous abyss, from which the spray rolls up like the smoke from a burning house. The shaft into which the river hurls itself is an immense chasm, lined by glistening, coal-black rock, and narrowing into a creaming, boiling pit of incalculable depth, which brims over and shoots the stream onward over its jagged lip. The long sweep of green water roaring for ever down, and the thick flickering curtain of spray hissing for ever upwards, turn a man giddy with their constant whirl and clamour. We stood near the edge peering down at the gleam of the breaking water far below us against the black rocks, and listening to the half-human shout which came booming up with the spray out of the abyss.

The path has been cut half-way round the fall to afford a complete view, but it ends abruptly, and the

traveller has to return as he came. We had turned to do so, when we saw a Swiss lad come running along it with a letter in his hand. It bore the mark of the hotel which we had just left, and was addressed to me by the landlord. It appeared that within a very few minutes of our leaving, an English lady had arrived who was in the last stage of consumption. She had wintered at Davos Platz, and was journeying now to join her friends at Lucerne, when a sudden hemorrhage had overtaken her. It was thought that she could hardly live a few hours, but it would be a great consolation to her to see an English doctor, and, if I would only return,

"I SAW HOLMES GAZING DOWN AT THE RUSH OF THE WATERS."

etc., etc. The good Steiler assured me in a postscript that he would himself look upon my compliance as a very great favour, since the lady absolutely refused to see a Swiss physician, and he could not but feel that he was incurring a great responsibility.

The appeal was one which could not be ignored. It was impossible to refuse the request of a fellow-countrywoman dying in a strange land. Yet I had my scruples about leaving Holmes. It was finally agreed, however, that he should retain the young Swiss messenger with him as guide and companion while I returned to Meiringen. My friend would stay some little time at the fall, he said, and would then walk slowly over the hill to Rosenlaui, where I was to rejoin him in the evening. As I turned away I saw Holmes, with his back against a rock and his arms folded, gazing down at the rush of the waters. It was the last that I was ever destined to see of him in this world.

When I was near the bottom of the descent I looked back. It was impossible, from that position, to see the fall, but I could see the curving path which winds over the shoulder of the hill and leads to it. Along this a man was, I remember, walking very rapidly.

I could see his black figure clearly outlined against the green behind him. I noted him, and the energy with which he walked, but he passed from my mind again as I hurried on upon my errand.

It may have been a little over an hour before I reached Meiringen. Old Steiler was standing at the porch of his hotel.

"Well," said I, as I came hurrying up, "I trust that she is no worse?"

A look of surprise passed over his face, and at the first quiver of his eyebrows my heart turned to lead in my breast.

"You did not write this?" I said, pulling the letter from my pocket. "There is no sick Englishwoman in the hotel?"

"Certainly not," he cried. "But it has the hotel mark upon it! Ha, it must have been written by that tall Englishman who came in after you had gone. He said——"

But I waited for none of the landlord's explanations. In a tingle of fear I was already running down the village street, and making for the path which I had so lately descended. It had taken me an hour to come down. For all my efforts two more had passed before I found myself at the fall of Reichenbach once more. There was Holmes's Alpine-stock still leaning against the rock by which I had left him. But there was no sign of him, and it was in vain that I shouted. My only answer was my own voice reverberating in a rolling echo from the cliffs around me.

It was the sight of that Alpine-stock which turned me cold and sick. He had not gone to Rosenlaui, then. He had remained on that three-foot path, with sheer wall on one side and sheer drop upon the other, until his enemy had overtaken him. The young Swiss had gone too. He had probably been in the pay of Moriarty, and had left the two men together. And then what had happened? Who was to tell us what had happened then?

I stood for a minute or two to collect myself, for I was dazed with the horror of the thing. Then I began to think of Holmes's own methods and to try to practise them in reading this tragedy. It was, alas, only too easy to do. During our conversation we had not gone to the end of the path, and the Alpine-stock marked the place where we had stood. The blackish soil is kept for ever soft by the incessant drift of spray, and a bird would leave its tread upon it. Two lines of footmarks were clearly marked along the further end of the path, both leading away from me. There were none returning. A few yards from the end the soil was all ploughed up into a patch of mud, and the brambles and ferns which fringed the chasm were torn and bedraggled. I lay upon my face and peered over with the spray spouting up all around me. It had darkened since I left, and now I could only see here and there the glistening of moisture upon the black walls, and far away down at the end of the shaft the gleam of the broken water. I shouted; but only that same half-human cry of the fall was borne back to my ears.

But it was destined that I should after all have a last word of greeting from my friend and comrade. I have said that his Alpine-stock had been left leaning against a rock which jutted on to the path. From the top of this boulder the gleam of something bright caught my eye, and, raising my hand, I found that it came from the silver cigarette case which he used to carry. As I took it up a small square of paper upon which it had lain fluttered down on to the ground. Unfolding it I found that it consisted of three pages torn from his note-book and addressed to me. It was characteristic of the man that the direction was as precise, and the writing as firm and clear, as though it had been written in his study.

"A SMALL SQUARE OF PAPER FLUTTERED DOWN."

that the letter from Meiringen was a hoax, and I allowed you to depart on that errand under the persuasion that some development of this sort would follow. Tell Inspector Patterson that the papers which he needs to convict the gang are in pigeon-hole M., done up in a blue envelope and inscribed 'Moriarty.' I made every disposition of my property before leaving England, and handed it to my brother Mycroft. Pray give my greetings to Mrs. Watson, and believe me to be, my dear fellow,

"Very sincerely yours,
"SHERLOCK HOLMES."

A few words may suffice to tell the little that remains. An examination by experts leaves little doubt that a personal contest between the two men ended, as it could hardly fail to end in such a situation, in their reeling over, locked in each other's arms. Any attempt at recovering the bodies was absolutely hopeless, and there, deep down in that dreadful caldron of swirling water and seething foam, will lie for all time the most dangerous criminal and the foremost champion of the law of their generation. The Swiss youth was never found again, and there can be no doubt that he was one of the numerous agents whom Moriarty kept in his employ. As to the gang, it will be within the memory of the public how completely the evidence which Holmes had accumulated exposed their organization, and how heavily the hand of the dead man weighed upon them. Of their terrible chief few details came out during the proceedings, and if I have now been compelled to make a clear statement of his career, it is due to those injudicious champions who have endeavoured to clear his memory by attacks upon him whom I shall ever regard as the best and the wisest man whom I have ever known.

"My dear Watson," he said, "I write these few lines through the courtesy of Mr. Moriarty, who awaits my convenience for the final discussion of those questions which lie between us. He has been giving me a sketch of the methods by which he avoided the English police and kept himself informed of our movements. They certainly confirm the very high opinion which I had formed of his abilities. I am pleased to think that I shall be able to free society from any further effects of his presence, though I fear that it is at a cost which will give pain to my friends, and especially, my dear Watson, to you. I have already explained to you, however, that my career had in any case reached its crisis, and that no possible conclusion to it could be more congenial to me than this. Indeed, if I may make a full confession to you, I was quite convinced